To Denise,
Enjoy your visit to...

An Island
A Novel of ARUBA
Away

[signature: Daniel Putkowski]

DANIEL
PUTKOWSKI

HAWSER
PRESS

HAWSER
PRESS

AN ISLAND AWAY Copyright © 2008 by Daniel Putkowski
All rights reserved. Printed in the United States of America.

ISBN 978-0-9815959-0-0

FIRST HAWSER PRESS TRADE PAPERBACK EDITION MAY 2008
10 9 8 7 6 5 4

danielputkowski.com

FOR
CHARLIE
You have to improvise.

☙ Language Guide ☙

THIS BOOK is written in English. However, to maintain the authenticity of the characters, portions of the text — particularly dialogue — appear in Papiamento and Spanish. Most of this non-English text is easily understood in the context of the story. The guide below serves as an additional resource.

(P) PAPIAMENTO   (S) SPANISH

Carlotta: (S) *pronounced "car-lote-tah"*
Hernán: (S) *pronounced "air-nan"*
Inez: (S) *pronounced "ee-nace"*
Jaime: (S) *pronounced "high-me"*
Jorgé: (S) *pronounced "or-hay"*
Luz: (S) *pronounced "loose"*
Marcela: (S) *pronounced "mar-say-la"*

---

acá, aquí: (S) *here*
allá, allí: (S) *there*
arriba: (S) *up*
bon dia: (P) *good day*
bon nochi: (P) *good night*
borracho: (S) *drunk*
buenas dias: (S) *good day*
buenas noches: (S) *good night*
choller: (P) *bum, street person*
claro: (S) *of course*
cuántos, cuántas: (S) *how many*
damas: (S) *ladies*
danki: (P) *thank you*
de nada: (S) *you're welcome*
Dios mío: (S) *my God*
dueña: (S) *owner*
felicidades: (S) *congratulations*
habitación: (S) *room*

hola: (S) *hello, hi*
linda: (S) *pretty*
lo siento: (S) *I'm sorry*
mami: (S) *mommy*
mucho gusto: (S) *nice to meet you*
nombre: (S) *name*
papi: (S) *daddy*
permiso: (S) *permission, permit*
pero: (S) *but*
playa: (S) *beach*
precio: (S) *price*
tal vez: (S) *perhaps*
también: (S) *also*
temprano: (S) *early*
todo, toda: (S) *each, every, all*
tú vives: (S) *you live, you're alive*
venga: (S) *come here*
verdad: (S) *true, truth*

BOOK I
San Nicolaas

CHARLIE LIVED in a place where the illegal was legal, where the immoral was moral, and where some people's fantasies were other people's realities. So, he lived every day in anticipation of the fantastic. And why not? It was the night before his birthday, the start of another marvelous year in a place where anything could happen.

Good times in mind, he surveyed the town of his birth with a careful eye. The buildings around him struggled up from the rocks and dirt of the southwest corner of his desert island nation. A cascade of them flowed over the hills and down toward the Caribbean Sea. Had the slope been steeper, they might have fallen into that sea. As it was, they stood fast and mostly upright against the constant trade winds that drove the waves upon the eastern edge of the island. Here on the western rim, the breeze swept the streets while the sun burnished the peeling façades that stood back from the curb.

Over his shoulder, beyond the shadow cast by a concrete wall, stood the oil refinery that created the town he now faced. Behind the wall, the bitter punch of South American crude cooked into innumerable products bound for markets to the north. Reliable winds carried the refinery's smoke and pollution away from the island's shore with such efficiency that handsome beaches fringed the facility's borders. Local children played on these beaches, and adventuresome tourists came to snorkel in less crowded waters than those on the north end of the island. The view from here, like everything on the island, offered a bizarre contrast. In this case, the industrial eyesore of the refinery abutted the ecological delight of pristine sea life.

Beneath the plumes of burning flare gas labored a mixture of islanders, guest workers, and a few *Norte Americanos*. There weren't so many as there had been, about a third of the number that had passed through the gate during the time of Charlie's father, Charles Brouns, Senior.

Half a century ago, the elder Brouns bought the bar over which Charlie now lived. It served ships' crews, refinery workers, locals, and most recently, tourists. His father would have despised the tourists, and Charlie was relieved his father wasn't alive to see them. They were an economic necessity in light of the diminished local workforce and the dwindling number of men serving aboard ever-larger ships that called less frequently at San Nicolaas. A Senegalese working in the refinery balked at a three-dollar glass of beer. Not a tourist. He thought it was a bargain. At his hotel bar, he paid four dollars and felt obligated to leave a dollar tip the way he would have in the United States. No one but tourists and fools tipped in this town. They were the only ones with enough money or the propensity to give it away. To keep them in the mood, Charlie told a few dirty jokes when the moment was right and hosted the occasional topless photo contest if the female patrons were in the mood for living dangerously. "All in good fun, all in good fun," he was quick to remind everyone. "Enjoy yourself! You're on vacation!"

Originally, there were twenty bars in the center of town. Then five were added. And then five more. And still a couple more, until Charlie could look down from his terrace and count thirty-two. If a man wanted to make a journey of his drinking it would be a short one, which would have been fine had there been three times the number of men working in the refinery. However, the payroll had been cut to a skeleton crew that picked the bones of parts gone bad to make patches for the good ones. Not only were there fewer workers, the salaries were significantly less than Esso used to pay. Esso paid, paid handsomely, and paid frequently, as Charlie's father had often reminded him. The company was never ashamed to be first class. Esso shipped in Americans, their families, their schoolteachers, their automobiles, and enough comforts from home to keep everyone in their colony living more or less the way they did back in the States. But Esso had sold the place to a less benevolent outfit.

"Those were the days," Charlie said to his cat, who dozed atop the parapet. "The milk and honey clung to your whiskers. You could have a taste whenever you stuck out your tongue."

The cat blinked slowly at the breeze and put his head up for a rub between his ears. Charlie obliged the animal. He admired cats for their appreciation of fine seafood and the luxury of a midafternoon nap, not to mention their all-night sense of adventure. What a life! It was similar to his own, which followed a routine not so regimented as reliable. He rose early, smoked his first cigarette of the day, and greeted the sun from his balcony. After half an hour of reflection on life and the meaning of the universe, to which he never dedicated more than a half-hearted effort, he descended to his business, the barroom bought by his father some sixty years ago. He examined his receipts from the previous day's sales, consulted with the cooks as to their needs, and drank a pot of coffee while calculating how much money should be in the old register that stood near the end of the bar. Before his barman arrived, he counted the money and separated it into two piles. The first pile, and what he hoped was the larger one, formed the deposit he made at the bank around the corner. The second pile he returned to the register to make change. Lately, that first pile was losing altitude when compared to the second. He pondered the meaning of that and what he could do to reverse the descent.

With his fiduciary duties fulfilled, Charlie spoke with his barman, Herr Koch, about the news of the day. At last, he drove his pickup truck four miles out of town, to a grove of Divi trees where he kept a house surrounded by some rental bungalows, a tiny painting studio, and a pavilion with an outdoor bar. His property fronted the ocean and featured a small pier, which was perfect as a swimming platform. Here he spent the rest of his morning and the early afternoon painting, talking with his friends, and finishing little projects. Then it was a short nap, a shower, and a drive back to town. He chatted up the tourists at the bar. They liked his bawdy jokes, his willingness to be photographed with them, his gently urging the ladies to take off their tops and drink for free as long as they remained disrobed.

His nights were something else. He closed his bar early, never later than ten. After ten, drunks and brawlers rambled about, looking for a place to puke, either in the bathroom or a less convenient place. With the bar shuttered, he had a choice to make. He could visit his girlfriend. He could stay home with his wife. Or, he could go out on the town, have a few glasses of rum, and meet a nice girl. He varied his choice with his mood, indulging in the sumptuousness of each one as often as the other but without any pattern. He believed it was impossible to live free without the challenge of random events. The possibility of bizarre happenings excited him.

"You have to improvise!" Charlie told his cat. This cat was named Screwball. His predecessors were named Snowball and Eight Ball for their colors. This one was something of a calico mixed with who knew what. The cat wasn't handsome, but he knew how to live, and that's what counted in Charlie's eyes. The cat stretched, yawned, and closed his eyes.

Charlie inhaled the last smoke from his cigarette. He never smoked in his residence. In fact, he despised the smell of tobacco smoke even as he pulled the last drag through his mouth. This contradiction explained much about his life and the island where he lived. The desire for vice and the pleasure of its enjoyment stood against the human insistence on regulating such things. Of course, when clever bureaucrats needed more money, they were quick to tax vice in the name of the greater good. Or, if they found themselves feeling righteous, either in the name of the Lord or human dignity, they would pressure the bars and brothels to operate in the darkest of corners and the latest hours of the night.

His Dutch ancestors, bureaucrats of the first order, thought themselves capable of administrating any enterprise. They turned out to be mostly talk and less action if judged by the current length and breadth of their empire. Charlie existed in an insignificant corner of that empire's remnants. Still, he was grateful to those who had gone before him. They were the ones who wrestled Aruba away from the Spanish, who stood up to the South Americans from time to time, and who were willing to leave the place to its own devices so long as they weren't too expensive.

Charlie took another look down at the street. It had two names: Van Zeppenveldstraat, the name given it by the original Dutch islanders, and Main Street, the name everyone called it. To his left were two of the oldest bars in town: Caribbean and the Chesterfield. The girls employed there, like every one of them working in this town, were from Colombia. They came to Aruba for a ninety-day "tour of duty," as he liked to think of it. When ninety days expired, they were shipped back to Colombia and were not permitted to return to work for an entire year or as a tourist for five years. So sayeth the law. However, some came back early, the ones who found reliable clients or who made a lot of money and wanted to do a repeat performance. They forged documents, stole a sister's passport, or paid an immigration officer to look the other way. If caught they were unceremoniously deported, a small risk compared to the reward of earning a month's salary in a single night.

He turned to his right where there were twelve more bars, among them: Copacabana, Ron and Menta's, Minchi's, China Clipper, Bongo, Java, Black & White, and Pianito. Twelve bars meant at least forty-eight girls, for with rare exception, each bar had governmental permits allowing four girls to work as prostitutes, which the bureaucrats euphemistically referred to as hostesses. The other bars were on streets to the east and west, within the Zone of Tolerance as the Dutchmen officially referred to it. If he wanted to, he could inspect all the merchandise and have a bit of a stroll while he was at it. There was nothing like exercise with a view.

At times, there were fewer girls in a bar than was permitted. The bar owners tried to avoid this situation. They charged a daily rate for the room in which a girl lived and worked. At present, that rate was fifty dollars. Charlie had to sell about seventeen glasses of beer to gross fifty dollars at his bar. The prostitute had to spend half an hour with a man to earn ten dollars less. The talented ones, the professionals, were able to complete the act in half that time, thereby multiplying their earning potential.

For Charlie, the idea of going back to the girl's room lacked any appeal. He never rushed anything, least of all his sexual exploits. Thirty minutes in a box with an old mattress, a worn-out sheet, and barely enough light to untie his shoes was not his thing. He enjoyed the romance of playing the charming gentleman, which wasn't so much an act as who he really was. A girl in these circumstances needed to relax, to experience a change of scenery, to have a quiet and nutritious meal. Then, when they had chatted about her part of Colombia, perhaps a bit about her child (most every one of them had a child or two and no husband), they moved to the bed, which was one of his preference: wide and firm and spotlessly clean. Since the girl knew him and his manners, she didn't mind a decent amount of light. He could see her body clearly and thereby add to his enjoyment and protect himself from the more obvious medical calamities.

His approach to this endeavor required patience. Not every girl was keen on leaving the bar. A girl working steadily might earn less money with one man than with the four, five, or more who might patronize her during the course of the night. Beyond that, he wanted a girl whose personality meshed with his in an easy fashion so the time leading up to the act was more courtship than a business transaction. Finding one like that took time and skill.

And yet, he never lost his sense of perspective. He kept tucked away, like an old coin in the back of a drawer, the thought that this was not about love or friendship or anything less than business. These girls came here to make money. If they wanted to do it for free, they would have stayed home. Therefore, while he was charming and they were accommodating, no one was a fool.

A car rolled beneath his balcony, flashed its signal, and turned right. Charlie watched his lifelong friend Sam park at the end of the block. He couldn't help but smile at the man's reliability and persistence. No one but Sam took the time to make his birthday a grand affair. Unfortunately, and despite Charlie's constant warnings, Sam fell prey to indomitable emotions with regard to the girls working in San Nicolaas and frequently found himself miserably heartbroken, a condition Charlie studiously avoided.

"Thanks to Sam, we're in for a nice time," Charlie said to Screwball. "Unless something else comes up. You never know. Eh? Let's hope we have a party and something else."

The cat shifted on the parapet, licked his forepaw, and once again put his head upon it.

Something else? Charlie asked himself. What could it be? Well, this town was named San Nicolaas and not for the Jolly Old Saint Nicholas the Americans called Santa Claus. Nonetheless, the town gave its gifts (such as they were) to one and all, Charlie included. Christmas was every night of the week, every day of the year, with the exception of the actual Christmas Day, New Year's, Carnival Saturday, and Easter Sunday. And on those days, too, an enterprising man need only walk the lane known as Rembrandtstraat, peek into the caged halls leading to the rooms upstairs, and call out. Someone would reply. Someone would unlock the door, lead the man to a room, and provide the service of the oldest profession. The experience could be another meaningless act, or it might change somebody's life. As he knew, the outcome depended on the man, the woman, and the people in between.

Charlie stubbed out his cigarette and looked over the street one more time. "Welcome to San Nicolaas," he said. "We're open for business."

CHARLIE'S FATHER had built the Lido in 1950, and it was Sam's first stop of the evening. After running it as a nightclub for twenty-two years, Charlie Senior sold it to two brothers from Holland who reduced it to a full-service restaurant. Sam liked to eat at the table in the back corner, where he could inspect the crowd and tell stories about the place before it was ruined by those tulip-pluckers. The brothers had done away with live music and dancing, a sin Sam never forgave, but the food was outstanding.

Sam belonged to an odd club of people known as Arucanos. Born in Aruba but to American parents, he enjoyed a sort of untidy dual citizenship: an American by nationality, an Aruban at heart. Like an immigrant pining for the old country, he never denied his love for Aruba, his childhood home.

Since the day he left for college, he longed to replace the rambunctious diversity of San Nicolaas. He tried to find it working on such varied projects as the Alaskan Pipeline and a highway through a remote corner of Australia. Neither one satisfied his taste for romantic overindulgence, but the worldly experience he'd earned in business management taught him to be a perceptive observer who saw through the nonsense to the real issue. In the end he settled in Miami, opened a one-man consultancy, and hired himself out as a troubleshooter to big corporations. More important, Miami was little more than two hours from Aruba, and thanks to the tourists, there were three flights a day.

Despite being separated by vast distances, Sam and Charlie never lost touch over the years. Since Charlie embodied all things Aruban, Sam honored his boyhood friend in a manner befitting a sacred idol residing in the holy of holies. As soon as he started earning a decent salary, he turned Charlie's birthday into a spectacle, which was never so much fun as when he and his merry bunch all showed up for a week-long binge in San Nicolaas. The trouble was Sam's "littermates," as he referred to the group of Arucanos that were close to his age, had fallen from the fold. One by one, they excused themselves with explanations about work, family, and old age. Sam believed fifty-five was too young to be giving up anything but more hours at the office. Just the same, he found himself hosting more locals and fewer Arucanos. It didn't matter because Charlie's birthday was a holy day of obligation for him, one he never missed.

Sam enjoyed cruising San Nicolaas to check for anything new that might have cropped up. Naturally, he sat at Charlie's Bar for a few hours, regaling tourists with tales of Aruba from years gone by. Inevitably, someone asked what it was like to live here. "Paradise," he said, "but not for amateurs." He never explained what that meant, but the implication was that a tourist who dreamed of living here was not so much unwelcome as unqualified. "In other words," Sam said, "if I have to explain it to you, forget it." It was his cue to exit the stage with an air of mystery behind him. He timed his response to the last sip of his drink. He paused three long seconds while everyone waited for him to say something profound. Instead of imparting any words of wisdom, he gave the audience a sly smile. At last, he drained the glass in a single gulp and slammed it on the bar. He pointed his finger at whoever had asked the question, winked, and walked out the door.

Herr Koch rolled his eyes at Sam's performances. He had seen the act so many times he could do a flawless imitation, but not until Sam was down the street. Then Koch took the glass, rinsed it in the sink, and winked at the stack of them on the drain board. He turned back to the crowd, and invariably someone wanted to hear about the mystery man. Koch waved a hand dismissively. "Local character," was Koch's standard answer. Had Sam heard the remark, he would have smiled at such a compliment. After all, he'd been born there and it was his life's goal to live on the island and nowhere else.

Living in paradise was one thing, but it would be a waste to do it alone. Thus, he had to find a suitable companion, and she had to be of a certain type. The thing for Sam was that he found most of the women he'd known, including his two ex-wives, lacking the combination of subtlety and drama he'd encountered among young women working in the San Nicolaas bars. He preferred smoldering Latina charm to the brash certitude of American women. As for those aggressive Aussie broads, they could stay a hemisphere away where they belonged.

Charlie chided Sam for falling in love with the San Nicolaas girls. He denied he actually fell in love, explaining that he simply enjoyed the experience as if the money he paid had nothing to do with it. Like a movie, he let himself believe the lie for as long as it lasted. He liked to find a girl who clicked, someone he found more comfortable than his old deck shoes. Depending on the length of his trip, he spent several days or as long as two weeks with her. If she was a particularly good fit, he would fly back to see her, call her in Colombia, or send a few hundred dollars to help her along. Charlie scoffed at this, but Sam relished the thrill of making a girl smile, especially one who appreciated his lifestyle. If she liked to soak up the sunrise after dancing all night, cook meals over an open fire, and swim naked, she was the woman for him.

On his way through the Lido's front door, Sam found himself standing face to face with San Nicolaas Police Chief Jules Calenda.

"Good evening, Sam," Calenda said.

"*Bon nochi*," Sam replied slipping into local patois to confirm his status as equal to Calenda's birthright.

"Tell me, how long is your visit?" the policeman asked.

"I'm home," Sam retorted. "I visit the other place, the one up north." He pointed in the general direction of the United States.

"Of course! I just returned from a visit of my own, a joint training course with the New York City Police Department. Fascinating work in community policing."

"I'll bet," Sam said.

Calenda donned his hat and asked, "Have you started to build your house?"

"Soon."

"I'm glad to hear it. I suppose you're ready for Charlie's party?"

"Everything but the girl," Sam answered.

"Don't forget," Calenda said on his way outside, "you can take a girlfriend anywhere on the island, but if money changes hands, be sure you're in San Nicolaas."

"Yes, sir," Sam acknowledged and headed for his favorite table.

Forty-five minutes later, Sam stepped out of the Lido and into the night. He felt like he was sixteen again, as he did every year when Charlie's birthday came.

He tugged at his shirt, flapping the fabric against his skin, wishing a breeze would draw the heat away from the island. Breeze or no breeze, he had his routine. He started at the beginning, walking to the east end of Main Street where he gazed at the frame of the half-finished hotel. It hadn't changed in five years, standing there like the bones of a dead whale, a home for vagrants, who were called chollers in Aruba. Over his shoulder was the first bar on that side of town. It was up thirty-two shallow, uneven steps. Before getting melancholy, he climbed the stairs and began his mission.

He passed through five bars without finding a girl who clicked. A few almost fit the bill. One blonde in particular caught his eye. She had a face that could grace the cover of any magazine and a set of legs that could only be seen on the inside pages. The problem was she had an attitude to go with the look. Sam didn't care for haughty broads and left without buying a single drink. A second beauty at Black & White Bar approached him from out of the blue. She was also blonde and came highly recommended by José, the bar's owner. Sam bought her a vino and chatted her up a few minutes. Then, in a whining voice, she begged for a trip to her room, thereby spoiling the buildup. That kind of aggression put him off like bad breath, warts, and rotten teeth. He was looking for a little class with a bit of sweetness, not a quick bang and a shove out the door.

He entered Java Bar, where he knew he could find a friendly face. Kenny, Java's bartender, had played host to Sam and his friends for the past twenty years, since he returned from a job as a pit boss at a London casino. His mother happened to own Java as well as the Chesterfield.

"Sammy, my man!" Kenny said slapping a coaster on the bar. "The usual?"

"*Bon nochi*, yourself," Sam replied sticking out his hand.

Kenny shook it and poured Sam a vodka tonic. "On the house," he said raising his own glass.

So it was that Kenny sold women like diamonds and Swiss Army knives. It depended on a man's desire or need: beauty or utility. He said, "The dark haired one in the corner is easy on the eyes, a little chunky, but friendly and sweet. Her friend over by the jukebox is good with her hands. I have one upstairs with massive breasts, absolutely massive. Because of circumstances beyond my control, I have one room empty."

Sam winced at Kenny's blunt assessment, wondering one more time what had happened to the gentlemanly ways of his youth. Bartenders used to let a customer have a drink or two, enjoy some gossip, and then casually mention a girl as interesting or pretty or fun. The lurid details were saved until much later and usually in the company of men exclusively.

"I just ran into Chief Calenda," Sam said, keeping his desire in check.

"He's been making regular rounds through town, checking the girls' permits, rousting drug dealers and kids who loiter in the alley alongside the bar," Kenny explained.

"Strutting his stuff," Sam remarked.

"It's good, Sammy. It's good. The girls have to work that alley. Better the cops run those pains in the ass out of there. The girls can get a few tricks before they go to bed. How else can they pay rent?"

"It's good if you say it is," Sam said. "Sounds like the trip to New York went to his head."

To change the subject, Kenny noted, "It's four weeks since Ricardo died."

Sam raised his glass again, this time in honor of the man who had owned Minchi's Bar, the next one down the street.

"He could have picked a better wife," Kenny commented.

Chuckling, Sam said, "We all could have. How about another drink and one for yourself?"

As he made the drinks, Kenny said, "I heard on the news from Curaçao that a boat sank in the storm which passed by several days ago."

Sam shrugged. "Boats always sink in storms."

"This was a tugboat, a big one. Sank just north of Curaçao."

"What was it doing there?"

"On its way to pick up a barge or something. I don't know if they found the crew."

"Probably dead. The ocean is no place to play, boy. I know. I remember when we brought Charlie's boat down from Lauderdale. We were in fifteen footers and damn near out of fuel. Charlie got us into Cuba. That took some doing, let me tell you."

Kenny knew the story. He'd heard it a hundred times, a hundred different versions of it, too. Sometimes the seas were rough; sometimes they were calm. One time they had no fuel. The other time they had no food. Some other time they had neither food nor fuel nor water.

"Ever wonder what you would do if you were shipwrecked on a desert island? Make yourself a little hut under the palms? Walk around naked? Shit where you liked?" Kenny asked.

"Unless it's this one I'd kill myself," Sam said.

Kenny noted a certain sullenness in Sam's attitude. No doubt this was the result of Sam's lacking a fitting companion. Kenny had to be careful which way things went. He didn't need a sad drunk at his bar, ruining the mood for everyone. Most of the time he liked having Sam around. He often bought a round or got things going with a dozen coins in the jukebox. He worked out the odds the way he used to at the blackjack tables, then said, "Why don't you check out the girls at Minchi's and come back and tell me what you found?"

Sam slapped the bar and pointed his finger at Kenny. "*¡Excellente!*" he proclaimed and strolled out the door.

Minchi's was only fifteen steps away from Java. The owner had been an old Aruban named Ricardo "Ricky" Cortés. Some time ago, he took up with Marcela, one of the toughest whores to come through town. He was known as "Ricky the Lion Tamer" until he married her and then no one said anything. Gradually, Ricky stopped tending personally to the affairs of the bar. He hired a bouncer named Spanner to do the hard work and a skinny guy named Pablo to pour drinks. His whore-turned-wife, Marcela, managed the bar's affairs, including the girls. She told Pablo how much liquor to put in a drink and how cold the beer should be. She cowed everyone but Spanner, and even he kept his mouth shut when she was in the bar. Sam had always wanted to ask Ricky what he saw in Marcela, but now the man was dead of a heart attack.

Sam passed through Minchi's swinging saloon doors at the same time as he lit a fresh cigarette. The effect was to enter the room behind a cloud of smoke, just like a gunfighter in the movies. He pulled it off perfectly.

Inside, he greeted Spanner with a handshake and a clap on the back. Pablo brought him a vodka tonic. Sam sat at the end of the bar without making eye contact with any of the girls. He knew they were there. He would get to them in his own time.

"I hear Calenda is making the rounds," he said to Spanner.

The bouncer looked over his mirrored pilot's glasses, put both palms on his chest and then turned them face up. He said, "*Policía* are *policía*, Sammy. We need them to take care of things, and they need us to have things to take care of. This is life. You should know."

"I know."

"Good. Then you know la Dueña is officially in charge," Spanner added.

"Ricardo's dead a month and you're calling Marcela the owner already?" Sam scoffed.

"It's true," Spanner replied seriously. "Ricardo is not coming back from the grave."

"What about his son?"

"Andrés is an artist. What does he want with a bar?"

"If it was his dad's, it should be his," Sam said.

Spanner wagged his finger. "The wife comes first. The child is second. You should know . . ."

Sam was tired of hearing about things he should know. He said, "Pablo, give me another and put some vodka in it this time."

Pablo made the drink the same way. Sam downed it in a single swallow before the bartender could turn away. When the glass hit the bar, Spanner put his hand atop it. He said, "Sammy, it's your first night. Why don't you go upstairs, man, take the pressure out of your vessel?"

"*Verdad, chico,*" Sam said and turned his back to Spanner. He looked at the girls. There were four of them, all dark haired, all wearing dresses. He liked when they wore dresses. It made them more ladylike. Lately, too many had taken to wearing pants, jeans even, like so many women in America. He didn't go for that unless the girl was particularly appealing in every other category.

Letting his cigarette lead the way, he sauntered across the room for a closer look. "*Buenas noches,*" he greeted them.

"*Hola,*" they replied, almost in unison.

"How many days in Aruba?" he asked. This was a critical piece of information. Any of these girls might be at the end of her tour. He didn't want another guy's hand-me-down.

One girl took the lead. She wore a strapless green dress and four-inch heels. Sam appreciated the look. The girl said, "A few days," in accented English. She didn't know it, but she had blown her chances with Sam. He didn't want a girl who spoke any English. She could understand everything he said, especially when he didn't want her to.

"*Excellente,*" he replied with a toothy grin.

"*Lo mismo,*" the next girl said. "*Somos amigas.*"

"*Excellente también,*" Sam said to her, knowing that she meant she was there the same number of days and was friends with the one in the green dress. His Spanish was passable when he was sober, which meant it was fine in San Nicolaas where most transactions required little explanation.

"*¿Amigas?*" he asked pointing at the other two girls.

They said, "No."

"*Por favor*," Sam prodded. "*¡Todos son amigos en San Nicolaas!*"

The girls looked at each other and grinned.

"Okay. *Comprendo. ¿Dias? ¿Cuántas? ¿Cuántas? ¿Cuántas?*"

The girl to his right said she had been there two weeks, and the other one, who wore a blue dress to her knees, said she was there less than a week, which was perfect. She understood the system, but not well enough to be comfortable. He took her hand and asked, "*¿Tu nombre?*"

"Luz," she answered looking at his eyes.

Oh, he liked that, the way she showed spunk in a shy way. He also liked the way she gently squeezed his hand. He took it to mean she appreciated contact that wasn't gross the way it was with most of the men who pawed over the girls. She knew he was a gentleman and honored him with the respect he deserved.

"*Ah, Luz. ¿La luz de la luna o del sol?*" The light of the moon or the sun, he wanted to know.

She smiled with one side of her mouth as she thought about the question. "*Los dos,*" she replied putting up her hand and wiggling two fingers to make the point.

"*¡Felicidades!*" Sam proclaimed, adding, "*Permiso, chicas,*" to the others. He steered Luz to a seat in the middle of the bar. The other girls went back to gossiping.

"Vino, Pablo," Sam ordered. "And another drink for me, with vodka, *por favor.*"

Pablo placed a tiny flute of sugary wine in front of Luz and Sam's drink beside it. He took a blue poker chip from a fishbowl beside the cash register and deposited it into a cup with the number three written on it.

"*¡Salud!*" Sam said raising his glass.

Luz met it with her own and sipped the vino. She looked at the man seated beside her and tried to size him up. He seemed to be in his midfifties. His hair was gray and neatly combed. He was thin but with a little belly that pushed out his shirt a couple of inches. The cologne he wore she knew cost more than most. His shoes were shiny and clean. She figured he had the money to go upstairs.

"A week," Sam began. "How do you like Aruba?"

"*Qué calor,*" she said fanning herself.

"Get used to it, sweetheart. When I was a kid growing up here, it hit a hundred ten degrees for three weeks in a row. We thought we would die!"

She believed him. The scenery of this desert island lent itself to what he was telling her.

"You must be from the mountains," Sam said. "*¿Bogotá?*"

"*Sí*," she answered.

"*¡Tan bueno!* I always wanted to go there. Maybe you can show me the city."

"If you come."

"Be careful what you wish for."

Without Luz's asking, he bought her another vino. This encouraged her. Any man who wanted to go upstairs had to buy at least two vinos, or pay for them, before he could go up. She watched Pablo put the second chip in her cup and raised the glass to her companion. She asked his name.

"*Samito*," he said. "*El Príncipe de San Nicolaas*."

"*Quien es el rey?*" she asked. If this man was a prince there had to be a king, though she sensed this was some kind of inside joke.

"Ah, *el rey, mi amor, el rey* is one great man, and he is the king of the entire island."

If he was such an important man, she doubted he came to San Nicolaas for this type of entertainment. Then again, it wasn't unheard of in the little bit of history she had studied.

"Charlie is the King of San Nicolaas and all Aruba. *Todo, mi amor*."

"Charlie," she repeated.

"*Sí*. You'll meet him. I'll introduce you. I've known him all my life."

She pretended to be impressed that Samito knew Charlie, the King of San Nicolaas and all the island. She took it as a good omen. So far, her stay had been barely profitable given all the expenses she had to pay. Maybe Samito would be generous. Maybe Charlie would be, too. She hoped so. She needed the money in the worst way.

"Pablo!" Sam called. "Keys!"

Pablo took the keys from beside cup number three and placed them on the bar before Luz. There was also a packaged condom.

"I'm not paying for the condom," Sam told him.

"Everyone pays for the condom," Pablo said. "It's the law."

"Calenda knows I bring my own."

Pablo stiffened. "Good for you, but I'm not going to tell Marcela that you didn't pay for one."

Sam dug deep into his pocket where he found two guilders. He tossed them at the bar. They bounced over his empty glass and landed on the floor. He turned his back and ushered Luz out of the room.

A staircase separated Minchi's from the next bar, Ron and Menta's. The straight flight of stairs led to the second floor landing, where there were two doors made of steel bars like the kind found in prisons. Luz used a key to open the door on the right. Her room and the other three for the girls in Minchi's were on that side.

When Luz opened the door to her room, a flood of cold air swirled around her and Samito. It refreshed her after the closeness of the bar downstairs. Sam hugged her from behind and kissed her ear.

"*Mucho frío,*" he said as he took a seat on the bed.

Luz locked the door and turned to face him. Samito looked her over from head to toe without hiding his lust. He wasted no time on her chest, but he lingered over her hips and legs. She turned her back to him because men seemed to like that side most of all.

Sam confirmed her assumption by saying, "*Tan linda.*"

Instead of tossing her clothes on the floor or a spare corner of the bed, she hung them neatly. The closet in her room had plenty of space since she'd brought only four outfits from Colombia. She opened the door and looked coyly at her client. He smiled and came to her side.

"Let's see what we have here," Sam said in English as he swung the closet door out of the way. A woman's closet was a goldmine of information. He immediately saw this chica wasn't lying to him when she said she had been in Aruba for only a week. She had a couple of dresses and a pair of jeans hanging on the rod. There were only two pairs of shoes at the bottom. Any whore with a set of legs as good as hers, and such a splendid attitude to go with them, would have filled every hanger by the end of the first month. He was willing to bet that in three weeks this space would be packed. Her makeup kit filled one drawer. The others were empty. She needed money, and if she treated him the way he liked, he would be happy to oblige.

"*¿Está bien?*" Luz asked when Samito turned back to her with a smile.

"*Perfecto,*" he grinned.

"*¿Amor?*" she asked with a hand toward the bed.

Sam looked at the bed, at the girl, and back at the bed. He didn't want to spoil the buildup. If he slept with her now, he wasted his chance to do it the right way back in Savaneta. The clock wasn't running in Savaneta. The bed didn't belong to someone else half an hour ago. He'd learned this method from Charlie, and the king knew best.

He picked up her hand and kissed it lightly. "Massage," he said. "Nude."

"*Cualquier tú quieres.*"

He disrobed, placing his shirt, pants, and shoes on a chair. Then he sprawled onto the bed without pulling back the duvet. The girl straddled his back, light as a leaf. Her hands kneaded his flesh and he nearly dozed off under her.

The clock beside the bed told Luz she had five minutes before time was up. She whispered in Samito's ear that they had to go. He moaned, rolled over, and pulled her down. He held her tight for a few seconds then released her. She got dressed deliberately but without haste. Samito watched her every move.

As she picked up the keys from the table beside the bed, her client put down two bank notes and a coin. One was a ten-guilder note, the other a twenty-five. The square coin she knew was worth five guilders. The going price for half an hour upstairs was fifty guilders, or forty U.S. dollars. She waited a moment for the other ten guilders. When Samito made no indication he was going to pay it, she took up the two bills and looked at his eyes.

"¿Señor?" she began then corrected herself with, "Mi príncipe, el precio …" She let the last word hang out there.

"I know the price. No amor, señorita. Massage only. That's a gift."

"Pero …," she protested.

He took her hands in his, kissed them, and continued speaking Spanish. "There will be more money later," he said. "You'll see."

What was she to do? She could complain to Pablo or to Spanner. They might mention it to Samito, or they might not. She'd heard about girls who complained. They got less and less business until they had to go home early with nothing but the clothes on their back, having sold the few garments they brought with them to meet expenses. It angered her that she'd spent the entire half hour with him, given him a good massage, which was not easy work, and had not been paid the full rate. She was told it was the rule that whatever the man did in the room he had to pay the rate. It seemed the rules were getting flexible and not in her favor.

"¿Promesa?" she asked Samito.

Now he had her where he wanted her. She wanted him to come back, and nothing was more gratifying than to be desired by a whore. The woman could have any man for the price, but she wanted him for what he promised. He silently nominated her as a candidate to be the one. This entitled her to attend Charlie's party, and if things went well, to an all expenses paid week on Sam's arm.

"Promesa," he said and tugged her hand toward the door.

As they descended the stairs he told her about the planned festivities and that he would pick her up at two o'clock.

"I'm not supposed to work outside the bar," Luz said, though she wanted to go to the party if for no other reason than to cut her expenses.

"This is fun, not work," Sam explained. "And don't worry about Chief Calenda," Sam replied. "I spoke to him less than two hours ago."

Luz reconsidered her initial impression of this client. Although he hadn't paid her properly, he seemed to have influence with the police. That is, if he was telling the truth. Then again, what was the worst thing that could happen? The police would arrest her and deport her back to Colombia. The way her stay in Aruba was going, that might be a blessing.

Back in the bar, Sam kissed Luz on the cheek and left her with the other girls. He strutted up to Pablo and Spanner, who were talking by themselves.

"Feel better?" Spanner asked him.

"Top of my game," Sam said.

"You're her first trick," Spanner said next.

Sam kept his composure despite the revelation. He knew the massage was not a mistake. It was proof he knew how to control himself, to follow Charlie's lead. He pointed his finger at Spanner, winked, and took his leave of the place.

"Business is bad, Sammy, why don't you go upstairs again?" Spanner called after him.

Sam went from one end of town to the other. Being a prince, he concentrated on his drinking and his old friends, all the while remaining cordial to the other girls. Since he'd found one who clicked, he wasn't going to waste time or energy in that area. Besides, he wanted to promote Charlie's party to ensure there was a critical mass of people to make it a full-blown celebration.

Every bartender knew him. Many of the regular patrons did, too. There were hugs and shared drinks, handshakes and stories, enough to take him through the night. He made a few new acquaintances, including an insurance salesman from Hoboken, New Jersey, named Barry. In Guadalajara Bar, he bumped into Roger, an old pal whose father had once been the chief of security for Esso. Roger's dad had chased Sam and Charlie on numerous occasions, incidents about which they laughed to this day.

"I'll be there," Roger assured Sam, "and my cousins Carlos and Manny, too, especially if you're doing the cooking."

Sam pointed his finger and winked. "I'm getting the fish from Old Man Juárez first thing in the morning."

"I can taste it already," Roger said, grinning.

"Bring your own girls," Sam advised. He was pleased the others would be in attendance. The party usually started off slow, just him and his friends. The crowd showed up later, in time for front-row seats to watch the sunset.

Having his fill of vodka, Sam checked his watch. It was just past one. If Luz had been working at another bar, he would have taken her back to his room at Charlie's in Savaneta. Most bars allowed a girl to leave before closing if the client paid the *molta*, a fee of twenty to one hundred guilders. However, Marcela demanded the girls work full shifts, which meant they remained in the bar until 4:00 AM. Sam thought this was stupid. It ruined morale, and morale was everything in this business. Girls who were tired, bored, or hungry turned lousy tricks. Sam wasn't about to explain this to Marcela. She was the type who could not care less how some Norte Americano thought she should run her husband's business.

Given that sharing the balance of the night with Luz was out of the question, Sam decided to head to another favorite spot, Chinaman's kitchen in the back of American Bar. He walked the long way so as to avoid passing Minchi's. He didn't want to see Luz there because it would mean she wasn't working and thereby was hurting for money. And if she wasn't there, he would also be chafed because she was upstairs with a man other than himself. His feelings were complicated. He knew they were prostitutes, that they serviced other clients, but he wasn't without a certain amount of feeling for a girl who caught his eye. He wanted her to do well, to have a better life. He could help make that happen so long as she followed his prescription for success, which was to act like a charming young lady. If she did that, he would be more generous than a rich man trying to enter the kingdom of heaven.

To avoid Minchi's, Sam walked down Rembrandtstraat. It was barely more than an alley. There were no sidewalks, just doors made of steel bars like animal cages that fronted the asphalt strip. A few odd shops nestled along the street. There was a lady who sold lottery tickets, prepaid telephone cards, and when she felt up to it, homemade sandwiches. One corner had rival minimarkets owned by two different Chinese families who brought their feud all the way from Guangdong Province. The rest of the doors led into the bars via hallways, off of which were the girls' rooms. During daylight hours or when a bar was closed, the girls loitered here to land clients. On paydays, the alley choked with traffic as men drove a loop which started at the south end of town and ran straight up Rembrandtstraat to the dead end at the hardware store, where it turned right. After two more blocks, it turned left onto Helfrichstraat to the point where it made a hairpin left onto Main Street. From there, it headed south to the starting point. The route was known as the San Nicolaas Five Hundred by those who used it. Some guys drove fifty miles a week on the San Nicolaas Five Hundred. Gas station owners and tire dealers loved it.

Halfway to American Bar a scrawny black man called out to him.

"*¡Samito!*"

Sam stopped short. The guy angling toward him had both hands in the air to get his attention. "Frankie!" Sam called back. "Take your time. I'm going nowhere, chico."

Frankie didn't slow down. He walked as fast as he could without breaking into a run. His shoes made this difficult. There were no laces and hardly any sole remained between his foot and the asphalt. He wore ragged cargo pants and a torn T-shirt. The government saw to it that his head was shaved every month. As it had been two weeks since the last cut, his hair was looking as disheveled as his clothes.

"How about a florin?" Frankie said as he rolled up to Sam. "I'm hungry."

"A florin, Frankie, for something to eat?"

"Come on. What's a florin to a big man like you?"

"A florin is nothing to me, Frankie, so I'll give you five," Sam said, fingering a square coin. "I'll give you five because you're the only choller who can beg in multiple languages."

Frankie snapped to attention and said in rapid succession, "*¡Sí, señor!* Yes, sir! *Ja, mein herr!*"

Sam remarked, "Save something for your dentist."

Frankie dropped his head in shame. It was true that his mouth looked like a drawer full of rusty nails but rude of Sam to point it out. He wiped a tear that wasn't on his cheek and tried to hand the coin back to Sam. "If you're going to be nasty, I don't want the money."

"Ah, shut up, Frankie. I've got a bum tooth, myself."

"Then you know what it's like," Frankie said and drifted back into the shadow where he waited for his next chance to beg a few guilders.

Sam crossed Main Street and walked through a passageway that led to the westernmost street in town, Rogerstraat, the one which bordered the refinery wall. He turned left and entered American Bar, where the Stars and Stripes hung on the wall and Budweiser was the only beer served. In the back was the kitchen and tiny dining room operated by Chinaman, who had no other name to anyone who knew him, including the two feuding families of Rembrandtstraat who sought him out to mediate their battles.

Flopping onto a plastic chair, Sam declared, "Anything Soup!"

Anything Soup consisted of a thin broth filled with noodles, a few vegetables, and other leftovers. It came in a bowl the size of a helmet. Sam was passed out in the chair by the time Chinaman served him.

"You wake up!" Chinaman said. "Soup here!"

Sam forced his eyes open. They were pasty and bloodshot. He looked down at the soup. Relief was in sight. Chinaman put out his hand. Sam slapped a five-florin coin into it.

"Six guilder. Six florin. Same thing."

"Since when is it six guilders?" Sam protested.

"Since two month ago," Chinaman answered.

He paid the extra money and dismissed Chinaman. The soup, a salty brine, flushed down his throat like hot seawater.

Bloated from a night of drinking and a late meal, he started for his car. He had a long list of things to do in the morning, enough for two people to do, which meant the perfect amount of work to keep his mind off more tempting distractions like the girl from Minchi's.

Was Luz *the one*? In other words, the one to join him in his house by the sea? She was definitely in the running. He'd been to the island four times in the last year and had not encountered another girl who showed the same strength and pluck that Luz had. He liked the way she challenged him about the money, how she looked into his eyes, and above all, how she held his hand and kissed his cheek. This girl was a charmer, not a vamp. He touched the medallion that hung from his chest and prayed silently she would not let the job turn her into someone like Marcela.

Whatever happened with Luz, there was work to be done. Old Man Juárez bumped the dock just after dawn. Sam was never second in line to buy his fish. It was the best or nothing for him, and he deserved it. He was *el Príncipe de San Nicolaas.*

SAM WAS on his feet before dawn. In an attempt to knock out a hangover before it began, he splashed a shot of vodka into a glass of orange juice, then spent a few shaky minutes making his bed and hanging up his clothes. As it was, his room was small. There was sufficient space for a twin bed, two nightstands, and one bureau but barely enough space to walk around three sides of the bed. The bathroom consisted of a tiled shower stall, a pedestal sink, and a toilet crammed into the corner. This combination of rooms Charlie let him have free of charge whenever he came to the island. They called it the Dog House. It had been an addition that shared a wall with the old Cunucu house Charlie had refurbished as the centerpiece of his Savaneta retreat.

Satisfied his room would be presentable for Luz's first visit, Sam headed to Zeerovers Fisherman's Wharf for the first catch of the day. He wasn't the only early morning shopper. There were two hotel buyers and a bunch of homemakers. He smiled as Old Man Juárez flopped a giant red snapper on the scale. To the dismay of the people behind him, Sam bought it and another one. Juárez made the others wait while he filleted the fish for Sam, which only added insult to their injury. They lacked the patience of the old tomcat that bided his time under the packing crates. The feline knew there would be guts and heads to feast on. He never so much as got his paws wet to catch a meal, but he ate better than any animal on the island, probably better than half the people judging by the size of him.

Sam iced the fish in a cooler and refused to let the now mounting hangover keep him from his appointed tasks. He blasted the air conditioner in the little Nissan he'd rented and set off in search of provisions. Jeweler Ivan Stansky, who once owned a store on the upper end of Main Street, brought a Cadillac to the island in 1956. It was the first car equipped with airco that Sam had driven. After washing and waxing the car for Ivan, he would drive the long way back to the jewelry shop so the airco could catch up with the heat of the day. Sam liked Ivan. The jeweler tipped well and taught him the fundamentals of business.

Here he was, decades later, driving a car less than half the size of that Cadillac. However, the airco worked perfectly, which was a blessing given his condition. He fought off the urge to vomit. Did he drink that much last night? He couldn't have. He was in bed by two o'clock, seven hours ago. Yet, he felt terrible. Could it be he was getting too old for this lifestyle? "No way in hell," he said aloud and switched on the radio.

He secured seven cases of mixers from Herr Koch, who doubted he would be able to get things together for the party. But the Prince of San Nicolaas was undeterred. He wrangled a pair of pork loins, a dozen strip steaks, and half a dozen racks of ribs from an ornery butcher. He busted his hump cleaning Charlie's out-door bar and pavilion. The barbecue was particularly challenging given the axle-grease-like substance on the grate. He wondered what the interlopers who rented the bungalows cooked that left muck like that. Wildebeest flanks? Whatever it was, he got it off and built a proper Boy Scout fire under it. After checking out the stereo system, he went to the storage room for the sets of white Christmas lights which he strung around the biggest Divi tree, across the patio dance floor, and finally to the porch in front of the apartments.

He repaired to the kitchen for the final phase of preparations. After blending a savory marinade from a secret recipe of spices, liquor, and molasses, he whipped up a pot of dry rub for the fish. He laughed aloud, remembering that Juárez fished every night but Friday because he believed Jesus multiplied the loaves and the fishes on a Friday and did not want to be so arrogant as to compete with the Savior when it came to feeding the masses. To the other fishermen, this made no sense given that Sunday was the Lord's Day. Juárez didn't care what fishermen or priests or cooks said. Who were they to tell him how things should be when he spoke to God while fishing under the stars as he did?

To celebrate completing a job well done, Sam walked out on the pier and stared down at the swimming hole in the sandy bottom of the ocean. He pulled off his shirt and leapt into the sea like a seven-year-old, a grin on his face and his fingers pinching his nose. The water broke around him, cool and soft. Coming up for air, he let the sun blaze through his closed eyelids. He flipped to his side and stroked a few laps around the pier, working the last of the hangover out of his system, then climbed up the ladder. He shook out a cigarette, lit it with the Zippo lighter given to him by Charlie twenty years ago when Sam had started his consultancy.

"What a great life!" Sam told himself. Sun, sea, and fresh air. Good friends on the way. Excellent food and happy times waiting for all. He wasn't worried about a thing — not that he was acting like a teenager nor that the consequences of his binges in Aruba might catch up to him. He had a plan, and he was right on track.

The plan was to build a house on the island, find the woman of his dreams, and after he used a one-way ticket south, hang his passport in a nice frame on his bedroom wall. He already owned the land on which his house would be built. He had most of the money he needed to retire early. As for the girl of his dreams? Well, Luz was available. Paradise, with all its accoutrements, was his for the asking.

He looked out at the waves breaking over the reef just a hundred yards from the end of the pier. The reef sheltered a stretch of beach that began at the west end of San Nicolaas and ended four miles later where Savaneta became another town called Pos Chiquito. Sandbars fringing the reef shifted with the currents that changed direction several times during the year. Hurricanes never made landfall on Aruba, but they came close enough to redirect the wind and with it the water. It was a fool who got caught up in something that powerful, just like the people who got wrapped up in careers they thought were the only important thing in the world. There was more to life than making money. Sam heard people say that all the time, but what did they do about it? They went to work every day as if there was nothing beyond the paycheck but a waiting grave, as if they didn't go they would catch cancer. Sure, they took vacations like the touristas who filled the hotels on the other end of the island, "the other side of the bridge," as he liked to say. They spent a week lounging by the beach, sipping fruity drinks, talking about how great it would be to live in a place like Aruba. But they never took the time to make it happen.

Feeling refreshed and confident Sam returned to his room for a hard-earned nap. He took a seat on the bed and mulled over how he was going to spring Luz from Minchi's for more than a Sunday afternoon. He needed several days of her undivided attention in order to determine if she was worth a significant investment of time and money. The trouble wasn't Chief Calenda, who was a letter-of-the-law type of guy. It was Marcela, who was a law unto herself. Despite his years on the streets of San Nicolaas, he remembered only a few facts about her. If he was not mistaken, she had worked at Las Vegas Bar. The last three weeks of her final tour she had lived with Ricardo, who bought out her contract. He flew to Colombia to marry her some months later. When the Aruban government fussed over the paperwork, he married her again on the island. These bits of information Sam received secondhand, and he had not known Ricardo well enough to verify them. No matter her history, Marcela's current reputation as an enforcer was one of brutal swiftness. Girls who broke the rules were fined. Girls who continued to break the rules were sent home on the next flight. Sam didn't want that to happen to Luz, not this early in her tour. He decided to take it one step at a time. The party came first. After that, he would improvise and come up with something that would make Charlie proud.

When he left his room two hours later, Sam wore a fresh cane cutter shirt and his most comfortable slacks. His hair was perfect, his teeth clean, and his eyes shined with excitement. He bee-lined for San Nicolaas with all due haste, praying Chief Calenda was busy with more important matters than speeding tickets.

He took Rogerstraat first. There were only three bars on that street, American, Caracas, and Tropicana, all at the end near the refinery gate. He slowed down but wished he hadn't. The girls on display wore too much make up and not enough clothes. He smiled and waved just the same.

He rounded the corner, passed Main Street, and turned left onto Rembrandt-straat. The first couple of doors were empty. The third, behind Pianito, featured two good-looking specimens of the type his old pals liked. Sam continued until he got to Minchi's, where he stopped and exited the car. One of the girls from the night before blocked the doorway.

"*Hola, mami,*" Sam said.

"*Hola, Samito,*" the girl replied.

"Where's Luz?" he asked.

"I don't know."

"*Perdóname,* but no bullshit."

She shook her head. "No bullshit."

"Okay, let me pass."

She turned sideways but didn't leave the doorway. He forced his way past, brushing her chest as he did. It wasn't a bad set of tits but not what he wanted just now. Upstairs, he looked around the common area where the girls shared their meals. He knocked on the door to room number three.

"*¿Quien es?*" came the reply.

"*El Príncipe de San Nicolaas,*" Sam told her.

Ten seconds passed before Luz opened the door and said, "*Señor,* I cannot leave the bar."

Sam barged into the room, picked Luz off her feet, and smacked her face with a dozen kisses. She put her arms against his chest and tried to pry out of his grasp. He didn't stop kissing her until he started laughing and then she giggled, too. They fell down on the bed, where he stroked her hair and kissed her ear softly.

"Come to the party," he said. "We're going to have a feast. Take a swim in the ocean. Do some dancing if you want. If you don't like it, I'll take you home."

"To Colombia?"

"No, back here."

"*Mi príncipe*," Luz said, "La Dueña does not permit us to leave the bar."

"When the bar is closed, you can go wherever you want. I'm not leaving unless you go with me." Sam peeled up the covers from the edge of the bed and rolled himself into them.

"This man!" she thought. He was playful enough, like a little boy, but he had to understand she needed to work the street. She would be in debt up to her ears if she didn't find paying clients soon. At the same time, she was hungry, and he had said there was going to be food.

"One hour," she said holding her finger up. "*Sesenta minutos. No mas.*"

"*No mas, mami*," Sam replied, unrolling from the duvet. After fixing the covers, he told her he would wait for her in the car.

Downstairs, Sam found Roger and his cousin Carlos passing by, each with a carload of girls. There were five packed into Roger's little Toyota, which made it look like a clown-mobile at the circus.

"See you at the party!" Roger called to him.

"Thanks for the warning!" Sam yelled back.

Luz appeared with a tiny bag over her shoulder and a pair of sunglasses atop her head. When she was safely in the passenger seat, he got behind the wheel and checked his mirror before pulling out.

When they were beyond the limits of town, he put his hand on Luz's thigh and said. "I hope you're hungry."

"One hour," Luz reminded Sam.

"Relax. You want to come back in an hour, that's what you do. No problem. Just make me a promise. If you have a good time, stay as long as the party lasts. Okay?"

Luz pushed her hair behind her ears and looked out the window. She suddenly worried that she would be trapped at the party with no way of getting back to the bar.

"Here," Sam said holding out his hand.

Luz saw the folded bill pinched in his fingers. A man had come to Minchi's with a roll of those hundred-dollar bills. He never gave her one, but he spent them on other girls and on liquor, too. Pablo complained whenever he changed them. Apparently, a lot of fakes were in circulation.

"Are you going to take the money?" Sam asked her.

She took it. That's why she'd come to Aruba, to make money, not to be a whore, although that's what she had to be to make money. She folded the bill into a small strip. When it was deep in the pocket of her jeans, she said quietly, *"Gracias."*

"Will you please smile?"

She smiled for him in her reserved way, the way that had charmed Sam into thinking she might be *the one.*

"That's it. Come on, it's Charlie's birthday. This is the most important day of the year."

"More important than Christmas?" she asked.

"Christmas? Whose birthday is that?"

"Señor," she said solemnly. "Don't say such things."

"Charlie is the King of Aruba. This is his day. It's my duty to make sure it is fantastic."

At Charlie's in Savaneta, he parked out of the way, where the car was less likely to be dented by a drunken reveler making an uncontrolled departure. This happened from time to time and was an expensive inconvenience.

"Introductions," Roger said as Sam walked up with his arm around Luz.

"You first, champion," Sam replied.

Roger stood up, cleared his throat like an emcee, and waved at the five girls standing at the bar. "Our first contestant is Juanita. She's from Cali. Then we have two from Bogotá. They are Jenny, a very un-Colombian name, and Dahlia, a pretty flower if ever there was one. Also from Cali is the lovely Maria, not to be confused with the Lord's mother. And finally, from a small town somewhere near the Venezuelan border, is Laura. Oh, and that last one over there is Carlos, but he's *ocupado* already." The guys laughed while the girls checked things out.

"This is Luz," Sam said to his friends.

"Mucho gusto," Roger said, putting out his hand.

Luz shook it gently. She didn't know what to make of these men, but they seemed to be enjoying themselves in harmless ways.

"Nice choice," Carlos stage-whispered.

"Watch it, chico," Sam said, "Get the girls some drinks while I fire up the barbecue."

"Yes, sir."

Sam took Luz to the barbecue, where he showed her the perfection of his Boy Scout campfire. He wasted no matches in the breeze. Instead, he used his Zippo. It ignited on the first try and stood up to the breeze like a flare at the refinery.

"Something to drink?" he asked Luz.

"*Agua.*"

"Water? *Mami*, please. How about a beer? No. Whiskey? No. Alright, maybe Baileys? Ah, I think I saw a smile there. Baileys it is." Sam poured a reasonable amount of Baileys into a cup with ice.

Luz sipped the drink. It was delicious in the heat of the day.

"Okay. Snacks," Sam said and went off to the kitchen. He drafted Roger on the way. When they were in the kitchen together, he said, "What do you think?"

"She's nice," Roger replied.

"Nice? Please, she's better than anyone I've seen in more than a year."

"Maybe she's *the one.*"

"We'll soon find out. Bring that tray of cheese and stuff, will you? And where's Manny?"

"On his way," Roger answered and took the tray, added an armful of cracker boxes, and headed outside. Sam hefted a bowl of salsa and two giant bags of tortilla chips. At the bar, he organized the food to make it appealing. He took a taste of each thing to make sure it was perfect. He told the girls to help themselves, spearing a cheese cube with a toothpick and pointing it at the nearest girl's mouth.

"Here we go!" Sam shouted and clapped his hands to the music. He turned the volume up a few notches. His dancing amused the girls. They pointed at his hips as he rocked to the salsa as if he were the Latin King himself. He came out from behind the bar and took Luz into his arms. She fell into the rhythm with him. Soon everyone but Carlos was dancing. He tended the fire and poured drinks so no one went thirsty.

"Oh, shit!" Sam cried suddenly. "I forgot the cake!" Without another word, he jogged to his car and sped off.

Luz accepted a second glass of Baileys from Carlos and chatted with Jenny, a girl she recognized from Rembrandtstraat.

"This place is pretty," Jenny said. She and Luz gazed at the pavilion with its outdoor bar, the nearby barbecue, and the surrounding bungalows that were tucked among Divi trees and wild foliage. All of it was less than fifty feet from a beach fringed with coconut palms.

"I'm worried." Luz said. "We're not supposed to work outside of San Nicolaas."

Jenny waved her concern into the breeze. "What are they going to do, arrest us all?"

Luz turned her head and took a taste of her drink.

"You came with Samito," Jenny said next. "I hear he has a lot of money."

Luz turned away from Jenny. Samito had given her a hundred dollars, but she wasn't about to volunteer that piece of information.

"Another girl told me he comes to Aruba all the time. She said he wanted to marry a girl and live here with her. Maybe you'll get lucky."

"Maybe," Luz said but kept her eyes toward the ocean.

"You like the ocean?" Jenny asked.

"I've never been in."

"Want to go for a swim?"

Before Luz could answer, Jenny pulled off her shirt and started walking toward a wooden pier that protruded into the sea. A car stopped at the pavilion. A man about Sam's age hopped out of the passenger side and ran up behind Jenny. He tugged down her shorts. She screeched and slapped him playfully then kicked off the shorts to reveal her thong bathing suit. Carlos whistled from the bar.

Jenny and the guy bolted for the end of the pier. She dove off the end, came up for air, and waved her bikini top over her head like a signal flag. Luz watched from the dock, turning every few minutes to see if Sam had returned.

"Come in!" Jenny called to her.

"Shark in the water," the guy said as he swam up behind Jenny. He cupped her breasts and nuzzled her neck. Jenny fell back on him, pushing him under. He came up, got in front of her, and kissed her neck.

Luz turned away. She didn't want to watch the antics of another couple. Just then, Samito pulled up trailing a cloud of dust. After the air cleared, he took a box from the back seat and carried it into the house. She followed his path toward the kitchen door. He met her on his way out.

"Having a good time?" he asked.

"Sí, gracias," she answered.

"¡Fantastico! Let's do some cooking." He took her by the hand and danced her across the patio to the barbecue. The fire needed about fifteen more minutes, just enough time for him to get everything outside. The two of them carried out the meat, grill utensils, and spices. She tied an apron around Sam's waist. He drew two pairs of tongs like six shooters and pointed them at her. "We're going to feast, mami!" he said.

His enthusiasm fascinated her. It was more like a professional athlete's than a child's. He was doing what he loved, and he loved doing it right. Each piece of meat underwent careful inspection. He dabbed more marinade on it then smacked it onto the grill. When it sizzled on the grate, he clapped his hands and sniffed the aroma. While the steaks grilled, he rubbed spices over the fish. He also salted the vegetables and wrapped them in aluminum foil. He budgeted the space on the grate effectively so all the food would be ready to eat at the same time.

Roger and Carlos brought trays to receive Sam's creations. He cleared the grill one piece at a time until everything was off except two steaks and two pieces of fish. He looked to Luz and winked. She smiled back at him.

They sat at the bar, where Carlos had plates and utensils set up. Jenny and her partner came running when they heard the food was ready.

Upon seeing the guy, Sam smacked the bar and shouted, "You lying sack of . . . When did you get in, Tom?"

Tom smirked. "About an hour ago. Manny gave me a ride," he said pointing his finger across the pavilion at Manny, who was acquainting himself with one of the girls.

"Why didn't you tell me you were coming?"

"Surprises are better," Tom answered.

"What about the other guys?" Sam inquired.

"Ah, you know, they have their excuses."

After a shrug, Sam raised his glass. "To our dear friend, Charles," he said. "May he show up soon."

Just then the man himself pulled to a halt in front of the house. He walked around to the patio and threw his arms in the air. "You started without me!"

"There's plenty," Sam said.

"I know," Charlie replied smiling. "Let's have the cake."

"First, I have one for you to meet," Sam told him. "This is Luz."

"*Mucho gusto,*" Charlie said to her, bowing slightly. He continued in Spanish, "I see you're with the Crown Prince of San Nicolaas. As the king, I must warn you, he's a terrible playboy. Don't fall in love."

Luz blushed at the joke. Maybe it was the Baileys that made her giddy. Whatever it was, she was enjoying herself at this place. She ate the steak and fish Sam had saved for her as well as some of the vegetables. It was a huge meal, enough to last her another day. The music was as good as the food, and no one seemed to care about anything except refilling their drinks.

A number of other people arrived after Charlie — couples, small groups, and even a few children. They wished Charlie a happy birthday, sampled a portion of Sam's cooking, and took a turn dancing. Everyone knew each other and conversed as best they could with the music blaring.

Then Charlie's wife, Rosalba, appeared, and the party stopped for a second. Rosalba took her time placing fifty-six candles on the cake while everyone watched. When she started to light them one at a time with wooden matches, Sam lost his patience.

"Here, *mami*," he said stepping up to help her. He took out his Zippo and lit four candles in his hand. He gave her two and kept two for himself. They went around the cake, lighting four at a time, until all fifty-six were burning.

With Sam conducting, they sang "Happy Birthday" to Charlie three times, in English, Spanish, and Papiamento. Charlie took off his glasses, leaned over the cake, and blew on the candles. He got them all out to the cheers of the crowd.

As the sun set, the party started to wind down. Little by little, Sam cleaned up the barbecue and bar area. He made a game of it, dancing his way to the kitchen door and back. He never took his eyes off Luz. He smiled, winked, pointed his finger-pistol at her, and kissed her constantly.

Luz enjoyed the attention. It felt genuine. But she grew more anxious as her hour-long commitment turned into six. Minchi's opened at nine, only forty-five minutes away. She wanted no trouble with la Dueña. She decided to ask Samito to take her back to town as soon as he could. He had no reason to complain. There wasn't much going on at the moment. His friends were settled over the domino table and their beer bottles. He could drive her back and return in time for the next game if he didn't dither. Of course, there was the question of what he expected for his hundred dollars.

She approached him near the domino table, where he was waiting for his turn. She took up his hand and kissed it lightly.

"*Señor*," she said.

"*¿Sí?*"

"A walk by the water?" she suggested.

"*¡Fantastico!*" Sam beamed as he led her toward the dock.

"Maybe a little time together," Luz said as they walked along the wooden planks, "and then you could take me to town."

Her subtlety impressed Sam. He accepted her proposal with a simple, "*Claro.*"

At the end of the pier, they sat on one of the chairs. She expected Sam to start kissing her or put his hands on her body. Instead, he sat with her in front of him, draped his arms over her shoulders, and one by one, pointed out constellations. He seemed to be restless but not in a hurry. To keep his hands busy, he rubbed her shoulders. Charlie was right about Samito. He was a prince. He fed her, gave her expensive drinks, danced with her, and now he was rubbing the knots out of her muscles. At some point, he was going to ask for sex. Why else would he have given her the money?

"*Vamos,*" Sam said rising from the chair.

It was time, Luz reasoned. He had a room here, and they were headed for it. But at the end of the pier, he turned to the right and led her down the beach. Did he want to have sex on the sand? That was only fun in the movies.

Music drifted with the breeze. She looked over her shoulder at the Christmas lights strung around the pavilion. She thought they were just as pleasant as the stars. A smile spread over her face.

"*Ah, tan linda,*" Sam said.

Luz blushed for the second time that night. He turned her to face him and started moving his hips with the music. Wasn't she just thinking about the movies? Yes, she was, and this was like a scene from one of those silly romances her sister liked. The moon was big. Music played softly. They stood close enough to the ocean to taste it. For a second, she forgot about why she was in Aruba and the hundred-dollar bill in her pocket. She put her head on Samito's shoulder. They danced a slow salsa in the sand, two lovers, a married couple, anything but a whore and a client.

Sam pulled back to gaze down at her. She opened her eyes to him. He felt the genuine affection she had for him at that moment. It was in everything about her. The way she held his hand. The way she pursed her lips to say something but didn't. The way she curved those lips ever so slightly to smile. It was only at the corners of her mouth, but it was a smile, one that meant she was happy. She wasn't worried about her family in Colombia, nor was she concerned with la Dueña or the police. And if it was only for an instant, so be it. She was living entirely in the present, in the exact second of joy he had prepared for her. A twinge of guilt nicked his ego. He paid a hundred dollars for something that was worth a million. Where else but Aruba could a guy have so much fun, never break the law, and for so little money? He didn't know and didn't care to find out.

He twirled her around on the sand so she was facing down the beach. Then his ears roared with the sound of her screaming. She spun into his chest and sobbed. Instinctively, he clutched her to his body. Lifting his head out of her hair, he saw what it was that had frightened her half to death. A man lay face down on the beach, the lower half of his body submerged in the lapping water.

4

DOCTOR VAN DAM heard a vehicle pull into his driveway, followed by loud voices and then pounding fists on his door. He looked from his office window and recognized the pickup down there. It belonged to Charlie. Charlie himself was in view. Beside him stood several other people. He knew only Sam, although the others were vaguely familiar. Then he saw that Sam had a person under the arms and was dragging him toward the entrance to the clinic.

"Damn these whoremongers!" he said to himself.

They enjoyed their parties and their drinking and their stupid antics. Inevitably, they showed up at Centro Medico, the hospital, or here at his clinic, where he served the general public as a family physician. There was a price to pay for having outrageous fun. It was only six months ago that they brought in a girl with a cut on her foot which required eight stitches. Sooner or later, someone was going to be seriously injured. By the looks of things, his prediction had come true.

Nonetheless, he was a physician who swore an oath to preserve life and provide care. He took it seriously even in cases of the stupid, the foolish, the reckless, and all of the aforementioned afflictions combined. He was hoping that someday there would be a vaccine or a pill which would lessen those maladies. In the meantime, it was up to people like him to do their best.

Despite the fact that it was Sunday and the clinic beneath his residence was closed, he wanted to look professional. He tugged on his white coat and draped his stethoscope around his neck. On his way downstairs, he muttered to himself about having to order more supplies, hire another nurse, and take a vacation to Holland or somewhere cold enough to need a coat. The constant sun and heat of Aruba wore him out. He arrived at the door, took a deep breath, and pulled it open. The sight on the other side made him gasp.

"Set him down," he ordered.

Sam eased the man onto the floor. "I found him on the beach," he said. "He's still alive."

"I can see that," Van Dam replied, putting his stethoscope to the man's chest. "He's obviously dehydrated, sun burnt, and starving."

"What can we do?" Sam asked.

"He must go to the hospital. Immediately. Put him in your truck. I'll ride with him in the back."

The men looked at Van Dam as if he had just ordered them to jump into a raging fire.

"Now! Are you so drunk you can't move?"

They snapped out of their trance that instant. Tom held the door open while Sam and Roger heaved the man onto the back seat of Charlie's pickup. Van Dam got in with the patient as Charlie took the wheel. Sam rode in the passenger seat.

"Lock the doors!" Van Dam shouted to one of the men standing in his driveway. He said to Charlie, "Drive as fast as you can, as safely as you can. I don't think a few bumps will do any more damage."

"You think he'll make it?" Sam asked.

"Who can tell? Was he conscious when you found him?"

"Barely. He mumbled something about drowning or not drowning. I couldn't understand it."

"He obviously didn't drown. If he dies, it will be from exposure or dehydration and such."

Sam held on as Charlie swerved around several cars waiting in line at the first traffic light. He said, "Kenny told me a tugboat sank somewhere off Curaçao. Maybe he was part of the crew."

Van Dam said, "If he drifted all the way from Curaçao, he's lucky to be alive."

Charlie checked his mirrors. No one, the police or otherwise, was following him. A green light glowed at the intersection for the airport. He dodged several cars there. The drivers protested with blowing horns and flashing lights.

Taxis and locals going to and from the center of Oranjestaad blocked the main road near the cruise ship terminal. The pickup bounced over the curb at the parliament building as Charlie navigated around the pavilion on the side. He slowed just enough to shift into a lower gear. A security guard ran inside, no doubt to phone the police. Well, he had a good reason for tearing up the greenery, and it was about time the security guard did something other than stand there and scratch his ass for the tourists all night.

To save time, Charlie drove the wrong way up Havenstraat. He was half on the sidewalk, half on the street. Horns blared. People shouted. He ignored them and concentrated on not crashing. At the circle on the far side of town, he got back on the highway. With enough room for him to get to full speed, he shifted up through the gears, barely letting off the throttle to work the clutch. He reflected on how his new truck charged like a bull. What a good selection he had made!

The sign for the hospital flew by. Charlie knew it was shorter to take the second left. He slowed to a safer speed to make the turn. The tires barked and the tail end of the truck started to slide. He steered into the skid, the tires caught, and he whipped the wheel back the other way. The truck shuddered then leapt forward toward the emergency entrance.

When Charlie came to a complete stop, Van Dam started breathing normally again. It had been a wild ride, as harrowing as one he'd taken in Sarajevo during the recent war there. He left his patient on the seat and ran into the hospital. Two orderlies were staring through the door with curious faces. "Is this a hospital or a beach club?" Van Dam said.

"Sometimes both," one orderly replied.

"Get a gurney! There's a very sick man out there."

The orderlies took their time gathering up the gurney. Van Dam bolted over, took the head end, and shoved it toward the door. They caught up with him at Charlie's truck. Upon seeing the man lying on the back seat, they set about doing their jobs as they had been trained. Van Dam supervised, keeping his eyes on everything at once.

"Come on," Charlie said, "It's in their hands."

"You have a cigarette?" Sam asked.

"Do you have a lighter?" Charlie replied.

Sam winked. They walked outside just as Tom and Carlos showed up.

"Is he alive?" Tom asked.

"He was when they took him," Sam said.

Tom put his head down. "I hope they don't kill him."

"What a night!" Carlos commented.

"Chico," Sam warned, "it's early."

"We dropped the girls off," Tom said. "They didn't know what to think."

"How was Luz?" Sam asked.

Tom thought for a second. "Stunned, I guess," he said.

"Poor kid. Tough start for her. Let's hope this guy makes it," Sam finished.

The smokers lit up and leaned on the truck, waiting for word to come from inside. To pass the time, Tom related a story from his days in the Navy, this one about a plane that was launched off an aircraft carrier directly into the sea. The pilot survived; the copilot died. As soon as the pilot was back on deck and in a dry uniform, he was forced to take off immediately.

"I guess you lose your nerve if you don't get right back in the saddle," Carlos said.

They all shook their heads, wondering if they had the courage to do such a thing. Then the group broke up. They admitted there was nothing they could do at the hospital. Tom and Carlos volunteered to clean up the remnants of the party. Charlie and Sam said they would stay and bring the good news as soon as it was available.

Less than fifteen minutes later, a police car pulled up to the hospital. Jules Calenda got out of the passenger seat. The officer driving followed closely behind.

"*Bon nochi,*" Calenda greeted Sam and Charlie.

"Greetings, Commandante," Charlie said lightly.

Calenda tried to smile, failed, and retained the grim look on his face. "I see you are here at the hospital, so there must be a reason for your dangerous driving," he said.

Charlie knew better than to taunt Calenda. Reckless driving wasn't close to murder, but policemen thought conspiracy lurked around every corner. For the most part, they were correct. It was just that the conspiracy was not always criminal. It was more a case of people having a good time and wanting to be left alone. At least that was how Charlie viewed the world. However, he respected Calenda's efforts in light of the fact that San Nicolaas was in dire need of a good spring cleaning.

"A man washed up on the beach," Charlie said.

"A man washed up on the beach," Calenda repeated, "and you did not call the police?"

"I'm sorry, Commandante. We took him to the clinic. Doctor Van Dam ordered he be brought to the hospital."

"Would you agree it has been an interesting weekend?" Calenda asked.

"Of course, and a full moon, too."

"Do you believe the full moon makes people do strange things?" Calenda asked seriously.

"The full moon and rum, Commandante, which is why I never drink under a full moon unless it is my birthday. Three negatives make a positive, you see."

Sam released a grin but turned his head sideways to hide it.

"I don't know if we agree completely on that. You will wait here while I confer inside?"

Charlie spread his arms. "Naturally," he said. "I have the night off to celebrate my birthday."

"You as well, Sam."

"At your service," Sam replied.

Calenda entered the emergency room, where he spoke to a woman behind the counter. She was mostly unhelpful in that the information she had was less complete than what Charlie had given him. She knew only that a man in serious condition was brought in. The patient was upstairs in the intensive care ward. She did not know who the attending physician was. She did not know if there were any facts of the man's identity. She did not care to look away from the tiny television playing a Venezuelan soap opera to relate these bits of data to Calenda.

As Calenda saw it, the problem with Aruba was that no one took anything seriously except leisure activities. When it came to enjoying oneself, hardly any nationality exceeded the Arubans. An Aruban is an expert at dozens of useless skills such as wind surfing, salsa dancing, and carnival costume design, to name a few. However, when it came to occupations critical to society's proper function, such as this secretary's, Arubans scored near the bottom.

If Calenda was bitter, it was because he believed his tiny nation should aspire to lofty goals as their Dutch conquerors once had. Holland was a tiny nation when compared to England or Germany or France. Yet, Holland once dominated world trade. Rotterdam was still the busiest port in Europe. The world thought the Netherlands was a quaint place full of flowers and people who wore wooden shoes. That was to overlook her contributions to medicine, engineering, and the arts. Sadly, Calenda's forgotten colonial outpost was never infused with the same work ethic as the motherland.

Perhaps it was impossible to concentrate on serious matters when every day planeloads of tourists came to laze their vacation time away. The natives caught the disease from the visitors. In the last ten years, as the refinery declined and the hotels boomed, Calenda's fellow islanders slid deeper into a miasma of thoughtlessness. Vehicle accidents involving alcohol were up. Deaths during the carnival season increased each year. Petty crime, nonexistent in Calenda's youth, was a growing problem in the hotel area. Jobs at the hotels used to be snatched up by local people who preferred pleasant surroundings to the industrial wasteland of the refinery. Now workers were imported from Colombia to fill the demand while native citizens subsisted on government largesse. Colombia used to send nothing but prostitutes. At present, Calenda couldn't tell the difference between the young women cleaning rooms at the Hotel Royale and the girls working in San Nicolaas. "How can you tell the difference?" his colleagues from that end of the island joked. "You mean there is a difference?" was the answer. That aggravated him most of all. There was a zone of tolerance in Aruba. It was in San Nicolaas, where it always had been and where it rightly belonged. When his colleagues looked the other way at prostitution in the hotels, they invited disaster. Not everyone had the same tolerant view of these activities, especially Americans. American mothers did not like their children exposed to tawdry scenes in the hallways or on the beaches. When word spread that women worked the same hotels that families used, tourism would go the way of the refinery. Then what would the island do to support itself? Ah, he almost forgot, they would call Holland for more money to fix things.

He didn't expect to change the course of history by himself. He would do his job the way it was supposed to be done: professionally, expeditiously, and with a conscience. His conscience bothered him most, and at times he worried it affected his ability to be an effective enforcer of the law.

At the entrance to the intensive care ward, Calenda found Doctors Van Dam and Sanial. He stood with his hands behind his back, employing his excellent memory instead of a notebook.

"It's not so often I get my patients from Charlie's parties, but once in a while," Van Dam said.

"This man they brought to you. Can you tell me anything about him?"

Van Dam replied with a shrug. "I don't know so much as his name. There was nothing in his pockets. However, we believe he will live. You can ask him all the questions you like in a day or so."

"Any signs of violence?" Calenda inquired.

"Nothing I would attribute to deliberate violence. He shows some bruises that would be expected in his circumstance. He's also dehydrated and probably hasn't eaten in many days."

Doctor Sanial agreed with Van Dam.

"Is he conscious now?"

"No. He won't be conscious for at least eight hours."

"Nothing more to add? Either of you?"

They both said they had nothing.

Calenda loathed a day of interviews at the Port Authority and the refinery. Perhaps they knew of a ship that had gone down. He should contact them immediately so word would spread. Better yet, he should assign someone to do this. Of course, the assignee would do a lousy job of it, not put a sense of urgency behind the effort. But he did not want to do it himself because talking to those bureaucrats was horrendously tedious. They would all want to have a cup of coffee. They would all want to know what was the purpose of his official visit. They would all exaggerate their position and the aid they would lend. Later, they would ignore his follow-up calls and ultimately issue a letter on fancy paper stating that they had turned up nothing to assist the investigation. It would be a complete waste of time. Or was he becoming as lazy as his countrymen about whom he liked to complain so much? He reminded himself what he had learned when he trained with the New York City Police Department only a few months ago. Use your resources wisely. Time is the resource you have the least of. Do not waste it.

"I'll return tomorrow. Hopefully, I can have a talk with him," he said to the doctors.

They were noncommittal but smiled.

Calenda excused himself and returned to the parking lot, where Sam and Charlie sat on the tailgate of the truck.

"Tell us, Commandante, how is the patient?" Charlie asked.

"The doctors tell me he will live."

"Well, then, a celebration! A drink on the veranda for you and Sam and me."

Calenda would never collect the drink. He noted the patches of grass stuck to Charlie's fenders.

"Be careful driving," he said and turned to leave. From the corner of his eye he saw a hearse pulling away from the building. There were only four hearses on the island. This one belonged to the Ad Patres Funeral Home of San Nicolaas. Without realizing it, Calenda had stopped to watch the car drive out of the parking lot and down the road. From behind him, he heard Charlie speak.

"Better a ride in my truck than one of those, eh Commandante?"

Calenda looked back and replied, "I was thinking of Ricardo Cortés. Did you know him?"

"Like me, he owned a bar," Charlie said.

"Not quite the same as yours," Calenda reflected.

"But on the same street in the same town."

"And his wife?" the policeman asked.

"She rules the roost now, doesn't she?"

"Not Ricardo's son?" Calenda queried.

"Not his type of business," Charlie said. "He paints with me sometimes."

"I hear he is very talented. *Bon nochi*, gentlemen."

Charlie and Sam departed the hospital and drove to Savaneta, where they found no one. With the exception of the twinkling Christmas lights, all signs of the party had been taken down, put away, or thrown in the trash.

"Going to town?" Sam asked Charlie.

"My wife and I are spending the night here," Charlie replied.

A dream come true, Sam almost said. His piece of land was only a few hundred yards away, and like Charlie, he would someday live in sight of the ocean with a wonderful woman.

Charlie said, "Tomorrow, we'll check on Jonah, whom the whale spit out. Isn't that the story?"

"I'll have to consult my Bible."

"Please do. And pray for me," Charlie said. "I'm a terrible sinner."

To clear his head, Sam walked to the beach, to the spot where he found the man at the water's edge. The breeze was picking up. It came from the east, which was the direction it was supposed to come from. That was reassuring in its normalcy. Sam was used to abnormalities but only in terms of outrageous fun. Exotic drinks, women with strange names, and theme parties all made sense to him. Murders, shipwreck survivors, things of that nature, were not amusing. They disturbed the joyful atmosphere of his paradise.

Near the edge of the horizon, a cruise ship approached the island. He couldn't imagine drifting around on the open sea for days on end. What did it take to keep your wits when there was no hope in sight? What did it take to not inhale a lungful of seawater and end the torment? He wondered if he had what it would take to fight to live in that situation.

On the sand in front of him, he saw the life jacket that had been around the man's neck. It was still inflated. He picked it up, turned it over, and noted the name stenciled on it in capital letters: *PATRICIA*. In smaller letters, down one side, it read, PHILA, PA. Sam couldn't remember the last time he had been to Philadelphia. Most of his days were spent in Florida and Texas.

He carried the life jacket back to his room, where he hung it over the doorknob. Sam hoped that the guy would donate it to Charlie's Bar, where it would hang amidst all the other junk left by sailors and tourists. It would be a hell of a conversation piece. "Let me tell you about this guy who washed up on the beach one night," the story would begin. He would point at the life jacket as proof.

He rinsed quickly, donned fresh clothes, and drove to San Nicolaas to maintain his reputation. He didn't pass a single person on the street as he drove along the refinery wall. He parked near the main gate, purposely away from Minchi's so he had time to have a few drinks with his pals before checking on Luz.

Sam walked into Java Bar, where his friends sat at one end of the bar. Kenny held court, slinging booze and shaking out cigarettes. Two working girls sat in the corner by the jukebox, gossiping and twisting their hair.

"You rescued Robinson Crusoe," Kenny said to Sam.

"We don't know his name yet," Sam replied.

"I told you I saw something on the television about a boat going down in that storm last week," Kenny reminded him. "The usual?"

"Yeah," Sam told him. "Do you remember the name of the boat?"

"No, but the rest of the crew was rescued from a life raft. They were picked up by a ship bound for Curaçao."

"Good for them," Sam said taking his drink.

His friends wanted to know how the guy was doing. Sam informed them that he was expected to live. Other than that, there was nothing to report. He raised his glass to the man and toasted his survival.

"Better him than me," Kenny said. "I'd rather die in a plane crash than let the sharks get me."

Tom said, "What if you crash-land a plane in the ocean and then the sharks get you?"

"Why don't you go upstairs with the one with the massive breasts over there and see if she can float you off the bed?" Kenny replied.

"If that guy makes it, I'll pay, and he can take her up. What does everyone think of that?"

They agreed the guy deserved a free one. Each man put ten dollars on the bar. Kenny scooped up the money and stuffed it in the jar used to keep track of the vino the girl sold.

"There," Kenny said. "He has a free jump waiting. Now who needs another drink?"

Several rounds of drinks took up the hours. Sam quit after his fifth. It was a long day turning into a longer night. He wanted to be reasonably sober for the early morning hours with Luz.

"Goodnight, gentlemen. See you on the porch," Sam said and headed for the door.

"Off to your pillow?" Tom said to his back.

Sam raised a pair of finger-pistols in the air and continued on his way. A few men trolled the street ahead of him. They peeked in the windows, made disgusting jokes to one another, and shuffled on. He stopped at the corner to get a cigarette from his pack when Frankie came out of the shadows.

"Franklin," Sam said, rattling the change in his pocket, "It's been an interesting night."

Frankie gestured toward Minchi's and said, "There was no funeral parade for Ricardo last month. If he didn't get one, who's gonna have one for me?"

"I will Frankie, a parade that's half a day long."

Frankie picked up his head and smiled with his rotten teeth on full display. "You're a man of honor. A gentleman. A caballero!"

"Okay, Frankie, cheer up. I have a girl to see."

"She's gone. Gone with the wind. Gone. Gone. Gone."

"What?" Sam snapped.

"She leave with the woman in the big car."

Sam barged into Minchi's and looked around. Pablo handed a fresh beer to a guy in refinery coveralls. Spanner sat at the far end of the bar with his arms folded over his chest. The other girls were occupied with a trio of high-school-age punks.

Sam crossed to Spanner and fired his cigarette. Before he exhaled the first puff of smoke, Spanner held up his hands.

"Save your words," Spanner said to him.

"Where is she?" Sam asked.

"She go with la Dueña."

"La Dueña?"

Spanner heaved himself off the barstool. He took a glass of ice from the cooler and dumped a few cubes into his mouth. "I told you before, Ricardo is dead. She is the owner."

Sam drew too hard on his cigarette. Hot smoke scorched his throat. He choked back a cough. After a long exhale, he said, "Andrés gets nothing?"

"Maybe Ricardo's boat. What's it to you?"

"What's it to me?"

"That's what I asked you. What business is it of yours?"

"None, but I would have liked an after-hours date with the girl."

Spanner chuckled. "First come, first served. There are three other girls here. If you don't like them, there are a hundred more in town."

Furious, Sam kicked the door open ahead of him as he passed onto the street. He spotted Frankie slinking along the wall. Seated against the tree that stood before Bongo Bar was Speedy, another choller, who thanks to years of drug abuse was about as fast as a dead rabbit.

Sam wasn't about to go back to Java, where he would have to explain why he wasn't with Luz. For a second, he thought about breaking his own rules and bedding a girl in another bar but decided his heart wouldn't be in it the way it would have been with Luz. He tossed his cigarette into the gutter and headed for his car.

The drive to Savaneta settled him with its monotony. He parked in the back and walked out on the pier. White lights on a fisherman's boat sparkled beyond the reef. He went for a swim the way he did as a kid, buck-naked.

The laps around the pier reminded him of a swimming meet he'd won when he was in elementary school. The coach gave him a plastic trophy that was a prized possession until he left the island for college. He threw it in the trash when he cleaned out his room. He was all grown up, heading out into the world to prove he could do anything. And what did he prove? Only that where he'd started was where he wanted to end. The stuff in the middle wasn't worth a handful of sand.

He floated on his back, watching the stars, waiting for something to appear. No divine revelation was forthcoming. However, an earthly one came to him in the form of a voice speaking from the dock.

"The Greeks had the right idea," Charlie said. "They only wore clothes when they had to, and that did not include athletics or swimming."

Sam climbed up the ladder and accepted a drink from his lifelong friend.

"What do you think?" Charlie asked.

"I think you're my best friend in the world," Sam replied.

"I can see you're alone and feeling sad, out here in the ocean with your manhood exposed to the sharks. Freedom has its risks, you know."

"Do you think Andrés will get screwed out of everything?" Sam asked.

Tilting his head, Charlie answered, "That depends on his stepmother, Marcela. Ricardo should have found himself a nice Dutch farm girl. She might have been plump as a milk cow, but she would have loved him for bringing her to the sun and treated his son fairly."

"And Marcela?" Sam asked.

Charlie stirred his rum with his index finger and licked it clean. "She's Colombian. What else can be known?"

"She has my girl with her."

The rum gave Charlie a moment to think. He sought the good things in people. It was his nature. However, a life gallivanting about the world, and Colombia specifically, had taught him that evil intentions nested in more people than he cared to admit. He sipped the rum, then said, "Marcela is the boss. What choice does the girl have?"

"She could have come home with me," Sam remarked.

Charlie shifted topics with a shrug. "A man lands on the beach over there. What a way to get a visitor, eh? Amazing."

"It's Aruba," Sam said. "Anything can happen."

"That's the spirit," Charlie said with a smile and raised his glass to the waning moon.

ARUBA'S ONLY hospital accepted its usual cases the next day. There were tourists with severe sunburn. A man broke his ankle at a hotel swimming pool. He was chasing his five-year-old son. Another man had a stroke after breakfast. Two children burned their mouths by trying to imitate fire-eaters who performed at the Carnival Spectacular Show. There were no overnight traffic accidents. No barroom brawls sent battered patients in need of sutures.

There was a man on the third floor who was one-of-a-kind. The upper portion of his body was sunburned like any of the tourists. He was dehydrated but much worse than the fools who drank too much and sat on the beach all day. He also differed from the tourists in that he didn't get to the island on an airplane or a cruise ship. He floated or swam. No one knew exactly how because he had yet to speak a single word.

His first two visitors were Sam and Charlie, the man who found him and the one who brought him to the hospital respectively. Doctor Sanial said the man absorbed fluids "like a sponge," and that he "probably" didn't have any organ damage. Sam wondered about his own damaged organs, specifically his liver, which processed vodka by the gallon, and his lungs, which filtered cigarettes by the carton. Charlie didn't care about these things, firmly believing that there was no way to prolong life or to prevent death. One had to live the way one wanted without watching the clock and constantly worrying how much time remained.

Sam and Charlie sat in chairs by the window. They reminisced about the old days as they took in the view. Before that building was built on that spot, we had a picnic there. That road heading into town, it used to be a mule track out of town.

A plane made an emergency landing on this stretch of beach in 1968. The pilot walked away without a scratch. A man found a gold nugget at the foot of that hill. The same guy won a thousand dollars the day the Royal Cabana Casino opened.

"Looks like he's coming around," Sam said after looking over his shoulder at the patient.

Charlie turned away from the window. The man's face was haggard. The hairs of his beard looked itchy. His lips were blistered. And his first sight was a couple of boozers staring down with sloppy grins.

"Welcome to Aruba, Captain," Sam said. "Permission to come ashore has been granted." He performed a lazy salute with the wrong hand to make the point.

The guy said nothing. He squinted at them and shifted in the bed. Charlie pulled the curtain halfway across the window.

"What's your name, Captain?" Sam asked.

The man swallowed and worked his mouth side to side.

Charlie was ready with a Styrofoam cup of ice water. He held it up to the man and positioned the straw close to his lips. He took a sip and sat back against the pillows.

"I'll get the doctor," Charlie said and handed the cup to Sam.

"You want another sip?" Sam asked.

"Aruba?" the man asked suddenly.

Sam smiled with his arms wide open. "Our island paradise. We'll have to stamp your passport later. We couldn't find it. Tell me whose name I should write on the manifest?"

"Nathan Beck."

"Of the motor vessel *Patricia*, correct?"

"Tugboat."

"Right, tugboat," Sam said. "The news reports that your boat sank somewhere near Curaçao. You drifted all the way to Charlie's beach."

"Who's Charlie?" Nathan Beck asked.

"He's the King of Aruba. Just a joke. He's sort of a local celebrity."

"Who are you?"

"I'm Sam. Charlie and I are best friends. I found you on the beach."

"What day is it?"

"Today would be Monday. You were out there in the deep blue sea for about a week."

Nathan Beck looked around the room. There was nothing but his bed, a table, a couple of chairs, and some medical equipment that was attached to his body.

Doctor Sanial entered with Charlie a few steps behind. "The patient awakes," Doctor Sanial said. "This is a good thing. Let's do a thorough examination and see what can be done to make you better."

"Drinks are on us," Sam said.

"He loves to give away drinks at my bar." Charlie added as they left the room, "We'll be back to see you later. Don't worry, we'll notify your family and the authorities and the Queen of the Netherlands, too, just in case she posted a reward."

"Get well," Sam finished. He winked and followed Charlie out of the room.

Doctor Sanial looked down at Beck. He took up his stethoscope and applied it to his patient's chest. After listening to the beating heart, he stood erect. "I never understand how some men survive and others do not," the doctor said. "How did you do it?"

It was shame that kept Nathan Beck alive, rather his fear of shame. He couldn't bear the idea he would die at sea. He was the grandson of a man who had survived three years of Atlantic convoy duty during the Second World War. His grandfather, Torsten Beck, had two ships blown out from under him courtesy of his distant German cousins. Nathan Beck wasn't going to meet his grandfather in the next world and have to explain how he'd perished at sea during peacetime in the balmy Caribbean.

A cook's assistant, Torsten Beck never slept in his bunk. No matter what the weather, he slept on deck, sometimes lashed to the rail under a pile of blankets topped with an oilskin. He washed dishes outside the deckhouse using a hose and a bucket instead of in the galley sink. He peeled potatoes and carrots and chopped meat and onions on a portable cutting board he made from crate wood discarded by stevedores back on the docks. These practices saved his life. The men who laughed at him never lived to tell the comedic tale of the boy so afraid of the dark that he had to sleep under the moon. It wasn't the dark that frightened him. It was the torpedoes, the deck guns, and his third cousins who knew how to use them. When his ships were hit, he was the first one in the lifeboat.

Torsten Beck survived the war and swore never to step foot on another ship. Just the same, he founded a waterfront restaurant with a clientele involved in the business of marine transportation. From the second-floor dining room, customers watched their ships, tugs, barges, and launches ply the Delaware River in Philadelphia.

It was sight of that river, and the stories Torsten Beck told after hours, that continued the Beck curse. He liked to play pinochle and drink schnapps after closing the restaurant. Beside him sat his grandson, Nathan, the one who ended up shipwrecked in the Caribbean. Nathan was there because his ambitious father, Viktor, dropped him off one afternoon, declaring that he never wanted to see the boy's mother again. This was a crucial time in Viktor's career, and a supportive grandfather promptly agreed to take care of his motherless grandson. That was the decision that led Nathan Beck to break the oath his grandfather had made after the war.

It was the stories that affected the youngest Beck the most. He was just a boy, too young to be up half the night the way his grandfather allowed. His drowsy ears soaked up a different kind of bedtime story. As the cards slid across the table, his grandfather and his friends inevitably talked about their wartime experiences. Tales of storms and battles, pranks and lost loves, exotic harbors and dangerous cargoes fired his imagination. He dreamt of being in the middle of the action. He saw himself aboard the ships he watched from his third-floor bedroom window.

Beck spent his first teenage summer aboard a launch that carried river pilots to and from ships calling at Philadelphia. During those three months, he saw his share of the nautical life. He liked the ships, the way they lumbered through the water and towered over the tiny launch. However, he loved the tugboats. Although compact vessels, they were stout and powerful. They wrestled ships to and from the docks. They seemed to dance around the river, rushing from one job to the other, their captains chatting with each other on in-house radio channels. It was like a social club whose small membership roamed a giant preserve bounded only by the banks of the river. After that summer, Nathan Beck decided he wanted to join.

His grandfather gave him only one piece of advice: "Always sleep on your life preserver!" His father told him that he was an idiot. His mother was nowhere to be found.

Doctor Sanial shined a light into Beck's eyes. It was a routine part of a physical exam. Still, Sanial was pleased to see the pupils react properly. He said to his patient, "Did you have a life jacket?"

An involuntary smile formed on Beck's lips. Of course he'd had a life jacket. It was the latest kind, a tube of reinforced plastic, inflated by a cylinder of compressed air. He kept it beside his pillow whenever he lay down to sleep, just as his grandfather had advised him.

He awoke on the floor with a splitting headache, and as *Patricia* took an unnaturally hard roll to the starboard, he reached for his life preserver. He didn't inflate it just yet because he was still inside his cabin. First, he had to make it outside.

The only light came from a battery-powered emergency fixture. Shadows confused the shape of the room. Two feet of seawater covered the floor. More water leaked through the vent in the bottom of the door to the passageway. The deck tilted toward the bulkhead, which meant the entire boat was listing to starboard at an angle steep enough to make him fear for his life.

The boat surged up, then plunged down again as if an angry parent had smacked a toy from the hands of a petulant child. Beck tumbled against the bulkhead landing with his arms tangled in the life preserver. He shrugged his head through the loop and worked to fasten the strap around his waist. Without the strap fastened properly, the preserver would pop off his body when it inflated. The boat rolled again, this time to the port side. He braced himself between his bunk and the bulkhead. Water swirled up the length of his body until he had to release himself and struggle above it to breathe. At this moment, he knew he had to get out of the boat or he would go down with it.

A moment of calm passed as the boat settled. Sensing that another roll was coming, he crawled to the door. He twisted the knob with both hands, and the door burst open under the pressure of the sea on the other side. Holding on, he swung with the door, floating in the water that sloshed into his cabin. The boat snapped back and the water rushed out, taking him with it into the passageway.

After colliding with the wall, he got to his feet. The water went flat as the boat settled again. He thrashed through it on his way to the port-side door that would release him from the deckhouse. It was easier going in the hallway. With his hands pressed on either side, he pitched with the boat but remained standing.

He arrived at the doorway spitting water. The door itself was already open, which meant the rest of the crew must have abandoned ship. The door slammed against the house, and the deck beneath him rose up so that he tumbled toward the other side of the boat, where he landed against the wheel of the starboard door. The fall knocked the wind from him. He sputtered, coughed, and clawed for a handhold. He found one on the wheel of that door. When the boat rocked again, he hung above the opposite door where the ocean flowed in unimpeded.

Trapped in the hallway, watching black water rush at him through the shadows, he nearly panicked. Every sailor fears drowning no matter what he says at his local tavern, and Nathan Beck was no exception. As dramatic as his fear was, the incredible sight rising toward him was mesmerizing. At this point, many a sailor surrendered to fate. The voluminous sound of surging water quenched bravery and brought death's relief.

It wasn't fear that Nathan Beck succumbed to or even panic. It was shame. Surely he would be dead and not have to explain, not to the living. But if there was an afterlife, his grandfather would want to know what had happened. That shame bore down on him with more weight than the tons of water filling his boat. His grandfather survived torpedo attacks, the cold North Atlantic, and a sea covered with burning fuel. Now his grandson was about to die in peacetime in the warm Caribbean without a lick of flame in sight. It was embarrassingly shameful.

Beck wasn't going to let that happen. Not this way. Not now. He timed his move with the rolling of the hull. It started to right itself, and as it did, he let go of the wheel and started for the opposite door. He was up to his hips in water, which made it impossible to run. The deck started to tilt. He leapt for the door and caught the edge just in time. Tons of water poured over him. He waited for the door to slam on his fingers. Luckily one of the levers blocked it, preventing the severing of his fingers into eight neatly cut sausages.

The boat was not righting itself anymore, which meant it was too full of water to float. He cursed as he pushed against the closed door, swearing he would not let himself drown.

The boat lolled and seemed to do a lazy pirouette, like a drunken ballet dancer. Beck felt his body sinking against the deck, which meant the pitch of the boat had declined slightly. He pulled his shoulder against the door, yanked his legs up, and pressed his feet out against the walls. Then he heaved against the door until his feet slipped. The door moved barely enough for him to shove an arm through the gap. More water gushed in through the wider space even as the door threatened to crush his arm.

At that moment, the boat tilted more in his favor. He knew what this meant. The keel was settling. *Patricia* was pointing her bow upward as her stern surrendered to gravity. She was bound to sink at any moment.

He clamored over the bulkhead and through the doorway onto the deck. The deck to his left sloped into the sea. To his right, it angled toward the sky. He threw himself into the sea, kicked furiously, and pulled with both arms to get away from the sinking tug.

A massive wave broke over *Patricia's* bow. It swallowed the hull for a second, then spit it out the next. As it passed, it carried Beck fifteen feet above the top of the wheelhouse, which was normally thirty feet above deck level. He rode the wave on his back. As he slid down the other side, he remembered the belt on his life preserver. He got it in both hands and tried to work the clasp. It took more coordination than he had at the moment. He settled for a simple double knot. He yanked the lanyard with a quick snap of his wrist. The tube inflated around his neck all the way down to his waist. It pulled his head and shoulders up and out of the water.

As he looked back, *Patricia* took another wave. This time it didn't cork above the surface. When the wave carried him up, he looked back into the trough as air whooshed from the hull. It was his last sight of her. She left only a few bubbles that were erased by the next wave.

He survived the wreck. Now he had to survive the storm.

Doctor Sanial asked Beck to hang his legs off the edge of the bed. He tapped both knees. The patient's reflexes were good. "You must know," he said to Beck, "that Aruba is the last island in the chain. The next bit of land is some possession of Venezuela or Colombia. If not, well, it's a long way to Central America."

Beck's first concern had not been where he would ultimately make landfall. It was the sea.

The sea carried him up toward the sky. It dropped him into its valleys. It dragged him without conscience over the tops of its waves. When it wanted to, it lashed him with spray driven into his skin by a wind the water seemed to pull over the horizon.

His life preserver kept his head and shoulders above the sea. His feet pointed down, his head up. He careened over the cliffs of the waves, dipping below the surface, but always popping up like an empty bottle.

He'd trained for this time, a time when his life was craved by an angry ocean. Through the courses of his captain's license, he watched videotapes of how to protect himself. These lively episodes featured clips from popular movies. He and his fellow students laughed at the actors who always lived to play another role. It was easy to laugh in the confines of the classroom, where nothing worse than a broken air conditioner could spoil the atmosphere. Here, in the infinity of the sea, there was no humor to be found. The drills they repeated in the calm waters of the river did nothing to prepare him for this type of torment.

The first thing he remembered was not to fight the sea. He rode the waves with his head back, his arms and legs out. The key was to float. Swimming required all the muscles of the body, which made it excellent exercise but guaranteed exhaustion to the shipwrecked sailor. It still required great effort to maintain position and avoid the clutch of colliding waves.

At least his stomach was full. He had eaten a large supper before climbing into his bunk. He was well rested, too. He'd been in a deep sleep when he was suddenly tossed from his bunk. That his head still ached meant he most likely struck it on something in his cabin. Just the same, he should have heard the general alarm. Surely someone had sounded it. There were eight men on that boat, and it didn't sink in such a hurry that none of them knew what was happening.

He wondered where the crew was. The life rafts in their drumlike containers should have sprung up automatically as the boat sank. They worked the same way as his life preserver, only they were a hundred times as big. As the boat sank, they would float upward, and when the tether came tight, inflate into an orange tent capable of holding ten men. There were two of them fixed to the top of the boat. He couldn't remember seeing them as it sank.

Of course, once the raft inflated, the sailor had to get aboard. In a wind as strong as he faced now, the raft would dash away like a kite on a broken string. Maybe the others were in the same position as he was, floating in life preservers, scattered by the waves, searching for him and their fellows.

He hoped this was the case. They were men he knew and liked, for the most part. He shared their company for weeks at a time in a space not bigger than a poor man's house, cut into so many pieces it felt like living in the pigeon holes of an old desk. They ate together, shared bunkrooms and a single bathroom, and worked as a team whether they were feuding or not. It took more than one man to do any job aboard a tugboat.

Fleeting thoughts of what could have caused the boat to sink passed through his mind. None of these lasted more than a moment because he was consumed with survival. It was best to lean his head on that plastic tube of air and focus on something else to keep his thoughts off the certain doom he faced.

He thought about his grandfather and wondered if the old man was pulling for him, begging God to let his grandson have another chance. If his grandfather was in heaven, was he there as an old man pleading for a younger one's life? Or was he there as a young man pointing at his own likeness bobbing one more time in the blue, shaking his head at fate's demonic tendency to repeat itself.

Doctor Sanial scratched a few notes on Beck's chart. "Did your life flash before your eyes?" he asked as he placed a blood pressure cuff around his patient's arm.

His life had not flashed before his eyes. He had been thinking about his grandfather, and then he considered what had become of his mother. He had no memory of her. He'd never heard from her. No one spoke her name nor answered his questions nor offered any scrap of evidence aside from his very presence that she even existed. It was as if he was left at the door by a passing stork that mistook one house for another. His father had taken him in, decided he was too much trouble, and dropped him with his grandfather to be free of the burden.

The most his father said on the subject was, "She's out of your life. More than that you need not know." It was his father's way of talking, formally, directly, just as he had been taught at the fine University of Pennsylvania. When this method was employed on a young boy's mind, he got the idea not to keep asking the question. The lack of a mother was problem enough that he didn't need to add his absentee father's scorn. He managed to forget about it, to set his curiosity loose on other topics, topics that his grandfather indulged liberally.

Such were the thoughts of a man recently stripped of his boat, given little chance to live, and yet who refused to surrender to what had to be a certain inevitability of circumstance.

"Perhaps you can tell me later," Doctor Sanial said, "After you've healed and had a few drinks with Charlie and Sam. They're quite a pair those two."

At the moment, Beck could not imagine having a drink of anything but cool, fresh, spring water. The sea had tormented his body. Its abuse occupied the better part of his mind through the initial hours of darkness and light. It relieved him of the responsibility of serious contemplation of what it would take to live to tell the tale.

After more hours than he could count, the sky lightened to a bitter gray. No color showed in any direction. It was simply more light than dark, as if the Bible had it exactly right when it proclaimed, "And then there was light." There was the light of the sky and the dark of the sea. The ocean clung to him, pulled at his clothes, and weighed down his hands and feet. But the coming light encouraged his will.

He knew the storm was moving away because the waves changed. They went from steep cliffs crashing into one another at odd angles to rolling hills moving in long, merging lines. Not that they were small, because they were at least twenty feet by his estimation. There was enough distance between them that he rose up and down like the lazy progression of a Ferris wheel.

The captain who had taught him everything was named Upton. He was a coarse man fond of cursing, lamenting the bygone days of tugboats, and smoking forty cigarettes a day. He was also an excellent mariner capable of doing more with less, the impossible with the impractical. He had an expression for every condition, every situation. For storms and the trouble they caused, he had a vast and ribald list of pronouncements waiting just behind his tongue. Had Upton been there, he would have said, "I'll tell you, Nate, she's howling over another man's grave. See the waves, all roly-poly like a fat whore in a wheelbarrow full of ice cream? You make it that far, and you can feel sorry for him who's grave is dug, not for yourself, because soon you'll be in the clear."

In the clear Nathan Beck was not. The sky was not clear, nor was he anywhere clear of danger. He was beyond the initial disaster. Still, he was far from saved. "Don't start complaining," Upton would have said.

Beck did not complain. He tried to figure out what had happened to his boat. He started at the beginning, which was really the end of the original voyage. *Patricia* departed Trinidad after delivering a new barge to the oil refinery there. She was light boat (that is, without another vessel in tow) and bound for Curaçao, where she was to retrieve another barge, which was completing repairs in the dry dock there, and return it to Philadelphia. Some 1200 nautical miles of water separated Trinidad from Curaçao. Given an average speed of eleven knots the trip should have taken about five days.

After checking the weather forecast, which was less than favorable, Captain Shahann, *Patricia*'s master, decided to sail anyway. The storm track was supposed to drift northward through the middle of the Caribbean, then turn toward Cuba. They would stay behind and to the south of it, where there would be an ugly sea running, but *Patricia* was no raft of twigs. She was a hundred twenty feet long, drew eighteen feet, and offered six thousand horsepower divided between her two propellers. Her fo'c'sle bow blunted the sea, keeping most of the water away from her low stern. In the wheelhouse, she had the latest electronics: two radar sets, a global positioning system, a chart plotter, and a single side band radio which allowed the captain to talk to his home office thousands of miles away.

All that being true, what had happened that *Patricia* found herself mortally wounded? What failure of man or machine caused the boat to find a permanent spot on the bottom of the sea? And why hadn't he heard the alarm? Why hadn't anyone come to his cabin screaming to abandon ship?

The last thing Beck remembered when he left the galley was his conversation with Captain Shahann. Shahann liked the midnight watch and spoke to Beck in his usual sarcastic tone.

"Sleep well, young master Beck, I'll get us through the night while you dream of your naked princess."

This was a double jibe. In the first place, it implied Beck couldn't handle the boat through the storm. Secondly, the "naked princess" of record was a woman named Nicole Reston. Beck made the mistake of mentioning he and Nicole had recently broken up. He paid for that mistake as Shahann went into a lengthy interrogation regarding her physical attributes (or lack thereof), her sexual appetites, and her unwillingness to cook, clean, and care for a sailor in dire need of womanly attention. Beck shut his mouth, ending the conversation by lying that he had only been getting to know her. The truth was he'd had marriage on his mind before she called it off.

"The forecast track shows the storm dipping south," Beck had commented to Shahann as they stood in the wheelhouse together.

"Hah! It may wobble a bit, but we're below any hurricane track known for the past three hundred years. We'll see some rollers. Nothing to fret about."

"We could slow down, let the storm outrun us," Beck had suggested.

"You a sissy? Afraid you'll toss your biscuits?"

Beck said nothing.

Shahann pushed against both throttle levers, which were against the stops, to make his point. "No little tropical disturbance is going to huff and puff and blow our house down."

"Well enough," Beck had said finally.

"Sleep tight, master Beck, you'll wake to a splendid morning," Shahann said as Beck left the wheelhouse after a final look at their present position on the chart plotter's cobalt screen.

What was that position? He recalled it as somewhere northeast of Curaçao, about half a day's steaming from their destination.

Shahann had been correct. Islands in the southern Caribbean benefited from being south of the hurricane belt. Natural forces steered the storms to the north so that they never took a direct hit. However, they sometimes felt the effects of passing storms. The trade winds (the prevailing easterlies of yore) blew steady across the lower latitudes just above the equator. They pushed a hurricane from its humble beginnings as a cluster of thunderstorms generated in the heart of Africa across the Atlantic to the Windward Isles. By the time the storm arrived, it usually developed into a low-pressure vortex blowing in a counterclockwise direction. The winds on the southern portion of the storm actually countered the trade winds themselves. Instead of a steady fifteen to twenty-five knots from the east, they dwindled to nothing or blew from the west when a hurricane passed through the central Caribbean at the longitude of Bonaire, Curaçao, and Aruba. The normally breezy islands found themselves sweltering in a sun as strong as the one that scorched the Sahara desert.

Beck sensed the first doubts attacking his resolve. A man adrift had five days, seven at most, to live. Dehydration was the obvious killer. Seawater would not slake the coming thirst. If the clouds dropped rain, he had only his open mouth to catch the drops. Insanity, shark attack, suicide, were all less likely culprits but equally deadly.

As the sky yielded to the coming night, he noticed the clouds were dissipating rapidly. The storm was gaining speed, moving away from him, probably to the west and north. An orange stain covered the horizon to the west. Higher up, a rampart of clouds broke here and there. A shaft of iridescent light, shifting from yellow to orange to red, pointed through a hole. Captain Upton's voice spoke to him. "It's the Devil's finger pointing. He's either coming at you or walking backwards because he never turns his back on an endangered soul."

Which is it, Beck wondered, coming or going?

"You need a few days here as my guest," Doctor Sanial said.

A few days of rest sounded wonderful to Beck. He harkened back to his thoughts of the devil and how relieved he had been at that moment. He had been confident that he had beaten Lucifer and dozed off, which was understandable given the physical exertion of the previous day.

He awoke to the entire firmament overhead. Constellations looked down on him. Individual stars shone in true color: Betelgeuse, orange; Polaris, distant blue; Deneb, white. Then, at the end of the world, a milky film spilled onto the sea. It started as a small blot that grew into a widening puddle. It expanded across his field of few. At last, the moon rose high enough to make out its oblong shape separating from the earth. He remembered that in three day's time it would be full. He studied the gray patches until his eyes hurt. Without realizing it, he dozed again, his head lolling against the life preserver.

Awake again, this time in sunlight, his face felt hot, his tongue dry, his throat sore. Using extreme care he took his shirt off and wrapped it around his head like a turban. Throughout the maneuver, he kept his life preserver securely attached to his body.

The wind was up again, twenty knots by his estimate. It was the easterly, bringing humidity from Africa to the Caribbean. It pushed the waves to about six or eight feet, him along with them. He considered holding his shirt up like a sail. He forgot the idea and went back to pleasant thoughts of Nicole Reston. She was the real estate agent who had sold him his row home. She said she'd never met a tugboat captain and that was enough to get them started.

While he entertained himself with memories of Nicole, Beck scanned the horizon for another vessel. Once in a while, he looked to the sky. He didn't know the availability or quality of search and rescue teams in this part of the world. Any vessel in trouble within a hundred miles of the United States had the good fortune to be under the eaves of the United States Coast Guard. The Coast Guard was well trained and equipped. They effected rescue operations in some of the most adverse conditions the world had to offer. They did it on a regular basis, too, because as Captain Upton had said, "There's no shortage of fools and unlucky bastards spinning the wheel of fate."

His spirits rose as he reflected more deeply upon the nature of his position. These waters were well traveled, especially by tankers. There were refineries in Curaçao and the dry dock, of course; there was also a refinery in Aruba. Aside from the tankers calling at those places, there were merchantmen headed to Curaçao for repairs. There were fast ships carrying refrigerated fruit and meat from Argentina, Brazil, and forgotten colonies to markets in the United States and Europe. Furthermore, tramp freighters hauled used cars, bulk rice, bagged cement, and whatnot to the islands. With his grandfather's luck, he would be spotted by one of them. He wouldn't mind a little adventure aboard a tramp for a few weeks before making it home.

Nothing came that day. No sight of ship, plane, or land. The sun left him. The moon returned. He slept. He woke to a blanket of stars. He sang himself a song he heard on the radio the day he left Philadelphia. He slept again.

The second full day passed as had the first. He maintained his routine of searching for a ship and fighting back hopelessness. Yet, he could not deny his thirst or his hunger. The sun roasted him from the shoulders up while the sea pickled him from his armpits down. Between the two, it felt like he would turn brittle and ultimately break in half.

In the evening, the wind slacked again. The sea settled to a low swell. Beck slept most of the night. He woke at dawn, floating in a flat calm, which rarely occurred in this part of the world. He wondered if there were currents pulling him in any direction or if he was simply bobbing in a millpond. Hot and angry, the sun came over the horizon. The shirt over his head wicked moisture from the sea but did nothing to stop the glare from scalding him.

His mind faltered. For how long, he wasn't sure, but he found himself thinking about nothing but cold water and drinking it from a glass filled with ice. When he regained his senses, nothing could take him away from the nagging reality that he was unlikely to live. He was going to shame his grandfather. It was time to face it.

He denied it with an angry shout at the sky. His throat hurt. His chest ached with thirst. His stomach cramped. The pain did him the favor of relieving his mind of dismal thoughts. Night came again, preceded by a spectacular sunset that cruise ship passengers lingered about deck to celebrate.

"So far so good," Doctor Sanial said. "A few more things and I'll leave you to yourself."

The full moon came to Beck two nights after that brilliant sunset. He missed its rise over the horizon. A stiff breeze pushed him and a choppy sea toward the west. The moon crept up behind him, a spotlight on his fate. Much later, he watched it settling toward the west, mocking him as a creature out of place.

Overhead, he saw flashing red lights that could only be airplanes. Sight of them gave him a bit of hope. The planes seemed to fly on a northwest to southeast heading, as he judged it from the position of the moon.

Most of the next day, he daydreamed of Nicole Reston. It was more than three weeks since he'd last seen her. She wore a white blouse that day and a long skirt. He was thinking about asking her to marry him. He saw the two of them standing before his friend, old Captain Wilkie, who could perform the ceremony. The only thing missing was a tugboat of his own, which was his life's goal. He was sure he'd wanted his own tug from the day he saw the first one lumbering down the river. Adrift in the Caribbean, it seemed that his dreams were going to drift away with the storm that had already claimed *Patricia*. Even if he survived, Nicole had effectively told him their relationship was over.

His schedule warped to the point where he slept most of the day and pondered the moon and stars through the night. At the end of his fourth day, he spotted a brilliant green light in the distance. Immediately, he knew it was the starboard light of a large ship. He squinted into the darkness and made out the range lights, one lower on the forward mast and one higher at the stern. The ship was moving quickly, traversing his field of vision, blocking out the stars at the edge of the horizon. That meant it was close, perhaps less than a mile.

Like a drunk meandering his way home, Beck paddled slowly in the direction of the ship. No doubt it traveled in the lanes leading to and from some destination. He splashed along to some invisible point where he collapsed against his life preserver.

"You must have been relieved when you saw the island," Doctor Sanial said.

When he first saw land, Beck had thought it was an illusion. It was dawn, and a mile or two in the distance he perceived what seemed to be cliffs. They stood above the sea, brown blotches with streaks of black among them. He stared with his itchy eyeballs for what felt like hours. When the cliffs grew bigger, he realized they were real.

He felt a smile crack the skin of his lips. He was close enough to swim for land. His muscles cramped, but he couldn't scream through his parched throat. Thankfully, his life preserver kept him afloat, or he would have sunk to the bottom like a rag-covered stone.

The wind lent him its assistance. It pushed him in the general direction of the cliffs. The waves steepened as they approached more shallow waters that led to dry land. As his body hopped along with the waves, he did his best to steer toward shore.

Late in the afternoon, he was close enough to see the surf pour over the rocks. Whether it was a blessing or a curse, he wasn't sure, but the currents pushed him parallel to the boulders. He heard the noise of rocks blunting the ocean. He saw birds playing in the updrafts at the edge of the cliffs. What he did not see was an appealing beach on which he could land safely. Those rocks would have shredded a man in excellent condition. After a week at sea, he would have felt only the first blow.

In the final light of the day, he realized he was passing by the tip of an island. It had to be Aruba because Curaçao had a lighthouse at its southern tip and Aruba did not. There was a beach in the distance, but it was tucked behind that fringe of nasty rocks. He drifted along, unable to swim against the current. Salvation had come and now it was going. The devil was laughing into the wind. He could hear his cackle echoing over the deserted beach.

As the sun fell, so did the wind. The seas settled to a casual swell. Beck labored to steer his course toward the shore. He tried a lazy backstroke, his head aimed at the black splotch of land sprinkled with lights. There were people going about their lives under those lights. They were eating their suppers, talking with their families, and making plans for the next day.

Suddenly there was a brilliant orange light leaping up from somewhere on shore. He knew immediately it was a refinery flare. He saw them on nights when he traversed the Delaware River, which fronted half a dozen refineries. Because his head was back against his life preserver, he stared at it upside down. In his demented existence, it poked at the ocean, not the sky. Maybe it was the devil pointing at him again.

He tilted his head up and saw another fantastic sight. The light of the flare carried over the water and illuminated a tanker with a tug hanging alongside by a single line. At last, he was going to be spotted! They couldn't be more than two hundred yards away. He read the name of the ship, *Athos I*. He put his arms up and waved. He thrashed for several minutes, but the duo continued without any sign of spotting him. Couldn't someone be looking out to sea?

He heard the engines from the tug as it drifted by. They were just above idle, putting out enough power to coast along with the ship. He waved his arms, beat the water around him, and made noises he hoped were shouts. No response came. He had no tears to cry and no voice left to scream. He suffered in silence as his second brush with salvation faded away.

The refinery flares lit up the night, as did the lights of the town on shore. It tortured him to watch them move. He hoped there were fishermen in that town and that they would be out soon. The moon would be up in a matter of hours. Didn't that make for good fishing? He wasn't sure.

The ship and her escort were in the distance now. Whistle signals called out between them. Only a few of the old docking pilots demanded whistle signals in Philadelphia. The radio did the job better than any combination of tweeters. The old-timers liked them, however, because they knew each tug by the pitch of her whistle. Those pilots were slowly disappearing.

Similarly, Nathan Beck was going to disappear from the earth. The crushing defeat of missing two chances at saving himself overwhelmed him. He cursed himself for not grabbing a flare or a chunk of metal or a mirror to use as a reflector.

No one would see his death as heroic. His father would think it stupid, reminding anyone who would listen that he'd warned his only son to stay away from the ocean, to go to college, and to get a job where nothing was more dangerous than a corporate consolidation. Nicole would be sad but relieved that she had left him before the tragedy. Jack Ford, the owner of Ford Towing and Salvage for which Beck worked, would be disappointed. He had promised Beck the master's position on the next new boat. It seemed that blessing would be bestowed on some luckier man. At least his mother wouldn't be upset. She had probably forgotten him years ago. All of them could say what they wanted. He would never hear their voices. A few more sunrises, three or less, and he would be dead.

The rambling state of his mind eased as exhaustion overtook him. He felt the strange urge to laugh out loud but his parched body denied him that pleasure.

A vivid illusion occurred some time later. He remembered seeing the island silhouetted before the growing moon as it climbed into the sky. The lights on shore looked like falling sparks as they twinkled below. Then he felt something firm against his foot. It bumped once and again and again. Entranced by the lights, he ignored it. All at once, he realized he was no longer moving. Whatever was bumping his feet was now touching his legs. Perhaps a whale had crossed his path and was going to surface with him on its back.

He dragged a few feet along the obstruction, eventually stopping after his body swung around like a wind vane in the current. He was sideways to shore. The refinery was off in space, somewhere beyond his feet. As his mind lapsed into unconsciousness, he thought he heard music.

He woke in the same reclined position. The refinery remained a fixed point. The music played on. He looked to his left and saw how close he was to shore. It appeared to be a hundred yards or so. Or was it a mirage? The lights were brighter than ever. Were those voices he heard or a delusional fantasy? The scent of roasting meat was also in the air. What he would do for a slice of steak!

His patient worked his jaws. Doctor Sanial liked the sight of that. It meant the man was testing himself, checking what worked and what didn't. "No solid food just yet," Sanial advised.

Beck was thinking how he could taste that grilling meat while he was stuck in the water. All he had to do was stand up and walk over there. Such a simple concept boggled his mind. How could he walk across the water? What the hell, he decided. It had been so long since he used his legs that he didn't know if they still worked. He rolled onto his belly and pulled his knees up. He found his hands pressing against the bottom. He clutched two fistfuls of sand, drew them up to his face, then released them into the water. He was on land! Not quite land, but he was on a bottom not so deep that he couldn't stand.

But he couldn't stand. He tried. He rose up on both knees and got his torso erect. Then he pressed one foot down, but as he lifted himself out of the water his leg collapsed. He toppled into the water with a soft crash.

Walking required more energy than he had left, so he crawled. He selected a point on shore, just as they had taught him in navigation school, and steered for it. He put one hand in front of the other and one knee after each hand. He lumbered half the distance to the lights when he suddenly plunged into a hole. His head dipped beneath the surface, but his life preserver brought him back up. He flailed like a snared animal until he found a new purchase for his hands.

The tumble sapped his last bit of strength. His breathing grew harder. The water lapped his chin. He rested against his life preserver and looked up at his destination. It was definitely no illusion. It was a heaven-sent reality. Upton had been right. The devil was backing away. The angels were calling him. They were beckoning with laughter and music. A few more yards and he would be in paradise.

Some of the time he was afloat, paddling like a dog. The rest of the time, he was on hands and knees. He was going to make it to shore or die trying. He may succumb to exhaustion, but he did not shame his grandfather by dying out there amongst the creatures of the sea.

Finally, he was head and shoulders out of the ocean. Only a few inches of water skirted the sand. The place he wanted to go was amidst a grove of low trees. He took another rest. It felt wonderful to be on solid ground. Looking at his bare feet, he wondered what the rest of his body looked like. He had to be a fright for whoever was going to see him first.

He sat up and stared in the direction of the music. Between the trees he saw shapes dancing. A man leaned over a bar. Beer bottles clanked as two guys toasted one another. Just a few more feet and he would be there among them. He would be safe, alive to tell the tale.

Forgetting his previous failure at walking, he tried to get up again. He heard voices, a man and a woman, very close. He looked up and there they were, a couple dancing on the beach. They stopped and the man turned the girl to face him. He kissed her. They were so close he could hear their lips smack. Why couldn't they see him?

He wanted to find out. He struggled against the all-powerful force of exhaustion that pressed down on his shoulders. His vision blurred as he wobbled upright. A screeching roar filled his ears. The distorted view before him tilted one way, then the other. He went light-headed, dizzy to the point of retching. He put his arms out to break his fall. The sound in his head increased in pitch until it blocked out all other sound.

He collapsed on the beach with his feet in the water. He caught a glimpse of the moon before it went black and took all the stars with it.

"I didn't drown," he whispered into the darkness.

Doctor Sanial said, "No, Herr Beck, you did not drown."

"THIS CALLS for some improvisation," Charlie said as he and Sam left the hospital.

"What do you have in mind?" Sam asked.

"We're not going to let the authorities phone the United States and all that crap just yet. The man has been through an ordeal. He needs to have some recovery time."

"He may have family who thinks he's dead," Sam said.

"If he's dead to them, what is the difference?"

"You're telling me you're going to let them go on worrying or making funeral plans?"

"I'm telling you it doesn't matter," Charlie said.

"What about Calenda and the doctors?"

"I'll take care of that."

"How?"

"My friend, we've known each other all our lives. I am a master of improvisation, am I not?"

"*Sí, señor.*"

Sam knew better than to ask Charlie what his plans were. It would take away the fun of the surprise. They drove to Savaneta listening to the radio. He left Charlie to his mischief and went to Oranjestaad. He had a surprise of his own. He found a flower shop, bought a sensible arrangement, and kept the air conditioner on full power to prevent the flowers from wilting in the heat. It took him an extra fifteen minutes to arrive at his destination. It had been a long time since he had been to Ricardo's neighborhood. He carried the flowers to the front door, eager to see who was on the other side.

It took two rounds of knocking before he heard the lock turn. Marcela opened the door. She wore the black dress perfectly but more like armor than a mourning garment.

Sam smiled humbly and said, "Sorry to hear about Ricardo. It's a little late but please accept my condolences and these flowers."

Marcela didn't look at the flowers but she took them in her hands. "Were you a friend of my husband?"

He put out his hand and introduced himself. "I went fishing with Ricardo," he said, although he had only seen Ricardo's boat and never actually fished with the man.

She put the flowers down at her feet and shook his hand weakly. "Many people went fishing with my husband," she said as if Sam counted for nothing among the multitudes. "I'm selling his boat today. So many expenses. With my husband gone it will be difficult."

Expenses for what? Sam wanted to ask. He held his tongue and shifted his eyes for signs of Luz. "Is there something I can do to help?" he inquired.

"I will manage."

Sam stared across the threshold at her. He recognized the eyes of a professional whore: hard, unyielding, and steady. He held her gaze long enough to give her the impression that he was not afraid. Then he shifted his gaze to focus on Luz who was seated on a couch in the background. The edges of his lips curved into a slight smile.

"Okay," he said. "Maybe I'll come back in a week to see how you're doing."

"Thank you," she replied and swung the door closed.

Sam didn't like turning his back to a witch so he walked sideways to his car.

Inside the house, Marcela spoke to Luz. "Do you know that man?"

"He was a client," Luz answered. "He was the one with me when I saw the man on the beach."

"You should have been at the bar when that happened," Marcela said.

"I'm sorry, señora."

"Do you know why he came here today?"

"No, señora."

"It was not to bring flowers," the owner said. "You have to be careful around their lies. You have to protect yourself."

Luz looked at her feet to avoid betraying her reaction.

Marcela continued. "Men like this client of yours, they tell you you're beautiful, you're sweet, I love you. They tell you these things as if you believe them to be true. They're little boys, every one of them. They never grow up."

Luz had heard enough. She said, "I should go back to the bar, señora."

"Soon, but first you can go with me to the marina and see my husband's boat. You like boats don't you?"

"I've never been on a boat," Luz admitted.

"It's a beautiful thing. I will miss it."

Luz wanted nothing more than to return to Minchi's where she could be alone with herself. So many things had happened in the past two days that she was exhausted. She needed to sleep and put the world in order before she lost control of the little piece of it in which she lived.

Marcela readied herself to go to the marina and told Luz to do the same. Luz followed instructions, then waited in the living room, watching the door as if Samito might burst in to rescue her.

They drove to the marina in Ricardo's Mercedes. As nice as the car was, it was nothing compared to the boat. The name on the stern was *Perfección*, and the boat lived up to its name. It was like a white cloud sitting in the water.

A Venezuelan man waited for them on the dock. He kissed Marcela on the cheek and looked at Luz. "Your assistant?" he asked.

"My protégé," Marcela said grandly.

"As pretty as the boat," he replied.

"Isn't she?"

Luz smiled as if she appreciated the comments. Hadn't Marcela warned her about that kind of talk less than an hour ago?

A man in a white uniform came down the dock. The Venezuelan introduced him as Captain Rodriguez. They all went onto the boat together. Luz sat on one of the chairs at the stern. She noticed that some of the other boats in the marina had similar seats. There were fishing poles sticking up like flag poles in front of the chairs.

Fifteen minutes later, Marcela returned with the Venezuelan. She said, "Señor Suarez would like to take the boat for a test. I told him you have never been on a boat and would enjoy his company."

Behind a smile, Luz gritted her teeth.

"Enjoy yourself," Marcela said, "I'll be here when you get back." She patted Luz on the shoulder and climbed over the gunwale to the dock.

The boat backed away from its mooring. Captain Rodriguez stood at the wheel, high above the deck where Luz sat with Suarez.

"A boat like this is wonderful," he said. "It leaps over the sea. You can put a pole there and pull in a fish that's twice the size of me. Can you imagine that?"

She could imagine it but had no urge to do it.

He made small talk, asking her where she was from, if she had brothers, if she liked Aruba. She told him she was from Colombia, a tiny town he wouldn't know. She had one brother and a sister. She didn't know if she liked Aruba because she had only been there a week and a half. He had been there many times but never to San Nicolaas. He liked the big hotels, especially the Hyatt.

"Have you been there?" he asked.

"No," she told him.

"Too bad. Let me show you the rest of the boat."

She knew what was going to happen. It went precisely as she expected it to. He made a big production of showing off the interior of the boat. There was the galley, the crew quarters, and the engine room. Then he took her forward to the "owner's suite." The bed took up most of the cabin. A small door led to the bathroom. Having proven his knowledge of all things nautical, he tugged her down onto the bed to demonstrate his sexual prowess.

He yanked off her clothes without ceremony. When she was naked, he stood back, unbuckled his belt and slid down his pants. His erection stood out from his loose underwear.

"Do you have a condom?" he asked.

She said, "I wasn't expecting this."

"No matter. Marcela tells me you're fresh." He stepped forward with his cock in his hand like a miniature sword. He forced himself into her and kept going. Luckily, he finished quickly. He used the bathroom, then told her to "wipe off," that they would be back at the dock soon.

She sat on the bed for a few seconds looking at him as he pulled on his clothes. When she heard the door in the hallway close, she got up off the bed. The bathroom was tiny, much smaller than the one she used at Minchi's. She cleaned herself as best she could with paper towels. The little shower was inviting, but she dared not risk using it. The controls looked complicated and her hair would never dry in time.

When she came on deck, Suarez was sitting beside Rodriguez. They looked down at her and shared a laugh. She went to the back of the boat, where she sat down and watched the water go by. She knew Marcela had given her away as an incentive to help sell the boat. Her face burned hot with anger and shame.

Rodriquez steered the boat into its slip without touching the wooden pilings on either side. He switched off the engines and hopped down to the deck. Suarez handed him the ropes, and they tied the boat fast. Marcela strolled up the dock. She wore a big hat which shadowed her face from the sun.

"Do you like it?" she asked Suarez.

"*¡Claro!*" he said.

"We won't argue over the price," Marcela said next.

Suarez looked at Luz and said, "Since you made it so attractive, I won't insult you by bargaining."

Marcela had her hand out. Suarez took it. She told him, "My lawyer is waiting for you. I signed the papers. You need only to pay him, and you can have the boat this afternoon."

"You won't invite me for dinner?" he asked.

Marcela tilted her head back to laugh. "I have other business, but I am flattered that you would expect my company."

For the first time since meeting Marcela, Luz realized how formally the woman spoke. She used the polite forms of address and employed complicated sentence structures. Luz also noted that Suarez appreciated it, as if Marcela were deferring to his importance, playing the role of obedient servant who speaks every word carefully.

"Luz and I must go now, Señor Suarez. *Buenas dias.*"

Marcela led the way to the Mercedes, which was already running. The interior was as cold as a refrigerator. Luz shivered in her seat.

"Did he treat you well?" Marcela asked as they drove on the main highway.

"He must be an important man," Luz answered.

"I'll tell you a secret. He was my lover."

Luz didn't know what to say so she looked out the window.

"It's okay. It was in the past, like so many things. I am sad to sell Ricardo's boat, but it's best to be rid of things that remind you of your loved ones."

The woman was incredible. Her husband was dead for only a month, and she was doing away with all references to him. Luz's mother still wept at the sight of Luz's father's photo, which was kept in a drawer to prevent such crying bouts.

"I'll take you to San Nicolaas now. Tonight, just before the bar opens, I want to have a talk with all the girls. Make sure everyone knows."

Marcela took her as far as the hardware store at the north end of town. Luz walked the last four blocks to Minchi's. Upstairs, she found Inez seated at the plastic table watching television.

"What happened to you?" Inez asked. "You look like you were scared to death."

"La Dueña wants to talk to everyone tonight," Luz said ignoring Inez's observation.

Inez changed channels on the TV. She said, "You're calling her la Dueña, too?"

Luz didn't want an argument so she replied, "She told me to make sure every-one knows."

"That she's la Dueña?"

Frustrated, Luz found the key to her door. "No," she answered. "She wants everyone to know she wants to talk to them tonight."

"Probably wants to complain we're not making any money, the bitch."

"Watch your mouth," Luz warned. Then she was furious at herself for defend-ing Marcela. Didn't Marcela give her away to that man to help sell the boat? Still, she was the owner and the position, if not the person, demanded respect.

"It's not our fault. The men in this town are either too poor to pay or else they're all gay."

"She will be here just before the bar opens," Luz said.

"Samito was here asking for you," Inez said.

After her morning with Marcela, an afternoon with Samito would be splen-did. "When?" she asked Inez.

"About an hour ago. I told him you were with *la señora de la casa*, that witch."

Luz stormed up to the table. She pointed her finger at Inez. "Don't talk about her like that. She's going to hear it, and we're all going to have trouble."

"Are you her little pet? *Sí*, you're her little bitch. The two of you are in the same bed together all night while we're working on our backs."

"Shut your mouth!" Luz retorted.

"I will, you lesbian. I'd rather fuck Frankie down there than touch that thing of hers."

Luz whirled around and rushed into her room. She slammed the door, went over to the window, and looked down on the street. No one but the occasional tourist searching for Charlie's Bar walked the streets at this time of the afternoon. Men from the refinery were not yet driving on Rembrandtstraat in search of a quick lay. She decided to take a shower and look her best. Maybe Samito would return. She hoped so. A hundred dollars didn't last long in San Nicolaas.

At quarter to nine that night, the four of them sat in the bar. Luz and Inez stayed away from each other. Carmen and Laura talked quietly. Spanner and Pablo filled the ice chest and placed extra cases of beer near the cooler. It seemed they were expecting a busy night.

Marcela came in at one minute before nine. She wore a black suit over a pair of black heels which made her taller than everyone but Spanner. Luz saw that her fingernails were freshly lacquered. A strong cloud of perfume floated around the woman, magnifying her presence. It filled the bar with a scent too sweet for the atmosphere. Luz wondered if Suarez persuaded her to change her plans for the night, or if another man would take that smell home on his clothes.

"Spanner," Marcela began, "bring me the book."

He handed her a ledger that contained a page for each girl working in the bar. Down the left column was the date. The second column held the number of vinos sold by the girl. The next column held the amount paid for the casa, or house, which was basically the girl's room rent. If it wasn't paid, the space was left blank. If partially paid, the balance due was written there. The final column was the number of times the girl went upstairs while the bar was open. It was Pablo's and Spanner's duty to keep track of the book during business hours. No one cared what the girl did after hours. Marcela ran her finger down each of the pages. She clicked her tongue several times.

"I want to know why you girls are not working. You are all very pretty and well dressed. But the men do not seem to want to go upstairs with you. Why?"

Inez glared at Luz.

"Maybe you think you are too good for the men in San Nicolaas," Marcela said. Keeping her fingers bowed to avoid chipping her nails, she slapped an open palm onto the bar. Luz jumped at the crack. Next came a pointed finger and a tone of voice Luz remembered from earlier in the day. "You're whores. Each one of you sells your body. It doesn't matter who the man is, what he looks like, how he dresses, or if he washes his face before he comes in here. What matters is if he has the money."

The girls stared at their boss.

"You want to drive a car like that?" Marcela said pointing to the window through which was visible Ricardo's Mercedes. "Do you?"

"I do," Inez said with her chin up.

"You do?" Marcela countered. "You went with only one man last night. Do you think one man is enough to pay for that car? You shake your head because that car costs more than you ever made in your life. And if you only fuck one man a night, you will never make enough to pay for it if you fuck every single day of your miserable life."

Luz looked to Spanner who was busy wiping a liquor bottle on the rack behind the bar. She wondered how many times he had heard this lecture.

"You think I don't understand what this is like? You are wrong. I was a whore, too. Ask Spanner. No, I will ask him." She said to Spanner, "Tell them I worked in this town."

"Yes," he said, "You worked in Las Vegas Bar."

"And what was my room number?"

"Number one."

"You see?" Marcela said. "Someday I will show you the page that was mine. It was full, absolutely full! Did I turn away from a man with rotten teeth or body odor or the stink of oil on his clothes? Not if he had the money."

Marcela rattled her fingernails on the bar. It was as if she were plucking hairs from each of the girls and delighting in the torment. She said, "You came here to make money like I did, so you better learn to work like I did. I see all of you are behind in your rent. How do you expect to make it up? How do you expect me to pay my expenses if you don't pay yours? Do you think I'm going to forgive it? Do you think the people who sell me beer will forgive it? Do you think the electric company will forget about the bill? The government will forget to collect the taxes? They won't. I won't. And all of you better not. My husband is dead. He didn't leave me a million dollars in insurance the way men do in the United States. I had to sell his boat today to meet expenses so this place could operate tonight. Isn't that true, Luz?"

Luz nodded that it was. She wanted to say that she had to give the buyer her body to improve the price.

"This bar needs to make money to pay for itself. If I'm lucky, and you girls start working the way you're supposed to, it will make enough to pay Spanner and Pablo and then, finally, a few florins for myself. Is that too much to ask?"

No one said it was.

"Luz," Marcela said, "Is that too much to ask?"

"No," Luz replied quietly.

"Good. You are the only one with an excuse. For helping me today, I'm going to forgive you two days' rent. The rest of you? You were here with less competition since Luz was absent. What did you do with the opportunity?"

If there was any chance of patching things up between her and Inez, it was now gone for Luz. Marcela's erasing the house rent doomed her. Carmen and Laura would take Inez's side. Luz was alone, without a friend in the place.

"I'm not going to waste my breath. You came here to make money. So make it. The bar is open." She slammed the book on the bar and walked out. There was no doubt in anyone's mind that she was officially la Dueña and that Luz was her favorite.

Sam saw the whole incident from the street. He intended to pop in the bar early, make a date with Luz, and pick her up at closing time. Marcela ruined that plan. He saw her wheel up in the Mercedes, or Nazi staff car, as he liked to call it. Her body language told him she was heading to an ass chewing. He leaned on the window frame, where he was out of sight to everyone on the inside. Marcela went through her spiel as he expected, all hellfire and brimstone, complete with slamming fists and pointing fingers. The only area that could have been improved was her exit. She needed someone to hold the door for her so she wouldn't have to slow down on the way out. He thought about tripping her, just for the laugh, but figured it would only make things worse for the girls. He backed into the side alley until she drove out of sight. Then he thought twice about entering Minchi's. The girls would be in a foul humor. Spanner and Pablo would also be on edge. There was no fun to be had there, but nor was he in the mood to swallow six drinks an hour with his pals. That would end badly, somewhere between a hangover and a drunken brawl.

He detoured to the far end of town, where he could find a comfortable seat and a friendly ear. A strong drink wouldn't hurt either, he told himself as he hit the door of Bar Sayonara. Here he felt at home as much as he did in Java. The place used to be owned by Max, an original Aruban with roots going back to the Arawak Indians. Max died about two years ago and left the bar to his common-law wife, Carlotta. Carlotta, like Marcela, had been a whore. She started in San Nicolaas at eighteen and didn't quit until she was fifty-two. Even when she was living with Max, she had clients on the side. She took care of Max through two bouts with cancer. The third time was too much for him. He died a miserable, suffering death. Against doctor's orders, Carlotta gave him brandy whenever he wanted it, which was about every half hour. "He's going to die," Carlotta had said. "What does it matter if he's drunk?" She renamed the place Sayonara in honor of Max, who used the word instead of *adiós.* "Sayonara, Max," she said at his burial and blew a kiss over his grave.

Sam squinted at the neon sign Carlotta had installed over the door, then leaned forward and pushed the door. He and his friends called the place Carlotta's or the Clown Joint. Carlotta had installed cheap paintings of circus clowns on the walls about ten years ago. There was the happy clown, the sad one, the goofy one. These faces stared out at the patrons from every wall. One time, a guy on a mean drunk went crazy at the sight of them. He swore they were staring at him, which wasn't entirely untrue. He started throwing chairs, cursing Carlotta, and swinging his fist at anyone who tried to stop him. Sam circled behind him, got him in a headlock, and pressed him into the floor. A couple of other guys jumped into the fray and dragged him to the street. It was a close call, but no one was seriously hurt, including the guy who started it.

Inside, Sam found Carlotta behind the bar. She wore one of her giant hats and a fancy lace dress. He smashed his cigarette into the first ashtray and leaned in for a kiss. She planted one on his lips, then pulled out a white linen handkerchief to wipe her lipstick off of him. He brushed her hand away and kissed her again, this time with more force. She broke away, fanned herself, and rolled her eyes.

"Oh, Samito! Please! Think of my heart!" she exclaimed.

"I was, *mami*," Sam replied with a wink.

Carlotta was immune to blushing, but she faked it for Sam. He was a good customer. "Look at these pretty girls I have," she said with a wave at a pair standing by the jukebox. "Save your energy for them."

Sam shrugged his eyebrows a couple of times. "*Gracias mami*, but I might have found *the one*," he said.

She batted her eyes at him. She knew what he meant, but she couldn't resist the chance to tease him. "Oh, Samito is getting married," she said. "Why not a girl-friend, too? Your new wife may have a headache tonight."

"You know my style."

She patted his hand. "How are you, Samito?"

"*Excellente*," he answered. "And you?"

"The same. Business is slow. The company that owns the refinery isn't spend-ing any money. Why don't you talk to them?"

Unfortunately, Sam didn't know anyone above the rank of foreman who worked on the other side of the wall.

"Two men died last month," Carlotta said. "Two men dead and one was a very good client. He was with Melissa, the redhead over there. She was very sad. She wouldn't work for three nights."

"Terrible."

"Terrible for business, Samito. I remember Esso. When they had the refinery, there were men through here day and night. There were Americans with money. Now? These people that work there, where are they from? Countries that are not on the map. I was here when the Americans were here. They knew how to spend money."

"So was I, *mami*, so was I. My dad was one of the originals."

"The new company has been here five years. What have they done?"

"*Nada*," Sam told her.

"*Nada de nada*," she repeated. "Look at my girls. No work for them. Look at my bar. No one to buy drinks."

"I see that."

"A blind man can see that. Why don't you find a big American company to buy that junk pile over there and make it safe again. Make it like Esso."

"I'll try, *mami*."

"Try harder, Samito, I'm getting old. I'm older than Ricardo was, and he died last month. He and my Max used to fish together."

Sam leaned over and kissed her on the cheek. "You always look beautiful to me."

She blushed honestly and poured him a drink. He paid her and she returned his change on a small tray. From behind the bar, she brought out a small crystal dish filled with mixed nuts. Bar Sayonara, despite difficult times, remained a classy establishment.

Carlotta enforced different standards than Marcela. She lectured her girls on all manner of subjects. First and foremost, no girl was to make promises in the bar she didn't intend to keep in her room. Second came the admonition to never ask for the money first. If a client didn't pay, the girl was to report it to Carlotta, who would deal with him. Then came the general rules about appearance and hygiene. Never was a girl to work the street or look like a tramp in public. She was to dress modestly and use facial expressions to charm a man, not the sight of flesh. The public knew what went on in San Nicolaas and left it alone so long as it wasn't ugly. Half-naked girls may walk the streets, but none of them worked in Bar Sayonara. When the cops did roundups, they sought girls who looked like whores, not girls who looked like their sisters. Her girls were to shower at least twice a day and keep their clothing washed and pressed. Their rooms, the common area between the rooms where they ate, and the staircase leading up from the bar needed to be spotless. Whereas Marcela's girls worked seven days a week, Carlotta gave her girls Sundays off. She liked to take them to the hotels, where almost no one would stare at them like the locals in San Nicolaas. To the tourists, the entourage looked like a nice grandmother out with her granddaughters. That's what she wanted them to think. Many of these girls had never seen a building bigger than the church in the little towns in Colombia where they lived. Here in Aruba, they could see a thirty-story hotel and a real windmill imported from Holland in the 1960s.

"Where does your girlfriend work?" Carlotta asked.

"Minchi's," he said after a sip from his glass.

"Are there nice girls there?"

"There's one," Sam said.

With a nod of her head, Carlotta poured more nuts into the dish. She helped herself to a few because she knew people felt uncomfortable snacking by themselves. She also knew that the only thing that sold more liquor than salty food was a pretty girl. Her girls were pretty this time, and thin, too. Her last batch was on the homely side, and there had been two heavy ones. She complained to the agent who complained back. Word of slow business in Aruba had spread to Colombia. Once the girls heard the bad news, they were reluctant to sign up to work on the island. They would rather try their luck in Panama or Spain or Japan. Carlotta wished Sam would spend some of his money with one of her girls. It would encourage them that an American had come in here and opened his wallet. She knew better than to force the issue.

"How was Charlie's party?" she asked.

"Unbelievable!" Sam crowed. "A man washed up on the beach. His boat sank and he drifted all the way from Curaçao."

"¿Verdad?"

"Verdad, mami," Sam confirmed. "Charlie and I took him to the hospital."

"Dios mío," Carlotta sighed. "Maybe he will bring us good luck."

"As soon as he's well enough, you'll meet him." Sam looked at his watch. "I have to go," he said. "Hasta mañana."

"Okay," Carlotta said, a little sad because there was no one else in the bar. "I think I'll close early. Let the girls sleep."

"Good idea," Sam told her on his way out. When he was two blocks down the street, the neon light over his shoulder went dark.

He headed due east to Caribbean Bar, where his pals liked to hang out when they weren't in Java. Once again, his instincts were right. Roger, Carlos, and Tom were in the bar.

"And we thought you were lost," Carlos said. "Where the hell have you been?"

"Dancing the night away," Sam replied moving his hips to a salsa beat.

"With the one?" Tom wanted know.

"Wouldn't you like to know," Sam told him with a wink. "Let's get the party started. One for me and a fresh round for everyone!"

The bartender poured out the drinks, including a vino for each of the girls. The friends toasted each other, and the fun began. A girl who had been upstairs with a client entered the room. She was a knockout by anyone's standards. When the client left, Carlos bought her a vino and another round for the bar. When these drinks were gone, it was Roger's turn.

The bartender could hardly keep up. After the fourth round, everyone was in the mood for a strip show. Each man passed twenty florins to the bartender and told him it was for the girls if they were willing to put on a great show. The bartender rattled on in rapid Spanish, and the girls were only too happy to oblige on such a slow night.

Tom locked the door then turned up the jukebox. The first girl was the foxy one. She danced with her arms out and her head back. She rocked her hips, kicked her legs over the men's heads, and stooped down to run her hands under their chins. The other girls took their turn until all four of them were stark naked on the bar. Everyone clapped to the music and started dancing. Before the bartender realized what was going on, the men were taking off their clothes. He waved his hands frantically to get them to stop, which they did, but not until they were down to their underwear. As they got dressed, they nuzzled the girls and drank three more rounds.

They poured out of the bar with their shirts half buttoned and a full load of alcohol in their stomachs. It was like the end of a war. They were shouting and laughing and slapping each other on the back. Other men on the street stopped to stare at them. "Cheer up!" Sam called down Main Street to no one in particular. "It's a beautiful night!"

They piled into Java, where Kenny did nothing to slow the drinking. He backed up the rounds until there were three coasters stacked behind each man's glass. Kenny's girls didn't appreciate the revelry. No other men dared enter the bar upon seeing the friends living it up. Kenny told them to work Rembrandtstraat, hoping they would turn a few tricks to pay the casa.

After they told each other stories that had all been heard before, the night started to wind down. They were yawning and looking at their watches. Carlos was the first to give in. He went around the corner and picked up the girl working for Kenny, the one with the big chest. He dared not drive back to Savaneta. He barely made it upstairs to her room.

Roger went home alone, risking the drive even though Kenny offered to call a taxi. Tom and Sam walked across the street with every intention of going into China Clipper. Sam pulled up short and suggested they first go to the Chinaman for soup.

They waited for their meal in silence. Their livers were overloaded with alcohol, and it was a challenge for their brains to work afloat in vodka and beer. Once the soup came, they were able to make small talk.

"You going to pick up *the one* tonight?" Tom asked.

"If the saints allow," Sam replied.

"I was thinking about one at Black & White."

"You pay your money; you take your pick."

Nodding, Tom asked, "You ever think of marrying one of these broads?"

It was time to infuse some of Charlie's wisdom into the situation. "Don't fall in love," Sam warned.

"This from the man who tells me he found *the one*."

"Might have and if she is *the one*, she's *the one* for here," Sam assured his pal.

Tom said mockingly, "So you have considered sticking with one of them."

"Maybe."

"I did," admitted Tom. "But, you know, I bet if you marry one of them and move her in, she'll probably turn out the same as all the rest. She'll be at the lawyer's office before the ink is dry on her green card."

Sam gave him a bored look. "That's what I'm trying to tell you when I tell you *the one* for here." He poked a finger into the plastic table to reinforce the point.

"It's a shame. We're all getting old and ..."

Sam interrupted him. "Speak for yourself, chico."

"You're not going to be running this town in ten years," Tom said.

After dropping his spoon into the bowl, Sam said, "I'm going to be running this town in twenty years."

"Give me a break. You can't keep drinking like this and expect to make it on the long haul."

"Why not?"

"Ah, shit. I'm too drunk to argue," Tom said.

"Who's arguing?"

"We are."

"No, we're not. I'm telling you something, chico. This party never ends. Very soon I'm hanging up my spurs and doing this full-time every day thereafter."

"Are you serious?"

"Serious as a heart attack," Sam said before he could stop himself from making a reference that might offend the recently deceased, namely Ricardo.

"I don't think I could do it. It's one thing to come down here and carry on like this for a week. Living here all the time would probably ruin it. You don't see Charlie out here like us."

"Charlie has his own thing going. He's not sitting at home watching TV."

"The girl in Lago Heights?"

"Among other enticements," Sam said.

"See, that's what I want. A nice girl, regular, someone I can count on to be there."

"Go find her," Sam told him. "There's a hundred in town."

"A hundred and five or something I heard. Ah, hell, I'm drunk and happy and full of shit."

They grinned at each other like two guys who had discovered a bag of money fallen from the back of an armored truck. San Nicolaas was the prize, and the best part was that they could win it any time they wanted. The odds were always in their favor. All it took was a few dollars and a little time.

"Hey, what about the guy from the beach?"

"He needs a couple of days in the hospital. Then we'll spring him and show him how real sailors live."

"I don't know if I can take too many nights like this."

Sam fired his finger-pistols and left Tom slumped in the chair. He walked up the pedestrian alley that led back to Main Street. At the curb, he stopped and gazed at Minchi's. The light was on in the marquis. He juggled the change in his pocket as he thought about what to do. The sound of those rattling coins brought Frankie out of his shadow.

"Samito, a guilder so I can get something to eat."

"Here's two," Sam said.

"Always a gentlemen. Always. Except the time you said that stuff about my teeth."

"Frankie, you can't hold it against a man when he tells the truth."

"The truth hurts," Frankie whined.

"Does it ever," Sam said. The truth that he was too drunk to think clearly hurt him as much as the fact that Tom was right. There was coming a day when he wouldn't be able to drink a quart of vodka, smoke a pack of cigarettes, and still think about a roll in the hay all in the same six hours. No matter what he said, it was going to catch up with him faster than modern medicine could hold it back.

"Chicken tonight," Frankie said, flapping his arms and clucking like a chicken for an audience of one.

Sam had to laugh. The choller maintained a sense of humor despite his squalid existence. His own sense of humor was something Sam had to keep an eye on. He also needed to keep track of what was real and what was fantasy in a place where he knew there was no line dividing the two.

He knew guys like Tom fell the wrong way for San Nicolaas girls. They fell for the sly ones, the ones who were too professional for their age or too cunning for their own good. They were Academy Award winners for the part they played in a movie called *Life*. They were after your money or to wreck your life out of spite. One or two were like Marcela. She wanted it all, and the fact that she got it from Ricardo, someone who should have known better instead of a gringo new to the action, was proof of how incredibly talented a girl could be.

Perspective required distance, and with that in mind, Sam left town. If he felt the same way about Luz in the morning as he did right now, well, she would have passed the test. If not, there were a hundred and four other girls in town.

SAM AWOKE in the condition he expected. The night ended with a sigh rather than a bang, but he suffered just the same. He had remembered to draw the curtains before collapsing on the bed, thereby sparing himself the full force of the morning sun. He rolled over, stuffed his head under the pillow, and told himself he'd get up in a few minutes. Waves lapping the shore hushed him back to sleep.

Two hours later, he arose to face a day that was already half over. A cold shower did nothing for his headache or his creaking joints, but it rinsed the paste from his eyes and mouth. What he needed most was coffee, but he settled for cold water from the bottle he kept in the refrigerator.

He found Charlie seated in the shade of his studio.

"Hallelujah! The dead arise."

"The jury's still out," Sam moaned.

"But the judge has already imposed the punishment."

"That's for sure."

"As a dear friend, I'm telling you to be careful," Charlie said. "Moderation in all things."

"That sounds like the pot talking to the kettle," Sam replied.

"Either way, while you slept with the angels, I was busy seeing to it that our shipwrecked sailor will not go naked."

It took Sam a few moments to register what Charlie was talking about. The scene before him came into focus. There were two large shopping bags, one on each side of Charlie's seat. Over his lap he had a pair of blue jeans and in his hand a scissor.

"Through my connections at the hospital, which are both legendary and mysterious, I found out the size of everything the man needs to wear down to his shoes."

"He wasn't wearing any shoes," Sam said.

"Precisely. However, a certain nurse, who shall go unnamed at this time because I think she has a foot fetish, was able to measure his feet just this morning and pass the information to me on this miserable invention, the cellular telephone. You know, there was a time when a telephone was something you didn't need on this island. Now we carry them around in our pockets as if our lives depended on them. Judging by the way you look, you may want to keep one handy in case you have to swap beds with the sailor."

Sam looked at his mentor in awe. No one but Charles Brouns, Junior, would think of such details as a man's shoe size. He went so far as to buy what looked to be a week's worth of clothes. He was clipping the tags off at the moment, no doubt in preparation for washing them.

"I'll take them to the laundry as soon as you finish," Sam said. "Did you talk to Doctor Sanial?"

"Yes. He says Herr Beck will be a guest for another day and then should be strong enough to go home." Charlie held up one of his trademark "Boozer" T-shirts. He said, "Not until after we initiate him into our club, eh?"

"I yield to your greatness," Sam said.

"So long as I'm directing the show, Herr Beck is stuck with my script. This calls for you to host him about town."

Hungover and famished, Sam wasn't ready, but he would be when the time came. For the present, he would take Beck's new clothes to the laundry and do whatever else Charlie wanted done to make the man welcome. However, there was one other thing he wanted to mention.

"I saw Marcela yesterday," he began. "She said something about selling Ricardo's boat."

Charlie tilted his head and said, "Be careful sticking your nose into the jaws of the lioness."

"She's not doing right by Andrés," Sam went on.

"Look, my friend, this is none of our business."

"I thought Andrés paints with you."

"He does," Charlie acknowledged, "and he's better than I'll ever be. But I'm not even his uncle."

"So Marcela takes whatever she wants? What kind of justice is that?"

"This is a topic as mysterious as the cosmos itself," Charlie warned. "I put it to you this way. Justice is like a boomerang. It flies crooked and has a way of coming back at you. So don't turn your back."

Tom staggered out of his room and called over to Sam that he was making coffee. They joined up on the porch of Tom's bungalow, where they drank two pots, one in silence and one in reliving the night's highlights. Both swore an oath to never drink so much again knowing full well it would be broken that night if not sooner.

Sam then set about his assigned duties. He drove alone to the laundry, dropped off the clothes and then turned a lap on the San Nicolaas Five Hundred. There were girls about, lounging in doorways, waving to passersby. He hoped to spot Luz, but luck failed him.

Ready to test his stomach, he parked across the street from Pueblito Paisa, his favorite restaurant for quick food, and took his seat at the counter. He ordered scrambled eggs and toast. No one needed to be told to bring him a pitcher of ice water. As he sat there eating, a number of workers from the refinery came through. They were of the late shift, having their supper when the rest of the world took breakfast. Sam listened to their conversation out of habit. He liked to know what was going on.

By the time he finished eating, he had learned the refinery was doomed. Operations had been cut to a minimum, more layoffs were imminent, and the rumor among the superintendents was that the place was going to close. Sam kept his reactions to himself, but he was shocked. He couldn't believe the place that had employed his father, the fathers of his friends, and a generation of men since then, was going out of business.

Sam did nothing but shake his head. What bothered him most was the effect the closing would have on San Nicolaas. The town relied on the workers and their families, as well as the contractors and suppliers to eat, drink, and buy their daily necessities. The bars would feel it first, the girls especially. It would take a while for them to realize the worst had come to pass. Girls would continue coming to San Nicolaas, expecting men to buy their time until word spread to Colombia that the well had run dry. Similarly, the town could not survive on the tourists who drank at Charlie's. Local men would continue to patronize the bars, but their budgets and time were limited by wives and girlfriends who tolerated bad habits in small doses.

What a sorry way to start the week! He decided to make the best of it, which was to get on with his chores. They weren't actually chores. They were favors, and he enjoyed doing them because it was part of the greater adventure of Beck's arrival. He bought more coffee for the porch at Savaneta. He wrote a few post cards to friends in the States. After retrieving Beck's clothes, he drove a few laps because the hangover had ebbed and left him feeling frisky despite bad tidings regarding the refinery.

The optimist in him said, "Never give up!" Another company might come along, one that sees the potential of the place, and rebuild the entire complex. It would be like the old days, when sailors roamed the streets twenty-four hours a day, when refinery workers spent entire pay envelopes in a single night, when men fought one another to see particular women. In other words, it would be just like it was when he was a teenager. The confluence of those golden ages, that of the refinery and that of his youth, made him the man he was today. The experience infused him with bold appetites and the drive to satisfy them.

At the hospital, he took the stairs instead of the elevator. He felt energized by the challenge of the refinery and excited at the prospect of having his first conversation with Nathan Beck. He passed the nurses' station with a wave and a casual "*Bon dia*." No one looked up. He entered Nathan Beck's room with a patented smile and an outstretched hand.

Beck sat in a chair looking out the window. He started to get up to shake Sam's hand, but his visitor pressed him back into the seat.

"I'll slide a chair over and join you," Sam said. "How're you feeling, Cap?"

"Tired mostly," Beck replied.

"If there was ever a place to recuperate, this is it," Sam told him. "You see that beach over there?"

Beck looked at the stretch of sand fronting what looked to be a series of one-story hotels.

"That's not so bad, but it's nothing like the one I'm going to show you." Sam stopped short of what he was going to say when he realized Beck might have had his fill of the ocean for the time being. He steered on to other subjects in which he was also an expert. "We have great restaurants, nightlife like you wouldn't believe, and cozy places to hang your hammock and take a snooze."

Beck smiled. The skin on his lips cracked. He felt drops of blood fill the grooves. After blotting it on the shoulder of his hospital gown, he asked Sam, "Did the rest of the crew make it?"

"The news reports every one of them did. God bless you all, Cap. There must be some very tired angels who were working overtime to bring you guys back to shore."

"The others landed here, too?"

"No, they were picked up off Curaçao by another ship."

"Directly from the water?"

"They were in a life raft, I think, but don't quote me."

Beck mulled that over. He saw images of *Patricia* going down, her emergency lights flickering.

"Something bothering you?" Sam asked.

"A little. I can't figure out what happened to the boat."

Ever curious, Sam asked him what he meant.

"*Patricia* was a strong boat, not new, but in good condition. I can't understand why she sank so quickly," Beck explained. He didn't say anything about the ordeal of being the last man to abandon her.

"That was no small storm," Sam reminded him.

"We were behind it, on the edge. Those were rough seas for any boat, but we should have made it."

Sam scratched his brow. "You'll be talking to your mates soon. Maybe they know something."

Beck nodded that Sam was correct.

"We got you some clothes. Make sure they fit."

The gesture stunned Beck. He didn't expect this kind of hospitality, not from strangers in another country.

The jeans and shirts fit, slightly big, but he didn't mind because his skin was raw from soaking in the sea. The shoes fit perfectly.

"You're a new man!" Sam proclaimed, adding conspiratorially, "You could assume a new identity and work for the CIA."

"I hadn't thought of that," Beck said.

"That's why we're here, to keep things interesting."

What interested Beck most was finding out what had happened to *Patricia*, which had been a favorite. He had sailed her from Philadelphia to Norfolk, from

Savannah to Boston, and any number of other ports. He learned how to handle the bigger barges using her. He graduated from lower horsepower tugs to her massive engines sooner than anyone wanted him to. She forgave his mistakes and made him look good when he should have been the fool. He would miss her rattles and squeaks and the things he left behind. What would Captain Upton have to say? "No shame in tears for a good boat gone down. Better than seeing her in the graving dock." Beck wasn't sure he would agree with that. It was the saddest thing of his life watching *Patricia* sink.

"I guess I'll get a plane ticket and be on my way home in a couple days." Beck wasn't sure what was supposed to happen when he left the hospital. He reasoned that he would call Jack Ford, who would make arrangements for him to fly home.

Sam leaned forward in his chair. "Let me make a suggestion, Cap, purely a suggestion. After we spring you from this joint, spend a few days here in Aruba. Stay in the shade to give that sunburn a chance to heal. Enjoy what the island has to offer. You will not be disappointed."

"Thanks," Beck said. "But I have to call the office." He also wanted to call Nicole. Although they were no longer dating, it would be a joy to hear her voice.

"They'll wait," Sam suggested, hoping Charlie had somehow planned for this possibility.

Beck did not agree. "The company has more work than ever . . . "

"I understand all that," Sam cut in. "We're both Americans, and making money is what it's all about. That said, you're here. Take a taste before you get on that plane. This way, when you come back, you'll have something to look forward to."

"When I come back?" Beck asked.

"Everyone comes back," Sam told him. "Tell you what, call down to Charlie's when the doctor releases you. Koch, the bartender, knows how to find me. I'll be across the bridge as fast as my wheels can spin."

What could Beck say? The man dragged him off the beach, got him to the hospital, and brought him clothes. He deserved the respect of a day or two of his time.

"Alright," Beck said. "What's the number?"

Sam was already on his feet. "Just tell the nurse you want to call Charlie's. Let us take care of the rest."

It was odd for Beck to receive this kind of attention from a stranger. He was used to being around people he knew and who knew him. He spent his days on the dock or the boat with the same men day after day. In his personal life, he rarely met new faces except during the occasional night out with Nicole. She had a list of friends and acquaintances that filled her address book. Well, if he managed to win her back he could tell her about someone new. "There is this guy," he would begin. "His name is Sam, and he found me on the beach."

Doctor Sanial came in late that afternoon. He saw the clothes piled beside the bed and wanted to know if Beck had left the hospital to do some shopping.

"No," Beck said, "Sam brought them for me."

"Very nice of him." The doctor went on to say that all tests were coming into the "normal range," whatever that meant. He thought Beck should start walking in the hallways for the exercise. Before he knew it, another day would be in the past and he would be on his way home.

That night and the next day did not pass so quickly. His stomach hurt when he ate solid food. The hallways were not as long as sea-lanes, and he grew bored by the time he got used to his new shoes. He found some books in the tiny gift shop. The English ones were of no interest. The Spanish ones were out of the question. He picked up an English-Spanish phrase book with the idea it would occupy his mind. It did for a few hours. After that, he wanted out of his cage and on to the first plane going in the general direction of Philadelphia, but there was no telephone in his room to make the arrangements.

Doctor Sanial pronounced him fit for travel the next day, recommending he visit his personal physician immediately upon returning home.

He felt vaguely like a prisoner getting out after a long sentence. He was wearing someone else's clothes and carrying things in a heavy brown shopping bag. He went downstairs to the lobby, where he told the woman behind the desk he wanted to call Charlie's. She handed him the phone and punched the number from memory.

"*Bon dia*, Charlie's Bar, Herr Koch speaking," the man on the other end answered.

"This is Nathan Beck calling."

"Of course, Herr Beck," Koch said. "You're waiting for your taxi."

"Sam said I should call."

"Yes, I know. He will be there soon. I'm looking forward to meeting you."

"Thank you," Beck said and hung up. He also thanked the receptionist and stood near the door. Less than ten minutes elapsed before a string of cars pulled up outside. A group of men, led by Sam and Charlie, piled onto the sidewalk and headed for the door like marauding Vikings.

"Here is the man of the hour," Charlie said. "Gentlemen, this is our guest for as long as he likes, and it is our sworn duty to see to it that he enjoys himself in a manner befitting a true sailor."

Beck met Tom, Roger, and Carlos. Then he was relieved of his bag and placed in the passenger seat of Charlie's pickup.

"We had to deliver you here in the back seat," Charlie told him with a thumb pointed over his shoulder. "The view is better up here."

Sam handed him a carton of orange juice. "Best to stay off the booze but have a drink anyway."

Beck took the juice and sipped it.

Charlie showed him the sights as they drove southward to Savaneta. "That's our little commercial port, as you can see from all the containers. There's the cruise ship terminal, which has us overrun at times with trinket trollers. There's the government house, but they're always on vacation."

After the airport, Charlie turned on to the road that fronted the ocean. He passed the electricity and water plants and whizzed through several neighborhoods until he arrived at his place. The boarding party gathered around the bar, where there were more cheers and handshakes. When everyone had a drink in his hand, Charlie proposed a toast.

"An old Dutch captain used to call here at San Nicolaas. He would come to the bar, back when my father owned it, and give this toast every night. He said, 'To friends old and new. To friends! Absent, present, and overdue.'"

"Here, here!" everyone called out.

Sam had the barbecue burning in no time. It wasn't the complete feast he had prepared for Charlie's birthday, but it was a substantial amount of food. Beck looked at the roasting chicken and steaks and felt his mouth watering. It was too much to ask of his stomach just then, but he intended to have a taste.

"Let me show you something," Sam said to Beck. They walked over to the beach where Sam pointed to a spot about a hundred feet from the inland side of the pier. "That's where I found you."

Beck looked at the nondescript area of sand. Then he tilted his eyes out toward the reef. From this vantage point the view was nothing short of idyllic. He must have drifted onto the reef and then made his way inshore. He could remember pieces of that struggle but not all of it. Farther in the distance, under the arc of the refinery smoke, he saw a tanker nosing in toward her birth. By some miracle, Beck had floated past a ship just like that one as well as the tug escorting her. Because the wind always blew from shore, the tug was on the leeward side of the ship. There was no point in having a tug on the windward side if the docking pilot knew what he was doing. That same wind should have pushed Beck away from Aruba until he washed up on the shore of Venezuela or beyond.

Sam must have been reading his thoughts. "The wind was different that night," he said. "The storm that knocked out your boat stopped up the trade winds like a cork. It was breezy in the morning, mostly from down there, the south. Then it went calm until late in the afternoon and then south again, and hard. There's a current that runs up along the beach this time of the year. Other times it reverses, goes that way. You got a double shot of help when the wind and the current worked together to get you here. On a day like today? You would have been gone."

Beck needed no one to remind him of his good luck. He wished that luck had held for *Patricia*.

They returned to the others, who were enjoying their drinks and playing dominoes. When the food was ready, Beck sampled the chicken and steak and had a little salad with it. Even those small bits made his stomach ache. The men around him wanted to hear about what had happened on the ocean. He told them he couldn't be sure, that he was off watch, that when he talked to the rest of the crew he would know more.

"I always wanted to know why boats were named after women. You have any idea?" Carlos asked.

Beck quoted the late Captain Upton. He said, "Boats and women give us the same amount of trouble. Might as well give them the same names."

Everyone laughed.

They talked about women and boats, and before he knew it, Beck had fallen in with the group. Several hours passed until someone realized they had other things to show Beck. Before this could be accomplished, they wanted to make themselves more presentable to the general public. Charlie gave Beck the key to room number six, which was on the ground floor at the end of the row. "Don't need you risking the stairs," he said. Inside, Charlie showed him the details of the room including some of his original paintings on the walls. "Here," he said, handing Beck a sheaf of money. "You'll need this for the rest of your stay."

Beck looked at the money. It was the local currency, in bills of several denominations, and a few coins including some that were square.

"Go on," Charlie urged him. "Take it and pay me back when you return. Hopefully you don't swim to my beach again, but whichever way you prefer."

The hospitality was irrefutable. Beck folded the money into his hand as Charlie patted him on the shoulder. "One more piece of advice and then nothing more. Don't fall in love."

Beck had no idea what the man was talking about.

"Okay," Charlie said, "I'm putting you in the hands of Sam, which may not be a good thing, but I have to pay a visit to my girlfriend, who I have been neglecting. If I don't see her tonight, she will be angry and it will cost me money to make her happy. Can't have that now, can I?"

"I guess not," Beck said, thinking of Nicole, who liked the better things in life.

"Good. See you tomorrow."

Beck went into the bathroom, where he found a new toothbrush waiting on the sink. He looked in the mirror and winced at the sight of his own face. Sunburned skin peeled around his eyes and ears. The weight he'd lost made it look as if his eyeballs were hiding deep in a cave under his brow. His cratered lips were scabbed. At least his teeth were intact. He went out to the bar, where Sam was waiting for him.

"Okay, Cap, I'm going to go easy on you because you've had a fright and need to recharge your batteries, but there's a few people you have to meet before you go off watch."

SAM AND Beck were half way to the car when they ran into Chief Calenda and his driver.

"Commandante," Sam said with a salute. "This is our sailor, Captain Nathan Beck."

Calenda extended his hand. "A pleasure to meet such a man," he said. "You will forgive me for not coming to see you at the hospital, but your situation didn't involve any violations of the law."

"The commandante is a top notch investigator," Sam put in. "He trained with the New York City Police Department."

"Herr Beck, I am informed by my contacts in Curaçao that your crew has returned to the United States. Fortunately, here in Aruba, we have so many tourists that American Customs and Immigration has a facility at the airport. I told them you will be seeing them soon."

"Thank you," Beck said.

"My pleasure. I hope you will come see us again under more pleasant circumstances."

"I think I will," Beck said honestly.

"Good. Should you have any difficulties you will contact me, yes?" Calenda extended a card embossed with the official seal of Aruba.

They shook hands again, and Calenda departed after a terse nod to Sam.

"With that bit of official bullshit out of the way, we can get on to better things," Sam said. "Hop in. I'll drive."

The sun had long since gone down, and the yellow flames of the refinery flares towered over San Nicolaas. Beck remembered seeing them as he drifted just off shore. They looked much the same from this perspective.

Sam parked in his spot at Charlie's Bar. He said to Beck, "We'll go there tomorrow, when the tourists are around and we can have some fun. I have another place that's a blast about this time of night."

They walked up Main Street to the hardware store, where they turned right and went two more blocks. Sam pressed the bell at Sayonara's door and winked at Beck when the buzzer released the lock. "Here we go," he said.

Sam took a seat at the bar and held out a stool for Beck. Beck sat down and looked across the bar at the woman coming over to Sam. She wore a giant hat with a silk ribbon around it. The elaborate layers of her dress and the costume jewelry around her neck made it look like she was ready for a night out in Manhattan sometime around 1928. She kissed Sam on the cheek and turned to Beck as Sam did the talking.

"Doña Carlotta," Sam said, continuing in Spanish, "I present you Captain Nathan Beck, the luckiest man to find the beach in Aruba."

Carlotta shook Beck's hand and smiled at him. *"Mucho gusto, Capitán."*

"Pleased to meet you," Beck said.

"Carlotta doesn't speak much English," Sam told him. "It doesn't matter. The woman worked on her back for probably as many years as you've been alive. She has a life story just this side of Hollywood."

"We should get together," Beck suggested.

Sam liked that. "She could teach you things," he said. "And you would like it."

At this point, Carlotta brought Sam's drink and asked what Beck would like. Sam told her to bring him a club soda, that he wasn't ready for anything stronger.

"*Claro*," Carlotta said. "*¿Tal vez*, Coca-Cola?"

Beside the drinks, she put a crystal dish of peanuts. Sam helped himself to some and pushed the dish toward Beck. "Put on your spectacles," he began, "and take a look at those nice young ladies by the jukebox."

Beck turned toward the music and saw several girls perusing the songs on the machine.

"They are all awaiting your handsome presence and are ready, willing, and able to serve. The price is fifty guilders and don't pay more than sixty no matter what they do for you because you'll screw up the local economy. *¿Comprende?*"

"Whores?" Beck said bluntly.

"I see your powers of perception have not been diminished by your recent calamity. Although we like to call them chicas, girls, and friends sometimes, they are what you say they are."

As his eyes adjusted to the light and the girls turned back and forth to the music, Beck saw they were rather attractive. In fact, he found one of them particularly appealing. She looked at him for an instant, then turned away.

"You see something you like?" Sam asked.

"Maybe," Beck said.

"Don't be shy, Cap."

"I think I'll wait a while."

"It's a good idea to find one that clicks. There's more than a hundred in this town. You don't have to tie your lines at the first dock."

"There are more places like this?"

"Nothing quite like this. Carlotta is special to us. Let's just say the other bars are similar. You'll find booze and girls and rooms upstairs or in the back."

"I get it," Beck said.

"Watch this," Sam said and waved the girl Beck was looking at over to them.

She approached slowly, not sure if she was bound for Samito or the guy with the damaged skin.

Sam put his arm around her waist and pulled her in close. He asked for a vino, and Carlotta set it on the bar. "You want to talk to them, you should buy a vino or two. It's good etiquette," Sam said, then asked the girl her name.

"Vanessa," she said.

"This is Vanessa," he said to Beck, then asked her what part of Colombia she was from.

"Bogotá."

Beck recognized the name of the city.

"You have to learn Spanish to make the most of the experience."

"I can see that," Beck said.

"But don't be fooled. Some of these girls speak English and never let on. Watch what you say. The girls don't like it when you treat them badly in front of others. It's bad for their self-esteem, which is already in the gutter thanks to their chosen profession."

"Hmmm."

"It's a shame for these girls," Sam went on. "They have a kid or two back home, a boyfriend, or an ex-husband who shafted them. Maybe their family is hard up for money. They come here looking to make big money. Some of them do; most of them break even or make a few bucks. A few go home with nothing for their trouble."

In his life on the water, Beck had heard sailors talk about whorehouses in far off places. The descriptions didn't seem to fit with this place. Furthermore, he never expected the women to be so young or as good-looking as the one in front of him. Since the vice never appealed to him, he hadn't considered exactly what it would be like. This version of it was not altogether disgusting. In fact, he could see the appeal of it in that the girls were dressed nicely, seemed to groom themselves well, and the atmosphere wasn't the least bit sleazy. Sam clearly enjoyed having him under his wing, showing him the ropes, and teaching him how to operate in this environment. Just the same, he was satisfied to look and not touch.

"Take another Coke," Sam said, releasing the girl to go back to the jukebox. "I don't like to drink alone."

Beck caught her looking back at him with a twinge of disdain. No doubt his appearance turned her off. He was probably as frightening as a Halloween costume come to life. But Carlotta smiled at him like he was no different than anyone else. She asked Sam some things. Beck tried to follow the conversation but quickly lost track. He noticed the sadness on her face except when she caught Beck looking at her. Then she dredged up a grin.

"What's she upset about?" Beck asked Sam when Carlotta went to pour a drink for another customer.

"These old dames don't need a reason to cry. They can do it on command," Sam answered. "But since you asked, a local guy died. He was a friend of her deceased husband's."

"Sorry to hear that."

Sam stirred the ice in his glass. "Okay, Captain," he said suddenly. "We're going to weigh anchor and find another joint to take our money."

"Lead the way," Beck said and waved good-bye to Carlotta.

They walked south by west, into the wind. Three blocks on, Frankie approached from a side street. He came up to Sam, but upon seeing Beck, reeled backwards like a character from a silent melodrama.

"He's uglier than me," Frankie said pointing at Beck.

"Watch your mouth, Frankie," Sam said. "He's a captain, and I'll give you a beating if you don't show him respect."

"That doesn't make him any better looking, does it?"

"Very witty, Frankie," Sam said. "Apologize before I get ugly with you."

Frankie folded his arm back in a salute. "Captain, sir! Request a guilder, sir."

Sam tossed the choller a coin. "Beat it and make sure you watch my back, or I'll give you a boot in the ass."

"Hah, catch me!" Frankie said and ran off to wherever it was that he hid when he wasn't begging for guilders.

"Local social terrorist," Sam said to Beck. "Frankie and his pal, Speedy, are harmless. Give them a guilder or two and don't be too friendly, or they'll hang on you like lice. There are some others that are trouble. Stay away from them."

"How can you tell the difference?" Beck asked.

"If it's not Frankie or Speedy, it's trouble. *¿Comprende?*"

"One down, one to go," Beck answered.

Sam clapped him on the back. "I like you, Cap. You have a way of getting to the point."

They followed an alley to Main Street. At Main, Sam swerved left and led Beck to Java. He successfully avoided passing the façade of Minchi's and, therefore, seeing if Luz was working or not. They entered Java, where all the boys were waiting. Drinks were already backed up. The music was American and as loud as a rock concert.

A cheer rose up as Beck came up to the bar. Everyone wanted to know where they had been. Sam told them Sayonara, to pay their respects to Carlotta. The next question was if Sam had held Beck's pants while he got laid. They laughed and downed their drinks.

"What's your pleasure, Captain?" Kenny asked. "It's on the house."

"Club soda," Beck said.

"Club soda it is. You sure you don't want a splash of something on top just to wet your whistle?"

"Johnny Walker would be fine but just a little. My stomach's taking its time getting back to normal."

"Hey, your stomach is like Kenny's prick," Carlos said. "It takes a while to get back to normal."

"You see what I have to put up with to make a few guilders," Kenny said to Beck. "This kind of abuse makes a man old before his time."

"How old are you, Kenny?" Tom asked.

"Not as old as your mother and still more beautiful," Kenny told him.

Beck saw it was all in good fun. Kenny poured a glass of club soda, then brought two bottles of Johnny Walker off the shelf. "Here's your drink, Captain," Kenny explained. "A splash of black, a splash of blue. I'll spend the night with that girl, and so will you." He nodded toward the one with the massive breasts. Beck joined the laughter as the girl jiggled her tits at him.

"We took up a collection, Cap," Sam said. "You can have any one of these girls you want. It's on us."

"Maybe I'll take her upstairs first," Carlos said leering at the one with the big chest, "just to make sure it's okay for you. What do you think?"

"Be my guest," Beck told him.

"I guarantee you, I won't be the first guest in that motel," Carlos added.

Sam put his hand on Carlos' shoulder. "Captain goes first, chico."

"That's okay. I'll save it for later," Beck said.

"Gentlemen, here's to peace, love, and happiness," Tom said.

They all toasted to that, except for Kenny, who looked at Beck with resigned eyes and a weak smile. "These assholes would be happy living in prison and buggering each other if someone poured the booze fast enough." Having landed the jab he raised his glass and joined them.

Sam and his friends kept the party rolling. Every once in a while one of them would slip out the door and return half an hour or so later. Beck figured they were going to other bars to see different girls. He stuck to club soda with occasional splashes of whiskey. After a couple of hours, the noise and smoke got to him. He needed fresh air. He stood up from his seat and stretched his back.

"Got somewhere to be?" Tom asked.

"Going for a walk," Beck said.

Sam came over from the jukebox. "Feeling alright, Cap?"

"Just need to stretch my legs."

"Sure. Tell me her name later, will you? Don't forget, tonight we're going easy on you. When you get your land legs again we're going to show you one hell of a good time."

Beck smiled. He had no desire for a wild party or a rendezvous with any of the girls. He hoped the door was still open with Nicole.

"See you back here unless you get otherwise detained. Watch out for sinking boats, eh?" Sam said and went back to the jukebox with his handful of guilders.

Via an empty sidewalk, Beck went to the end of Main Street, where he stopped to stare at the half-finished hotel. Flickering light from the refinery flares gave the place the ambience of a bombed-out building. To his right, he saw the refinery gate with two flagpoles. The Aruban flag flew at the top of both. The flags cracked in the breeze, pointing due west. Beck estimated the wind at fifteen to twenty knots.

He turned left after passing Rembrandtstraat. A brief look down that alley was all it took for him to keep going. He saw two ugly whores, like the ones in the movies, waiting in the first doorway. There was also a knot of tough looking men talking over the back of a pickup which was parked in a dirt lot. He moved beyond these scenes without slowing until he got to Hollywood Bar. Men strutted around the felt of a pool table in there, taunting each other, making or missing shots, while a crowd looked on.

He followed Helfrichstraat northward toward Sayonara, where he and Sam had begun. He figured he would travel in a loop and eventually end up back at Java. For a few blocks, there were no bars. Instead, there were commercial buildings, storefronts, and the odd house stuck in between. In front of a tiny restaurant, a group of people sat on plastic chairs on the sidewalk. They stared at a TV mounted high on the wall inside. While a heavy-set man cooked over a griddle, they cheered or booed a baseball game broadcast from the United States. No one paid any attention to Beck as he walked by.

About two blocks on, he heard music. This wasn't blaring rock and roll like the stuff on the jukebox at Java. It was a live performance, what sounded like a couple of guitars, a violin, an accordion, and some percussion instruments. He detoured off the street, along a dirt track until he came upon a wooden house without a single right angle in the entire structure. It was as if the wind, always from the same direction, was slowly pushing the house over. The door and window frames were hopelessly skewed. The front steps looked like something out of an amusement park fun house. But the people gathered outside played as if they hadn't a care in the world, including whether or not their house made it through the night.

A man with a tattered violin led the group. The case was scratched, the finish worn through on the neck, but it was in tune. He tapped his foot to start the next song and was promptly joined by two other men, one with a guitar, the other with an accordion. The woman had a collection of percussion instruments strewn around her chair. She picked them up or put them down as they were called for. The violinist pointed at one of the guitarists who promptly took over the melody. While his partner had the lead, the violinist reached for a bottle under his chair. He balanced the violin on his shoulder while he tilted the bottle for a sip. Then the bottle was back on the ground; he nodded his head to recapture the tempo and joined in with the song. His bow hopped over the strings in a staccato beat, accented by woodblock taps coming from the lady.

When they finished the song, the woman waved Beck over. He eased up to the group. They tried to talk to him in Spanish and Papiamento, both of which left him at a loss. At last, one of the guitarists went in the house, got a chair, and put it by the others. The woman handed Beck a set of castanets and showed him how to play them between his hand and his thigh. Before he knew what was happening, they started playing again. He had the rhythm down, a simple beat, back and forth. Of course these people needed more than that. The woman syncopated the wood block and a cowbell between Beck's basic drumming. The song wound up with a dramatic display of guitar playing. When it was over, they all cheered Beck's musicianship as if Carnegie Hall were his next stop.

Liberal swigs from the bottle preceded another tune. This one was more serious. The woman sang a lamentation that could only be about lost love. The violinist did most of the work, with the guitars playing a soft counterpoint. The tension of the song was not to last. The woman jumped from her seat and shouted, "¡Basta!" The men all started clapping, and she danced around the circle several times before reaching under Beck's arms to get him out of his seat. He rose up and was mimicking her dance as best he could. The men added music and words, singing in a round that had unlimited verses. The tempo continued to increase until they were practically running in place, kicking up a cloud of dust as their shoes smacked the dirt. Beck was breathing hard, trying to keep up with the woman. As the song ended, he flopped down on his chair in a coughing fit. The nearest man passed him the bottle, but Beck waved it off. The guy took a long swallow for himself. It was the last one. He lobbed it into a steel drum. It smashed atop what sounded like several other empties.

Beck caught his breath a couple of minutes later. He couldn't say thank you in any language but English. He did that, patted them on the shoulders, and waved good-bye. He retraced the path to a paved street. His feet felt heavier than ballast rocks. He may have been released from the hospital, but he was foolish to think he was completely recovered. He leaned against a wall for a few minutes, holding his gut, thinking it might have been the wiser choice to stay in the room Charlie had given him. Then he heard feet shuffling toward him. When he looked up, Frankie stood there with one hand on his chin and the other pointing at him.

"You are a scary man, Captain," Frankie said.

"I'll take that as a compliment."

"You look like you're not feeling good."

"Some cramps," Beck told him, thinking that he never would have had a conversation with a street bum in Philadelphia.

"You eat from the garbage can like me, you get more than cramps," Frankie told him.

"I believe you."

"Believe me because it's true. A guilder and I won't have to be in pain like you."

"Give me a minute," Beck said to him.

"I watch your back, hah, your front. Don't want a choller coming along and getting the best of you when you're already in a bad way."

"Thanks, Frankie," Beck said and handed him a coin.

"Let me ask you a question," Frankie said then.

Beck straightened up, took a deep breath, but still felt awful. Following Sam's advice, he started to walk away from Frankie.

"A simple question," Frankie called after him.

Beck felt slightly dizzy and paused a second time. "What is it?" he muttered.

"Sam told me you swim all the way from Curaçao. How did you do that?"

"I was too ashamed to die," Beck said and turned down the street.

Suddenly, he was exhausted. He had not eaten enough to restore his strength. His stomach wouldn't allow the big meals he enjoyed on the boat. The splashes of whiskey were probably a bad idea as well, not to mention the dancing.

All he had to do was get back to Java. It wasn't more than four blocks, and they were small blocks at that. He looked around to see if anyone was watching him. His vision was blurred around the edges. He scanned back and forth, the way he did when he was steering through a fog bank. No one appeared to be nearby.

He pushed off the wall and started to walk. The first block went by easily. The breeze refreshed him as it took the sweat off his forehead, but he crashed into a set of metal gates as another dizzy spell overtook him. He held on so as not to fall on the sidewalk. The muscles in his arms trembled and gave way. He slid down to the pavement, where he lay still for a few minutes.

All at once, there was a roar in his ears, and he nearly blacked out. The next instant, his head cleared. His vision was perfect. Every sight, sound, and smell from the street rushed into his brain. He propped himself up on one elbow and wiped his forehead on the back of his hand. The hand came off dripping with sweat. He stood up as a group of men came around the corner. When they entered another bar, he started again for Java. He traveled another block without difficulty. Then he felt a wave of nausea coming on. It was like being seasick but worse. He wondered if the doctors on this island knew what they were doing. He fought on, making progress one step at a time. The last thing he wanted was to collapse on the street in a town like this.

He paused at the next corner. There was Frankie again, begging a couple of guys for a guilder. They gave him nothing but curses and raised their fists. Frankie cowered. When the men moved away, he taunted them for a fight. They turned back and laughed. Beck wanted to give Frankie a hundred-guilder note to help him to Java.

Before he could call out to the bum, another person came into view. It was one of the girls, dressed in a knee-length skirt. She was carrying a plastic bag with a Styrofoam container inside it, the kind for take-out food. She crossed the street in front of him, moving swiftly, her heels clicking on the asphalt. She gave him a quick glance, looked away, then turned a second time. He saw that she recognized him, but that was impossible. He didn't know anyone in this town. For some reason, delirium perhaps, he smiled at her. She smiled back and walked up to him.

"*Tú vives,*" she said.

"I don't know," he replied.

"*Encontramos en la playa,*" she went on, pointing with her free hand toward something far away.

"I'm sorry," he said, "I don't speak Spanish."

"*Ah, no habla español.*"

They stood there in silence for a few seconds. At last, the girl took the initiative. She said, "*Mi nombre es Luz,*" and stuck out her hand.

Beck wasn't sure what she was telling him, but he understood the handshake.

He grasped it weakly.

"*Soy Luz. Mi nombre. Luz,*" she said pointing to herself.

He got it now. "Okay, your name is Luz. Mine is Nathan."

"Nay tan," she said to him slowly.

"Right, Nathan."

"*Mucho gusto. Qué horrible cuando te veo en la playa,*" Luz told him because she had been terrified when she saw him on the beach. Samito dragged him out of the water and shouted for help. She knew this man had been alive when they took him away, but she did not know if he had lived after that. No one was talking about him. Ricardo's death dominated the conversation since it was directly related to San Nicolaas.

Beck staggered backwards until he had his back against another wall. He held his stomach with both hands. "I don't feel well," he told Luz.

"*¿Borracho?*" she said, tilting an imaginary bottle up to her lips. "*¿Mucha cerveza?*"

"No, no. I'm sick."

"*¿Enferma?*"

"Tired. I have to rest."

"*¿Cansado?*" She tilted her head into her palm as if putting it on a pillow.

"Yes. Sleep."

Luz stared at him for several seconds. His flaking skin and sunken eyes were frightening. He had survived some tragedy in the ocean and earned a second chance at life. She didn't want to be the one to deny it to him. To be sure, she put her face close to his and looked into his eyes. The pupils were clear. She smelled no alcohol on his breath. Besides, she'd done a favor for Spanner and Pablo by walking to the Chinaman to get their food. Closing time was coming soon. She could take this man upstairs, put him to bed, and then have a snack herself. In the morning, if he stayed that long, she could point him toward Charlie's, where people spoke English.

There was only one problem. She didn't have the keys to her room. Pablo kept them until a man paid the two guilders for a condom. After Pablo had logged the trick in the book, he would hand over the keys.

While she tried to figure something out, Beck started to breathe heavily. She saw him holding on to the wall. Perhaps it was best to tell Spanner someone was ill and needed help. Then again, why would Spanner help someone he didn't know? The bouncer would think the man was drunk or on drugs and not worthy of his time. He tossed men out of the bar for reasons like that. But she knew better. What this man was doing in San Nicolaas instead of the hospital or back where he came from was beyond her comprehension. It was like the night she saw him on the beach. He simply appeared from nowhere.

"*Vamos*," she said reaching for him.

"What?"

"*Vamos a mi habitación.*"

"I'm sorry."

"*No importa*," Luz told Beck and put her arm around his waist. He eased away from the wall and walked without leaning on the girl but was thankful to have her righting his balance.

Just before the door to Minchi's, she stopped and spoke to him. "*Señor, necessito un poquito dinero.*"

"Please," Beck said, "My friends are just down the street. I think I can make it." He pointed in the direction of Java.

"*No, señor. Trabajo acá. Tú duermes en mi habitación esta noche. Pero sin dinero, no es posible.*"

He decoded none of the words but "*dinero*" and the phrase, "*no es posible.*" He assumed the girl wanted money to take him to his friends down the street. Given his condition, he didn't much care about the money. The girl was helping him, and in light of her profession, a few dollars (or guilders or florins or whatever they called the money here) was something she had a right to ask for. He put a hand in his pocket and took out the money Charlie had given him.

"Here," he said, handing her a hundred-florin note, "Let's go."

Luz palmed the bill as politely as she could but very quickly. She didn't want anyone on the street to see it for fear they might try to take it. This man was in no condition to fight one of the chollers. A hundred guilders paid the casa for one night and left her money to eat for two more. She wasn't going to give it up easily.

The door to Minchi's swung open. Several men walked out, and Luz steered Beck to go in. He pointed down the street and said something in English. Luz tried to push him into the bar, and as he resisted, she felt his strength draining away. Finally, he gave in and entered the bar.

The bartender came over and took the plastic bag from Luz. Beck tried to speak to him in English. The man ignored him and put the bag on a shelf.

"*El no habla inglés*," Luz said to Beck.

He groaned and put his head down on the bar. If this continued, he was going to pass out right there.

Luz handed Pablo the hundred-guilder note. "*Mis llaves,*" she said. "*Y cambio también.*"

"Your keys?" Pablo asked.

"I'm going up with him."

"This ugly drunk?"

Luz had had enough. La Dueña had ruined her chances at friendship with the other girls. She had been given away to the Venezuelan who bought the boat. Spanner was nowhere to be seen, which meant he was most likely playing backgammon with another bartender. Then there was this man who showed up twice, once nearly dead and the second time in poor condition. Amazingly, he was giving her good money, so she decided to stick with him.

"Listen to me," Luz said to Pablo. "This man is a mariner. No, he is a captain."

"He looks like an ugly drunk to me," Pablo said to her laughing.

"He's going upstairs for the rest of the night," she insisted.

"But we don't close for two hours and ten minutes," Pablo said jerking his thumb at the clock.

"What's a couple of hours to you?" she asked.

"Then give them to me for free," he said leering.

"Give me the keys," she told him. Pablo didn't move. He fixed his nasty smile on her. Luz wanted to murder him but knew she could do nothing but try to outwit him. "The Captain is going to call his men," she said quietly. "They're going to come here and drag you into the street, where they'll whip you like a dog."

This gave Pablo something to think about. He remembered a time when some American navy men were in town. They fought with each other over girls, billiard games, and drunken wagers. Pablo figured this guy was also an American because he spoke no Spanish. He appeared to be drunk out of his mind, but there was the possibility he could still use the telephone.

"You want to go up with this ugly bastard?"

"You will call him Captain," she fired back.

"Captain Ugly, then," Pablo said. "You go. Go for all night. Don't call me if you have trouble."

Beck made no sense of the conversation except for the word *capitán*. How did they know he was a captain? It wasn't important, but it perplexed him. All he wanted was to lie down. He knew if he took a rest for half an hour he would be able to walk all the way back to Philadelphia.

"*Vamos*," the girl was saying to him as she scooped her keys and some money off the bar.

He pushed away from the bar and followed her toward the door. Instead of going out through the entrance, they used another door. After it, they turned right and faced a long staircase. The girl wanted him to go to her room. Somehow she thought he wanted sex.

"*Vamos, Capitán*," she said, "*Arriba. Mi habitación está arriba. Tengo una cama grande.*"

He thought of taking his chances on the street. How far was it to Java? Two blocks? Three?

"*Por favor, Capitán*," Luz said. "*La escalera y no mas.*"

"*No mas*," sounded wonderful to Beck. No doubt the girl had a bed. Wasn't that what he wanted? What if Sam wasn't at Java? What if the other guys were gone? If he could make it up the stairs and get into the girl's room, he could lie down and not worry about a thing.

At the top of the stairs, Luz waved him into the room. He sat on the bed. As he reached down to loosen his shoes, blood rushed into his head. Dizziness returned. He fell over onto the mattress. The will to fight left him. He took the deepest breath he could as his head sank into the pillow like a lost anchor. The last thing he heard was the girl's voice.

"*Duermes bien, Capitán*," Luz said.

FOR THE third time in a week, Nathan Beck awoke in the strangest of places. It was not the ocean or the hospital this time. He was lying on a bed with a flat pillow under his neck. This bed was not the one in his home, nor was it his bunk aboard *Patricia*. The oddest thing was the smell. His bedroom had a faint dusty odor because he rarely slept there. His cabin aboard the boat always had overtones of diesel fuel. This place had a hint of perfume and not the kind worn by Nicole Reston.

A slice of brash sunshine cut through a window on the other side of the room. He rubbed his eyes and turned away from it. The first thing his gaze settled upon was a tall glass cylinder with a candle burning inside it that stood in the corner. It was a votive candle, the kind he recognized from cemeteries and shrines. Propped behind the candle was a card bearing the image of a saint, which seemed to be peeking past the side of the candle.

He remembered the previous night to the point where he couldn't take off his shoes. Beside him lay the girl to prove it had not been a dream. Her hair was tied in a long braid that stretched down the valley of blanket between them. The voice of Captain Upton was in his head.

"Told you that storm was blowing over another man's grave," Upton said. "What a beautiful sight you lived to see."

Beck thought the girl was pretty enough. Just the same, his stomach ached and he wanted to fill it with solid food. If it killed him, he was going to eat a huge breakfast. He wanted eggs and bacon and no less than four pieces of toast. With that as his goal, he sat up and looked for his shoes.

He saw them on the other side of the room, placed neatly at the foot of a bureau. As carefully as he could, he eased from the bed and crossed the room. After tying his laces, he glanced back at the girl. She had her eyes open and was staring at him. He smiled and shrugged like a guilty boy, although he had done nothing wrong — not that he could remember anyway.

Luz felt herself smiling at the man whose name she had trouble pronouncing. Nay-tan, she said to herself. Nay-tan. El Capitán was easier. She shielded her eyes from the sun and sat on the edge of the bed. When her feet were in the sandals she wore indoors, she stood up and looked down at the street. There was no one there. She picked up her keys from the bureau and said to him, *"Te levantas muy temprano."*

Beck gazed at her. What was he to say? He tried, "Sorry to wake you."

"Nos vamos," Luz said to him. She pressed her lips together. No smile came this time. It was the reality that she had to face another day in a life that was nothing like it was supposed to be. This man's troubles were over. He was going back to his world, where he would probably receive a hero's welcome. She would be lucky to return home without anyone knowing where she had been and what she had done to earn the money in her purse. The story she told her family was that she was going to Aruba for six months to work in a hotel. Her plan was to come back early with a story about the job ending suddenly. The other part of the plan was to return with enough money to live without working until her son attended primary school. She'd heard stories about girls who came back with their purses bulging. They got

themselves out of the poverty that drove them to prostitution in the first place. Some bought a house or a car. She wasn't sufficiently naïve to believe everything in those stories, but if they were half or even a quarter true, she would be okay. At the moment, however, she had her doubts.

She unlocked her door from the inside and then the one that was made of steel bars in the hallway. They descended the stairs to the landing, where the final cage required a last turn of the key. She swung the gate, then gazed up at the man who had shared her bed.

"*Soy Luz,*" she said. "*No me olvide, Capitán.*"

"Thank you," Beck replied, adding, "I won't forget you," which was exactly what she had asked of him. He remembered the hundred guilders he'd given her last night and decided it was sufficient payment for the night's sleep, saving him from embarrassment, and keeping him safe on the street. Reflexively, he bent down, kissed her cheek, and hugged her lightly. It seemed like the right thing to do.

"Goodbye, Luz," he said and stepped out onto the sidewalk.

Beck looked right, then left, and saw that he was hardly a full block from Java. To his right, he saw the sign for Charlie's Bar. He strolled up the street, thinking a little about the girl and much more about breakfast. A familiar voice hailed him.

"Good morning, Captain," Charlie said from his balcony. "I see you found a nice place to sleep."

"Better than a sinking boat," Beck replied.

"You're a quick learner. Well, my cat and I have had our morning cigarette. What do you say to some coffee?"

"If breakfast comes with it."

"Even better. I never pass up a meal. Use the side door."

Beck went to the side of the building. The door was another steel gate affair, which seemed to be very popular in San Nicolaas. He entered through the storeroom. There were cases of beer and soda all around him. An ice machine chugged away in the corner. He followed Charlie through the narrow path until they entered the bar area, where he took a stool on one side and Charlie on the other. There was an old telephone between them. Charlie slid it to one side and asked him what he wanted for breakfast.

"Scrambled eggs, bacon, toast, and juice, if it's not too much trouble."

"I love trouble," Charlie said. He turned his head toward the kitchen and shouted, "*¡Huevos revueltos, salchicha, pan tostada, y jugo!*" To Beck, he spoke in English. "The bacon is no good here. You'll have to settle for sausage."

"As hungry as I am it won't matter."

"Good. Tell me, did you enjoy your night?"

"I did. Sam took me to meet a woman, Carlotta I think her name was, and then to another bar for drinks. I ended up going for a walk and saw some people playing music on the other side of town."

"That would be la Familia Arends," Charlie informed him. "They play at the hotels sometimes."

"Excellent musicians."

"They should spend some time on their house before it falls down. Maybe use some old guitar strings to tie it together."

"I noticed that. Then I had a dizzy spell on my way to Java. I should have sent that bum Frankie to get someone, but I pushed my luck. Ended up at another bar. Can't remember the name. I met a girl who seemed to know me, although I can't imagine how that's possible."

"Do you remember her name?"

"Luz, or something that sounds like that."

"She is the one who was with Sam the night the whale spit you out."

"Really? Amazing. She was talking to me in Spanish, and I didn't understand two words of it. She got me inside the bar, and I gave her some money because I thought she was going to take me to Java. She had an argument with the bartender. I almost passed out right there. The next thing I knew I was upstairs trying to untie my shoes and then I did pass out."

"My friend, you have had a beautiful experience. If you're not careful, I'm going to toss you back into the sea before you threaten my status as a living legend."

They both started laughing because all's well that ends well.

"So, the girl treated you perfectly," Charlie said.

"She took off my shoes because I woke up without them."

"There you go."

"She let me out this morning."

"Also a good thing. You don't want to be a woman's prisoner unless you're into that kind of thing."

"And here I am."

A woman brought their plates to the bar. She set them down between the men and retreated to the kitchen. Charlie followed her. He soon returned with pitchers of juice and coffee.

Beck shoveled the food into his mouth. His stomach filled completely for the first time in nearly two weeks. It ached but in a good way. He swabbed the butter from the plate with his last piece of toast. Half a glass of orange juice washed it down.

"You leave nothing for the dogs," Charlie commented.

They heard the side door rattle, and a moment later Sam walked in. "There you are," he said to Beck. "I thought you were lost at sea again."

"This man has a knack for survival," Charlie said. "He's in town one night, and already he's sleeping over with a girl and getting someone to make him breakfast."

"Tell me," Sam said, his eyes twinkling. "Which one?"

"Luz," Beck answered.

Sam slapped the bar. "Pablo told me she was upstairs with a drunk guy, that he paid her for the whole night. That was you?"

"I guess it was me."

After lighting a cigarette, Sam said to Charlie. "I save this guy's life, and he takes my girl."

"Timeshare only, Sam," Charlie said, "You know that."

"Sorry," Beck said. "I tried to get to Java but didn't quite make it."

"So you go upstairs with a girl?" Sam said incredulously.

"Wasn't my first choice, but I needed to lie down in a hurry."

"You found a good spot, Captain, with the best one in town." Sam pulled hard on his cigarette. "Happened to be the one with me."

Confused by Sam's tone, Beck said, "I apologize, Sam. I didn't know she was yours. All I did was sleep there."

"If you want to run this town, you have to remember one thing," Sam said. "A good fireman never steps on another fireman's hose."

Beck asked, "Is that like a good deckhand never stands on another man's line?" He was confused by Sam's possessiveness. As a prostitute, wasn't it the girl's job to sleep with other men?

"More coffee?" Charlie asked to diffuse the tension.

"I'll have some," Sam said and went to the kitchen for a mug.

Charlie looked at Beck. "Don't let him bother you," he said. "I told him many times, just as I told you, don't fall in love. No sooner than I warn him than he's ass end over shoulders for a chica."

Sam returned with his mug, and Charlie poured the coffee. "What's on the agenda for today?" he asked.

"Bad news," Charlie said abruptly. "Herr Beck is leaving very soon."

"I am?" Beck said.

"Yes, you are. I held them off as long as I could but that turned out to be not so long at all. I think the commandante had something to do with this turn of events. Anyway, there is a plane ticket, first-class of course, waiting at the airport. Unless you care to smuggle something home, there is no need to talk to customs. In other words, my friend, say your good-byes. I'll take you to the airport in a little while."

"We'll take him to the airport," Sam said.

As pleased as he was to be going home, Beck was cheerless at leaving these people who had been so good to him. He wanted to do more than give his thanks and be on with his life. They had welcomed him as one of their own without knowing more than his name, and no one had said he owed anything. Nonetheless, there was a debt, one he intended to pay when he figured out how.

Herr Koch walked in and stuck out his hand. "You take a week to arrive and already you're leaving," he joked.

"Wish I could stay," Beck said.

"Come back under better circumstances. I won't tell Charlie your first drink is free."

Charlie snorted. "So many thieves, so little money."

Koch gripped his shoulder. "Takes one to know one."

"The Captain is going to think we're all bandits, whoremongers, and wastrels," Charlie said.

"That may be true, but you've all done right by me," Beck said.

No one said anything for a long moment. Coffee was sipped. Cigarettes burned. A rag mopped the top of the bar. It was as if they were forgotten soldiers at some far off outpost and their commander-in-chief had made a sudden appearance to hand out medals.

"Okay," Charlie said getting up. "We go to Savaneta for some things and then off to the airport. You can use the telephone at my house to call your office. They're desperate to speak to you, Captain."

"I'll see you in a little while," Sam said and left on his own.

In Savaneta, Charlie gave Beck instructions for dialing the United States and left him to make the call.

Beck sat at the table with the telephone. He imagined what the people on the other end were going to say to him. That was easy. They would be joyful at his survival. But what was he to say to them? How was he to explain why he hadn't been in the life raft with the others? Why hadn't he responded to the general alarm?

Why hadn't he gone down with *Patricia?* How did he manage to get to that beach in Aruba? These were difficult questions. Good luck and bad were the easy replies. While Beck believed strongly in luck, he felt it had more to do with the odds in a casino than with any incident at sea.

He picked up the receiver and dialed as Charlie had told him. Before the first ring ended, the call was answered. "This is Nathan Beck calling. May I speak to Jack Ford, please?"

In his painting studio, Charlie searched among his masterpieces. He flipped through a stack of paintings done in his abstract style with automobile paint. After rejecting them all, he pulled open a drawer where he kept the smallest ones, most of them not much bigger than a note card. Normally, he gave these out to tourists at his bar. If someone told him a particularly good story or joke, he rewarded him with a free painting. It was a fair exchange and an excellent promotional device. None of these satisfied him either. Then he saw one propped on his windowsill. It was of a Divi tree pointing from the left side toward the right, with the sun setting in the upper right corner. Rays of sunshine danced on the water in acrylic brilliance. The subject Divi tree used to stand outside the window. It grew heavy enough to pull itself over one day in a particularly strong wind. He missed the tree, so he painted the little picture and put it where he would see it whenever he looked out the window. He held it up one last time, confirmed the view was accurate, and walked outside.

Beck met Charlie on the patio.

"How was the connection?" Charlie asked.

"Perfect."

"Another miracle. Well, they know you're alive, and the party comes to an end."

At these words, Beck was surprised at the images that crossed his mind. He had a vision of himself standing at the bar just a few feet away. He was holding a drink, talking with Charlie and his friends, waiting for Sam to finish on the barbecue. Several girls from San Nicolaas danced to music played by the Arends Family. Roger and Carlos smacked dominoes on the table under the Divi tree. Sitting on a seat, looking at the ocean, was Luz. She turned and smiled at him. "*Tú vives,*" she said.

"Captain?" Charlie was saying to him.

"Sorry," Beck said. "I was distracted."

"I know what you're thinking," Charlie said. "My friend, let me tell you, this place is much more than it appears to be, but so full of nothing that it overflows."

Beck looked past Charlie at the pier and the sea beyond. He considered

Charlie's words. The inherent contradiction puzzled him, but the vision was still there.

"A Divi tree was over there," Charlie said, pointing to a vacant spot of land behind his studio. "I painted this picture to remind me. Take it with you. Maybe you can find a dry place for it."

Beck took the picture. He held it up to the space where the tree used to stand. "Thank you," he said.

Sam pulled into the lot. He waved to Charlie and Beck and then stepped onto the porch to roust his friends. They came out one by one, slightly hung over and generally disheveled. Like a shore party sent by Blackbeard, they assembled around the bar. There were handshakes and backslaps, words of caution and wishes for good luck. Beck thanked them all one last time before getting into Charlie's pickup. Sam took the back seat.

Workers at the airport all seemed to know Charlie and Sam. They made sure everything went smoothly, from a place to park to getting Beck's tickets to passing him through security with Sam and Charlie by his side. The three of them sat at the gate until the plane started boarding.

"May the wind be with you, Captain," Charlie said. "Next time you come to Aruba use an airplane."

"All the best," Sam said shaking hands. "See you again down here sometime."

Charlie stepped up and added, "If your office wants to know what took you so long to call in, improvise. Tell them you had amnesia or something."

"I will," Beck assured him.

After going through the safety procedures, the plane pushed back from the gate. The pilot taxied to the end of the runway, turned the nose into the wind, and applied full throttle. Moments later the plane was in the air, bouncing lightly in the choppy winds that had brought a sailor from somewhere east of Curaçao to a stretch of beach in Aruba.

Nathan Beck looked down at the island. He could make out Charlie's place in Savaneta, including the ramshackle pier that stuck out toward the ocean. His eyes traced the smoke from the refinery back to the complex itself. He saw the streets of San Nicolaas winding between the buildings as clear as lines on a well-drawn map. The plane banked to the port side, stealing his view. He reclined in his seat and closed his eyes. In his head, a quiet voice said, "*Tú vives.*"

THE STREETS of San Nicolaas fell silent in the late afternoon. There wasn't an actual siesta time in Aruba the way there was in nearby countries. There had been too much American influence during the Esso days to allow work to stop. However, after the first shift change at the refinery, the town settled down for several hours. Rum shops closed. Shopkeepers dozed behind their cash registers. Even Herr Koch at Charlie's Bar eased through the lull by taking a seat in the corner and perusing the newspaper.

There was no traffic on Rembrandtstraat. The girls did chores they couldn't do earlier or later in the day because they were either sleeping or working. They walked in pairs to Hop Long Laundry. They darted in and out of Western Union to send money home to their families and make phone calls. A few window-shopped along Main Street making mental notes of the clothing they would buy if enough money found its way into their purses.

Luz carried her bundle of laundry from Minchi's to Hop Long by herself. Since the night la Dueña forgave her debt, the others barely talked to her. Satisfied the machines were working properly, she departed for Western Union's office. She had no money to send home, but there were three phone booths against the wall. The cheapest phone calls to Colombia were possible from these phones. She paid the woman behind the glass and provided her home number. A minute later, she picked up the handset and listened to the ring. Her sister answered.

"It's Luz," she said trying to sound as upbeat as possible.

"How are you over there?" Anna asked.

"Work is hard but better than nothing."

"Have you made any friends?"

"No."

"Why not? I thought there were other Colombians there."

"There are, but I have no time to chat. It's all work and then I'm tired and go to bed."

Luz wanted to tell her about the night she found the man on the beach. If she did that, she would have to explain what she was doing at the beach and the party, who she was with, and so on.

"How is my boy?" Luz asked next.

"Growing," Anna told her.

Luz pinched her nose and squeezed her eyes shut to stop up the tears.

"He eats plenty and sleeps good."

"I miss him," Luz said after coughing to clear her voice.

"Are you ill?"

"No, it's just the air conditioning in the hotel that makes my throat dry."

"Put lemon in your water," Anna advised.

"I will," Luz assured her. "How is our brother doing?"

"Looking for work. He went to a lumberyard yesterday, but they weren't hiring. Today, I don't know what he has. Tomorrow, he's supposed to go to the garage and see about working on trucks or something."

"That sounds good," Luz mumbled. The garage Anna mentioned was the one that had employed their father, before he was attacked by rebels while delivering a truck. He was killed in the incident, leaving the family in debt to his employer, Jorgé, who had loaned him the money to purchase the house they lived in. For six months, Jorgé allowed the family to skip payments. However, six months of mortgage-free living was the extent of his sympathy. He wanted them to start paying or to get out.

"Is Mother home?" Luz asked.

"She went to pray. She'll be home soon."

Luz could see her mother on her knees, bent over the pew in front of her. She prayed often and with great devotion. Despite her piety, her life never improved. Luz sometimes wondered if her mother was praying for the wrong things or to the wrong saint. Her husband was dead. Her son was unemployed. Her older daughter had no prospects for marriage. Her younger daughter was a prostitute with an illegitimate son. Although Mother didn't know the true story of the younger daughter's son, God certainly did.

The line clicked, which meant she had fifteen seconds before her money expired. "I have to go," Luz said. "Kiss my boy."

"I will. Be careful. We miss you," Anna said.

Luz returned the phone to the cradle. When she didn't get up immediately, another girl knocked on the window.

She made her way back to Hop Long. The washing machine spun her clothes back and forth. A few girls with bundles under their arms waited on the long bench that divided the washers from the dryers.

Luz didn't want to talk to anyone just now. She was feeling bitter and angry and resentful. She wanted to blame her father for doing the favor of delivering that truck for Jorgé. If he hadn't done that, he wouldn't have been found dead by the side of the road with four bullets in his body. He would still be earning a good living as the excellent mechanic he had been. But he was an affable, willing man, eager to do favors for his boss instead of sticking to what was safe. And her brother, he hung around Jorgé's garage too much when he should have been working his way up through one of the construction trades. There was nothing wrong with his desire to be a mechanic like his father, but Jorgé wasn't about to pay him a skilled wage for journeyman's work. Her mother, too, was responsible. She attended church almost every day but refused to work even a part-time job, believing that working outside the home was a man's duty. Anna did her part, setting up her food stand at the corner of the park, taking Hernán with her when Luz had a job. Yet Anna found every man who approached her not quite good enough even as she complained about her lack of dates.

She knew she wasn't being fair to her family and felt a terrible combination of guilt and sorrow deep in her soul. It was her own fault she was sitting in an over-heated laundry, in a crumbling boomtown, waiting to go back to work as a whore. It was the culmination of a long list of mistakes that began when she fell for a sweet boy from Medellín named Carmelo Vicuña who had come to Bogotá on a temporary assignment for a mining company. She followed him back to Medellín because he was promising marriage as soon as he got his next promotion. She believed him, thereby compounding the first mistake. When she told him they had to get married soon because she was pregnant, he literally threw her out of the apartment with nothing but her clothes and bus fare to Bogotá. Thanks to a newspaper article about a coal mine explosion, which happened to include the name Vicuña among the dead, she was saved from complete embarrassment in the face of her family. She was graced with a healthy baby boy, whom she named Hernán in honor of her grandfather.

She went to work sewing shirts in a garment factory until the contract was canceled and moved to China. Unemployed again, she made another mistake by going to one of the agencies that supplied cheap labor to the hospitality industry around the world. She chose one named Union Caribe because she liked the sound of the word union. It hinted at a strong group that she could join. There was the added appeal of the Caribbean with its sandy beaches disappearing into clear blue water.

If not her family, Luz could have blamed the people at Union Caribe. They were the ones who spoke genially about working the way she now was. It began with the moment she entered the building. The woman who handed her an application said, "You're a pretty young lady. You may be better suited to other things. Wait here a moment. Can I get you something to drink?"

"No, thank you," Luz replied.

The woman returned with Señora Álvaro, a slender, elegant woman wearing an expensive business suit. Upon seeing her, Luz stood up out of respect for someone who clearly held an important position.

Señora Álvaro put out her hand. "Tell me your name," she said.

Although intimidated by Álvaro's presence, Luz managed to say her name clearly without her voice's breaking. "Luz Meri Revilla."

"Come to my office, Luz," Señora Álvaro said.

Luz was ushered into a plush office. Señora Álvaro placed herself in an office chair behind a desk bigger than Luz's bed. Framed photographs covered the wall behind her. They were all of people who looked like different versions of herself, except that all of them appeared happy.

"These people found employment through my agency. I have drawers full of photographs like these," Álvaro explained. "I hope to have one of you to go right up there," she added pointing to a blank spot high in the corner.

The warmth of the woman surrounded Luz like a favorite blanket. Here was someone who cared about her, who wanted her to do well.

"What brings you here today?" she asked next.

"I want to find a job. I want to help my family."

"Of course! We Colombians believe our family is the most important thing in the world. Tell me about your family."

"I live with my mother, my sister and brother, and my little boy."

"How nice that you are all together. What about your husband?"

Though Señora Álvaro's eyes bored into her, Luz risked a lie because it was the truth of the story she had told her family. "He died in an explosion."

"In the war?"

"No. It was a coal mine."

"How terrible! Well, you have your son to remind you of him. That's a blessing."

"Thank you. I'm grateful to God that he is healthy."

"These are difficult times," Álvaro said. "Here in Colombia we are forced to suffer at the hands of our own as well as outsiders. Fortunately for people like you, for people like the ones in these photos who want to work hard, we can make life a little better. That's why you're here, isn't it? You want to do the right thing to keep your family living as best you can."

How well this woman understood her! In a few sentences she was able to sum up exactly how Luz felt and thought.

The first woman entered with two glasses of iced tea. She placed one on the desk before Señora Álvaro and handed the other to Luz. She left without saying a word.

"Help yourself," Álvaro said taking a sip from her glass.

Luz tasted the tea. It was delicious, exotic. At this point, she should have known that coming to Union Caribe had been a mistake. The people were too friendly, too accommodating. But she was caught up in the moment and was carried away by the positive energy which swirled around her.

Álvaro said, "What you need to remember is that you are trying to help your family, your little boy. How old is he?"

"He'll be three soon," Luz said.

"Such a tender age. Well, it is true a little boy needs his mother, but a family needs an income if it is to survive. You came here looking for work and that proves you are serious about providing for everyone's needs. You're not one of these selfish girls who runs off with a boyfriend and forgets about her mother and father. No, this is not you."

Luz stared into her glass. She wondered if this woman knew her story, if she could smell lies.

Álvaro said, "I see you worked in a sewing factory. *Dios mío.* That is hot work, and they unfairly reject so many pieces you're lucky to pay for your lunch."

At this reality, Luz nodded her head.

"Would you like more tea?"

"No," Luz said.

Señora Alvarez moved around the desk and took the glass from Luz, placing it carefully on her blotter. She said, "I could place you in any number of jobs because I am certain you are a hard worker. You could be cleaning hotel rooms, serving at a restaurant, or perhaps working as a secretary in an office. These are good jobs. The trouble is, they pay much less than you're worth. You're a pretty girl, Luz. You know it. Your husband, God rest his soul, knew it."

Luz wished she had the glass of iced tea to gaze at instead of Señora Álvaro's brilliant eyes. The woman had her trapped like a priest in the confessional.

"If you are going to leave your family for many months and do hard work, you deserve to get paid the most you possibly can. That is why I'm going to tell you about a job you won't see advertised on those posters in my window."

Luz waited patiently to hear about this special job.

"To the point. You can work as a hostess at some places in the Caribbean. The surroundings are pleasant, the clientele is oftentimes American. I have long-standing relationships with these businesses. I would not send you to a dangerous place or to one without opportunity. If you do well in this capacity, you can make enough money to purchase a home, or at least a car, here in Colombia. This work can be difficult in some ways, but the money is much better than you will earn for scrubbing toilets and washing someone's dirty underwear."

Again, Luz should have realized she'd made a mistake, thanked Señora Álvaro for the tea, and walked home. Instead, she said quietly, "*¿Una puta?*"

"Please! Whores work in those awful hotels on the other side of Bogotá. This is different. There are no gangsters like the ones who control so much of our beautiful country. In these places, the business is legal and controlled by the government. The governments have their shortcomings, but they generally do their duty. There is medical care, and the police are available should a problem arise. Some girls meet a nice man who asks her to live with him for an extended period, a week or as long as a month. He pays for everything, and she lives more or less like a wife without having to take care of babies."

The stories Luz had heard concerning prostitution centered on the terrible things that happened to the women. They were murdered or involved in drug trafficking. However, Señora Álvaro was painting a different picture.

"Let me show you a couple of photographs," Señora Álvaro said. She pulled a binder from one of her shelves and opened it on the desk in front of Luz. As she flipped the pages, she watched Luz for a reaction.

Luz carefully examined the photos in the book. They showed the façades of what were apparently bars or restaurants. The next bunch featured various interiors. There were polished bars with sparkling bottles of liquor behind them. Fancy billiard tables sat in the middle of the floors. A few small dining tables stood around the edges of the room. In one picture, a pair of girls danced with men with fair complexions. Were they the Americans Señora Álvaro spoke of? Why was it important to mention that Americans were there? She answered her own question; Americans were the richest people on earth. The final photos showed rooms with neatly made beds, bureaus for clothing, and clean bathrooms with large towels.

"You see?" Señora Álvaro said. "You can work in a place like this."

"Just like that?" Luz asked pointing at a photo but looking at Álvaro.

"Exactly that place. It is called Minchi's. It's on the island of Aruba."

"Aruba?"

"A small island in the southern Caribbean. The beaches are beautiful."

"Maybe I should work in a hotel," Luz said.

Álvaro closed the book. She returned it to the shelf, then found her way behind the giant desk. She said, "If you work in a hotel cleaning or cooking, you will make perhaps two hundred dollars per week. After you pay for your plane ticket, your living expenses, and so forth, you will probably come home with about two thousand dollars for six months' work. That is roughly eighty dollars per week. For someone like you this may sound like good money or not. I don't know all the details of your life. In comparison, if you work as a hostess you will be paid no less than forty dollars per client. This rate is fixed as a minimum. You may be paid more depending on the client, but never less. Yes, you have expenses. You have to pay fifty dollars per day for the room, fifteen dollars per week for medical examinations, and you must eat and such. It sounds difficult, but with a few good clients, you can easily make these expenses as well as a fair profit. Instead of coming home with eighty dollars per week, you could come home with three or four times as much."

"I see."

"Good. So it's less time for more money. Whether or not you want to do it is a separate issue. Tell me you understand the arithmetic."

"I understand," Luz said.

"Let me be clear. There is no opportunity to earn more in the hotels. This is very important, and other agents may not make this as plain as I have. Without the potential to make more money, your worth is limited. On the other hand, a successful hostess has unlimited potential. I won't lie to you. Some girls make nothing. This is mostly their fault. The majority of them do well when they settle down and discover how they fit in. A few hit the jackpot. They meet an American who falls in love with them. These men dump money into a girl's purse. This happens on a regular basis."

"How regular?" Luz asked.

"At least several times per year. While you are there, you will meet girls who have experienced this. It is the reason they return to the same place for the same job. They encounter the same men over and over. They actually form a relationship."

This perplexed Luz since her idea of a relationship was something based on love or family, not money.

"As I said before, you are a beautiful girl. This is a great asset in the business. Let's be honest, men want to be with a beautiful woman. Who can blame them? You can take advantage of this gift of God and make it worth more than the whistles and catcalls the boys give you in the street."

She experienced her share of that, but it never bothered her. It was common in Colombia, part of being a woman who was worth looking at.

"Go home. Think about it," Álvaro said. "It's not an easy decision. I respect you, whatever your choice. If you have any other questions, ask for me personally."

"Thank you," Luz said and stood up. She turned away from Álvaro and walked out of the room in a daze.

She should have forgotten about Señora Álvaro and her clever talk about whores being hostesses instead of what they really were. There was no shame in working as a cleaning woman. It was honest work. It had to be done, or the world would drown in its own filth. No one pointed at maids and said they were shameful women the way they did at whores. However, Señora Álvaro, a woman who clearly dressed and acted like someone who knew what she was talking about, explained that to be a maid was to limit Luz's potential. The logic was clear. After all, if being a whore was so shameful and a maid such an honor, why did the whore earn more money? Apparently this was true to the extent that what prostitutes did with their bodies was despicable. Yet, for that activity society was willing to grant a higher pay grade than someone who toiled with a bucket and mop.

As she walked down the street, Luz studied the men she passed. Sex wasn't something new. She had a son to Carmelo, and before him, there had been a few others with whom she had broken the Commandments. But was she really considering this? Would she have sex with the stranger wearing the blue jeans and the T-shirt? How about that policeman over there? What about the guy driving the truck stopped at the traffic light? Would she? Would she do it for forty dollars?

She was silent at the supper table. The conversation centered on everyone's lack of work. She listened to her brother complain about the government, how nothing was done to create more jobs. Her mother told them all that they should attend church more often and pray for God's guidance. Anna stayed mostly quiet, searching Luz's face, which was downcast through the meal.

The sisters washed dishes when the table had been cleared. Anna took the opportunity to find out what was wrong.

"I'm worried about us," Luz said.

"We'll be fine," Anna replied. "Rudi still has some work, and I had a good weekend at the stand. I made enough to pay for groceries this week."

"There are other bills, Anna, and Jorgé is looking for a payment. He won't let us live under this roof much longer."

"I know, but you worry too much."

"I don't want to go back there," Luz said without naming their old tenement, which had no running water, intermittent electricity, and reeked of sewage and trash.

"No one does, but if we do, at least we can say we had it better for a little while. Besides, it wasn't so bad."

"Yes it was," Luz said. "We barely had shoes."

"We were happier."

"That's because we were children. We didn't know what was going on."

Anna put a stack of plates into the cupboard, then put her arms around her sister. "Your baby is healthy. Be grateful for that. Things could be worse."

Anna's simple view of life left Luz frustrated and hurting. She went outside, where she sat on a rough bench Rudi had made from scraps at one of his construction jobs. Her father had worked so hard to give them a better life, to get them out of that slum. She felt it was her duty to see that what he had given them wouldn't be lost. Was becoming a whore something she should seriously consider?

The question haunted her for another week before she made the decision. Nothing tragic happened at the end of that week. No specific incident sent her running to Señora Álvaro. Rudi continued working, Anna set up her stand, and her mother went to church. However, there was no improvement in their collective situation. She walked to Señora Álvaro's office, determined to do something to make a secure life, something to keep herself free of desperation, to preserve what her father had given them.

Señora Álvaro was busy speaking with another girl who looked to be a few years older than Luz. The animated conversation involved plenty of laughter. Were they talking about the things Luz was pondering? That kind of fun couldn't be had discussing the high points of housekeeping or prostitution, could it?

After twenty minutes, the girl stood up, embraced Señora Álvaro, and walked out. She smiled at Luz and left the building. When Álvaro saw Luz seated in the waiting area, she waved her in hurriedly.

"Please, please, come in. Something to drink?" she said.

Luz noticed her makeup was stained with tears from laughing so hard. Despite being slightly disheveled, Álvaro still appeared magnificent in her spiffy suit. She tugged down the jacket and seated herself behind the desk.

"How can I help you today, Luz?" she asked brightly.

The details were fleshed out for her one more time. The plane ticket and her initial expenses on the island would be fronted by the bar where she would be working. They would have to be paid before she received any profit for herself. There was also the commission for Señora Álvaro.

"A pretty girl like you has nothing to worry about. You'll make that the first week you're there. The rest is for yourself," Álvaro said.

Luz was advised to return the following week with her passport. One of Álvaro's assistants would fill out the paperwork, including a contract with the specific bar and all the immigration forms required by the Aruban government. Álvaro told her she should consider how she was going to breach the subject with her family. Luz said she was going to tell her family she was working in a hotel.

"Show them this," Álvaro said sliding a folder of glossy pictures across the desk.

Luz opened it. There were shots of a fancy hotel with guests by the pool. On the other side were descriptions of jobs with smaller photos of workers happily doing them. Not one of the photos showed the name of the hotel. She prayed her family did not ask.

"There's another thing you have to consider," Álvaro said next. "If you are successful, and I believe you will be, you must be careful what you do with the money."

"What do you mean?"

"You can't come back with thousands of dollars without people noticing. If this happens, come to me. I will help you hide it."

She fantasized about having money that needed to be hidden. She was temporarily distracted from what she was going to have to do to earn it.

"The young lady who just left," Álvaro said, nodding toward the door, "I am like a bank for her. She has worked as a hostess three different times, once in Aruba, twice in Saint Maarten. She doesn't need the government or bandits or ungrateful people sharing her money."

Luz remembered the casual air about that woman, how light she seemed on her feet. She began to think she was taking all of this too seriously. She needed to relax. She had made up her mind to do it. Now she had to make the best of it so as to maximize her gain.

The paperwork went smoothly. Photos were taken of Luz in her favorite dress. When she made her final trip to Señora Álvaro, she was told she would be working in the very bar she pointed out in the binder, Minchi's. Luz took this as a sign of good luck, and that night she unleashed her lies. She told her family she was going to work in Aruba at a fancy hotel. Her mother and sister were stunned. Rudi asked harshly, "Do you know what you're doing?"

Late in the evening, just before going to bed, she spoke with Rudi in private. She asked him why he was angry.

"You're going away to work when I don't have anything here," he said. "You're making me look bad."

With memories of her experience with Carmelo still in her mind, Luz was careful how she replied. She said, "It's better this way. You won't feel pressured to take whatever comes along. You can get a job you really like."

He wouldn't look at her. She put her arm around his shoulders and kissed him on the cheek. "You're as good as papa, Rudi. He would have been proud of you."

They sat together for a while and then she stood up and went to bed. She dreamt of hiding money behind the sink in the kitchen.

She arrived in Aruba two weeks later. Upon exiting the plane, she was met by Francisco, a bony man, blind in one eye and missing most of his teeth. His shaved head bore scars from what could only have been brain surgery or a hatchet wound. He crossed her name off a list and told her to wait against the wall. Two other girls were already standing there. Eventually, the group totaled twenty-two. Luz checked them out and noted with pride that she was among the best looking of them. If this was her competition, she had the advantage Señora Álvaro had told her she would have.

Francisco ushered them through the immigration line as a single unit. The officer looked at each passport, stamped it, and made a notation in his computer. When Luz passed by his booth, he looked her over carefully. "Minchi's, eh?" he said and handed Francisco her work permit.

The girls were squeezed into three minibuses. Luz sat in the front, sharing the seat with a girl from Medellín. A few miles from the airport, she spotted the smoke from the oil refinery. As the bus drew closer to San Nicolaas, she saw the orange flames pointing west with the wind. The place looked like a version of hell described in the Book of Revelation. That couldn't be where she was going. It was nothing like the pictures in Señora Álvaro's binder. How could a lady as nice as Álvaro have lied to her?

It turned out to be exactly where she was going. The bus drove down Main Street, made two left turns, and doubled back along Rembrandtstraat. As she passed the bar façades, she recognized them from the photos but realized the pictures had been taken up close. There were none from a distance to put the place in context.

The bus stopped, the girls got out, and their luggage was piled in the street. Francisco spoke to them in a wretched voice which was difficult to understand. It was as if someone were trying to strangle him as he talked.

"Tomorrow, you must be here at eight in the morning. You will be taken to the hospital for tests, then brought back here. Do not work until your tests come back, which will be on Thursday. If you do work and are caught, you will be deported. Do not write lies on the paperwork, or you will also be caught and deported. Tomorrow! Eight o'clock, chicas, do not be late!"

Luz stood there as a few of the girls took their bags and moved off. Someone asked her where she was working, and she answered, "Minchi's."

"Two blocks that way," the girl told her.

Luz found her suitcase in the pile and headed in that direction. She came to a man standing in front of an iron door. "Is this Minchi's?" she asked.

"Go see Pablo," he said pointing farther down the street.

She met Pablo a few minutes later. He gave her a set of keys and told her if she lost them it would cost her three hundred dollars. If she had any questions, she should ask them on Thursday night before she started working — if she passed her exam and was permitted to work.

She went to her room, sat on the bed, and put her chin in her hands. God is punishing me for telling lies, she thought.

The next morning she was squeezed into an autobus and delivered to the hospital. The routine was perfunctory. Each girl put on a robe, went through an exam, was x-rayed and told to get dressed. None of the girls were rejected at this point. Francisco was happy about that. He gave each of them a soda from a cooler.

"No lies on the paperwork. No working before Thursday," he admonished them one more time when they were dropped off. Some girls laughed and dodged around the corner.

Luz had very little money with her, so she checked each of the small groceries nearest the bar for the best prices. Ye Fang Store had bananas a little cheaper. La Bonanza sold expired bread at half price. She ate just enough and tried to learn as much as she could about her environment.

Minchi's did a steady trade with men from the refinery. They came in their coveralls. Luz watched them walk up the street from the main gate, usually in pairs, sometimes in larger groups. Noise rose from the bar through the floor to her room. She heard bottles smashing in the trash can, music from the jukebox, billiard balls cracking, and the constant laughter of the perpetually intoxicated.

Another set of noises passed through the walls. These were the sounds of people having sex. Her room was one of four on that side of the staircase. It shared walls with two other rooms, one occupied by Laura, the other by Carmen. Once in a while Luz peeked out her door to see the men these girls brought upstairs. She wanted to see if the faces matched the voices. Sometimes they did, sometimes not. The event was the same every time. First came the sound of the metal door banging downstairs. Then there was the clicking of high heels on the stairs. The second door clanged with a higher pitch than the first. Keys jangled in the room's lock. Most times there was a squeal or a giggle as the impatient man put his hands or mouth on the girl. The door swung open, then slapped shut. Keys dropped onto the bureau. Shoes clopped onto the floor. A toilet flushed. More giggles turned to moans, grunts, exclamations. "¡Sí, papi, sí!" Usually there was a minute or two of silence before the process was reversed. The toilet flushed and water ran in the sink. Heels tapped across the room where keys were snatched off the bureau. The door opened, slammed shut, and was locked. Clangs and heel clicks alternated until the girl and her client were downstairs. The ritual repeated itself through the night. All Luz could think about was that her turn was coming to experience this first hand … if she passed her tests.

Of course she passed them! Francisco handed her a paper that was in another language. He told her, "Congratulations, señorita," and walked down the street to the next bar. That night she put on her blue dress, the one she wore for the photographs in Señora Álvaro's office. It was about fifteen minutes before nine o'clock. Pablo and Spanner were in the bar, getting it ready for business. It was then that she met Señora Marcela, la Dueña now that her husband was dead, for the first time.

Marcela entered the bar without greeting anyone. On her way across the room, she glanced at the jukebox and the billiard table. She took one of the cue sticks from the rack and made sure it was straight. At last, she went behind the bar, where she inspected the bottles of liquor and coolers.

"Pablo," she said, "starting Monday you will keep the cue sticks behind the bar. If someone wants to use them, they have to give you a deposit of twenty guilders. They get it back if they return the stick in good condition."

"*Sí, señora*," Pablo replied.

"Now let me see the new girl," she said looking over at the quartet of young ladies.

Luz smiled at her carefully. She sensed this woman was more of a dictator than a friend. That is, she seemed much less caring than Señora Álvaro.

"Tell me your name," Marcela said.

"Luz."

"I'm Marcela, and now that my husband has died, I own this bar."

"I'm sorry for your loss," Luz said.

"Yes, well, life goes on," Marcela replied. "Let me tell you some of my rules. The rest of you should listen, too. It never hurts to be reminded."

The girls tightened their group until they were practically touching shoulders.

"Always pay your casa on time," Marcela began. "If you are late, I will get the impression you are lazy and stealing from me. Do not use drugs or bring drugs to your room. If you do, I will send you home immediately. Sell as many vinos as you can. If you do not sell ten per night, again, I will think you are lazy and a thief for not doing your job. Keep your room spotless and the common area the same. Do not hang your laundry anywhere in sight. Do not let your garbage pile up and stink. Do not leave the bar with a man during regular hours. Tell every man you meet that you want him to play your favorite song on the jukebox. Leave your problems in Colombia; do not share them with me or each other. And most importantly, when a man is inside you and ready to burst, scream like it is the best orgasm of your life." She smacked her hand on the bar and laughed hysterically.

Luz didn't know if Marcela was serious or not. The other girls giggled.

"*Vamos, chicas*," Marcela said and left the bar.

That night, Luz stuck to the background until Samito came in. He hadn't paid the fixed rate but asked only for a massage. She was angry but held her temper, which was a good thing. He took her to the party and honored his promise by giving her the salvation of a hundred-dollar bill on the way. At the gathering, the food had been plentiful and tasty, the music pleasant. The other girls talked nicely to her. She danced a little. Samito asked her for nothing but smiles and a walk on the beach. Once again her world exploded when she saw that man at the water's edge. There he was, certainly dead. Would her torment never end?

As it turned out, the man wasn't dead. He came to San Nicolaas later that week to prove it. He gave her a hundred guilders and a hug. She wasn't positive, but she believed he was an American. He had money in his pocket, the way all

Americans supposedly did.

A bell sounded in the dryer that held her clothes. Luz snapped out of her trance and reached in for her things. She couldn't blame her family or Señora Álvaro or anyone else for what she had done. A little more than ten weeks remained until her contract expired. If something didn't change, she was going to have nothing to show for her lies and mistakes. She put herself into this mess. It was up to her to fix it. She hoisted her laundry bag off the bench and lugged it to Minchi's.

❋   ❋   ❋

Inez and the other girls grew chatty as Friday evening approached. They gabbed about how much they were going to ask if a man wanted to take them home. Luz stayed out of the conversation but found the others' optimism contagious. She needed to snare several men if she was going to get out of this place with enough money to take care of her family. She wore her blue dress again and tied her hair in a complicated braid that kept it away from her neck. A previous resident of her room had forgotten a bottle of perfume in the back of a drawer. It was a delicate scent with a hint of orange. She dabbed it behind her ears and on her wrists. The heat of her body released more of the scent into the room.

She got to the bottom of the stairs at five minutes to nine. The other girls peeked through the windows at the street as if they were waiting for friends. Inez told Laura she was expecting a rich client any minute. He had taken her away to a hotel and was coming for her a second time.

Luz gave her keys to Pablo, who took them without looking at her. She waved to Spanner, who sat behind his sunglasses and folded arms at the end of the bar. His head bobbed in reply. She took a seat just as the other girls scampered back from the window.

"Here she comes," Inez hissed.

Spanner was on his feet in a second. Pablo stood up straight but kept his eyes on the floor.

"*Buenas noches*," la Dueña said as she entered the room. "I see we're all ready for a busy night." She walked directly to the girls without first making her inspection. "You look very nice, Luz."

"*Gracias, señora*," Luz said.

"Let's talk for a moment."

Luz felt the heat from the other girls staring at her as she crossed the room to the billiard table. She was so frightened she almost tripped over her own feet.

"I have a special client coming tonight," la Dueña began. "I'm going to introduce you to him in a few minutes. He is American, but he speaks Spanish very well. I told him you would be delighted to meet him."

"*Claro,*" Luz said.

"If he likes you, he will take you to his hotel on the other side of the island."

"But not until after the bar closes, no?"

La Dueña put her hand on Luz's arm. "For him it is okay to leave whenever he wants. Don't talk about money with him unless you are in San Nicolaas, and stay away from the police. By the way, this man will pay for la casa as well."

"*¿La casa también?*" Luz questioned before she could check herself.

"I see you're excited by that. Yes, he will pay, and he will want to stay several days in the hotel. You have nothing to worry about. He will treat you better than any man you've ever met. He's not a handsome man and a little heavy. If you are good to him, he may give you some gifts, too."

"*Gracias, señora.*"

"Don't disappoint me," la Dueña said, squeezing Luz's wrist. "Oh, here he is."

A man wearing a linen shirt and loose pants came through the door. He looked at the three girls first then crossed the room to la Dueña and Luz. As he approached, Luz saw that his stomach hung over his belt a few inches. Still, he was not what she would consider overweight. His face must have been pocked by acne when he was young because the telltale scars remained. His hair was combed neatly to the side, and he was clean-shaven. He wasn't ugly as she had expected. He was simply a man on whom adolescence had taken its toll.

"Martin," la Dueña gushed. "How are you?"

He kissed her on the cheek and told her he was "*Fantastico.*" He held her with both his hands on her shoulders and his eyes fixed on hers. Luz saw the look they exchanged. It was one shared by people who knew each other intimately.

"*Entonces …*" la Dueña drug out the word like a game show host. "*Te presento Luz.*"

"Luz, a pleasure," Martin said.

"For me also," Luz told him.

"Call me when you can," la Dueña said to Martin. She strutted out of the bar to the curb where her car waited.

Martin's first question to Luz was the same as Samito's. How long had she been in San Nicolaas?

"Less than two weeks," she told him.

"The town seems very quiet. Has the bar been busy?"

"Not really."

"And you, have you been busy?"

This was a tricky question. She was not such a good liar as to do so with conviction. She said, "I haven't found the right people," which was the truth.

Martin raised his eyebrows. "Is that so?"

"*Es verdad*," Luz replied. "It's why I usually sit alone by the bar over there." She turned her head and saw Inez was glaring at her.

"Maybe I can do something about that," Martin said next.

"I hope so. I don't mean to be impolite, but I'm a little bored here."

"Come on," he told her. "We'll go to a restaurant if you're hungry, or to a bar I know by the beach. How does that sound?"

"I would be delighted."

"You should pack some clothes, your cosmetics. I'll wait here, but don't be long. I may be distracted."

"Please," she said, "I will hurry."

Inez never took her eyes off Luz as she marched across the room like a one-person parade. Luz darted up the stairs, then fumbled with the key to her door. Inside, she shoved some clothing, what few cosmetics she had, and several condoms into her small bag. She was back in the bar not three minutes after leaving it.

When she reentered, she found Martin talking to Inez. He was pleading with her, but Inez wouldn't look at him. When he saw Luz, he tried to kiss Inez on the cheek. She pushed his face away. He left her there to pout.

"Ready?" he asked Luz.

"*Sí*," she said.

He waved to Spanner and ushered her into the street. They walked half a block to his car, where he opened the door and held her hand as she seated herself.

Frankie turned the corner from the American Bar and spotted Sam at the other end of the block. In pursuit of another guilder, he rushed past Luz getting into the car. He was only two short of a fresh sandwich, not one made from pieces out of the trash.

"Two guilders, Samito! Two guilders and I'll have a full belly."

Sam ignored Frankie, seeing nothing but Luz getting into the car. He recognized the guy with her but couldn't remember his name. His reputation was unforgettable. He came to Aruba several times a year, sometimes living in one of the big hotels for as long as three weeks. From him, money flowed more freely than bullshit at Charlie's Bar. He bought girls out early and paid them too much to live with him. Sam wondered how stupid the guy could be. If he wanted to spend that much money to play house, he would have been better off marrying them and paying for a divorce. When a guy paid that kind of money, it screwed up the local economy. The girls grew high expectations. They wanted mucho dinero for a day at the beach or a night on a different bed. They got bitchy when the normal rate wasn't bumped with a ten-guilder tip. It diminished the whole experience to nothing more than getting laid. That was for newbies and fools, not the Prince of San Nicolaas.

This girl didn't know what she was getting herself into. She could spend her days with this guy, soak up his largesse, and maybe earn a good week's pay. When it ended, she would be sorry. Every forty-dollar trick would feel like she was doing it for free. After all, if he was willing to pay more, why shouldn't the next guy? But the next guy wouldn't pay. The next guy knew better. He knew what it was really worth. It was worth forty dollars, and it was worth less than that on the street after hours. It was a hard landing on the sidewalk after a week in the penthouse.

Sam felt genuine sympathy for her. She could have spent the time with him, earning a little less money, having the time of her life. It would have been genuine loving, not make-believe like the Hollywood sets those big hotels were. She was going to trade the real thing for so much less.

"Two guilders is all I'm asking," Frankie pleaded.

"Shut up, Frankie," Sam said, "or I'll split your head with an ax."

11

BEYOND ORANJESTAAD, past the hospital, was new territory for Luz. Martin signaled as he turned off the highway onto a secondary road which led to a tall, narrow building standing with its edge into the wind. This was a high-rise hotel larger than many buildings in Bogotá. They passed a few similar hotels until they came to an entrance bordered by stone walls. The car climbed the grade until Martin stopped under an awning. Instantly, a man in a white uniform stood beside Luz's door. He smiled, pulled the door open, and offered her his hand.

"*Bienvenido al hotel Hyatt,*" he said.

"*Gracias,*" Luz replied and stared at the building behind him. Half a dozen stairs led up to the open-air lobby. She found herself in the center of a grand hacienda that might have been a set in the novella her mother and sister watched. The ceiling of the lobby was so far above her it could have contained her family's house without touching the roof. Massive columns supported the ceiling. Surrounding each one were clusters of low chairs with tables in between. Wrought iron light fixtures with fancy electric lights designed to look like torches hung from the columns. Well-dressed people sat on the chairs and moved through the lobby.

She caught herself gaping at the luxury of the place. Suddenly, she felt small and nervous, as if the uniformed employees were all watching her. She clutched Martin's arm.

"*¿Te gusta?*" he asked.

"*Tan linda,*" she breathed.

"Let's put your things in my room," he told her.

They crossed the lobby to a bank of elevators. The people coming out laughed at something. They were the happiest people Luz had ever seen. She wondered what they did here that made them so joyous. She considered that with money to live like this what was there to make them unhappy?

Martin's room was at the end of the building, on the top floor, facing the sea. It wasn't a single room but a suite, complete with a salon, a bedroom, one full bath, one half bath, and a kitchenette with dining area. Her tiny bag hung in the closet like a lonely ghost in an abandoned mansion. She excused herself to use the bathroom. She took in the massive bathtub, separate shower, and twin marble sinks. This was like living in a novella. She couldn't wait to tell her sister all about it, except she would have to say she cleaned the place, not that she came with a man who paid her for sex in the bed that was almost as big as the entire room she shared with Anna.

When she came out of the bathroom, Martin was seated in the salon paging through a magazine. He stood up immediately and crossed the room, moving carefully, smoothly, as if he was afraid of startling her. He touched her on the shoulders with the tips of his fingers. Applying the gentlest pressure, he drew her to him and kissed her on the forehead. She felt his lips there and forgot she was doing this for money. This man was not a brute who simply wanted to enjoy her body. He cared for her. He was sensitive to her needs. His actions proved it.

"Are you hungry?" he asked quietly.

"A little," she said into his chest.

"Let's have a snack."

From the lobby they descended a stone staircase through tropical foliage to an outdoor bar disguised as a thatched cabana. They found a table in the corner. A waiter with a nametag that read "Janson" came over and took their drink orders. Martin suggested a glass of wine. Luz declined because it reminded her of the vino at the bar. She asked for a Baileys.

"Look there," Martin said with a thumb pointed over his shoulder.

Luz followed his gesture. The grandeur of the building could not be appreciated except from this distance. There were waterfalls and ponds, all lined with tropical trees and plants. Stone walls divided the natural areas from swimming pools that were also illuminated. More electric torches ringed an outdoor restaurant where people dined at the water's edge. The hotel loomed behind it all like the painted backdrop of a stage show. It was a magnificent sight for a girl from her barrio.

"What would you like to eat?" Martin asked her.

She was nervous about eating in front of him and said the drink would be enough.

When the waiter brought their drinks, Martin ordered a grilled chicken salad, as well as two plates and an assortment of dressings.

Until the food came, Martin made small talk. He asked her about her family, where she lived, did she have any brothers or sisters. These things were easy for her to talk about. She knew them well. It relaxed her a little, and she began to forget about where she was and the real reason for being there. Bravely, she asked Martin about his profession.

"I'm an investment banker," he said. "Very dull."

Luz couldn't imagine handling large amounts of money was dull. "Maybe you should do something else," she suggested.

"I could buy a farm in Colombia," he said.

Her face flushed hot at the idea and with the help of the Baileys. A man with money to stay at this hotel could live like a conquistador in Colombia. She saw herself living with him in a beautiful house. Her sister would come to visit. He would hire her brother to work on the farm machinery.

"Someday," he said. "What about you?"

"Me?" she said leaning forward.

"Yes. What would you like to do?"

Lightheaded from the elegance of the experience, her tongue tripped her up.

"I would be happy raising my son. Seeing him grow up, go to school, become a man." As soon as the words were out, she wished she hadn't said them. Now he knew she'd held something back. He was going to think she was like every other silly girl who got herself pregnant by a pimply-faced lover who promptly abandoned her.

It surprised her when he said, "The world needs more people who think like you. Too many children are neglected."

She flushed again, this time from her chest up to her chin. A sense of pride overcame her. She thought of her son, his miniature nose and fingers, how he used to sleep in the crib Rudi built for him. Simultaneously, her confidence grew in the decision to work as she was. She was doing it for Hernán, her little boy. Whereas the boy's father was too much of a coward to accept what was rightly his responsibility, she had risen to the challenge. Here was an American, an investment banker, whatever that was, telling her the world needed more people like her.

Janson delivered their food with the assistance of a uniformed woman who was definitely Colombian. Luz wondered if she had passed through Señora Álvaro's office. Janson placed the salad on the table with an elaborate flourish. With his other hand, he positioned a tray of dressings between the plates. He enjoyed his work. It showed in the way he did everything as if it were a choreographed maneuver. Luz thought it would be fun to be his helper.

"Anything else at this time?" he asked.

"Fresh drinks," Martin told him.

The waiter took their glasses and went off for refills.

Using an oversized fork and spoon, Martin mixed the salad until all the ingredients were evenly distributed. Then he made a small pile in the center of Luz's plate. When she tried to wave him off, he clucked his tongue. He finished by placing a dollop of each kind of dressing around the edge of the plate. She waited while he did the same for himself.

"*Buen provecho*," he said, picking up his fork.

The food was delicious. She wanted to gobble it up like a wild dog, but she forced herself to eat slowly. She savored the experience, taking her time with every forkful. She didn't know when she would be eating like this again. When her plate was empty, Martin split the last of the salad between them.

After four Baileys, she'd had enough. Alcohol made her warm, and she didn't want to sweat too much. Martin appeared to be feeling the same way. He sat in his chair with his head tilted up to the sky.

Martin snapped out of his daze and leaned over to her. He kissed her forehead, looked into her eyes, and whispered for her to come with him.

He held her hand through the lobby. Luz watched other couples coming from their cars. All of them looked dreamily tired. Their smiles were slack, their eyes watery. Some women leaned against their men for support. Their dresses were twisted and wrinkled. One woman carried her shoes in her hand. Luz would never think of doing that in such a place. A jealous pang gripped her for a minute. These women had men that loved them. They were vacationing in a beautiful hotel on a Caribbean island. Most of them were pretty, too. The stylish clothing made them even more attractive. Well, she was there with Martin, the investment banker. She decided to play at being his wife, at being one of these women, clearly some of the most fortunate in the world.

In Martin's room, Luz expected he would be ready for sex. He went to the bathroom, leaving her in the salon by herself. She wasn't sure what to do. It was easy to mimic the women she'd seen in the lobby, but how was she to know what they did in the bedroom?

He returned from the bathroom wearing a set of men's pajamas. "Let's go to bed," he said as a suggestion more than a command.

She slipped off her shoes, set them neatly beside the bed, and reached for the zipper on her dress. Martin's hand was there. He eased it down. The touch of his fingers made her jump. It wasn't that she was nervous. It was that a man so kind, patient, and sensitive had to be a fantastic lover. She found herself anticipating the pleasure it would be.

As she did in her room at Minchi's, Luz hung her dress neatly in the closet. At that moment, Martin switched off the overhead light. Only the light from the bathroom fell into the room. She hung her bra over the dress and paused at the closet.

"Is something wrong?" Martin asked.

"I'm cold," she said.

"Then come to bed."

Her flesh puckered against the cool sheets. Martin rolled her on her side and arranged the pillows so that he could place his head close to hers. He put one arm over her hip with his hand resting on her thigh. The heat of their bodies melded into a single being. It felt perfectly comfortable. Luz waited for him to touch her.

"Do you want to make love?" she asked quietly.

"*Mañana, señorita.* Tonight we sleep."

She struggled with a sigh, then took her breaths evenly, trying to stay awake in order to prolong her contentment. The warmth of the bed, the drinks, the food, it all conspired against her. She was asleep in minutes, dreaming of life at Martin's hacienda in the hills of Colombia where her grandparents were born.

She awoke on her back and alone. She thought her trip to Aruba had been a dream until she saw the heavy curtains over the windows and the huge expanse of bed around her. This was not the room she shared with her sister nor her room at Minchi's. She slid out of bed and stole into the bathroom, where she peed as quietly as she could. Then she slipped back into bed and pulled the covers to her chest and waited.

Martin entered the room carrying a cup of coffee, over which he blew gently. "*Café con leche,*" he said.

"*Gracias,*" she told him and sat up to accept the cup.

"Come," he said holding out his hand. "I have a tray of fruit for breakfast."

She padded into the salon, where one of the small tables had been draped with a cloth. On it sat a tray of assorted fruit, tall glasses of juice, and a coffee carafe. They had been eating for ten minutes when she realized she was topless.

"*¡Ahiiie!*" she chirped and ran to the bathroom where she remembered seeing a robe. She returned to the salon wagging her finger.

"You're cute," he told her with a smirk.

Her modesty restored, she helped herself to some grapes.

"Let's go shopping this morning," he said.

"What would you like to buy?"

"Something for the beach and a couple of outfits for nighttime. How does that sound?"

"Very good."

"Maybe you have a pair of jeans you can wear."

"I do."

They finished their breakfast and dressed quickly. Martin held her hand again. She liked that. It made her feel like his girlfriend. As she crossed the lobby, she told herself she was his girlfriend. It may be temporary, but it was real while it lasted.

The first store they entered featured nothing but swimwear for men and women. The mannequins wore bikinis and shorts in all colors and designs. She perused them, waiting for Martin to make his selection. She was looking at a one-piece suit that featured a thong back when he came up to her. "Did you find anything you like?" he asked.

"There are so many I like!" she gushed. "How about you?"

"Me?" he asked.

"You said you wanted to buy clothing."

He laughed quietly with his hand over his mouth then pulled her into a hug. "Pick out a bikini here, and then we're going to buy some dresses. And don't forget shoes. You have to have shoes."

She pried back from his hug and stared at him. "You're serious?" she asked.

"I'm a boring man, a banker, for the sake of Christ. I never make jokes."

Luz noticed the sales clerk watching them. The woman gave her a knowing smile. This wasn't the first time Martin had come here with a girl who needed something for the beach. Luz pecked Martin on the cheek and said, "I like this one."

"But it's not a bikini," he replied.

"All the same, I like it."

With the one-piece suit and a sheer wrap to put over it in a bag, they left the store arm in arm. He guided her through several other stores. The clerks welcomed him with smiles and offers of good value. The clothing ranged from dramatic to silly to just right. Luz had a hard time making up her mind. She didn't want to jump at the first thing that fit or caught her eye, nor did she want to be a pig and have Martin buy everything he thought she liked. That would be taking advantage. While she might never see him again, she wanted him to remember her as someone who was worthy of his affection, not a whore who had cleaned out his wallet.

They went back to one of the first stores they'd entered after the bikini shop. Martin bought her a skirt and top she thought would look good with the linen pants he had worn the night before. Then, in the last store on the block, she spotted a pants suit that reminded her of the one Señora Álvaro wore.

"I like this very much," she said to Martin, "but it's not a dress."

"Try it on."

The pants were a little long and the jacket slightly too wide across the shoulders. "It doesn't fit," she said heading back to change.

"Nonsense," Martin said catching her wrist. "They'll alter it."

The clerk pinned the pants and marked the jacket. She told Martin it would be ready late tomorrow afternoon. "Send it to the Hyatt, please," he said, placing an extra twenty-dollar bill on the counter.

At the hotel, they lunched American style until the sun's afternoon rays had softened. They changed in Martin's room. As they rode the elevator down, she examined his body for the first time. He was heavier than he appeared in less revealing clothing. His chest was soft, too. If he ate a little less and took some exercise, he would have an appealing figure. Maybe managing money took all of his time, or maybe he didn't care. She certainly didn't mind. He was such a gentleman that any physical defect, like the size of his belly or his acne scars, never came to her attention.

They set up camp under a palapa on the beach. Martin cautioned her about the sun. She listened to his wisdom and moved her chair into the shade. An hour later, they were both sweating. They frolicked in the sea, splashing and taking turns chasing each other. Martin lifted her out of the water and planted his lips on her cheeks. Aside from a few nights dancing with Carmelo, this was the best time of her life. After what Carmelo had done to her, those memories no longer counted.

"Let's have a nap and get ready for dinner," he said and carried her to the beach.

As they gathered up their things, Luz noticed the other men checking her out. The ones she thought were American tried to be sneaky, but she knew they were staring. To tease them, she patted the sand off her butt then draped the sheer wrap around her hips and knotted it slowly. When she lifted her head, she saw that Martin was also staring. She kissed his cheek. This time she took his hand and led him back to the room.

Again, she expected him to make love to her, and again he did not. They showered together. She soaped her hands and stroked his erection gently. He held on to the side of the shower and groaned. After a few minutes, he asked her to stop and rinsed himself off. She was sorely disappointed and began to worry he would never have sex with her. Did he think she had a disease? She might have caught something from the Venezuelan who bought Ricardo's boat, but she doubted it.

They dressed for dinner, he in one of his linen suits, she in a new outfit. In the mirrors of the elevator, they looked like husband and wife. Actually, they looked like husband and second wife. Luz was a bit young to be his first wife by the standards of the people around them.

He drove her to the northern tip of the island, up a meandering road to the base of a cylindrical lighthouse. The light at the top shined out to sea. She looked up at it until her neck hurt and then out at the blackness that was the ocean beyond the sand dunes. She saw a pair of white lights on the sea. The lights moved slowly to her right, away from the island. She thought of Nathan, the Captain, and caught a sudden chill at the frightening thought of being alone in the water.

The restaurant served Italian food but nothing like the Italian food she knew. Instead of plates of pasta with tomato sauce, there were cream sauces, lots of cheese, and large cuts of meat. She understood why Martin's belly was over his belt. He ate with pleasure, chewing his food thoroughly, swallowing slowly. He drank half a bottle of wine before the main course and finished it before dessert. Luz tasted it to be polite but found it didn't suit her. Martin was not offended. He asked the waiter to bring her a Baileys. Dessert was a pastry concoction, the name of which made no sense to her. There was no sharing a dessert this good. Martin wanted his own, and she surprised herself by eating all of the one before her as well.

Janson served them a nightcap in the Hyatt's lobby as they watched people coming and going. This life of leisure impressed Luz. People with money liked to sit and do nothing. She couldn't imagine not working for an extended period of time. A week, or maybe two, would be sufficient. After that, it was best to get back to earning what it took to put food on the table and a strong roof overhead. Good times are short times, her mother always said.

Martin stood up and put his hand out to her. She rose from her chair, feeling the drinks but steady on her feet. He had his arm around her as they ambled toward the elevator. A couple passed them in the middle of the lobby. The man looked at Luz, then at Martin and smiled. Luz told herself that the man was giving his approval to Martin for his fine choice in women. Then again, he might have been making fun of Martin, knowing that the banker bought his women in San Nicolaas. Luz didn't care. As far as she was concerned, she was Martin's girlfriend. He was with her because he liked her. The fact she was hired for the purpose was irrelevant. The woman on that man's arm didn't come cheap. She may not work in a bar in San Nicolaas, but she wore clothes, shoes, and jewelry that were worth more than Luz would make in ten years. Someone had to pay for that. Besides, what would that woman do if she were left with a child and no husband? What would she do if her father was dead, her brother without regular work, her sister selling food at the park? What choice would she make? She didn't have to make that choice because she was an American, one of the richest people in the world. They had so much money that they built buildings that touched the sky, lived in mansions, and drove expensive cars on gigantic highways. American children all went to college because they didn't want to work with their hands. They hired immigrants, such as Mexicans, to do that kind of work. In between it all, they vacationed from their luxury at places like the Hyatt Hotel in Aruba, which was just a different version of America. That's what she thought of Americans. Her experience confirmed it more or less.

Despite this line of thinking, she was not bitter. In fact, she was inspired. As the elevator door closed on the lobby, she decided America was her new goal. When she left Colombia, the idea had been to make enough money to cover expenses until Rudi found a better job. Now the concept was evolving into a grand plan. Why stop with a good job? Why not go for it all? The only place where everyone had it all was America. Hadn't Señora Álvaro told her that?

In Martin's room, she repeated her undressing ritual. This time he helped her. Only when she was completely naked, did he start to take off his clothes. She pushed him down on the bed and untied his shoes. She undid the buttons on his shirt and eased it over his shoulders. She hung the garment properly and returned for his pants. With a friendly pat on his belly, she slid them over his hips and off his legs. Then came his undershorts. She was delighted he was already hard.

Martin took the initiative away from her. He pulled all the covers off the bed, then pressed her down on it. His hands caressed every inch of her body, front and back. After so much of this that she wanted to scream, he started to do it with his lips. It made her frustrated and hot and aching for him to be on top of her. His fingers traced the inside of her thighs up to her sex. She felt him probe into her wetness. She watched him smile as his finger slid in with no resistance. Her breath came quickly as he moved away. A smile of relief spread across her face as she watched him place a condom over his penis. She tilted her head back and let her eyes slowly close. She felt the weight of him on her body first and then the fullness between her legs as he entered. It felt better than it had the last time with Carmelo. She did not have to make believe the way la Dueña had told her to.

Martin woke Luz by gently stroking the side of her face. They made love under the covers, then dozed another half hour. After breakfast, Martin asked her if she minded sitting alone by the pool. Of course she didn't mind, but she wanted to know where he was going to be. "Business," he said and told her to enjoy herself.

She walked cautiously out to the pool. With Martin, she had all the confidence in the world. Without him, she felt like an imposter. Halfway to the pool, she considered hiding in the room. There was a television there and some magazines on the table. But she didn't want to make him angry. She stopped beside the pool and dipped a toe into the water. It was cool to the touch and felt delightful in the hot sun. She looked for a chair that wasn't occupied. There were none to be had until Janson came to her rescue.

"Señorita Martin!" he called to her.

She didn't respond until he was beside her, touching her arm, and smiling.

"Señorita Martin," he repeated. "I was calling to you."

"I'm sorry," she said. "I was looking for a chair."

"It would be my pleasure to get you one."

"Close to the pool," she said, although she wasn't really sure.

"Perfecto." He carried a chair over his head as if it were no heavier than a palm frond. He set it down, looked at the sun, then repositioned it.

"Thank you, Janson," Luz said.

"*De nada,*" he replied. "Let me get you some things."

Luz sat on the chair to take off her shoes. She surveyed the women lounging there. They were oiled for the sun, reading books under umbrellas, or dozing with towels over their faces. One of them had her top off.

Janson brought an insulated bucket filled with ice. There were bottles of water in it, and he showed her with a sly grin a tiny bottle of Baileys. "Our secret," he said with a finger over his lips. He also had a satchel of Spanish magazines. "If you get hungry, just order whatever you like."

"*Gracias,*" she said.

Luz fell into the routine of the other women. After half an hour on her belly, she turned over. When the sun got too hot, she slid into the pool. As she dried off, a tall American woman tried to speak to her. The American was blonde and taller than Luz by at least six inches. Luz was stunned that the woman would be talking to her. Couldn't she see Luz was a Latina? "*Lo siento,*" Luz said with a smile, "*pero no hablo inglés.*"

Janson rescued her a second time. He explained to Luz that the woman wanted to know where she had bought her bathing suit. Luz was so happy the woman thought she had good taste that she ran on in rapid fire Spanish, as if the woman were her sister, who understood everything she said before she finished saying it. Janson asked her to slow down, then translated for the woman.

"You look stunning in it," the woman said directly to Luz.

After Janson said it in Spanish, Luz blinked away tears. "*Gracias,*" she said. "You're very beautiful."

Martin arrived early in the afternoon. He appeared happier than ever. Business must have gone well, Luz thought. He kissed her cheek and sat himself across the table.

"Not too much sun?" he queried.

"No," Luz answered, adding, "An American woman wanted to know where I got my suit. I told her in the center of town, but I didn't know the address."

"Your English must be very good to speak to an American," Martin chided her.

"Janson translated."

"He's a good man. I'm glad you made a friend of the woman," Martin told her. "Just watch out for her husband."

"I'm only with you," Luz said to him without blinking.

The pattern continued for the next three days. They dined in elegant restaurants, walked along the beach, and after late night drinks in the lobby, retired to the bedroom, where Martin made love to her. The American woman waved to her at the pool. Luz returned the greeting, then hid her face in a magazine.

After lunch on Thursday, Martin took her to the room, where he satisfied himself with total passion. He didn't have to tell her their time together was over. She knew it by the tightness of his face. He seemed as sad as she was when he patted her hand and looked down at her in the middle of the bed. She saved him the trouble of saying it by pulling his face down and squeezed him with all her might.

She had nothing in which to put her new clothes. She hated to shove them in with her old stuff. Martin solved the problem by calling the front desk. A bellman brought a plastic garment bag. He neatly hung her old dress inside with the new one and the pants suit.

The ride to San Nicolaas passed in silence. Luz wanted to tell Martin how happy she'd been during the four days with him. She wanted to thank him for everything, but each time she looked his way, the words jammed up in her throat. Soon they were approaching town. How ugly it seemed after the magnificence of the other side of the island. Flames and smoke poured from the stacks. She had forgotten how the place smelled, a mixture that stank of old urine and new paint. She held her nose for a second, then took her hand away. It was time to get used to it again, the smell and a bunch of other things: Inez and her dirty looks, la Dueña and her moods, the bar and its noise.

She looked out the side window as they climbed a rise in the highway. The sea was out there, clean, blue, and infinite. To keep her spirits up, she reminded herself of the American woman's compliment. It meant she had a chance of fitting in with people of that class. Her circumstances may not be the best at the moment, but she had shown her ability to mingle with her betters.

San Nicolaas drew them in. Main Street steered them past the gas station, beyond the ramshackle shops with goods out on the sidewalk, and into the heart of the Zone of Tolerance. Tourists at Charlie's Bar sang songs to the jukebox. The corner restaurants were full of men coming off shift at the refinery. Martin doubled back along Rembrandtstraat and stopped at Minchi's door.

He held her hand for a moment. He told her he had a splendid time with her. He hoped she enjoyed it. She said she would never forget it in all her life, which was true. He reached in his pocket and handed her a wad of folded American money.

"There's six hundred dollars there," he said.

There was no way to stop the tears at the sound of that. Luz allowed herself to cry. Six hundred dollars was more than half of her debt. She felt this was a turning point, the end of the beginning. She thought the rest of her trip might go better than she ever thought it could, that the lies might be worth it.

"*Gracias*," she said one last time and got out of the car. As she climbed the stairs, Luz hoped the other girls were napping. She wanted to avoid meeting them with her arms full of Martin's gifts. She got as far as her door when she heard one of the others open behind her. In a flash, she was inside her room. She tossed the clothing onto her bed and swung the door as quickly as she could. As it shut, she noticed Samito passing through the iron door at the top of the stairs. When she looked across the common area, she saw Inez staring directly at her.

Inez turned up the middle fingers of both hands, laughed hysterically, and slammed her door.

12.

SAM DESCENDED the stairs without looking over his shoulder. He was tempted to knock on Luz's door to see if she was back from Disneyland. He decided it wasn't worth the trouble. He knew Inez hated Luz for sliding into the sweet spot with Martin. It took him less than two minutes to assemble the facts of that case. He saw Luz leave with Martin in the big rental car. He entered Minchi's thirty seconds later and found Inez in the middle of a hissy fit. Sam stuck his head into the lioness's mouth when he told Inez she was ruining the atmosphere for everyone. Inez rose to the challenge, telling him that if he thought of himself as a big enough man to give the orders, he should go upstairs and prove it.

Less out of revenge and more to teach Inez a lesson, he climbed the stairs without wasting five minutes for two vinos. He didn't argue with Pablo over the condom either. He was frustrated with the chase and eager for a score. He practically dragged Inez behind him. She fiddled with the keys a moment too long. He shoved her out of the way, flipped the lock, and shouldered the door out of the way. Charlie's rule no longer applied.

Although a little scared, Inez clung to her arrogance. She strutted into the room, spun around to face Samito, and fell backwards onto the bed. Since he was already unbuckling his belt, she hiked her skirt and slid the crotch of her panties to the side. When she heard the condom package tear, she pulled up her legs. A second later, he was on top, pushing into her and grunting. Determined to show him she could do it better than Luz, Inez worked her hips back and forth, up and down, and in small circles. She groaned and panted. She palmed his buttocks and pulled as hard as she could. His rhythm became steady, a hard, quick pace that all her clients did before their climax. She prepared herself for his collapse. But Samito wasn't ready yet. He pulled out and told her to stand up and bend over. She did as he told her, placing her head over her folded arms on the bed. The smell of their sex filled her nose. It excited her that the mess was a result of her stealing Samito from Luz.

Sam entered a second time, thinking Inez had a great body but no class whatsoever. The sex wasn't that good in the sense that she acted too much like a pro, thereby erasing his passionate illusion. She forgot that not every client wanted a furious orgasm. Some of them, especially him, wanted an experience that transcended the mechanics of the situation. It was a mind game, not a physical sport. Luz clicked with him so well that at the party he easily forgot he was paying for the privilege of her time. It felt like it did in high school, like it was a brand new discovery.

After a while, the position bored him because he couldn't see the girl's face. A girl's expressions added to the thrill, especially if he believed she was really enjoying it and not faking. He knew Inez was as phony as a three-guilder note with Frankie's face on the front. The fun here would be seeing her go through the motions. He stepped back and caught his breath. She looked over her shoulder then fell onto her side.

He gave her a minute to rest. He knew he was being rough, rougher than he normally was. Then again, Inez had said she wanted him to demonstrate how much of a man he could be. He pulled her legs apart and slid her to the edge of the bed. He noticed her eyes go wide then quickly back to normal. Yes, she was nervous. It wasn't supposed to go this long. He was supposed to lose it when she did that trick with her hips, or certainly from behind when he was in so deep it felt like his whole body was inside. He wanted to tell her that those stunts worked for newbies, amateurs, and muchachos who knew nothing. He had control. He mastered this craft when her grandmother was on her back.

He plunged back into her. Her face contorted for him, and he admired her talent. She licked her lips, pressed her eyes shut, and gasped every once in a while. She even managed a smile or two when he held it in deep. He tried to think of Luz, to put her face over the one on the bed. It didn't work. He only saw her getting into the car with Martin. He started to go soft.

There was one way he knew he could finish. He sat down on the bed with his legs over the side. Inez started to get on top. He pushed her away and told her to put it in her mouth.

Inez smiled crazily, as if fellatio was her favorite thing to do. It was a trick another girl had told her about while they worked in Panama last year. This was her first opportunity to use it in Aruba.

It took Sam less than three minutes to climax. The burning heat rose from the seat of his pants toward the end of his prick, and he gritted his teeth. He fought the urge to squeeze his eyes shut. He was rewarded by the sight of her jerking back when he spurted. She kept going until he couldn't stand it anymore. He popped out and pushed her away.

Inez went to the bathroom where she spit in the sink. She rinsed her mouth, gargled, and wiped herself between the legs with paper towels. Samito sat on her bed puffing. He belonged to her now. Any man for whom Inez did that had to have it again. She would put up with him pounding between her legs like a blind carpenter. At the end, however, he was in her mouth, which was her domain. She had showed him just who was the master and who the slave. She knew he couldn't hold back. She knew it because another man had told her so. He begged her to do it like that. He paid her a hundred dollars for five minutes of that. Samito would be back just like the rest of them. Luz had lost him forever.

Inez was right. Sam came back every day. He arrived in the afternoon like many of her clients. It saved the cost of vinos and condoms. Inez didn't care when they decided to climb the stairs. She was paid the same, more or less. She didn't like the vino any more than they liked paying for it. As for condoms, she bought them by the gross.

Sam exited through the iron door on Rembrandtstraat and squinted at the bright sunshine. He had achieved satisfaction one last time with Inez only to realize he was tormenting no one but himself. He'd violated his own code of conduct and not for a good reason.

To make his final point in high style, he looked up at the second floor of the building to the window he figured was Luz's. He blew a kiss at the bars protecting the glass. He turned his back and walked down the street. Herr Koch had a drink waiting for him at Charlie's. There were tourists there, too, eager to hear local stories, and he had just enough time to tell them a good one before heading to the airport.

Luz watched Samito disappear around the corner. It didn't bother her that he was with Inez. The days she'd spent with Martin were fantastic. Her only regret was that she had no one to talk to. She couldn't discuss it with the other girls at the bar. They would be like Inez: jealous, angry, resentful. She couldn't tell her sister or her mother either. She realized what a lonely business this was. Success created contempt, yet failure had a million friends. It was backwards, stupid. Was that why it paid more than regular jobs?

It took her fifteen minutes longer to get ready that night. She'd had plenty of rest with Martin, so she didn't take a nap. She dawdled over what to wear when she knew damn well she was going to wear one of her "old dresses," as she thought of them now that she had the new outfits from Martin. Finally, she put on the black dress she brought from Colombia, but she wore the new shoes Martin had bought.

La Dueña arrived only moments after Luz handed her keys to Pablo. She inspected the bar, then examined the book. One by one the girls paid the casa. When Luz put three hundred dollars on the book, la Dueña counted it twice. She pointed with her pencil as she said, "Martin is very generous. You must have done something to make him angry."

Luz was horrified. "No, señora, I swear. We got along fine. He bought me these shoes."

"He did?" la Dueña asked with an exaggerated expression of surprise. "They're very nice shoes, but you have only three hundred dollars. He was with you four days. Are you telling me he paid you with shoes instead of dollars?"

"No."

"Then what are you telling me?"

"Nothing," Luz said.

"Nothing is what you're giving me, Luz. I gave you an opportunity to make a lot of money with a nice man. He wasn't one of those boys from the refinery with oil on his prick."

"No."

"Okay, he wasn't like that. Maybe he lost all of his money at the casino. Did you go to the casino?"

"No."

"If he didn't lose his money at the casino, why did he give you half of what he paid Inez?"

"I'll get the money."

Luz cried all the way to her room. She dug the money out of her bag. What a thrill it was going to be to show her brother one of those hundred dollar bills! Now she was going to hand every one of them over to la Dueña, the woman who had given her away to the Venezuelan. Luz had less than fifteen dollars left, barely enough to eat for two days. She wiped her eyes and fixed her makeup before returning to the bar.

"You must hide your money well," la Dueña commented. "It takes you a long time to find it."

"I'm sorry," Luz said as she laid Martin's cash over the book. She watched the money disappear into the envelope, which subsequently vanished into la Dueña's purse.

"I'll forgive you," the owner said. "Just remember to pay what you owe me first. What did you think you were doing holding back like that?"

Luz didn't venture an answer.

"With Martin gone, how are you going to pay the rest?"

"I'm going to work," Luz replied with her head down.

La Dueña cupped her chin and tilted her face so there was no way to avoid making eye contact. "That's right. You're going to work. This pretty face and that tight ass will make many men happy. The money they give you will make you happy, too. That's why you're here, to make money. Unless you have something else in your head."

"No, señora."

"You don't want to find a nice husband? A man like Martin? Hmmm?"

Luz blinked quickly to keep her tears from spilling out. She wanted to smack Marcela's hand away from her chin.

"No, not yet," la Dueña said. "You have things to learn before you're ready for that." She released Luz.

The meeting ended. Pablo took the book from the bar. Spanner dumped a bucket of ice into the beer coolers. On her way out the door, la Dueña dimmed the lights.

Around ten o'clock, a fresh group of men came in. They wasted no time at the pool table. They looked over the girls, ordered drinks, and started small talk. The usual first question was asked, "How long have you been in Aruba?" It was followed with the second most asked one, "Is this your first time working this way?" Everyone answered it was their first time even though Luz knew Inez had worked in Panama and probably other places.

"San Nicolaas virgins," one of the men said.

"Not quite," his pal said.

"I feel like a virgin," the first one said.

The guy called for Pablo to bring Luz a vino. He told her his name was Gilbert and that he lived on the island all his life. He managed a business in San Nicolaas but didn't tell her which one. The watch on his wrist and the bracelet beside it were gold and looked expensive. After the second vino, Gilbert waved to his friends, who were talking to different girls.

"I'm going up," he said, then motioned to Pablo. The bartender came over. Gilbert ordered, "A shot and a condom," and then laughed hysterically. He gulped the whiskey and palmed the condom.

On the stairs, he grabbed her ass like a teenager. She brushed his hand away, and he reeled back like a naughty boy. There was nothing appealing about him but his playful nature. She focused on that as she worked the key in the lock. At the same time, she tried not to think about Martin.

He took off his shirt and tossed it on her chair. Three heavy gold chains hung around his neck. He began to take off his pants, and Luz slid out of her dress. He saw her breasts and went wide-eyed. He lay back on the bed waving to her impatiently.

"We don't have much time," he said.

She climbed up his body. His hands met her boobs, which fascinated him. After caressing them, he kissed them around the nipples then flicked his tongue over the pink flesh. The whiskey on his breath met her nose.

Gilbert had enough of her tits. He put her down on the bed. "The condom," he said bluntly.

She took it out of the package and fumbled it.

"This is your first time," he said, chuckling at her clumsiness. When he pushed into her, he stopped giggling and started to grunt.

Luz was grateful for the lubricated condom. Her body refused to warm for Gilbert no matter how much she thought about Martin or the nights when she had danced with Carmelo. As Gilbert worked his body back and forth, she rubbed his back and his upper arms. He quickened his strokes. He pushed deep and held. Luz felt him swell. "Aaahhhhh!" she moaned. Gilbert convulsed and joined her groan.

He was out of her quickly. She waited while he used the bathroom. She saw him yank off the condom and drop it in the little trashcan. He washed his cock in the sink then patted it dry with paper towels.

"Your turn," he said coming out of the bathroom with his penis wagging at her.

She closed the door before she used the toilet. After wiping herself as best she could, she dressed under his watchful gaze and anticipated the money he would pay her. He pulled a wallet from his hip pocket. The bills in there were jumbled together. He selected two, both of them twenty-five guilder notes.

"*Gracias, señor,*" she said.

"*No, gracias a ti,*" Gilbert said, adding, "Nice boobs."

In the bar, Gilbert had to wait for his friends. They came down one by one until all of them assembled a little apart from the girls. They slapped each other on the back as each of them made gestures to describe how the girl looked naked or what they had done with her.

"How was she?" someone asked Gilbert.

"She's new," he answered. "I think I made her come."

They laughed together over another round of drinks, then left the bar to continue their night of revelry.

Just after midnight, the bar filled up. Each of the girls went upstairs at least two times. The second man for Luz was a middle-aged guy who asked her name, bought two vinos, and said nothing else. In her room, he was quiet and shy. He looked away as she took off her dress. He asked her to turn off the lights before coming to the bed. She touched his penis to be sure he was ready for the condom. A second later, she felt his semen squirt onto her hand and arm. He cursed himself and got up from the bed. They sat in the room for fifteen minutes, listening to the radio until he decided he could go downstairs without anyone making fun of him. She felt sorry for him.

The bar closed at four. The other three girls stood in the doorway on Rembrandtstraat. Luz retired to her room. After four wonderful nights with Martin, she'd lost her stomach for the filthy work of servicing men off the street. She had money to pay the casa and a little extra to eat and do her laundry.

Friday and Saturday were busier. Men flocked to San Nicolaas in greater numbers than her previous two weekends. She went upstairs with four men each night, including one eighteen-year-old Dutch marine. The boy's skin was red from sunburn, and his eyes were bluer than the Aruban flag. He practically glowed in the dim light of her room. The language he spoke to her was the strangest thing she'd ever heard. It sounded like a cross between vomiting and coughing.

The worst experience to date happened late Saturday, just before the bar closed. She went upstairs with a man who told her to leave her clothes on. He took her standing up, pulling her dress up over her ass. He went twenty minutes in this position and complained he couldn't finish. He told her to use her mouth. After a few minutes like that, he pushed her back, pulled off the condom, and told her to get back to work.

"Not without the condom," she said.

"Shut up," he told her.

"But …"

He grabbed the back of her head and shoved her face into his prick. Lubricant from the condom smeared over her cheek.

"In your mouth!" he ordered. "Or you're not getting a single florin."

Thankfully, it didn't take long to get what she expected. As soon as his semen gushed out, Luz pulled off. She realized it was a mistake only afterward. His spunk dribbled off her face onto her dress. His body shook and another glob of sticky fluid landed between her breasts. He looked down at her, pleased at what he had done.

She made him wait while she wiped his mess from her body and clothes. She couldn't sit in the bar with another man's stain on her. The dress would have to be dry-cleaned.

"Let's go," he said. "I'm not paying the bar extra."

"It's your mess," she fired back at him.

For a second, she thought he would be angry and make a scene. Instead, he laughed and said, "What a fine mess it is."

After entering the bar, she took her revenge. When the guy was about to rejoin his friend, she took his hand and spun him toward her. She went up on her tiptoes and kissed him full on the mouth. With her eyes on his, she poked her tongue through his lips. He pried her away by placing his forearm against her chest. It was her turn to laugh as he barreled out the door with his friend close behind asking what was wrong.

On Sunday morning, she ate some crackers and juice for breakfast, then walked the length of town to church. She sat at the end of a pew, near the middle of the congregation, where she hoped no one from town had a regular seat. In her parish church in Colombia, everyone sat in the same places each week.

A few minutes before the service began, two women walked up the side aisle. One wore a hat with a wide brim and a bright yellow ribbon which trailed down her back. The other woman wore a standard black dress that every woman in Colombia bought sooner or later for the purpose of attending weddings, baptisms, and funerals. They passed Luz, turned to slide into the next pew, but stopped short. The one with the hat smiled at Luz, seemed to recognize her, and excused herself as she entered the row.

The organ began to play. The congregation rose as the priest and his entourage entered from the rear. The woman with the hat sang the hymns in a lovely voice. Luz mumbled along so as not to taint the sound. A homily about the joys of God's love for all left the faithful feeling welcome and content. After the service ended, Luz turned to exit the church, but the woman with the hat asked her to stay.

"I'm Carlotta," she said.

"Pleased to meet you," Luz replied.

"What is your name?" When Luz hesitated, Carlotta put her hand on her arm. "Don't worry. God won't strike you dead. He's busy with other things."

"Luz."

"I thought so," Carlotta said tilting her hat back a little. "You know el Príncipe."

The word made Luz smile, not because she thought of Samito, but because she had Martin in mind.

"Let's have lunch," Carlotta suggested.

If for no other reason, Luz was willing to have lunch with Carlotta for the opportunity to cut expenses. Carlotta might offer to pay. It would be strange that a woman she didn't know would do this, but nothing was normal in Aruba, especially what happened in San Nicolaas.

The three of them left the church together, using a side door in order to avoid greeting the priest. Carlotta took the passenger seat in a four-door car while the other woman, whom Carlotta called Gigi, got behind the wheel. Luz sat in the back for the drive to a restaurant on top of the bluff at the south edge of San Nicolaas.

The simple menu offered the usual fare at modest prices. Carlotta drank hot tea. Gigi had a glass of lemonade. Luz stuck to water. It was free.

"Thank you for bringing me to lunch," Luz began.

"It's nothing. I like to talk, and Gigi knows all my stories. Maybe you can tell me one."

"I don't have any stories," Luz said. What could she possibly tell a woman with Carlotta's way of dressing? Clearly the woman had style and had seen her share of the world.

"Yes, you do. Samito told me you were with him when that man washed up on the beach."

Luz told her what little there was to tell about that.

"I thought you left Samito for this man," Carlotta said at the end of the story.

"That is not true. The Captain was sick, probably not recovered from his ordeal. He went to my room and fell asleep. Nothing else happened. I have not seen him since."

Carlotta stared at her suspiciously.

"Please, this is the truth."

"I believe you," Carlotta said after their food came. "Samito is a boy in a man's body. He was upset the Captain spent the night with you and then another man took you to a hotel. I tried to tell him he should know better, that a girl must work. She can't turn down every man, especially an American. Besides, I'm sure you would have been with Samito had the Captain not come there the way he had."

"*Claro, señora,*" Luz said with conviction, though she was more pleased to have the hundred guilders from the Captain than to massage Samito for forty. She got the idea that Carlotta and Samito were close friends. How else would she know all these details?

"These men," Carlotta sighed. "Sometimes they forget what they're paying for."

Luz shrugged. She was content to listen and learn.

"How is Marcela?" Carlotta asked. "Since Ricardo died."

"Fine," Luz answered because she could not honestly say la Dueña was sad. "She sold her husband's boat to pay some expenses."

"Expenses? Hah!" Carlotta said, "Ricardo and my own late husband used to fish in that boat. God rest both their souls in heaven."

Gigi made the sign of the cross.

For dessert they had small cups of ice cream. Carlotta washed her hands in the bathroom then spoke to Luz alone while Gigi did the same.

"Listen to me," Carlotta said evenly. "I own Bar Sayonara, at the very end of town."

"I walked past it on the way to church."

"That is the one. I'm telling you this because you are a friend of Samito and he cares about you."

Luz waited for Carlotta to give her some message from Samito, but what came next completely surprised her.

"Marcela is an evil woman who has found a place among us."

"*Por favor, señora,*" Luz pleaded. She didn't want to hear bad things said about Marcela lest she herself be associated with them.

"Hush, girl. I'm three times your age. I know how these things work. Like you, and Marcela herself, I was once on your side of the bar, until Max took me as his own. I loved him for it and cared for him until the day our Lord took him to heaven. Marcela does not have my love or my patience. She has the devil's greed."

If she could have, Luz would have run from the restaurant all the way back to Minchi's. Carlotta scared her with strong words about life, death, and God. But the woman had her full attention with her wrinkled hand clutched to her arm.

Her gleaming eyes bored down as she said, "How many days do you have left on your contract?"

"Nine weeks to the day," Luz said.

"You have no money. The best you can do is to be careful. Do not draw her attention. Work with the men. Pay the casa. Keep to yourself. Be very careful of your friends."

It was too late for that, Luz thought. La Dueña had arranged for her to be on the boat the day the buyer came. She had set up the date with Martin. Clearly, la Dueña had Luz at the fore of her mind.

"Hard times are coming to San Nicolaas. The refinery is a pile of junk. Two men died last month, and more are going to die before that place is condemned. When it closes, there will be no work for the girls. Hah, there will be nothing for me."

"What will you do?" Luz asked.

"I have no debt and money saved. If I have to, I can go back to Colombia and end my life where it began. Gigi can take care of me. That is not such a bad thing."

"No, it's not."

Carlotta reenergized her speech. "Make all the money you can. Don't come back to San Nicolaas. There will be nothing here for you but trouble."

This warning came across more ominously than was necessary. Luz had made it through some odd and treacherous events, from Carmelo's mistreatment to finding the Captain on the beach to what the men off the street did to her in her room. Most of it was physically repulsive but not inherently life threatening.

"You know where I am," Carlotta was saying. "If you need something, come to see me."

"Thank you, señora."

"How many children do you have?" Carlotta asked out of the blue.

"One. Hernán."

"He has a good mother. May the Lord bless him and you."

Gigi stopped the car on Helfrichstraat, two blocks from the door to Minchi's. Luz got out after thanking Carlotta for the advice, lunch, and her blessing. She walked back to Minchi's, where Inez stood in the doorway.

"*La princesa regresa*," Inez breathed. She bowed and swung open the door.

At the top of the stairs, Luz heard noise coming from the room next to hers. Someone was in there having sex, grunting, moaning, and swearing. She unlocked her door and entered her room. The first thing she noticed was that the candle in the corner was getting low. She needed to buy another one before the light of her saint went out.

※   ※   ※

Two weeks later Carlotta's prediction came true. There was an explosion at the refinery that claimed three lives. Flags hung at half-mast. Men muttered over their drinks. They went upstairs with girls lest they leave the planet without that last measure of fulfillment.

The brisk business put money into Luz's purse. She paid off her debt and had a hundred fifty dollars hidden inside the cup of a torn bra. La Dueña was happier than ever. None of the girls were in arrears. Beer and liquor sold in record amounts. On Friday and Saturday night, la Dueña appeared at midnight, emptied the cash register into a bag, and left without a word.

Having frequent sex made Luz's body ache. She wanted to pack her groin in ice at the end of the night. At her weekly medical exam, she told the doctor how it hurt. He handed her a tube of lubricant and told her to use it every time, even with men who excited her. It helped, but there were still bruises on her thighs as well as her arms where men squeezed her when they ejaculated. She wished for Martin to come back and take her to the Hyatt. The Captain was also welcome to sleep in her bed. If he wanted it to himself, she would sleep on the floor. As for Samito? She had a place for him, too. They were welcome so long as they were gentle.

During this period, she also landed three regular clients. One was a married man who came in the moment after la Dueña left. He went directly upstairs, where he struggled to be patient but always ended up rushing the act. Luz guessed his wife expected him home at a certain time. The other two clients had different versions of the same kinky behavior. One asked her to watch him masturbate. He sat against the headboard of her bed wearing nothing but his socks. He demanded all the lights were on. With a liberal amount of her lubricant, he stroked himself while she watched. The last guy reversed the roles. He positioned himself at the edge of the bed. As she touched herself, he directed her to do this or that, turn over, or get up on her knees. For these services, she was paid steadily and well. Each of them gave her seventy-five guilders no less than three times a week.

By the end of the month, the three dead men were forgotten. A crew of foreigners, mostly from Venezuela, came to make repairs caused by the explosion. There were also a few Americans. The talk on Rembrandtstraat was that the Americans stuck to Java Bar, where there was a jukebox full of music they liked. Why didn't Marcela put some discs with American music in her jukebox? Luz decided to make the suggestion the next time she saw la Dueña.

Six weeks remained in her contract. Luz had one thousand three hundred twenty-five dollars and some guilders. She hated to sacrifice the twenty dollar fee to send the money via Western Union, but she didn't want to have it stolen either. She decided to transfer five hundred dollars to Colombia. When the transaction was complete, she called home and spoke to her sister.

"You can go to the office and ask for the money," Luz told her.

"Thank God for you," Anna said. "Rudi hasn't worked in two weeks. He is still helping out around the garage for next to nothing. I told him to go for something else, but he wants to be like Papa. Maybe you can talk to him."

Luz agreed with her sister. If their brother spent less time loitering at Jorgé's garage and more at a construction site, he would have some money. However, she understood what it was like to do something she hated.

"Your boy is happy," Anna told her. "He giggles at me all day. You won't believe how big he is."

"Kiss him for me, will you? Right now. Kiss him so I can hear it." Luz held the phone until she heard kissing noises.

Anna came back on the line. "Come home soon," she said.

"I will." Then Luz told the lie that was the groundwork for her early departure from Aruba. "I'm cleaning some houses on the side. The houses are big, and they pay good money to have them cleaned. If I make enough over the next month, I'll come back as soon as I can get a plane ticket."

"That would be wonderful," Anna said.

"Don't tell mother. I want to surprise her. And Rudi, too. I love you, Anna. Tell the others."

"I will. Be careful, Luz."

Her heart ached at thoughts of her growing son. When she returned to Colombia, she would have money in her purse to throw a party. She would celebrate his birthday early.

She committed an extravagant sin that afternoon. She went into Giordano on Main Street and bought herself two outfits. One was a skirt and top, both embroidered in the Dutch style that was popular among the Arubans. The other was a long dress but slit from the ankle to her hip. The waist of her panties would peek through the slit. She knew men loved a glimpse of flesh under lace.

In her room, she couldn't suppress a guilty tear that she had spent money on clothes when her family was still in debt to Jorgé. But it was her money, and she had more hidden away in different places around the room. If someone wanted to rob her, they would have to demolish the building to get it all. She decided to wear the skirt that night since she looked incredibly sexy in it. Her regular clients would appreciate the change. They might even tip her.

The night turned out to be a bust. The bar and the street outside were empty. The repairs at the refinery had been completed. Two charter flights took away the guest workers because the company didn't want the expense of keeping them in cheap hotels. The Americans were on their own, camped out at Java Bar. At least this is what Luz heard Spanner tell Pablo. When Luz told la Dueña about the American music, her boss stared at her for a long moment, then said it was a good idea.

She had to dip into her reserves to pay the casa for the rest of the week. Her regulars were less regular, and new clients were nowhere to be found. Saturday night she put on her Giordano outfit again because she was feeling terrible about having wasted money on it. It turned out to be a good omen in the worst possible way.

Two guys in their midtwenties came in. They spoke English to each other and bad Spanish to the girls. "Chuck" liked Luz's dress. His friend, "Tony," wanted to be with Inez. This was no problem, but the guys huddled with each other at the end of the bar for a long time. At last, they spoke to Spanner, who laughed so hard that he had to take his glasses off and wipe his eyes. The guys enjoyed the humor for a few minutes, then spoke earnestly to the bouncer. Spanner listened, shook his head, and finally waved Luz down to the bar.

When she got there, Spanner was still waving. It took her a second to realize he was gesturing for someone else to come. Inez sauntered across the room. Standing shoulder to shoulder, Spanner spoke to them.

"These boys would like to go upstairs with you," he began.

"No problem," Inez said quickly.

"Wait a minute. They want to take you both into a room and watch you be with each other."

"No," Luz said and took a step away.

Inez got in front of her and put a finger to her face. "Wait a minute," she said, then asked Spanner, "How much?"

"I told them three hundred," he said.

Inez made a show of being disappointed. "Each?" she said.

Spanner raised his eyebrows and told the guys. They said that was too much, but they didn't leave. Luz shuddered at the thought of Inez touching her, even for that much money.

"Come on," Inez said sweetly. "They're rich Americans. They can afford it."

The guys conferred and offered two hundred for each girl but they wanted an hour. Spanner told them it was up to the girls. However, they had to pay for eight vinos, which cost forty more guilders, in order to satisfy the bar. Tony put four ten-guilder notes on the bar without a word.

"Two hundred each?" Spanner prodded the girls.

"*Un momento*," Inez said to Spanner and hauled Luz over to the corner by the pool table.

Luz looked her in the eye. She said, "No."

Inez blew out a lungful of air. "Listen to me. We're not friends. We don't have to be friends. We can hate each other, but we have to make money."

"No."

"Luz, calm down. Forget it's me. Think about Marcela."

"I'm not a lesbian."

"Okay, I'm sorry I said that," pleaded Inez. "We're talking about two hundred dollars, and we don't even have to see their pricks."

"I can't do it."

"Okay," Inez said. "I'll do it." She moved closer to Luz, so close her nipples brushed the fabric of the Giordano dress. She knew the guys were watching. "I'll put my hands on you and my tongue and whatever else these guys want. You only have to lay there and pretend you're enjoying it."

"They'll figure out I'm faking."

"So fake it good. Make them believe."

"But …"

"We had a terrible week here. If we do this, we'll pay the casa and have extra money. What are you worried about?"

"They'll want me to do it, too, and I can't do that. I can't."

"Let me talk to them," Inez said. "But if they agree, you'll go up with me, right?"

The trap closed around Luz. Spanner and Pablo were growing impatient over the dealing. The guys stood there like fools. They had the money on the bar. There was no going back.

Inez talked to Spanner, who talked to the guys. At first they were disappointed. Then they said, "What the hell," and shook hands.

Inez helped herself to the money, which she split with Luz on the way up the stairs. As they went into her room, she said to Luz, "Don't worry. I won't hurt you. I'll be nice. Who knows? You may like it."

Inside the room, Inez switched on her CD player. A smooth salsa played. The guys sat cross-legged on the floor while Inez danced for them. She ran her fingers around their faces and wiggled her hips at them. Luz joined her in the routine, keeping her hands on the men. When the second song began, Inez got behind Luz and ran her hands from her ankles all the way to her ears. She cupped each of her breasts and massaged them lightly until Luz's nipples hardened. The guys moaned at the sight.

Inez broke away to unclip the neck of her dress. She let it fall to her waist, exposing her chest to the guys. They nudged each other at the view and made comments in English. Next, Inez slid the dress past her hips, revealing a narrow lace thong. Taking her cue, Luz pulled her dress up over her head and hung it on a chair. She continued to dance to keep her body moving and her mind off what was about to happen.

For most of the third song, Inez and Luz rubbed their bodies over the men. It was a close-contact striptease that had the guys red-faced and panting. They didn't bother to look at each other for comments. They couldn't take their eyes off the flesh. Each one took his turn feeling up the girls and tugging at their thongs with his teeth. Never could they have something like this in the States for four hundred dollars.

The time came for Inez to earn the money. She led Luz to the bed and eased her back carefully. Luz gazed up with trepidation. Inez smiled sweetly, tilting her head the way she would to talk to a baby. She took off her thong and tossed it at the guys.

Luz felt her heart thudding. She turned away as Inez slid up the length of her body. The soft skin of another woman against her own was not entirely unpleasant. It was the thought that it was a woman instead of a man that bothered her terribly. But Inez was gentle. She used her fingertips to stroke her thighs and tweak her nipples.

Soon Inez had her face up close. She nipped Luz's earlobe then blew circles over the thin skin over her collarbone. She saw goose bumps pop. After spending some time around the nipples, she put a hand over Luz's mound. She then put a hand down to her own sex, which was rapidly heating up.

The guys stood up for a better view. The girl on the bottom clutched at the other's hair and gasped. The guys fought off the urge to drop their pants and do these girls the way nature intended.

For a few moments, Luz thought she had passed out. She felt a little dizzy and very confused. She heard the guys talking and tilted her head toward them but couldn't focus. At the same time, she couldn't make sense of her body. It didn't hurt, but almost.

The scent of Luz, the feel and sight of her pudenda, as well as the sounds of the guys watching drove Inez crazy. Her own vagina was so wet she hoped one of the guys would fuck her without asking. She needed relief. She stayed up on all fours and put her tongue back on Luz. She put a finger into herself. Then she took Luz's hand into hers and added another finger.

Inez felt hot lava spread down through her vagina as her orgasm struck. She imagined it was like getting hit with lightning. She couldn't help but pull her head away from Luz and scream. She shoved their combined fingers as deeply into her body as she could. Her thighs shook as she lost all control. She collapsed onto the bed with Luz's hand buried under her body.

Luz felt the heat radiating from Inez's body. It was a moment of sudden clarity during the event. She couldn't get out from under Inez, so she touched herself with her other hand. Her sex was as hot and swollen as if she had been with a man. As the song ended, she worried Inez had converted her to lesbianism.

The guys clapped for them. Inez expected them to join in, but they didn't. She got off the bed when her strength came back and looked at Luz, who had done a good job given her protest in the bar. If they worked as a team, they could make more money this way than letting these filthy men poke them. To end the show appropriately, she leaned over Luz and kissed her full on the lips.

Luz let her do it. It made no difference at this point.

It took them ten minutes to put themselves together. The guys paced like caged tigers until Inez released the door. Both of the men bounded down the stairs, having no patience left for women in high heels who had to take the steps with care.

Chuck and Tony paid Pablo for four more vinos and two condoms. They took Carmen and Laura upstairs before Pablo could pour the first round. Fifteen minutes later, they were in the bar again, shaking hands with Spanner, telling him he had the job of their dreams.

Luz and Inez had two hundred dollars each. Both Carmen and Laura earned fifty. The bar sold twelve vinos, two condoms, and six bottles of beer. Spanner watched two fools blow their money. Pablo dozed forty-five minutes while it happened. The guys enjoyed the time of their lives. Everyone was happy.

IT TOOK a week for word to spread around San Nicolaas that two hot girls put on a hell of a private show at Minchi's. The Americans thought it was expensive but worth it. The locals told each other they would never pay that much for two girls to get it on with each other. Many of them did pay and denied it despite Spanner's sworn word that he saw them go up. Girls at other bars started to imitate Luz and Inez. A round of bickering started among the men as to which couple was sexier, although they all refused to admit paying more than sixty guilders for anything upstairs.

Luz and Inez made peace the week after their first show. It happened before they went to the doctor for their weekly checkup.

"Let's walk together," Inez said to Luz as she locked the door to her room.

Immediately, Luz knew this was about more than having a companion. She greeted her housemate with blank eyes and a one-shouldered shrug.

"I'm sorry, Luz," Inez began as they descended the stairs.

Luz took each step carefully, as if Inez might trip her.

"I've been in this life longer than you," Inez continued. "I should know better."

This admission didn't shock Luz as much as it amazed her. Inez worked hard at being a whore. She juggled clients so that one saw another as rarely as possible. She professed divine love for one man in the front doorway while another went down the back stairs. No one sold more vinos than her. She prodded her clients to quench her thirst, sometimes with Baileys or other drinks that the girls weren't supposed to have. She had a kickback system in place with Pablo. Then there was the lesbian show she'd started, which only proved just how far Inez would go to get money from men. For her part, Luz pretended as best she could, which must have been convincing enough because they had done the show six times in the past several days. She had twelve hundred dollars to verify the score. It no longer disgusted her, yet she didn't exactly enjoy it. It's for the money, she told herself.

"Besides," Inez was saying, "we work well together. We're making a fortune."

"We are," Luz said as they turned a corner.

"We're making more than if we went to the hotel with Martin," Inez added. "The best part is we don't have to take these men in our mouths or between our legs. Don't misunderstand me. I like men, and I know you do, too. After so many, I think it's nice to have a break."

Luz nodded. Psychologically it was more difficult to be with Inez. Physically it was as easy as masturbating. However, Luz still serviced men between the shows. They used her how they wanted to, in the methods Inez had mentioned. None of them were like Martin. None of them treated her kindly or with sincere passion. They did their thing, pulled out, and left. When she returned to Colombia, she wasn't going to think about sex for a long time. She remembered meeting Carmelo and how flushed she'd felt when he rubbed against her on the dance floor. After three months in Aruba, it would take a man sexier than singer Carlos Vives to excite her. And if he wasn't sweet and gentle and patient, she would walk out the door.

"I have two and half more weeks here. I want it to be a happy time." Inez sighed. "I wish I could stay longer. We could make so much money together."

In her room, tucked away with five one-hundred-dollar bills, Luz had her ticket. No matter what happened, she was going to be on that plane bound for Colombia. There was also money in her purse, as well as hidden under a dresser, in a shampoo bottle in the shower, and wedged in a slot between the bricks in the wall. If she didn't turn another trick for the duration of the contract, she could still pay the casa, eat, and make it to the airport by taxi. Just last Sunday, she had prayed the building wouldn't catch fire.

"Why don't you come to Saint Maarten with me?" Inez suggested. "We could meet at the airport in Bogotá and fly together. We can do this from the beginning."

Luz said, "Don't you think there are girls doing it already?"

"No one did it here until we did," Inez replied. She paused for a second then said, "We have to be careful when we go. The cruise ships are busier certain times of the year. That's when there are more Americans with their fat bellies and thick wallets."

For Luz, this experience was a once-in-a-lifetime event. Señora Álvaro had told some of the truth: a lot of money could be made at this. Luz had accomplished that. She didn't want to do it again. She had enough to take care of Hernán and help her family for many months. In that time, Rudi would find work and she would, too. They would have two incomes, small ones, but put together it might be enough to keep the family secure.

"Let's trade numbers before I leave," Inez said. "That way we can talk on the phone and make plans in Colombia."

Luz told her that was a good idea, but she had no intention of giving Inez her number. The girl talked too much. No doubt she would slip up, and Luz's family would find out what she had done in Aruba. Thankfully, they arrived at Doctor Klein's office before Inez could push the issue.

✺   ✺   ✺

Domestic harmony reigned over Minchi's. Together the four of them walked to Hop Long with their laundry. They shared meals and chatted easily in the doorway as men drove the San Nicolaas Five Hundred in search of something that caught their eye.

The following week, as they waited their turns at the doctor, Luz learned just how the girls of San Nicolaas talked. Her previous visits to the doctor had lasted only half an hour. Each girl was given a number the morning of her exam. The number corresponded roughly to the time she would be seen by the doctor. Luz consistently drew low numbers so she was among the first group of girls to go through the process. This time, Luz as well as Inez, Carmen, and Laura, all drew high numbers. They would have to wait until the end of the day. Inevitably, the doctor fell behind. Other pressing cases showed up at his door, and the girls' weekly exams were delayed.

The four of them sat outside in the sparse shade provided by a Divi tree behind Doctor Klein's office. There were benches and a water fountain but no other comforts. Girls sat on the low wall dividing Klein's property from a row of stores on the other side. Some of them brought blankets or heavy towels and sunned themselves until their number was called. After an hour of silence, the nurse called three numbers. The girls shifted position as three spaces were vacated.

Inez looked at her token. "We'll be here another hour," she complained. "Does anyone want a drink?"

"I do," Carmen said.

"Me, too," Laura agreed. "I think I'll never get used to this sun." She was from the mountains outside Bogotá, where the climate was more temperate than in Aruba.

"How about you, Luz?" Inez asked.

"You go. I'll save our spot," Luz said. She spent no money on soft drinks. When she was thirsty, she drank water, including with meals. The only time she had a fruit smoothie or something else was when Inez or a man bought it for her.

"I'll bring you something," Inez said.

The trio walked around the wall to the stores. Before going into Bocodillo Grande, a sandwich shop which had a cooler so cold the sodas and juice sometimes froze, they peeked into a photography store that developed film and sold cheap disposable cameras. They looked over the frames, albums, and colorful boxes of film. Inez bought a camera, then led her friends to Bocodillo Grande for drinks.

While they were gone, Luz kept to herself. She listened to girls describe their San Nicolaas experiences in minute detail. One had a regular client who wanted her to wear a fake penis and slap him in the face with it. Another had a guy steal her underwear while she was washing up in the bathroom. Two girls had been to the beach with two brothers. They had sex with both of them at the same time.

Two other girls, who were sitting on the wall, started talking about Minchi's. Luz snapped to attention. She realized she was being obvious so she rubbed her neck and turned her eyes away but her ear toward the girls.

"Minchi's has two hardcore lesbians. They won't go with men anymore."

"Seriously?"

"They go upstairs and let the men watch while they lick each other like dogs."

"The men watch?"

"They do and then they want to fuck, but these girls won't let them. The men have to come downstairs and go find a real woman who knows what to do with a cock. They're ripping the clients off. They should fuck the men. It's what they get paid to do."

"I don't believe you."

"It's true. The problem is, I have a client who wants me to do it."

"Maybe we should try it."

"Are you a lesbian, too?"

"No, but if the men want to pay …"

"Ugggh. What a man does down there doesn't bother me. He can put his tongue in it if he likes, but I'm not putting my face between a girl's legs. The Bible says it's wrong."

"It does?"

"Are you stupid?"

"Why are you angry with me?"

"I'm not. I'm pissed off because these girls are ruining it for us. The more you give, the more the clients want. It's bad enough we have to put up with their rotten breath and dirty hands all over us. Now they expect us to be gay. It's too much."

The nurse appeared in the doorway and called out two more numbers. The gossips went in. Luz looked at her token. Only a few more to go and it would be her turn.

Inez handed Luz an ice-cold Coca-Cola. Luz reached into her pocket, but Inez told her to forget it. Luz would be sure to return the favor. She owed no one at this point in her life, not Inez, not la Dueña, not Señora Álvaro.

Doctor Klein saw her forty minutes later. He went through a list of perfunctory questions, the same ones he had asked the week before. She answered all of them in quick succession wanting to get out of there as soon as she could. Then Klein initialed the card that remained at the bar should the government want to verify she had been examined according to the law. It occurred to Luz that not since her initial exam at the hospital had Doctor Klein given her a proper gynecological work up. She only knew how the proper one should go because the doctor who delivered Hernán was a caring man. Unexpectedly, she felt panicked as she remembered the Venezuelan who did it to her without a condom. What if he had given her a disease? Then she thought about the other things different men had done to her. She wasn't bleeding. She ached a little here and there. But what if there was something that was less obvious? She couldn't ask Doctor Klein. Only a curtain hung between them and the next girl, who happened to be Inez.

Worry plagued her as she walked to Minchi's. Carmen and Laura joked the whole way back. They were giggling about something they had seen on the television a client had given Carmen. Before they went upstairs, Inez asked them to pose for a photo in front of the bar. Luz didn't want to do this since it would be evidence of where she had been. She offered to take the picture. When she had taken two of Inez by herself and one of the three of them together, Inez told Carmen to take one of Luz.

"No, save your film," Luz said.

"I want a picture with you," Inez begged. "We'll look back on this and laugh our heads off."

Luz managed a smile. Carmen had the camera up and snapped one of Luz by herself. Inez chastised her and said she wanted to be in it. After a little more encouragement, Luz relented. Inez put her arm around her shoulders and pulled her close. "My little sister," Inez said just before Carmen pushed the shutter.

Upstairs, the girls went to their rooms for the nap they routinely took before getting ready for a night in the bar. Luz sat on her bed, her mind racing over what type of disease she might have. Too many men to count had been inside her. Then there was the business with Inez. She was unsure if the way they touched transmitted disease. It bothered her to the point where she couldn't sleep. She had to ask someone what to do before she went insane.

She washed her hands and face, pulled on her jeans and left the building as quietly as she could. She used the front door and walked up Main Street. If anyone had heard her leave, they wouldn't be able to see the direction she was headed. She passed Western Union and began the next block when she stopped short at the sound of her name.

"¡Luz! ¡La luz de mi vida!" a man called to her.

She looked across the street. Charlie stood in the doorway to his bar.

"Venga," he said gesturing for her to come over to him.

She didn't want to be rude after the wonderful hospitality she had enjoyed at his birthday party. She smiled and crossed the street. He kissed her on the cheek and asked her if she would like something to drink, "On the house."

"Gracias, pero no."

"Smart girl. Rum brings out the devil, but since the devil is my friend, I have nothing to worry about except for God, but I think He is busy with other things."

"Don't say things like that," Luz said with mock horror.

"Of course you are correct. I should be a pious man, go to church, stay away from loose women. But I am weak. I need salvation. Can you tell me where to find it?"

Luz appreciated his acting and joined in the comedy. "I think they sell it at Lucky Store. Two blocks that way," she said pointing toward Helfrichstraat.

Charlie chortled at her response. "I like you," he said. "You have class. You know how to take a joke. And," he added looking over his glasses, "you have good taste in men."

By this time, she had forgotten about her body and was trying to figure out what he meant by this last comment. Did Charlie know one of her regular clients? Perhaps he knew Martin. Oh, she remembered, he was talking about Samito, the Prince of San Nicolaas.

However, Charlie wasn't talking about Samito. He said, "You managed to spend the night with our shipwrecked captain. What good timing you had!"

Without knowing why, Luz found herself smiling happily. Every moment of that night came back to her as if it had been a movie. She saw the Captain stumbling on the street. She heard him talking to her in English. She smelled Pablo's fetid breath as he argued with her over the time. She woke up, and the Captain was standing there looking for his shoes.

"I think he will be back to see you," Charlie was saying. "A captain never forgets a friendly port."

"I hope he comes soon. I leave before the end of the month."

"People have a habit of coming back to Aruba. This place is like a tornado. It sucks you in and spins you around and around. You cannot escape."

Luz looked at him for a moment without knowing what to say. Charlie saved her further consternation. He said, "Sorry to bother you. There's no one in the bar at this moment, and I was getting lonely. Go on to your errands. Have a nice day."

It took her a few seconds to remember where she was going. Then it came back and she was off at a hurried pace to the edge of town. However, when she arrived at the door of Bar Sayonara she did not enter. She was going to beg Carlotta to take her to another doctor. But the presence of a woman who possessed so much confidence made her feel silly, like a little girl who'd lost her doll.

She turned away from Sayonara and started for Minchi's. After a few blocks, another idea occurred to her, one that could make her final weeks a bit easier.

Lucky Store sold thousands of items in every category. Luz had been inside several times. She bought hair clips, a nail file, some underwear, and soap. It was only a few blocks from Sayonara. She roamed the aisles for half an hour but nothing seemed appropriate for her purpose. She gave up and headed toward Minchi's.

She used a different route than the one she had used to get to Sayonara. Five blocks from Lucky Store, she came upon a florist. The florist was different from the one beside the nearby funeral home in that fresh flowers were not on sale. Only the dried variety filled the shelves in the window. It was the perfect thing for Aruba's hot climate.

Luz entered the store, certain she would find something. In less than five minutes she saw it, an arrangement of red roses with other flowers stuck between in a low, globular vase. The clerk told her the arrangements on that shelf were thirty dollars. The pensive look on her face must have struck the clerk because the price fell to twenty-five without another word. To make that much money took her the better part of half an hour upstairs with a man. But if it bought what she wanted, it was worth ten times as much.

The clerk wrapped the flowers carefully in fancy paper and placed them into a heavy bag with big loop handles. Luz left the store hoping the other girls were not yet out of bed. She didn't need them questioning her about what was in the bag.

In her room, she put the bag under her bed where no one would see it. Since the flowers would not wilt, she had time to develop a plan. She stretched out on her bed, content with the path that lay before her. The weeks behind her no longer seemed so difficult, and the three weeks ahead felt like only a few days. She settled into her mattress and fell asleep.

She dreamt the devil was chasing her down Main Street. To escape, she bolted through the refinery gate. This turned out to be a mistake. The refinery was the devil's lair. Fire shot from pipes and burned in trenches along the ground. Everywhere she turned, the devil was waiting. She saw a patch of blue sky between the streaks of smoke. She dashed for it, the taste of rotten eggs in her mouth. At last, she came to the water's edge. A blue sky was in the distance, over the ocean. The devil approached her from land. Without another thought she dove into the water. Instantly the flames disappeared, along with the smell and taste of hot crude oil. When her face broke the surface, she looked back at the refinery. It was gone. In its place, a little wooden dock stuck out from the land. She recognized it as the one at Charlie's in Savaneta. She climbed up the ladder. A heavy towel hung from the railing. She dried off and padded across the planks. At the end of the dock, she peered at Charlie's pavilion. People were there, having a party: dancing, laughing, and cooking. The scent of the barbecue was unmistakable. She couldn't wait to have a taste of the food and a tall glass of ice water.

Luz woke with a terrible thirst. She had slept beyond the length of a good nap. She was grumpy and disturbed by her dream. She went through the motions of showering, applying makeup, and getting dressed for the night. When she was ready, she sat down heavily on her bed. Her mood had swung so far below where it had been she thought the whole day must have been part of her nightmare. She dreaded going down to the bar. She contemplated telling Spanner she was ill.

At eight fifty-nine, she descended the stairs. As quietly as possible, Luz handed her keys to Pablo, who carelessly dropped them. It sounded like a stack of china hitting the floor.

Marcela took her time crossing the room and held her eyes on Luz as she did. "It's exactly nine o'clock," she said, and with a glance at the clock above the whiskey bottles added, "Oh, now it's one minute after."

Luz cursed herself for delaying the inevitable. Why hadn't she come down five minutes early? It wouldn't have killed her to sit on a bar stool before handing off the casa money. She was back on la Dueña's bad side. She had to stop acting like a little girl. She had to act like a woman, maybe a little like la Dueña herself. No, she had to be like Señora Álvaro and Carlotta. They were women who faced the world for what it was.

"I haven't checked your rooms in a long time. Let's go up together," Marcela said setting off for the door.

She went through Inez's room first, then Carmen's and Laura's. Each girl received high praise for her cleanliness. The girls stood uneasily around the table in the common area. They tried not to look at Luz as she opened her door for la Dueña.

Luz stayed in her bedroom while la Dueña poked around her bathroom. She slid the florist's bag from under her bed and placed it on the nightstand.

"You should wipe the sink after putting on your makeup," Marcela said. "The powder clumps around the porcelain. If it builds up, you'll have to scrub hard to get it off."

"You're right," Luz said rushing for a roll of paper towels. She cleaned the sink then returned to the bedroom, where Marcela was staring at her closet.

"You don't have many outfits. I would have expected you to buy some more clothes. The men are going to see the same thing every night and skip over you."

"There are some tops in my drawer," Luz said.

"I'm sure there are, but you should get a couple more dresses. Men like to see women in dresses."

Marcela scanned the room for some other defect. She spotted the bag on the nightstand. "Why is that bag there?" she asked with her finger pointing at it.

"It's a gift," Luz answered.

"From a client?"

"It's for you. I wanted to give it to you at a better time, but I suppose now is just as well."

La Dueña pried open the bag with her fingernail. She saw the flowers and dipped her hands in to extract the arrangement. It took her a few seconds to peel away the wrapping paper. Holding it up to the light, she rotated it back and forth until she saw every side. "It's beautiful, Luz," she said. "I'm touched you thought of me."

"With what happened to your husband, I'm sure you are upset and very busy. Through all that you have been good to me. I want you to know I appreciate your help."

The arrangement went back in the bag without all of the wrapping paper. Luz folded the paper and shoved it into a drawer.

"I'm going home this minute and putting it on my table," Marcela said. "By the way, I have someone for you to meet. Next week, Tuesday or Wednesday. I will let you know. Let's keep this person between us."

"*Claro*," Luz said, hoping it was another client like Martin.

In the common room, la Dueña told her girls what a good job they were doing. She thanked them all for paying the casa on time and stressed the need for them to continue doing so. She paid special attention to Inez, who would soon be leaving. Like soldiers, they were dismissed to go back to their post at the bar.

"What was in the bag?" Inez asked Luz.

"Something she wanted," Luz said.

Before Inez could ask her another question, a guy came up to them wanting to know about their show.

The night went faster than any other. Luz and Inez performed their special show twice, which took up two hours plus the time spent negotiating the price. The second time they got less than the standard two hundred dollars each. Inez let the price fall because she was drunk on Baileys and talking about how soon she would be going home. In the middle of the second show, Inez had a giggle fit that almost brought it to an end. When she wouldn't stop laughing, one of the men got angry and slapped her on the ass. Inez rubbed the spot then asked him to do it again. He smacked the other cheek, and she dove between Luz's legs in earnest.

Luz went with no men that night, but she managed to sell ten vinos. She talked to the men who bought her drinks. As soon as they asked the questions of how long she had been there and how many times had she worked in this way, the conversations petered out. Luz figured that the men had their own way of hedging their risks. They wanted to be with a girl who was new, fresh, who hadn't had time to be with their friends. It was a sort of race to see who could have sex with whom first. The race lasted ninety days for the locals since they lived there and had the luxury of observing the girls through the entirety of the contracts. Americans on vacation or working a short contract at the refinery had a different time frame. The clocks started on the day they arrived or the day a new girl started working. For them, it was a mission of discovery and conquest before retreating to their regular lives, which were where the airplanes took them. This group competed with each other to find the best-looking girls with the least amount of time in Aruba. Naturally, the make-believe rules were forgotten when anyone had enough to drink.

After not servicing a single man that night, Luz figured she had to do two things. First, she had to start lying again. The next man who asked her how long she had been in Aruba was going to get a different answer: "Three weeks," instead of, "Eight weeks." Secondly, a new haircut would set her apart from her old look. The regulars who came to play pool would know it was her. A casual visitor would be less certain. She may be able to fool him into thinking she was a new girl. Maybe la Dueña was right. A couple of new dresses might do some good.

As she brushed her teeth, she counted up her various packs of hidden money. The total came to two thousand one hundred fifty dollars and some guilders. She had sent five hundred home. If she spent twenty dollars on her hair and another two hundred on clothes, she would still have plenty of money to take home. If the investment in her new look paid off, she might make a dozen times what she'd spent. Why had she doubted Señora Álvaro? The way things were going, she would leave Aruba with nearly three thousand dollars, about ten times what she would have made in Colombia. She couldn't understand why people thought whores were bad people. They provided a service and were paid well for it. What was wrong with that?

Luz went to bed listening to the sounds of the street. Tires screeched as young men showed off the power of their cars. Girls laughed and yelped as men propositioned them on Rembrandtstraat. High-pressure gases hissed out of the refinery. A beer bottle smashed against a wall. Moments later a couple of men started shouting at each other. More voices joined in until it sounded like a soccer match. Sirens cut through all the noise.

When the blue lights streaked her window, Luz got out of bed for a look down at the street. Police cars blocked both ends. The brawling men were trapped. Four policemen exited each car. They carried clubs in their hands. Another policeman with an officer's cap on his head jogged in from the north end. He raised his hand and waved his men on. The brawlers closed ranks into a close knot with a common enemy. They were no match for trained policemen with batons. The cops rushed them, their officer shouting orders and warnings. In five minutes, only the policemen were standing. The rest of the men were laid out along the walls like fallen bowling pins. The officer took off his cap, wiped his brow, and placed it back on his head. Luz saw it was Chief Calenda. He put his hands on his hips and surveyed what his men had done. He seemed pleased. Luz was, too. If she had to, she knew she could trust him.

AS SOON as she got out of bed, Luz knew where she was going. The salon was called Jaime's and was located beside Charlie's Bar. She believed Jaime would be more honest with her than a female stylist. Besides, Jaime's was spotless, had framed photos of beautiful women on the wall, and there were always people waiting.

She went to la Bonanza for apples. Listening to the radio, humming along to the music, she ate her breakfast. She overflowed with positive sentiments. Her future was going to be better than she ever thought possible. In two years, she and Hernán would be walking together, him to start primary school, herself to finish high school. After that, she would decide what she wanted to do.

Carmen and Laura came out first. They told Luz a couple of guys were taking them to the beach. A horn blew on Rembrandtstraat not two minutes later. They hustled down the stairs, hardly taking the time to say *adiós*. When Inez appeared, Luz poured a glass of orange juice for her.

"Did you see the fight?" Inez asked.

"No," Luz lied. She didn't like to talk about violent things since her father had been killed.

"These guys were fighting in the street. The police came and beat the hell out of them. I saw a guy with his head split open. There's a puddle of blood in the street."

"Uhhg," Luz said and covered her eyes.

"I was standing in the doorway. I couldn't look away."

Luz waited a minute for Inez to settle down. When the orange juice was gone, she said, "Let's get our hair cut today."

"That's a great idea!" Inez said. "Where?"

"I was thinking Jaime's."

"You don't know how smart you are, do you?" Inez said.

Luz didn't know how to take the comment, so she smiled.

"When you come out of Jaime's looking better than ever, you'll be walking past Charlie's where all the tourists hang out. Some American guy with a grumpy wife will see you. He'll get what he can't get at home and give you a hundred dollars for it. I'll be happy to join you. We're partners, aren't we?"

In reality, Luz was after nothing but a good haircut to change her look for the men who entered Minchi's. At the same time, she recognized she was clever, not always on purpose, but she had a way of putting herself in the right position at the right time. She excused herself to get ready.

At the bottom of the stairs, Inez promptly took Luz's arm. They paraded up the street like royalty, on the way to their haircuts and the possibility of landing a fortune.

Jaime's had the usual crowd. Three stylists worked steadily through the line of people until Luz and Inez were next. They spent the time scrutinizing magazine photos, asking each other what they thought of this cut or that one. Luz said she wanted to do something completely different. Inez cautioned her not to go too far. In terms of her life, she had gone beyond all comprehension. Something as insignificant as a haircut was nothing to worry about, especially considering that it would grow back.

When her turn came, Luz had the luck of the draw. She sat in Jaime's chair, a little nervous but mostly excited. He asked her what she wanted to do. She told him whatever he thought would be best. He spun the chair back and forth studying the shape of her face.

"Let's take it all off," Jaime said.

"¡Dios mío!" Inez cried. She put her hands over her face.

Jaime looked at Inez. "Don't you trust me?" he asked.

Inez shook her head. She couldn't bear to watch.

As a professional, Jaime loved a challenge. This girl had the long, straight hair every Latina liked to let hang to her ass or braid over her shoulder. While that had a certain elegance, it lacked creative flair. Jaime saw himself as an artist bent on doing the exotic with the average. He unleashed his scissors, hacking away strands of hair seemingly at random. It cascaded over the apron, piling up on the floor around the chair. He never slowed down, not even when the friend peeked between her fingers at his work and sobbed. These girls, what do they know? Their whole lives they have their mothers and sisters cut their hair. They never get to enjoy real style, high culture, what a pretty woman deserves. Today they had come to the right place.

After the cut, Jaime washed Luz's hair thoroughly so he could demonstrate his styling technique. He dried it and applied gel, tugging out the ends in a radical statement of his artistic mission. He explained to Luz exactly how to do each step. He told her it was easy. A spot of gel between the palms, rub them together, stroke it through the hair, tease out the extra. Repeat if necessary. Be random. Grab a clump here and there. Don't be timid. He made her do it a couple of times. He didn't want her going home and messing up his good work. People would ask her where she had that done, and she would tell them Jaime's. He would be shamed. She followed his instructions. She was a good student but not quite the professional he was. She had only one head to work on while Jaime did ten per day, sometimes twelve.

When Luz saw the finished product, she gripped the arms of the chair to keep herself from jumping into Jaime's arms. He'd given her exactly what she'd wanted, something she would never have done on her own. In these circumstances, it was possible to break the rules, not that there were any rules in San Nicolaas.

"I can't believe it," Inez said.

"Do you like it?" Luz asked.

"It's wild."

"I love it."

Jaime gave her a tube of hair gel, a special brush, and more words of advice. If she had trouble with it, she was to come and see him immediately so he could help. Luz promised she would.

Inez was finished half an hour later. She stuck with her regular style, freshened up by Jaime's partner. Inez couldn't stop staring at Luz. She marveled at the difference the haircut made in her appearance. It gave the illusion she was taller. Her face seemed more angular. Since her neck was completely exposed, she gave off an elegant and formal air, like the wife of an important man. If they hadn't made so much money together, Inez would have been jealous. As it was, this would only enhance their earning potential.

Eager to find out what kind of reaction they would get, Inez hurried out of Jaime's salon. She wanted to strut past Charlie's Bar. No, she wanted to charge in there, order a drink, and let the men see what they had been missing.

Herr Koch saw them cross the threshold and caught himself gaping. In his fifteen odd years behind the bar, he had seen both sides of countless females as they passed in and out of that door. It had been a long time since a pair like this ventured in for a drink.

"*Damas*," Koch said, "How can I serve you?"

"Baileys with ice," Inez told him.

"Right away."

To her disappointment, there were no other men in the bar. Inez toasted Luz's new haircut and their recent financial success. Just then, Charlie came from the stock room.

"What a pleasant surprise," he said to the girls. "I was afraid the tourists had run off to Cuba, and yet here are two beautiful women to share my day."

Luz and Inez smiled at him.

Charlie took stock of them and concluded that his previous assessment of the smaller one had been absolutely correct. She had class, class enough to get herself a real haircut. The average whore lost track of the little things, Charlie knew. She concentrated on the thing between her legs instead of the thing between her ears. If those two pieces of equipment were in perfect synchronization, the woman made a tremendous amount of money. Men, on the other hand, could never synchronize their equipment. Due to a mischievous act on the part of a wicked God, the nerves of the penis did not connect to the nerves of the brain. Or so Charlie believed. Yet, he couldn't fault a man like his friend Sam for falling for such a girl. The same mischievous God provided such tempting fare that even a man as worldly as himself occasionally lost his footing and fell into the morass of enchantment. However, he never fell in love. That was the hardest landing of them all. It was the mistake Sam frequently made, thinking he could change the leopard's spots. Thankfully, Sam had plenty of company, or he would have been miserable and lonely.

"Tell me, ladies," Charlie said, "Why aren't you married?"

Feeling bold, Luz tilted her head and touched Charlie's arm. "I'm waiting for a man like you," she said.

The man with a million comebacks leaned back on his stool. This girl had something he couldn't precisely describe but definitely recognized whenever he saw it. It was a combination of style, charm, good looks, and bullshit. They were qualities he possessed himself, ones he had cultivated all his life. Here was a girl not half his age and already she was a master sorceress able to manipulate the magic potion of interpersonal communication.

"Well," Charlie said, "I'm sad to say I'm already married, and my friends are not half the man I am."

"What am I going to do?" Luz pressed, her eyes big and sad in front of the spectacular haircut.

"Best to buy a dog," Charlie advised her. "Dogs are more loyal. They don't live long enough for you to grow tired of them the way you can of a husband. Best of all, they shit outside."

The three of them laughed. Inez wanted to get on with the day because there were no potential clients in Charlie's. She suggested to Luz that they go to Giordano. To reward them for being such good sports, Charlie gave each of them a T-shirt with his logo on it. They paid with a kiss on his cheek and headed down Main Street.

Inside Giordano, Inez took her turn at playing the game. "Let's make this fun," she began. "I'll pick an outfit for you, and you pick one for me. What do you think?"

Feeling brave, Luz said, "Let's do it."

They split up and walked through the racks. Once in a while, one peeked over the top to see what the other was doing. They waved back and forth trying to dissuade each other from ruining the surprise. After half an hour, Luz went to the register to purchase the outfit she had selected for Inez. It was a very simple dress, in a Roman style with a rounded neckline and a narrow belt to hold it snug. When it was in the bag, she went to the front and waited by the door.

Inez held her choice for Luz against her body. She whispered to the clerk what they were up to. The clerk liked the idea. It was something she'd never thought of doing with her girlfriend.

"Let me see!" Inez said when they were on the street.

Luz darted to Minchi's door with Inez close at her heels. The common area became their dressing room. They took off their street clothes, then handed each other the Giordano bags. Luz opened hers slowly. She took hold of the hanger and pulled up. The dress unfolded out of the bag until hanging before her was a sequined shift which sparkled in the overhead light. It was the most expensive thing in the store. Luz had looked at the tag a couple of weeks ago. She had wanted to buy it, but only if she won the lottery first.

"Put it on," Inez said.

In bare feet Luz looked stunning in the dress. She went to her room for shoes. When she came out, Inez was wearing her dress.

"Do you like it?" Luz asked her.

"I love it," Inez said. "What about you?"

In the tall mirror by the door, Luz stared at herself. Three months ago, a dress like this was something she looked at in windows. Now she owned it. "I hate to think about working in this," she said.

"That's what it's for, to get you work," Inez replied. "Men won't be able to stay away from you tonight."

"I can't wear it tonight."

"Why not? I'm wearing the one you bought me." Inez approached Luz so the two of them stood side by side in the mirror. Inez touched the side of Luz's face. "Your hair is great," she said.

"Thanks."

Inez leaned in and kissed her on the mouth. At first it was soft, just a brush of the lips. Then she pressed in firmly, cupping Luz's head with her hand.

Luz allowed herself to be kissed. It felt pleasant, and she was used to it. Inez held her for a long moment, the way Martin held her the first night they'd made love. Something broke the spell. Inez withdrew, smoothed her dress, and started to gather up the bags and wrapping paper. She said over her shoulder, "I'm going to miss you, Luz."

On her fingers, Luz ticked off the days. Inez had nine before her contract ended, which meant Luz had twenty. In less than three weeks, she would be on the plane. Her boy would be in her arms. She would have money to buy him clothes and toys. She would pay Jorgé to leave them alone. Aruba would be in the past.

Carmen and Laura came back with their men. They were drunk and had noisy sex that woke Luz from a pleasant nap. She rolled back and forth on the bed before giving up. It was too early to get ready for work, so she completed another errand on her list of things to do.

At Western Union, she handed the cashier five hundred twenty dollars to send to Colombia. She paid another five dollars for use of the telephone.

Anna was shocked. "Five hundred more? What do you eat?"

"I have plenty to eat. I think I gained a kilo since I've been here."

"That's so much money. I wish I had gone with you," Anna said breathlessly.

Luz shuddered at the thought of her sister working in San Nicolaas. Anna embodied all that was perfect about a woman in the Colombian culture. She put nothing before her family or God. She spoke humbly, cooked superbly, and spent frugally. She adored children but had none of her own for lack of a mate.

It hurt to lie to Anna, but Luz had to keep it up. "It's the private houses," Luz said. "They pay better than the hotel. The hotel covers my expenses. On weekends and at night, I make extra."

"You must be dead tired working every day of the week," her sister commented. "Do you at least go to mass?"

Luz answered that she went to mass with a friend, which was true. It was also a fact that Luz was exhausted. The naps in the afternoon helped, when they weren't interrupted. But staying awake until four in the morning and getting up after only a few hours of sleep to do laundry, go to church, and take care of the little things of life was a heavy burden. The bursts of energy that came and went were mostly fueled by the sugary vino. Each day her body felt a little heavier. Walking to church and the doctor seemed to take longer and longer. When she got home to Colombia, she was going to curl up with her boy and sleep for an entire day.

"I pray for you," Anna told her.

Luz said she had to go back to work, which was one of the few truths of the conversation.

La Dueña did not appear to collect for the casa. Her absence lifted the mood in the bar. Carmen and Laura were still drunk from their afternoon jaunt. They played several games of pool. The regular players enjoyed grabbing their asses and dancing with them between shots. Pablo and Spanner let them keep drinking so long as the guys were buying. The backgammon board stayed out of sight because the bar was busy from the time it opened until closing.

The reason for the surge in business was Luz. Her haircut and sequined dress brought men in off the street. They took one look at her and had to stay for a drink. She sold twenty vinos and four Baileys. While she chatted with one guy, others would sit at the opposite end of the bar waiting for their chance. Spanner ejected two unruly idiots who tried to barge in on her conversations.

She went upstairs six times in as many hours. Captivated by her new look, the men stared down at her as they worked themselves up to an orgasm. One guy insisted she keep the dress on as she bent over a chair. She argued with him for five minutes before he said he would give her an extra fifty guilders if he ejaculated onto it. She told him he wasn't getting near her unless she saw the money first. He put a hundred-guilder note on her bureau and slid the chair into the center of the room. He lasted less than ten minutes and did not make a mess. He let her keep the hundred guilders and said he would be back tomorrow.

Spanner and Pablo didn't close the bar until four fifteen that morning. With the girls selling so many vinos and the busy pool table, they had a register full of money. Being the larger of the two, Spanner counted out the revenue and stuffed it into a paper bag. He drove with the bag directly to la Dueña's house.

After six clients, a quart of vino, and several Baileys, Luz felt sick to her stomach. The only thing she hadn't done that night was a show with Inez. She vomited, wiped her sink, rinsed her body, and tore the sheets off her bed. From her bureau she took out a clean set, which she fitted around the mattress. The street was busy with the usual characters spinning their tires, hollering, and laughing. Fortunately, there were no fights or another reason for the police to come calling. She fell asleep just after dawn. The sun cutting between her open curtains did nothing to disturb her.

Saturday was a repeat performance. Luz fixed her hair, wore the dress Martin had bought her, and serviced six men, including the guy who came back to see her in sequins. She hardly saw Inez and the other girls. One man paid Luz for a full hour and the others wanted her undivided attention as they bought her drinks in advance of climbing the stairs. The refinery might have burnt to the ground, and Luz would not have seen or heard anything of it. She set her alarm so she would wake in time for mass. When it sounded she switched it off and slept until noon.

Sunday afternoon Luz ate with Inez at Pueblito Paisa because their regular spot, Rincón, was closed. For a little while, she worried Carlotta would be angry with her for skipping church. Then again, Sayonara was probably as busy as Minchi's the past several days.

"This is my last week," Inez said as they ate.

"I bet you can't wait to get home," Luz said.

"Not really."

To this point their conversations had been of a professional nature. Luz knew little of Inez's personal life in Colombia. She was reluctant to ask. After Aruba, she didn't plan on seeing Inez again.

"My brothers are donkeys. My mother is a drunk," Inez said as she stirred her fruit smoothie. "My poor father, he's the good one. I give him money when I can. He lets mama have some of it, but she only buys Aguadiente and shouts at the television all night."

Luz didn't know what to say. She sipped her drink and silently thanked God for her family, which sounded perfect compared to Inez's.

"One day, I'm not going back," Inez continued. "I'm going to get one of these guys to marry me. If not, I'm getting a plane ticket to America and taking my chances there."

"I thought they didn't give visas to Colombians," Luz said. She heard stories that the airlines wouldn't sell tickets to Colombians who didn't have a visa to get into the United States.

"They don't, but I'll find a way. You meet people in this life who can fix things. I'll bet Marcela knows people who can do it. All it takes is money, Luz."

She knew it well. For the right amount of money, she had sex with strangers, acted like a lesbian, and let a man watch her masturbate.

"It's not fair," Inez complained. "We're beautiful women. I'm not being arrogant. Look at us. We are beautiful. You see how we have to live?" She pinched her eyes but failed to stem the tears that seeped out. A heavy sob wracked her body.

The sudden display of emotion startled Luz. She saw Inez as a hard woman. She was the one who practically attacked Luz over Martin, who started the lesbian show, who rushed into situations Luz would run away from. At the end of her contract, a time when she should have been overjoyed to go home, if not to her family at least away from this job, she was overcome with sadness.

"I don't understand why Colombia has to be so bad for us?"

"There are problems everywhere," Luz reflected.

"Where have you been to say that?" Inez said, her voice bitter.

Seeing a glimpse of the old Inez frightened Luz. She wished she had kept silent instead of trying to be sympathetic. Her straw offered an escape. She put her lips on it and drew in some of her drink.

"I've been to places you haven't dreamed of," Inez said. "People don't machine gun each other in the streets. They don't have guerillas attacking buses on the highway. The government isn't fighting a civil war since their grandparents were children. The narcotrafficantes don't rule the countryside."

Luz didn't need a list. Like any Colombian, she knew her country's problems well. Although her father was a victim of those problems, she saw her country as a beautiful place, full of wonderful things, but plagued by a few bad characters who someday would be vanquished. Since she was young, a woman, and poor, she felt she could do nothing to bring about positive change aside from minding her own business and doing the best she could to avoid tragedy.

"You know what some of the Americans say?" Inez asked as if Luz had a dozen American friends. "They say the only thing better than Colombian cocaine is Colombian pussy. That's what they think of us. *Coca y cuca.*"

Luz winced at the last word. No woman liked to hear her pudenda referred to as a cunt. Whether or not Inez's claim about the Americans was true, Luz couldn't be sure. If it was true, she couldn't fault the Americans. Why wouldn't they think that way when Colombia was so willing to export these things?

"I hate Americans," Inez said finally. "They're fat and they're rich and they take advantage of us."

Luz did not agree. Martin was an American. He treated her like a princess. He was fat and he was rich, but he didn't take advantage. He paid her well and bought her clothing and fed her at restaurants in which she would have been lucky to wash dishes. More importantly, he respected her. Of course, Inez had more experience than Luz. Maybe she had met more Americans of the other type.

Inez tempered her mood. She wiped her eyes and mouth with a napkin and crumpled it atop her empty plate. "We made a fortune, didn't we, Luz?" she said.

Unlike the previous two nights, Sunday brought few clients. Carmen and Laura nursed hangovers, at one point falling asleep with their heads on the bar. Pablo and Spanner played several games of backgammon. Inez and Luz studied the jukebox until a man came in and asked them about their show. Normally, Inez would have engaged the man. She would have run her hands over his chest, tickled his ears, and stroked his thigh as she described just how fantastic the show could be. This time she spoke to him like she was reading off the specials of the day at Rincón. She told him in a flat voice that it was two hundred dollars for herself, the same for Luz, plus eight vinos for the bar. The guy didn't want to pay that much. Inez turned brusque and Luz stepped in to see if she could convince him it was worth it. It turned out he was from Holland and had learned his Spanish during frequent vacations in Spain. He was in Aruba for the first time. Luz found out he was married and had two children living in Amsterdam. His wife was at a hotel casino. A pit boss at the casino had told the Dutchman about the show at Minchi's.

The word casino inspired Luz. If the man had enough money to let his wife gamble the night away alone, he had plenty to spend for an hour watching two girls together. She imitated Inez's moves one at a time. She twisted the hair behind his ear. She nuzzled into the spot where his earlobe met his neck. He smelled clean, as if he had just taken a shower. When her hand touched his thigh, he fell into her trap. His head tilted toward her shoulder. His lips pressed onto her clavicle. She heard him take a deep breath of her perfume. Luz closed her eyes and stroked his back. When she opened them, she saw Inez staring at her. Luz smiled slightly, just a twist at the side of her mouth and a tiny squint of her eyes.

The man paid Spanner for the vinos that would be skipped and also the con-doms. Inez took her keys from Pablo and the trio went up the stairs. Carmen and Laura woke up, saw what was happening, and promptly put their heads back down on the bar.

In the room, things got off to a slow start. Inez failed to take the initiative. She lay on the bed, her body slack and her eyes closed. Luz concentrated on the man for several minutes but it became clear he expected the girls to put on the show. Seeing Inez wasn't going to play her regular part, Luz took over. She undressed first, then pulled Inez's dress up over her head. Her hands went to every sensitive area of her partner's body. The gasps and soft moans coming from Inez had an eerie quality since the street was quiet and the radio was off. After a while, Luz felt the heat ris-ing from between Inez's legs. She knew her friend was genuinely aroused.

At this point, Inez put her arm around Luz's neck. She clutched her tight and nipped her ear. "I want to feel good," she whispered. "Make me feel good."

Luz let her fingers drift over Inez's body. Inez held on tightly and started to pant. "Harder, Luz," she said. "Harder. Make me feel it."

When her fingers slid into Inez, Luz knew the other girl was lost in a fantasy. The words coming from her made no sense. Her eyes shifted behind closed lids, watching a scene conjured by a delirious mind. Her body tensed and shook until it squeezed tight around her hand for the final release. Inez sucked in a breath, held it, choked off a yelp, then exhaled a long stream of whistling air.

Luz noticed the man had his clothes off and was putting a condom over his stiff penis. Inez opened one eye, saw him, and nodded to Luz. "Let him put it in me," she said, opening her legs.

Inez turned her head so she could see Luz. "I love your haircut," she said, then pinched her eyes shut as the man plunged into her.

The night ended after the show. Inez didn't bother coming downstairs. She closed her door, and Luz heard the lock slam home. The man took Luz by the hand. In the bar, he bought her a drink, and then Spanner told him they were closing. Luz was thankful for getting to bed a few minutes before four o'clock.

MARCELA LOWERED the passenger window and told Luz to get in. Luz obeyed the order.

"I'm glad I saw you. We're going to meet those people I told you about."

"But I'm not dressed nicely, and I haven't eaten."

"You'll survive," la Dueña barked. "We have an appointment."

The air conditioning in the big Mercedes was enough to make Luz shiver. She rubbed her shoulders to warm up. Her stomach rumbled as they passed the snack shops on the way out of San Nicolaas.

"I'm introducing you to my attorney," Marcela said when they were on the main road to Oranjestaad. "Then you will meet a young man named Andrés, my late husband's son by another woman. I think you will like him."

Luz looked out the window, wondering if Marcela expected her to service the attorney to reduce her legal fees or perhaps her stepson for a different purpose. After what happened on the boat, she had every reason to expect so. Her stomach exchanged hunger pangs for knots.

Without waiting for Luz, Marcela barged into the office and announced herself to the receptionist. Luz caught up after checking her hair and attempting to apply a little powder to her face. As soon as she stepped out of the car into the gritty breeze, her efforts were defeated. Given notice, Luz would have fixed her hair the way Jaime had taught her, the way that turned heads in the bar.

Marcela's lawyer was named Beltran Salinas. He was a prissy man compared to what Luz was used to. His hair and skin were perfect, like a woman's. When he shook Luz's hand, his grip was light and soft. His office gleamed with polished metal and lacquered wood under track lighting, which did nothing to warm the place against an air conditioner stronger than the one in the Mercedes.

"Andrés will be here in a few minutes," Salinas said.

"Let's get to business," Marcela told him.

"Okay," Salinas drawled. He turned to Luz and said, "Andrés is a nice boy. He's much younger than me, probably close to your age."

Luz thought she knew what was coming. They were making a deal to loan her body to this young man in exchange for something between themselves. She seethed at this possibility, but she sat with her back straight and her eyes gleaming as if they were telling her she had just been accepted to the National University in Bogotá.

"As it is in life," Salinas said with his hands spread wide before his two guests, "each of us can help each other. For example, I sort out various legal issues for Marcela, and she pays my fee. This is an honest and fair relationship, the way it should be."

"Get to the point," Marcela said.

"Marcela tells me you have been very successful working in San Nicolaas. I'm here to offer you something not every girl who comes to San Nicolaas deserves. This is reserved for the special ones, the ones like you."

Here it comes, Luz thought.

"No doubt you'd like to leave Colombia and go to America," he said.

Her composure slipped. She hadn't expected him to say something so bizarre. "I love my country," Luz said reflexively. "My family is there, my little boy, too." She bit her lip to prevent saying anything else.

"*Claro, claro.* But you know how difficult Colombia can be. Wouldn't you like to go to America? Wouldn't you like to have a job there? Maybe as a secretary for a big company? Then you would come to a place like Aruba on vacation with your husband, a man who appreciates your beauty for what it is. If you lived in America, your next husband would be an American, right? The pot of gold, eh?"

Two months in San Nicolaas had taught Luz the difference between dreams and reality. This fussy man was pitching the former, not the latter.

"I know you're thinking this is impossible, that I'm trying to convince you of something that can never be. That is to say, it can never be given the present status of Colombians with regards to traveling and living in the United States."

Luz tried to relax. Marcela shifted in her chair and sighed loudly in an effort to prompt Salinas to move faster.

"This is where Andrés comes in," Salinas said, folding his hands. "He is a native of Aruba. He can travel anywhere in the world with his passport because we Arubans are as harmless as sheep."

At this point, Marcela broke in. She blurted, "If you were married to him, Luz, you would have the same status."

Luz felt all the air leave her lungs. Why would she marry a man she'd never met and then go with him to the United States? While she had thought of making

America a goal, her thoughts of going there were nothing more than a passing notion. With the money she'd made, she could pay Jorgé and therefore stay exactly where she belonged, in Colombia with her family.

Salinas clarified. "After two years, you can divorce Andrés if you want to. You may want to stay married and have a baby. You never know. The key point is after two years of marriage you will also be an Aruban, and you are free to travel and live in a way that is not available to you now."

She understood how that might be valuable for someone like Inez but not for herself.

"What do you think so far, Luz?" la Dueña asked her.

"It's interesting," Luz managed to say.

"Best of all, it's cheap," Salinas added.

"Cheap?" Luz questioned.

"Sí, barato. You may be offered the same opportunity by others. They will want a significant amount of money up front and higher monthly payments."

"Monthly payments?"

"Yes. I propose to offer you a marriage of convenience to Andrés for only three hundred dollars per month, thirty-six hundred dollars per year. You made double that working in San Nicolaas so far, didn't you?"

Hardly, she wanted to say but suspected these two were capable of smelling lies.

The lawyer continued, "And as long as you work in San Nicolaas you can continue to earn this much money, which has to be a hundred times what you ever made in Colombia."

With each second that passed, she found it harder to maintain her cool smile and friendly gaze. These people wanted to make her a slave. No, it was worse than being a slave. They wanted her to pay for the right to work. It disgusted her more than what her clients did to her. At least those men were honest about their desires. They paid fifty guilders for the half hour. There weren't any complicated arrangements for the privilege to travel or become a citizen of another country or a two-year waiting period.

"You wouldn't have to live with Andrés," Salinas said, "unless you wanted to. This is your choice."

Marcela stood up. "Where is he?" she wanted to know.

"He's coming," Salinas informed her. "Luz, tell me your feelings on this matter."

Luz wanted to run out of the building, straight to the airport. Instead, she asked herself what Carlotta would do. She said, "I need some time to think."

Salinas pressed her. "So you'll consider it?"

"You have less than two weeks on the island," warned Marcela. "I suggest you make up your mind soon."

There was a knock on the door, and everyone's attention turned to a young man who entered the room. He was the plain sort of man, without any distinguishing characteristics. He wore a pair of pressed slacks, a white shirt, and carried a baseball cap in his hand. He barely needed to shave.

"Come in, Andrés," Salinas said. "Meet Luz."

Andrés held his shoulders back and his chin up, but Luz could tell he was nervous. She recognized his false confidence. He behaved like some of the men at Minchi's. In the presence of their pals, they could do anything. Alone with a woman in a darkened room, they were bashful and awkward unless they had enough to drink. Then they became heroes again, out to prove their manhood in despicable ways.

Andrés seemed as eager as Luz to be out of the room and on to other things. Luz noticed he had dried paint on his hands. He picked at it while he stood there. He didn't so much as say hello or shake her hand. She felt sorry for him. He was probably a nice boy.

"Now they have met," Marcela said. "There's nothing more to it other than the fact that, if you marry Andrés, Luz, you'll be part of my family."

Luz squeezed her hands to keep from shouting.

Marcela stood, gathered up her purse, and took Luz by the arm. "I will call you, Beltran," she finished.

Luz nearly fell through the door, propelled into the lobby by Marcela's harried gait.

Marcela stopped a block north of Hop Long. "Think about the offer," she said before unlocking the door. "A time will come when you'll wish for this opportunity. It may not be available. A man can marry only one woman at a time. Do you understand me?"

"*Sí, señora.*"

A thunk sounded as the lock released. Luz pulled the latch and stepped out into the warm breeze. Her skin crawled until she entered her room.

After double-checking her door and putting a chair under the knob, she prized open each of her hiding places and took out her money. The cash on her bed totaled three thousand eight hundred fifty-five dollars. She counted out six hundred fifty, which was what she owed for the casa until the end of her contract. That left three thousand two hundred five. She took out an envelope in which she kept her guilders for the doctor, the laundry, and food. She had enough to pay for two more doctor visits and still have thirty-seven guilders remaining, probably less than the cost of a taxi ride to the airport and a small meal while she waited for the plane.

She'd earned more money in ten weeks than her father ever made in a year. She clutched the stack of bills and fanned them back and forth. It should have been no surprise that she accomplished her goal. After all, she worked at it every night. There was no reason for her to start dreaming of America or to get into an arranged marriage.

She heard the metal door clang and scrambled to hide her money. As Carmen, Laura, and Inez came up the stairs, she mussed the bed so it looked like she had been sleeping. A soft knock came just as she kicked off her shoes. She padded to the door.

"I was worried about you," Inez said.

Luz grimaced and said, "I'm not feeling well. A man did it in my mouth last night. It made me sick to my stomach," Luz explained.

"If you can get used to it, they tip more."

The thought of doing that on a regular basis made Luz genuinely ill. Inez handed her a plastic bag.

"I brought you a sandwich and a bottle of apple juice," she said.

"Thanks. I'll see you tonight."

"Try rinsing your mouth with club soda afterward. It works for me, and Spanner doesn't charge you for it," Inez added and retreated to her own room.

A week passed. La Dueña collected the casa money every night. The girls worked enough to meet their quota of vinos but not much more. Spanner and Pablo took up cards over backgammon. Luz and Inez performed no shows, but there were several inquiries.

On Friday afternoon, Luz called her sister. They had the usual exchange about Luz's work, the family, and Hernán.

"I'll be home soon," Luz told Anna.

"Another three months," Anna said. "It feels like you've been gone a year."

"Maybe I'll come home sooner," Luz said previewing her surprise.

"But you're paid so well. Don't do something that will make them angry," Anna warned.

"It'll be okay. I'll let you know."

When Luz disconnected, she started to formulate a special set of lies to explain how she had ended a six-month contract in three and was still on good terms with her employer.

Saturday night was the last one for Inez. Luz thought she shouldn't have to work. The girl earned piles of money for the bar. It only seemed right that there should have been a party for her. It didn't have to be a grand affair. Maybe a small cake, some Baileys, and half an hour of her favorite songs on the jukebox. When Marcela rolled in for her nightly inspection, it was clear there would be no celebration.

La Dueña skipped the bar and went straight upstairs. She entered Luz's room first, then Carmen's, Laura's, and ended with Inez's. They were in there a long time until both of them stormed out in a shouting match.

"I never smoked marijuana in my life!" screamed Inez. "You brought that with you."

"Shut your mouth!" la Dueña hollered back. "I can have you put in jail for this." She tossed a hand-rolled marijuana cigarette onto the table. "I think I'll call Chief Calenda this moment."

Inez closed her mouth, but the pressure built behind her eyes. Her hands formed two tiny hammers that were ready to strike.

"Look at this," la Dueña said to the others. "I give you a nice place to work. It's clean. It's safe. It's the best bar in town. How does this one repay me? By bringing drugs into her room. You were all warned that women who worked here were not allowed to have drugs. What am I supposed to do?"

No one ventured a suggestion. Luz kept her eyes on Inez. If Inez made to hit la Dueña, Luz would pull her off to save her from further charges. It would also make her look good, as if she were protecting her boss from a crazy woman. Of course, she was ashamed of her own diabolical thinking, but she had to make it through the next eight days without a problem like this.

"Am I to make an exception and look the other way?" la Dueña was saying. "Would that be the right thing to do with someone who has taken advantage of me?"

Again, no one said a word.

"That would tell the whole world I'm weak, a foolish woman distraught over the death of her husband, someone who can be abused."

Marcela's charges were false and everyone knew it. Yet there they stood, listening closely, fearing their own fate. Luz glanced at Carmen and Laura. They clutched their arms around their chests as if they were about to be beaten with a belt.

Marcela lowered her voice. "I'm not without compassion. I know you some-times need comfort, so I'm going to be reasonable. Inez, since it is your last night and you'll be leaving tomorrow, I'll ask that you pay a fine of a hundred dollars."

"She has the devil's greed," Carlotta had said. Luz wondered if the devil could be a woman.

While they waited, Inez marched into her room. She came out with a canvas purse, one Luz had never seen. Slowly, she pulled back the zipper and turned it over. A small avalanche of money fluttered to the floor. "Take what you want," she said.

La Dueña charged in close, delivered an open palm slap to Inez's face and kicked her foot at the money. "Pick it up!" she screamed.

Inez began to cry. La Dueña cocked her hand for another slap, but Inez bent down to the money. She put clumps of it into the bag until it was all off the floor. With a shaking hand, she placed a single hundred-dollar bill onto the table and stepped out of la Dueña's range. Carmen sobbed and Laura pinched her nose. Luz stared at the money.

"Good luck, Inez," Marcela said. "When you learn to do as you're told, you'll do better in life. Then you'll want me as your friend."

One by one, the girls went to the bar. Inez came down last. Spanner poured her a drink without being asked and put his arm around her. She covered her face with her hands, and Spanner sat with her until a group of thirsty refinery workers entered.

Inez failed to service a single man that night. Luz went upstairs twice, and Carmen and Laura saw their regulars. Each time they passed through the door, they stole a glance at Inez. No one dared to talk to her. She was a leper, someone to avoid lest her bad luck rub off on them. The men felt the same way. They looked at her, saw her expression of combined grief and defeat, and steered to the pool table or the other girls. It was the longest night Luz had lived through since she made the decision to come to Aruba.

The next morning, Luz went straight to Pueblito Paisa where she bought break-fast sandwiches and fruit smoothies for everyone. She was determined to give Inez a happy sendoff. She assembled Carmen and Laura around the table and knocked for Inez. Inez came out looking groggy and beaten.

They chatted as best they could, each girl taking a turn talking about her child or her family or what they were going to do when they returned to Colombia. Luz said she wanted to spend a week of days in the park with her son. Carmen remembered the joy of her daughter's first step. Laura had no children but said she hoped to one day if she met the right man. Inez only joined in at the end. She asked if Luz would help her pack.

In Inez's room, Luz saw firsthand that Inez earned more money than she imagined possible. The other times she had been in Inez's room, it was dark and things had been put away. On the day she was leaving, every drawer, closet, and box gaped open. The closet overflowed with clothes, including enough shoes to cover the floor. She also had a tiny television, a boom box radio with CD player, and a portable radio with headphones. Her makeup kit required a separate case of its own for all the bottles, tubes, and brushes. Luz couldn't help but gawk at Inez's possessions and wonder how it was all going to fit into the suitcases that lay open on the bed.

To make the money required to buy these things, Inez must have serviced twice as many men as Luz. Luz hardly worked the doorway, while Inez rarely missed the hours before the late afternoon nap or after the bar closed. Luz feared working that way because there was no one to call if she had a problem with a man.

Luz believed she could earn as much as Inez. However, she didn't see herself as a professional prostitute. She wondered if that was a mistake. If she was going to do it, why not make the most money possible in the least amount of time? One way to ensure she never came back to this life was to make enough money so she wouldn't have to. The theory made sense. She thought she would try the doorway on Monday to see how it went.

Her daydream ended when Inez asked her to bring an armload of pants from the closet. Inez folded her clothes neatly, then pressed each item flat on the bureau. Piece by piece she squeezed them in. She didn't talk much through the process. Luz realized Inez had a system for packing, that she had done this many times before. It still took three hours to get to the point where they struggled to close the zippers.

The last thing Inez did was to divide her money into several stacks. She made no attempt to hide the amount from Luz. There had to be six or seven thousand dollars and another thousand guilders. "Be careful when you go home, Luz," Inez said as she wrapped rubber bands around the bills.

"I will," Luz replied.

"I mean with your money. There are men watching for you at the airport. They know we come here to work, and they wait to see who gets off the plane. They can tell by the way you dress, or maybe they can smell the money on you. I don't know, but they'll rob you just the same."

"In the airport?"

"Just outside, while you're waiting for the bus or a taxi. They grab you and stuff you in a car and take whatever you have. A friend of mine rolled her money up and stuck it inside a condom. She inserted it into her vagina just before the plane landed. They got that, too."

"What can I do to avoid them?"

"Dress poorly. I have too many suitcases so they'll be watching me from the moment I collect them. But I have someone to pick me up."

Luz hoped Rudi would be able to meet her.

"Come with me to Western Union. I'm going to send all this to myself in Colombia."

Luz was curious how much money Inez had sent home during the previous weeks. "Why didn't you send this home earlier?" she asked.

Inez looked at her. "I thought I might need it if I went to the United States."

"You would go there?"

"I would go there right now if I could, Luz."

As they walked to Western Union, Luz mulled over telling Inez about the arranged marriage that had been offered to her. She had nothing to go home to the way Luz did. But what if it was another of Marcela's traps?

The clerk at Western Union hardly glanced at the pile of money Inez shoved through the slot under the heavy plate window. She counted it, initialed the form, and gave Inez a receipt. She managed a weak smile but no further emotion.

"Francisco will be coming soon," Inez said. "I'm not hungry, but we can get something to drink."

"I'll buy," Luz volunteered.

"I will," Inez insisted. "Let's go to Charlie's."

Charlie's had yet to welcome the tourist crowd, but Herr Koch waved them to a booth in the corner. He brought them glasses of ice and two bottles of Coca-Cola.

"I think I'm finished with Aruba," Inez announced. "I was going to come back here next year, but this is probably not the place for me."

Luz wanted to say she wouldn't be returning either but thought it best to let Inez have her say.

"Martin will be back. He practically lives here. If you see him again, tell him 'thank you' for me."

"I will," Luz promised.

"Maybe when you come back you'll get to spend a whole week with him. I did that. It was my first week here. It was like heaven."

Luz didn't have to imagine that it was.

"You meet men like that," Inez went on. "They're not sweet. They're good. Do you understand the difference?"

Luz shrugged. The men she met in her life were typical. They seemed to tolerate women more than appreciate them. Her brother was like that, and so was Carmelo in the end.

"Boys are sweet," Inez was saying. "When they do something special like buy you flowers or tell you you're pretty, that's sweet. Martin is different. He's a good man. He doesn't care about how we work. He cares about us. You know why he bought you the clothes? When he takes you to those fancy restaurants, he wants you to be comfortable. He knows how women are. He doesn't want you to be judged as a whore by the other women, so he dresses you properly. You have a chance at being equal."

"He told you that?"

"No, but I can tell. He keeps you away from embarrassing situations. Janson took care of you at the pool, right?"

"*Sí.*"

"He pays Janson to keep an eye on you in case something happens."

"What could happen?"

"You never know. Maybe a policeman who recognizes you from San Nicolaas shows up and asks for your permiso. Maybe a jealous wife catches her husband looking at you and complains to the manager. They can throw you out. Then what? That's why I always keep some money tucked away. I slip it inside the sole of my shoe or in a slot in my belt."

That piece of advice Luz would never forget.

"Martin is a good man," Inez repeated. "I'm going to miss him. I hope he remembers me."

"He will," Luz said wondering how many girls wanted Martin to remember them.

At Minchi's, it took both of them, one on each end, to carry the biggest suitcase down the stairs. Carmen stood with it while Luz and Inez went back for the other two. On Rembrandtstraat, there were a dozen girls with suitcases. Few of them had as many as Inez. None looked as heavy.

The driver of Francisco's bus stopped down the block, behind Java Bar. The girl there heaved her suitcase into the back and took her seat. A girl came up from Black

& White Bar and repeated the sequence. Inez and Luz dragged her suitcases down to the bus because Inez didn't want them on the roof for the trip to the airport. One time she had seen them fall off, break open, and scatter clothing everywhere. The driver never stopped. That was in Panama. She said she was never going back there. Her next stop was Saint Maarten.

The driver cursed Inez for her heavy bags, but he squeezed them in. Inez kissed Luz on the cheek and took her seat.

When the van was gone, Luz noticed there were a number of men standing around the corners of Rembrandtstraat. They drank beer and nudged their pals as they pointed at different girls getting into the vans. Departure time was a spectator sport for them. They enjoyed replaying the sad farewells and sordid moments spent with the girls. One guy got down on the sidewalk, rolled on his back, and spread his legs wide. He humped an imaginary lover to show his pals just how well he had been serviced.

Just before Luz turned away, she saw two men in uniforms stride up. She recognized one as Chief Calenda by the hat he wore. He bent down, grabbed the man by the front of his shirt, and yanked him upright. The man dropped his beer bottle, which smashed on the sidewalk. Calenda cursed him for the breaking glass and threw him against the wall. The junior officer held his baton up at the others who might dare to move toward the senior man. They backed down like scolded dogs. Calenda turned his quarry to face Main Street and kicked him squarely in the seat of his pants. The guy spun around, but before he could utter a syllable, the cop had his baton pointed at his nose. The idiot put his hands up and backed away. The two cops stood on the corner until the rest of the men faded down the alleys. After seeing the incident and remembering the fight from the previous week, Luz decided the cop was the best kind of man. He boldly waded into a melee of brawlers. He wasn't afraid to set things right. It gave Luz hope that there were other good men, that she could find one of them worthy enough to be her boy's father.

She had seven nights left in Aruba.

16

THE NEW girl's name was Diana. Compared to Inez, she was chubby, loud, and unbearable. She promptly broke all the rules Francisco announced in the street. Before the sun went down, she walked into the heart of San Nicolaas, came back a short time later leading a man by the hand, and took him to her room. Their moaning and banging woke the others. She stood naked in the doorway when the man left and tried to pinch his crotch as he kissed her good-bye. She made no attempt to apologize to the other girls and seemed to have no fear of being caught by Marcela or the police.

Luz ignored Diana. She knew trouble when she saw it. In the best case, Diana would draw la Dueña's attention, giving Luz cover to escape the pressure of the arranged marriage. In the worst case, la Dueña would be in a permanent rage and take her frustration out on all of them. Luz dreaded the coming of each nightly inspection. She thanked God when Spanner collected the casa money. It meant la Dueña was doing something else.

The bar remained empty during the early part of the week. Every night that Luz paid the casa, a little chunk was removed from her pile. She felt like it was slipping away. She had gotten used to the enormous income generated by shows with Inez. Now that she was back to fifty guilders for half an hour, it seemed like she was working for free. She considered and reconsidered working the doorway but ultimately decided not to.

The last visit to the doctor was also a bad joke. She expected him to be more thorough and actually conduct an exam for a change. After all, wasn't it important that a girl left the island knowing she was healthy or not? Clearly, it wasn't. He signed her card for the last time and dropped it on her lap without asking a single question.

While waiting her turn at the doctor, she overheard a conversation between the same two girls who had discussed her shows with Inez. Since they had that story half right she believed the majority of their second tale. This one centered on a girl working at the Chesterfield. Supposedly, she met a guy from Europe, either England or Germany. He paid the casa so she could stay with him for two weeks.

This was not unheard of. Luz had done it with Martin. Anyway, the guy fell in love with her and paid off her contract to the amount of four thousand dollars. He bought tickets to Saint Maarten, where they were to be married on the coming Saturday. A third girl sitting under the Divi tree confirmed the story. Every girl but Luz jumped into the conversation. They argued over what was the best way to trick a man into doing the same thing. Luz didn't want to trick anyone; she wanted to be home with her family.

La Dueña returned to her regularly scheduled visits on Thursday night. She wasted no time admonishing Diana about the rules. After collecting for the casa and making sure the bar was in top shape, she asked Luz to go for a ride. They took the Mercedes out of town to a spot with a view of the refinery.

"Have you thought about the offer that was made to you," la Dueña began.

"*Sí, señora*," Luz said.

"And?"

"I think it's best if I stay with my family," Luz explained.

"You could still benefit from the marriage," Marcela told her. "You could make a deposit now from the earnings you made on this trip. After visiting your family, you could pay the balance by returning here to work."

"I hope to have another job in Colombia."

Marcela fiddled with the air conditioner controls. She said, "I have a family in Colombia, too. I had to leave them."

"I'm sorry to hear that," Luz replied.

"Don't be sorry. They were bad for me."

This violated every tenet of Luz's life. Her family was everything. Actually, her family was the only thing. Aside from the tiny house they lived in, they had no significant possessions, nor did they have any education or a claim to a title that would get them respect. No one had served in the military or in a governmental or ecclesiastical capacity. They were ordinary people who clung to each other for identity and security. It was how God ordained life to be for His children. So said the priest in her parish church when he blessed the children and the mothers in the name of the Holy Family.

"Do you know why my family was bad for me?" Marcela asked.

Luz shrugged her left shoulder.

"I came to Aruba, much the way you did, through an agent who got me a place at Las Vegas Bar. And, like you, I sent money home for them. I worked hard, that is no exaggeration. I won't be angry if you ask Spanner about me. I have no secrets."

At this Luz suppressed a cough.

"I was with ten men in one day and not everyone entered me the way nature intended. I'm not here to tell you about how I suffered. I'm here to show you a way out of that kind of life. It took me several trips to Aruba to realize I was supporting my entire family. I was sending money home so my sister could go to school, so my brother could buy a car, supposedly for him to get to work, and so my father could have an operation on his eye."

To Luz, those were perfectly good reasons to send money home. Helping your family was a way to help yourself, she believed.

Marcela read her mind. She said, "I should have sent money home for those purposes. But don't you think they should have contributed like me?"

"*Claro, señora.*"

"Well, I discovered the more I worked, the more they let me work. The more things I paid for, the more they asked for, until it got to the point where I was on my fifth trip to Aruba and still there were things they wanted me to buy."

Luz agreed that five trips to Aruba were enough for any woman. Furthermore, if Marcela earned proportionately what Luz had during each of her trips, then her family should have had enough money for all the necessities of life.

"My fifth year in Aruba, that was when I met Ricardo. He took me to his house and we were lovers, real lovers."

This part of Marcela's story Luz knew to be factual because Carlotta had told her an identical version.

"Of all the things I am grateful for, I am most grateful to Ricardo for explaining how stupid I was being."

"I don't think you were ever stupid," Luz put in.

Marcela smiled, a rare sight. "That's nice of you to say, but I was stupid. I was doing a difficult and dangerous thing as you well know, and I was doing it for the wrong reason. I wasn't doing it for my son the way you are. I was doing it so my family could sit on their asses while I had my legs spread for the men coming out of that refinery. That's what Ricardo made clear to me. He said I had paid a debt I never owed. He showed me how I could work for myself, for my own benefit."

Luz's situation was different. Rudi worked whenever he could. Anna took care of her son, and her mother held the family together as a bridge to previous generations. Luz wasn't sending money for them to live a casual lifestyle.

"Part of my change was marrying him. Do you understand?"

Luz nodded. "*Sí, comprendo.*"

"I don't think you do," la Dueña countered. "So long as you are a Colombiana, you are trapped. You can go nowhere or do anything without someone else's permission. You are a prisoner the jailor doesn't have to feed."

"But I love my country," Luz protested.

Her contention was dismissed with a wave of la Dueña's hand. "A country is a line on the map, some cities, a bunch of people that call themselves by a name. Do you love the guerillas who murder us? Do you love the government that taxes us to death? Do you love your neighbors who steal from you?"

Luz's neighbors didn't steal. They were good people, looking for work, trying to keep their families together.

"What about the narcotrafficantes? Do you love them? They make our country the joke of the world."

Marcela neglected to mention all the good things about Colombia, and Luz thought it best not to do so either. She would be happy to walk back to Minchi's if Marcela would unlock the door and let her out of the car. It was not to be. La Dueña had more to say.

"A country is meaningless shit taught to little children so when they're adults they will obey. Fortunately, you have met someone who can make it clear to you, as Ricardo did for me. The way he should have to that boy, Andrés."

If Ricardo was that kind of man, Luz was glad she had never known him.

"I want you to think very carefully about what I have told you. This is not a marriage like you were promised when you were a little girl. Your mother, the old women, the priests, they tell you about love and the sacrament of Holy Matrimony. Bah! Men invented this concept to make us their slaves, so they can have a monopoly on what's between our legs. You know well enough no woman is entitled to exclusive rights on what hangs between their legs."

The trouble with listening to Marcela was the fervor with which she delivered her speech. She was as sure of her message as a priest was of the Gospel. She believed it to be the only version of reality, and based on her experience, it fit perfectly. Luz came from a less cynical environment, a place where love existed and could be counted as a blessing.

"Enough," Marcela said suddenly. "It took me a while to understand. Never forget what you have learned here. Don't think of this as a job or anything less than an education. Here in San Nicolaas you have become a different person and all for the betterment of yourself."

With that la Dueña put the car in gear and drove toward Minchi's. As they came down the hill into town, she delivered her benediction. She said, "I won't ask you about this again. If you want to do it, you must come to me." From a slot in the dashboard, la Dueña removed a business card. She handed it to Luz as she stopped at the corner where Charlie's Bar stood.

"*Gracias, señora,*" Luz said and pulled the door latch.

"One last thing," la Dueña said before releasing the lock. "Tell none of the others about this. Do you understand?"

"*Sí,*" Luz replied knowing she would not say word. She never wanted to unleash Marcela on anyone, including Diana, who needed some discipline for her own good.

"*Buenas noches, Luz,*" la Dueña said and pulled away even before the passenger door was closed.

Luz hurried down the block. Frazzled by her conversation with Marcela, she wanted no more problems on the street. There were men about, looking in the windows, laughing, shoving each other the way boys do on the playground.

Frankie came out of the alley and saw her. He stopped in the middle of the sidewalk and held his chin to think like the famous Rodin sculpture.

Luz slowed her pace, trying to decide which way she was going around him. She knew Frankie was harmless, but she wasn't in the mood for the hassle. It was amazing that someone who spoke four languages as well as he did was reduced to begging in the street. If she spoke four languages, she would have been working in a spiffy office translating documents.

"I won't ask you for a guilder," he said. "You work as hard as I do." The choller then bowed deeply, like a courtier, and smiled with his rotten teeth on full display. Just before Luz entered the bar Frankie called out, "Don't forget me when you're married to a rich man! Find a dentist!"

Frankie's joke erased her anxiety. Luz waved to him and entered the bar.

Only one man came to see her that night, the one who liked to watch her masturbate. At the end of his half hour, he asked her when she was leaving for Colombia. She told him Sunday. He gave her ten extra guilders and said he would see her one more time.

She slept very little that night since Diana worked until dawn. Diana's clients were the worst kind: drunk and boisterous. From the noises that echoed through the building, there might have been a wrestling match going on in the room. Luz longed for the days when she and Inez ate breakfast and lunch together. It was a pleasant way to spend the hours. As much as she was ashamed to admit it (because it confirmed one of the things Marcela had told her), Luz had learned a lot from Inez. She learned how to tolerate men's desires, to play to them, and to deceive them into believing their fantasies were reality.

As soon as Hop Long opened, Luz delivered her bundle of laundry to a washing machine. She decided against waiting until Saturday, her normal laundry day, because if the place was busy with other girls she may not have her things washed and dried in time to pack. Returning to Minchi's, she spotted Charlie entering the service entrance to his bar.

"*Hola, señor,*" she called to him.

"*Buenas dias.* What a wonderful sight so early in the morning. Would you like a cup of coffee?"

She didn't drink coffee but accepted his offer because she enjoyed his company.

"This way," he said waving her in.

He pulled a bar stool out for her, the one at the pass through, where he always sat by the cash register. Luz seated herself and waited while he went in the back. He returned with two cups and an old tin pot.

"Tell me something," Charlie began. "I lived in Colombia for many years, and I am a student of every culture I encounter. Without sounding arrogant, I must say I have benefited from all of this observation and study. And yet, there is something even I cannot figure out. Perhaps you know."

Luz could not imagine she would know something this man did not. She offered to try.

"Colombia produces the best coffee in the world. In the United States there are advertisements on television bragging about the excellent coffee from Colombia. And this is true. I've had it. However, the coffee you drink in Colombia, I think they make it in the sewer. Why is that?"

"I don't know," Luz admitted. What he said was true. Coffee was not so good in Colombia.

Charlie said, "Another mystery for me to ponder for the ages. That and where is the Ark of the Covenant. Did you see that movie?"

She pointed at him with a smile. "*¡Sí, tan bueno!*"

"Yes. I liked that one myself. Adventure! Love! A little bit of God and the demons just to keep us nervous." He patted her on the hand to make his point.

"*Gracias,*" Luz said out of the blue.

"For what?" Charlie asked.

"You always make me laugh when I walk past here. I enjoyed your birthday party even though that man drifted onto the beach."

"He was lost and you found him. And a second time, too."

She blushed, then said, "I go home on Sunday."

"How terrible! We were only getting to know each other." Charlie then told her about his daughter who lived in Holland. She worked for a pharmaceutical company. "Hopefully she invents a pill to cure cancer before I get it from these cigarettes, eh?" he said.

"Why don't you quit?"

"A filthy habit, I know, but addiction is a terrible price we pay for a little bit of pleasure. I think the tiger will sooner change his stripes."

She thanked him again for his kindness as she rose off her stool.

"Stay away from men," he admonished her in the doorway. "And don't fall in love."

❋   ❋   ❋

Friday night brought its usual assortment of salary men out for a good time. Luz wore her sequined dress. Diana prattled on about the dress for more than an hour before Luz finally told her to shut up. There were two nights left on her contract, and it was bad enough she couldn't sleep for all of Diana's antics. She didn't need a second dose in the bar. Despite the busy crowd and her fancy dress, Luz only went upstairs twice and neither client tipped.

Saturday morning she headed to Western Union to send the bulk of her money to herself in Colombia. To her horror, Western Union was closed. A sign on the door announced no business would be transacted due to computer problems. There was another place farther up Main Street that wired money. She went there but got a bad feeling just looking through the window. It appeared less official than the Western Union office. The cashier was a man in a T-shirt instead of the better dressed but impersonal women with whom Luz had become familiar. At Minchi's, she put the money back into hiding.

She decided to pack early. Following Inez's method, she opened all the drawers in her bureau, the doors to her closet, and the mouth of her suitcase. In just over an hour, her possessions were neatly contained by her suitcase and the new garment bag. Only two outfits remained. The one she had on, which she was also going to wear tomorrow, and the dress she was going to wear tonight, the one that Martin had bought.

She looked at her watch. It was after one. Carlotta would be at her bar, having just opened it for business. Luz set out for Sayonara relieved her packing was finished but worried that she would be robbed of her money when she left the airport in Colombia.

Following Helfrichstraat, she passed familiar sights she would soon be leaving. There was Pueblito Paisa with the two women who always smiled no matter how difficult the customer. There was Hollywood Bar across the street with its doors open to the breeze. Up the side street a few blocks was Lucky Store. There was Moderna Nail Palace, where Inez had gone for manicures, a luxury in which Luz never indulged.

At Sayonara's door, she paused for a deep breath, then pushed forward.

"*Hola*," Carlotta said from behind the bar. "Come, have a seat with me."

It took her only a second to enter the warm embrace of the woman who brought her so much comfort. She held on to Carlotta for a long moment, letting her nervous energy dissipate amid the strong perfume. Then she sat down against the wall with Carlotta by her side.

"I'm excited to see my boy," Luz began. "My sister tells me he's talking more every day."

"They're so precious. I wish I had one of my own."

"*Gracias*, Carlotta, for everything."

The madam put her hand on Luz's leg. "You'll be a fine mother."

"I wanted to buy you a gift, but I couldn't find anything that was right. Can you forgive me?"

"You came here to see me today. That is enough. Buy a present for your little boy. He needs it more than me."

They talked for a while about Colombia and Carlotta's province of Riseralda. Luz asked if Carlotta ever returned, and Carlotta said it had been more than ten years since her last visit.

"There's nothing there for me now," Carlotta said. "My parents died a long time ago, and my brother and sisters have their own families. I was here with my Max. He was my family. He is dead, but I have the business and Gigi. We're like sisters. The girls, sometimes they are like daughters. They're good and bad, as you would expect."

It was time to say good-bye. Luz cried. Carlotta sniffled. Luz promised to call to let Carlotta know how she was doing in Colombia. She exited the bar into the heat of the afternoon. Her tears dried instantly, two salty tracks over her cheeks.

The excitement of going home precluded an afternoon nap. She returned to Western Union where the sign had been moved to the cashier's window. The telephones could be used, but no money transfers would be permitted. She paid for what would be her last call.

She asked Anna if Rudi was home.

"No, but it's for a good reason. He has work. He'll be at a construction site all weekend."

This was good news for them but bad for Luz. She would have to get home from the airport on her own and with a purse full of money.

"Is something wrong?" Anna asked.

Luz sighed. "Don't worry about it."

"What else has happened?" her sister prodded. "In three months you haven't told me much about this island."

The reason for that, Luz knew, was because she had barely ventured out of San Nicolaas. She had been to Charlie's in Savaneta and the Hyatt Hotel. Other than that, her life passed within the Zone of Tolerance, which was the center of San Nicolaas. She didn't want to do it, but she made up some stories for her sister. She told her about a giant house she cleaned for a woman. The woman gave her a pair of dresses, but they didn't fit. She traded them with another girl for a different dress and a pants suit.

"Oh, and I cut my hair," Luz said next.

"You cut your hair?"

"Very short."

"Oh, *Dios mío*. What will our mother say?"

"I hope she likes it."

"You have time to grow some of it back," Anna suggested.

Much less than you think, Luz wanted to say. She gave her usual salutations and rang off. No one wanted to use the phone. She brooded in the tiny enclosure. How she wanted to tell Anna she would be home tomorrow! She ached to be there with her family and away from the place that gave her its money but stole her dignity. She marveled at Marcela's doing this five times and Carlotta's doing it for most of her life. It wasn't always physically demanding, but it stretched the limits of self-respect. It left her guessing not what she would do for money but what she wouldn't do.

Her room looked different, empty, like one in a hotel that hadn't been used in a long time. She peered out the window at the street. A few cars passed. Diana tried her luck with the men and failed.

Luz suddenly felt the need to talk to God, to pray, to ask for forgiveness for this part of her life. She prayed to her saint, the one on the card behind the candle in the corner of her room. She vowed to put twenty dollars into the collection basket at her parish church in Colombia.

She readied for work in the usual way. As if she could make the time go faster, she went down the stairs half an hour early. Spanner was in the bar alone. He stacked cases of beer and logged them into the book. He greeted Luz and asked her if she was ready for her last night in San Nicolaas.

"I hope it goes quickly," she told him.

"Don't wish that, girl," he warned her. "Soon you'll be older than me and wanting to go back to your youth."

He was right, and she recanted. "Just this night," she said. "After that, time can stop."

"I think the new girl is going to be a problem," Spanner lamented. "When la Dueña catches her, !Dios mío!"

Luz shrugged and looked out the window. As if Spanner had conjured up the devil simply by mentioning his name, Marcela's Mercedes pulled up to the curb on the opposite side of the street. Luz watched as a man got out of the passenger seat and entered China Clipper.

"That's her new boyfriend," Spanner said. His voice was so close to Luz it made her jump.

"You scared me," she said holding her chest.

"Sorry. That's Alex Montoya. He owns China Clipper."

Luz figured he was collecting for the casa just as Marcela did every night. The bar owners were wise to keep a close eye on the money. Similarly, their presence lent an air of authority over the bar. It let the girls, the bartenders, and the patrons know the boss was aware of what was happening.

When Montoya returned to the street, Marcela exited the car. The two of them walked across to Minchi's, where they entered one after the other, Montoya holding the door for la Dueña.

"Hola, Luz," Marcela gushed. "Meet Señor Montoya."

Montoya stepped up with his hand out. Luz shook it. "Pleased to meet you," she said.

"Let's get this over with," Marcela continued. She took out the book and turned to Luz's page. With the money in one hand and a pencil in the other, la Dueña marked the final day paid.

"We can go to my room," Luz suggested in anticipation of the final inspection. She hoped she did not get the same treatment as Inez, but she had an extra hundred dollars ready just in case.

"I trust you, Luz," was Marcela's reply. "You're not like the other girls, are you?"

It was another of la Dueña's tricks, an attempt to get Luz to speak ill of the other girls. Luz recognized it for what it was and changed the subject. "*Gracias*," she said, "For your help and kindness."

"You see," Marcela said to her boyfriend. "This girl is something special. She's going to make someone a nice wife."

Montoya grinned but said nothing. Maybe he was her lover the way she had confessed the Venezuelan to be. Luz worried he may have a shortened life like Ricardo's, but she quickly shut her mind to the subject. She would never see these people again. What did it matter what they did with each other?

"Don't forget," la Dueña was saying, "Call me whenever you like. I wish I had four girls like you."

"*Gracias*," Luz said for the compliment.

Carmen and Laura appeared, each clutching fifty guilders. They laid their money on the bar and smiled nervously. Like Luz, they were waiting for a room inspection that ended in a shouting match and a fine. But Marcela was anxious to leave. She put the money into her envelope and asked where Diana was. No one knew. With a hideous smile, la Dueña said, "She will learn not to be late."

On cue, Montoya pulled open the door, and Marcela walked out. Luz was relieved she would be in Colombia when Diana faced la Dueña's wrath. Carmen and Laura might not be so lucky. They had a few more days to go.

Men came in soon after the behind-the-scenes business of the bar ended. They looked over the girls, ordered drinks, and settled into rounds of billiards. Spanner and Pablo stuck to their routine of card games interrupted by drink service. Luz hoped none of the men selected her. She would be happy to pass six or seven hours staring at the jukebox or watching the pool table. One of her regulars, the married man as she thought of him, came in and ruined the possibility of a tranquil night.

They wasted no time sharing two vinos. He told her he had missed her the last couple of weeks. Upstairs, he took his time since he "wanted to make their last night together special." For Luz there was nothing special about it. He pressed on top of her, stroked in and out, grunted, and then went to the bathroom. Aside from the smudge between her legs, there was no evidence he had even been there.

A new guy bought her a vino and played a game of pool with the regulars. He came back for the second vino after losing a game. He won three games in a row after that and was clearly thrilled with himself. To celebrate, he took Luz upstairs. It started off on the wrong note when he asked her how much to do it without a condom. She told him she wouldn't do it without a condom no matter how much he offered.

"A million dollars?" he asked sarcastically.

In the same tone, she replied, "Let's see it."

"Okay. A hundred?" The bill hung between his fingers.

"No."

He tried to stare her down. When she wouldn't give in, he rolled the condom on. She straddled him and started bobbing. He didn't like her technique so he rolled her over and pumped away like every other boy who thinks only about his own pleasure. He gave her sixty guilders, which meant he must have enjoyed himself.

Two more men took their half hour with Luz. They both mentioned this being her final night. The last man to come in was the one who paid her to masturbate. She found herself in a strange mood as he positioned the chair to watch her. She decided to give him a hell of a show. Instead of waiting for him to direct her, she posed on her own, touching her body in the places she knew he wanted to see touched. Strangely enough, she found herself enjoying it. At one point, she opened her eyes and saw him staring at her face. His expression was not a disgusting leer but one of desperate longing. It turned her on to the point where she arched her back, felt her body contract, and let out a sharp cry as she climaxed. When she looked over at him, she saw that he had ejaculated. She wondered why he did it in his hand when he could have done it inside her. He left a hundred dollars on her bureau and exited before she came out of the bathroom.

Spanner closed the bar at five minutes past four. Luz carefully inspected her dress for any sign of the way it had been used. It was only wrinkled; there were no stains. She discarded her underwear and took a shower. She put on clean panties from her suitcase and slid under the covers.

Surprisingly, she slept late. By the time she arrived at Pueblito Paisa for breakfast, the place teemed with both refinery workers and girls. She ate hurriedly and on the way back to her room saw Carmen and Laura get into a car. They didn't notice her approaching and drove off. It hurt Luz that they didn't stick around to say good-bye, but she couldn't blame them. They had to earn what they could.

She watched the street to pass the time until the first autobus rolled up

Rembrandtstraat. After checking her purse to see that all her money was there, she zipped it closed and tucked it inside her shirt. She hefted her suitcase and went to the stairs. The last thing she did at Minchi's was put her keys under the door to the bar.

The autobus driver told her to sit up front, the same seat she had on her first day in Aruba. One by one, the bus picked up other girls until it was full. The driver turned onto Helfrichstraat, which connected to the main road to the airport. As they passed the police station at the end of town, Luz saw Chief Calenda standing beside a patrol car. She waved, but he didn't see her.

At the airport, the immigration officer looked over her passport. "See you next year," he said with a smile and turned to the next girl.

On the plane, the excitement of leaving the island overcame her. It felt like she was going on a grand vacation, not a trip home. Her boy would be waiting for her, and they could play in the park together. How surprised her family would be! They would need an explanation for her early return, and she had it ready, that one and a hundred other lies. She didn't feel guilty about not telling the truth. She was proud. She was going to get Jorgé off their backs. The family would be able to settle into the regular rhythm of living. It would be as if they had made it through a terrible storm the way the Captain had. They would be together again, the way the Captain must be with his own family.

When the plane left the ground, Luz struggled to look down at the island. She spotted the beach in Savaneta, then traced the sand toward San Nicolaas. Charlie's pavilion was clearly outlined on the shore. She could see the reef a short distance off the beach.

"Tú vives," she said to herself.

THE RHYTHMS of Aruba's refinery were as much the soundtrack to Charlie's life as the salsa he adored. He had watched it from the day of his birth to the present day and had missed very few in between. As nothing but a glorified pressure cooker, Aruba's oil refinery made all the same sighs, wheezes, and belches as its tiny counterpart. In reality, Charlie knew the refinery was significantly more than that. The refining system was a chemical process which required ingredients beyond South American crude and some heat. It necessitated smart people doing difficult jobs and less smart people doing even more difficult jobs.

It was a Tuesday night turning into Wednesday morning. Midweek days were laborious for Charlie. Midweek nights were interminable. The only thing cavorting on Main Street was dust caught up in the breeze. On this night, however, he felt as if the hours had scurried past him like his cat pursuing one of the tiny lizards that invaded his upstairs lair from time to time. Charlie looked over at Screwball, who rested on the western parapet with his forepaws tucked under his chest.

The cat's ears twitched, and Charlie gave him a rub on the chin. Screwball turned away from his owner and stared out over the refinery wall. As he did, one of the flares switched off. It wasn't just the main body of flame that faded but also the blue torch that served as an igniter near the nozzle from which the waste gas emanated.

"That's something different, eh?" Charlie said.

Screwball cocked his ears again. Another flare went out, followed by a low moan, like a giant tire going flat.

"Maybe another explosion?" Charlie asked.

Restless, Screwball jumped off the wall, pranced around the veranda a few times, then hopped onto Charlie's lap, which was at such an angle he had to use his claws to hold fast. Charlie placed him back on the wall, but Screwball stayed close.

Several police cars turned into the refinery and parked just beyond the gate with their lights flashing. Charlie couldn't actually see the face of the man standing slightly apart from the others, but he could tell by his posture and the glint off his shoes that he was the commandante. As he stood there petting his cat, Charlie discerned a continuous reduction in the noise coming from the complex. It got to the point where he could hear the breeze first and the refinery second.

"I think this is trouble," he announced to Screwball, who already knew that it was.

A long line of men passed the cluster of police cars at the main gate. Some of them greeted each other as friends. Most ambled through the gate and into town without so much as a "bon nochi."

"Now we'll have some action," Charlie said. His voice rose a little at the possibility of a fresh batch of revelers entering the bars. He was disappointed to see the majority of them get into cars and drive away. Those who lived in town didn't seem to have the lift in their step that meant they were headed for drinking or screwing. This made no sense to Charlie. Whatever was happening at the refinery, good or bad, it was a reason to drink. It was either a celebration or a lamentation, and both were good for the soul. So sayeth the Good Book according to Charlie's interpretation. Didn't Jesus lay on the food and wine at that wedding celebration all those years ago when prophets were prophets and oil refineries didn't exist but whorehouses did? Of course!

After a while, Charlie realized the entire staff was abandoning the facility. A private security group showed up in cars newer than the ones Calenda and his men drove. They wore smart uniforms, too. These men were not from this part of the island if they were from the island at all. They looked more like the Dutch marines from the base located outside San Nicolaas. They were fair skinned, light haired, and too well built to have gone to seed in the lazy island lifestyle. Whoever they were, they stationed themselves at different points around the refinery including the office, the gate, and near the wharves. Charlie assumed they were also in control of the areas near Roger's Beach. That was a good place to be. From there it was possible to catch couples swimming naked at this time of night.

Calenda's men patrolled for twenty minutes, but no one loitered for them to harass. They rolled out of town in a single-file convoy without taking a turn down Main Street to see the sights. Their chief was not in such a hurry. He exited the passenger side of the last cruiser, then waved the driver off. When the car was gone from sight, he strolled to the end of Rogerstraat, where the unfinished hotel showed no signs of further progress.

Charlie switched from the east side of the veranda to the west as Calenda passed into town. Screwball remained where he was, sniffing the breeze for a clue to what had happened on the other side of the wall.

A few minutes later, Charlie spotted Calenda strolling up Main Street. He stopped to peek into closed shops and open bars. He detoured through the pedestrian alley by American Bar and up the little corridor that linked Main Street with Rembrandtstraat and Helfrichstraat. This was the place where the drug dealers had once operated their open-air pharmacy.

"Good evening, Commandante!" Charlie called out when the cop was within easy shouting distance.

"*Bon nochi*, Charlie," Calenda replied with a formal wave.

"It's a lonely night," Charlie continued. "Come up for a cup of coffee." He saw the police chief hesitate for a moment's consideration. To his surprise, Calenda nodded his head and crossed the street.

The door at street level was never locked, though the one at the top of the stairs always was. Charlie thought of this as his portcullis, a trap for anyone who wanted to rob him. Of course anyone robbing him was such a remote possibility he entertained this concept only for its delusional effects. He had nothing to steal but a fine cat and a decent wife, both of which no thief would comprehend as valuable. His money was in the bank next door where it belonged. The booze was downstairs in the bar, also where it belonged. Why would anyone take the trouble to break the lock only to find half a pack of cigarettes in the pocket of a man who needed to lose thirty pounds?

He met Calenda with a proud salute and a broad wave onto the veranda. "Welcome, Commandante," he said. "The coffee will be ready soon."

"*Danki*," Calenda said. He perused the space, then crossed to the parapet near Screwball.

"Be careful," Charlie warned. "He is a man-eating tiger, and this is his jungle."

Calenda grinned as the cat pressed its head against his hand.

"Okay, maybe a special breed of friendly, man-eating tigers," Charlie added. "A tiger, nonetheless, with fangs and claws and sometimes a bad attitude."

Calenda sat on the wall to wait for his coffee. When they both had a cup in their hands, Charlie said, "Maybe a little something for flavor?"

Seeing the bottle of whiskey in Charlie's hand, Calenda said, "This is good."

"This is better," Charlie replied and splashed an ounce of liquor into his cup. He tasted it, smacked his lips, and stifled a burp. "Tell me what the hell is going on over there. It's turned my tiger into a pussycat and my town into a mausoleum."

"The refinery has been closed," Calenda told him.

"How could that happen and I didn't know about it?"

Calenda shrugged. "Our government has hired a firm from Holland to secure the facility until a buyer has been found."

"They don't trust you?"

"They don't trust anyone."

"Their only good idea in the last ten years."

"They did reform the Carnival Queen voting system," joked the new chief.

That Calenda could find humor at a time like this impressed Charlie. He said, "We still try to rig it now and then. Anyway, I heard there was a buyer but the deal fell apart."

"We all heard that, and I think it was the truth. Official people came here to look at it," Calenda said, also knowing the newspapers would publish a statement from the Prime Minister stating that another buyer would soon appear. A week later there would be fancy drawings of the new resorts that would be built on this end of the island. A month later, it would be forgotten on the northwest side of the bridge that there was the hulk of an industrial estate rusting away on the southeast side. Someone from Holland would be down to investigate when the request came for money to pay the unemployment benefits. Another team would ponder redevelopment possibilities. In the meantime, Calenda was left with a town fallen on times harder than the difficult ones they were used to.

"The question is," Charlie was saying, "what are we going to do about it?"

"My job is to keep the peace," Calenda replied. "I know nothing of the oil business."

"Neither do I," Charlie said. He lit a cigarette to buy time to think.

"We have the tourists," Calenda said next.

"Thank God for them. I would be begging for guilders like Frankie and Speedy if not for them. Look at the lifestyle they give me. I have a pet tiger and a view that's the envy of people at the Hyatt Hotel. Don't forget the cellar full of booze under it all. What more could a man want?"

Calenda glanced at the refinery. There were only a few lights on, one in the lobby of the office building, one at the main gate, a smattering in the middle of the plant. Like Charlie, he had grown up with the refinery. He never knew it when it was a glorious source of wealth in San Nicolaas. Still, he understood how the town and this part of the island depended on it. Unemployed men, their frustrated women, and their roaming children presented him with difficult police work. He wasn't lazy. He would take on the challenge the same way he'd beaten the drug dealers out of Rembrandtstraat. San Nicolaas was not headed for bedlam. At the same time, it wasn't on its way to grandeur.

"These will be interesting times," Charlie declared waving his finger.

"It's why I do this job," Calenda told him.

Charlie considered the policeman's statement. He realized he and the chief were from different generations and different sides of the street, but it was the same street, in the same town, on the same island.

Calenda reverted to type and started asking blunt questions in the form of commands. "Tell me about Marcela," he said.

Charlie squinted at the sight of Minchi's Bar down the street. He faced Calenda and said, "She is difficult to know."

"Why?"

"She lives on the other side of the bridge, in the middle of Oranjestaad. Here, in my town, I spy at will. Up there? I can't peek up her skirt without looking like a pervert."

"I found her permisos. She worked at Las Vegas Bar some years ago. She worked there several times."

"Our government hasn't lost those records yet?"

"They're very good at filing paper. They don't find it so quickly, but they have it."

"We have nothing but time here in our island paradise," Charlie said after a sip.

"Marcela is selling arranged marriages. She offered one with her stepson to a girl working at the bar."

"Andrés told me, too," Charlie sighed. "He wanted to know if it was a good idea."

"And you advised him?"

"That to have a woman supporting you can be dangerous."

Calenda adjusted his tunic. "But not illegal," he noted.

"You're the expert on that," Charlie said. "All I know is if he wants to take a girl's money so he can get to art school, he couldn't find a better girl than that one."

"So you met this girl who Marcela tried to broker."

"Several times, and I will tell you this, my friend, I am a specialist in the human condition. I can relate to people of all walks of life. It is the only thing I am really good at, which is why I own a barroom. It is the only place where this skill has any value except …"

"I was asking about the girl."

"Let me finish. I was going to say this rare skill also has value two other places, which are politics, where so few quality practitioners exist that we are nothing but bored with their lousy performances."

"And the other place?"

"The whorehouse!" Charlie beamed from the pinnacle of his argument. "The whore who convinces a man the experience has nothing to do with money is a queen. She rules him."

"And you think this girl is one of these queens?"

"She is the queen of queens, and she doesn't even know it. Sam fell within minutes of meeting her. He's not the best yardstick to measure the field, commandante. However, I was also enchanted by her. I am a connoisseur of the art, a man who should know better, and still I nearly made the mistake."

"Fascinating," Calenda interjected.

"Precisely," Charlie said. "I am not so cynical as experienced. In all my experience, it is rare that I see someone like her."

Calenda reduced the diatribe into a single sentence. "She'd make a fine wife."

"*¡Exactamente!*" Charlie confirmed.

They sat in silence for a few moments before Calenda asked, "Do you think we'll see the girl again?"

"She's better than this job," Charlie answered with a wave of his hand down at Main Street in general and Minchi's specifically. "In another world, say America, she would be doing a job with those looks and that personality that doesn't involve removing the clothes."

"I see. And Marcela, would you issue the same opinion of her to her new boyfriend, Señor Montoya?"

After he stubbed out his cigarette, Charlie said, "Montoya should think about Ricardo's recent passing before making any vows."

"I'll take one more look around town," Calenda said, rising from his seat. "Thank you for the coffee."

"Thanks for the company," Charlie replied. "Please come again. I may have many more lonely nights ahead of me."

"You have your pet tiger," the cop said pointing at Screwball.

"That's true," Charlie said with a smile. He saw his guest through the door and waited until he was out on the street. Leaning over the parapet he called down, "Be careful, Commandante. Don't fall in love."

Calenda saluted and walked up Main Street toward the police station.

When Charlie turned back, he found Screwball with his nose in the bottom of his coffee cup. He chuckled and said, "You have to improvise, Screwball. You have to improvise."

BOOK II
Here & Now

THE PORT OF PHILADELPHIA — A southwest breeze pushed islands of muck across the river. Among the tree branches and leaves were plastic and glass bottles, bits of Styrofoam, and the occasional old tire. Every rainstorm rinsed Philadelphia's streets into drains which ultimately emptied into its two rivers, the Delaware and the Schuylkill. It had been a drenching spring, and both rivers were logjammed with trash.

Captain Nathan Beck grimaced at the mess and looked at the painting Charlie had given him. It was a bright spot compared to the gloomy scene outside the wheelhouse. He stood at the helm of *Katie*, the smallest boat in Ford Towing and Salvage Co.'s fleet. *Katie* was only sixty feet long. On her best day, she put out eight hundred horsepower. A lesser man might have taken this assignment as a demotion. Not Beck. *Katie* had been his first boat, the one on which he learned how to handle barges. "She's frisky as a horny pup," Captain Upton had said, and Beck soon learned he was right.

A small tugboat was a joy to operate, especially around the harbor. There were any number of construction rigs to be moved, barges to shuffle, and quick jobs that required nimble deckhands and a captain who knew how to direct them. This was the type of work Beck had watched as a boy. His bedroom had been three stories above the street, just high enough to have a view of the river. It was the sight of that river and the stories his grandfather told which drew him to the mariner's life.

Despite nearly losing his life at sea, Beck was happy to be aboard a tug. Taking *Katie's* wheel was like coming home. His crew consisted of two men who'd worked with him aboard *Patricia* and one new guy. Syd, *Patricia's* chief engineer, tended to the engine room with the help of Ramirez, who'd hired on with the company only a month ago. Tony had worked as a deckhand on *Patricia* and stuck to the same job on *Katie*. Beck was glad to have them, especially Syd. It was Syd who landed himself in a heap of trouble for returning to the sinking *Patricia* to search for Beck, who had not appeared with the others to abandon ship.

The investigation into *Patricia's* demise was closed. For the official record, Captain Shahann stated a rogue wave had swamped the boat. Given that a hurricane was in the vicinity, this was entirely plausible. The wave stripped the boat of her radar and communications antennae. It also took her lifeboats. As the boat crested the wave, her propellers were suddenly free of the water. Without any resistance, the engines spun too fast. Before Shahann could pull back on the throttle, the port shaft snapped and the engine on the same side exploded. Shahann felt the racket all the way up in the wheelhouse. As *Patricia* slid down the other side of the next wave, her propeller windmilled free, dragging the shaft out of the boat. Abramson, *Patricia*'s other engineer, saw water gushing into the hull. On its way out, the flailing shaft destroyed the port generator and shorted out the electrical system. There was no way to control the flooding. Abramson reported to Shahann that they had better abandon ship. Luckily, there was an extra life raft stowed in the upper engine room.

Shahann and Abramson told all this to the insurance company's investigator, a fellow named Carter. An argument ensued between Shahann and Syd because Syd claimed that no general alarm was sounded. Abramson swore he'd heard it. Tony couldn't remember because he'd been so seasick from the heavy weather that he could hardly think straight. The other deckhands said there had been so much noise from the engine room and the storm that the alarm could have been difficult to hear. Whatever the case, everyone was in the lifeboat but Beck.

Syd refused to shove off without Beck. Shahann had been within his rights when he told Syd they had to get away from *Patricia* if they were to make it themselves. In spite of the danger, Syd leapt the gunwale and tried to reenter the boat. Shahann caught him at the door, practically knocked him out, and heaved him back into the lifeboat. In light of the fists that had been exchanged, Jack Ford kept them apart, assigning Syd to work with Beck aboard *Katie* and putting Shahann on a boat running between Boston and Norfolk. And that was the end of the matter, which was almost a year in the past.

Katie rounded the horseshoe curve in the Delaware River at the former Philadelphia Navy Yard, where Kvaerner Shipbuilding had taken over operations. Jack Ford had a new tug being built there. The boat was big enough to fit *Katie* in her engine room. If things went Beck's way, he would be master. Jack had promised him the senior position on the next new boat that was built. Sadly enough, that new boat was born out of *Patricia*'s death.

Beck denied himself a peek in the direction of the Navy Yard. Instead, he focused on the towers of the Walt Whitman Bridge. A stream of cars flowed in both directions as people made their way to and from Philadelphia. He continued up the river, past new condominiums built on old piers. At Penn's Landing, he saw tourists climbing over the Spanish-American War flagship *Olympia* and other historical attractions. He cruised under the Ben Franklin Bridge and turned toward his first stop of the day.

Alliance Dredge and Dock was located about half a mile past the bridge, on the New Jersey side. They rafted more than two dozen pieces of floating equipment together. Their superintendents joked they had more real estate afloat than fast land. Beck angled *Katie* toward the crane barges, one of which he was supposed to take up the river. He could see men loosening lines and looking in his direction in anticipation of the move. Beck lowered the starboard wheelhouse window so he could speak directly to his men on deck. Just then, he heard them shouting. Syd and Ramirez pointed up the river at a boat that trailed a plume of black smoke.

Beck instantly recognized the boat. She was *Petrel*, a tug about twice the size of *Katie*. *Petrel* moved a barge between the Sunoco Refinery at Girard Point and a chemical factory on the Delaware River at the end of Allegheny Avenue. It was a regular run, three times a week, the kind of assignment that kept the boat in the harbor every day of the year. Beck hoped to find such work when he had a boat that belonged to him.

Without a second thought, Beck pushed the throttles forward and turned *Katie's* bow toward *Petrel*. Syd and Ramirez didn't have to be told to arm themselves with fire extinguishers. The next time Beck looked down, he saw them each holding an extinguisher at the ready. They had another one waiting against the gunwale. Tony looked less assured than the two engineers. It was then that Beck remembered the contents of the barge. He didn't know the flashpoint of the chemical. The words "NO SMOKING" painted across the deckhouse were all the clues he needed to guess.

Before he had time to reconsider, the wheelhouse door opened on *Petrel's* port side. A man climbed over the rail and leapt into the river. He wore a bulky life jacket which made it hard for him to swim away from his drifting boat. Two more men appeared on *Petrel's* stern. They looked at the river, back at their burning boat, then down at their comrade who was now waving for them to jump. Only one of them had a life jacket, but they both jumped.

Petrel lost headway and started a slow spin to the east. If the pair made half a turn, the breeze would blow the flames directly over the deck of the barge. Beck pushed hard against the throttles, hoping to gain a few seconds, but they were already against the stops.

He grabbed the radio tuned to the company channel and hailed Captain

Wilkie, who he knew would be sitting in the wheelhouse of *Marlena*, the boat Jack Ford reserved for harbor work.

"*Marlena*, standing by," Wilkie replied.

Beck summed up the situation. "*Petrel's* on fire off Penn's Landing. We're going to lend any assistance we can. Call the Coast Guard and the Philadelphia Fire Department."

"Roger that, Nate. You know what's in that barge?"

"I'm close enough that it won't matter."

The first thing Beck wanted to do was push the bow of the barge to the west so the flames would blow away from the barge. *Katie* charged ahead at full power. When he was almost even with the bow of the barge, he put the rudder over hard and cut the starboard engine. *Katie* rolled steeply, then righted herself as Beck centered the rudder and eased off the port engine.

The bow fender bumped the barge a moment later. Beck put both throttles ahead gently. Too much power would cause the barge to spin in the other direction. As soon as the barge started to move, he shifted to neutral. He looked across the deck at the fire and realized he had to do something quickly or he might kill his two best men and the new guy, too.

"Syd!" he called down. "I'm taking us around to the other side. Get the ax. Cut her loose."

Beck maneuvered *Katie* around the bow of the barge with no room to spare. Her upper railing folded over when it caught under the barge's rake. He approached *Petrel's* bow and noticed he had bumped the barge hard enough to turn it too far toward the wind. It was too late to back away. Syd went over the stem carrying his ax toward *Petrel's* lines. Ramirez followed him, but Tony stood fast with his eyes fixed on the flames and smoke.

"Catch a line there!" Beck ordered Tony.

Tony stumbled with a line, then found his footing and tossed the eye over the H bit on *Petrel's* bow. He made it fast to *Katie's* starboard quarter bit and looked to Beck for further direction.

Beck searched for Syd and Ramirez. After Syd chopped the bow line stretching between *Petrel* and her barge, he had disappeared into the smoke, which was now rolling down the deck and over the top of the barge. Beck glanced down at Tony and issued his orders. "As soon we slide down the barge, get over there and find the anchor. Drop it when I'm clear."

Tony looked at the barge, then back at the burning tug. The deckhand wanted nothing to do with that barge or the burning tug. Like it or not, he was tied to it. He had made the line fast himself. He was left with a choice between jumping in the river or doing as he was told. He clambered up the bent railing to the same level as the deck of the barge. He looked at Beck, whose hand eased down on the throttle.

Beck felt *Katie* surge forward against *Petrel*. *Petrel*'s bow separated from the barge.

Tony took his chance and leapt over the gap onto the deck. A few seconds later, the boats were at right angles to each other. Then the stern line came taut, and *Katie*'s momentum carried her forward so she was side by side with *Petrel*. The flames that had threatened the barge now turned on *Katie*. The last thing Tony glimpsed before going to the anchor was Syd swinging the ax at *Petrel*'s stern line.

A roasting heat surged into *Katie*'s wheelhouse, followed by blinding smoke. Beck coughed into his sleeve and pulled back the throttles. Tears flooded his eyes as he tried to peer through the windows to see where he was and what was happening. He may have saved the barge, but now he had to save *Katie*. All he could do was put the rudder over and hope the boats would turn back into the wind. He cranked down the windows on both sides in an attempt to clear the wheelhouse.

Beck didn't know how long it took, probably a minute, maybe two, but eventually *Katie* was upwind of the fire. He heard voices and saw Syd and Ramirez darting around *Petrel*'s deck. The smoke rendered him speechless as he coughed it from his lungs. He steered *Katie* down river with just enough speed to keep her straight. He looked back at the barge. It was impossible to tell if Tony had dropped the anchor or not.

Almost at once, the smoke turned from black to grey to white. Syd and Ramirez had found the flames with their extinguishers. Syd rushed back to *Katie*. He waved up at Beck, white teeth grinning through his soot-smudged lips. He reappeared on deck with a length of fire hose. *Katie*'s fire pump was not very powerful, only enough to fill a two-inch line. Syd screwed the fittings together, then dragged the hose through *Petrel*'s forward door. A second later, he was back to open the valve. The smoke diminished to nothing.

Syd came out of the deckhouse. "Fire's out!" he called. He spun the valve closed with one hand while he wiped his face on his shirt. Ramirez joined him on deck. The two slapped each other on the shoulders for a dangerous job well done.

"We have it under control," Beck said to Wilkie over the radio. "I left Tony on the barge. You may need to bring him a clean pair of underwear."

"How about you?"

"Wouldn't be a bad idea," Beck said.

"Any other casualties?"

"Three in the river. We're going back to look for them."

"Coast Guard is on the way," Wilkie told him.

The Coast Guard relieved Beck of the responsibility of finding *Petrel's* crew. Half an hour later they were out of the river and on their way to hot showers.

"The fire was in the companionway," Syd explained to Beck. "Climbed up the paneling. Made a trail all the way to the wheelhouse."

"You guys okay?"

"Filthy," Syd said.

Ramirez nodded.

"I guess we'll take her back to the dock and see what her owners want to do."

They eased down the river at a casual pace. Syd and Ramirez checked through *Petrel* to make certain the fire was out and that there were no other threats. They found no further damage, no leaks, nothing smoldering. Aside from cosmetics, the boat was in good mechanical condition. However, she needed to be remodeled from her galley to her wheelhouse.

Beck brought *Katie* to her space at the pier. Syd and Ramirez tied her off while everyone from the office watched. Beck met his crew on deck.

"That was brave work," he said. "We'll split the salvage money."

Ramirez and Syd seemed nonplussed, as if rushing into a burning boat was part of their daily routine. "I have to shut down the mains," Syd said and ducked into the engine room.

Ramirez stood there looking embarrassed. Beck clapped him on the shoulder. "Do you think you can patch her up by the end of the week?"

After scanning *Katie's* bent railing, blistered paint, broken lights, and scorched windows, Ramirez said, "Maybe next Monday."

"Good," Beck said and stepped ashore.

Captain Shahann, recently back from Norfolk, was there to meet him. "No one cares if you die an orphan," he said, "but the other men's wives might not feel the same way."

Beck caught the reference to his lack of a mother. It was an old wound, one that wasn't bothering him at present. But to imply he was reckless was something else. That was like saying he didn't give a damn about his crew. It wasn't he who had left a man on *Patricia*, not he who might have panicked and not pulled the alarm.

"I'm not half the coward you are," Beck said and moved forward, fists at the ready.

"It's easy to be brave with other men's lives," Shahann retorted.

"Or to forget about them when yours is in danger."

Ramirez jumped between them. "*Capitán*," he said. "*Venga*. Come with me. To the office. Jack wants to see you."

Retreating a few paces, Shahann said, "It's getting to be a regular United Nations around here."

Jack Ford waited at the office door. "Looks like you put the salvage back in Ford Towing and Salvage," he said. "Nice work, Nate."

"Thanks," Beck replied. "I wasn't alone out there."

"Now do me a favor," Jack said, "Keep your fists in your pockets. I'm short of captains just now and don't need Shahann or anyone else in the hospital."

Beck agreed to let the matter go. He went home, where he packed an overnight bag for a weekend with Nicole. Since he had returned from Aruba, they had been seeing each other off and on again. Things weren't back to normal, but he believed he was headed in the right direction, that given the opportunity he could charm her into marrying him. If he was lucky — and he figured he was, having survived the *Patricia* disaster and more recently the *Petrel* incident — they would have a son or maybe two. After all, he would need crewmen for his boat.

To his surprise, *Petrel* was the top story on both the six and eleven o'clock news broadcasts. A tourist on Penn's Landing had videotaped his actions on the river. At ten past eleven, his phone rang. It was Nicole. She had seen the report.

"I can't go with you this weekend," she said.

"Why not?" Beck wanted to know.

"You promised me when you got back from Aruba you wouldn't be doing things like that," she said.

It was impossible to explain to someone who didn't work in his environment that he hadn't been reckless or foolish. The odds were not as bad as they seemed, especially after he saw the footage from shore. From the perspective of the video, he could see the flames stayed away from the barge the whole time.

"It's how things are done on the river," he replied.

On the river, although adjacent to a major city, a rescue took time. If *Petrel* had waited for the Coast Guard, she most likely would have been a total loss. The barge and its cargo would have been a bigger catastrophe. Mariners were obligated to lend mutual assistance and were rewarded accordingly. He knew firsthand what it was like to be alone, with little chance of anyone coming to help. He wasn't about to leave *Petrel*'s crew in a similar position.

He said, "I'm going to get the captain's share of the salvage money for *Petrel*. It'll put me that much closer to my own boat."

"That's why you did it?" Nicole asked accusingly. "You risked your life for money to buy your dreams?"

That wasn't true nor was it fair. He felt his anger rise but checked it when he remembered that he loved Nicole and she deserved his patience. She was upset, he figured, and saying things she didn't really mean. Gathering his courage, he said, "We have to go. It's too late to cancel the reservations."

"Please, Nate," she moaned.

"I love you, Nicole," he said.

"I know you do," she replied. "It's just that I never understood how dangerous your job was."

"My grandfather survived worse things than I did. He had someone looking over his shoulder, and now he's looking out for me. Let's keep those reservations. What do you say?" In his head the words sounded great, but after he said them, he felt awkward, especially when Nicole didn't answer immediately.

At last, she said, "Give me some time to think, okay?"

He settled for that and hung up. Still, her words left him hurting, and he had nothing to occupy him on his days off.

He slept fitfully until dawn. Then he grabbed his sea bag, the one that was always packed for his time aboard the boats, and headed for the pier. Chances were Jack had something for him to do.

"I have just the thing," Jack said, "if you don't mind being away for a while."

"Perfect," Beck said, thinking it would keep him from haunting Nicole. He knew the surest way to ruin the progress he'd made was to call her too often.

"The thing is, I need the rest of your crew," Jack said next. "You think you can persuade them to come in on short notice?"

"They'll do what I ask," Beck said confidently.

"If they're on board, you sail *Kathryn* at noon."

Shahann was *Kathryn*'s current master since Beck's friend, Captain Wilkie, was only working the harbor aboard *Marlena* until he recovered fully from heart surgery.

"Where are we headed?" Beck wanted to know.

"To a place you've been before," Jack answered, adding, "But you have to go to

Houston first."

Beck liked the sound of that. Houston was a long tow through the Atlantic and the Gulf of Mexico. The sea was where he belonged, even if it was in the company of Shahann. He hoped his grandfather was still looking over his shoulder.

"And Nate," Jack continued, "no hurricanes, no shipwrecks, no fist fights. Okay?"

BOGOTÁ, COLOMBIA — Luz and the family celebrated her mother's birthday in high style. They ate together at a restaurant, which was the rarest of occasions. Anna had wanted to have the party at the house, but Rudi insisted they go out. He had money to pay for the meal, for gifts, and some left over to put in the bank. Luz wanted to ask him where the money had come from but decided not to risk ruining the mood.

Nine months ago, she had scampered through the airport clutching her purse as if she carried the Holy Grail inside. Every dollar she'd made in Aruba was in that purse. Inez had warned her about bandits lurking outside the airport, but Luz had seen no one who looked like anything worse than a wary passenger anxious to get home. Less than an hour after landing, a taxi dropped her at the curb in front of her house.

No one was home. She had time to hide her money, some of it under the kitchen sink, the rest beneath a loose tile in the back of her closet. Later, the family had been overjoyed to see her and greatly relieved when she handed Jorgé their overdue payments. When all the bills were paid, Luz had more than a thousand dollars remaining. She took a week for herself and Hernán. Then she spent a month looking for a job. She found one, working for Señor Garcia at a grocery store which had opened around the corner from a quartet of brand new apartment towers. She earned enough to pay her expenses and have a few pesos to buy Hernán's toys. Thanks to Rudi, she didn't have to use her savings from Aruba to pay Jorgé's regular demands.

Rudi had sponsored their mother's birthday party, and the celebration was as much about him as about Mother. He talked of his adventures on the highway, delivering parts for Jorgé in different barrios of the city as well as the surrounding countryside. Everyone at the table seemed to forget that this was how their husband and father had been killed.

When the meal was over, Luz took Hernán to the park. While her son played in a pile of dirt with his trucks, she sat on the grass with her shoes off. She pondered what had happened in her life and couldn't help but feel cheated. Part of the problem was that her family didn't know how she had earned the money to keep them together in the place their father had bought for them. It had been more trying and sometimes more painful than giving birth to Hernán. It had been as nerve wracking as the time of her father's death. Yet her mother said nothing of her strength and perseverance the way she did of Rudi's. Anna gushed over Rudi's pay but treated Luz's like a minor allowance.

Luz had returned home with her head up like a soccer champion. She had defied the odds. She'd won. She had prize money to prove it. But no one hung on her words the way they listened to Rudi's stories. They didn't ask her for details about her time away. They gave her thanks for dealing with Jorgé when he showed up at the door with a hard face and an empty palm. For covering their overdue payments and one in advance, they should have given her the kind of respect and honor they regularly gave to Rudi. But they quickly forgot how desperate they had been when her brother started up his stories of clever shortcuts and near misses on the highways.

Luz felt more than petty jealousy. For their disregard of her accomplishment, she harbored a growing resentment. Then she remembered la Dueña's comments and found herself crying. She couldn't blame them for what they didn't know. Hernán heard her sobs. He left his truck in the dirt and sat in her lap.

"You're a good boy," Luz said to him. "I know I can count on you to become a great man."

Later that week, when her mood had not improved, Señor Garcia spoke with her.

"Luz," he said, "is there anything I can do to help?" He was sincere, though he held a strong sexual desire for her. In spite of his attraction, or maybe because of it, he genuinely cared for her. She shrugged with one shoulder, an act that brought a length of her hair forward. She shook it back and used both hands to tuck it behind her ear.

"My son," she said but added no explanation. She had carefully avoided Señor Garcia's subtle advances. She wasn't about to put her job in jeopardy by way of an affair.

It was always the son, Garcia thought. These young mothers struggle with boys who inevitably grow up to be like their fathers, disrespectful and absent. "He's well, isn't he?" Garcia asked.

"Yes," Luz answered. "A little small for his age."

"I was like that," Garcia said. "Look at me now. Growing wider every month." He welcomed her smile and wished she would put her fingers on his shoulder the way she used to. For the first time since meeting Luz, Señor Garcia reflected that having another woman in his life might not be worth the trouble.

On the bus home, something happened which put Luz in an entirely different frame of mind. A young man she'd seen dozens of times sat down beside her and introduced himself.

"My name is Abel," he began. "We see each other twice a day but never talk."

Luz was flustered, and for some reason she said, "I work at the grocery," instead of introducing herself.

"For Señor Garcia?" Abel asked.

"He's a nice man. Do you know him?"

"Only that he is the manager. I applied for a job there."

"He's a good boss. Very progressive."

"I'm sorry," Abel said. "I don't know your name."

Luz blushed. It had been too long since she had looked at a man and considered him for a date. Abel appeared to be a decent guy. He reminded her of Rudi in that he was well built and not afraid to make himself known. "My name is Luz," she said.

The ride passed more quickly than usual because they chatted the entire time. Abel worked as a repairman in one of the new apartment towers. He lived with his parents and a brother a couple of stops past where Luz got off the bus. He asked if they could have a snack one day after work.

Although she wanted to accept, Luz found herself explaining that she couldn't. She thought it was better to tell Abel straight away she had a son and that she had to be home as soon as work ended. Her sister Anna did the favor of watching him, and Luz didn't want to ask more of her sister than was necessary.

"I could come to your house," Abel suggested.

"Let's see how things go," Luz replied. Her experience in Aruba had taught her to evaluate a man quickly. Abel seemed like her type, but she wasn't going to introduce him to her family until she was sure.

"See you tomorrow," he said as she got off the bus. He waved to her from the window as the bus merged into traffic.

Luz entered her home to find her mother and Anna sorting through clothes. They had everything out of the closet and spread out on the beds. Before asking what they were doing, Luz peeked down at the tile under which her money lay hidden. It appeared undisturbed.

"Here she is," her mother said to Anna. "Who is Marcela Cortés?" she immediately asked her other daughter.

Luz nearly collapsed at mention of la Dueña's name.

"This card was in with your clothes," Anna said.

That instant, Luz was back in the frigid car with her old boss. The card Marcela had given her must have gotten mixed up with her things when she packed.

"Minchi's Bar," Anna said flatly. "Where's that?"

Luz avoided the second question and answered the first. "She was a business woman who owned a big house. I worked cleaning it. She was the one who gave me some of her clothes."

Anna handed the card to Luz.

"We need to find something for Anna to wear," mother said. "She has a date."

Luz felt herself smile. She was happy for her sister.

Then her mother said, *Dios mío.* If she gets married it'll be you and me, Luz. Two old maids."

Luz resisted the urge to scream. She wasn't an old maid; she was younger than Anna. She wasn't ready to give up hope she could find a man who would love her. Hadn't Abel approached her on the bus? He hadn't blinked an eye at mention of Hernán. And there was always Señor Garcia, whom she knew to be smitten by her. Although he was married, he may be contemplating divorce. He may want to start a new family. He may find her more attractive and interesting than the woman he had married.

Her anger flared. This was her mother and sister, not la Dueña and Inez. She deserved the same consideration she gave them. The telephone rang just as she opened her mouth.

"Answer it, Luz. You're closer," her sister said.

It was Rudi. He was making a delivery for Jorgé and wouldn't be home until tomorrow. He was calling so no one would worry. As Luz relayed the message to Anna and her mother, her rage drained away. It was on just such a job that her father had been killed. What did her gripes matter in light of the danger her brother might be in?

"I would have liked to talk to him," her mother huffed.

"He sounded like he was in a hurry," Luz replied. "And long distance calls cost money."

"He's been making more than ever, as much as Papa did," Anna told her.

"I think this will fit you," Mother said. In her mother's hands was the skirt Martin had bought for Luz.

Anna held it up to her torso.

"You've kept your figure better than your sister," mother said. "Put it on, and let's have a look."

Luz accepted defeat. She left the house wishing she had a number for Inez. She missed their lunches. Inez had been to other parts of Colombia and different countries, too. She talked about interesting people she met in those places. They prattled on for an hour, sometimes two, before Inez went to work in the doorway and Luz retreated up the stairs to wait until the bar opened. In a way, things had been easier for her in Aruba. She hadn't been worried about her brother or frustrated by her mother. She was singularly focused on making money. Little things didn't matter.

There was a person who understood her choices, and Luz visited her the following week.

"What a handsome boy!" Señora Álvaro gushed. "You're blessed to have him."

Luz basked in the woman's compliment. Her boy stood by her knee while she held him at the waist.

"Look at his bright eyes. I'll bet he's going to be a doctor or a lawyer."

Luz felt her cheeks warm. She turned her boy to look at his face. Señora Álvaro was not just saying something to make her feel good. Hernán was a good-looking boy with smart eyes, a strong chin, and a perfect nose. He was a tiny replica of his father. Although Luz had no way of knowing what Hernán would make of himself, she was absolutely certain he would never treat a woman the way his father had treated her. She was going to raise him to respect every woman (including herself, his grandmother, his aunt, and his future wife) as if she were the Holy Virgin. He wouldn't be getting them pregnant and slapping them or going to Aruba and having his way for fifty guilders.

Señora Álvaro sipped her tea, then continued. "I've heard about your time in Aruba. *Dios Mío*. You should have told me these things months ago."

Luz felt guilty about not seeing Señora Álvaro sooner. She'd come to hear a friendly voice from someone who believed in her but found herself doing much of the talking. It would have taken hours to relate what happened in Aruba. She kept the stories short, adding the finer points only when Álvaro asked for clarification. Instinct told her Álvaro was a sympathetic ear, but she said nothing about Marcela or Ricardo's death. To her surprise and relief, Hernán behaved himself, eventually settling onto the other chair in front of Álvaro's desk and falling asleep.

"A man washed up on the beach. It sounds like something from a telenovela," Señora Álvaro said when Luz finished. "I wish I knew someone at a production company so you could sell it to them."

What a great idea! Luz wanted to shout. She kept her composure and shrugged with one shoulder.

"And how is Señora Mendez?" Álvaro asked next.

Luz said she hadn't met anyone by that name.

"I meant Marcela Cortés," Álvaro said, correcting herself. "When last I spoke to her, Ricardo had just died."

"She's well," Luz said, hoping more details would not be required.

"Save your money," Álvaro advised over a wagging finger. "You worked hard for it. Don't waste it on silly things. Your boy is counting on you."

Luz looked down at Hernán, knowing she would provide whatever he needed.

"You know you can call on me," Álvaro said finally. "My door is always open. Please come back to visit. Bring Hernán. He's a joy." Then she pointed to the blank space high on the wall. "I need a photo of you, Luz, to go up there. I won't give that space to anyone else."

Luz looked at the spot and grinned. She gathered up her son, nodded one more time to Álvaro, and made her way through the office. As she passed by the receptionist, she saw a young woman seated in the same chair Luz had used when she first came to Union Caribe. Luz sensed the nervousness in her eyes and hands. She wanted to tell her all the things she had told Álvaro, as well as many things she had not. Luz knew exactly what Señora Álvaro was going to say when the girl was in her office. "See that one with the handsome boy on her hip? She came to me just like you. She made a hard choice, but in the end, she did the right thing." And so the speech would go on, and another Colombiana would be bound for Aruba or another place where the brothels operated. Still, Luz said nothing. She backed through the door to the sidewalk. She was on her way home to do the most normal of things, which was to get ready for supper.

✻   ✻   ✻

Her mother always attended the early Sunday mass with the other old women of the barrio. Luz went with her, bringing Hernán so he would learn the traditions of his faith. Each week, she fought the urge to stay in bed another hour and go to the second mass. It was important she go early out of respect for her mother as well as to honor her promise to live a less sinful life. However, her life in Aruba had permanently affected her sleeping schedule.

Hernán was as grumpy as she was. He wouldn't let her put his arms into his shirt. She struggled with him for ten minutes until he finally relented. His face was blotchy red from crying, and he fidgeted all the way to church. Once inside, he calmed down. The other women in her row cooed over him until the service started.

The offering baskets were passed from the center aisle toward the outer walls of the church. Since Luz sat at the end of the pew, she was the first to put in her money. While in Aruba, she had promised God twenty dollars as proof of her commitment to a holy life. She had put very little into the basket over the past several months, certainly not the twenty dollars she had promised. After she paid Jorgé, only a third of her earnings from Aruba had remained, and she had been uncertain of the future. Today she felt more secure. Rudi was doing well, and she worked at the grocery.

No one in her congregation used dollars, and Luz was not about to draw attention by placing an American bank note among the pesos. The equivalent of twenty dollars was forty thousand pesos. She held the bills tightly in her hand. Then she set them into the basket and leaned back so it could be moved on to her mother. Her mother spotted the money and glared at Luz. Luz didn't understand why she was angry. She should have been happy. After all, she was the one who went to church every day and thoroughly read each pamphlet handed out by the priest. She should know it was important to support the church financially.

Thankfully, her mother liked to sit near the front, among the first to receive communion. Luz took her turn after her mother, who held Hernán for her. As the priest placed the wafer onto her tongue, she looked into his eyes. She had never confessed to this priest, and as the wafer dissolved, she decided she wouldn't begin now. She preferred to speak directly to God.

Luz returned to her spot and kneeled to pray while the remainder of the congregation received the sacrament. She encircled Hernán in her arms, folding her hands on the other side of his growing body. Her lips moved as she issued her appeal to the Almighty. In proper fashion, she thanked God for the many things He had given her: her healthy boy, her family, and the strength of her constitution. She asked the favor of God that the future be better according to His will. She concluded by asking him to watch over Carlotta and Charlie and even Inez, wherever she might be and whatever she might be doing. She began to rise up when she suddenly remembered the girl waiting to see Señora Álvaro. Luz issued one last request, that God protect that girl and forgive the sins she was about to commit. The girl had her reasons, and they were good ones.

The service ended with the recessional hymn. The congregation exited the building and grouped together in their families and cliques. Luz's mother hustled away from the steps, bound for their house in a rush. Luz hurried after her, bouncing Hernán against her hip.

"Slow down," she said. "I can't keep up."

Her mother whirled around. "I've never been so embarrassed!" she hissed.

"What are you talking about?" Luz pleaded.

"Putting all that money in the basket! What are you trying to prove?"

Stunned, Luz couldn't answer.

"People know you were away, working in a strange place. They're going to think you struck gold."

"Why would they think that?" Luz asked.

"Are you stupid? Everyone saw you give forty thousand pesos. I wouldn't be surprised if Jorgé comes this afternoon looking for everything we owe."

Luz found that possibility ridiculous. She doubted anyone saw the money other than her mother. If they did see it, let them think what they wanted. What bothered her most was that her mother didn't appreciate the gesture. She should have been proud of a daughter willing to give so much.

The jostling had annoyed Hernán. Luz stopped to comfort him. Her mother continued without looking back. When Hernán settled down, Luz started again for home, trying to forget her mother's criticism. When she arrived at the house, her sister picked up where her mother had left off. Didn't she think about the taxes that were coming due on the house and the payment Jorgé was expecting? Had she forgotten about the clothes Hernán would need? Yes, it was important to give to the church but only so much as they could afford.

Hernán's crying distracted her. She lifted him off his chair. As she bent over, her tears splashed onto his face. He loved her in his innocent way. He was her boy. He had nursed at her breast. He still slept in her arms. He didn't care what she did or how much she gave to the church. He only wanted the affection of his mother.

She took one of his blankets and led him out the front door. She didn't care what her mother or sister thought.

She sought a corner of the park where she could be alone with her boy. Her barrio was known for its green spaces. They were well maintained and used frequently by the citizens whose small houses had little room for large gatherings. It was one of the reasons her father had chosen the area for them.

Luz sat on a patch of grass with Hernán between her legs. She stretched out on her back, holding him up to the sky. The clouds drifted across the blue field beyond his head. "You'll be a good boy, won't you?" she said. Hernán twisted his mouth as if he were answering her. "I know you will," she told him. "You'll be a man people respect."

Her stomach grumbled, and Luz realized that by this time her family was sitting down to the big lunch Anna prepared every Sunday. Hernán wasn't making a fuss, but he was probably hungry, too. "Let's have a snack," she said. "Would you like that? Sure you would. Let's go."

She carried him to a café that fronted the park. She ordered a large fruit smoothie for both of them. It brought back memories of Aruba. They took alternate spoonfuls and watched the people. The men looked her over, but once they realized Hernán was her son, they didn't bother with a second glance. Luz was pleased to be undesirable for a change. After the months in Aruba, where she was on display like hanging meat at the butcher's, it was a relief to be nearly invisible. Her boy was barely as tall as her hip, and already he was protecting her. It wouldn't be long before she could count on him to act like a real man.

She paid for the drink and started for home. She passed a few shops and businesses where she had looked for a job. Her limited skills had not been in demand at any of them. Still, her job at the grocery was good enough. It paid for her necessities. She would like to go to school, to study business so she could work in a pleasant office. No doubt her family would see that as another selfish act.

She'd had enough hostility for one day. Regardless of the fact her sister and mother might be angry, Luz wanted to be home before dark. They were her family, disagreements and all. She held Hernán's hand, guiding him along, pointing out sights and asking him what they were. He answered in his uncertain way, screwing up his face, struggling to say the words.

At home, the mood improved. Rudi spoke excitedly about working at Jorgé's garage. He had fixed something the other mechanics couldn't. Jorgé gave him a small bonus, which Rudi gave back as payment on their house.

Later that evening, when Hernán was asleep, Luz went outside where Rudi sat paging through the newspaper.

Rudi said, "Jorgé is looking for more money on the house."

"Already? You just gave him your bonus."

"The more you give," Rudi muttered, "the more he takes."

"It won't be long before you're his best man. You'll be working in the shop full-time, and he won't worry about getting his money."

"There may be another job for me."

"Really?"

"At the refinery."

"Which refinery?" Luz asked.

"The one in Aruba."

Her heart sank. Her brother could not be serious.

"I went to one of those agents, like you did. They said there's going to be a lot of work at the refinery there. The whole place is going to be rebuilt."

"It's dangerous," Luz warned. "Some men died while I was there."

"I'll be careful," he assured her.

"You won't have to. Jorgé will need you. We'll stay together the way a family should."

"You think so?"

She put her hands on his shoulders. "You know I do," she said, thinking that if Colombia were filled with men like Rudi it would be a glorious place. Why did there have to be the guerillas and the narcotrafficantes and the crooked politicians? Why couldn't they all be men who just wanted an opportunity to work hard and support their families?

"Thirty million pesos," Rudi said getting up. "More or less, that is what we owe him."

Thirty million pesos equaled roughly fifteen thousand dollars. Luz had a thousand dollars hidden in the house. If things didn't work out, it was enough to pay the mortgage Jorgé held, but only for about six months.

Rudi smiled and kissed his sister on the cheek. "You would make a good wife," he said. "I hope to find a girl like you."

Her brother's approval gave Luz more pleasure than anything except the sound of Hernán laughing.

LUZ HADN'T seen Abel in weeks. She worried that he'd lost his job and that they'd never see each other again. She should have jumped at the date he'd offered her. Instead, she'd been shy, stupid, and worried about the wrong things.

She trudged home feeling more disappointed than bitter. The sour sentiment vanished as she approached her house. Hernán was in there, and he always cheered her up. Señora Álvaro said he looked like a doctor or a lawyer. Luz intended to see to it that he had everything he needed to reach his goals. After all, she had given him life. What was a few pesos for school?

Just as she opened the front door, ready to greet her little boy with a hug and a kiss on his cheek, she was overcome with blinding fear. Sitting at the kitchen table with Hernán on her knee was Inez. Luz nearly collapsed over the threshold. She stumbled forward, her arms out for her boy. Her vision went blurry before she reached him, and she pulled up short. Anna rushed to her side.

"Are you okay?" her sister asked, taking her arm.

Luz felt the air leave her lungs like a popped balloon. She leaned on Anna, who eased her into a chair.

Inez said, "I knew you would be excited to see me."

Hernán giggled, and Luz snapped out of shock. She needed her wits to control whatever damage had been done. She puffed like she had just run a marathon but found a smile for Inez and Hernán. "I see my boy likes you," she said.

"He's a handsome one. I wish I could have met his father," Inez replied. She helped Hernán to the floor where he retrieved a toy truck and drove it toward his bedroom.

"If I had known you were coming," Luz put in, "I would have met you."

"This trip came up at the last second," Inez said. "I like to surprise people."

Luz knew all about Inez and her surprises.

"I was telling your sister how hard we worked in Aruba. What a bitch that woman was!"

Luz almost fainted again.

"At least we got a couple of nice dresses out of it."

"We did," Luz croaked and stole a glance at her sister who stood over the sink. Anna started preparing supper for the rest of the family, which gave Luz a chance to redirect Inez. "How long can you stay?" she asked.

"Only a little while." Inez checked her watch. "I have an appointment in about an hour."

"That's a shame. You could have stayed for supper." Luz got up and moved to her sister's side. "I can help you while I talk to Inez."

"Don't be silly. Why don't you two chat outside?" Anna said.

"Let's go," Inez said quickly.

Luz gathered up Hernán and his truck and followed Inez to the backyard. Hernán liked the change of scenery and set to moving miniature piles of stone with his truck.

"You didn't tell Anna anything about Minchi's?" Luz whispered to Inez.

"Had you worried, didn't I?" Inez replied.

"Please, Inez, tell me you didn't say …"

Inez cut her off. "We're friends, Luz. I wouldn't do that to you. I knew from the first moment I met you that you were a good girl, that your family could never know what you did."

"*Gracias a Dios*," Luz said, crossing herself.

"Thank me, not God," Inez retorted. "You're lucky I was able to find you. You never gave me your number. Señora Álvaro told me where you live."

"I'm sorry," Luz said with as much sincerity as she could conjure up for a person she once regarded as the devil. She shivered at the thought of the hateful stare Inez had given her when Martin took her from Minchi's, and Luz reminded herself she had to be careful around this girl.

"After what we've been through," Inez told her with a wave of the hand, "I can forgive anything."

Luz noticed the gold bracelet on the wrist below that hand. The gold had the correct tone to be authentic, as did the rings and necklace which completed the set. As if the jewelry were not enough, Inez sported exotic sunglasses, a fancy dress, and shoes that were as practical as high heels on a sandy beach. From head to toe, the outfit cost more than two million pesos. No one who cleaned houses in a far away country dressed like that. Anna must have been pondering just what it was her sister had been doing with this stranger on that island. Anxiety overcame Luz to the point where her ears began to ring.

"Are you listening?" Inez prodded her.

"Sorry," Luz said again. "I was just thinking that Hernán has to go to the doctor tomorrow."

"He doesn't look ill."

"No. He's due for another vaccination."

"Oh. I don't know anything about children except that men like to practice making them." Inez laughed and slapped the table in front of Luz.

"You were saying something about ...," Luz prompted her former co-worker.

"Saint Maarten, Luz. Think about it, another island with lots of horny men."

"Keep your voice down."

"Sorry. Think about those great big cruise ships that will come there this time of the year. Those ships are full of men with dumpy wives and grouchy girlfriends. They ask the sailors and taxi drivers where they can find some pussy."

Luz cringed at the English word that she knew was understood in most every language around the world. Pussy and fuck were universal. She figured in the middle of the Sahara desert was an Arab who would know those two words.

"You let the little things get to you," Inez chided her. "You have to have a thick skin if you want to make real money."

All Luz could do was nod her head in agreement.

"Anyway, this is the high season for the cruise ships. We have to get there in the next two weeks. I have a friend who is already there, and she says there are so many Americans it's like being in New Jersey. She should know; she lived there for a few months."

"I can't go to Saint Maarten," Luz said.

"Sure you can. Think of the money we'll make."

"Please, Inez, I don't want my sister to hear."

Inez put both hands up. Luz saw a ring on her right hand that held an emerald the size of a garbanzo bean. "You're right," Inez said. "I need to calm down. It's just that when I think about the money we made doing the private shows at Minchi's, I get so excited I could scream." She squeezed Luz's hand so hard the ring dug into her flesh.

Money from those shows lay hidden under the tile in the back of Luz's closet. What was once under the sink had been spent on Hernán and the family.

"Let me put it this way," Inez continued. "Wouldn't you like to have some new clothes? Wouldn't you like to get another haircut? A real one, like you got in Aruba, by a guy who knows what he's doing? No, forget that stuff. They're trinkets. With the amount of money we got paid to act like lesbians you could buy a car or even a house."

Luz turned to Hernán for protection. "I have to save money for my boy," she said. "I can't waste money on expensive haircuts."

"Exactly. You know what school is going to cost. You know he'll need books and uniforms and supplies."

"I know," Luz sighed.

"All the more reason to go. He's still young. He won't even miss you. It's better if you do this now. That way you can be here for him when he needs you most."

Hernán needed her now as much as he would a year from now and ten years from now. So many children ran the streets that it was a national epidemic in Colombia. Luz knew she could count on Anna and the rest of her family, but Hernán was truly her responsibility. She accepted that burden with joy, and she wanted him to have a father, too, a man with honorable traits that would be imprinted on her son.

"We're doing very well right now," Luz explained. "Rudi and I both have work."

Inez leapt off her seat like a scalded cat. She paced around the table a few times, then sat down and spoke to Luz in a harsh whisper. "When are you going to learn?" Inez demanded. "You can never count on a man. Do you hear me?"

Hernán pushed his toy truck past the table. Pebbles overflowed from the back. Luz watched him and forced a smile.

"Pay attention," Inez was saying. "Men are good for two things: a cock and a wallet. The first thing makes a mess, and the second thing pays to clean it up. The sooner you accept that, the sooner you'll live the type of life you deserve."

Hernán wasn't going to be what Inez thought men were. Luz was going to instill a sense of dignity in him that would keep him from turning into a hooligan. He was going to have pride in himself. He was going to respect women. He was going to care for his family.

"If you learned anything in Aruba," Inez said, "you should have learned that. Look at how stupid those men were! They paid us to act, to make believe. They thought we were lesbians, that we get off that way."

Luz remembered several times when Inez had a real orgasm during their time together upstairs.

"I thought I was coming here with an opportunity for you," Inez said. "I could have gone to see any number of other girls. I wouldn't have had to track them down. They gave me their numbers. I came to you because I thought you needed it more than them."

"I appreciate …" Luz started to say.

Inez cut her off. "No you don't. You're still a little girl, Luz. You believe all that silly shit they told us when we were in elementary school. I'm disappointed. I thought you were smarter than that."

The insult soaked in like a stray raindrop that landed in her eye. Just as she had done in Aruba, Luz gave Inez time to deplete her fury. Inez went on for several minutes about how much money she would lose, how hard she would work at the grocery for nothing, how stupid she was being. Then, slowly, Inez began to accept that Luz was not going to Saint Maarten.

"If that's what you want to do," Inez said at last, "I'll have to live with it. It's going to be harder on me than it has to, and it'll twice as hard on you here. You'll have those rich people looking down at you at the grocery when you know you could be shopping there instead of waiting on them. But you are your own person. I hope one day you come to your senses."

Just then Anna appeared in the doorway. "Are you staying for supper?" she asked Inez.

Inez immediately turned on the charm Luz had seen her use in Minchi's. She twisted her watch around to see the face and announced, "I'm late already!" She made a production of finding her purse, putting on her sunglasses exactly right, and kissing Luz on the cheek.

"It was good to see you," Luz said.

"I'll be back in three months or so," Inez told her. "Nice to meet you, Anna. Next time I'll be sure to stay for one of your meals. Luz told me how good they are. I want to meet your mother, too." Finally, she bent down and kissed Hernán on both cheeks.

Inez pranced away, toward the boulevard where she was sure to find a taxi to take her to her appointment. The appointment was certainly with a man who paid for the time. Luz hoped her sister was merely suspicious and had not figured out exactly what Inez had done to pay for her ensemble.

Luz picked up Hernán and carried him back toward the house. "Truck," he said. "A truck."

"You lost your truck?" Luz asked her boy. "Let's go back and get it." She set him down and started for the rear of the house, where he had been playing.

"No," he said pointing toward the end of the street. "Truck."

Luz saw a large vehicle coming down the block. "Yes," she said to Hernán. "That's a truck." She smiled at her brother who pulled to a stop and set the air brakes.

Hernán ran to greet his uncle. "Big truck!" he shouted with his miniature voice.

"Do you like it?" Rudi asked as he climbed down.

Rudi swung Hernán off his feet and set him on the seat where the boy went to work jogging the steering wheel back and forth.

Luz asked Rudi why he brought the truck home.

"Jorgé asked me to take it to a customer," Rudi answered.

"That's what happened to Papa," Luz commented and went in the house without another word.

Of course Jorgé asked Rudi to drive the truck to the customer! It was a dangerous job the other men working in the garage didn't want. And how could Rudi refuse when Jorgé held the mortgage on the house? Wasn't Jorgé doing the family a favor by giving Rudi work so he could pay the mortgage? He was, but in a way that only indebted them further.

Before they sat down to supper, Luz spoke to her brother. "You're not taking the truck tonight," she said.

"Early in the morning."

"Good," she said and kissed his cheek to show her approval.

"This may be my last two weeks on the job," Rudi continued.

Luz felt her eyes widen. "Why?"

"The refinery in Aruba," Rudi said quietly. "I talked to the agent on the way home. He said there's a new company taking over."

The combined stress of Inez's visit and the possibility of Rudi's going to Aruba left Luz exhausted. She wanted to show more phony excitement for her brother, but she was played out. She knew better than to warn him about working in Aruba. He was bent on showing the family he could do more than her. Her biggest fear wasn't that he would be killed but that he would discover she had worked at Minchi's.

"Why don't you help Hernán wash up," she suggested and retreated to the kitchen. She helped herself to a glass of orange juice and set the table. Her mother showed up first. The eldest member of the family was thrilled to hear Rudi's news. She rambled on about her hardworking son, how he was going to make more money than his dear father. She knew it would only be a matter of time before they would need a bigger house because surely a young man like Rudi, who worked a dangerous job far from home, would be more attractive than ever to the young ladies. Marriage was the next logical step and, God willing, a little baby.

Neither Luz nor Anna said anything. Luz knew her sister was angry because Anna hardly said a word while they ate. She pecked at her plate and avoided Luz's gaze. When it came time to clear the table, Luz said a silent prayer for her brother.

At the sink, Luz asked her sister what was the matter.

"You were away for three months. Now Rudi is going away. I've had one date in two years. If I could get out of this house, maybe I could find someone for myself," Anna said. "If not a boyfriend, at least a girlfriend to talk to."

Luz put her hands into the dishwater and prayed some more.

Two weeks later God issued His replies to her prayers. Rudi's agent told him the company that was supposed to buy the refinery had backed out. Rudi felt betrayed. Luz was grateful. Anna was indifferent. The good tidings made Luz wonder if all her mother's days in church were starting to pay off.

※　※　※

"I'd like to see you in my office," Señor Garcia said in a tone that drew the attention of the other women. They all looked at Luz with an expression that revealed their concern. What had she done to raise Señor Garcia's ire? Luz approached his door cautiously, hesitating before she knocked. He must have heard her coming because he had the door open before her knuckles touched the surface.

"Come in, Luz," he said. "I'll be with you in a minute."

She watched him sort through several papers, place them in folders, and then tuck everything into the side drawer of his desk. "We're going to have lunch together," he told her. "I want to discuss some things with you."

Normally, Luz ate in the stockroom room at the back of the store. Not once had Señor Garcia joined the employees there. She often saw him eating at his desk. Sometimes he left the store at midday, but rarely, and never with another employee.

Garcia looked at his watch. "We can leave now," he said. "There's a place I know just a few blocks away." He was out of his chair and at the door before she could rise from her seat. "Come on, Luz, I want to beat the crowd."

The restaurant was a place Luz recognized. She passed it going to and from work. The front window revealed a number of tables in the space behind. Garcia pointed to one farther back, where a waiter stood with menus in his hand. He sat facing the window so Luz had a view of a wall, which left her with nothing to look at but Señor Garcia himself.

"Order whatever you like," he said opening the menu.

Upon taking her seat and measuring Señor Garcia's demeanor, her suspicions were confirmed. This meeting was a prelude to only one thing, and Luz struggled to find a clever way out of it. She never suspected Señor Garcia would approach her like this. He was always a gentleman and keenly interested in operating the store properly. She expected him to be more discreet.

To her relief, Garcia spoke about the store while the two of them ate spoonfuls of soup. He updated her on the company's plans to install new scanning machines at each register. The clerks would no longer have to enter the price of each item. The system eliminated nearly all mistakes. It also would interface with a computer in his office. Each day, a report would inform him what had sold and thereby what had not. Eventually, his store would be connected to computers at company headquarters, and ordering would be conducted automatically.

"It's a brilliant system," he said when the waiters brought their entrées.

Luz agreed and told Garcia it would make his job much easier.

"I'll have more time to spend in the store with the customers and employees," he added. "That's what counts."

Then the conversation drifted to the vacations Garcia had taken. He had been to Colombia's Caribbean island of San Andreas. He said it was primitive compared to Bogotá, but he liked it that way. He also had a small cabin in the mountains near a town so remote even the guerillas didn't bother with it. He asked her if she had traveled anywhere.

"No," Luz lied.

"You know, there's a huge convention for grocery companies. It is held every year in the United States, in Las Vegas. You know, Las Vegas is the gambling capital of the world."

Luz didn't know that, but she was impressed Garcia did. She hadn't figured him for a gambler.

"I like to make a bet once in a while," he said, flashing a smile. "Sometimes on a horserace, and one time I won a million pesos in the lottery."

"*Tan bueno*," Luz cheered. She remembered that a pair of men had paid nearly that much for the show at Minchi's.

"Yes, it was," Garcia said.

The waiter cleared their plates, and Garcia settled back in his seat. He put his hands on the table and tapped his index fingers. Then he looked Luz in the eye and spoke to her in a lower tone.

"It is Thursday, Luz. Everything at the store is ready for the big push tomorrow. I would like to have some fun tonight before all that work. What do you say? Would you like to join me?"

If the circumstances were different, she would have taken his offer. If she believed he loved her, she might have overlooked the fact that he was married and her boss. She doubted Señor Garcia loved her. He may be infatuated, but his lust would evaporate as soon as he grew bored with her the way the men in Aruba grew bored with a girl who had been there more than a month. He would drop her just as quickly as he disposed of the rotten fruit in the container behind the store.

There was no way for her to get out of the situation without losing her job. Because she was trapped, she considered playing the whore. No matter what happened, she was going to be unemployed with no reference. It may take a month or two or three, but in the end, Garcia would find a reason to terminate the affair and her position at the store. Her time in Aruba sold for forty dollars the half-hour. She had no idea what men paid in Colombia. She assumed it was significantly less. Still, she could be discreet and available at his whim given their similar schedules. How much was that worth when combined with her youth and beauty?

Before she could ask, she came to her senses. She was not a whore. She was never a whore. She was a young woman who had done something to help her family in general and her son specifically. She cursed herself for allowing such thoughts into her mind.

The problem was how to get out of the situation as delicately as possible. Señor Garcia had been good to her. She did not want to offend him, even though he'd turned out to be no better than an ordinary cad. She decided to act as if she had missed the point of his question.

"I would love to," she said. "But there's a meeting tonight for people with children who will be going to school in September."

"September is two months away," countered Garcia. "There will be other meetings."

"I'm afraid if I miss it, it would be bad for Hernán."

"I see."

Luz watched his jaw flex as he conjured up a new tack. His eyes flitted as a waiter approached with the check. No doubt he was trying to figure out if she were truly oblivious to his intentions or if she were hiding behind a lie. Luckily he didn't know Hernán wasn't old enough to start school for another year.

"We should get back to the store," Luz suggested, putting the strap of her purse over her shoulder.

Garcia placed some money atop the check and rose out of his chair. He put his hand out to help Luz up. She accepted it, and that touch gave him a glimmer of hope. He knew her son was the most important thing in the world. He couldn't blame her for thinking of him first. At the same time, her gaze was too steady for her to be unaware of what he expected of her. She was a Colombiana of an age to have had experience with men.

In Aruba, all but the most hardened men who came downstairs with Luz always wore a peculiar look. They appeared part embarrassed, part ashamed, and a tiny part proud of having been in bed with a woman they had paid. It was an awkward time when they arrived in the bar, where the man's friends usually waited for him. Luz remembered how Spanner had handled this. He took the tension out of the moment by calling out in a loud voice something the man or his friends would respond to. "Come on, man, your boss is waiting," he would say. Or, "Pablo has a fresh drink here." Or, "It's your turn at the pool table." The man relaxed immediately. He forgot about what he had just done, except that it had been a pleasure, and moved on with his night.

Luz waited until she was in the presence of the waiters near the front of the restaurant. She put her hand on Señor Garcia's shoulder and pointed at the ancient cash register. "Do you think they will ever have a computer here like the one you're talking about for the store?"

Garcia looked at the antique machine and shook his head.

"Their loss," Luz said and made her way to the street. "You know," she continued when they were outside. "When you first asked me to come to your office I was worried I did something wrong, that you were angry with me."

"No," Garcia assured her. "But there is one problem. This new system may be so good that we need a few less clerks. I can count on you not to mention that."

"Silencio."

Because she mentioned the computer system, it was the topic of choice for the walk back to the store. Garcia bored her with details. As they waited for a traffic light to change, her boss took Luz's arm. They stepped off the curb, and when Luz looked up, she saw Abel crossing from the other side. She smiled at him as they passed in the middle of the avenue. He ignored her.

Back in his office, Señor Garcia flopped into his seat. He rubbed both eyes with his hands. He could not decide if Luz was incredibly stupid or brilliantly clever. Perhaps she was neither. Could it be she simply thought he brought her out to discuss the computer? Probably not. It was more likely she understood exactly what he wanted. Yet she had found a way for him to save face and extricate herself without giving cause for anger. She did not make a scene, nor did she insult him with a rebuke. His machismo remained unoffended.

He found himself laughing out loud. As funny as all this was, he could not deny the lust he had for the girl. Sooner or later it would have to be satisfied or she would have to go. Maybe after the new computer was installed. Then he would have a reason to celebrate, a motivation to try his luck again with the girl who drove him crazy. If that didn't work, he could always fire her.

Luz waited for the bus home. If the tension with Señor Garcia had not been enough, the look on Abel's face surely was. She longed to scream her lungs out but couldn't. Not in public and not when Abel might show up on the exact same bus.

She needed relief, something to drain away the stress. She remembered the day of Charlie's birthday party, how she had given in to Samito's pushiness and ridden to the party where he poured her that first glass of Baileys. She hardly tasted the alcohol, but after the second one and on her way through the third, she felt it.

She boarded the bus and took her seat. Abel did not get on. She opened her purse. Deep in a hidden pocket she located her emergency money, the bills Inez had warned her to keep hidden. This was an emergency, after all, so she was not bothered at spending it. She left the bus one stop early, found the liquor store, and bought a bottle of Baileys. The store had only the large one, which was more than she required. She practically jogged the rest of the way home.

Anna and her mother had the table set. Her boy made engine noises as he played with his toy trucks. Luz took a glass from the shelf and put ice into it. Her mother and Anna gasped as she filled it. Before either of them could remark on the cost of the liquor or how much of it she was about to drink, they heard the sound of a real truck outside.

"Your brother is home," her mother said.

Luz looked through the window and saw Rudi step down from the cab. When he closed the door, she saw that Jorgé's name was painted on the side in fancy script. It was a magnificent vehicle. Luz toasted Jorgé's taste in trucks and asked the Lord one more time to look after her brother who drove them. She was glad she had poured herself a double.

LUZ DRANK several large glasses of Baileys before she ate supper and another one after and one after that. The last thing she remembered was Hernán's blowing the horn on the new truck, which brought the neighbors out complaining. To placate them, Rudi offered rides that lasted long into the night. She thought it was a waste of expensive fuel but could hardly protest in her condition.

She slept in her clothes, awoke hungover, and had barely enough time to get ready for work. She panicked when she realized Hernán was not with her. He was asleep beside her brother, a tiny truck in his hand. The two of them snored softly as Luz went about getting dressed. Looking down on them she was reminded of the Captain. Her mind went back to the night when he collapsed on her bed. He was an ugly sight with his peeling skin, cracked lips, and tousled hair. The memory made her smile. It was one of the good ones from Aruba.

As she rode the bus to work, she vowed to grow up. Getting drunk for silly reasons was childish. Dealing with Señor Garcia was nothing compared to what she had coped with in Aruba. The worst that he could do was fire her. She had found the job at his store; she could find another one. She needed to accept that her brother was capable of providing for the family. It was important that she supported him, that she not act like a teenager by drinking too much and neglecting her own responsibilities. As for Abel, she had plans to find out what he was thinking.

That Friday, Señor Garcia closed the grocery early. Technicians were coming to install the new scanners. Garcia asked Luz to stay, but she begged him to let her go with the others. He made the mistake of asking why. She said she had a date. Both disappointed and relieved, Garcia relented, and she rewarded him with a kiss on the cheek which made him forget all about what the technicians were doing.

Luz walked to the building where Abel worked. She waited near the service entrance until she saw him come out. The surprised look on his face satisfied her as much as Hernán's laughter.

"I'm off early," she said. "We could go somewhere."

Looking down at his stained shirt and pants, Abel replied, "You want to be seen with me?"

She thought back to the men from the refinery in San Nicolaas and considered that Abel was a handsomely better sight than any of them. She said, "Don't worry about it." As Abel eyed her carefully, Luz shrugged her left shoulder. He smiled at that, and she knew she had him.

Abel insisted on changing, telling her he had clean clothes in his locker. He came back and took Luz on the first date she'd been on in years.

Although it was risky, Luz said she'd like to go to the same restaurant where Señor Garcia had taken her. She was careful to let Abel know she couldn't stay late because Anna planned to go out with a girlfriend. They had time for a snack and a couple of drinks. He agreed because he had a project to work on with his brother, something they were building at their house.

Luz ordered a small Baileys and Abel took a beer. He explained that his schedule had changed. He worked from early in the morning until just after lunch. Luz never mentioned Señor Garcia, and Abel seemed to have forgotten he'd seen them together.

"Maybe Anna would like my brother," Abel suggested. "We could go out together next week."

Excited at a new prospect for Anna, Luz told him, "She would love that."

"Let's see how it goes," Abel replied mimicking what Luz had said to him a month ago.

Her cheeks grew warm because she liked the way Abel talked to her. He had an easy manner that was casual but also confident. She inquired about the people who lived in the building where he worked. He told her most of them were agreeable. They tipped him when he fixed something in their apartments. She was tempted to ask him if he could get Rudi a job, but it was too early for that.

After they finished their second drink, Abel looked at his watch. "We better go," he said.

Luz was grateful he didn't try to keep her out and that he hadn't asked about Señor Garcia. If he had been Samito, she would have had to make an escape. As it was, their time together continued on the ride home. Before getting off the bus, she gave him a quick kiss to let him know she liked him and wanted their relationship to go further.

"See you tomorrow," he said the way he had said it when they used to see each other every day.

The back door was unlocked, which meant Anna was still home. Luz rushed in to tell her that Abel had a brother who may be interested in a date.

Anna sat at the kitchen table, the telephone at her elbow. The look on her face told Luz her outing had been delayed, if not canceled. Still, Luz smiled brightly and started to talk excitedly about Abel. Her mother put up a hand for Luz to be quiet. It was then that Luz noticed Hernán sitting on a third chair with his head down. None of his trucks were in sight.

"What's wrong?" Luz asked.

"Rudi's missing," her mother announced.

"Jorgé is looking for him," Anna said.

"Looking for him where?" Luz asked.

"I don't know," Anna murmured. "Jorgé has the truck, but he says Rudi is gone."

"Tell me what's going on," Luz insisted. She feared the worst, that her brother had been killed like her father.

Before Anna could answer, Luz heard a car stop in front of the house. Jorgé got out with two other men. She watched them stride up the walk and enter the front door without stopping to knock.

Jorgé was an ancient man, maybe seventy-five years old, but he moved with the power of an angry bear. He waved for his two men to search the house. When Luz opened her mouth to protest, he pointed at her and told her to shut up. She turned to her sister and mother. Anna's tears overflowed the space of her forearm and puddled on the tablecloth. Her mother prayed silently.

Jorgé's men came out of the bedrooms shaking their head.

"Where are you hiding him?" Jorgé asked. He controlled his rage, but barely.

"Why would we be hiding him?" Luz shot back.

"Because he's a thief!" Jorgé shouted.

Astonished and confused, Luz said nothing.

"I gave him a chance to make good because of his father. That's gone now. He stole from me, and he's going to pay for it. You all are." With that declaration Jorgé exited the house.

Luz chased Jorgé to his car. "¡Por favor!" she begged. "Tell me what happened. I know Rudi would never steal from you. It's a mistake."

Jorgé stared her down. "These past months I sent Rudi on deliveries. He was a good driver, always on time, always where he was supposed to be. Sometimes a customer complained things were missing. What do you think happened?"

Luz sucked in a breath. "How do you know it was him?"

"It was him," Jorgé insisted. "How else could one of my customers have his own goods sold to him by someone else, goods that Rudi was supposed to deliver." When Luz didn't reply Jorgé added, "Simple, isn't it?"

Luz refused to show weakness before Jorgé. She tilted her head up, looked him in the eye, and held his gaze.

"I'm finished with all of you," Jorgé said.

"Wait here," Luz said.

"You expect me to ..."

She jogged into the house without pausing to argue with him. Inside, she rushed to the closet, where she retrieved the money that waited under the tile. On her way, she noticed that neither her sister nor her mother had moved from the table.

Jorgé was still there. His men had taken seats in the car. They appeared bored, as if they had been through this routine before.

"I don't know what you think my brother stole or how much it was worth, but ..."

Jorgé cut her off. "I know what he stole and exactly how much it was worth."

Putting her hand up, Luz said, "I only have enough money for three payments on the house. I would appreciate it if ..."

"You would appreciate it," Jorgé snorted. "I want you out of here tonight."

"What will that get you?" Luz asked.

"My grandson can move in tomorrow," Jorgé answered.

"How much will he pay?" When he didn't say anything, Luz answered the question herself. "Nothing," she said. "Take this money. Give us three months. After that we'll be gone." She saw him look at the money then back up at her. She prodded him again. "Whatever my brother did, it wasn't the fault of my mother or my sister or me. Take the money."

Jorgé looked at the money a second time. He wasn't used to young women standing up to him. He wasn't used to anyone standing up to him. But he couldn't argue with this girl's logic. He snatched the money from her, counted it, and said, "I'll give you three months and not a day more."

"*Gracias*," Luz said.

When Jorgé was in the passenger seat, he said through the open window, "Your brother should pay his debts the way you do."

Back in the house, Luz found her sister and Hernán at the table by themselves. She heard something rattle and fall in her bedroom. She followed the sound of curses and found her mother on her hands and knees in her closet.

"What are you doing?"

"Searching," her mother replied.

"For what?"

"Money."

Luz stood over her mother a second later. "I earned that money," she said. "And it's all gone."

"Why did you hide it?" her mother asked. "Why did you keep it a secret from this family? Rudi risked his life and you were hiding money. Why?"

"I wasn't keeping it for myself."

"You weren't? Who were you keeping it for?"

"Hernán." It felt good to speak the truth for a change.

"He's only four years old. What does he need with money like that?"

"What about school? What about clothes? What about ..."

Her mother cut her off. "Bah!"

"You won't find any more," Luz told her. "I gave the last of it to Jorgé."

"What good will that do?"

"It will keep us in this house for three more months."

"Then what?"

Luz pointed at the street. "Would you rather be out there tonight?"

Her mother made herself clear. "Now you try to fix what you broke and play the hero. A baby with no husband. A job in a fancy store in the rich part of town. Hiding money. Look what you got us with your ambition."

"All because of me?"

"Who else? It's your fault Rudi got into trouble."

Luz left the room then shot back in when she remembered her mother had left her clothes from Aruba lying on the floor. She scooped up the dress and the pants suit and smoothed them over their hangers.

"I'm going to sell those," her mother assured her.

"No you're not," Luz said. She hauled out her suitcase from under her bed and started putting things into it by the handful.

"Running away from home?" her mother asked.

From the corner of her eye, Luz saw Hernán staring from his seat by the doorway. That he was witness to this strife saddened her. Nonetheless, she smiled at him lovingly. While he didn't return the smile, his eyes displayed a calm trust in her. There was no way he could understand exactly what was happening, but Luz knew he felt her love, that he had confidence in her.

Luz faced her own mother with a less affectionate look. "No, Mother," she said. "I'm going to sell those clothes in a place where they'll bring a lot more than they do here."

SAM SLID his hand along the top of the doorframe. When his fingertip touched the key, he smiled and the cigarette fell out of his mouth. He stomped out the Marlboro, stuck the key into the lock, and entered the Dog House. He tossed his bag in the corner, cranked open the windows on both sides of the room, and flopped back on the bed. He was home.

He had his work cut out for him. Before he got on to the usual San Nicolaas follies, he had to find out what was going on at the refinery. When Charlie told him it had closed he nearly collapsed. He remembered the conversation he'd overheard in Pueblito Paisa and knew the place was in terrible condition. Still, he never thought he would hear the word closed. He ran up a three-hundred-dollar phone bill in pursuit of details. No one had solid facts other than the one about foreign security guards keeping an eye on the place. Sam tried to follow that clue. He played it several different ways: as an old friend of a past refinery president, as a former employee looking for a job, and as a potential new employee. Nothing worked.

He neglected his work in a way that would have given cause for firing from a regular job. Being self-employed, he answered only to his bank account. Despite recent distractions, he had done well over the past year. In fact, it had been his best, thanks to a corporate scandal he had unraveled for a grateful board of directors. He wasn't worried about the financial ramifications of a slack month, especially if it were spent in San Nicolaas.

He started going out late, training himself for the coming all-nighters in Aruba. Latina faces at the bars and clubs in South Beach reminded him of the girls working in San Nicolaas. He attempted to chat them up, but they were too distracted by young descendants of émigrés escaped from Castro's island castle. Besides, he preferred Colombianas. They appreciated his energetic interpretation of salsa dancing and his well-honed skills in the kitchen. On top of that, three drinks cost more than a tank of gas. Like a wounded veteran denied a pension, he sulked around

Miami for another week until the day of departure arrived. He couldn't have been happier to leave.

He sat up, looked at his bag, and resolved that his clothes were staying here. Charlie kept this room for his exclusive use. It was about time he moved in. His closet in Miami was full of business suits and clunky shoes required to impress the corporate world in colder climates. The cane-cutter shirts, slacks, and loafers in his bag rarely saw fresh air. Here in Aruba, they were his nighttime uniform. For daylight hours, he had a pair of swimming trunks, a few T-shirts, and some jeans.

A nap was what he needed, but a trip to town was what he had to have. Nothing seemed out of order on Main Street. A cluster of cars filled the lot in front of the police station. The usual closed stores sat back from the curb. A couple of rummies squatted on a bench down the block from the White Star Store. Sam slowed to a crawl as he passed Charlie's Bar. Tourists occupied a few stools. Herr Koch leaned over their glasses. They could wait, he decided.

Turning left in front of the still unfinished hotel, he put the refinery's main gate in his rear view mirror. He accelerated away, buzzing through neighborhoods, only slowing at stop signs to make sure no one was coming. Eventually, he climbed the hill at the east end of town, entering the area known as Lago Heights. Charlie's girlfriend lived here. It was also an excellent vantage point for viewing the refinery. At a familiar spot, he pulled half onto the sidewalk and left the car.

It was from this place that he and his littermates had mapped out their childhood excursions. World War II had ended twenty years earlier, but they developed a strategy to protect the refinery from the Russians and the Venezuelans, both of whom Sam was certain would take the island sooner or later. As boys, they knew commandos would inevitably parachute out of the sky. However, the enemy had plans of their own. The Russians did their damage in Yugoslavia and Vietnam. The Venezuelans were too busy fighting with themselves to bother with Aruba. Sam grinned. He knew if they had taken their shot at his piece of paradise they would have gotten more than a bloody nose courtesy of his youth brigade.

The refinery spread out below him like a ship dashed on the rocks. All of it had been rotting long before this day. It pained him to think of how it had once been a proud example of American engineering. His father and his fellows never would have tolerated what had become of the place that supported them for their entire careers.

Sam spotted one of the security vehicles rolling through the complex. The guys on the other side of the wall were not even caretakers. They guarded a graveyard in a place where robbing the dead was not a profitable vocation. As far as Sam was concerned, the place needed only a couple of padlocks instead of this high-priced bunch of rent-a-cops. He snorted, pinched out his cigarette, and tossed it on the ground.

Back in town, he cruised Rembrandtstraat. At the very beginning of the street, where it butted up against the unfinished hotel, he saw the food stand was open but lacked customers. He felt sorry for the girl working behind the counter.

He continued up the street. Vacant doorways yawned at him. The drug dealers had not returned, either due to a lack of business or Calenda's vigilance. Sam figured a little of both did the trick for those idiots. At the end of the street, he doubled back for another lap just in case he'd missed something. The result was the same. The place was a ghost town.

He parked on Rogerstraat against the refinery wall. Jessica sat on a stool in front of Hop Long Laundry. He waved to her just before rounding the corner into Charlie's Bar, where Herr Koch offered him his favorite stool. "*Bon dia* to you, too," he said without a trace of American accent.

"I hope you're not looking for a job," Koch said.

"Only a drink," Sam replied.

"Drinks we have. Jobs, sorry, but no." Koch stood Sam's drink on a coaster and tapped the bar with his fist indicating this one was on the house.

"*Danki*," Sam said and sipped the booze.

"Have you found a girl?" Koch asked.

"Just got home," Sam told him, "but I'm always on the lookout."

"I hear there are fewer than usual."

"I'll say. You can fire a howitzer down Rembrandtstraat and not hit a soul."

"Grape shot?"

"Grape shot, buck shot, bowling balls if you have them."

"Carlotta is open," Koch said.

"*¡Excellente!*" Sam declared. He had planned to see Carlotta but not until he ran circles around a few touristas. The pairs at the bar looked uninspiring, as did the ones at the tables on the other side of the room. They peeked at the junk hanging around the bar, checked their watches, and asked about taxis or when the next bus would come to take them back to the resort area. He downed the drink and made his exit.

"Come and chat sometime!" Koch called after him.

On the way to Carlotta's, Sam hoped to see Frankie or Speedy. He had a five-guilder coin ready. Neither choller was on the street. The lack of their presence unnerved Sam more than anything else. He knew Calenda wasn't interested in rousting them. The cop focused his attention on drug dealers, illegal parking, and other petty crimes that nagged the citizenry.

"*Hola, Samito,*" Carlotta greeted him. "Have you come to rescue me?"

"I'm here, *mami,*" Sam said. "Ready, willing, and able." He clutched her in his arms and danced her around the jukebox until the current song ended.

Carlotta made his drink and set out cashews for him. Sam raised his eyebrows at the upgrade from peanuts, pleased that Bar Sayonara's standards had remained high. His hostess came from behind the bar and sat on the stool next to him.

"Look at my girls," she began.

Sam checked out the three Colombianas seated together at the end of the bar. They smiled at him. Despite the friendly attitude, he saw that every one of them was critically flawed, either too fat, too ugly, or both.

"How are these girls going to make money?" Carlotta asked.

"On their backs," Sam said without his usual compassion.

"Who is going to be on top?" Carlotta shot back. "There are no men in this town. I hear the refinery is going to reopen. When? The government has done nothing but make promises. Promises are not accepted at the bank."

"Something good will happen," Sam assured her.

Carlotta feigned a heart attack. "Something good. Nothing good has happened in this town since Esso said adiós."

"*Basta, mami.* Think of all the good times we've had."

"Always a party for you, Samito, but not for us here in San Nicolaas."

"I live here, too," Sam said without hiding his anger.

His tone was not lost on Carlotta. She twisted her handkerchief, then took a different approach. "You know what it was?" she asked.

"What was it?" Sam asked as he finished his drink.

"That witch from Main Street," Carlotta told him pointing toward Minchi's. "Marcela brought her evil spirit to this town, and we have suffered for it."

"She can't be responsible for everything."

"Poor Ricardo left this earth early didn't he? That's enough proof for me."

Sam shook his head. Marcela was a rotten character, but Ricardo had dropped dead of a heart attack, something that happened a million times a day.

"God is punishing us, Samito. We must atone for her," Carlotta finished.

Sam was tempted to agree, but instead of stoking the fire, he quenched it.

It was what Charlie would have recommended. He put his hand on Carlotta's and looked into her eyes for a long moment.

"*Mami*," he said, "you have survived a life that would have killed a conquistador. You're strong enough to make it through this."

Tears fell from her cheeks. She squeezed Sam in an embrace that pressed her perfume into his clothes. After she broke free, she went behind the bar for a shot of brandy and then took two guilders out of the cashbox and gave them to the nearest girl. "Play the music you like. The stuff that makes people dance," she said.

"That's what we need!" Sam declared. "More dancing!"

He took turns with the girls and bought each of them a couple of vinos. Seeing Carlotta in better spirits, Sam felt he had done his good deed for the day. He'd spread some joy and proved that Charlie knew best. Still, he left Sayonara Bar feeling as if he had escaped a plane crash.

In Savaneta, Sam found Charlie in his studio, painting a picture only slightly larger than a matchbook. He had a magnifying glass in one hand and a brush in the other.

"I'm in my miniature period," Charlie informed him. "I must control costs."

Sam squinted at the image. He saw it was an underwater scene with colored fish set against gray coral. Looking at the tiny brush in Charlie's hand, he said, "You'll go blind doing that."

"Great artists suffer," Charlie replied. "That's what makes our work so good."

"I think our town has suffered enough," Sam said.

"Don't be glum, my friend," Charlie continued. "The sun is shining, our bellies are full, and neither of us has cancer unless that's what you came to tell me."

"No."

"See that? A reason to celebrate." Charlie put down his painting tools and reached for a bottle of Barbancour rum. He poured two thumbs' worth into a pair of glasses and handed one to Sam. "To the future," he said. "It's all we have."

They touched glasses and sipped.

"Did you buy me something interesting for my birthday?"

Sam grinned. "The man who has everything is asking for a birthday present?"

"Why not? We have telephones in our pockets, computers in our watches, and cameras on the end of a pencil. There has to be a gadget out there just for me."

"How about a lovely young woman?"

"You have my attention. For all our technology and sophistication, it is the simple pleasures we love most. These are the things we need to live: good food, excellent booze, fine friends, and female company! The rest of it? All crap."

Sam raised his glass a second time and swallowed the drink. Charlie did the same.

"What about the refinery?" Sam asked. "I can't get the story from anyone."

"There is no story. The place is closed. I hear it has been sold, but that was the story before they shut the doors. Maybe this time it is true, maybe not. Either way, something good is bound to happen because there's nothing bad left. Eh?"

"You got that right."

"This is the Lord's day, a day of rest. Go take a nap before you get depressed. Set your alarm for six o'clock."

"Why six o'clock?" Sam wondered aloud.

"I'm disappointed in you," Charlie groaned. "At six o'clock nothing is going on except that your sad ass will be rising from that bed. You'll be in the shower for a few minutes, maybe on the toilet, too. You will shave. You will brush your teeth. You will dress appropriately, and then you will drive to the airport, where twenty-five beautiful Colombian women will be arriving at ten past seven on the Avianca flight from Bogotá."

Sam slapped his pal on the shoulder.

"Feel better?" Charlie asked him.

"Like a prince," Sam replied and backed out the door.

"Don't forget who is your king!" Charlie retrieved his brush and magnifying glass and returned to his work. He liked these little pictures. The concentration forced his mind off other things, like the closed refinery, the decline in tourists at his bar, and the general lack of quality talent in the whorehouses. He took comfort in Sam's arrival; his friend was a lucky guy. He beat the casinos when he wanted to. He dodged the cops better than Robin Hood. His greatest defect was his intense passion for life, which left him with unmet expectations. However, Charlie was coaching him through the rough spots. So what if the refinery was closed and the girls were below par? A lull in the storm gave brave sailors a chance to repair.

Charlie dabbed a spot of paint above the waterline in his picture. It was a boat coming over the horizon, an incongruous element in the otherwise completely natural scene.

As Charlie ordered, so Sam obeyed. He took his nap, his shower, his shave, and dressed for the night. He arrived at the airport early, in time to gossip with old friends who worked for customs. They told him big things were going to happen at the refinery. Expensive cargo bound for the refinery was scheduled to appear.

When Sam pressed for details, they swore they were too low on the ladder to know any more.

Francisco pulled up in the lead autobus with three more behind him. The cops allowed him to park at the curb, where no local or tourist dared to stop. Sam drew hard on his cigarette. The hot smoke burned his throat and gave him a coughing fit. He tossed the cigarette into the gutter, vowed to cut back, and entered the terminal. He promptly bought a Coke and took a seat to wait for the show to begin.

Half an hour later, Sam perked up at the sight of Francisco leading a pack of chicas, each of them dragging suitcases across the tiled floor. The ones closest to Cisco left much to be desired. They were the newest of the newbies. He could tell by the way they stuck close to each other and Cisco. The second half of the group looked more comfortable. They laughed when a suitcase toppled. They waved to married men who clearly were not potential clients, then giggled when the wives shot their husbands angry looks. Sam chuckled at that stunt.

Suddenly, he clamped his jaw shut at the sight of a particular girl near the end of the pack. Even at this distance, he could see she was harried and tired. He also knew her name. It was Luz. She had been *the one* until unforeseen events overtook him: Nathan Beck washed up on shore; that guy had taken her across the bridge to Aruba's version of adult Disneyland; and Sam ended up playing third chair in a sour concerto with Inez. As much as he was thrilled to see Luz, it pained him just the same. By the look of her, she was back in Aruba for all the wrong reasons.

"This time," he swore aloud, "you're mine."

As an experienced whoremaster, he approached carefully. He circled wide, staying out of Francisco's view and clear of anyone who might recognize him. He didn't want to blow the revelation. Surely Luz would remember him, and he wanted the moment of recognition to be a total surprise. The ones in the know helped themselves to seats in an autobus. The true newbies picked up the idea and took turns heaving their suitcases into the back of another vehicle.

Luz waited her turn with her eyes fixed to a spot on the ground. Just as she was about to step into the bus, Sam charged forward. He took hold of her bag with one hand as he held the other up to Cisco. Luz glared at him for half a second. Before a smile came to her lips, Sam embraced her with his free arm.

"¡Felicidades!" he said into her ear.

Luz managed a sigh for him and let go of her bag.

"I'm taking her," Sam said to Francisco.

Chafed by the loss of the ten-guilder fee for transporting a girl to San Nicolaas,

Cisco said, "Julio Calenda is checking permisos. Have her there soon, or he will be looking for her."

"I know the drill," Sam promised. He took Luz by the hand. *"Venga, mi amor, a mi coche."*

All the rules Luz had followed on her first trip to Aruba she was now prepared to break. She understood she was supposed to go directly to Minchi's. She knew her paperwork was to be inspected by the police. She remembered the anger Marcela had loosed on her and Inez. She recognized the risk of going with Samito, and yet she didn't hesitate. Samito escorted her to his car, where he held the door as she lowered herself into the passenger seat. He kissed her on the cheek and began telling her how glad he was to see her. As difficult as it was to act like the sweet girl he wanted her to be, she did it. She held his hand. She freshened her smile whenever he looked over. She laughed politely at his poor Spanish. She did these things for one reason. There was money in his pocket.

Her behavior wasn't a total fraud. After her troubles in Colombia, Sam's was a welcome face. Her sister cried day and night over their missing brother. Her mother wouldn't talk to her. Hernán asked incessantly when Rudi was coming home to play with him. Jorgé, whom she had called before departing for Aruba, vowed to kill her brother if he found him.

And then there was Samito, a tall, grinning American with hundred-dollar bills in his pocket. Luz remembered the fun he'd had at Charlie's birthday party, how he worked the grill, how he danced, how he kept the party going. His was a charmed life, free of disasters, full of merriment.

"We'll go to Minchi's. You can unpack and have your permiso checked. After that, we go to my place."

"If la Dueña permits me," Luz hedged.

"I'll deal with her," Sam asserted with his finger pointed at the front window.

She let him make his boast and took in the sights. The darkness limited her view, but she caught sight of the movie playing at the drive-in theater. She pointed it out to Samito, and he asked her if she had ever been to a drive-in movie. She told him no, and he said that when he was boy, it was the thing to do. She imagined it was and that it involved taking girls there to have sex with them in the car while the movie played. As they approached San Nicolaas, she noticed the absence of flames emanating from the refinery. Although it was a Sunday, she expected to see more traffic and more people on the streets. Something had changed, and Señora Álvaro had not mentioned it when she made the arrangements for Luz to return.

Sam turned serious. "The refinery is closed," he said, adding quickly, "But it's only temporary."

In an instant, Luz connected herself to the situation. Her lack of education didn't interfere with her ability to understand the economics of San Nicolaas. With no pay envelopes, there would be no men in the bars. She felt a headache creeping from the base of her skull toward her temples.

"It won't affect you," Samito said. "You're in good hands."

He sounded like the immigration officer who stamped her passport. The man with the blue pen and inkpad had recognized her from the last time. "Minchi's, right?" he asked. When she nodded affirmatively, he said, "I thought you would be back." The officer, like Samito, made it sound like she was on vacation.

"I'll help you with your suitcase," Sam said as he switched off the car. The autobuses pulled in behind him. Francisco wagged a finger at them. He lugged her case up the stairs, then told Luz he had to move his car. He took it around the block and parked in his spot at Charlie's Bar.

In the common area, Marcela's hand smoothed a fresh page in her ledger. "Luz," she said, "Give me a kiss."

Luz bent over la Dueña and pressed her lips to the woman's cheek.

"You wasted no time finding Samito," Marcela said.

"*Bon nochi*," Sam said to the owner.

Luz left them there. She let the door to her old room hang open to keep an eye on what was happening.

Sam got straight to the point. He spoke authoritatively, like a soccer coach laying out the game plan. He said, "She's staying with me until she gets her diploma from Centro Medico."

"I see," Marcela said. "You must have connections with the police. You know it is their policy that the girls don't work until after they have passed their tests."

"Jules knows me."

"He must if you can use his first name. I thought we were supposed to address him as Jefe Calenda."

"Commandante," Sam corrected her.

"As you say. Well, he'll be here in a few minutes."

"Good," he said with confidence.

"I must say, Samito, I am a little offended you have not congratulated me," Marcela said next. She clasped her hands together so that the diamond on her fourth finger could not be missed. "Señor Montoya asked me to marry him."

"*¡Felicidades!*" Sam said and pecked her cheek.

"We haven't picked a day, but that's not important is it?"

"Only to the law," he answered.

At that moment, Chief Calenda entered the room with two cops, one of whom was a female.

"*Bon nochi, Commandante,*" Marcela said to him and held out her hand.

Calenda shook it and took a step back. "These two will be checking papers tonight," he said.

"*¡Chicas!*" Marcela hollered. "Bring your permisos and passports immediately!"

The cops made a point of being polite to each of the girls, returning their documents in a neat stack with a shiny paperclip keeping them together.

"Commandante," Sam said, "Luz will be staying with me for the next several nights."

"The law is very clear," Calenda began.

Marcela smirked at his words. She anticipated the chief putting Sam in his place.

"She cannot work until she has passed her medical exam," the policeman continued.

As if on cue, Marcela rose from her chair. She gave Sam a consoling pat on the shoulder.

Calenda finished by saying, "However, the law does not specify where she must sleep."

Luz heard the commandante speak, and the crack of the ledger as la Dueña slammed it shut.

La Dueña said bitterly, "Thank you for your well wishes on my engagement." The scene ended with the sound of high heels and heavy boots descending the stairs.

In the same drawer, Luz found the twice-forgotten bottle of perfume. She applied some to her wrist. Sam stepped forward and pulled her arm toward his nose. He inhaled the fragrance and flashed back to the night he first met her, when he had the nude massage on that very bed. He fought off the urge to have her. Calenda's simultaneous admonition and reprieve was not to be violated. It had been a brilliant move on the chief's part, and Sam thought the man might somehow get rid of Marcela and thereby relieve San Nicolaas of her curse.

"Don't unpack," he said. "Just bring a few things."

She tossed a pair of clean jeans and a casual top into a plastic bag along with spare underwear and a few toiletries.

"You need another suitcase, a small one," Sam said as he took hold of the sack.

They strolled hand in hand up Main Street. He soaked up the pleasure of walking with a pretty girl, thinking of those second-generation Cubanas back in Miami and how they had ignored him a week ago. They were nothing compared to this Colombiana. This was *the one*, the real thing, the kind of young lady that in different circumstances would have had it all.

As they stopped beside his car, he heard Charlie call out to him.

"I told you good things were coming," Charlie said.

"I bow to your greatness," Sam replied and bent at the waist like a common servant.

"Don't fall in love," Charlie repeated and disappeared behind the parapet.

Off the beach in Savaneta, Sam and Luz swam naked for half an hour. She allowed herself to exist in the moment with Samito, to let him tell her a childhood story in his bad Spanish, to indulge his innocent handholding, to float on her back and look at the stars. This kind of phony romance made her forget about her family and Jorgé and what she was going to do for the next three months. Soon enough, Samito would deliver her to Minchi's, and she would be servicing men with more vulgar demands. She would be at Western Union, sending money those men had paid her. But for now, it was a quiet evening with a friendly man who entertained himself by entertaining her.

Later, as they walked toward the pavilion, Luz stole a glance at the darkened beach. It was a year ago on a similar night that she had seen the Captain lying at the edge of the water like a piece of moldering driftwood. Less than a week after that, he had collapsed on her bed. The next morning, he had gone down the street and out of her life. Charlie had told her the Captain would return, but there were no ships out there, only the blackness of the sea.

SINCE MEETING Luz the first time, Sam had been to Aruba twice. Both times, he'd encountered girls who clicked, more or less. Yet they lacked certain elements that overflowed from Luz. She possessed a sad side that was endearing, not annoying. Her smile was lovely instead of goofy. She spoke reservedly without being obtuse. He never felt he was leading her along but that she was at his side, which was where she belonged.

Luz being who she was, Sam knew it wouldn't be long before her client list stretched around the corner. He would have to put the word out that she was to be treated well or there would be serious consequences. Normally, he was above that type of chest beating. However, due to their serendipitous second meeting, Luz was well on her way to being *the one*.

This was a direct violation of his master's orders. The King had warned him just the night before, "Don't fall in love." Sam admitted he felt love for Luz but denied that he was falling in love. As much as Charlie chided him for losing his mind with the chicas, he never lost sight of the reality that they were whores and he was a client. He paid money for their affection and for access to sex, too. With Luz, it was more complicated. It didn't seem like business, nor was it blind affection. It was a form of appreciation and caring that could not be summed up by the phrase "falling in love."

It was impossible for him to know if his money bought sincerity. And yet, he knew if he showed Luz how life would be with him, there was no way she would continue to be a whore or go back to her tragedy, whatever it was, in Colombia. She would stick with him because it made the most sense, and that was good enough for him.

These things Sam had on his mind as he sat on the pier watching the sunrise. Like Charlie, he relished his first cigarette of the day, the view out over the ocean, and the caress of the rising breeze. Tourists gushed over island sunsets, but sunrise was the more beautiful of the two. Princes like him knew the difference and rose early for the show.

A tranquil feeling overcame him with the warm rays of sunshine that saturated his skin. He forgot about Charlie's advice. Aruba was the place he wanted to spend the rest of his life, and the next several days would prove what he already suspected, that Luz was the one to spend it with him.

Before the sun grew too hot, Sam left the pier for the shade of the pavilion. At the bar, he smelled coffee but couldn't remember putting it on. He heard the clink of china from Charlie's house and rose to investigate. He came through the door to find Luz in the kitchen.

"*Buenas dias*," he said brightly and kissed her from behind. "How did you get in?"

"All the keys are above the doors," she explained.

She was resourceful and by the looks of it wasn't afraid to make herself at home. If it got better than this, Sam wanted to know where and with whom.

"After we eat, we'll go to town for some shopping," he said as they sat down to breakfast.

"*Medico primero.*"

"*Correcto.* Medico first, then shopping. Your closet is still empty."

Luz shrugged one shoulder and chewed her food. "I don't need a lot of clothes, especially here. Does it ever get cold?"

"Not like the mountains of Colombia."

"No skiing here?"

Sam shot his finger-pistols at the ceiling and laughed. He told her about his time on the Alaska pipeline. Halfway through his contract, a group of welders who had been ejected from a local bar came back with chainsaws and cut their way through the wall. After that, they drank whatever they wanted, wherever they wanted.

"You were lucky to get out alive," Luz said wide-eyed.

"They haven't made the bullet for me," Sam said. "Not yet, not ever."

"What about chainsaws?" Luz joked.

He gave her a kiss for that one, then washed the dishes while she took her turn in the shower. He waited at the bar, hoping Charlie would show up, but it was too early for the King to paint.

Luz left her hair damp. She did not want to keep Sam waiting. Once she started working at Minchi's, she would get it cut at Jaime's again, but not until a month had passed and she needed a fresh look. She wasn't going to change anything until some of those hundred-dollar bills were in her pocket. Given a choice between shopping and taking the cash, she would have taken the cash. He wasn't offering it that way. So, she touched his shoulder, took his hand, and let him drive her to the hospital for her tests.

At the hospital entrance, Sam handed her off and palmed a twenty-dollar bill into Cisco's hand. "She goes to the front of the line," he said.

Francisco laughed and patted him on the back.

Sam waited barely an hour. Luz came out with an envelope full of official paperwork and a bandage inside her elbow, where they had drawn blood. "Now we're going to start this day out right," he told her.

The long way to Savaneta was a road that ran up through the hills to a town called Santa Cruz. From Santa Cruz there were routes in all directions, including a dirt track that led east through Arikok National Park. Sam was an excellent guide. He knew the history of all the churches. Who gave the money to have them built, the names of the priests, and who was buried in their graveyards. He explained that people made their fences of cut cactus stalks because they were free and the spines wounded ill-intentioned trespassers. He stopped at one of the oldest Cunucu houses on the island to show her how thick the walls were. It was those thick walls which kept the heat out, just like a cave deep in the earth. The shape of the roof, a steep triangle atop a shallow one, also circulated air more effectively than a single-pitched roof. When a sign for the gold-mine ruins went by, he said the roads they were driving on had been paved with spoils from the mine. In those spoils were bits of gold the older processes could not remove. Therefore, the streets of Aruba were literally paved in gold.

"How about that?" Sam queried.

"*Tan bueno*," Luz said. The streets of San Nicolaas were asphalt like anywhere else, but the men who walked them spilled their money onto the bars and into the purses of whores at a regular rate. For Luz, the only place where the streets could disgorge more money was in the United States. The entire country was full of people like Samito, people who made as much in a month as her entire family earned in a year. Inez had told her about America's incredible buildings, its big cars and massive highways, its luxurious lifestyle. "Americans complain about taxes," Inez had said.

Luz had replied, "Imagine making so much money you have to complain about that."

Then Inez had added, "I wish," and Luz seconded the motion.

Now Sam was saying, "I have a piece of land not far from Charlie's. It's not big, but it is on the beach. The owner is an old man who promised it to me years ago."

"He's going to give it to you?" Luz said.

"No. I won it."

This was too much to believe. "You won it?" she asked.

"The man who owns it was a friend of my father. They used to play cards together all the time, a whole bunch of them. I wanted to play, but since I didn't have any money, I said I would bet my bicycle."

"Your bicycle?"

"It was a nice bicycle, too. I washed cars for a year and a half to save the money for it. Anyway, the guy who owns this property said any kid brave enough to risk his bike ought to be let in the game. My father stepped out because he wouldn't play against his son. Let me tell you, I took all their money."

"How did you get the land?"

"The guy couldn't meet my bet. He didn't have enough cash on the table. He also had a good hand and didn't want to fold. So he pledged me the land but said I couldn't have it until he died. As a kid, I didn't care about the land; I just wanted to win the game. I agreed, and we turned up our cards. He had a flush but I had a full house."

"What's that?"

"It's poker. It's a combination of cards. My hand won, and he said with my father as a witness that the land was mine upon his death."

"Is he dead?"

"Not yet, thank God. He needs to sign the papers. We'll have a picnic there tomorrow. Okay?"

She agreed to the picnic just as they parked the car. She recalled this part of Oranjestaad from her visit with Martin. Samito took her to shops selling clothing that was less formal, more comfortable, and more affordable than what Martin had bought. The type was not important to Luz. She appreciated Samito's lifestyle. He liked the beach, cooking his own meals, and drinking the night away with his friends. There was nothing wrong with that.

After dinner, he took her to the drive-in movies. He paid ten guilders to watch two American comedies with Spanish subtitles. Luz missed most of the jokes, but the slapstick kept her grinning through the night. At intermission, Sam bought popcorn and sodas and told her this was what kids did in the United States all those years ago when he was a kid in Aruba doing the same thing. He rambled a little, telling her one of the reasons he loved Aruba was that he could still go to a drive-in movie and share popcorn and a Coke with a beautiful girl. She kissed him for saying that. She also gave herself a bellyache by eating too much popcorn. They slept together as they had the night before, side by side and mostly naked.

There were no official visits to be made on Tuesday. Luz, like the other prostitutes, waited for her test results. She did not have to appear in person until Thursday morning, at which time her results would be given to her and the immigration authorities simultaneously. This way, if she failed the test, the immigration officer would put her on the next plane to Colombia. The first time she worked in San Nicolaas, those four days had felt like a month. With Sam they flew by.

Their second day together was spent at the beach. Sam packed a cooler with food and drinks and loaded snorkeling gear into the trunk of his car. He went so far as to smear sunblock all over her body. While he applied the lotion, he educated her on the aloe plant, which grew abundantly in Aruba. Only a few fields remained of the plantations that once grew it. According to Sam, the best aloe came from those fields.

They drove only a short distance to Sam's future homestead. Piles of coral marked the boundaries. To Luz the parcel seemed to be about twice the size of the lot on which her own house sat. In other words, it wasn't very large. However, her house did not have a view of the ocean, nor a sandy beach with blue water lapping over it, nor the backdrop of a desert island.

Sam sensed her appraisal of his delightful piece of paradise. He found a stick and used it to outline his house in the sand. The kitchen and a powder room were back to back on one end. This gave him a view of the sea while he cooked. In the middle was an open living-room/dining area with double doors in each side to let the breeze through. The northwest part of the house was a pair of bedrooms with a full bath in between. Of course, he would sleep in the bedroom closest to the ocean.

Luz asked, "What about your work in the United States?"

"I'm about finished with that," Sam answered, "I'd rather be here for the rest of my life."

Luz thought the island was a small place for someone who lived in the expanse of a large country, who spoke fondly about the wide-open spaces of Alaska, and who drove as if gasoline were free.

"Have you ever snorkeled before?" Sam asked as he threw the stick into a cluster of cactus.

Luz looked at the ocean. "No."

"You'll love it!" Sam declared. "This is the perfect place to learn."

He helped put the fins on her feet, then fitted a mask over her head. After donning his own equipment, he showed her how to adjust the snorkel tube. Like a couple of giant penguins, they waddled into the water until they floated even with the surface. Sam demonstrated the process by lowering his head into the water. He swam several circles around her, then advised her to start by letting him hold her in his arms.

Luz proved herself to be a quick study. She swam beside Sam as they explored the shallow depths along the shore. There were fish she had never seen before and some old bottles among the coral. It was only after they came up on the beach that Luz realized what good exercise swimming could be. She pulled off her mask and fins and sat back on the warm sand to rest. In minutes the sun dried her skin. She felt a shadow cross her face. When she opened her eyes, Samito was descending on her. He kissed her forehead, the tip of her nose, and the edge of her ear. He made out with her the way boys did in junior high school. It was sweet and romantic. It was exactly what she knew Samito wanted.

They ate their picnic lunch in the shadow of a Divi tree. Soon after they had started the second bottle of wine, they were in the water again, splashing like kids, racing each other to the bottle, then back to the sea. It took a couple of hours to exhaust themselves, but they did it thoroughly, laughing at things only children and drunks find amusing.

The wine, the sun, and the swimming caught up with them once they were inside Charlie's house. Sam fell asleep in a chair and Luz on the couch. At some point after dark, they crawled into his bed. Neither of them awoke until the next morning.

Sam said, "These sheets are covered with sand." They laughed one more time and took turns in the shower.

Dressed, Sam went out for a cigarette and found Charlie seated outside his studio painting one of his miniature pictures.

"I don't think there is a happier man on the island," Charlie said. "Let me take your picture for the tourism board. You can be our poster boy."

"How much does it pay?"

Charlie recoiled. "You want us to pay you? You're the one who is so happy to be here. You have to pay us. And let me tell you, a place like this doesn't come cheap. Tell me you are not neglecting my birthday."

"A momentary distraction," Sam said.

"It looks like more than that to me. I saw you playing by the sea yesterday. You looked like a couple of dolphins out there. You never heard me blowing the horn on that beautiful truck of mine."

"You were there?" Sam asked.

"I was there, and I was hoping for a better show. Some nudity would have been appreciated. I'm talking about the girl, not you."

"You pervert."

"Not perverted, my friend, jealous. You have a real gem there. What is on the agenda for today?"

"I think we'll do some visiting. Maybe go to the casino."

"Do something real," Charlie advised. "Go dancing."

"*Excellente,*" Sam said. He turned to see Luz coming from his room. She looked better than ever.

They spent four hours cruising about and never seemed to be on the same road twice. Samito drove her from one side of Aruba to the other and from one end to the other. He stopped by rum shops and filling stations, private homes and odd businesses. The most bizarre place was a gravel quarry cut into the side of a large hill. Sam knew one of the men who operated the machinery. The people in these places greeted him with handshakes and smiles. They asked him about her, and he introduced her as, "*Luz, la luz de mi vida.*"

She was pleased Sam skipped the casino. "There simply isn't time," he said. It was okay; she knew casinos were places that took people's money. Still, he told her about the time he won five thousand dollars in a slot machine. He celebrated by closing Java Bar and hosting his friends in grand style.

That night, the nightclubs in Oranjestaad filled with locals as well as tourists from a cruise ship docked in the harbor. Luz saw Sam tip the doorman at the club the way he had Francisco. The man waved them in and held his hand up to the rest of the line.

Having abstained from liquor the whole day, it was time to catch up. Without her asking, Sam ordered Luz a Baileys. He took a vodka tonic himself. "To the night," he said raising his glass.

"*La noche,*" Luz seconded and sipped her drink.

She soon discovered Sam danced exceptionally well. He moved her around the floor better than Carmelo had. There were other men who were just as good as he was, and they didn't shrink from the challenge Sam presented them. One offered to trade girls for a song. Sam said, "If you dare," in a light but serious way. The next thing Luz knew, she was in the arms of the other guy. When she looked around, she saw that Samito never took his eyes off her, which wasn't right. He should have been concentrating on the other girl. Her partner's less frisky style gave Luz a chance to catch her breath. The DJ changed songs and she was back with Samito. "I taught her a few things," he said.

The night evaporated into the breeze until the DJ announced that cruise ship passengers had to hurry or they were going to miss the boat. Twenty minutes later the club closed. Sam hated to leave. This was his last night before Luz went to work in San Nicolaas. He wanted to make it last. But they were both tired, fairly drunk, and reality refused to yield.

They walked along the promenade that fronted the seaport. They were the only ones in sight when the streetlights switched off. Sam plopped onto a bench and pulled out a cigarette. He thought back to the time when there was nothing here but a few fishing boats tied to rocks. Now it was a full-blown terminal, complete with a customs checkpoint, every tourist trap a factory in China could fill with junk, and a smattering of local business to lend some authenticity. He only came here for the dancing, which he could no longer get in San Nicolaas.

Luz put her head on Sam's shoulder. Like him, she knew this was her last night before work began in earnest. For a moment, she forgot about the money, the hundred-dollar bills he used to pay for dinner, and the change with which he bought their drinks. She thought about the friends he had, the places where he was welcome, and the gusto he put into everything he did. In a way it was inspiring. She hoped some of his energy seeped into her pores. When her family was together again, she wanted to live more vibrantly and less in a state of desperation. He'd given her a fantastic time, but it was exactly that, a fantasy. It was ending just as this night would end with the coming dawn.

The cruise ship, its passengers back aboard, drifted away from the dock. Luz watched the crew pull the lines off the bollards along the wharf. She expected a horn to blow or maybe a whistle. There was no sound at all, just the breeze passing between the buildings of Oranjestaad. A tugboat came around the front of the ship. A stream of smoke spouted from its stack as it maneuvered against the bigger hull.

"Is that boat like the one that sank last year?" she asked.

"I don't know," Sam answered sullenly.

A few moments later, he crushed his cigarette against the bench and ushered her to the car. The ride to Savaneta passed in silence, and Luz realized she should not have mentioned anything about the incident which brought that suffering man to her room.

When she awoke the next morning and Samito wasn't with her, Luz panicked. She worried he'd held a grudge. She put the clothes he'd bought her into a neat pile and stuffed it into one of the plastic sacks the grocery used. She peeked out each window and didn't spot him. She continued her routine by showering and dressing for the day. After sitting on the bed for fifteen minutes, she decided to go out and find him or another way back to San Nicolaas.

To her relief, he was outside talking to Charlie. She stayed back for another five minutes, watching them to gauge the mood. It seemed they were jovial as ever. She stepped into the conversation with a smile and touched a fingertip to Samito's shoulder.

Sam pulled her close and pointed at Charlie. "Don't say it," he said. "Don't say it."

"All my life I have known this boy," Charlie said to Luz. "We are talking about more than half a century. I try to teach him the way a man tries to push a chain. He never learns until you wrap it around his neck and pull!"

The three of them laughed.

"Take her away," Charlie said. "Do it now before jealously overcomes me!" When Sam and Luz were in the car, Charlie had no one to say it to, but he said it anyway. "Don't fall in love."

Luz passed her tests, received her official work permit, and Sam delivered her to the door behind Minchi's. He took her bag of clothes and carried it to the trunk of the car. He opened the lid, worked inside a few moments, and came out with his carry-on suitcase.

"You can have this," he said. "I don't need it anymore."

"*Gracias*," Luz said and allowed him to carry it up the stairs.

Inside her room, she thanked him for everything. She noted the sadness behind his eyes and the weakness of his smile.

"Until tonight," he said with surprising confidence.

"*Hasta la noche*," she repeated. When he was gone and she took her things out of the suitcase, she discovered three hundred dollars rolled up in the pocket of her jeans. Considering she would not have earned anything those first four nights, it was an excellent way to start her second excursion to Aruba.

She met the other girls, one of whom had been on the plane. Her name was Alison. The other two were Elizabeth and Christina. Luz knew she was the only one using her real name. The other girls picked ones they saw on American television shows. They wanted to know where Luz had been, especially the two veterans who had been cowed by la Dueña. She told them she had been with a friend and that he hadn't paid her nor did they have sex since it was illegal to work before they passed the medical exam. No one believed her. Luz feigned a serious rage. She never intended it to put them in their place, but that was the effect it had. They apologized and swore that they followed the law and la Dueña's rules to the letter.

Although it had been her routine with Sam, she couldn't sleep that afternoon. She made a trip to the laundry and to Lucky Store. She considered a visit to Carlotta but decided to surprise her another day. After a shower and putting on the dress Martin had bought for her, she was ready to face her first night at Minchi's.

Marcela showed up early. La Dueña gave Luz a twisted grin and no other greeting. The girls were waiting. The two veterans had their money out. Marcela took it first, then marked Alison as four nights unpaid. She had a blank page for Luz.

"Well, Luz, I suppose you'll be four nights unpaid, too."

"No, señora. I have the money," Luz said.

"You do? How could you have the money? You were not supposed to work until tonight."

"I brought it with me from Colombia," Luz lied. She placed two hundred-dollar bills over the blank page.

"Two hundred dollars. I'll have to make change."

"Perhaps I can pay for tomorrow," Luz suggested.

"*Perfecto*," la Dueña said and marked it in the book. "You see, girls," she said to the others, "Luz knows how to show respect. You can learn a lot from her."

On top of what had transpired that afternoon, this exchange put Luz far above them. She knew that after the next visit to the doctor, every Colombiana in San Nicolaas would know she was able to do whatever she wanted. They would infer that she was protected by Marcela, a bar owner and known tyrant.

"To work!" la Dueña announced.

They filed down the stairs.

"Stay here, Luz," la Dueña said. She paused until the other girls had gone through the lower door, then added, "There's someone here to see you."

"*Muy bien*," Luz said without a trace of the fear she felt. Her first thought was back to the Venezuelan on Ricardo's boat. It would be la Dueña's way of getting back at her for spending four nights with Sam.

Marcela kept her eyes on Luz, trying to break her gaze, but Luz wouldn't look away. "He's waiting downstairs. Act surprised," she said.

"*Claro*," Luz replied, fearing she had escaped one torturer for another.

In the bar, she saw no one but the girls, Spanner, and Pablo. Continuing with her act of showing respect, she gave the two barmen kisses on the cheek and asked them how they had been. They kept it short, surely because Marcela's car was still in front of the bar. Spanner put a coin in the jukebox and picked a trio of songs.

The door opened before the first song ended. Luz, along with the other girls, turned to see who it was. Martin stood there with his arms out. Luz scampered across the floor to him. As la Dueña had ordered, she gasped with surprise, hugged him for dear life, and told him how much she had missed him. To her own ears it sounded genuine. Martin loved it.

"Let me settle some business with Marcela. Then we'll go," he said. "By the way, I love that dress."

She modeled for him until he waved her up the stairs. She used the case Samito had given her. She was beside him again in less than five minutes.

Martin held the door, taking her suitcase as she passed through to the street. Outside, it was so quiet she could hear the hum of the neon lights.

"Do you know the Hyatt Hotel?" he asked.

"Please, show me," she said.

Sam stepped out of Java at quarter past nine. He tugged at his shirt, flapping the fabric against his skin. He had several drinks with Kenny without revealing how he had spent the previous four nights. He stuck to the subject of the refinery, on which Kenny had no new information. A better secret had not been kept since the Manhattan Project. Sam was less interested now that Luz was on the island.

He walked two blocks to Minchi's, paused on the doorstep for a fresh cigarette, and entered the bar like a gunfighter. He nodded to the three girls, then stepped up to Spanner and Pablo, who had a backgammon game in full swing.

"A drink would be nice," he said.

Pablo made it for him.

"Where's my friend?" Sam asked Spanner.

"She go away," Spanner said without looking up.

He would have coughed the drink had he sipped it. Luckily it was still on the bar. "She's gone? Since when does Marcela let anyone leave during working hours?"

"She told me something just tonight," Spanner replied. "She said, 'Tell Sam he started a trend.' I don't know what that means."

Sam threw his drink across the room. It smashed against the wall where it ran down to the floor.

Spanner shouted, "Cool yourself down! Go for a walk!"

"Tell Marcela *buenas noches*," Sam said and walked out. He pounded up the street, crushing the cigarette in his hand. He dropped it in the gutter, then looked up at the sound of Frankie's voice.

"Samito!" Frankie called from down the block. "I need a guilder to ..." Before he could finish the sentence, Frankie found himself under fire. A handful of guilders hurtled toward him. He couldn't decide whether to duck or to try to catch them. He attempted both at the same time. One bounced off his head. Another struck his hand. The rest landed on the sidewalk and rolled away. He scrambled for them as Sam sped down Main Street.

From his veranda, Charlie watched the scene unfold. He sat down on his chair and looked to Screwball for interpretation. "If the wages of sin are death," Charlie said to the cat, "the wages of love are eternal agony. What do you think of that?" The cat hopped off the parapet and climbed onto his lap.

He reflected on Sam's broken heart and his own birthday. He was going to be fifty-seven this time. "How many cat years is that?" he asked, but Screwball was already dozing. Charlie put his head back and dozed himself.

He woke around four o'clock in the morning. He knew what time it was because the lights at Minchi's went off just after he stood up. The other bars had closed hours ago.

Charlie turned to the west, gazing out at the refinery. For several months, no sound had come from over there. It disturbed him the way the empty streets of San Nicolaas disturbed him. Both sides of the wall were supposed to be bustling places. There should be men working over there and women working over here. Ships should be taking fuel away from the refinery, and trucks should be bringing booze into town. Things were out of synch. Someone needed to do something.

"Not me," he said to Screwball. "I'm a philosopher, not a tycoon."

The cat turned his face into the wind and folded his forepaws under his chin.

Ready to go to bed, Charlie took a last look toward the sea. It was then that he discerned something different within the cluster of structures in the refinery. A brilliant red light stood out among the more subdued white ones in the buildings. The red light moved slowly, ducking behind the pipe racks and reappearing on the other side. Maybe because he was groggy or just getting old, it took him several minutes to make sense of what was happening. A ship was coming into Berth Number Two. How could that be? The refinery was closed, and there were no tugs to help it to the dock.

Suddenly, floodlights were illuminating the vessel. Charlie saw how close the hull was to the dock, less than twenty feet. A tall mast stuck up from the bow. On it flew the Stars and Stripes.

"No worries," Charlie said to Screwball. "The Americans have come to save us."

BECK STOOD at the helm, one hand on the rudder, the other split between the throttles. He'd arrived offshore at half past three in the morning. The run that began in Philadelphia took him to Houston, where he picked up the barge *Caribbean*. Jack Ford then instructed him to tow it to Aruba, where there was some finished product remaining to be moved. Above all, he wasn't supposed to tell anyone but the crew where they were going.

"What's the big secret?" Beck had asked.

Jack had said, "The people who buy and sell refineries and the leftover oil in them don't like other people talking about their business."

With the lines made fast, Beck told Syd to shut down the main engines. He noted the time in the logbook: Four eighteen. Behind it he wrote: Arrived Aruba. Berth Number Two. All secure.

"I never figured you krauts as good boat handlers," Shahann said from the bench at the back of the wheelhouse. It was as close to a compliment as he could muster.

Beck switched off the chart light. He said, "That's because I'm an American, just like you."

"John Paul Jones and all that. Don't give up the ship."

"I have not yet begun to fight. Better write that down so you don't forget."

"Lend me your pen, Captain. I'm just a poor swabbie," Shahann said.

Beck ignored him as he descended the companionway. His head was filled with bits and pieces of Spanish Ramirez had taught him during the voyage south. He was going to visit Charlie, stop by the Arends Family, and ultimately have a few drinks at Java. Maybe Sam and the other guys would be there.

He stretched out on his bunk, looking forward to the weeks ahead in the wheelhouse. Jack had a contract to take this bit of oil to Philadelphia. After that, he was sure *Kathryn* and *Caribbean* would be motoring the Atlantic Coast on a run Jack had snatched from the competition. It was logical that the new owners of the Aruba refinery would have given the company other contracts.

Thoughts of having his own boat filled his head, as they always did when he saw how much available work there was. If *Kathryn* were his boat, he would be making the money to pay for her instead of its going to Jack. He didn't resent the man. On the contrary, he admired Jack as the type who did things right, aside from keeping Shahann on the payroll. He paid well, kept his equipment in top condition, and did what he could to keep the crews happy. Beck wasn't there for the money. He was there because he loved standing in the wheelhouse, operating a handsome piece of machinery, and living a legacy that was fast disappearing. Just before he fell asleep, he touched his life preserver. It was there, beside his head, where it belonged.

Several hours later Beck was dressed to go ashore, complete with a leather holster Syd's brother had made for his radio. There were two pieces, a belt where the radio hung, and a shoulder strap that supported the microphone just to the left of his chin. This way his hands were mostly free to operate the boat or catch a line or hold on when things were rough. Few things on a boat could be done one-handed.

Beck spoke to Syd in the galley, explaining that he was going ashore to visit his friends. He would have the radio on the house channel if anything came up. Syd said *Caribbean* was being loaded and that Shahann wanted Beck to respond to a request for a meeting with Mr. Herzog, the refinery's new chief superintendent.

On the other side of the gate, Beck surveyed the town. He expected Frankie to appear from one of the alleys, but the bum was out of sight.

He jaywalked across the street to Charlie's Bar. The steel door was closed, with the lock hanging in the hasp but in the open position. He slipped the lock, let himself through the door, and returned it to the same position as he'd found it. Charlie sat on his stool wearing no shirt, his false teeth out, and the telephone to his ear.

Charlie hung up the phone, put both arms in the air, and shouted, "We surrender!"

"*Buenas dias, señor,*" Beck said and put out his hand.

"We say '*bon dia*' here," Charlie replied. "That's because we speak a bastard's language. With no father, no decent mothers, and lots of undisciplined children, you have to expect this." He called for breakfast as Beck sat on the stool opposite him. "You look like a storm trooper."

Beck adjusted his radio. "I come in peace," he said.

"In that case, we'll take your money, give you booze, and get you laid. A fair deal, right?"

"What more could a sailor ask for?" Beck replied.

Charlie put on one of his trademark "Boozer" T-shirts. "Don't want to be out of uniform," he said. "So, tell me, what kind of trouble did you get into that you were sent back?"

"No trouble at all," Beck said. "There's oil to be moved."

Raising his mug, Charlie said, "To oil. Without it, everything would squeak."

As they ate breakfast, Charlie asked Beck about the refinery. Beck could only tell him that Jack Ford had given orders to keep his mouth shut. Charlie accepted that and told a few stories about the old Esso days. Then Sam arrived.

"Don't you recognize our honored guest?" Charlie said.

Sam saw it was Beck sitting at the bar. He shook his hand and formally welcomed him to San Nicolaas. "You don't have to worry about us fighting over the same woman," he said. "She's gone over the bridge with that millionaire."

"I hear violins playing," Charlie sighed.

"You can have her if you can afford her," Sam said finally. He went to the kitchen for the coffee pot.

When Sam was out of earshot, Charlie said, "The girl who found you on the beach is the love of his life, and she's gone to a hotel with another man."

"I remember she was a pretty girl."

"More than that, my friend, much more than that," Charlie said. "And please don't indulge Sam's misery. It's my birthday. Let's celebrate another year away from the grave."

When Sam returned with the coffee, he poured each of them a fresh cup and announced, "I have someone else."

Charlie perked up. "If the horse throws you, the best thing to do is to get another horse."

Without laughing, Sam went on. "This one is straight off the shelf. She arrived a couple days late to Sayonara."

"Carlotta must be happy," Charlie said.

"Overjoyed. I think it has more to do with rumors that the refinery is cranking up than anything else."

"Rumors, my ass. Captain Beck is proof that real things are happening," Charlie put in.

Beck put his hands up. "I can't confirm that."

"You don't have to," Charlie told him. "I can smell it. When you come back, bring a ship full of booze."

"Barge," Beck said.

"That's a barge you have over there? Looked like a ship to me last night."

"I have the tug in the notch at the stern. It works just like a ship but handles much better."

"Hmmm. Let's talk about something more important. Sam, are you ready for my birthday?"

"I have something planned you don't want to miss. We'll see you there, right, Captain?"

"Tell me when," Beck said.

"Tomorrow. It usually starts after two and runs until we're out of food and booze and other ways to kill ourselves."

Beck said, "I'll be there."

"Don't wash up on the beach," Charlie said. "Once in a lifetime is enough of that."

Sam went to the other side of the bar. He used a chair from one of the tables and climbed atop it to retrieve Beck's life preserver from where it hung on the wall. "Take this just in case," he said to Beck.

Beck laughed. "I have a new one."

"Suit yourself," Sam said. "Just stay away from the new girl at Sayonara."

"She's all yours," Beck assured him.

With less enthusiasm than the year before, Sam collected the provisions for Charlie's party. Marci, the new girl from Sayonara, accompanied him. She was all smiles and as helpful as he could have expected, but she was not Luz. Although in her midtwenties, Marci acted like a teenager. She laughed too easily, asked too many questions, and talked too much in between. However, she had a body that satisfied his eyes and his loins. He didn't give her a four-day pass in that department the way he had Luz. He took her upstairs last night, had sex with her, and then did it again after breakfast at Charlie's just to make sure it was worth the money he would be paying. When it came to the physical part of sex, she probably had Luz beat. He tuned in to that mode of thinking, acting a little like a teenager himself to put Luz somewhere in the back of his mind.

When they arrived in Savaneta, he put things in the proper places. With Marci's help, he blended his spices, cleaned the bar, washed the tables and chairs, and stocked the coolers. Then he took her for a swim as a reward for her diligent assistance. He used her body for the third time in twenty-four hours, proving he was more of a man than Luz deserved to have.

Sam resolved to fly solo the rest of the day. After they showered together, he drove Marci to Sayonara and told her he would see her that night.

"*¿Promesa?*" she asked.

"*No hay promesas en la vida,*" he said and drove off.

Using *Kathryn*'s satellite phone, Beck called Nicole. She didn't answer. He left a message that he missed her and would be home in about two weeks. He hoped they could get together.

After supper, Beck updated the log and told Syd he would not be back for several hours. He had his radio fully charged and on his waist. If anything happened, Syd was to hail him without hesitation.

"Don't worry about her. She's our boat, too," Syd said.

This sentiment reminded Beck that he sailed with good men. Independent of their paychecks, they were loyal to the boat, which they thought of as something more than a place to work. It was their home and their temple and a source of pride. They protected it with their lives.

"Don't forget this," Syd said handing Beck a black case.

"Send it over when I'm on the dock."

Once Beck was solidly on land, Syd lowered the case over the gunwale. Beck saluted the security guard at the main gate and headed for the Arends Family.

The family, or the band, or both, had grown. Two guys played trumpets and another one a saxophone. A teenage boy sat beside one of the guitarists. Beck was welcomed like an old friend. He tried some of his Spanish, didn't get very far, and handed the black case to the violinist. He opened it and took out the guitar Beck had purchased in Houston. The others showed their approval with a round of applause. They passed the guitar from one to the other until it finally reached the youngest member of the group. He tuned it by ear, then exchanged a few chords with his father. The violinist counted down, and the music began in earnest.

Although in perfect health, Beck waved off the bottle they passed. He played the castanets, danced with the only woman there, and tried to sing along with the songs. The boy showed off the guitar during a solo. However, Beck thought he should have found them a carpenter to fix their house instead of giving them the guitar. The building was bound to collapse any day.

He left them to their music and headed for Helfrichstraat. To his right flashed the neon lights of Sayonara. He thought about a stop there but stayed on course for Java. He was looking forward to meeting Sam and his friends. Two blocks later, he saw Frankie leaning against a wall.

"Captain!" Frankie called out.

"How are you, Frankie?" Beck asked.

"Not as good as you," Frankie answered. "Last time, you were sick and looking ugly. Now it's my turn."

"What's wrong?"

"I got two problems. I have a tooth that has to leave my head."

Beck thought all the teeth in Frankie's head needed to go. He asked, "What's the second problem?"

"Samito is like an angry dog! He threw five guilders at me. He nearly put my eye out. What happened to him?"

After a moment to think, Beck said, "He fell in love."

"Charlie says, 'Don't fall in love.' Look at me," Frankie said slapping his chest with both hands. "I never fall in love, and I'm the happiest man alive."

"Except for that tooth."

Frankie coughed. "You make a good point."

"I only have dollars, Frankie."

"Legal tender for all debts public and private so help me God!"

Beck gave him a dollar. Frankie snapped to attention. After Beck returned the salute, the bum said quietly, "Be careful, Captain. A flying guilder can put your eye out, too."

Around the corner, Beck saw Speedy dozing in a doorway. He folded a dollar bill the long way and slid it into the neck of Speedy's open shirt. The guy didn't move a muscle.

"Come in, Captain," Kenny said when Beck appeared at the door to Java. "We need paying customers."

As Beck entered the bar, he saw everyone was there. The raucous welcome they gave him sounded like the crowd at a football game. Sam shouted for a round, and they all toasted the safe return of Captain Beck. Kenny took a wrinkled envelope from under the drawer in his cash register. "I've kept this a whole year."

"What's that?" Beck asked.

"It's fifty dollars we collected for you the last time."

"Fifty dollars?" Beck said not remembering.

"Yes. It costs forty dollars to go upstairs with one of the girls. There's an extra ten in here just in case you're that well hung. Now take your pick. They haven't had a trick all night because this place has become a gay bar."

The guys all laughed as Beck looked at the girls. Two of them appealed to him in a physical way, but he wasn't the type to consort with whores no matter who was paying. After all, he still loved Nicole. "Let's drink it," he suggested.

"Another queer," Kenny said, crestfallen. "How are these girls supposed to make any money to pay me the rent when nothing but gays and paupers come here?"

Carlos crossed the room. He snatched the envelope from Kenny's hand, quick-stepped over to the closest girl, and took her by the arm. "I've been converted," he said over his shoulder and passed through the door.

During the half hour while Carlos was upstairs, Sam and his friends took turns updating each other and Beck. The guys wanted a ride on *Kathryn*, which Beck said he would be happy to give them if they didn't wait too long.

"When are the workers going to arrive?" Kenny asked Beck.

"I don't know," Beck replied. "According to Herzog, the chief superintendent, as soon as the paperwork is done."

"That will take forever," Roger said to Kenny.

"Just when I had my hopes up high," Kenny moaned.

Carlos returned with the girl, and she joined the other whores.

"Drink up," Sam said, "We have plans."

"Oh shit," Carlos said and swallowed the last of his beer.

Two hours later, everyone was beyond inebriated. They left Java to prowl San Nicolaas like a pride of drunken lions. They dodged parked and moving cars alike. They stopped to peek into various windows, then pissed against the wall on Rembrandtstraat where the drug dealers used to congregate. Less experienced packs of revelers avoided them.

When they arrived at Las Vegas Bar, Sam took charge of the escapade. "In honor of Captain Beck," he said, "we're going to play an old sailor game." He waved them into the back room, where there was a makeshift casino.

Each man took his place around one end of the craps table. The dice passed to Sam, and he shuffled them gently over the felt as his friends placed their bets. He released the dice, sending them in a tumble against the far bumper. It was a seven. They cheered as their money was doubled by the croupier. Sam threw five more times, hitting various numbers without crapping out.

"Give me a number, Cap," he asked Beck.

"Four," Beck said. "The hard way."

Sam fired the dice. They came up five. "Next time," he said.

Beck took him at his word and wagered ten dollars that a pair of two's would come up on Sam's next throw. When the dice stopped, he had won.

"See that," Sam said over a grin. "Anyone else need some money?"

"Shut up and throw," Carlos said.

And so it went. Sam survived thirty-two passes until he finally crapped out. No one cared except the owner, who was happy to see them back in the bar spending their winnings on drinks and girls.

Inspired by his victory at the table, Sam continued his antics at the bar. He bought drinks for everyone in the place, cranked the jukebox up as loud as it would go, and took a turn dancing with every available girl. To escape the noise and madness, Roger took a girl upstairs. It wasn't long before Manny did the same. Beck took the remaining girl off her stool and out to the dance floor, where Sam was doing a shirtless salsa.

At last the bartender turned down the music. Roger and Manny returned a few minutes later to find Sam, Carlos, and Beck catching their breath at the bar. Since everyone was now present and accounted for, they paid the tariff and blasted through the door like cannonballs, landing in the street against cars, street lamps, and barred windows.

"The night is young," Sam said to his crew. "There's more to be had."

Beck checked his radio. He saw that the girl hadn't changed any of the settings.

"Put that thing away," Sam said. "Your mom won't be calling."

No, Beck's mother would not be calling, not on the radio or the telephone. For a second, he wondered what his life would have been like had he been raised in a regular household instead of in the backroom of his grandfather's busy restaurant.

"Better a crooked keel than a leaky hull," Upton's ghost said.

For this fact of his life, Beck blamed his father, not his mother. And then he realized he might owe his father a word of thanks. If his mother had been there, if he had not had a bedroom with a view of the river, if he had attended the University of Pennsylvania, he would never have been a tugboat captain. He would have had a boring job in a building that looked like a thousand others.

"Steer your course or get away from the wheel," Upton reminded him.

Beck had steered his course and was proud of where he was headed. Whatever it took, he was going to have a boat of his own. In the same vein, he was going to convince Nicole to marry him.

"You okay, Cap?" Sam asked.

Beck felt none of the alcohol, nor any of the distraction caused by the girls. "I'm heading back to the boat," he said.

"Already?" Carlos said. "We're just getting started. Let's go to Sayonara. I hear there's a girl there named Marci …"

"Watch it," Sam said. His finger-pistol was loaded and cocked in Carlos's direction.

"I thought the other one was *the one*," Roger put in.

"You, too," Sam glared.

"I'll see you guys tomorrow," Beck told them. A determined feeling replaced his happy, crazy one of earlier in the night. He kept his head back and his arms at his side. He was deliberate when placing his feet over the curbs. At the refinery gate, the guard saluted him and he replied in kind.

Gazing up at *Kathryn*, Beck knew she was the kind of boat he dreamed of. He loved her lines, the way the wheelhouse curved where it met the lower deckhouse, and the bow, which was high enough to break waves and still fit in the notch, but sufficiently low to see over when handling her on the hip. Her elliptical stern gave the boat a sleek appearance which betrayed her true speed. Beck climbed over the gunwale, thinking the only thing he would do differently was name her after his mother, whoever she was.

Charlie was impressed. Captain Beck apparently knew when to call it a night. The man was a sailor, but he was of the new breed that navigated with computers and didn't risk a flogging for sneaking booze onto the boat. That kind of person often took an overdose of San Nicolaas that left him wrecked physically and mentally. When the refinery was first sold by Esso, the new owners had sent several dozen American managers. Five of them ended up divorced twice, once from their wives, and a second time from the whores they married. Nonetheless, Charlie was pleased the Captain had fallen in with the boys. Their carousing was mostly harmless, at least to others. As for themselves, well, that was their problem.

"Sam needs to take it easy," Charlie said to Screwball. "A little taste, maybe a bite or two."

Captain Beck was a little smarter. He tested the water one toe at a time. Of course, it didn't mean he wouldn't eventually fall in. It wasn't the first step that was slippery; they all were.

MARCI KNEW the deal. Sam told her she would be sleeping at his place. In the morning, if he felt like it, they would take a swim, have sex, and then nap. A communal shower would come before they set up the party. Once the party started, she would be the star attraction with the man who made it all happen: Samito, el Príncipe de San Nicolaas. The way he said it made her giggle. The hundred-dollar bill he gave her made her gasp. She'd heard about guys like Samito from the agent who got her the place at Sayonara and was thrilled to have met one.

The sun came up before Sam. He got out of bed only to pull the shade. He managed another hour of sleep before waking to find Marci was no longer there. Apparently, she'd misunderstood last night's lecture. She was in Savaneta to be with him, not to meander around in search of another client. He skipped his first cigarette of the day and left the room to lay down the law.

He made it as far as the domino table, where Marci nearly bowled him over. She flew out of nowhere, started pecking his cheeks with dozens of tiny kisses, and prattled on about a surprise that was waiting for him. She took his hand and dragged him to a tattered Styrofoam cooler tucked in the corner of Charlie's outdoor bar.

"So what?" Sam said. He was irritated at having to put up with her when he should have been taking it easy with Luz. His chest hurt, a good reason to skip his first cigarette, but it was now time for the second Marlboro. Pain or not, he had to have nicotine. On top of it all, this chica wanted to play show and tell.

"A man came," she explained. "He said he would put this here for you. He told me to make sure you get it."

"I'll take care of it later," Sam said and started for the bedroom.

"Don't you want to know what's inside?" she asked.

You're a pain in the ass! Sam wanted to scream. His plan for the morning had been to have a light breakfast, then a swim and a lay. That went out the window when he woke up with a malicious hangover. He needed to recover in order to enjoy Charlie's party. A full recovery required more sleep and lots of orange juice with a little vodka. "I'll check it later," he said and turned again for his room.

"You promised we would go swimming," Marci whined.

Sam glared. He stepped over to the cooler, kicked it with his foot, and watched the contents spill onto the floor. Two slabs of Bonita flowed out with a small avalanche of ice. Since Sam hadn't shown up to make the purchase, Old Man Juárez had brought it to him. It was another reason he wanted to spend the rest of his life on this desert island; there were people like Juárez, who remembered what was important. They were there to remind Sam that the little things were biggest of all.

"Let me clean this up," he said to Marci. "Then we'll have a swim."

"I'll get my suit," she said.

"You won't need it."

After three days with Martin, Luz felt fat and lazy. He fed her too much and abandoned her at the pool while he conducted business. Janson brought her magazines and drinks. The most exercise she got was walking between the shops and the half hour of sex each night. She longed for the hours she spent playing with Hernán, but she couldn't complain. Martin had treated her with respect and as if he were madly in love with her.

Of course, he was not madly in love with her. She was his entertainment for the time being. Late Sunday afternoon, the time being ended abruptly. They were sitting on the balcony waiting for the sunset with glasses of wine. On the beach below them, tourists returned their towels and gathered up their things from the sand. Overhead, an airplane descended through the clouds on its way to the airport. His cell phone rang. After he hung up, he didn't look at her for several minutes, not until her glass was empty. He tugged the bottle up from the ice bucket, saw it was finished, and carried it inside. When he came back, he took the glass from her hand and set it on the table.

He said, "We're going to San Nicolaas." He used the same tone as when he told her "We're going to the lighthouse for dinner" or "There's a new shop I want to show you." It was light and pleasant but direct. She resisted the urge to cry. To keep her cheeks dry, she thought about the real reason for her sadness. It wasn't the end of luxurious days spent in the company of an agreeable man. It wasn't the delicious meals that would be replaced by plastic containers from Pueblito Paisa or Rincón. Nor was it a halt to the shopping excursions. Money brought the tears. The money came easy, too. He gave it without bargaining, without demanding sex without a condom or disgusting lesbian acts.

"A few minutes to pack?" she asked.

"*Claro,*" he said.

She did not keep him waiting. Into Samito's suitcase she placed both the outfits she had brought with her from Colombia and the new items Martin had purchased. There were also two boxes that contained shoes. Fifteen minutes later, the bellman rolled his cart into the room. He stacked her shoeboxes atop the suitcase and offered to carry her purse. She said she would carry that herself. Martin extended his arm. She took it and walked with him to the elevator.

During the drive to San Nicolaas, they passed a pair of autobuses Luz recognized. The second one was blue with a white stripe. It had taken Inez away last year. Luz hummed to the radio, wondering what kind of night it was going to be. Would one of her old clients be in? Would she get to know the other girls the way she had Inez? Would one of them propose they do shows to make extra money?

Martin took her to the gate on Rembrandtstraat. He handed her ten fifty-dollar bills. She closed her hand around them and kissed him on the cheek. He started to apologize, saying he enjoyed his time with her, telling her he hoped they could do it again. She put her finger over his lips the way she did to Hernán when she wanted him to stop crying. She kissed him one more time on the cheek and let herself out of the car.

In her room, she tossed the boxes and suitcase through the door, then pulled it closed. As fast as she could, she went down the stairs leading to the bar. At the bottom, she peered out into the street. Frankie and Speedy sat under a tree in front of Bongo Bar.

Luz twisted the handle on the door leading into Minchi's. To her surprise, it was unlocked. She entered the bar and was hit with the smell of stale cigarette smoke. She went to the window, stopping a few feet from it so anyone on the street could not see her in the darkened room. After several minutes, she was ready to give up on her hunch when Marcela's Mercedes stopped in front of China Clipper. Again, Luz stepped back from the window. The trunk popped open and la Dueña stepped out of the car. A chica exited the passenger side and came around to the back.

Frankie called out to Marcela for a guilder. She screeched back at him to leave her alone. He made a comment Luz couldn't hear, and Marcela charged him. Frankie retreated quickly, but Speedy was too delirious to move. Marcela kicked him in the thigh. He yelped. She returned to the chica, who watched the exchange with a suitcase in her hand. Frankie got Speedy under the arms and dragged him out of sight.

That Martin was driving the next car to appear did not shock Luz. He stopped in front of the Mercedes and left his motor running. Marcela greeted him and introduced the chica as Connie. It was another American name, Luz noted. By the smile on his face, she saw Martin found Connie to be perfect. He put her suitcase into his trunk and helped her into the passenger seat just as he had done for Luz. He thanked Marcela for "Always finding me exactly what I like."

"You're a dog," Marcela replied. She paused to point her finger at his nose, then shooed him back to his car.

Her suspicions confirmed, Luz left the bar. She reminisced a little, trying not to blame Martin for trading her in. It was his money and, therefore, his choice.

It was the end of her first week in Aruba and she had earned eight hundred dollars. Her closet was full of new clothes. If she wanted to take them with her, she required a suitcase three times the size of the one Samito had given her. She wasn't planning on a trip, not yet. Her family needed that money in case Jorgé changed his mind and took their house.

She was about to get a few things at la Bonanza when she remembered that Samito had said it was Charlie's birthday.

❋   ❋   ❋

Sam struck his lighter, touched it to the paper, and dodged a column of flame that would have made NASA proud. He was deliriously drunk, thanks to Marci, who possessed encyclopedic knowledge of mixology. She stood behind the bar, surrounded by his pals and the girls they had carted up from San Nicolaas. They called out names of drinks. She obliged with a confident hand on the bottles. Each new drink was a round for everyone.

Sam took a break from the fire to see what Charlie was doing. He found his friend seated under the awning of his studio. Two easels were set up, one for Charlie, the other for Ricardo's son, Andrés. Both of them were painting the same scene, a harbor view with a ship at anchor. Charlie, using acrylic automobile paint, took an abstract approach. His wide brushstrokes and bright colors gave the picture an exotic feeling. Andrés's work couldn't have been more different. He meticulously blended his paint to achieve realistic hues which he placed on the canvas with precision touches of the brush.

"Andy Warhol meets Rembrandt," Charlie said to Sam.

"I know talent when I see it," Sam said with a wink to Andrés.

Andrés smiled briefly at Sam and immediately returned to his work.

"Serious work, too," Sam added.

"Precisely," Charlie said. "Let the geniuses create."

Sam retreated past a stage Charlie had constructed in front of his studio. The Arends Family wasn't due for two hours. Sam could hardly wait. He was in the mood to dance. Live music under the stars was the best way to do it. Actually, live music under the stars and barefoot on the beach was the best way to do it. He was satisfied keeping his shoes on, Marci in his arms, and all his pals around him. He thanked God for not revealing this place to the tourists. It was still pure, still original. Here the future was kept at bay by a present that never surrendered to the past. It was as it had always been, the same since his childhood, renewed now that the refinery was back in business.

It was his turn to show off. He gathered the food and his utensils and set to work over the fire. Marci tied an apron around his waist. Her hand found its way to his zipper, but he wasn't ready for that kind of action, not yet. He had steaks to grill, chickens to roast, and a slab of fish to fry that would make Screwball go bonkers.

Roger and Carlos put several tables together. They stretched a single bolt of cloth over them. For a change, they used real china, flatware, and honest-to-God glasses. The seat at the head of the table was reserved for Charlie. The opposite end was held for their esteemed guest, Captain Beck. In the center was enough room for everything Sam cooked, as well as pitchers of water, beer, and liquor.

Half an hour before sunset, Sam unloaded the grill. Manny and Carlos ran a shuttle between Sam and the table. His friends put on a courtly air. They held chairs out for the girls, waited for them all to be seated, and then sat down themselves. Just before they started attacking the platters, Charlie rose and said, "Attention!"

Nathan Beck strolled up to the table as the other men rose and saluted him. "Permission to join you for supper?" he asked returning the salute.

"Permission granted," Charlie said. "Now let's stop this bullshit and eat."

They ate like royalty. Though drunk, their manners were impeccable, their conversation polite. The girls giggled at the exaggerated courtesy shown them by this brotherhood of jesters. When they left Colombia, none of them had expected to encounter men so intent on entertaining themselves in such a silly way. It was ridiculous but risk free, aside from all the drinking. In their profession, it was the most they could hope for.

To do their part, the girls cleared the table. They set up an assembly line to wash, dry, and stack the dishes. Sam and the boys took a break from the booze. They smoked cigars at the table, speaking in code about the girls. They asked Beck when he was going to take his turn.

"I have a lady in Philadelphia," he said. "If I can talk her into it, I'd like to get married."

"Done that," Sam commented.

"Twice," Carlos reminded him.

Charlie tapped a cigarette out of a pack. "A married sailor is a lonely man," he said.

Beck nodded his head and blocked Charlie's comment from his mind. He'd spent many days away from Nicole, but he had never been lonely. The anticipation of being with her again excited him.

Before anyone knew it, the Arends Family appeared on stage. They added microphones and amplifiers to their collection of instruments. In the meantime, Charlie's wife placed the birthday cake on the table. She put two candles in the shape of a five and a seven atop the cake. Tom switched off all the lights. Only the candles and the stars overhead illuminated the scene. The Arends boy played the guitar Beck had given him. They sang "Happy Birthday," and Charlie cut the cake. Gone were the fancy dishes. They were down to paper plates and plastic forks. "The way it should be," Charlie said. "Nothing to wash!"

"*Bon nochi, bon nochi! ¡Nosotros somos la familia Arends!*" The senior member of the family put the violin to his chin, tapped his foot, and began the musical portion of the evening.

"Let's dance!" Sam yelled. He took Marci's hand in his and spun her to the music. The others joined him, aside from George, who had just begun a game of dominoes with a latecomer to the party.

Beck found himself standing at the bar with Charlie.

"The guitar you gave that boy," Charlie said. "That was a nice gift."

"I think we should build them a house. He can't live in the case," Beck replied.

"This is true," Charlie acknowledged and handed Beck a drink. "Look at these guys. They eat. They drink. They dance. They have the time of their lives. I wish them good health and long life and ask them not to block my toilets."

"Better dig a latrine," Beck said.

"Good idea," Charlie said. "If you'll excuse me, I have to greet my guests. It always amazes me how many people can smell free booze."

Beck looked around. The party had grown substantially since the sun had gone down. There were at least fifty people clustered around the property. A string of cars lined the dirt road that paralleled the beach. He finished his drink and headed for Charlie's dock, where half a moon and a sky full of stars waited for him.

"This is not Charlie's," the cab driver said.

"I know," Luz replied.

The driver grumbled at having to make change for the fifty-dollar bill, then left the girl by the side of the road.

Luz could hear the party, which was more than a soccer field away. She did not want to make a bold entrance. She thought it would be better to approach slowly to see what was going on before revealing herself. Instead of using the road, she walked along the beach. She expected to see someone on the pier or perhaps atop a blanket on the sand. As she came closer, she saw a man cross the strip of sand and step onto the boards of the pier. He went to the end, where he stood looking out at the sea. Because she was watching him and not where she was going, she stumbled over a lump of coral. The little yelp gave her away. The man turned but did not come toward her.

A touch of fear spurred her on. She walked more quickly. Though Samito and his friends meant her no harm, she was less sure about others who might be about. She didn't stop until she was close enough to see the band on stage. To her relief, Samito and a girl danced among the crowd. Charlie and his wife stood behind the bar. A bunch of men played a noisy game of dominoes. Groups of people congregated under the Divi trees and on the backs of pickup trucks.

"*¡Hola!*" a voice called out behind her.

She turned to see it was the man from the pier. He walked steadily toward her. Being close enough to the party to call for help, she waited for him. When she saw who it was, she backed up until she bumped into the side of a car.

"*Tú vives,*" she said.

"*Sí, yo vivo,*" Beck replied. "*¿Como está?*"

"*Y hablas español, también.*"

"*Poquito,*" Beck said.

"Ah, a little," she repeated in English to show she had learned a few words of his language, too.

They stood there looking at each other for a moment.

"*¿Tu barco?*" Luz asked.

"*Mi barco,*" Beck replied. "*En* the refinery."

"*¿En la refineria? Pero tu barco hundió.*"

"*¿Hundió?*"

She flattened her hand and gestured toward the ground. "*Sí, hundió.*"

"Oh, yes. *Hundió.* It sank. *Otro barco.*"

"Ah," she sighed.

"*Sí, otro barco,*" Beck repeated. "*Grande y bonito, como tú.*" It sounded stupid, but when she smiled he was glad he'd said it.

The conversation halted there. Luz turned toward the party. She was hungry, but she also thought the music was delightful. She looked at Beck again. "*¿Baile, Capitán?*" she asked. By the look in his eyes, she knew he didn't understand. She sidled up to him, took his hand, and started to dance. "*¿Baile?*" she asked again.

"*Sí,*" Beck said with gusto. "I'd love to."

"*Muy bien,*" Luz replied. She looked down at his feet. "*Un momento.*"

When the girl untied his shoes, Beck started to laugh. It might have been the drinks or the light touch of her hands on his feet. Whatever it was, he was suddenly giddy. He tugged off his shoes, set them on a rock, and took her in his arms.

The Arends Family was in top form. Beck and Luz rocked to salsa and merengue for nearly an hour. Dancing was a language they both understood. Though slightly clumsy in the sand, Beck picked up the Latin rhythm quickly. Luz laughed as he twirled her across the beach.

When the musicians took a break, Beck gestured toward the party.

They walked to the bar where Charlie stood talking to some people in Dutch. His face lit up at the sight of Luz. "You found him again," Charlie said to her in Spanish. "This captain needs a better navigator."

"*Sí,*" Luz said. "*Como está, señor?*"

"*Bien. Muy bien.*" Then to Beck, Charlie said, "Take her inside. My wife will make a plate for her."

"How do you know she's hungry?" Beck asked.

"These girls are always hungry," Charlie answered. "Especially when they get to the party late."

They entered the house together. Rosalba sat at the kitchen table with a friend. She spoke to Luz but looked frequently at Beck. She told Luz she was lucky to catch a captain, and an American, too.

As they rejoined the party, Beck noticed the music had changed. The song was more romantic, one with a drawn out melody played between the violin and guitar. At the bar, they found Charlie had been replaced by Sam and Marci.

"Again you're with my girl?" Sam said to Beck. "You don't give up the ship do you?"

Beck sensed the underlying anger in Sam's comment. He was helpless since there was nothing he could do to change the situation. "We're all friends," he said.

"No problem, Cap. You're new here. If one of those other guys did it to me," Sam said with a thumb pointed over his shoulder, "there would be hell to pay. Understand?"

It was a warning, and Beck took Sam at his word. Just the same, Sam's anger made no sense. Beck had told them all about his woman at home. Although Luz was a joy to be with, he had no intention of taking her to bed or keeping her from doing so with Sam. She was a prostitute, and he would take no offense if she left him that minute to earn her living.

"I have the perfect thing to mark the occasion," Sam said and disappeared from the bar.

The Arends Family stopped playing to refill their bottles. A few seconds later there was a series of sharp cracks. Everyone stopped what they were doing to watch Sam's fireworks display. The sky lit up with multicolored explosions as he ran back and forth along the road, touching his cigarette to fuses. Roman candles fired into the air. Rockets shot high overhead and burst into balls of color. One toppled over, launched down the road, ricocheted off someone's car, and landed in the water. The display continued for ten minutes, until Sam ran out of breath and things to ignite.

He was leaning against his car, panting, when Chief Calenda drove up in an official police cruiser.

"A twenty-one gun salute," Sam puffed.

"Careful, Sam. We don't want any injuries," Calenda said.

"Only one wild round," Sam admitted. "No apparent damage."

"Let's keep it that way. You look like you need a rest."

"Just another drink and the love of a beautiful woman."

Calenda continued down the road shaking his head. He had come to tolerate what happened at Charlie's. Charlie was good to the department, the community, and his friends. The soccer field in town had bleachers, goal posts, and equipment thanks to the bar owner. Calenda could remember when Esso paid for things like that. If San Nicolaas was lucky, it would soon be like the old days. If not, well, it wouldn't be any worse.

Sam received the praise of his audience from the stage. He took several bows, then the Arends Family was up there with him. The music resumed, along with the drinking and dancing.

"You take my girl," Sam said to Beck. "I'm going for a spin with yours."

"Sure," Beck said and coupled with Marci for a dance.

In Samito's arms, Luz felt less comfortable than with the Captain. He was too drunk, too frenetic, to stay with the beat. She tolerated him because he had been a good client and deserved to be treated with patience.

"Stay with me tonight," Sam said boldly.

"But you are with Marci," Luz told him.

"Tell me you'll stay the night and I'll take her back to Sayonara right now."

"Samito, you know that would be wrong."

"Wrong? What's wrong with that?"

Luz turned her head to make sure they weren't going to crash into anyone. She saw Marci and the Captain at the edge of the dance area. If she could only switch partners! But she couldn't walk away from Samito without causing a scene.

"I'm waiting," Samito prompted.

"Think about what Martin did," Luz said.

"Who is Martin?" The words slurred together like a smear of paint.

"Martin is the man who took me to the hotel. He paid la Dueña, and I was gone before you had a chance to come to the bar."

"So what," Sam said too loud for how close they were.

"*Tranquilo*," Luz said to him. She contemplated an escape, but there was none. The Captain was facing away from her. Charlie was nowhere near. Sam clutched her tightly enough to leave marks. "How did you feel when you came to the bar and I was not there?" she asked.

"I was angry as hell."

"Now you want to leave Marci for me. How will Marci feel when you do that?"

"I don't care," Sam said quickly.

Luz broke free. She put her hand on her hip and poked his chest with the other. "You told me you were the Prince of San Nicolaas. You sound like something else."

Stunned by the assault, Sam let his jaw drop. His brain swam in alcohol, unable to sort out his emotions. He was furious at the rebuke, embarrassed his friends may have seen it, and yet enthralled by this girl. He felt like a dog that tracked mud across a clean carpet. It wasn't his fault; it was his nature. He was just doing what a dog did, which was rush into the arms of his master regardless of what was on his paws. How could he explain that to Luz?

Before Samito's anger flared, Luz pulled him into an embrace. She whispered into his ear. "I appreciate what you did for me those first four nights. I am happy you want me to stay with you again. But you are a good man. You will spend the night with Marci because you must have promised it to her. I know you will keep your word."

Sam drew her hand to his lips and kissed it lightly. What hurt most was that a girl with the bravado to speak like that was the type of girl he wanted for the rest of his life. But if he dropped Marci, he would be unacceptable to her. He would be banished as another whoremonger not worthy of true affection.

As she held on to Samito, Luz felt the tension leave his shoulders. "The Captain is a good man, too," she continued. "He did not come looking for me. We met over there by accident just like the first time. You must not blame him."

"We'll have another chance," Sam said.

They left it at that. Sam released Luz at the end of the song. He crossed to Beck, slapped him on the back, and said, "I'd sail with you anytime."

SAM KEPT the booze flowing long after the music stopped. He rustled his friends away from the domino table for a round of whiskey shots. When Manny complained he'd had enough, Sam sent him for a walk with one of the girls. Roger and Carlos never let up.

The ash from Sam's cigarette fell into the glass as he poured in the vodka. He gulped the drink, ashes and all, then made a fresh one for Carlos. "How about you, Cap?" he asked.

"One more," Beck said pushing his glass forward, although he'd had enough to flood *Kathryn*.

"Here we go," Sam said reaching for the whiskey. "Anybody see Marci?"

"She's sleeping," Carlos informed him.

"Sleeping? When we were twenty-one, this kind of party was a warm-up. Wasn't it, Manny?"

"I don't know. I was in Vietnam," Manny said.

"You know what I mean," Sam said to no one in particular.

"I want to know when we're getting a ride on that boat," Carlos asked Beck.

"You better get on board," Beck told him. "I expect to be leaving soon."

"You just got here," Sam moaned.

"Boats that are tied to the dock don't make any money."

"What you want to do," Sam said, "is buy a place here. You don't have to worry about pulling out until you're ready."

"The boat is my place," Beck said laughing. "I'm a captain."

Sam squinted across the bar. He didn't like it that Beck found his suggestion funny. He could not comprehend why anyone wouldn't want a house in Aruba. Besides, captain or not, the guy was young enough to be his son, and when Sam was that age, he had taken all the advice his elders could give. These days, he sold that wisdom to major corporations.

"Do what you like," Sam said. "You may have to do it for the rest of your life."

"That would be fine with me," Beck said.

"The rest of my life is going to be spent right here," Sam vowed.

"Come on, Sam. We all know what you're going to do. Just tell us when you're going to do it," Carlos put in.

"Sooner than you know, chico."

"What does that mean?"

"The math would confuse you."

On that note, Beck stood up, stretched his back, and announced he was going to the boat.

"Don't forget your date," Sam muttered. "Take good care of her. I may want her back when you're done. Untarnished."

Beck never intended to raise Sam's ire. He wished Luz were staying with Sam, but she had asked him to take her to San Nicolaas. Charlie translated so there would be no confusion. "She's here with you," Charlie had said. "She expects you to take her home. It's how things work with them." Naturally, Beck accepted the responsibility. However, considering how much he had drunk, the last place he belonged was behind the wheel, especially in a car loaned to him by the refinery superintendent.

Beck faced Sam, stuck out his hand, and said, "I'm only giving her a ride home."

Inebriated as Sam was, it took him a few moments to register that Beck was making him a promise and extending a hand to seal it. He gave a lazy salute and said, "Aye, aye, Skipper. Go tend to your boat."

Beck crossed the pavilion to the domino table, where Luz sat with another girl.

She said good-bye and took his arm.

"*Yo conduzco,*" Luz said, then remembered he didn't speak Spanish. She put her hands on an imaginary steering wheel. "*¿Está bien?*" she asked.

"*¿Qué?*" Beck asked.

"*Dáme las llaves,*" she said putting her hand out.

Before he could say, "*No comprendo,*" she reached for the keys. Letting her have them was the smartest thing he'd done all day. If he'd been a little smarter, he would have stayed on his boat where he belonged.

Luz silently thanked Rudi for teaching her to drive. She prayed he was safe, wherever he was. She glanced at her passenger and said, "*Tú eres el Capitán, y yo soy tu chofer.*"

"*Sí,*" he said, "*El Capitán, with no boat and no mother.*"

He was vaguely aware of her humming as she drove. Other than that Beck had no memory of the drive to San Nicolaas. When next he opened his eyes, the car was parked across the street from Minchi's. Luz had the keys dangling over his hand. She lowered them slowly, then closed his fingers over them.

"*Tu barco, está allá,*" she said pointing toward the refinery.

All of a sudden, Beck experienced one of those odd moments of clarity that come like bursts of sunshine through storm clouds. He was amazed as he saw the same appeal in Luz that Sam had seen. Yes, she was a prostitute, but if he had been sitting in a car with her on a street in Philadelphia, no one would be the wiser. She didn't have her tits out or her skirt up over her ass. She wasn't wearing thigh-high boots. She was dressed like anyone else would be in Aruba, or Philadelphia, or Colombia for all he knew. Beyond that, she kept them out of danger by taking command of the car, driving skillfully so as not to disturb his sleep. Furthermore, she negotiated her way around Sam like a world-class diplomat. He realized that more than anything he needed to put himself in his bunk aboard *Kathryn* before that type of thinking ran its logical course.

"*Pagas despues,*" Luz said when Beck tried to hand her two fifty-dollar bills.

"*Es for tiempo,*" he said.

"*No, Capitán. No dinero.*"

"Take it," he said and tried to put it into her hand. She frustrated him by making fists and folding her arms. "*Por favor,*" he begged.

"*No. Si quieres dáme dinero, tienes que dormir conmigo arriba.*" She pointed to the second floor again.

"No. I don't want to go to bed with you," he said. He thought for a second then added. *"No sexo. El dinero es for bueno tiempo with you."* Idiots made more sense than he did between the two languages.

"Duermes conmigo," Luz repeated. *"Entonces, en la mañana, dáme el dinero. ¿Está bien?"*

He let the money fall in her lap and got out of the car. After closing the door, he turned to see her coming toward him at full speed. She put the folded bills up to his face and started speaking in Spanish so fast it sounded like machine-gun fire.

"¡Capitán! ¡Escúchame! Es mi trabajo y estoy contento por el dinero pero no es correcto. En esto trabajo un hombre paga para sexo y otras cosas pero el no paga para nada. Nada de nada. ¿Me entiendes?"

If she hadn't been so serious, he would have laughed in her face. However, as Captain Upton had said, "When a woman has her face the color of the port light you keep the humor to yourself."

"El dinero for you," Beck said somberly.

Luz took a deep breath. She looked at the ground then up at the Captain. *"¿Dinero para me? Entonces nos vamos."*

Beck felt his arm yanked hard as a heavy barge on a short hawser. He stumbled to the side, caught himself, and tried to resist. She was the more powerful boat in the block. He followed her across the street until he was able to get her to stop. "I'm not going up there," he said shaking his head. "I'm going to my boat."

With all the conviction of a harbor pilot talking to a foreign helmsman, she pointed at the row of windows above the bar's sign. *"Ahora, mi habitación,"* she insisted, then switched her hand toward the refinery. *"En la mañana, vas a tu barco."*

He was at a loss why this girl refused to take his money. If he spoke Spanish perfectly, he would tell her that he enjoyed dancing with her and that he would love to do it again. Maybe they could have dinner together. He would also say he found her very attractive. However, he was trying to hang on to a wonderful woman with the same headstrong mentality. Finally, he had sworn to Sam that he was going back to his boat, and he meant to keep his word.

Luz lost her patience. Men were driving her insane. If it wasn't Samito's infatuation, it was the Captain's reticence or Martin's fickle taste. She knew any of the other girls would have taken his money and let him go on his way. Inez would have laughed herself silly at the scene. But Luz understood if she took his money for nothing it would come back to haunt her. His friends would tell him how stupid he'd been. He would be resentful, and it would cost her more lost business than it was worth.

At last, Luz put her back to the Captain as she fished out her key. It took her a few tries to fit it into the lock. She got it in but turned the lock the wrong way. She reversed the action until the catch slid free.

Frankie called from down the street. "Hey! Captain! My tooth is fixed. Good as new."

Both Luz and Beck watched as Frankie bowled down the street like a circus clown on his floppy shoes.

"My choppers," Frankie said pulling back his lips. "White as clouds." There was only one white tooth in there. The rest were broken reeds in a muddy stream.

Luz recoiled from the sight of Frankie's mouth. "Frankie!" she said with such force the bum slammed his mouth shut. "Tell the Captain I won't take his money unless he goes upstairs with me."

Frankie hesitated.

"Tell him!"

"She says she won't take your money unless you go upstairs with her," Frankie said to Beck in English. "I think you should go," he added sounding like the Oracle of Delphi.

"I don't want to get laid," Beck said. "I just want to give her the money because I had a good time and she drove me here."

Frankie's eyes fixed on the fifty-dollar bills. "Give me a hundred dollars. I could get another tooth and chew my food!"

"Tell her," Beck ordered.

Frankie cleared his throat. This time he spoke Spanish. "He says he doesn't want sex. He wants to give you the money because he had a good time." Tears welled up in his eyes as he thought about a hundred dollars for having a good time. These girls were incredibly lucky to have men like the Captain and Samito giving them money the way his teeth gave him pain.

Luz cocked her head. "I didn't tell him we were going to have sex. I told him we were going to sleep upstairs."

This time Frankie translated immediately.

"Like the last time?" Beck questioned.

"You slept with her before?" Frankie asked. "What about Samito? She was his girl."

"Just ask her."

When Frankie put the question to her, Luz nodded her head that it would be like the last time.

Beck surrendered. He took Luz by the hand and started for the stairs.

"Ahem!"

"What?" Beck said glancing over his shoulder.

"Something for the effort, Captain," Frankie said.

Beck tossed one of the fifty-dollar bills at him. Luz followed it across the threshold. She pointed her finger at Frankie. "If you tell anyone he gave you fifty dollars, I'll have you arrested. And if Samito finds out, I'll kill you myself." She ran her finger under her chin to reinforce the point.

"*¡Silencio!*" Frankie said. "My tongue is tied." He moved his hands to form an imaginary knot, then jogged out of sight.

"*Ahora,*" Luz said calming down. What fools these men were! They paid to sleep in strange beds and gave vagrants fifty dollars because they couldn't learn another language. They would be better off spending the money on a tutor the way she was going to do for Hernán. Her son was going to learn English and speak like the Queen of England. Never was he going to stand in a country not his own and depend upon bums to do the talking. As bums went, Frankie was the best kind, but he was still a bum.

Beck sat down on the bed and unlaced his shoes. Luz was on the other side of the room. Unexpectedly, he felt like chatting, probably because he was used to talking to Nicole before they went to bed.

Wearing a nightshirt, Luz approached the bed. Her guest still wore his pants. It was now clear to her what puritans some Americans were. She understood the Captain was not going to have sex with her. Just the same, he didn't have to sleep with his pants on. She pulled the covers back from the pillows, then faced him.

"No sexo," she said waving a finger to make it clear. "*Pero tu pantalones. No necesario.*" She pointed at his legs. She mimed the action of pulling off her jeans.

He got it. "*Pero …*"

"*No espere,*" she said casually waving her hand as if he were a lifelong girlfriend spending the night. Without waiting to see what he did, she slid under the covers and put her head on the pillow. If the silly Captain wanted to sleep in his pants, let him.

Sleeping fully clothed was nothing new or uncomfortable for Beck. During busy nights in the harbor he undressed only to shower. In between shifting barges and assisting ships, he slept atop the blankets, removing only his radio, which hung over his bunk and within arm's reach.

"*Apaga la luz,*" she said, pointing at the ceiling.

He glanced up, saw the light fixture, and made the connection. He walked to the switch, turned off the light, and returned to bed. He then found the courage to take off his pants. With it came the nerve to lay beside Luz with his arm over her hip. She put her hand over his.

"There you go," Upton whispered. "A captain never sleeps better than in the arms of his favorite whore."

"She's not my whore," Beck heard himself say.

"Damn the details," Upton retorted and sailed over the horizon.

FOR THE first time in his life, Sam wished he had a bathtub. He grew up in Aruba at a time when fresh water was scarce and baths were reserved for infants. He saw his first tub in a New York City hotel when he was six years old and on his way to see his maternal grandparents. After Esso built the island's desalinization plant, fresh water flowed like the Mississippi. Still, he never cared about bathtubs. A shower with plenty of pressure was perfect. Today, however, he needed more. He longed to soak in a pool of hot water until the booze leached out of his body.

Staring at the corner where Charlie had installed the shower, Sam saw there was no space for a bathtub. Two people could stand under the nozzle if one was as small as Marci and the other was no larger than he was. His place on the beach was going to have a tub the size of a swimming pool, just in case he wanted to jump in from the doorway.

He staggered out of the bathroom thinking this hangover was a record-breaker. He felt more dizziness than pain. The bed was only a few steps away, but he didn't make it. He slid down the wall and sat on the floor. A deep breath ended in a coughing fit that woke Marci. She rolled over, looked at him with bright eyes, and asked if he was okay.

"*Estoy bien,*" he lied. He wasn't well at all. As much as he wanted to get up, he remained in the seated position. The floor felt cool. It drew the heat down from his chest, which burned as if he had a raging ulcer.

Marci saw him rub a spot in the middle of his ribs. She swung out of bed, padded around him to the bathroom, and drew a cup of water from the sink.

"*Gracias*," Sam said. He swallowed slowly, then dropped the cup when the pain in his chest expanded to the point where he doubled over on the floor.

"I'll call a doctor," Marci said.

"No!" Sam barked. With his face the same level as his feet, he suddenly felt better. Shallow breaths of cool air diluted the pain. Marci petted his mussed hair. The soft tips of her fingers on his temple distracted him from his suffering. You did it to yourself, he admitted. You drank like an amateur; you smoked like an idiot. Yet, until this moment, you never made a fool of yourself. You were a champion. Didn't the crowd love those fireworks? Weren't your friends in awe at the food you spread out for them? Could any of them dance like you? Not one of them dared. He impressed the Arends Family, his friends, the locals — everyone, including Charlie. He ruled the night! The morning? That was for newbies who didn't know how to live under the moon.

He forced himself into a sitting position. Marci got to her feet and went to the window. He finally took notice of her nudity. What a glorious sight! She reminded him of another girl her age. He had been fifteen when they met. The things she did with him he never managed to repeat with the same intensity. As he sat there on the floor, he recognized his body's appendages were mostly numb, including his loins. A repeat performance of his teenage thrill was out of the question.

"I'm going swimming," Marci said. She pulled a bikini over her twenty-one-year-old hips, snapped the waistband, and took a second to examine her breasts in the mirror. Having confirmed her girlish mounds hung perfectly on her chest, she left the top on the bureau.

Going swimming when he was hurting like this demonstrated an unforgivable lack of class. Instead of bouncing her way to Charlie's pier, she should have been getting a cold washcloth, a couple of aspirin, and a glass of orange juice. A drop or two of vodka would be nice, too. When he was finished with that, she should have helped him onto the bed, where she would rub his shoulders for half an hour until he fell asleep. Then, when he was snoring softly, she could sneak out for a dip in the ocean.

Luz would have taken care of him. She had more class than a New York socialite. It was no fault of his that she got herself tangled up with Martin and Captain Beck and therefore missed out on more incredible nights with the Prince of San Nicolaas. Nonetheless, he refused to blame her. She was doing her job. He didn't like it, but he understood the system.

Marcela was the one screwing up his program by not catering to the clients who really mattered. La Dueña? Hah! Ricardo made that bar what it was, not her.

Charlie altered his routine to avoid Savaneta for the entire day. He was disappointed in Sam the way a father was disappointed in a good son. He understood Sam's character and appreciated the man's love of fun, but there were limits to excess that Sam, of all people, should have known better than to exceed. The price to be paid for going too far was the scorn of those closest to you. Thus, Charlie didn't want to see Sam with his glazed eyes, his vomit-tinged aftershave, and his rattling cough.

He assumed Sam's duties at the bar, which meant entertaining the tourists with tales of Aruban glory and as much booze as they could afford. Tuesdays were usually good days. The time-share people were on the move. The all-inclusive crowd grew bored with their buffets and watered-down drinks. The more adventuresome types, Scuba divers, German hikers, and American mountain-bike riders, were always in attendance. They needed a master of ceremonies. Charlie, in honor of Sam, obliged them. The whole time, he never touched a drop of booze in observance of the eleventh commandment: Thou shall not drink in your own bar.

The midday heat settled things down. Koch pointed at the empty stool near the wall and shook his head. The only one missing was Sam.

Luz had accepted Captain Beck's hundred dollars. Through pantomime and a few Spanish words she understood he had many things to do with his boat. She was in the same position. There was her laundry, a phone call to home, and possibly a visit to Carlotta.

The Captain received her kiss on his cheek the way her brother used to. She wondered if this man would ever desire her in an intimate way. Before she could search his face for clues, his radio spoke to him. He turned the dial, spoke into the microphone, and waited for the reply. Moments later he was gone.

After depositing her clothes at Hop Long, Luz strolled down Main Street and soon met Alison in the Giordano store.

"You're back," Alison said.

"*Sí*," Luz replied. It was only the second time they had met, but Alison started talking like Inez, as if they had been together for months and had done things that made them closer than sisters.

"Be careful," Alison warned. "La Dueña has raised the rent."

"How can she do that?" Luz asked.

Alison was shocked that Luz didn't understand la Dueña's powers. "You should know," she said. "She does what she wants. A girl from Las Vegas Bar tells me the owner of that place heard about it and also charges more for the room."

"How much more?" Luz wanted to know.

"Ten guilders," Alison answered.

Luz calculated how much she owed la Dueña. The increase was about the same as what it cost her to eat every day.

"I also heard the party was unbelievable," Alison was saying. "Is it true there were fireworks?"

"Sí," Luz said, remembering Samito's display.

"What holiday is it?" Alison wanted to know.

"Charlie's Birthday," Luz told her.

They window-shopped along Main Street, passing the time with idle conversation. Alison said that after finishing her three months in Aruba, she planned on terminating her career in the business. Luz shrugged and turned her head. Her first tour of duty was also to be her last. She knew better than to make simple declarations like that. It hurt terribly when she had to go back on them.

As they continued to talk, Luz learned that their stories were remarkably similar. Alison's father was a lawyer. He found himself on the wrong side of a corrupt judge. He lost his job and was now working as a factory clerk. They were having trouble making the payments on their house, which had been purchased when times were good.

On the way back to Hop Long, Luz pointed at Jaime's salon and explained how short her hair had been cut.

"That was over a year ago," she said. "I'm going to do it again. Maybe next month."

"Your hair is beautiful," Alison told her. "Why would you ever cut it?"

"Something different." She told the lie in an attempt to protect Alison from the realities of the profession. Maybe this would be her only trip. Maybe her father would find a position at another law firm, and Alison would be off to college or on to a husband.

They separated upon arriving at Western Union to send money and make their calls home.

"How is Hernán?" Luz asked her sister when the connection was made.

"I think he has a cold," Anna said.

"Does he need the doctor?"

Anna sighed. "He'll be okay. We'll all have it before the week is over."

Luz wanted to ask if Anna had heard from Rudi but didn't. In the week leading up to her departure for Aruba, she had called various truck-repair garages around the city. The ones that had been willing to talk to her said they had no one named Rudi or anyone fitting his description working for them. She had known it was a long shot, but she had to do something. Her mother and sister were paralyzed.

At risk of sending her sister into a crying fit, Luz asked, "Have you heard from Jorgé?"

"He stopped here yesterday."

"What did he say?"

"Nothing. He's a rotten man."

Luz bit her finger then said, "He has his money. He should leave you alone." She cursed herself for not playing things differently with Samito. She should have leapt into his arms, promised him undying love, and let him throw Marci to the boys prowling San Nicolaas. After all, she was with him first. If he wanted her, it was her right to claim him. If Marci made a fuss about it, she would have had to take it up with Samito, who at the time would have told to her to leap into the sea.

"I have to go," Anna was saying. "Phone calls are expensive. We need to save the money."

"You're right," Luz said, and they both hung up.

Hearing Alison laughing in the next booth did nothing to improve Luz's mood. She longed to forget about everything the way Alison seemed to do. It would be nice to live one day at a time without fear of the future.

Charlie drove to his studio, where he continued work on the harbor scene he'd started with Andrés. Around three o'clock, Sam's girl entered his studio. She appeared fresh from the shower.

She said, "Can you take me to Bar Sayonara?"

"I can, but where is Samito?" Charlie asked.

"He is sleeping."

Marci waited a minute as Charlie went to the Dog House to kick Sam out of bed. He didn't bother knocking on the door. He barged in to find Sam on the floor. A moment of panic struck Charlie as he thought Sam might be in the middle of a serious medical emergency.

Sam opened his eyes and managed a weak smile. He regretted his condition in the presence of his patron, but it could not be improved with such short notice. "Do your crown prince a favor, Charles," he said. "Take that girl to San Nicolaas."

"It's going to be expensive," Charlie said. "You're taking the night off, and that is a royal decree."

"By your command, my lord," Sam said and closed his eyes.

As he returned to Marci, Charlie eyed her suspiciously. Girls like her were quick and clever and as dangerous as a leaky boat in a heavy sea.

"Let's go," he said to her without ceremony. "The bus is leaving for San Nicolaas."

Luz told her housemates to have their casa money ready, to be polite no matter how mean la Dueña was to them, and to smile frequently but not like a crazy person. Her explanation was, "You have to forgive her. Running a business like this is very difficult. The men make a mess of the bar. People steal. There are bills to pay and taxes to the government."

The others accepted her logic with wary nods. Elizabeth, who had been there the longest and most likely suffered through a few of la Dueña's terrors, seemed the least certain. Luz looked at her and said, "Think of your worst client, the man who wants to do it without a condom or the one who is so drunk he can't finish. Well, every one of your bad clients is also her bad client. Now multiply that by four. Add the guys who break the billiard cues, who throw up in the bathroom, and who give Spanner and Pablo a hard time. It's enough to make anyone nasty."

A clang sounded downstairs. La Dueña's heels tapped on the stairs. She was in the room with them before Luz's words had dissipated into the walls. "*Buenas noches, chicas,*" she said.

Almost in unison the girls replied, "*Buenas noches, señora.*"

Taken by surprise, Marcela sat down with a smile. She opened the book with her left hand so each of them couldn't miss her giant diamond atop the black cover. "Luz, there has been an increase in the casa," she began.

"*Claro,*" Luz said, "I'm sure you have many expenses."

"More and more every day," la Dueña sighed. "The government is talking about raising the fee for permisos. As if they don't take enough from you girls already!"

With that the complaints ended. La Dueña accepted their money. She wrote their payments into the book using a gold pen Luz had seen in the jewelry store in the lobby of the Hyatt. She wondered if Martin had given her the pen as a gift.

Her business concluded, la Dueña issued a warning. "Stay away from the police," she said. "They are looking for reasons to send you back to Colombia. You don't want that to happen. You'll lose whatever you paid the agent plus the chance to make good money here. Luz will tell you what the police are like, won't you, Luz?"

"*Sí, señora,*" Luz said and fixed her face into a serious stare.

"Good luck tonight, chicas." La Dueña dismissed them except for Luz, whom she asked to accompany her to her car.

Luz had no choice but to tag along like a little girl. She dreaded that icebox of a vehicle.

"I have something to ask you."

"Anything," Luz said.

"This would mean very much to me, and I hope you'll accept."

The second lie came as easy as the first. "*Claro. Por favor, pregúntame.*"

"I would like you to be a part of my wedding."

It was the last thing Luz expected to hear. She heard herself say, "*Gracias.* I would be honored," as she worked through the logic. Of course la Dueña wanted her to be in her wedding. She had disowned her family in Colombia. Her personality kept others from being friends.

"Wonderful!" la Dueña crowed. "I'll reward you for this."

"That's not necessary," Luz said.

Without hesitating, her boss added, "Have you thought about marrying Andrés? We could make it a double."

The forced smile came harder than the lies. "*Sí, pero no,*" she said.

"You know he's an artist? He paints with Charlie."

Under raised brows, Luz widened her eyes and her smile. "I should go, señora. I'm expecting a client early tonight."

"*Tan bueno.* I'll give you the details another time."

Luz could hardly exit the car fast enough. The warm breeze thawed her body, but her soul was still frozen. She feared all her mother's prayers would not get her into heaven. She would have to give Hernán to the church. Her boy would have to be a monk to save his mother from the devil's pitchfork.

✸   ✸   ✸

After checking the weather and conferring with Shahann, Beck called Jack Ford for instructions. Jack wanted *Kathryn* to sail for Philadelphia as soon as the barge was loaded. Beck was glad to hear he only had twenty-four hours to wait. He was anxious to be at sea, off the island with all its temptations and petty rivalries.

Since there were few private places on the boat, Beck went to Herzog's office and used the phone there to call Nicole.

"How is Aruba treating you this time?" she asked.

"*Muy bien,*" he answered lightly. "Sam, the guy who found me is here."

"Again?"

"I understand he wants to live here permanently."

"Sounds like a small place," Nicole said. "Won't he get tired of it?"

"With people from all over the world," Beck told her, "it makes it feel bigger."

"Interesting."

"It is," he said. It occurred to him that a woman like her was not a "sailing wench," as Upton would have put it. She danced in expensive shoes on polished floors, not in bare feet on the sand. She didn't share her bed easily. She avoided bums with rotten teeth. Hard drinkers and whoremongers were not among her circle of friends.

"Are you there?" Nicole was saying.

"Sorry," he replied. "I'll have some days off when I get home. Let's make up that weekend."

"We can talk when you get here," Nicole said.

"I'd like that," he said and hung up.

He passed the day touring the refinery with Herzog, who was assessing the facility's urgent requirements. They took a launch around the natural harbor along which the complex had been built. Herzog pointed out places where the piers needed repairs and asked Beck's opinion. Beck told him what he thought should be the highest priorities and what could wait.

"I think we'll have the first unit on line in no time," Herzog said. "Then the tankers will start coming, and I'm going to need a tug to help them to the dock."

"What about the one that works with the cruise ships in Oranjestaad?" Beck asked.

"Lots of mechanical problems," Herzog replied with a roll of his eyes.

Another opportunity for a captain and his boat was sliding past Beck.

In light of his pending departure, Beck decided to go into town for a few hours. He checked in at the boat, making sure everything was secure. On his way through the galley, a deckhand asked him what girl he was going to see.

Shahann answered for him. "He's a love-sick man. He doesn't consort with whores. Isn't that right, Master Beck?"

"I'll have a look, but I don't need to touch," he said.

"See that boys. He's tied to a whipping post that may belong to another man when he's not in port."

Instead of rising to the insult, Beck exited the room. The breeze came hard out of the east-northeast, pressing his shirt against his skin as he walked toward Java Bar. It would have been the death of him had the breeze been from that direction when he drifted away from *Patricia*. He pulled up short at the sight of Frankie.

"Thanks to you I have an appointment with the dentist," Frankie said. "I'm getting another tooth to match this one."

"Good for you," Beck said.

"Maybe a guilder for something to eat, Captain. I need my strength to face the pliers."

Beck gave him a guilder and a few minutes later he passed Charlie's. The man wasn't on his veranda. However, the cat sat on the parapet looking down at the street. Beck continued on, not slowing as he walked under the sign for Minchi's. He ducked into Java before the idea of hiring Luz as his Spanish teacher took root.

"Another paying customer," Kenny said to greet him. "The usual?"

"Have I been coming here long enough to have a usual?" Beck asked.

"Here a day is a week, a week is a year, and a year is a lifetime," Kenny explained. "You can meet a girl, fall in love, and break up in the space of a single evening. A usual drink comes with the territory."

"Charlie warned me not to fall in love," Beck said.

"I should have taken that advice. I fell in love with one of these whores, went to Colombia, married her there, brought her back here, and you know what happened?"

"I can't imagine."

"You don't have to imagine because I can show you the evidence. Her husband, the one she was still married to when she married me, came to collect her. He smashed my nose, too. Cheers, eh?"

"Where is everyone?" Beck asked next.

"They're probably at the Cunucu. It's a fried chicken joint at the east end of town. They like to eat there to keep their cholesterol level high enough to protect them from all the booze they drink."

"Does that work?"

Kenny laughed. "I hope so. If not, I'll soon be losing my best customers to cirrhosis of the liver. Meantime, what do you think of my girls?"

Beck looked them over. "They look pretty enough."

"Not a bad crew," Kenny said, "I'm hoping this refinery brings about two thousand of you Americans here. These girls will have to sleep on their stomachs because their backs will be sore."

They had two more drinks before Beck excused himself to go for another walk. On the other side of the street, he saw Frankie panhandling and Speedy slumped against his tree near Bongo Bar. He broke his previous oath to stay away from Minchi's.

There were a dozen people in the bar. Four men stood around the pool table. They played a noisy game and lined their empty beer bottles along the windowsill. Several more sat at the bar with the girls. A middle-aged man with some gray in his hair was beside Luz. Beck saw a crystal bottle next to her flute of vino.

"Up here, Captain," Spanner called from the end of the bar. "You're just in time."

"What's that?" Beck asked when he was beside the bouncer.

"This man with your girl."

"She's not my girl," Beck groused. "She's Sam's."

"She's the one who found you. That makes her your girl."

"Okay."

"This man was her client last year. The problem for him is a jealous wife. So, he brings the girl the same perfume his wife uses. Now when he goes home, he smells like his wife and has nothing to worry about. The man is a genius." Spanner laughed hysterically, and Pablo couldn't keep a straight face as he poured Luz another vino.

Beck watched Luz look up at Pablo, then down the bar at him. He smiled with the side of his mouth. She focused on the client without giving him any sign of recognition.

"There he goes," Spanner said as quietly as if they were watching a golf match.

As Beck turned his head, Luz slid her keys off the bar with one hand and took her client's arm with the other.

"The man is smarter than all the men in San Nicolaas, don't you think?" Spanner said.

"Smarter than most," Beck agreed. He nearly said "smarter than me" because the man knew what he wanted and had found a way to get it with the least amount of trouble. Beck, on the other hand, didn't want Luz as a sex toy, the way the guy with the perfume did. He wanted her for something else. Exactly what that was he wasn't sure. He'd like to have her as a sister of sorts, someone he cared for and about, someone to stay close to. It wasn't logical, but it made him bitter to see her go upstairs with another man. What right did he have to feel that way? Just because she found him on the beach didn't make her his ward. He slept two nights in her bed. These things entitled him to nothing. Yet he sat at the bar, glaring at his half-finished drink, wondering what would happen if he bolted up the stairs after her. He decided he had to go to sea before he humiliated himself. He left the drink behind and headed for the door.

On the sidewalk, Beck encountered two guys threatening Speedy and Frankie. The bigger one had his fist up. He poked it at Frankie, who cowered in the face of a man who had never skipped a meal. Speedy crawled on all fours. The smaller guy kicked him in the ass, then cackled over the bum's sprawled body.

Beck crossed the street without looking. He slid between two parked cars and around the tree Speedy used as a chair. The smaller guy saw Beck's movement. Turning too late, the guy flew against the wall when Beck shoved him out of the way and zeroed in on the bigger one.

"You don't look like his brother," the bigger guy said with a heavy accent and pointing at Frankie.

Wasting no time, Beck landed a right cross on the guy's jaw. He followed it up with a solid left to his stomach. The guy reeled back, tripped over his own feet, and landed hard on the seat of his pants.

"This isn't America, you fucking gringo," the smaller guy said.

"I'll show you where America is," Beck said. He reared, spun on his heels, and caught his second victim in his left hand. He held the guy's shirt and jabbed him three times with his right fist. When he released his grip, the guy slid down the wall with blood oozing from his nose and mouth.

Neither of them had anything more to say.

Beck looked for Frankie and Speedy, but the chollers were gone. He wiped his hands on his pants and headed down the street. At the alley that crossed to Rembrandtstraat, he ran into Shahann, who was leaning on the corner of the building.

"You might be part Irish," Shahann said to him. "You fight like it, anyway."

"You want to go a round?" Beck growled. It was the right time and place to settle the score.

"That would be assaulting a fellow officer," Shahann replied and sauntered down the block.

Beck let him go. It was the wise thing to do. He headed for the refinery gate, where the comfort of his boat waited on the other side.

Naturally, Charlie and Screwball saw the whole thing from the veranda. He was late getting back from his girlfriend's but early to his ringside seat.

"Fists fly for two reasons," Charlie said to Screwball. "Love or money, and I suspect that sailor already has a boatload of money."

LUZ COULD not decide which was worse, the interminable hours of the night spent waiting for clients or the endless afternoons whiled away pondering what type of night it was going to be. She thought about going to the hotels to see if there were jobs there and, if so, how much they paid. She also considered buying a cell phone. She overheard several girls talking about how convenient they were compared to waiting for a booth at Western Union. At last she decided to visit Carlotta, whom she had not seen since returning to Aruba.

"¡Niña!" Carlotta squealed when Luz came up to the bar. "You look beautiful."

Luz stopped, looked down at herself, then back at Carlotta. The older woman had her arms wrapped around her a few seconds later. A cloud of perfume nearly choked her, but Luz kissed Carlotta's cheeks and sat down on a low chair against the far wall.

"This job can ruin some girls," Carlotta said, "but you look perfect, like the day you took your first communion."

The comment sent another wave of guilt over Luz as she thought about the vow she'd made upon her return to Colombia, the one about living a clean life. The idea of confession came to mind. Carlotta, better than any priest, knew what this life was like. Luz told her a few facts about her return. When she finished, Carlotta patted her knee.

"I only wish you had come to work here," Carlotta said. "Here you have a friend. At Minchi's you have a master."

Luz had thought of working at Sayonara. She worried it would have ruined her friendship with Carlotta, just as having an affair with Señor Garcia would have been a problem. And if la Dueña had discovered that she intentionally chose a different place, who knew what trouble she would cause?

"I'm sorry. The agent never mentioned you had an opening," Luz lied.

"It's okay. You come to see me when you could be at the beach with a high-paying client. But listen to me when I tell you, that witch is dangerous."

"I know." Then, without thinking, she let slip a comment that a moment later she regretted. "She's going to marry a man named Montoya."

Carlotta slammed her foot on the floor. "Montoya!" she shouted. The girls and customers spun to see what she was yelling about. "He owns China Clipper!"

For the next ten minutes, the woman experienced a mild seizure as she ricocheted around the room, smacking her hand on the bar, slamming chairs under tables, and chopping the metal scoop into the ice cooler. A few men sitting in the corner laughed at her, but none of the girls dared a smirk. They stared into their vinos and urged the men to take them upstairs. Finally, Carlotta stopped in front of the sink, drew a glass of water, and drank it without stopping for a breath. Seeing her lipstick smudged on the glass made her chuckle. She rinsed it clean and returned to her chair beside Luz, who had chewed half the nail away from her index finger.

Carlotta gently pushed the hand away from Luz's mouth. "You're a beautiful girl. That habit makes you look ugly."

"I'm sorry, señora."

"Marcela has him trapped the way all men are trapped. The man is not at fault; he is acting like a man. She is the evil one. She takes advantage of his weakness. She could give him love, babies, a home to be proud of. But what does she do?"

Luz knew better than to interrupt with the answer.

"She steals from the dead," Carlotta whispered, adding the sign of the cross. "Let me guess, she will have Ricardo's son, that poor boy, at her wedding with Montoya. She needs another person, too, a woman."

Luz covered her face and wept. She felt as if she had betrayed Carlotta, her dear friend who gave her excellent advice that made her life endurable. She wanted to run out of the bar and hide with Frankie and Speedy. She felt the madam's hand rubbing her back.

"I know," Carlotta said. "You must do what she tells you." She got a clean towel from behind the bar and gave it to Luz. "Ricardo's boy, Andrés, he's a good boy. He wants to study painting in Holland, where all the great painters came from except the ones from Spain. Charlie is helping him, but Charlie told me himself there is no one who can teach the boy what he already knows."

"Have you seen any of his pictures?" Luz asked.

"No. I only hear about them from Charlie."

They both stared into space for the next several minutes. Luz considered her options to make a graceful exit. She carried the towel behind the bar, where she put it neatly on the pile with the other dirty ones.

Carlotta got to her feet. "Come back to me," she said. "Tell me everything that happens. These men, they cannot see the fire that burns at their feet until it touches their whiskers. We must look out for them. Do you understand?"

"I understand," Luz replied. She stepped into the afternoon sun thinking about the Captain. She had taken care of him, hadn't she? Turning south on Main Street, she mulled over how to teach Hernán to be a man who could perceive reality for what it was and deal with it accordingly.

The beach curved inland like a crescent moon away from the sea. About a hundred yards out, a slight chop dimpled the surface. Between the two clusters of mangroves, Sam's cove was as calm as the water in the giant bathtub he was going to put in his new house. He proved to Luz that this was the perfect place to swim, to snorkel, or to put your feet in the saltwater as the sun went down. It was time to make it habitable.

"I made eighty years two months ago," Hans Krauss said to him.

"You should have called me. I would have thrown you a party," Sam told the man from whom he had won the land.

"Ahch! I heard about those parties," Krauss said pointing toward Charlie's pavilion. "Something like that is too much for an old man like me."

"I remember some wild card games back at the Esso Club."

"That's why we moved them to your father's house," Krauss explained. "They threw us out of the club."

"I know the feeling," Sam added.

"You know my daughter lives in Orlando, Florida. She has two boys of her own. They've never been to Aruba."

"They don't know what they're missing."

Krauss took off his hat, wiped his forehead, and plopped the cap back over his bald head. "Maybe it's better," he said. "We lived in a different time."

"It's the same as ever," Sam put in.

"That may be true. I haven't been to San Nicolaas in years. Not the way we used to go."

"I still go," Sam reminded him.

"My daughter, her husband, her sons, they don't want to live here. It's too small, they say. They see an oil refinery and they think it's ugly, dirty. I loved that place. It gave me a good job. I earned big money as a young man. I traveled to Europe. I bought a house and this piece of land and I still had money in my pocket for a night out with my wife or my friends. Now? I don't know. My grandsons turn their noses up at places that make smoke and noise."

It was men like Krauss who had influenced Sam's childhood. He witnessed the trajectory of their lives. He saw that it was a steep arc, one which spanned the geographic hemisphere as well as the distant reaches of human experience. Sam followed the same path. His life began in Aruba, stretched out to the United States, and went over the borders of several continents. It was time to return to the beginning. This house and Luz were part of the homecoming package. It was the place in the sunset, and she was the girl. They were the hero's rewards for noble deeds done in the face of insurmountable odds.

"I'm glad you're building here," Krauss said. "I hope I live to see it."

"You can cut the ribbon," Sam told him.

"Tell my doctor that," Krauss scoffed. "He says this is wrong with me, that is wrong with me."

"What does he know?" Sam asked.

"Only what the tests tell him." Krauss examined a pile of rocks Sam had stacked at one corner of the property. "Don't let the government tell you a word about what you build here," he said. "The deed is unrestricted. You can do what you want. You can put a pier out in the water there and tie a super tanker to it if you want."

"Just a little house," Sam interjected.

"Make it a nice one. Traditional. A Cunucu house with thick walls, louvered windows, and the kitchen on the end."

"*Exactamente.*"

"You always listened to reason, Sam. Drive me home. I think I was supposed to take a pill or something."

They got into Sam's car and drove into the hills where Krauss lived alone. Sam sorted the bottles of pills, found the right one, and shook out a tablet for the man who had been one of his father's best friends.

"The lawyers will do the paperwork?" Krauss asked after swallowing the pill.

"They always do."

"Good. Let them earn some money for moving the pen instead of their mouths for a change. Bring it to me, and I'll sign it whenever you like."

"The transfer tax is on me," Sam said. "A belated birthday present."

"*Danki*," Krauss said. "It's probably money you won from a high-class casino on the other side of the bridge."

The money was actually from his savings. He hadn't been to a casino in months. He sat with Krauss until the old man dozed off. Before taking his leave, he looked around at the home. It was precisely what he wanted to build.

☀   ☀   ☀

"The Lord has sent us an angel!"

So deep in thought was Luz that she'd lost track of where she was. She stopped short, looked to her right, and saw Charlie seated with his back to the bar. His smiling face and open arms expunged her worries. She accepted his welcome, saluting him with a kiss on the cheek.

"You must have been with my honorary wife, Carlotta," Charlie said. Her perfume is a rare type brought from distant India. I would know the scent if I stood in the middle of a million Colombian roses."

Luz searched his eyes to see if he was serious.

"You can also buy it at a tourist shop in Oranjestaad."

Charlie, Koch, and Luz shared the laugh. Sensing Luz was still distracted by something serious, Charlie offered to share a cold drink with her.

"Have a seat in the booth over there," he told her in Spanish. "The one in the corner that the newlyweds always take. I'll get us a Coca-Cola and meet you there."

Luz took the seat Charlie offered. She smiled at the couples in the room. They looked like the Americans she saw at the Hyatt Hotel. Most of them were sunburned and overweight. They seemed so happy they might explode with joy. She vowed to someday visit America if only to see what a place was like that produced people like this.

On his way to the table, Charlie glanced out the window that fronted on the street named after his father. He squinted to be sure the person out there was the one he thought it was. There was no mistake. The man had a radio on his hip and a serious scowl on his face.

"Screwed again," Charlie said quietly. He put the Cokes on the table in front of Luz and said he would be right back. At the door he met Captain Beck. "Come in, Captain," he said. "Your table is waiting."

This was the type of greeting Beck wished his father would give him someday. Or even Shahann. With them, it was always an uneasy process of breaking the ice. With Charlie, it was a salutation for the prodigal son.

"I was coming to say good-bye," Beck said.

"This I already knew," Charlie said. "You see, we are linked telepathically. I can hear what you are thinking." Sly as the Judas goat, Charlie steered Beck into the bar, around two tables, to the booth where Luz sat sipping Coca-Cola. He said to her in Spanish. "You don't mind sharing the table?"

Luz glanced up, saw Beck was as surprised as she was, and started to rise off her seat.

"You don't have to get up," Charlie said. "He may be a captain, but his boat sank, which makes him nothing but a castaway."

Luz smiled nervously. She lowered herself onto the bench as Beck took his place.

As he sat with Luz, Beck couldn't help but think what a fool he was. He had no business drinking himself into oblivion, sleeping in the same bed with whores, and protecting bums from thugs. San Nicolaas was not his home port. Luz was not his woman. He was not the protector of the weak. Philadelphia was where he belonged; Nicole was his woman; and there were policemen to handle assault and battery. Then he heard Upton's ghost laughing at him.

"Captain or not, the sailor's life is yours," Upton said.

It only took another glimpse of his knuckles to damn Upton's ghost. Upton had come up half a century before Beck. It wasn't a time of pirates and wenches, nor was it akin to Viktor Beck's social club at the University of Pennsylvania. Upton drank, whored, and fought in every port from Bangor, Maine, to Brownsville, Texas. In between, he had his five marriages, never sired a child that he knew of, and left his final and first wife (who happened to be the same woman) enough insurance money to forgive him. For Beck, it was completely different. He worked around boats as an adolescent. He was exposed to Upton's stories and people who confirmed them as true. However, he never lived that way. He earned excellent grades in school, went to work for Jack Ford, and when he encountered Nicole Reston, was sure he would marry her someday. Furthermore, as much as he enjoyed Sam's company, Beck recognized the guy lived in an alternate universe, one that Beck had found interesting to visit but too intense in which to remain.

Upton's voice was back in his ear. It said, "If you're going to sail into the wind, you better learn to tack."

Looking at Luz, Beck figured it was best to enjoy a few minutes of her company and make a polite escape. She deserved his respect, and as a captain, he was happy to honor her with it. They spoke formally, exchanging a few phrases that they both understood.

"*¿Y cuando regresa?*" Luz asked, wondering if he would want to share her bed again when he returned.

He interpreted the words without exactly knowing them. "*No se,*" he said. Luz's words blurred together, and he put no effort into figuring them out. They finished their drinks quietly, under the mindful eyes of Koch and Charlie. Then Luz looked at her watch. It was nearly four o'clock, and she needed at least a nap if she were going to make the most of the coming night.

"*Tengo que ir,*" she said. "*Gracias por todo, Capitán.*"

Beck rose from his seat. He stood rigidly, the way his father did on the few occasions he saw him. As inappropriate as it was, he reached to shake her hand. But she was too close, already rising on her toes to kiss his cheek. He savored the touch of her lips on his skin.

"*Ciao, Capitán,*" she said. "*Hasta luego.*" On her way out the door, she waved to Charlie and Koch.

Beck heard a woman at another table say, "What a nice couple." He was pleased with himself for not getting caught up with Luz one more time. For a change, he was thinking clearly. But there was a part of him that had rubbed off Captain Upton and clung like thick fog over warm water. Every time he thought he had a clear view, a swirl of intrigue and desire socked him in. Thankfully, he had avoided the trap. He was leaving in a matter of hours, heading back to Nicole if she would have him.

Charlie came up beside him.

"I'd like to put that girl out of my mind," Beck said to him with a hand toward the now empty booth in the corner.

"Get another one," Charlie instructed. "That's what Sam did."

"What if the next one is better than this one?" Beck inquired.

"I am a professional," Charlie declared. "Call me immediately."

A cold shower invigorated Sam to the point where he was ready to speed into San Nicolaas for a look around. His pals had to be there, probably at Java or Caribbean. If someone else kicked it off, they knew how to keep the party going, but they were no good at getting it started. Fortuitously, he was in the mood to prime the pump. He donned his cane cutter shirt, put both legs into his pants at once, and slipped into his loafers before grabbing a fresh pack of cigarettes off the bureau.

The refinery flares weren't there to guide him in, but he made a perfect landing. He parked directly below Charlie's balcony. There was no better place in all of San Nicolaas. A late night rendezvous with Luz was just what he needed to celebrate his deal with Krauss. In a flash, he was out of the car. He slammed the door, pressed the button on the key fob to lock it, and took a step toward his idea of the perfect woman.

"You're just in time," Charlie called down to him.

"Just in time is right," Sam called back.

"Come up here. I want to show you something."

Sam held back a grimace of frustration. If he made it to Minchi's in the next ten minutes, he was guaranteed a night with Luz, either in her room or back at his. If he dithered with Charlie, there was a chance another client would take her away. However, he could not deny the King. He hurried up the stairs and greeted Charlie with a bow.

"So young and full of energy," Charlie said. "You must have made a deal with the devil while you were dead."

"Not dead yet," Sam said.

"I thought maybe you were."

"What is it you wanted me to see?"

Charlie pointed out beyond the refinery. "There's a man out there who knows what he's doing."

In the distance, Sam saw *Kathryn*'s navigation and deck lights. He thought back to a time when he had been on the veranda with Charlie's father. The old man liked to watch the ships come and go through a pair of giant binoculars.

"He's got that barge in the channel now. Can you figure out which way he's headed?"

"I know port from starboard," Sam said. He glanced down the street and was glad to see Minchi's had not yet closed.

"I wasn't sure."

Charlie's tone was not lost on Sam. The trouble was, he felt too good to commence an apologetic appeal. He wanted to hop, skip, and jump down the street to Minchi's. If he passed Frankie or Speedy along the way, he would give them ten guilders just to share the joy.

"He'll be rounding the point of the reef in a few minutes," Charlie announced.

Sam tapped out a cigarette then offered the pack to Charlie.

"No," Charlie said, "Screwball wants me to quit. He says the stink never leaves his fur."

"Beck's boat is the only thing passing the anchorage," Sam commented.

"Not for long. Already there are people in town I don't recognize. Behind them will come the ships. With all due respect to Captain Beck, his barge is not big enough for this business. This is the age of the ultralarge crude carrier. The bigger the better."

"The more the merrier," Sam added.

"Not in every case," Charlie corrected him.

This time Sam did not return fire. He knew it was not a night to push his friend. They stood there together until *Kathryn* was fading from sight.

"That's the end of the show," Charlie said when only the white stern light of the tug could be seen.

"Good evening, Charles," Sam said and went down to the street, noting the bright lights at Minchi's.

"Take your car," Charlie said from the balcony.

Having finally lost his patience, Sam retorted, "I don't need my car!"

"Yes, you do. You need to take your car, stop at the corner, look both ways, and make a left turn. Where that street ends, make another left turn. Follow that to the little snack shop and make a right. Go two more blocks, then make another left …"

"I know the way home," Sam protested.

"You forget sometimes," Charlie said and withdrew from the parapet.

For a few seconds, Sam stared at the sky behind the space where Charlie had stood. In the absence of the refinery flares, the stars shone brightly. Over his shoulder, the lights were on at thirty-two bars.

He leaned on the hood of his car to finish his cigarette. The town of his birth surrounded him like a venerable old museum. The alleys were its cloisters; the streets were grand galleries. The artwork on display here meant more to him than anything he'd seen at the Met during those summer trips with his parents. San Nicolaas was a place where patrons like him lived what day-trippers only imagined. They sat at Charlie's, listened to his stories, and sighed. "If only …," they said. If only they could live in a place like this. If only they had a house on the beach where they could toast the sunset every night. If only they could find a way to leave it all behind. He didn't need to find a way. It was his birthright.

He tossed the finished cigarette into the gutter. It occurred to him that more than a year had passed since he'd met Luz. She was in her second tour of duty, which didn't bode well for her life back in Colombia. Every chica had her reason for coming to San Nicolaas. Not all of them were tragedies. He hadn't discovered much about Luz during her four nights with him. They were too busy having fun to dwell on life's tribulations. The thing was, if she wanted him to, if she allowed him to, he would make every day like that. Charlie liked to kid him about his habit of falling for particular girls. Those affairs were petty dalliances compared to his feelings for Luz. He had hosted private picnics, snorkeling trips, and club-hopping evenings in Oranjestaad, but no one had visited his personal slice of beach except for Luz. She deserved it since he expected sooner or later she would be living there with him. If that was his objective, he needed to get to work. He wasn't leaving an executive suite for the Dog House or a tent on the beach. A house that took six months to build in the United States required two years in Aruba. The permits alone sat on various desks for more than half a year. Then there were the inevitable delays for Carnival, Navidad, and midsummer vacations. The time between now and his one-way ticket seemed much shorter when he put it in this context.

As Charlie had instructed, Sam stopped at the first corner, looked both ways then turned left. He accelerated around the second turn, letting the dirt fly from his tires. The sooner he got out of town, the sooner he could come back.

29

THE NEXT day, Sam suffered through two hours of waiting at the notaris, a quasi government official that handled land transfers, for an unscheduled appointment and another hour filling out the paperwork. To put himself in the right frame of mind, he stopped at Charlie's. He needed at least two vodka tonics to erase his built-up aggravation. At the bar, Herr Koch slapped a coaster down and didn't bother asking if he wanted the usual. Sam was showing all the signs of a man ready to launch himself into his favorite pastime. His smile was on full power. His body rocked to Charlie's salsa music. He lit off more jokes than a stand-up comedian.

Tourists piled in. Sam rang the bell that hung over the bar, thereby granting a free drink to everyone on a stool. It cost him fifty-six dollars, and he didn't care. Since he already ruled the night, it was time to conquer the day. The tourists thanked him, then returned the favor threefold.

Two buses full of men drove down Main Street.

"There they go," Koch said.

"Who?" Sam wanted to know.

"Another group of workers for the refinery. Colombians and Venezuelans."

"What about the locals?"

"I hear the ones they want are already inside. The others? I don't know. There are about two-dozen Americans. They came when you were in the recovery ward."

"I'll have to offer my services," Sam said. "They'll need a guide, or they'll be lost in this jungle."

"The company has rented those last couple houses in the old colony," Koch went on, waving his hand toward the area known as Seroe Colorado, where Esso had originally built an entire town for its American employees.

"What's old is what's new," Sam said. He turned on his stool and delighted a pair of couples with tales of his childhood. He washed a dozen cars a day for money he gambled on card and dice games. He escaped his father's curfew and crawled over the wall to avoid the guards at the main gate, all so he could visit a local girl who lived in Lago Heights. The girl's brother caught him one night. He sprinted through town and scrambled over the wall just in time to escape the beating of his life.

"And just think," Koch said, "You're still doing it."

Sam fired his finger-pistol at the bartender and rang the bell again. A cheer circulated through the bar. It was loud enough to be heard down the street, where a caravan of tourists was asking a local guy for directions to Charlie's Bar. The local pointed up the street at Sam, who had moved to the sidewalk with a drink in his hand, a cigarette in his mouth, and a look on his face that said, "How dumb can you be?"

The clerk at Western Union counted Luz's money twice, checked that her form was correct, and then used her computer to print Luz a receipt. Her transaction complete, she sat on a plastic chair until a telephone was available.

Through the window, she watched the tourists at Charlie's. She saw Samito standing on the sidewalk. He was drunk and drinking more. She wished she had seen him earlier. He might have offered her lunch or a trip to Savaneta for a swim. She laughed to herself when she realized Samito had given her as much money as Martin and nearly as many gifts, but he had yet to have sex with her. She had seen him in town but not in Minchi's.

In those intervening days, Luz had secured her regular clients. The married man came twice, and another guy she suspected of having a wife also went upstairs with her three times in four days. From a health-risk standpoint, she preferred married clients. They were less likely to have a disease and never questioned the use of condoms. The other men that came through the bar bought her a few vinos, chatted if they spoke enough Spanish, or felt her up if they did not. She earned money to pay the casa but not the fortune she had made with Inez.

There were Americans who had come in, too. They fell into two categories: the kids in the candy store and the nervous husbands. The first bunch rushed upstairs; the second group paced around the bar trying not to get caught staring lustfully at girls who were the same age as their daughters.

One American, Patrick, seemed more comfortable than the rest. He talked with the bartenders, the locals, and the girls. He was *"tranquilo,"* as Luz had told Alison when she asked about him. Alison taught her a word the Americans used for someone like that. "Cool," she said. "He's cool." Luz repeated the phrase. She found it difficult to shape her mouth properly in order to pronounce it as well as Alison.

Patrick bought her vinos for an hour and a half. He asked her if she wanted to play pool. She said she would rather dance, but he didn't know how. They compromised by sitting at the bar telling each other little pieces of their histories. He had worked at refineries around the world, including Mexico and Venezuela, where he had learned Spanish. He had been in Aruba only three days and had a ten-week contract. She told him she had been at Minchi's a short time. She said nothing of her previous trip.

He turned her down for a trip upstairs, saying he'd like to go to his house. She said that sounded wonderful but she was forbidden to leave the bar while it was open. La Dueña's rules were back in force now that Martin had gone, Charlie's party was over, and Calenda had checked everyone's permisos.

"Perfecto," Patrick said. "I'm starting the night shift. I finish around three in the morning. I'll pick you up when the bar closes."

Luz neither accepted nor declined. Instead, she shrugged with one shoulder the way she always did. She was used to a hundred dollars per night. If he wanted to pay that, she was willing to give it a try. For nothing more than a different bed, the possibility of breakfast, and the pleasure of his company? She was going nowhere for that.

Anna answered the phone in the same dejected tone she used since Rudi had left them.

"I sent a hundred ninety dollars," Luz informed her. "It may be two weeks before I can send more."

"We'll stretch what you gave us."

"Did Rudi call?"

"No."

"Maybe you should call the police?" Luz suggested.

"We thought of that," Anna shot back.

"I'm sorry, Anna. I'm trying to help."

"I'm here taking care of your son, and you don't know how much work that is! This job never ends!"

"Listen, I only meant …"

"We don't have a man in this house, Luz. Mother and I are alone here. We wait by the phone for Rudi to call. What if he's dead? What are we going to do then?"

At a loss for words, Luz took a deep breath. "Maybe mother could watch Hernán, and you could go to work for Señor Garcia. I could ask him to hire you."

"Don't start giving orders," Anna retorted. "We can do what we have to."

Luz doubted they could. Rudi was the center of their universe. With him gone, they were lost.

"I'm not giving orders, Anna," Luz pleaded. "You have to listen to me."

Anna cut her off. "What's the sense," she said.

It took Luz a few seconds to realize the line was dead. She stared at the receiver and wondered what she had done.

She left Western Union bound for the electronics shop that sold cell phones. A teenage boy named Harry managed the store. He bored her with the depth of his knowledge. He explained the features of every phone, the pros and cons of their battery lives, and how to change the ring tones to something catchy. She was lucky, he told her, because the phones he sold would work in Colombia as well as Aruba. All she needed was another microchip, which he would be happy to sell her. After an hour, he got down to the price. The phones ranged between seventy-five and three hundred dollars. Prepaid cards added calling minutes to the phone. A call to Colombia cost fifteen cents per minute, exactly the same as it did at Western Union.

"With one of these," Harry said, "you don't have to wait in line. If your family or your boyfriend wants to reach you, they simply dial. Get a nice leather case and wear it on your belt like this." He twisted to show her how the phone hung at his waist. It reminded her of Captain Beck's radio except the phone was much smaller.

She needed several more clients before she could afford to buy the phone. "*Gracias,*" Luz said and left the store.

She retrieved her laundry, picked up a few things at la Bonanza, and bought a fruit smoothie from the stand at the end of Rembrandtstraat. She fretted over her family and her son and if she would make enough money to pay the casa. Without a new client she would be broke in two nights. Why had she wasted her time looking at cell phones?

She tossed the empty cup into the trash and sat down on her bed. Once again, she thought of the money she had made with Inez. She considered doing shows with Alison, but the other girls were already leery of her because la Dueña treated her like a pet. They would take the idea of lesbian shows and extrapolate it into her being Marcela's lover. Well, there were Americans in town, and Samito was still on the island. She had two chances there and maybe a third with Patrick.

Rather than closing the blinds, she pulled a pillow over her head. In four hours she would find out who it was going to be: Samito, Patrick, or someone new. She wished the Captain were on the list, but she knew he was gone with his boat. She refused to hold out hope he would return. Too many men had let her down.

The tourists reveled in Sam's magnificent reenactments of island exploits. They plied him with drinks that Koch watered down. Sam started making them himself, and after six hours he could hardly stand. Koch cut him off and promised not to tell Charlie if Sam would leave.

Sam left.

He meandered through town until he happened upon Frankie.

"You look *borracho,*" Frankie said. "Drunk as a skunk."

"How drunk are skunks?" Sam replied.

Frankie scratched his chin. "I don't know, but that's what people say."

Sam swayed back and forth before finding a convenient wall to lean against.

"A guilder is all I need," Frankie was saying.

"If you get me to Sayonara, I'll give you ten."

"Let Frankie be your guide." He hooked his arm around Sam's waist and pulled him off the wall.

"Don't touch me you smelly bastard!" Sam hollered.

At this criticism, Frankie jumped back. Sam nearly fell over, catching himself just in time.

"A man in need can't choose his helper," Frankie said. He ducked around the corner, leaving Sam to get to Sayonara on his own.

He made it. Barely. Had it not been for an alert driver who hit the brakes just in time, he would have been splayed over the hood of a car. For Sam's part, he gave the guy the finger before stumbling up to the door at Sayonara.

Inside, Carlotta put him in a seat at a corner table. The booze on his breath was enough to make her woozy. By the time she got to the ice chest, he was on his feet again. He dropped three guilders in the jukebox and punched buttons without looking. The girls winced at the songs that came out of the machine.

He hauled the nearest girl off her stool and tried to dance with her. It was an exercise in keeping her feet from being crushed beneath Sam's. To the other patrons, it looked like she was jumping on hot coals. Sam found it hilarious. The girl attempted to make light of it, but Sam caught her big toe under his heel. She yelped in pain. The door opened, and a well-dressed man came in. She rushed into his arms, her tear-streaked makeup staining his shirt.

Before Sam could cause any more trouble, Carlotta got him to sit down for a drink. She told him it was vodka, though it was only tonic water with lemon juice. He gulped it, then kissed her hard on the cheek.

Patting his chest, Carlotta said, "Go upstairs. Take a siesta."

"Not alone!" Sam declared. He was off his seat in a flash, but he tangled his feet and landed flat on the floor. Getting up was harder than it had ever been. His arms weren't strong enough to push his chest off the floor. He remembered a time when he used to do forty-five pushups in a minute. He rolled onto his side and noted the clown painting on the wall. It was the happy clown, a laughing mouth under squinting eyes. He laughed, too, and tried again to get up. This time he was able to rise to his hands and knees. A few moments later, he got one foot on the floor, then the other, and then he pressed down at the floor and saw himself rise to eye level with the clown. He pulled his finger-pistol and shot the clown twice for good measure.

"Let me see him give you any more trouble," he said to no one.

Carlotta stood beside him with a plastic bag filled with ice. She said, "Put this on your head."

"What for?" he wanted to know.

"You fell. You hit your head. Put ice on it."

He knocked her hand away. "You can't keep a good man down!" he shouted to the room. He hurtled toward the door, which someone opened a split second before he would have crashed through it.

The gods were smiling upon him at that hour. He careened from the bar into the street, and there was not a car moving in either direction. He stood on the white line, twisting his head from side to side in search of his next destination. He couldn't decide, so he reached for his cigarettes. He peered at the mangled pack for several seconds before tossing it down. This made up his mind. He had to get more smokes.

He turned in the direction of la Bonanza only to face a car that rolled to a stop barely five feet from him. The driver got out, as did the passenger.

"Sam," Chief Calenda said, "there's a welt on your head."

"Why does everyone keep saying that?"

"It seems like you're disoriented, too. Let me give you a ride to Doctor Van Dam."

"That quack!" Sam hollered.

"No need to shout, Sam. Let's have a closer look at that mark on your head."

The driver shined what seemed to be a laser beam on Sam's face. He held up his hands to shield his eyes, but Calenda pulled them out of the way.

Calenda said, "Doesn't look too bad. Not as bad as you're going to feel in the morning for all the liquor you've had."

"I drank more on my sixteenth birthday than you'll ever drink in your life," Sam told him.

"I'll give you a ride to Savaneta just the same."

Calenda took one side and his driver the other. They lifted Sam off his feet, carried him to the car, and shoved him in the back seat. During the ride to Savaneta, no one said a word. When the car stopped, Sam didn't wait for them to help him out. He caught the latch, kicked the door open, and escaped into the night.

Weaving between the palm trees and Charlie's landscaping was one last challenge. He stopped at the door to the Dog House. As drunk as he was, he knew he couldn't be caught here in the morning. He took deep breaths until he heard the police car drive away. When he thought it was clear, he picked his way to the dirt road that led up the beach.

He staggered along the track until he came to the piles of coral that marked the corners of his house. He wanted to pass out in his own home for a change. With that thought in mind, he sat down with his back against one of the piles. He felt the pressure of the rocks against his spine but no pain. His head tilted back slowly until all he could see were the stars.

"*Bon nochi, Luz,*" he said. "*Hasta mañana.*"

☀   ☀   ☀

After paying the casa, getting a stern lecture from la Dueña about how the Americans in town were to be treated, and admonished to sell more vinos, Luz and the girls took stations around the bar. The place was not exactly jumping, but it was more crowded than when she had arrived from Colombia. Spanner and Pablo no longer played backgammon or cards during the first part of the night. They served a steady stream of mixed drinks and beer and tracked pool cue deposits.

Luz serviced her two married men early. Afterward, she circulated with the pool players. Without their asking, she cleared away their empty beer bottles and brought fresh ones. Working the room helped pass the time and kept her moving, which meant on display to the men who came and went.

Around eleven o'clock, the boy from the electronics store came in. He sat at the bar and drank Heineken. Luz stroked her hand down his back and asked his name as if they had never met.

"Harry," he said, grinning and playing along.

She sensed his nervousness. To make him more comfortable, she asked him what phone he thought was the best. He went into one of his long explanations, during which she managed to get him to buy her two vinos. She asked if he wanted to go upstairs.

"Sí," he said, "But …"

"¿Pero?" she asked in a comely way that put him off balance.

He put a phone on the bar. It was the best model. He told her earlier in the day that it cost three hundred dollars. A second chip for use in Colombia was another fifty.

He said, "I could give you this phone."

She replied, "It's beautiful."

"So are you," he said awkwardly.

As she faked a blush for him, she figured out his proposition. She asked him bluntly, "One time and you give me the phone?"

"Six times," he said without looking at her.

She needed cash more than the phone, although it would be convenient to have it. In light of the risks, she bargained. "Three times," she said with her finger pointed at the ceiling. "For the phone and the chip that works in Colombia."

He shook his head and kept his eyes on the phone. He twirled it on the bar.

"Four," she said as she rubbed his leg.

"Nos vamos," he answered.

He insisted on having the lights out. Luz requested permission to take off her dress first. He sat on the bed as she hung it neatly on a hanger. He turned his head when she took off her bra, then looked back for a glimpse of her breasts. From that moment on, he could not avert his eyes. She switched off the lights and waited by the door until she heard his belt buckle clank on the floor.

She felt her way to the bed, holding the condom in her hand. He twitched when she glided her free hand up his leg. His penis throbbed as she rolled the condom over it. Satisfied it was on properly, she asked him if he wanted to be on the top or the bottom.

"Bottom," he said.

Keeping his member in her hand, she swung her leg over his hips. She eased herself down, pointing him at the correct spot. The lubricated condom made entry smooth and easy. He gasped, pulled down on her hips, and thrust up hard enough to lift her off the mattress. She felt him swelling inside her. He pushed back and ejaculated with a moan.

Luz gave him a minute to enjoy the pleasure of his orgasm. As she felt him go soft, she rolled off and found her way to the bathroom. When she had wiped herself clean, she peeked into the room. Harry sat on the edge of the bed, staring at the floor.

Before he left, Harry gave her the original box for the phone and mentioned that prepaid cards were for sale at la Bonanza.

"*Gracias,*" she said and shook his hand the way Señora Álvaro would have, with a firm grip and steady eyes.

During a lull in business, Luz stood in the doorway looking up and down Main Street. She hoped Samito would pass by. While she knew exactly what to expect with him, Patrick's offer was less certain. All of a sudden, Frankie bolted around the corner by Charlie's. He headed straight for Luz, but she couldn't see anyone behind him. He ran past her without a witty comment. Then he pulled up short, stumbled over his peeling sole, and landed in a pile of rags near Java Bar. A police car had turned the corner by the unfinished hotel and was driving the wrong way up Main Street. Frankie gathered himself together and got back to his feet. He hustled sideways toward Luz, his head ratcheting back and forth. An ambulance approached from the correct direction. Another police car blocked the street at Charlie's.

"Hide me!" Frankie cried to Luz.

She reeled into the doorway, but he was already beside her.

"They're coming for me!" he shouted.

Luz followed his gaze as he looked over his shoulder. The ambulance bumped over the curb in front of Bongo Bar. Two paramedics got out of the vehicle. They snapped latex gloves over their hands.

"*¡Por favor!*" Frankie screeched. "Don't let them take me!"

"They're not coming for you," Luz said, seeing that the paramedics were not interested in her side of the street. They brought out a stretcher, laid it on the sidewalk, and waited. Chief Calenda walked up the block from his car. Another cop was at his side, the one who had checked Luz's *permiso.*

"*¡Dios mío!*" Frankie continued. "Let me in!"

"Frankie!" Luz hollered. "Settle down."

"I only have two teeth. They come to take them back. *¡Por favor!*"

The authorities were not there for Frankie's teeth. Calenda stooped down as he spoke to Speedy. Speedy's head rolled back and forth before he toppled onto the sidewalk. With a wave of Calenda's hand, the paramedics put Speedy onto the stretcher. A moment later, they slid him into the back of the ambulance. There was hardly enough time for people in the other bars to see what had happened.

Frankie sobbed against the wall. "They took Speedy," he said. "I'm next. They want my teeth."

Luz said, "Don't worry. They'll leave you alone."

"You have powerful friends," Frankie retorted. "You have men to protect you. Me? No one. Samito? I can't find him. The Captain? He left without me. What am I going to do?"

If Frankie hadn't been crying, Luz would have laughed. But he was genuinely distraught, the way her sister had been when their father had died, when Rudi had left. She heard herself say, "I'll tell Chief Calenda to leave you alone."

"Can you do that?"

She had no influence with the policeman. However, if she happened to see him, she would put in a good word for Frankie. "I will tell him you are no trouble to anyone."

While Frankie scratched his chin, Luz studied his face. A mind of some power lay behind his scruffy features. After all, Frankie spoke three languages, as well as Papiamento.

Frankie stepped back, bowed deeply, and said, "*Gracias, mi princesa.*" He backed away without raising his eyes, fading around a corner to one of his hiding places.

Various groups of locals as well as a few Venezuelans working at the refinery came to Minchi's. They were more interested in drinking than going upstairs. Luz overheard them talking about how the Colombian workers preferred Las Vegas Bar, which meant the chances of encountering someone who would go back to her barrio, talking about having seen someone who looked just like her, were small.

The last hour was always the hardest. If no one was there, Spanner and Pablo played cards or backgammon. The girls gossiped or dozed. If there were people in the bar, it took tremendous effort for Luz to concentrate on appealing to the men. She anticipated the comfort of her bed and the simple pleasure of sleep. The last thing she wanted was to work at coaxing a man up the stairs. He usually would be exhausted and more than likely drunk. There was the possibility she would be stuck with him until morning. This had yet to happen to her, but she heard about it while waiting for the doctor. One time a man had passed out for the night. The next morning he vomited on the floor, left the mess there, and walked out without paying.

Just when she was ready to find a spot to nod off, Patrick came in with two other Americans. He smiled at her, paid the deposit for a trio of pool cues, and went to the table, where his pals had racked the balls. Patrick's presence reenergized her. She and Alison brought them a round of Budweiser. Christina and Elizabeth were too busy talking about their children back in Colombia.

Patrick's friends didn't speak Spanish. They were polite with Luz and Alison, offering to buy a vino each for the pleasure of their company. Patrick told them he would take care of Luz, that they would have to fight over the other one. As his pals chuckled, he translated for Luz.

The three men rotated through several games of pool. Patrick played like a professional. The other two took turns losing to him. He let them break, gave them several free balls, and offered to play left-handed. It didn't matter. He won every time. He knew how to perform trick shots, jumping one ball over another, to the delight of everyone, including Spanner.

"Boy," Spanner said, "you play like Wisconsin Fats."

"Minnesota Fats," Patrick corrected him.

Spanner laughed, then announced it was closing time.

"Come home with me," Patrick said to Luz. It was a command, not a question.

"What about your friends?"

"They'll stay in their rooms," he answered.

She wanted to have Alison or one of the others with her in case she needed help.

"Why don't they take a girl for themselves?" she insisted.

"They don't speak Spanish, and I don't want to translate."

She looked at her watch. "What time tomorrow afternoon?"

"Work starts at three. I'll have you here by two-thirty."

"I can stay in your room?"

Patrick sensed her trepidation. He said, "Only with me. If those guys touch you, I'll club them with this stick." He touched it to the side of his pal's head to make the point.

"Two o'clock?" she asked gently. "I have things to do tomorrow."

"I'll meet you out front."

Not knowing what the day was going to be like, Luz packed only a change of clothes and a few toiletries. When she appeared at the door, Patrick's friends got in the back of his car. As she helped herself to the front seat, she saw Charlie leaning over the parapet of his balcony. She was relieved when he waved to her. Someone knew where she was going.

Sometime around dawn, Sam staggered back to the Dog House and collapsed on the bed. A prolonged nightmare wracked his mind and body. He tried to get up several times without success. At one point, he felt as if he was suffocating. He gasped, thrashed on the bed, and struggled to figure out if he was dreaming or awake. He threw up over the edge of the bed and was powerless to roll away from the rising stink of his own puke. Pounding noises rattled the walls around him. It sounded like slamming doors or hammers beating against the Divi trees. His body ached everywhere. His head felt as if it might explode like the fireworks he'd set off at Charlie's party.

A voice he recognized came to him. It repeated his name over and over. He ignored it as part of the nightmare, but it didn't go away. Then a tidal wave struck his face. He screamed as icy water ran down his chest. When he was doused a second time he bolted upright, wrenching his spine in the process. He yelped at the pain, collapsed on the bed, and mumbled incoherently as the voice continued to call his name.

The torture continued. There was another gush of water. The hammers wouldn't let up. His face turned white hot under what could have only been an open palmed slap. Instantly, he turned lucid. His eyes focused on Charlie, who stood at the end of the bed.

"There you are," Charlie said, "I thought the devil had finally taken your soul."

"What the hell happened?" Sam said. His brain registered that he was incredibly hungover, soaking wet, and shivering.

"You nearly killed yourself," Charlie informed him.

How could I have done that? Sam thought. I had a great time at the bar and then chatted a few minutes with Carlotta. How did I make it out of town? Did I drink so much I blacked out and can't remember? Was I in a car wreck? Did Charlie pull me off the beach like Captain Beck? Is that how I got wet?

"What happened?" Sam repeated without knowing exactly what he was saying.

"You came in here, made a mess of the place by pissing and puking everywhere and letting me catch you at it. I nearly murdered you, and only by the divine intervention of your saint is it that you're alive."

"Which saint?"

"The one who looks after drunks, assholes, and best friends," Charlie said.

"They have one for that?" Sam wanted to know.

"They must or you would be dead. Get in that shower and find some clean clothes when you're finished. You have to be at the airport in less than an hour."

His brain cleared enough for Sam to compute that he had at least four more days before getting on a plane. "It can't be Tuesday. Can it?"

"Call it whatever day you want," Charlie said, "Your seat is waiting on the plane that just brought a bunch of gringos here to get some sunburn and sand in the cracks of their asses." Before Sam could protest further, Charlie exited the room and slammed the door behind him.

After making himself as presentable as possible, Sam sheepishly approached his old friend, who was sitting at the bar. "I don't know what it is," Sam began. "I can't drink like I used to."

"You don't drink like you used to," Charlie said. "You drink too much. You drink too often. This makes you a pain in the ass. Get in the truck."

Charlie got behind the wheel and started the engine. Sam took his spot on the other side. He resisted the urge for a cigarette. He waited to see if Charlie was really taking him to the airport or if he was just trying to scare him. Charlie was not kidding. He drove directly up the main road without slowing until he came to the traffic light at the airport.

"Your ticket is at the counter," Charlie said.

"Charles," Sam said. "I'm sorry. Take me to Savaneta. I'll clean up the room. I'll pay you for whatever I ruined."

"Sam, you need to go home."

"This is home," Sam insisted.

"Not yet."

"Krauss has signed over the land."

"Good. When you come back, you can act like a civilized human."

It made sense to cut his losses and get on the plane. When time passed, Charlie calmed down, and he had an opportunity to visit with a good doctor, Sam could make his apologies and return to the fold with a few black marks on his report card but still a favorite son. After all, the only thing he did wrong was to enjoy himself a little too much. That wasn't a crime here in Aruba the way it was in the United States.

Charlie said, "Have a nice flight."

UNLIKE SAMITO, Patrick had no interest in cooking. He ate cereal with milk while he studied a thick manual for a piece of equipment that was on its way to the refinery. Luz helped herself to half a bowl of cereal, which tasted like pure sugar. When they finished eating, he put the dishes in the sink and led her to the bedroom.

Though a confident lover, Patrick lacked the romance of Martin. At the same time, he wasn't coarse like many of her previous clients or quick the way Harry had been. He liked to watch her perform fellatio. He cupped the side of her head with one hand and held her hair out of the way with the other. With the midday sun approaching its zenith, he laid her down on the bed, put on a condom, and pushed inside her with no foreplay. When he finished, she showered, pulled on her jeans, and found him in the living room with his manual on his lap.

In an attempt to earn as much money as possible, Luz rubbed his shoulders. He told her she was good at that and also at what she did in the bedroom.

"I can cook a little," she offered.

"That's what restaurants are for," he replied. Then he gave her the remote control for the television, which was located in another room.

She took the hint and left him to his reading. Television interested her less than the guide for her new cell phone. It was in five different languages including

Chinese. The instructions baffled her as she tried to decipher them to operate the phone's features. She resigned herself to asking Harry when he appeared for one of his next three sessions.

Patrick touched her shoulder sometime later. He was ready to go to work. He said nothing about money until they turned the corner at the fruit drink stand where Rembrandtstraat began.

"*¿Cuánta vale?*" he said using a phrase that implied a negotiated price more than a fixed one. He was asking her literally, "What's it worth?" as opposed to, "How much?"

"A million dollars," Luz wanted to say. She perceived his test, which fit with his technical personality. She decided to ask for what she had been paid before. If he balked, she would take what he gave her and not go with him a second time.

"A hundred dollars," she said as he stopped behind Minchi's.

"*Bien,*" he said. He paged five twenty-dollar bills from his bankroll.

"*Gracias, señor,*" she said and stepped out of the car.

"See you around the same time," he said through his open window.

She responded with a noncommittal wave, turned her key in the lock, and went through the door.

Harry recommended Luz to his friends and programmed her cell phone during his three follow-up visits. She noticed each of his pals owned not only a cell phone but also several other electronic gadgets. As young as they were, she wondered where they got the money to pay for them as well as her services.

Each Sunday, she met Carlotta at Mass and had lunch with her afterward. The subject of Marcela's pending wedding hung between them.

"And what about Samito?" Carlotta inquired. "He didn't kiss me good-bye. When did he leave the island?"

"I don't know," Luz answered.

"Samito brought us good luck," Carlotta went on. She crossed herself and looked up to heaven. "*Gracias a Dios.* There are Americans here, *niña,* and they spend money like no one else in the world."

This Luz knew to be true. Patrick was paying her four hundred dollars a week. Alison had steady clients paying sixty dollars for half an hour. Christina and Elizabeth seemed happy on the occasions they went upstairs with non-Spanish-speaking Norte Americanos.

"You should have seen this place when I was your age, when Samito was a young man. Every business on Main Street was busy, including the jewelry store. Charlie's father had sailors lined up for drinks at the bar, and his nightclub was full every night but Sunday. It was fantastic."

At that moment, they seemed to have the same thought.

Carlotta said, "And that man you found on the beach. A friend tells me he left with his boat."

Luz suggested, "Maybe Samito went with him."

"Samito is no sailor," Carlotta scoffed. "I know a sailor when I see one, and that man was a real sailor. One of my girls tells me he got into a fight with two men outside Bongo Bar. He beat them bloody."

The same story had made its way to Luz. "Do all sailors fight?" she asked.

"No. I didn't mean to say he was a ruffian. He's not a coward is what I meant."

Luz agreed and believed that Chief Calenda was also a brave man, albeit in a different way. The conversation drifted to Marcela's wedding, a subject Luz had tried to avoid.

Carlotta said, "It will be you and Ricardo's son at Marcela's ceremony. It might be good for you to marry that boy."

How did Carlotta know about la Dueña's proposal for Andrés? Stunned as she was, Luz attempted not to react. She squeezed her fingers into her palms.

"I wish I had married Max," Carlotta said. "The Mass can be a beautiful thing."

Luz thought back to the photos of her parent's wedding. Her mother had described it as a small affair but dignified by the priest and attending congregation. Luz hoped to have the same thing, someday, but with a man she loved, not with one she had to pay or who had paid her.

Again, Carlotta read her mind. She said, "You're young. You'll meet a man who cares about you. I found my Max; God bless him. He would have liked you."

On her way to Minchi's, her cell phone rang. Only her family had the number. She was amazed that the screen displayed the incoming call, which was the number of her house, including the country code.

"¿Luz?" Anna said.

"Sí," Luz answered brightly. She was proud to have the phone and to be able to take her sister's call whenever it came.

"Jorgé just left," Anna continued. "He wants all the money. He says if we don't have it in a week he will throw us out. Can he do that? I thought you paid him."

Luz hesitated to answer. No doubt there were papers her father had signed, papers she had never seen. Even if there weren't, they did owe the money, and what

Rudi had done only made the situation worse.

"Get me the number for Jorgé," Luz said.

"You're in Aruba. What can you do from there?" Anna asked.

"I'll go to Western Union right now. I'll send him what I can. But you have to get me his number."

"It was Mother who spoke to him," Anna whined.

"What does that matter? You have to get me his number." Luz wanted to scream at her sister. Instead, she forced the issue. "I'm going to hang up so you can look for the number. Call me back right away." She closed the phone and looked around to see if anyone had overheard her conversation. No one was near her, not even Frankie.

Luz scrambled up the stairs at Minchi's. She took the money from her hiding places and counted it on her bed. It totaled two hundred thirty dollars. There were twelve florins as well, all coins. Having eaten with Carlotta, she could skip supper, and the twelve florins were enough to buy her meals the next day. She would have to miss a night's casa payment, which would put la Dueña into a fit. No, she would work the street, the way Inez used to.

She ran to Western Union. Before the ink was dry on the transfer form she called her sister.

"Give me the number," Luz demanded.

"Mother said she was going to handle it."

"Anna, please, give me the number. You know it will be better for everyone."

"Hernán is outside. I have to go watch him."

"Tell Mother to watch him!" Luz shouted. She took a deep breath and asked one more time for the number. She heard her sister crying. Through the sobs, she got the number. "Call me if Jorgé shows up or calls you. Can you do that?"

"Can't you come home, Luz?" Anna howled. "Can't you find Rudi?"

"I'll be home as soon as I can," Luz promised. Before she hung up, the sound of her mother shouting echoed over the line. It was something about her traveling daughter, the one with the expensive clothes.

Luz collected herself before trying to call Jorgé. She rinsed her face and brushed her teeth. She sat on a chair in the common area and listened to the street for fifteen minutes. Then, when she felt ready, she opened her phone and dialed his number. It took three tries to get through.

"This is Luz, Rudi's sister," she said when Jorgé answered.

"The one with the money," Jorgé replied.

She began by staying off the topic, the way she did with the men who came in to Minchi's looking for sex. She knew what they wanted. They knew what they wanted. However, for some reason, it was critical not to address it immediately. A girl who got straight to the point was unlikely to get an affirmative response. It was better to let the momentum build, to create some excitement.

"I was thinking of you, Jorgé," she said. "Here in Aruba, there is a guy with a garage just like yours."

"There are garages everywhere because there are trucks everywhere," he said impatiently. "What were you doing there?"

At this point, Luz thought she had made a small gain. Jorgé's tone had softened. Whatever he had thought when he first answered the phone was now in the back of his mind. So, what was she doing at this imaginary garage?

She said, "I clean the house for his wife. She was giving me a ride, and we had to stop there first. She's a nice lady and takes good care of her husband."

"That's her job," Jorgé put in. "Are you going to tell me something I don't know?"

Feeling she was losing ground, Luz tried a new tack. "I have a surprise for you."

"Let's hear it, chica. I have work to do, and your sister and mother need to get out of that house."

Her chest tightened, but Luz held her voice steady. "I have your money. I sent it to your name."

"A surprise I would have never expected," Jorgé said.

"You promised me you would wait three months, Jorgé. Can't you give us that? After all, it is what you agreed to. I paid you for it."

"I had to pay for what your brother did," he said. "My customers were not happy."

"A month has passed already, can't you hold on for two more? Eight weeks?"

"Why should I?"

"Because I just sent you some more money."

"Oh, just some money, not all the money."

"It's all I have," Luz said quietly. She hoped he could hear her over the cell phone.

Jorgé said, "The money you sent is going to be rent."

It was Luz who was surprised at this point. "Rent?" she asked.

"Rent. That house belongs to me as of tomorrow morning. My grandson needs a house and that one will be fine. Because you gave me some money and because your father was a good worker, I'll let you all live there for a month before I throw you out. Unless more trouble comes from that brother of yours."

Luz cut her losses. "Jorgé, you're a fair man to make such an offer. Since I'm going to be in Aruba for two months, can you give my family some extra time? Can you wait until I come home and then they'll have help moving?"

She could hear him breathing, thinking, which meant he wasn't as evil as la Dueña, who would have rejected her offer out of hand. "Forget about Rudi. We had nothing to do with that," she pleaded. "The house is between us."

"I'm going to find him," Jorgé said.

"You can settle what he did with him. Take what I sent you today as a month's rent for us, for my mother and my sister and me."

"You said you needed two months," he corrected her.

"I do. You know I'm on a contract here."

His snort came through the phone as clearly as if his lips were beside her ear. "I know exactly what you're doing in Aruba. I expect next month's rent on the first. Don't be late or your family is in the street."

"You'll have it," Luz promised.

"I don't want any trouble when the last day comes."

"There won't be any," Luz said. "We'll be gone the day before. Is that good enough?"

"I'll believe it when I see it."

She disconnected from Jorgé and dialed her sister. After she explained the situation to Anna, her mother came on the line. "This house was bought by your father. I'm never leaving!" her mother shouted. Before Luz could calm her down, the phone went dead. Her prepaid minutes had expired.

What her mother said meant nothing. Although it seemed contradictory, Luz expected Jorgé to honor the deal because it was an excellent bargain. He was collecting rent, and the tenants were well known to him. Just like la Dueña, he would squeeze her again because he could get away with it. There would be more calls from Anna to relate his demands, and Luz would meet them.

If she wanted to avoid losing everything, Luz had to find her family another place to live. If she were in Bogotá, she would already be looking for an apartment. The next time she called home, she would tell Anna to do just that. Mother would have to mind Hernán.

Whatever happened in Colombia, Luz needed to work the street to pay the casa. She descended the stairs to the back door where Alison, Christina, and

Elizabeth sat on plastic chairs. A few cars went by. Then a trio of men stopped to talk. Luz stayed in the background. The men, straight from the refinery, stank like rusted metal and old grease the way her father had when he came home from working in Jorgé's garage. They left after a few minutes and the street turned quiet. Her housemates went upstairs, leaving Luz to stand alone in the doorway.

She paced back and forth to stretch her legs. At the end of the block, people stopped for a fruit drink and chatted with the girl working there. In doorways behind the other bars there were girls just like her. They stuck their heads out once in a while to make sure they missed nothing.

A familiar truck came around the corner, a red pickup with a driver who smiled at her as he squeaked to a halt.

"I've never seen you working the street," Charlie said putting his hand over hers.

She kissed his cheek and said, "Only when I have to."

He turned her hand over, put a crumpled piece of paper into it, and said, "Not today." A moment later, before she could see what he had given her, Charlie drove down the block.

Luz waited until the truck was out of sight, then looked into her palm. An American fifty-dollar bill was there, folded to look like a bird. She marveled at the gift, wondering if Charlie had meant to give it to his girlfriend or his wife or maybe a granddaughter she didn't know about. Either way, it was enough to pay the casa.

Screwball sat on Charlie's favorite chair. Growling at having to move, he skipped a pat on the head and went straight for his food. The cat knew if he emptied the bowl Charlie would fill it again. The fine for disturbing a comfortable feline was a fresh ration.

"One tragedy begets another," Charlie huffed on his way to the cupboard where he kept the cat's food. Inside his home, he contemplated the choice between a cigarette and a glass of rum. After feeding Screwball, he chose both and returned to the veranda with one in each hand.

Seeing Luz in the street put him in the kind of vile mood he had not experienced in years. He was as disgusted as he had been when the government closed the bridge over Pirate's Cove, thereby taking away one of his favorite places to pass by with a new girlfriend. The new road ran farther inland giving a view of a muffler shop and a warehouse.

Of course, he couldn't blame the government for Luz's being in the street. For that he held Sam accountable. Because Sam claimed to be first in line, he was automatically obligated to take care of the girl. But he had gotten himself smashed, literally and figuratively, to the point where he needed to be exiled for his own good. This girl was supposed to be *the one*, but she was without her patron, which made her the last one.

The consequences of Sam's action had been catastrophic for Luz. She was in the street, where boys and fools trolled for discount tricks. A girl of her caliber deserved a stable of reliable clients who paid top dollar and treated her like a queen. While there were good things happening at the refinery, there was not yet the density of men flush with cash to provide for her in that manner. Therefore, it was up to Sam, and to a lesser extent Charlie himself, to see to the welfare of the chosen few.

In an effort to relax, Charlie distracted himself with the pleasure of his vices: tobacco smoke that the Americans fretted over as if they might drop dead at the very mention of it; rum, the relief of sailors for half a millennium; and endearing thoughts of the lovely women who had passed through his life. Therefore, with modest exertion, he forgot the tribulations of the day and attained that most sought after of all conditions in life: happiness.

PHILADELPHIA, PA — The idling engines woke Beck. He shifted in his bunk, listening for another change in vibration. *Kathryn* rode her own wake, pitching slightly from bow to stern. He thought about how well the boat had performed. She responded eagerly, like a boxer on his toes during the first round. She was exactly the kind of boat he wanted: plenty of power and good looking, too. His share of the *Petrel* settlement was barely enough to purchase the steel in *Kathryn's* hull. Just the same, he knew he would someday own a boat like her. It was the single focus of his life.

He swung his feet off the bunk, reached for his pants, and glanced back at his life jacket. The lights were still on. The deck was level. The alarms were silent. His life was not in danger. By the time he tied his shoes and shrugged into his radio harness, there was a knock on his door. He told whomever it was to come in.

Syd stood in the red light from the passageway. "Welcome to Philadelphia," he said.

After a few stops in the city, Beck was at home, sorting his mail and contemplating his approach to Nicole. She had been distant on the phone, and he was prepared to do something to show her he was committed.

Captain Upton's voice said, "The best way to face a rough sea is to put your nose into it."

He picked up the phone, dialed Nicole's number, and told her he had a week off. She said she was between showings and would see him in an hour.

Beck repacked his bag with a week's worth of casual clothes. Since he'd had plenty of regular sleep on the boat, he was ready to do whatever she wanted after he made his proposal.

Nicole arrived looking washed out. "I can't take a week off," she sighed. "I have a closing on Wednesday."

"How about a long weekend somewhere?" Beck suggested.

She looked away for a few seconds, then moved across the room to the kitchen counter, where she put down her purse. Beck took that as a good sign.

"We could stay here, order in, sleep late," he said.

"What are you going to do, Nate?" Nicole asked.

"This weekend?"

"Not this weekend," she said, "for the rest of your life?"

"I'm going to buy my own boat, work this harbor, and I'm going to marry you, Nicole," he said. To prove he meant what he said, he took out the ring he'd bought that morning.

Nicole held the ring up to the light. It was a handsome solitaire, simple and beautiful.

"Try it on," Beck said.

"Nate …"

"What?"

"Are you going to be home tonight?" she asked.

"Sure. I have the whole week off."

"And then?"

"Then I'll go back to wherever Jack has us going."

"That us doesn't include me, Nate."

"What do you mean?"

"You're talking about yourself, the boat, the men on the boat. I'm here, and you're out there. I want us to be together."

"We will be together. We'll be married."

"But you'll be on the boat."

"It'll be my boat, Nicole. Jack's going to retire sooner or later, and I'll be first in line to buy one of his tugs."

"When, Nate?"

"I don't know," Beck admitted.

Nicole set the ring beside her purse. "I'll be waiting for weeks on end to see you a few days. I don't know if I can do that anymore."

"Once I have my boat, I'll be in the harbor more often. I'll have a regular schedule, maybe hire a captain or two. We'll have plenty of time together."

"Hardly that much," she corrected him. "A week here, a few nights there. It's less than I think I want."

Beck felt as lost as he had when *Patricia* had gone down. Things had been on and off with Nicole, but now she was telling him the relationship was over, that she wasn't going to put on the ring. For the first time since surviving *Patricia*, he wished he had gone down with her. If he hadn't been sleeping with his life preserver. If he hadn't made it to Charlie's beach. If Luz hadn't seen him there. If Sam hadn't carried him to the doctor. If any of those links had been missing from the chain of events he would have died and thereby been spared the pain of this moment.

As fast as *Patricia* had disappeared, so Beck wanted to be gone. There was no need to prolong his suffering the way he had been tortured during that week adrift. He hefted his bag off the floor, turned the doorknob, and looked at the woman that he had expected to marry.

He said, "Keep the ring, Nicole. And since you're in real estate, maybe you can sell this place for a good price." He went through the door and down to the street. He was determined to make a life to his liking with people who had the same purpose.

Jack Ford saw Beck crossing the parking lot. He wasn't expecting one of his best captains for six more days. Just the same, he was glad to have him at the pier. As frequently happened in the world of marine transportation, the schedule had changed.

"The new boat is going to be finished this week," Ford said. "I'm pairing her with that behemoth of a barge, *Caribbean*, and putting them on a run between here and New York. You'll be master."

It was the kind of job Beck had been telling Nicole about. With his own boat and a relief captain, he would work two weeks a month, spending the other two weeks driving her crazy. But it was too late for that. While he appreciated Jack Ford's enthusiasm, New York was too close to Philadelphia.

"What else have you got?" Beck asked.

The new tug was supposed to be Beck's boat, and Jack was giving him the kind of run every captain dreamed of. He eyed Beck for a second, waiting for what surely had to be a punch line.

"Did you ever think about retiring and selling me one of these boats?" Beck asked his boss.

"Only when people like you piss me off," Jack said. "You want to tell me why you don't want the New York run?"

"Does it matter?" Beck asked.

"Only if it's going to embarrass me with the Coast Guard. And if you don't take that run, I'm handing it to Shahann, and he'll keep it until he dies."

"Let him have it," Beck said.

Jack Ford feared the worst. Whatever had happened to Beck, it was severely impairing his judgment. "What the hell, Nate?" he asked. "Let's hear it."

"Just send me out of here. Don't you have a wreck we can tow to the scrappers in India?"

"I have something you might like," Jack said, "but it'll shuffle the whole deck."

Hearing rumors that Shahann was going to be master on the new boat, Syd, Ramirez, and Tony jumped ship with Beck, swearing loyalty to him over Shahann. Jack cursed all of them for screwing up his schedule to the point where he tore up the pages of his planning book and left them on the floor of his office. He wanted to fire them all, but he had too much work to do that.

Captain Wilkie made the peace. His crew was more than willing to go aboard a brand new boat on an easy run that was close to home. Wilkie himself was an old-timer who didn't much care where he went or what he did, so long as there was water under his keel. Knowing Beck and his men were capable sailors, he was happy to go with *Kathryn*, serving as mate so the responsibilities would be on Beck's shoulders.

"That solves it," Wilkie said to Jack. "My old crew is now on with Shahann, and Beck and his men can take me south with them."

Jack shouted at the five of them, "I hear one complaint about you being far from home, away from your women, on an old boat doing a boring job, and I'll beat every last one of you with a marlin spike!" He ran them out, kicked the door closed, and tried to put his scheduling book together.

It was twelve hours later when *Kathryn* passed the sea buoy where the Delaware Bay met the Atlantic Ocean. The sweeping V of her wake rolled out from the point of her bow. The sea buoy rocked back and forth over the wave, like a finger wagging at the stern of the tug and her troubled captain, Nathan Beck.

32

"WHAT A nice phone," Marcela said.

They were at the dress shop. Luz had put her cell phone atop her purse before going into the changing room. "*Un regalito*," Luz said.

Marcela replied, "You must have a client with more money than Martin if he gives you gifts like that."

"*Un amigo*," Luz said thinking of Harry, who liked to talk to her so much. She didn't fault him for taking her upstairs in exchange for the phone. Nothing was free.

"Friends are expensive," her boss was saying. "Stick with clients. They pay your bills."

Charlie and Samito were also friends who supported her. Then there was Captain Beck. He was mostly a stranger, but she had bonded with him when they slept in the same bed without having sex. Whatever their connection, he had given her money, and she appreciated it.

As Luz inspected the dress, she reflected on the time she and Alison had been spending together. They were friends of a different sort than she and Inez had been. For Inez, the most important thing had been money. She'd had three suitcases full of clothes, more pairs of shoes than she could wear in two weeks, and jewelry worthy of a pirate's chest. She talked about Panama, Saint Maarten, Japan, all the other countries she could go to work as a prostitute and make more money. Luz couldn't understand why she continued to sell herself when she had everything money could buy. Alison was more like Luz. She wanted to help her family, to get them through a difficult time. Her father was actively searching for another job, and her mother was looking after her daughter. But Alison, like Luz's brother, was impatient. She behaved recklessly, admitting to sex without a condom and getting drunk to the point where she couldn't remember what had happened.

"But it's with an American," she had said one day at lunch. "He's married but said he wants to divorce his wife. I told him he could live in Colombia and no one would know he was married. We could live forever on the money he makes at the refinery. It's enough to have an apartment in Centro. Wouldn't that be great?"

"It would be great," Luz had replied. She had similar thoughts about Martin and to a lesser extent Samito. When Samito had shown her his land, she thought it would be wonderful to live by the beach, snorkeling when she felt like it and enjoying an endless string of sunsets. However, she learned from her experience with Martin that when another girl came along, one the man preferred over her, the fantasy dissolved in a matter of minutes.

Unlike Carlotta, Luz dispensed no advice. She listened to Alison, made pleasant replies, and focused on maximizing her earnings. Thanks to Patrick and her other clients, she sent home enough money to keep Jorgé satisfied.

The dress fit perfectly, but Luz took her time examining it because she knew Marcela liked to dither in the store while the staff waited on her.

Having heard so much about Alison's neighborhood, Luz considered moving her family there. A decent apartment rented for the equivalent of two hundred dollars per month. A house could be had for three hundred fifty. The dollar was the only currency in which Luz thought. It was a part of Inez that had rubbed off on her. Inez could calculate exchange rates faster than she could have a client up the stairs. Aruban florins, or guilders as they were called, counted for nothing in Colombia, and pesos quickly lost their value. The dollar was reliable, portable, and the only money the recently arrived Americans cared to use. Using pencil and paper and the calculator feature of her cell phone, Luz figured she was paying la Dueña one thousand five hundred dollars per month to have a room to work and sleep in. She wondered what fifteen hundred dollars bought in central Bogotá. It didn't matter because she had no way of earning the same money in Colombia that she did in Aruba. What did matter was that her family had a place to live and work.

Before slipping out of the dress, Luz established her goal for the rest of her time in Aruba. She needed to save six month's rent, eighteen hundred dollars more or less. Half a year was sufficient time for her family to settle in, find jobs, and get on with life. It worked out to one or two extra clients per day. If someone like Samito or Captain Beck came along, it would be less.

"Let's go, Luz," Marcela said. "We have business to do."

Being Monday afternoon, Luz had no idea what business la Dueña was referring to. They drove to San Nicolaas, where they parked in front of China Clipper.

To her surprise, Francisco was there with two girls. La Dueña unlocked her bar and went inside with everyone behind her. A few minutes later, the other two girls working at China Clipper entered the bar followed by Alison, Christina, and Elizabeth.

"There is a change," la Dueña announced. "From tonight on, Luz will collect for the casa."

As she had recently taught herself, Luz remained expressionless. Collecting for the casa was a dreadful responsibility. When girls didn't pay, it would be her problem.

"As for you two," la Dueña said to the girls who had come with Francisco, "you were supposed to be here yesterday. You're going to pay for last night and you're going to pay whatever it costs to go to the hospital tomorrow. Is that clear?"

The girls nodded it was.

"If Luz tells me there is a problem with any of you, I will come here myself and put you on the next plane to Colombia," la Dueña said next.

Luz had heard Diana was sent home, so the threat was real.

"Remember why you are here," la Dueña continued. "To make money. There are men here with money in their pockets, and you have to get it from them. They want what you have between your legs. Give it to them. Give it to them until they beg you to stop. Then you can help yourself to what's in their wallets."

This lecture grated on Luz's nerves every time la Dueña gave it. It failed to inspire the girls. It only reminded them how obscene and difficult their lives had become. What they really needed was a set of pointers to guide them through the tricky maze of prostitution. They were bound to be more successful with a little coaching than with the constant beatings of a slave master.

"Leave us alone," la Dueña said. "I want to speak with Luz in private."

The girls left in pairs, except for Alison, who was without her partner. Luz gave her a quick look, and Alison took her turn through the door.

"My wedding is Saturday. Andrés will pick you up at five thirty. You can dress at my house," Marcela began. "I won't charge you for the casa that night, and I'll give you two free nights per month for collecting from the girls."

"*Gracias*," Luz said with as much gratefulness as she could muster.

"*De nada*," la Dueña replied. "Don't let this bunch take advantage of you. If you have any trouble, use that phone of yours to call me. I also want you to watch Pablo and Spanner. Let me know if they are stealing."

"*Sí.*"

"I have other business these days with Señor Montoya." She sighed, tapped her fingernails on the bar, then looked around the room. "This place needs to be remodeled, don't you think?"

"Perhaps some new paint," Luz suggested.

"Perhaps the wrecking ball." With that, la Dueña was on her feet, in a hurry to get out of the bar as if the building were on fire. At her car, she handed Luz the ledger for Minchi's and a second one for China Clipper. "I will come for the casa money tonight. Look for me in the street at nine fifteen."

"Si, señora," Luz said and headed for Pueblito Paisa to eat a lunch that her twisted stomach begged her to skip.

Collecting for the casa went better than she expected. She began the night at China Clipper, where her face was less familiar. The bartender stood to the side as she took cash, made change, and marked the book. Coming out the door, she noted a police car parked at the end of the block. She crossed the street with China Clipper's ledger under her arm and entered Minchi's with confidence. Spanner, contrary to la Dueña's suspicions, was a great help. While Luz stood behind the bar, he sat in front with his arms folded and his eyes hidden behind his sunglasses. The girls had to stand directly next to his intimidating form as they paid. To her credit, Luz never appeared mean or disrespectful to them. She smiled, thanked them, and wished each one good luck. Whenever it occurred to her, she gave a compliment on some attribute she thought might be appealing to a potential client. It was her way of helping the cause, seeing to it that the girl accomplished what she had come to San Nicolaas to do.

During her first week as la Dueña's assistant, more men came to work at the refinery. Luz overheard them talking about what was happening on the other side of the wall. The Spanish conversations were mostly about things she didn't understand, and the English ones were completely indecipherable. But there was no mistaking the excited tone. She saw crane booms sticking up in the air. Trucks roared through town, bringing in supplies and taking away junk. In between, the nightlife in San Nicolaas boomed. On the night before Marcela's wedding, Luz serviced seven clients in eight hours and had to tell Patrick she could not go home with him. If she wasn't exhausted and hurting, she would have gone with him and thereby achieved a personal record for money earned in a single day.

Andrés had grown a narrow beard since she had last seen him. It ran along his jaw line and up the center of his chin. A thin mustache bordered his upper lip and connected with the beard. It gave him a sleek look which complemented his intense eyes and slightly distracted countenance.

"Have you ever been to Holland?" he asked before they turned the first corner on their way out of San Nicolaas.

"No," she replied.

"I asked because some of the girls have been there."

"Sorry. I have only been here and Colombia."

"Holland used to own this island. They took it from the Spanish."

Samito had told her that bit of history.

"We're not exactly independent," Andrés went on. "But who cares? We're just a place no one thinks about."

While not exactly thrilled to be going to Marcela's wedding, Luz still wanted to be as cheerful as possible. She asked, "Is Holland a big country?"

Andrés chuckled. "Bigger than Aruba but smaller than most of the states in the United States. America is big. My father and I went to Miami to look at a boat."

"You would rather go to Holland than the United States?"

"Only to study art. The schools are better, but when it comes to living, America is better."

"Why is it better?"

"I don't know. It just is."

She dropped the subject and let him drive her the rest of the way in silence.

Since Marcela asked for no help, Luz dressed quickly and waited in the living room, just down the hall from where Ricardo had died. She focused on Hernán's kisses and the questions she wanted to ask Alison about living on her side of Bogotá. The few words she exchanged with Andrés convinced her that moving was the right thing to do. If he longed to go to Holland and then America, there was nothing wrong with her shifting locations in Bogotá.

"Ready," Marcela announced.

"*¡Tan linda!*" Luz exclaimed appropriately. Her boss did look magnificent, but any woman would have wearing such an expensive dress tailored to hide her imperfections.

"This isn't my first time," Marcela said, "but I think it will be my best."

Luz feared adding anything to that kind of statement.

"Drive us to the government office," la Dueña ordered Andrés, who had been sitting at the kitchen table drawing with a pencil and paper. He took his time rolling the paper, which he tucked inside his jacket.

Montoya waited in the reception area of the government office. A photographer chatted with him. He kissed Marcela lightly on the cheek when she came through the door. Luz thought he genuinely looked happy. It amazed her that he truly wanted to marry a woman she found so detestable.

The ceremony took longer than Luz expected. The presiding official spoke in Dutch. Then, because Marcela had insisted beforehand, everything was repeated in Spanish. The marriage document was also in both languages. Montoya and Marcela signed at two places so there could be no confusion as to what they were agreeing. The photographer took their picture, pens in hand, government man in the background. Andrés and Luz were not invited into the picture. They were present as witnesses, to sign as such, and were kept out of the way. She suppressed an angry comment about spending so much money on a dress that wouldn't even appear in the wedding album.

"Long life and lots of luck," the official said to end the service.

As they descended the stairs toward their waiting cars, Marcela whispered to Luz, "In that dress, you'll drive those refinery workers crazy."

Luz turned away from la Dueña and gritted her teeth. Without saying good-bye, she rushed to meet Andrés. She helped herself into the car, slammed the door, and stared straight ahead. Being angry made her ugly, but she despised Marcela and could not help herself. What disturbed Luz most was that she had to face her every night of the week and act as if she liked it, as if she were talking to Jessica at Hop Long or Charlie at his bar.

Andrés gave her the impression he was above it all. She figured he was probably dreaming of Holland, pretty blond girls, and wooden shoes. He drove her to the unfinished hotel in San Nicolaas. Luz was about to scream at him to take her directly to Minchi's front door. He preempted her by handing over the paper from inside his jacket. She unrolled it and gasped. Under the dim streetlight, she saw he had drawn her figure while she was seated on the couch in Marcela's house. He had started with her face, then worked his way down, elaborating the detail of her dress. The lower portion was not finished so it gave the impression she was floating in space. The quality of his work was unmistakable.

"Go to Holland," she said, "and then America. They have money to pay for work like this." She tried to give him back the paper.

"It's for you," he said.

She forgot where she was and got out of the car, pausing to look at herself a second time. Although only a drawing, she was enthralled by the picture. He had an eye for detail that astounded her. Every bead on her dress was there, as was the little mole near her ear. It was like looking at a photograph.

She glanced up to check the street, saw it was clear, and crossed. Farther on, she spotted Frankie talking to a man who didn't have his fist or foot headed in the bum's direction. Frankie saw her coming. He grinned with both his teeth and pointed at her. With his filthy right hand, he pushed on the man's shoulder to turn him toward Luz. In front of her stood Captain Beck.

"You owe me a hundred guilders," Frankie said to Beck.

Luz noted a gaze of pleasant resignation on Beck's face.

Frankie said in Spanish, "I bet him the most beautiful woman in San Nicolaas was coming. Now he knows I'm right."

She smiled at Frankie's flattery. "*Tú vives,*" she said to Beck.

"I'm still alive," he said, at a loss for more Spanish words.

"*Mira,*" she said, proudly holding the drawing out for him to see.

"The Mona Lisa!" Frankie proclaimed.

"Beautiful," Beck seconded.

"Ah, hah," Frankie said. "When I have my teeth, my portrait will hang on the wall next to this one."

Beck shook his head. He couldn't fault Frankie for his optimism. Having been in port less than an hour, he had no guilders and settled the bet with dollars.

"*Venga, Capitán,*" Luz said looping her arm in his. He fell into step without the slightest hesitation. Something had changed in the previously reticent captain.

❧33❧

"THESE AMERICANS never give up," Charlie said to Screwball. "If only the French were like that, eh? We wouldn't have had that second problem with the Germans. But then my mother wouldn't have come here to meet my father, and I would never have been born. I suppose it all worked out for the best. What do you think?"

Screwball hopped onto the parapet to see what his owner was talking about.

It was half past seven in the morning, and Captain Beck was leaving Minchi's. He held the hand of a girl whom Charlie coveted and Sam cherished above all others. The body language was clear. Beck's kiss to Luz's cheek was a millisecond too long. He held her hand too gently. They were not lovers, but they were not brother and sister. It was a magical time, a critical point in the relationship where it either ended abruptly or swept them into something they would not be able to control. Beck didn't know it, but Charlie did, and the King of San Nicolaas would do his best to rescue the innocent from the error of their ways. It was too late for Sam, but there might be hope for Captain Beck.

"We have a visitor," Charlie told Screwball. "Try to look your best."

Downstairs Charlie greeted Beck at the door. "Come in, my friend. Tell me about your evening. I've been staying home these days and need some inspiration to get me back on the street. If I don't come home smelling like strange perfume my wife will suspect I've become a homosexual."

Beck gave Charlie a bewildered look.

"Actually, I'm jealous. Please tell me about this girl so I can live every moment through you."

While they drank coffee, Beck related the events of the previous night. The trip from Philadelphia had been through uncomfortable weather, which had left him anxious for solid ground and a strong drink. He put *Kathryn* in the hands of Captain Wilkie and came into town for that drink. No sooner had he rounded the corner on Main Street than he ran into Frankie.

"A luckier bum never walked these streets," Charlie interrupted. "They took the other one, Speedy, to a rehab clinic. Who knows if he'll make it?"

Beck continued his story. Without thinking, he had taken Frankie's bet because he thought he would be in Java Bar before the next girl appeared. Frankie turned him to face Luz and it was all over.

"Over? It was just the beginning!" Charlie snorted.

It was the beginning. He went to Minchi's, where Luz changed her clothes. On the way out the door, Spanner pointed at Beck and gave him a thumbs-up the way Sam would have. She led him to Sayonara, where Carlotta hosted them in grand style. The lady herself served drinks and snacks.

"Personal service like that is hard to find," Charlie said. "Except here, of course, where I come on bended knee."

At Sayonara, Beck did his best with the Spanish Ramirez had been teaching him. Then they went to the Arends house. "I see they made a few repairs," Beck noted.

"What choice did they have?" Charlie said. "If they don't do more work they'll be living in cardboard boxes."

"There are enough crates at the refinery to build a mansion," Beck said.

"Don't tell my cat! He'll be over the wall tonight."

As had been his custom, Beck spent the night with Luz. It was a platonic situation, he added quickly. They shared the bathroom and the bed but nothing more.

"You can't bullshit a bullshitter," Charlie said even though he believed what the Captain had told him.

"It's not like that," Beck said.

Charlie rolled his eyes. "And you call yourself a sailor."

"If I spoke more Spanish, I'm sure we would be good friends."

"If you spoke more Spanish, you would be at the altar."

Beck wasn't convinced he was on his way to the altar with anyone. He'd lost Nicole, and marrying a prostitute seemed like a dodgy proposition.

"Don't fall in love, my friend," Charlie warned. "Or, you'll be in worse shape than Sam."

Beck wished he'd heard that advice years ago. He asked, "How is Sam?"

"He had to leave the island," Charlie replied, "for medical reasons."

"Nothing serious I hope."

"No. He went crazy. He'll be back when he comes to his senses. Now tell me your official reason for being here," Charlie demanded in a friendly way.

Beck told him half the story. "The man I work for landed a contract to dock the ships bringing parts for the refinery and then the tankers. Tomorrow, I sail for Curaçao to bring a pile driving rig back here."

"Just like old times. When is the first tanker due? I want to organize a celebration. I may have to release Sam from the asylum to act as master of ceremonies."

Beck shrugged. "I'll talk to Herzog today, but at the rate things are going, I would expect in a month or so."

"Tankers in a month," Charlie reflected. "What's on the agenda for today?"

"Not much."

"Idle hands do the devil's deeds, especially at night. I'll give you the day off to rest and meditate, but I expect you to join me for the evening."

"What do you have in mind?" Beck asked.

"Something civilized," was all Charlie would say. "Find a white shirt with epaulets. That'll impress the women."

The Captain had given Luz a hundred dollars. She considered him her best client because he paid like the rest but asked for nothing aside from her company.

He was slowly learning Spanish and was a good dancer. Unlike Patrick, he liked to be active. This trait was most appealing to Luz since she had trouble reading and found television boring. She felt like an ignored stepchild when she waited for Patrick to get in the mood for sex or to finish his studies before he took her to Minchi's.

The way Beck ushered her around town surprised Luz. Nothing distracted him, not even the whistles from other men. He couldn't miss the guys leering at her while they munched Carlotta's food. He had to understand that they wanted to have their turn with her and most likely would when they discovered she worked at Minchi's. Still, he wasn't like an overly protective brother the way Samito would have been. It was as if he were concentrating on her and the others were no bother. Luz basked in his attentiveness, especially since it wasn't focused on the space between her legs.

She put Beck's hundred-dollar bill atop the other money she was sending home. The total came to three hundred fifty dollars after Western Union's fees were subtracted. Her family would be secure until she returned home. Now she was working toward their new place, where they would restart their lives.

She finished her business at Western Union by purchasing three phone cards, then dialed home.

Her sister got straight to the point. "Mother is furious with you," she said.

"How can she be upset with me when I'm not there?" Luz asked.

"Jorgé was here. He told us about the deal you made. How could you sell us out like that?"

"He wanted to throw us in the street. I bought us another two months."

"Us?" Anna wanted to know. "We're here, but you're over there. What do you have to worry about?"

Her face hot with rage, Luz said deliberately, "I have to worry about paying debts that aren't mine."

Her sister was quick with a reply. "Now you're blaming Papa for what those criminals did to him, and Rudi for doing what he had to do."

Luz took a breath. "I'm not blaming anyone, but I'm the only one making any money."

"You should hear yourself, Luz. It's only you who cares. It's only you who tries. Who do you think is watching Hernán this afternoon?"

At the sound of Hernán's name, Luz felt her hands go cold. She missed her boy terribly. She was desperate to have him with her, but it wasn't as if her current environment lent itself to raising children. How long would it be before her son heard from one of his schoolmates that his mother was a whore? Then again, he was a smart boy. He would figure it out on his own when his mother left the house every night and did not return until just before dawn.

"Are you there?" Anna was saying.

"I'm here," Luz replied. "I just sent more money. Sooner or later Jorgé will come looking for it."

"When Rudi comes home and hears what happened, he'll kill Jorgé."

"Don't say that!" Luz cried. "Things are bad enough without our brother in jail."

"It's not like a hundred people aren't killed every day in this country," Anna retorted. "What's one more loan shark?"

While Anna was correct, Jorgé was not completely at fault. He had loaned their father money in good faith. It was only right it should be paid back.

Anna said, "Mother is not leaving. She says since Father bought the house, she's the only one with the right to sell it."

It was senseless to explain that it didn't matter what her mother said. Luz stared at the overweight tourists loitering in front of Charlie's. They laughed, toasted each other, and slapped each other on the back. Despite already sunburned noses, they weren't smart enough to go inside. It was as if they needed sunshine to power their fun.

Suddenly, Luz was aware of her sister's calling out her name. "Calm down," she said. "I'm here. Sometimes these cell phones don't work right."

"How can you afford a cell phone when we don't even have a house?"

A lie was the only thing that would save her. "They're cheap here," Luz said.

Anna scoffed at the idea. "Now that you're making all the decisions, tell me where we're going to live when Jorgé throws us into the street."

She wanted to sound the way Captain Beck sounded when he spoke into his radio. The English words made no sense, but his tone was firm and clear. He was giving orders, issuing instructions. He expected them to be followed. "*Quintas de Santa Barbara*," Luz said.

"SANTA BARBARA?" Anna screamed.

"Stop yelling," Luz told her and continued to lie. "I have a place in mind. When I fly home, I'll check it out."

"When I fly home," her sister repeated condescendingly. "You're a jet-setter, too."

Luz ignored the remark. "If it's good enough, I'll rent it. We can move that week."

"¡Dios mío! You really did sell your dresses, didn't you? You only wear pants, like a man."

"Anna, I don't want to fight with you. You're my sister, and I love you. I want us to have a good life. I'm working harder than you could ever imagine to make that possible. Please, work with me."

"What can I do?" Anna asked. "I'm nothing but a nursemaid for a boy who's not mine."

If Luz had been in Colombia, she would have a grabbed Hernán and run out of the house. Unlike the last time, she wouldn't go back. On her way out the door, she would tell her sister, and whoever else happened to be there, that she had been a whore for them, that she had spread her legs for strangers so they wouldn't have to live in a slum. She would let them live with that for the rest of their lives. But she wasn't in Colombia. She was a thousand miles away in Aruba, where she would soon be getting ready to look her best for those men who were waiting for their half hour with her.

She said without a quiver in her voice, "Anna, I will call you in a couple days." Just as Harry had shown her, she closed the phone gently so as not to damage its inner workings.

Beck met Charlie at the main gate and immediately noticed the gleam in his host's eye.

"We are cultured men," his host said. "Where are your epaulets?"

"I don't have epaulets," Beck answered.

"But you're the Captain?"

"And you're the King of San Nicolaas. Where's your crown?" Beck joked.

"In my vault," Charlie said, "with the rest of the crown jewels. Naturally, I keep the family jewels right here where they can be of use from time to time. You know, from these loins sprung a woman who today is working to cure cancer."

"Your daughter?"

"That's her, Captain. I hope she's working overtime. Like Sam, I don't want to give up my cigarettes."

They drove to Oranjestaad and made several confusing turns before parking in an expansive lot.

"You'll like this place," Charlie said. "It's our version of the Waldorf-Astoria."

"Lead the way," Beck said.

They entered through frosted glass doors with "Hotel Victoria" etched into the center panel. Inside, Beck found himself standing on a plush carpet and surrounded by urns stuffed with flowers. To the right was an old-time reception desk with numbered pigeonholes for keys and letters. On the left was a staircase. Directly ahead was another pair of doors.

Charlie nodded to the reception clerk and led Beck farther into the building. The next room welcomed them with more unexpected elegance.

"This is my friend, Captain Beck," Charlie said to a liveried maitre 'd.

"A pleasure, Captain Beck. I am Armando, welcome to the Hotel Victoria."

Beck asked if he was underdressed.

"In this climate that is impossible," Armando said tugging at his collar. He ushered them to a table near the edge of the room.

"Here there is more spit and polish, more illusion than San Nicolaas," Charlie said.

Beck looked around, noted some well-dressed young women at the bar, and turned back to his host.

"First, I'd love to tell you some stories that everyone else has heard," Charlie went on. "Then we'll do some dancing, and I don't mean you and me."

"Steady as she goes," Beck replied.

"I used to own the best whorehouse in Bogotá," Charlie began. "It was bigger than this place and more grand, if you can believe that. My place smelled like a florist shop. They came by the truckload. There was a live-in doctor, a seamstress on call, six runners who changed sheets and stocked the bar, and a kitchen staff that numbered a dozen."

"Quite a business," Beck commented.

"It was like a cruise ship," Charlie said after taking a deep breath.

He selected his girls not only for good looks but also for having the right attitude. "I'm a psychiatrist," he said. "Back then, I pried into their minds before I let someone into their bodies."

His girls had to have the right constitution to deal with the rigors of the job. They regularly received offers of marriage, huge monetary gifts, and trinkets that ranged from diamond rings to motor scooters. "These things confuse the girls," Charlie explained. "They get the idea that everything is theirs for the asking. When they start asking? Trouble! The client gets resentful. He drops them like yesterday's dirty underwear and finds a fresh one. After all, none of these offers is real."

"I see what you mean," Beck said.

"That's only half of it," Charlie continued. "I taught those girls how men think. Just as they are enigmas to us, so are we to them. The ones who listened, who learned, they made enough money to have whatever they wanted without asking anyone for anything."

"The ones who didn't?"

Charlie put out his cigarette. "They made money, too, but it was a job like any other. How do you say in America? A grind?"

"Why did you give it up?" Beck asked.

"I had to. Colombia changed. The country had been fighting a civil war for longer than anyone could remember. You gringos started buying drugs by the shipload. The narcotrafficantes, they had more power then the conquistadors. They had money to buy all the cheese in Switzerland."

"They bought you out?"

"Sort of. The offer of my dreams. I took the money and came home to Aruba, where I turned my father's bar into a tourist trap. It had to be done. Waiting on you sailors to come back? I would have starved."

"You had the money from your place in Colombia."

"I did, but that's for a rainy day."

"Aruba's a desert," Beck commented.

Grinning, Charlie said, "And when it rains we get flash floods that take away everything."

"Better get a boat," Beck advised.

"I'll leave that up to you. Let me tell you another story about my father. He came to Bogotá one day. He gets into a taxi at the airport and asks the driver to take him to the best whorehouse in town."

"He came to your place?"

Seeing that his son was the owner, Charlie's father promptly installed himself in one of the rooms. He ordered up food, drinks, and girls. For two weeks, he never left the building.

"I said to him, 'Papa, you have to go. I'm on the verge of bankruptcy!'"

They laughed together.

"He was the only man I've known to rival Sam."

"That's a tough act to follow."

"The toughest," Charlie finished. "I see the band has arrived."

The musicians were better dressed than the Arends Family. They played an organized repertoire which flowed from salsa to merengue.

As if on cue, a pair of young women came up to their table. They were Jazmin and Ingrid, both from Caracas, Venezuela. Their appearance was more European, as they were both blondes and stood as tall as Beck.

"To friendship," Charlie toasted.

"*Amistad*," Beck seconded, demonstrating he knew some Spanish.

The girls touched glasses with them and sipped. Charlie led the conversation by telling the girls that Beck was an American, a captain of a massive vessel. He also loved to dance with pretty women.

"We're here," the girls said.

"*Exactamente*," Charlie added.

Beck paired with Jazmin, who moved more like Nicole than Luz. She kept her back straight and her hand primly on his hip. Luz was not afraid to touch his back, or once in a while, let her hand drift to the side of his neck. Still, dancing with Jazmin was not unpleasant. She was a beautiful young woman with a figure that tempted a man who'd recently been dumped by his girlfriend.

There were no clocks in the ballroom. Beck lost track of time in the course of the drinks, dance sets, and jokes Charlie told. Finally, the bandleader announced the last song would be next.

"Don't insult me by asking to pay for everything," Charlie said to Beck.

"Just my half," Beck said.

They paid and kissed the girls good-bye. In the truck, Beck saw it was three o'clock in the morning. Charlie pulled out of the lot and headed for San Nicolaas. "Just enough time for a nightcap," he said.

"Those girls are for hire just like they are in San Nicolaas," Beck said when they were on the main road.

"They are," Charlie answered. "We paid more for their time on the dance floor than we would have had we gone upstairs for an hour."

"I see."

"It's not all about the sex," Charlie told him. "Any man with a stiff prick can have sex. That's not for me, and I suspect it's not for you either. That's why I took you there. We're all lonely, but we don't have to suffer. We can meet someone new. We can have a good time."

"I don't know if we're all lonely," Beck put in.

Charlie waved his finger. "That's where you are wrong, my friend. Loneliness is the greatest affliction of the human race. We all want affection. It comforts us that someone cares."

Beck kept his mouth shut. He was thinking about Nicole, wondering if she was thinking about him.

"When someone cares about you, you are no longer alone. You have a companion. They may be in your arms or on the other side of the world, but if you believe they care about you, they are with you. If not, well, you're lost."

"That may be true," Beck said. "But these girls are paid to act like they care."

"Ahhh, we arrive at the duplicity of reality."

Charlie seemed to have developed a grand hypothesis, complete with its own vocabulary. He said, "A man pays one of these girls for sex, or for her time on the dance floor the way we did. It's a business transaction, correct?"

"Right," Beck affirmed.

"Incorrect! You may forget this girl. You may forget that one. However, if you keep putting yourself into a place like this ..."

"Like what?" Beck interrupted.

"Like San Nicolaas," Charlie said. "Reality will trick you. You will forget they are whores. You will rationalize the money you pay them. You and the girl will agree it's a gift, not payment for services rendered. You will deny you care, the proof being the time spent with other girls. Yet you'll drift back to the same one again and again. And then you are in danger. You are on the edge of the black hole known as love. That is the point of no return, Captain, the abyss. Eternal suffering."

"Unless you find the right one," Beck put in.

Charlie shook his head. He said, "The best defense is offense. Recognize you care. Admit it to yourself. Deal with it early before it confuses you. And by dealing with it I mean keeping it far enough away that you don't burn your fingers."

The solution was not entirely clear to Beck. He struggled to understand his experience with Luz in the context Charlie presented, but it wasn't as if he were contemplating a relationship with her like the one he'd had with Nicole. If he happened to think of Luz or care enough to give her a call or send her a few dollars, so what? That was ordinary life. Charlie was making too much of it.

By this time, they were parked around the corner from the bar. Beck accepted the invitation for one last drink on the veranda. As Charlie unlocked the door, Chief Calenda came down the street.

"Is the ferocious tiger locked in his cage?" Calenda asked.

"No. He is resting, conserving his energy for the hunt. Join the Captain and I for the final drink of the night."

The three of them climbed the stairs and found seats around the table. Charlie poured rum for Beck and himself. Calenda accepted a glass of club soda. Screwball eyed them from his perch on the parapet.

"I think that cat knows more about what goes on in San Nicolaas than anyone else," Calenda commented.

"Naturally," Charlie said. He reached over, stroked the cat's fur, and added, "The monkeys may laugh at the tiger, but they stay in the trees, eh?"

Beck chuckled at Charlie's unlimited supply of wisdom. If Captain Upton had lived to meet him, the two could have gone on for days exchanging witticisms, draining liquor bottles, and discussing their adventures.

"Town is safe?" Charlie asked next.

"For the most part, and Speedy is drying out."

"Poor bastard," Beck said. He hoped Calenda didn't bring up his brawl with the guys who had attacked the bum.

"And Frankie is up to four teeth," Charlie said.

It was Calenda's turn to laugh. "He thinks I'm going to abduct him and take them out. It's Señor Montoya who has to be careful."

"Who's that?" Beck inquired.

"Marcela's new husband," Charlie replied.

"Getting married is as dangerous in Aruba as it is in America?" Beck asked.

"In a different way," Charlie told him.

"So it is," Calenda remarked. "And what of the refinery, Captain? When will it be operational?"

"Soon is the word everyone uses," Beck answered.

"Better than never," Charlie commented.

"It's late," Calenda put in, "even for San Nicolaas."

"But not for Screwball," Charlie said. "He's about ready to make his rounds."

"I think he's ready for bed," the Chief reflected.

"Aren't we all," Beck said. "If you gentlemen will excuse me, I'm going to my boat."

When Beck was about to go down the stairs, Calenda said, "Be careful at Minchi's, Captain."

Beck hesitated on the first step. The combination of the late hour, Charlie's lecture, and Calenda's warning had his head swimming. At that moment, he concerned himself with safely descending the stairs.

A block farther, he slowed as he saw Luz come out of Minchi's. There was a car parked in front of the bar. A guy waited for Luz to get in the passenger seat.

"Where was I going?" Beck asked himself as he stood at the corner. He remembered he was going to his boat and that he would sail for Curaçao, where there was a pile-driving barge waiting for him. It was exactly how it had all begun last year. He reminded himself to sleep on his life jacket, which would keep him afloat until he drifted back here one more time.

LUZ ROLLED away from the sunlight that cut through the blinds in Patrick's bedroom. He was asleep on the couch in the living room, a loose-leaf binder over his chest. If he stuck to his routine, he would be awake in about two hours. Then he would wash his hands and face, make a cup of instant coffee, and do some more reading. Around one in the afternoon, he would take her to the bedroom. After sex, he would shower, wait while she did the same, and then drive her to San Nicolaas. For Luz it was no different than being a dog waiting to go for a walk. She decided then and there she would never own a dog.

She missed the cool, rainy beginnings of her days in Bogotá. She would lay in bed with Hernán, feeling him squirm into a comfortable spot. His warm body against her was the simplest pleasure and something she cherished as a gift of motherhood.

She craved real affection. In lieu of that, she wouldn't mind Samito's convivial charm or Charlie's gentlemanly hospitality or Martin's flattering generosity. If she had her choice of the men she met in San Nicolaas, she would pick Captain Beck for his unpretentious cordiality. The Captain behaved naturally, not as if he was trying to charm her like a lover or impress her with how much money he had in his pocket. When Alison had asked her what he was like, she answered, "He's a good man." Alison had asked, "If he wanted you to go with him on his boat, would you go?" Luz had replied that she didn't like boats but had not explained why. Captain Beck's boat, the part of it she could see, was more like a ship. Still, the memory of what Suarez had done to her was still fresh. But what if Beck asked her to go with him? She shrugged because he hadn't asked her, and he probably wouldn't. She suspected he had a wife in the United States and that he was like that puritan class of Americans Inez talked about. They were afraid to have mistresses and actually obeyed the Commandments. While she was curious what kind of lover he was, Beck had asked for nothing, which meant to her that he was content in another relationship. She would be no different than la Dueña if she spoiled that. At the same time, she needed money, and Beck had proven a willing customer, eager to pay for whatever it was he got from her.

There were other potential clients: young Dutch marines stationed at the base, more Americans at the refinery, the locals, a few red-faced Englishmen from cruise ships that docked in Oranjestaad. They all brought money to San Nicolaas.

Before letting herself fall back to sleep, she thought of her family. She wanted them to be together, to live a comfortable life. She didn't expect to have luxuries, nor did she want to lay awake every night wondering how she was going to pay the electricity bill. A decent life was a fair reward for hard work. She wasn't afraid to work hard, to struggle, but being a prostitute wasn't like that. She listened to men talking about how easy it was for the girls in San Nicolaas. "All they do is spread their legs," they said, but had no comprehension of what it was like to have another person thrusting into your body, someone you didn't know, you didn't care for, someone you prayed would pay you when they finished. She would like to see them act as if every woman they met was as charming and glamorous as the ideal specimen. She would like to see them stay erect after the clothes were on the floor and the frightful flesh was exposed in the dim light shining through a crack in the bathroom door. Then there were the smells, the sticky substances, and the comments spoken in public. If that was an easy job, she prayed she never had a difficult one.

But she had accepted Señora Álvaro's offer, and for that reason she was lying in a stranger's bed trying to avoid the mistakes of the past by making good decisions about the future.

Sometime later, she awoke to what she thought was Patrick's touch. As she opened her eyes, she recoiled at the sight of Patrick's housemate, Bill. He was grinning at her as she held the thin sheet over her chest with one hand and wiped her eyes with the other. He placed two twenty-dollar bills at her side and covered his closed lips with a finger.

"No, señor," she whispered. "No es correcto."

"Sí, forty dollars," he said. "You and me. Now." He pointed at the bed.

"No," Luz repeated. "Tu amigo es mi cliente."

Bill struggled with the few Spanish words he knew. "Media hora," he said putting his hand over the money.

"*Señor Bill, gracias pero no es posible. No es correcto.*" She watched his eyes turn from frustrated to angry to disappointed. She tried not to notice the erection in his underpants. Finally, he snatched up the money and walked out of the room.

Later, Patrick came to her as he always did. They had sex, showered, and left his house.

On the ride to San Nicolaas he asked, "Why didn't you fuck Bill?"

She kept her eyes straight ahead. "You are my client," she said, "not him."

"The whores are very loyal here in Aruba," Patrick commented.

"Some," she said quietly.

"You could have made another forty dollars, nearly fifty percent more than I pay you for the night."

Luz said, "I'm hurt that you think I only come home with you for the hundred dollars." When he didn't have a quick, mathematical reply, Luz knew she had caught him off guard. She was proud of herself at having bested him in this small way. Simultaneously, she was saddened at having manipulated him. She thought of herself as an amateur, as someone who was doing something only because she had to, and therefore without too much thought about improving her skills. On this morning, as the car approached Rembrandtstraat, she realized she had become a professional.

Through the windshield, she saw directly into the main entrance of the refinery. Not two hundred feet past the open gates was the pier where Captain Beck's boat stood. Patrick stopped the car as he waited for the workers on the back of a trash truck to dump the cans. It gave her a minute to watch the goings-on at the pier. The boat was backing away and Captain Beck was bound for sea one more time.

"I'll get out at the gate," she said to Patrick because she wanted to see the Captain leave. Maybe he would notice her and wave. She could tell Hernán she knew a captain and that he was her friend.

"Let me take you to Minchi's," Patrick replied, the contrition in his voice obvious.

Luz knew she had broken him and refused to accept this meager offer. She exited the car, checked for traffic, and crossed to the other side of the street for a better view of the departing tug.

The guards would not let her in, and she didn't try to pass the gate. But she did stand as close to the line as she could, barely a toe's width away from where the iron gates met the asphalt. It was easy to see into the guts of the refinery and the water beyond. Silhouetted against the distant blue sky, she saw Beck's figure through the open windows of the wheelhouse. He leaned out, called down to his men, and returned his attention to the controls inside. The men on deck scrambled over the lines.

"Here," Patrick said at her side.

She ignored him.

"It's a hundred and fifty dollars."

Luz closed her hand over the money. She kissed his cheek, said, "*Gracias, cariño,*" and started for Minchi's.

"I'll see you tonight?" he called after her.

She shrugged with her left shoulder and didn't look back. From that day on, her nightly price was one hundred fifty dollars, not a penny less.

☀   ☀   ☀

Bar Sayonara idled during its first open hour. Once the refinery workers had eaten their lunches and sought something extra for dessert, there would be no time to chat. Two chairs sat against the back wall of the bar. This was where Carlotta received visitors. She brought Luz a glass of orange juice and sipped something stronger herself.

Luz got straight to the point but took a careful route. She flattered Carlotta by mentioning her memory of the woman's advice with regard to marrying Andrés. She said she wanted to go through with it, but only if Carlotta thought it would be good for her future. Similarly, she sought counsel regarding the legalities and pitfalls of such an arrangement.

Carlotta looked into her eyes as she spoke. She outlined a plan that would protect Luz from the worst that could happen, though there were still risks. Her lawyer, one Herr Boedeker, would write the marriage contract and interface with Marcela's lawyer. No doubt the two were familiar with each other, and once Marcela's lawyer knew that Boedeker was involved, he would not try anything stupid.

To become an Aruban citizen, Luz would have to remain married to Andrés for two full years. If subsequently divorced, she would retain citizenship and have all the rights and privileges of a natural born Aruban. This was not a new concept on the island, Carlotta said. Some lazy Aruban men married three times in ten years. Thanks to the contract, Andrés could not divorce her in less time, or he would be in default and have to return the money.

"Collecting it is another matter," Carlotta sighed. "Forget about that. I think Andrés will stick to his end. He has things he wants to do, and you will be helping him get them done. It is Marcela who must be watched."

Luz thought that so long as she worked at Minchi's, paid the casa, and caused no trouble, Marcela would be tamed.

The bell rang and three men entered the bar.

"Is there anything else?" Carlotta asked getting up from her chair.

"My son," Luz said. "I want him with me."

"That is more complicated. Let me talk to Boedeker."

On this point, Carlotta seemed less confident. Yet Luz left the bar feeling upbeat. It wasn't that she was looking forward to an indeterminate time working as a prostitute. It was that the decision had been made.

35

"YOU'RE A smart girl, Luz."

The tone surprised Luz more than the words. Sarcasm and condescension were absent from the comment. Luz expected la Dueña to be perturbed if not downright angry, but her boss sounded genuinely impressed with her. Of course, there was a catch.

"As for your boy," la Dueña said. "This is something you have to work out with Boedeker and Salinas."

La Dueña was seemingly agreeing that Luz's son could come to live in Aruba if Boedeker were able to make it part of the contract. Luz wanted all or nothing. Either Hernán came to live with her, or she would take her chances in Colombia. She chose her words carefully and spoke in a clear voice that didn't break.

"We have both lost husbands. I don't want to lose my son."

"Lose him?" la Dueña questioned.

"Remember how you told me about your family, how they abused you? I want to learn from this. I want my boy to know me as his mother, not a cash box."

"I hear what you're saying."

"If he is not going to be with me, then coming to Aruba was a big mistake. It's like you told me last year. What am I working for? The answer is that I'm working for him. It only makes sense that he is with me."

Marcela pointed her finger at Luz's chest. "It will be difficult for you," she said. "His friends at school will tell him what his mother is. They will hear it from their fathers and on the streets. And who will take care of him while you're working all night? That will be expensive."

Luz had spoken with the ladies at Pueblito Paisa, and they knew other women who would babysit Hernán for a reasonable daily rate. As for his finding out his mother was a prostitute? She would tell Hernán she was a hostess at a fancy restaurant and the men who said bad things about her were angry because she rebuffed their advances. By the time he was old enough to figure it out, she would be living in Colombia again, doing a job she wouldn't have to lie about.

"I think your important friends can find a way for Hernán to be with me," Luz said with confidence.

"Let me talk to them," la Dueña said too quickly.

"The refinery is busy," Luz said. "The Americans will pay my expenses."

"They're good for that," la Dueña agreed.

Those same Americans would support her family until they found a way to make their own living in Barrio Santa Barbara. The way Alison spoke of her neighborhood, it would be no time before Anna had a job. Perhaps she would meet a nice man who would marry her. If things went very well in Aruba, Luz could return home in a couple years with money to buy a house. Then they could start over without people like Jorgé or Marcela making demands.

"*Gracias, señora,*" Luz finished. She stepped out of the car and entered Minchi's, where Spanner kept a close eye on the pool table. She saw that Patrick and Bill were in the middle of a heated game. The mood had changed since the morning she had turned away Bill and his forty-dollar offer. Patrick now paid her one hundred fifty per night, and she limited him to three nights a week, not because she had other clients but to give the impression that she did. It kept Patrick hungry for her company. He read less, paid more attention to her, and was irritable with any of his friends who happened to be in the house when she was there. The tension frightened her, but she risked a brawl in exchange for that kind of money, which covered the casa, meals, and her doctor visits.

She saved the cash from her other clients. Since her last argument with Anna, Luz visited Western Union less often. She used her old hiding places. It was getting to the point where she worried about someone burglarizing her room. She was going to ask Carlotta to keep some of it but decided not to when she realized that after her marriage she would be able to open a bank account.

"How are things?" Spanner asked in English.

Luz replied, "Okay." She had requested he speak to her in English as much as possible. She learned common phrases. "How are you?" "What's your name?" "Are you married?" "Would you like a drink?" The men who came to the bar were surprised whenever she used them. She wasn't afraid to show off a little, even when it got her into trouble. If she started with an English phrase, the man always came back with one. If she didn't know what he meant, she would laugh and smile. Sometimes they knew she was faking it and made a fool of her. She couldn't wait for Hernán to begin school. She'd heard that Aruban children learned Dutch, Spanish, and English, as well as Papiamento. She would learn these languages side by side with him.

"La Dueña is happy?" Spanner asked.

"*Muy feliz*," Luz said, adding quickly, "Very happy."

"Why?"

"I marry," Luz said shrugging her left shoulder.

Spanner's sunglasses slid down his nose. He used Spanish so he could find out what she was talking about as quickly as possible. "You're getting married?"

"To Andrés, her stepson," Luz replied.

"Ricardo's boy?"

"The painter," she said with pride.

It took Spanner a few seconds to digest the information. It had been a long time since one of Minchi's girls had married a local. Spanner never figured Luz for doing that. She was too independent to tolerate the yoke of a lazy man who wanted a free and regular woman for sex in addition to the steady payment. He pushed his glasses up, took a glance at the pool table, and then looked back at Luz. He had seen prettier girls come through San Nicolaas. He had spoken to ones more clever, too. But he had never seen one capable of taming la Dueña, of marrying a local, and of learning some English in such a short amount of time.

"Congratulations," he said. "Soon I'll be working for you."

"Thank you," Luz replied, switching back to English. In light of the fact that she needed money to pay Boedeker, she made her way to the pool table. She timed her arrival with a break in the action. When Patrick stepped away to let another guy take a shot, she rubbed her hand down his back.

"*Hola*," he said.

"Lonely," she told him.

"You're lonely?" he asked.

"I miss you."

"Let me play a few more games. Then we'll go," he said.

Luz smiled for the one hundred fifty dollars she knew would be in her hand the next morning.

❈   ❈   ❈

With Carlotta by her side, Luz listened carefully to Herr Boedeker explain the contract he had drafted. There were two copies, the official one written in Dutch, as well as a Spanish translation. She followed along as best she could. Occasionally, Carlotta pointed out a key paragraph and asked a question.

"In order for your son to remain here," Boedeker clarified, "Andrés is acknowledging that he is the father. We all know this is not true."

"*Claro*," Carlotta interjected.

"This document makes it true for the sake of the Office of Immigration. Andrés is essentially adopting the boy."

"But if the boy is his why must he adopt him?" Carlotta asked.

"Because he was not born here, and the Office of Immigration knows that documents in Colombia are forged all the time. If he is adopted, his parentage is irrelevant."

Blunt talk about such chicanery made Luz uncomfortable. At the same time, she was glad it was out in the open. She was beginning to understand why la Dueña spoke the way she did. It was how business people communicated, directly and economically.

"I would like to have my own bank account," Luz put in.

Herr Boedeker said, "My friend at Caribbean Mercantile Bank would be very pleased to have your business." He handed Luz a card.

During the ride to San Nicolaas, Carlotta offered Luz advice regarding her banking.

"Don't tell anyone about your account," Carlotta said. "That is your affair and has nothing to do with your husband, your family, or your friends. Not even me."

"I understand," Luz said.

"Good. You'll do very well in this world, *niña*. I wish I had a daughter like you, but God gave you to someone else."

Never had Luz heard kinder words.

*   *   *

The lunch crowd tired Charlie out. He wished Sam were there. Sam was inexhaustible when it came to entertaining tourists. However, Charlie had banished Sam from the kingdom and, despite the current crisis, was not prepared to repeal his order. He loved Sam, but the man needed to learn when enough was too much.

"There's smoke coming off your shoes," Charlie said to Koch.

"But I think we get a break soon," Koch told him as they passed each other in the kitchen.

When Charlie returned to the bar, he saw that two tables had been vacated. Every stool at the bar was occupied, but no one waited behind those with seats. He tapped three glasses of beer, collected payment from a cute couple from Arizona, and asked a pair of Dutch retirees if they wanted another round. They declined, took a photo of the bell hanging over the bar, and waved good-bye.

Three quarters of an hour later, Charlie and Koch were alone. They perused the newspaper, checked their lottery numbers, and chatted about progress in the refinery. Charlie excused himself to go upstairs to wash his face and don a fresh shirt. He planned to steal a few minutes' sleep if things remained calm.

After patting his face dry, he went out on his veranda to check Screwball's bowl. It was full, but the cat was nowhere in sight. As he turned to get a clean shirt, he noticed a flash of color down on the street. Carlotta approached the bar from the west side of town. She traveled under full sail with one of her trademark hats fixed to her head, this one lime green. Carlotta's personal appearance in the bar meant a serious issue needed to be discussed. Instead of a clean T-shirt, Charlie slipped his arms into a freshly pressed oxford. The bar's logo was embroidered on the pocket.

"Doña Carlotta," he greeted his honored guest in the bar. "Would you like a drink?"

Carlotta gave him a tight smile. "A white wine," she said.

He made a show of selecting a special glass and opening a fresh bottle of California chardonnay. He placed the glass on a tray and invited Carlotta to join him at the table in the farthest corner. Koch raised an eyebrow, and Charlie replied with a look that told his bartender to keep an eye on him in case the tears started to flow.

"There is something we must do," Carlotta began.

"For you I am always available," Charlie assured her.

"It's not for me," she continued. "It's for her." Her finger was pointed down the street.

Charlie took a moment to consider which particular her it could be. Kenny's mother, who owned Java and Chesterfield? The woman who worked in the restaurant on the corner by China Clipper? The wife of the old man building the hotel that would never be finished? Not Marcela, whom Charlie knew to be an archenemy of Carlotta, nor any of the hundred or so girls in town because Carlotta had been dealing with them for years and had run out of sympathy long ago. On second thought, there was one girl, and it took Charlie only a quick glance at Carlotta's eyes to know he was right.

"She will marry Andrés next Saturday. We are going to be her witnesses."

"Andrés said nothing to me," Charlie said, more surprised than doubtful about the truth of Carlotta's statement.

She put her hand over his wrist. "He finds out today when Marcela and her lawyer tell him."

Charlie looked lovingly at the glass of wine in Carlotta's hand even as he prayed for something stronger. However, he was in his bar, and within its walls he did not indulge his weakness.

"She'll be fine with this arrangement as long as she has us looking out for her," Carlotta finished.

This was true. Marcela attacked the weak, the foolish, and the unsuspecting. She stayed away from the strong, the wise, and the wary. Carlotta and Charlie were all of that and more. Their presence at Luz's wedding would leave Marcela with no doubt that the girl had their protection.

"I'll be sure my suit is pressed."

"Wear a blue tie," Carlotta said, "It goes well with your eyes and will match my dress. Is Samito here?"

"No."

"*Gracias a Dios*," Carlotta sighed.

Charlie might have added that Captain Beck was gone as well.

Carlotta finished her drink and shared a hug. When she was gone, Charlie sat at the end of his bar. The place was empty except for Koch and the women in the kitchen. He looked out at the sun-bleached street. The White Star Store was closed. A few cars passed by. The guard from the bank carried his lunch back to his post.

"This one's on me," Koch said placing a fresh glass of ice water before Charlie. "*Danki*," Charlie said and sipped the refreshment.

He could hardly remember the last time he felt such a confusion of emotions. It was probably when his daughter went off to Holland. She told him, "Papa, I'm going to university, and then I'm going to get a job." He was elated. "Good!" he said proudly. She said, "I plan on living in Holland for the rest of my life. I hope to meet a man, maybe get married." It had to happen this way. As much as it hurt, it made him happy. His girl was moving on with her life, escaping a small island for a small country on a small continent, but a step up nonetheless.

Luz's marriage was something else. He had no reason to care about her. He wasn't Sam. But he did care. He had hoped her first tour would be her last. When she appeared a second time, he had been apprehensive, but his contacts told him she was doing well. Now that she was marrying a local, he had renewed cause for concern. She would have to be a whore for at least two years just to pay the contract. If the job wasn't in her blood already, it would be when the contract ended. She would be a professional's professional, skilled at the art, proficient in the tricks of the trade. Charlie had seen girls develop this way in his own place as well as in San Nicolaas. Some of them seemed born for the job. Others struggled through it. It wasn't that he thought Luz couldn't do it but that he thought she was worthy of something better. It was as if she had a winning hand but someone had stolen her cards. He saw what Sam saw in her: grace and charm, honesty and sincerity. These four qualities were scarcely found among modern girls. His own daughter lacked them. People of her generation were too anxious to get to the point. They failed to appreciate the subtleties of life. They shouted when they should whisper.

So long as he was being completely honest with himself, he admitted he was slightly jealous. Andrés had the talent of an old master. He touched his brush in a daub of paint, moved it to his canvas, and a scene was suddenly rendered in brilliant detail. He made it look easy, which was the truest sign of genius. On top of this gift, Andrés was getting Luz. Simply being in the girl's company was a joy. With her for inspiration, Andrés was destined to exhibit in the Louvre. That she was paying him made the situation completely ridiculous. It was as if he had a wealthy aunt supporting him. How could Charlie not be envious of this combination?

Eventually, Charlie's jealousy dissipated. He knew it was a negative emotion. He was too old to waste energy on stupid thoughts like that. Before putting the matter out of his mind, he reflected on what his life would have been like had he the talent of Rembrandt and an angel for a wife. The fantasy gave him cause to smile. He got up from his stool, washed his glass, and told Koch he was going to Savaneta for a rest.

"Give Screwball some water," Charlie said on his way out the door. "It's hot out there today."

It was one week to the day after Carlotta's visit that Luz stood before the desk where she would sign the marriage contract.

Of all the things that should have been on her mind, Luz was preoccupied by how she was going to tell her family she was married. She imagined their reactions: her mother would faint. Her sister would think she was making another mistake. Hernán? He was too young to understand. Rudi? He was still hiding.

She had three weeks to come up with a story. Barely two weeks of her ninety-day tour remained. When that was finished, she was flying to Bogotá with Alison. She would use the third week to find a house. Alison had called her father, who talked to another man who was also a lawyer. This lawyer would work for Luz as Herr Boedeker had and make sure she had an honest lease. This man knew real estate brokers and had already talked to them about places she could afford.

For the time being, she refocused her attention on the matter at hand, her marriage to Andrés. Refusing to show any deference to Marcela, she wore a dress she bought secondhand at a store in Oranjestaad. Carlotta and Charlie stood behind and to the right of her. La Dueña and Montoya were in place to the left of Andrés. The Registrar read through the *marriage ceremony* with all the excitement of someone checking his grocery receipt. When he finished, Luz signed her name; Andrés signed his; and the four witnesses took turns signing theirs. After Carlotta kissed her cheek and Charlie shook Andrés's hand, it was over. She was married.

"Welcome to the family," Marcela said.

"*Gracias, señora*," Luz said. She swore never to use the word mother when referring to her boss.

"We'll leave you two so you can enjoy your honeymoon," Marcela said. She turned to Montoya and tugged his sleeve. "Give them the keys."

Montoya dropped a set of keys into Andrés's palm. Luz caught Marcela's smile. The newlyweds were expected to pay five hundred guilders a month for the use of his old house. It was a bargain compared to her room at Minchi's. In exchange for working at the bar, la Dueña cut the rate on that room to seven hundred fifty guilders. Her basic cost to live and work in Aruba was exactly the same as before. She still needed a full slate of clients to meet her expenses and provide for her family.

Andrés drove her to the house in San Nicolaas. The place was empty aside from a thin film of dust. The only furniture was an old twin mattress atop a box spring in the corner of the back bedroom. Andrés put her suitcase beside the bed, where he had dropped a plastic bag containing a few of his things. Andrés asked her if she wanted to go to the beach.

"It's late for that," Luz replied.

"I like the light," he said. "Carlotta gave us a basket with some wine and food. We should use it because we don't even have a refrigerator."

"Okay," Luz said reflexively.

After changing into casual clothes, they rode out of town, through the vacant streets of the old Esso colony, to the tip of Roger's Beach. Andrés laid out a blanket he kept in his car, using rocks to hold the corners. They drank wine from the bottle and took bites of cheese sandwiches in between.

"I won't be in the house very often," Andrés told Luz. "I work in Oranjestaad at an auto body shop."

"Do you like it?" she asked.

"No. Once in a while a guy wants his car painted with something special. That saves me from total boredom."

She understood the need to get paid.

"I've been saving money to go to Holland. I guess I should thank you since I'll be able to go sooner now that we have our arrangement. If my stepmother wasn't keeping her half, I would be gone by the end of the year. I'll probably have to wait another year."

"Where will you live?"

"Amsterdam," he answered. "My father was going to send me, but he died and Marcela kept the money from his boat. She said my father would have wanted me to work for my rewards."

"I understand," Luz said, saving him the trouble of explaining how la Dueña had stolen his dream.

He looked up at the sky, scanning back and forth as if searching for something. He got up, went over to his car, and returned with a painted board and a battery-powered lantern. "Tell me what you think," he said handing it to Luz.

Luz gazed at his picture. It was an exact copy of the scene which spread out before her. The beach curved to the right. A spit of rocks stuck up from the sea on the left. Above the rocks hung a three-quarter moon, casting faint rays that were caught on the waves below. Her fingers stuck to the edges in paint that wasn't completely dry.

"*It's beautiful,*" she said, but the word she wanted to use was moody. Judging by the wet paint and current phase of the moon, he must have finished it the night before. She was ignorant when it came to art and the logic behind it. Yet Andrés's work called out to her. It struck her as authentic.

He put the painting away, and they finished the wine and sandwiches. He asked her about her family. Despite feeling guilty about deceiving someone who displayed such honesty in his work, she told him the lie about her husband dying in a mine explosion and leaving her with a son, the son Andrés had agreed to adopt. As she repeated it one more time, she thought that it was the only thing Hernán would ever know. She would never tell him the truth about his father. Her son deserved better than the stigma of a foolish mother and a rapacious father.

"He'll like Aruba," Andrés said. "Send him to the International School here in Seroe Colorado."

"I was going to send him to the Catholic school on the north end."

"That's good, too," he said, "but the International School is run for the Americans. Aside from language study, they take education very seriously."

She didn't have time to ask how much it cost before Andrés solved the problem for her.

"One of your American friends can sponsor your son. Any American working full-time at the refinery can send two children to the school free of charge. It was set up that way many years ago when Esso paid for everything."

"The Americans are very generous."

"They can afford to be," Andrés told her. "They're the richest people in the world."

She nodded her head, thinking about what Inez had said about America.

Andrés apologized after a yawn. "It's the wine," he said. And stretched out on the blanket. She settled in beside him.

"Thank you," Luz said.

"For what?"

"For helping me," she answered. "For adopting Hernán."

"I'm an artist, not a saint."

"I'm neither," she said and put her head down on his shoulder.

36

LATE IN the afternoon, just as Luz was putting away her cleaning supplies, Andrés arrived with two friends. One of them was Harry from the cell phone store. They greeted Luz cheerfully, telling her how good the place looked.

"We're going to paint the walls," Andrés said. Harry and the other guy carried gallon cans of paint into the room.

"Okay," Luz said, wondering what colors were in the cans. She was no artist, but she had a sense of style that she hoped to express in the house.

"If you don't mind, stay at Minchi's for the next couple of days. That way you won't be bothered by the smell."

Luz wrinkled her nose.

"Don't worry. I'll be finished before the week is over. After that, the place is all yours."

"You're not going to live here?" she queried.

He sounded apologetic when he explained. "My apartment is close to my job."

Luz was comfortable living in her room at Minchi's, which wasn't necessarily the safest place, but living in a strange house among neighbors she didn't know made her stomach clench. Hernán and the babysitter would be alone while she worked through the night.

Andrés took a screwdriver from his pocket and pried open the lid of the nearest can. The liquid inside was pure white. The odor was strong but not awful. Andrés seemed to love it.

"You and Hernán each get your own room," he said. "Which one is his?"

"I was thinking the one back there," Luz said, pointing to the other side of the house.

"That's where I'll start," her new husband said and carried his paint in one hand and a roller in the other.

Harry followed Andrés with a pan and roller of his own. He winked at Luz and gave her a thumbs-up, which reminded her of Samito.

Luz juggled clients the way a circus clown juggled flaming torches. None of them could meet lest she ruin her earning potential during the last two weeks of her tour. Between Patrick, two married men, a Dutch marine named Franz, and new clients, she had enough business to fill her hiding spots with fresh cash. She kept the men satisfied yet longing for her by limiting their time to strictly one-half hour upstairs. Patrick was the exception. She went home with him on alternate nights. For his one hundred fifty dollars she permitted him to sleep with her until nine-thirty the next morning, to a half hour of sex, and to a communal shower, which saved the time of taking turns.

By quarter past eleven, she was sharing an early lunch with Alison at Pueblito Paisa. During these sessions, they planned their return to Bogotá over the day's special, for which Luz paid in exchange for valuable information.

"I spoke to my father this morning," Alison said. "He found a house for you only ten blocks from where we live."

Before asking about the house, Luz inquired about the price.

"He says they'll rent it for sixty-five thousand pesos per month but they want a lease for one year."

Sixty-five thousand pesos, or three hundred ten dollars, was the limit of her budget. She asked for the details.

"It sounds like our house," Alison said. "It has three bedrooms, kitchen, a combined dining and salon area. There's only one bathroom."

Her family only had one bathroom at present.

"The houses are close together, but my father said there is a yard in front. Nothing much behind it."

"That's okay," Luz said. "Tell him I'm very interested."

"I thought you would be. I told him to make an appointment with the agent for the day after we get back."

That would be a Monday, and Luz could hardly wait. The sooner her family was out of their present house the better off they would be.

"How far is the nearest church," Luz asked thinking of her mother.

"Our church is a ten-minute walk. From this house probably another five."

"Perfect."

"I told my father that since your business is so good here in Aruba you might want to buy the house."

Luz dropped her fork. "My business?"

"I had to tell him something, Luz. How else could you afford a house?"

"What type of business?"

"A restaurant and bar. I told him I've been working for you and that you're a great boss. It's enough truth that we can keep it straight if he starts asking questions."

Whether she liked it or not, Luz was stuck with this lie on top of all the others. She modified it slightly in order to make it acceptable to her family. "We'll tell him it's my new husband's business."

"It should be," Alison said quietly.

"What do you mean?"

"I heard how la Dueña gave Andrés nothing that was his father's."

"Don't repeat that," Luz warned.

With a hand over her mouth, Alison shook her head.

Half an hour later, Luz unlocked the door to Casa Montoya, as she came to know her rented home. The interior gleamed. Andrés had whitewashed every wall. With no drapes to curtail the sun, the place was as bright inside as out. How was she going to sleep in there when a quarter moon would light the room like a soccer stadium? She had a month to make the place habitable before Hernán arrived.

Patrick made Luz a proposal on the last Thursday of her tour. He offered to pay the bar fine, or *molta* as it was called in Spanish, for Friday and Saturday nights so she could be with him exclusively. His plans included a trip to the other side of the island, where someone he knew owned a timeshare. They would spend two days and nights together, walk on the beach, see a show, and eat at tourist restaurants.

"I have to ask permission," Luz told him. "La Dueña expects me to collect for the casa every night." While this was the case, she needed time to calculate how much she would gain or lose by going with him.

Like a fool, Patrick said, "My job is finished here. By the time you return from Colombia, I'll be somewhere else."

"The United States?"

"Maybe. I also have an offer from a company in Japan. The pay is double what they're paying me here."

"Do you speak Japanese?"

"No, but there was a time when I didn't speak Spanish. Ask la Dueña tonight. Okay?"

"I will," she replied without missing the plea behind his eyes. She had controlled him since the day Bill tried to bed her. As badly as he wanted her and in light of his future earnings, she concluded that three hundred dollars per night plus one hundred fifty for the molta was an appropriate figure. If both la Dueña and Patrick agreed, she would have nearly two month's rent in hand.

That afternoon, she phoned Colombia.

"You know we have to move," Luz began. "I need you to help me, Anna."

"I'll do what I can," her sister said.

"Through a friend, I think I have a place in Barrio Santa Barbara on the other side of Bogotá from where we live now."

"You mentioned it before. I hear it is a good neighborhood."

"It is, and it will be better for our family. I need you to help me convince Mother of that."

"What about Rudi?" Anna asked.

"When he comes back, he should have no problem living with us," Luz explained. "He will be away from Jorgé, and there are more jobs than anywhere in Colombia."

Anna interrupted. "Mother doesn't want to move."

"Tell Mother you think it's a good idea. Talk to her about it several times."

Anna's hesitation revealed her ambivalence.

"Have you spoken with Jorgé?" Luz asked.

"He was here yesterday. He only said that he wants us out of the house without any trouble. He didn't ask for money."

"There won't be any trouble," Luz said. "We'll have a place to go. Can you find someone with a pickup truck to move our things? I have money to pay for it."

"I don't know," Anna said lowly.

"There's more I have to tell you, Anna, but now isn't the time. Tell Hernán I love him and will be there a week from Sunday. Don't forget about the truck."

She spent Thursday afternoon transferring her things from Minchi's to Casa Montoya. It took several trips using Samito's little suitcase. She also commandeered a few cardboard boxes from behind the White Star Store. These served as her dresser and bureau. Only her toiletries and one outfit remained in her room above the bar.

That evening, la Dueña arrived early, fifteen minutes before nine. Spanner and Luz chatted at the bar with the account book between them, waiting for the girls to come down.

Luz asked about leaving with Patrick. "I have a special client," she informed her boss. "He wants to spend two nights with me on the other side of the island." To her surprise Marcela smiled broadly and clapped her hands.

"Very good, Luz, very good," la Dueña complimented her.

"I told him I had to ask your permission."

"And you can tell him you have it. Of course, he must pay the *molta*."

"*Sí, señora*," Luz agreed. "I have your blessing?"

La Dueña blew her a kiss. "You have it, *niña*."

It irked Luz that Marcela called her daughter. This term she reserved for Carlotta, whom she trusted like a mother, perhaps more than her own mother.

"You're as smart as I was at your age," her boss was saying. "You will need clients like this to support you. I'm impressed you have one already."

"*Gracias, señora*," Luz said.

"Spanner, you collect for the casa until Luz comes back."

Spanner nodded his head.

At that moment, Alison and the other girls entered the room. Each of them greeted their employer and promptly paid their bill. Nothing made la Dueña happier than an envelope of money, and she left with a full one at that.

Patrick hardly blinked at three hundred dollars per night. He paid the fine to Spanner and then proudly handed Luz her six hundred in advance. He told her to get her things, that they were going directly to the hotel. She was expecting this but told him she needed half an hour. She took her time to heighten his desire.

The first night, they went to a show at the Royal Cabana Casino. The dancing was average compared to what Luz had seen in Colombia. But the tourists loved it, and Luz was caught up in their enthusiasm. After the show, Patrick treated her to a couple of hours in the casino. He gave her chips to play at the blackjack table. He bet recklessly, lost consistently, and didn't notice that Luz had slipped most of her chips into her purse. After losing a thousand dollars, he took her back to the timeshare, where he had sex with her on the balcony overlooking the pool.

They spent the next day dozing by the same pool. When the sun set, they showered and drove into Oranjestaad to a restaurant where they dined American style on steak and baked potatoes. "There won't be much of this in Japan," Patrick said. "Only fish and rice there."

Although Inez had talked of working there and how much Japanese men paid for western women, Luz had no desire to find out for herself.

After dinner, they went to a bar located on the beach. There she had her first experience with karaoke. Everyone sang in English. The worse their singing, the more everyone laughed. "This is very popular in Japan," Patrick informed her.

Luz wished she were able to sing. She thought a beautiful singing voice was one of the greatest gifts God could give a person. She always kept her voice low, even in church, because she knew the limits of her talent. A young woman whom she thought she recognized took the microphone. The music coming from the speakers was familiar, too. The song was *Monton de Estrellas* and she loved the salsa version of it. After the introduction, the girl sang in a wonderful, clear voice, words that Luz knew by heart. The crowd fell silent until she finished, at which point they gave her a loud round of applause. It was then that Luz remembered seeing her in line at the doctor's office. She couldn't recall her name but was certain she worked at Caribbean Bar. As Luz got up to leave with Patrick, she exchanged glances with the singer. They both smiled in the comfort brought on by well-paying clients.

Patrick drove her to Minchi's the next morning. He talked about packing his things, trouble getting the flights he wanted, and the hassles of negotiating an employment contract with a multinational corporation. Since it was Sunday, Rembrandtstraat was a lonely place, which would have made it a romantic one in which to say good-bye. However, the sun was too bright, the wind too strong, and Luz had her mind on nothing but her family. Patrick was equally distracted. Though he helped her out of the car and gave her a generous hug, his words were rushed and sounded flat.

Standing in the doorway he put his hands in his pockets. "We had a good time," he said.

It was a lame statement, one Luz wished he hadn't made. They both knew it wasn't true. The good time had been his. He used her for his pleasure between doing his job at the refinery and reading books. Aside from last night at the karaoke session, there was not a single moment Luz could remember.

"*Gracias,*" she said, adding, "*Buena suerte, señor,*" because a one-word good-bye seemed rude.

"*Adiós, Luz,*" Patrick said and headed for his car. "Don't forget me."

On her way upstairs, she thought about what she would remember and what she would not. Patrick meant little to her, less than the married men she serviced or Harry, who had the patience to explain how her cell phone worked. She wouldn't remember what he looked like or that he went to work in Japan. She would remember that he paid her three hundred dollars per night. She would never forget that. Nor would she forget to ask a client for more than she ever thought him willing to pay.

She knocked on Alison's door. Alison opened it a crack, saw it was Luz, and stepped back into the room.

"Have you packed?" Luz asked.

"Some things. Francisco says the autobus will not be here until two thirty this afternoon."

"That's right," Luz said, "but we're taking a taxi. I'll pick you up at three."

"Francisco will be angry when we're not here."

"Why should we pay him twenty florins each when the taxi will charge only twenty for both of us?"

Alison put her arms around Luz. "I told my father you were really good at business," she gushed.

That evening, Charlie swept his stairs. A thin layer of grit had filtered in through the gaps around the lower door. He was careful with the broom because he knew how slippery fine dust could be. It had been two weeks since the last rainfall. This was the curse of his desert island. From the air, it looked like paradise, an opal set amid lapis lazuli. However, from ground level, without a drop of fresh water under the blazing sun, it was like an Egyptian tomb: hot sand, dried flesh, and clever artifacts, many of which hung in his bar.

Charlie never worried about dying of thirst. If anything, he would end up pickled in rum, which wasn't the worst way to go. It would save the undertaker a bit of trouble and maybe his daughter some money. If she was so inclined, she could install him in a glass case on a shelf behind the bar for all to see. It would be like Lenin's mausoleum in Moscow, creepy but one hell of an attraction.

On the balcony, he promptly retrieved his bottle of Barbancour and a chilled glass from the refrigerator. Screwball's bowl contained barely a puddle of water. He wondered if the cat might like rum but decided not to find out. Screwball had more of a dry wit than a ribald sense of humor, and that made him a whiskey drinker. The feline was like the Dalai Lama. He could smile like a fool because he'd already achieved total consciousness. Charlie wasn't there yet. Although he had a long way to go, he was making steady progress. For example, this night he perfected the art of accepting things the way they were, which was no minor accomplishment for a man so used to action. His daughter had called from Holland to let him know she had moved in with a young man he would never approve of. Charlie disliked the guy not because he was a bum but because he was a bum without style. He let the woman keep him when he should have kept her.

There was nothing he could do but wish her well and wonder what was wrong with these young people. They had the world at their feet with their educations, good paying jobs, and opportunities for more of both. And yet they talked to each other more via computer than in person and conducted sex separately, before two cameras connected by a satellite. How could that be any good at all? They'd never have the pleasure of waking in each other's arms after a deeply satisfying physical experience.

Ah, but who was he to judge? He was a glorified bartender, teller of stories, and half-assed painter. If he had Andrés's talent, he would be exhibiting at The Hague, bedding princesses, and not saying a word to tabloid reporters.

Screwball gave him a look that indicated great displeasure with the empty water bowl. Before making his own drink, Charlie rinsed the bowl, refilled it, and dropped in two ice cubes. When he finished pouring the rum, he heard a low whistling sound.

Screwball pulled back his tongue, pricked his ears, and sniffed the air. He jumped onto the parapet on the west side of the veranda, then paced back and forth a few times before looking at Charlie and releasing a hearty growl.

"Tell me, my friend," Charlie said, joining the cat at the edge.

Beyond the refinery wall, Charlie spotted what held his cat's attention. One of the flares near the center of the complex sputtered before the pilot torch caught and burned with a solid blue flame. The whistle's pitch increased slowly as the pressure of the main flare rose. After about a minute, it achieved the steady note Charlie and Screwball knew so well. The flare ignited. A belch of yellow flame plumed into the sky like a ragged sun. It took shape in the breeze, pointing west over the ocean, and illuminated the rare fisherman who plied the island's western lea. This was a beautiful and welcome sight.

Charlie simultaneously raised his glass and petted his cat's head. The refinery had been resurrected, brought back from the dead by strangers who would sooner or later be his friends. He downed his rum in a series of gulps and then refilled the glass. He would sleep well tonight, better than he had in months.

And there was more to the show, something he had to see before going to bed.

"Let's take a closer look," Charlie said. He went into his house and returned with an ancient pair of binoculars. They were massive and heavier than lead bricks. An American veteran of the Second World War had presented them to his father. "Keep a sharp eye for German subs," he had said. At least that was the story

Charlie's father had told. His father had been a notorious bullshitter, and Charlie was similarly inclined. At any rate, he put the binoculars up to his eyes in order to have a front row seat to a show he enjoyed every time he saw it.

A tanker approached from the north northwest, the way they always did. A cascade of water poured through her anchor port just in case something went wrong and they had to drop the hook. Charlie saw that the ship was on the perfect heading, its bow pointed straight into the wind, which was out of the east southeast and steady at what he estimated to be ten knots. Up to this moment, he thought the assisting tug was the one that serviced the cruise ships in Oranjestaad. However, when he focused his binoculars on the smaller vessel he realized it was another boat. She ran out from the east, turned toward the tanker and seemed to hold still until the tanker eased ahead. Just before the larger hull obscured the tug, Charlie caught a splotch of color flashing from the upper house of the tug. It was the Stars and Stripes, cracking in the breeze.

"*Bon nochi, Herr Beck!*" Charlie called over the parapet.

THE RENTAL agent was a pleasant woman named Teresa. She took her time showing Luz the features of the house. The neighborhood was secure and quiet according to Teresa. Luz knew that already. There was an elementary school within walking distance. This didn't matter; Hernán was going to Aruba. He would attend the International School courtesy of a yet to be named client of hers. The paved parking space was useless since her family did not own a car. The house appealed to Luz because the rooms were larger than the ones in the house they were leaving. The kitchen appliances were newer, and the single bathroom was brightly lit by lights overhead and around the mirror. What few pieces of furniture her family was bringing would easily fit inside.

"Tell me what you think," Teresa said as they leaned against the kitchen counter.

Luz combined Señora Álvaro's charm with Captain Beck's confidence and added just a hint of la Dueña's condescension. She said, "The house is fine, but I would like an option to buy it."

"*Bien,*" Teresa replied. "I will ask the owner if he is interested."

"My lawyer, Señor Guzman, has drafted this lease," Luz said placing the document on the counter. "It applies ninety-five percent of my rental payments against the sale price. I have one year to decide to buy it. After that, the rent is only rent and does not apply to the purchase. Will the owner agree to that?" This speech Luz had rehearsed with Alison's father, and it came off more as a demand than a request.

Teresa took a deep breath, picked up the lease, and thumbed through it. "I see you are well represented. I can't speak for the owner, but I will give this to him."

"You can recommend it," Luz suggested. "It gives him a five-percent premium every month that I rent."

"I understand and will mention that. It is still his decision."

"Of course," Luz agreed. "I'm counting on you to show him the good part."

Teresa eyed her carefully. Luz met her gaze and held it the way she did the eyes of the men who came into Minchi's. She added a slight smile to show she had the maturity not to get angry over something like this.

"Here's my number," Luz said giving the number for the second chip Harry had installed in her cell phone. "Call me tonight."

"I don't know if he will make the decision so quickly," Teresa said.

"But I can," Luz replied. "I have two other houses to look at today. I'd like to rent this one." She shrugged for effect. "You never know." She rummaged through her purse in order to give Teresa a view of two more copies of the lease that were in there. She pulled out her cell phone, opened it, and said, "A full battery. Good. You know how these things are, always going dead when you need them."

Teresa saw the expensive phone in Luz's hand and wished she had shown a more expensive house. If the girl could afford that phone and the purse in which she kept it, she could afford another ten thousand pesos in rent.

Luz ate supper with Alison and her family at their home. Alison's father, Gio, was a pensive man who rubbed the bald spot on his head. He was clearly relieved his daughter was home. That she brought a successful friend with her added to his solace.

"I'd like to meet your husband," Gio said.

"He's always off painting," Alison told him before Luz had a chance to comment.

"Painting?" Gio queried.

"My husband is an artist," Luz explained.

"Luz runs the business while he's at Charlie's with his brushes and paints," Alison put in.

Luz wished Alison would keep quiet and not make it any harder to perpetuate the lie they had started upon their return.

Gio wanted to know who Charlie was.

"A friend of my husband's. He has a studio where they paint together."

"It's beautiful," Alison said. "A little building by the sea where they chat and drink and paint pictures."

"You manage the restaurant by yourself?" Gio asked. He was skeptical because Luz appeared barely old enough to be out of high school more than two years. He reminded himself of the self-assurance she possessed in Señor Guzman's office. Still, she was young to be in charge of anything.

"I have the help of two capable bartenders," Luz answered referring to Spanner and Pablo.

"Every business is only as good as its worst employee," Gio said, and that put an end to the conversation.

Teresa did not call. Luz slept fitfully. She worried she would have to find another house in a neighborhood where her family would be complete strangers instead of close enough to Alison's family to feel welcome and accepted. She had five days to accomplish this before Jorgé put them in the street.

The next morning, Alison took Luz around her part of town. She showed her shopping districts, pointed out restaurants, mentioned clubs where sexy young men could be found, and clarified the transportation systems. Luz displayed her enthusiasm as best she could. She would have preferred to look for another house or an apartment for her family. Alison told her not to despair, that it would all work out for her the way it had in Aruba. Things hadn't worked out as well as Alison thought. Luz had effectively sold herself into bondage. Andrés was a friendly young man, but he expected to be paid, and Marcela would be sure of it since Luz paid her and then she gave Andrés his share. This was a two-year contract, not a three-month stint. Her expenses were no less than they were when she worked directly at Minchi's.

Luz opened her cell phone, checked the battery indicator, and closed it.

"Put that thing away," Alison said. "Let's go to a movie."

They went to a movie, during which Luz fell asleep. Luckily she awoke before the end, and Alison was none the wiser.

"How about supper out?" Alison asked. "I know a place where we may run into some Norte Americanos."

Alison's tone suggested they find clients. Luz was appalled she would do this in her home city. It didn't matter that six million people lived in Bogotá. There was the chance that one of them would know someone who knew someone else who knew her family.

"I don't want to spend too much money," Luz said. "Let's buy some things and eat at your house."

"That's boring," Alison whined. "Come on, you can't fool me. I know what you made in Aruba."

Luz had forgotten how girls in San Nicolaas watched each other, how quickly they spread gossip, how jealous they could be. She stuck to her position regarding the evening meal because every peso mattered.

After some coaxing, Alison agreed to supper at home. Having worked for Señor Garcia, Luz knew her way around grocery stores, and the one not far from Alison's house was gigantic. She selected the things she would have for her own family. They each carried two bags to Alison's mother, who was shocked that her daughter had been so thoughtful.

After supper, she stepped outside to call her family. Anna had proposed the move, but Mother had ignored her. Mother wanted to know how they could move without knowing where they were going and also insisted on calling a lawyer.

Luz refused to rise to the argument. "I'll be home on Sunday afternoon," she said at last. "We need to be gone by noon on Monday. Have you found a truck to bring our things to Santa Barbara?"

"I did."

Luz nearly collapsed at this revelation but said, "I knew I could trust you, Anna."

"I do my best, Luz."

She rang off and decided to find another real estate agent to show her houses and apartments. She knew the money in her purse spent as easily with them as with Teresa. Before going to bed, she informed Alison she would be going to see a new agent in the morning.

"You won't have to," Alison said and rolled over. In minutes, she was snoring softly into her pillow while Luz lay awake staring at the wall.

At Señor Guzman's direction, Luz opened a bank account the next day. Money she transferred from Aruba to Colombia would now go from one bank to another. She would avoid Western Union and save half the fee. When the paperwork was complete, she reunited with Alison in the bank's lobby. As they stepped outside on their way to another real estate office, Luz's phone rang.

Teresa said, "The owner would like to accept your offer with a small change."

"What change?" Luz asked.

"They want ninety percent of the rent to apply to the purchase."

"That's acceptable," Luz said. She heard Teresa let out a long breath. "If we can sign it tomorrow," Luz added before there was a chance of the deal's slipping out of her hands.

"I'll meet you at two o'clock," Teresa said.

"Told you," Alison said. "Let's celebrate."

"Not yet," Luz told her.

Alison smacked Luz with her purse. "What's wrong with you!" she shouted. "Everything goes right for you. You make more money than any girl in San Nicolaas. You end up married to a guy who isn't bad looking and can paint. And you get a great deal on a house. All you do is worry, worry, worry. I'm so angry with you!"

Stunned by the outburst, Luz said, "I'm sorry."

"You're going to get drunk and have a good time," Alison said.

And they did. They went to a crowded place full of people their age. Somehow they found their way home but not until they had danced with several guys and Alison had gotten sick in the back of a taxi.

Teresa brought a signed copy of the lease and two sets of keys to the house. They shook hands, and Luz returned to her family's new home alone. She went from room to room, opening the closets, imagining where she would put things, as if she were going to live there instead of in Aruba.

Considering the time required to move her family, she would have less than a day with them before going back to work. She had wanted to stay longer, but airline tickets were cheaper during the middle of the week, and every day she was away from San Nicolaas cost her money.

That night, she thanked Gio for his help and told him Rudi was an excellent worker, just in case Gio heard about jobs that might be available. He said he would ask around and let her know. She never mentioned that her brother had been gone for months.

"I also want to thank you," he said, "for giving my daughter a job and looking out for her. I wish she was a little more serious, a little more like you."

Since he had no idea what he was saying, Luz smiled and squeezed his arm. "She's lucky to have you as her father," she said and excused herself from his company.

"Luz!" Señora Álvaro called from her office.

Luz couldn't help but rush past the other desks to embrace the woman. She felt genuine affection in Señora Álvaro's arms, the kind she used to share with her sister, the kind she now shared with Carlotta.

Álvaro pointed to a spot high up on her wall. Luz saw a photo of herself there in the space that had previously been empty. It was the one Inez had taken of her in front of Minchi's.

"You're at the top of the list," Álvaro said. "You've done great things for yourself."

"I hope so," Luz said.

"You're married now! Before you know it, you'll be in the United States, living in a mansion, speaking English, and driving a Cadillac. Don't forget me."

Blushing, Luz assured her she would never forget her.

Álvaro then asked, "Did your friend find you?"

"Friend? Which one?"

"The one who took the photo, Inez."

Horrified at what Inez might have told her family, Luz said, "I haven't heard from her."

"I told her you were in Aruba and coming home soon, but not exactly when. She said she would find you there. It's a small island, right?"

"It's a small island," Luz repeated.

"Give me some more good news," Álvaro said. "You're one of my favorites. I love talking to you."

"Well, my family is moving to Barrio Santa Barbara," Luz replied. "I found a house for them."

Tears came from Álvaro's eyes. "Good for you. I see plenty of girls go to places like Aruba, only to return and waste their money on stupid things. You will be living in a mansion. You're smart enough to make it happen."

Full of pride, Luz rose from her chair. She thought about Alison's admonition. Things were going well for her. She did have the money to rent a good house in a better neighborhood. She might call Abel and invite him for a visit the next time she was here. She would own that house if a year or two passed as profitably as the previous three months had. Soon, she would have a Dutch passport for herself and her son. She could go anywhere she wanted, Europe, the United States, anywhere. She might even find a job to support herself and Hernán without taking off her clothes.

She left Señora Álvaro's office and walked through familiar streets to her house. This was going to be the last night she slept there. Tomorrow, it would belong to Jorgé. She prayed to her dead father, asking him to accept her decision to leave it behind. She knew how hard he had worked to move his family from the slums to this house. She remembered how proud he had been when they first settled in. He used to read the newspaper at the table for hours. Sometimes he would stand in the front doorway, staring at the street without saying a word. She and Anna chased each other through his legs.

Passing a bus stop, she remembered Abel and wondered what her life might have been like had their relationship continued.

She worked out the words to tell her family they were all going to live well in their new neighborhood. It would take some getting used to, but soon it would be just like this place. Feeling confident, she stepped up to the front door and walked into the house.

Inside, she found them waiting for her. Anna sat at the table. Her mother was on one end of the couch and Hernán the other. Stacked against the wall were boxes of various sizes, taped closed and bearing the family name. Hernán slid off the couch and slowly crossed the room. He embraced her leg but didn't look up. She glanced around the room and saw that no one wanted to speak.

"We're in your hands," her mother said at last.

It was then that Luz knew how her father must have felt when he brought his family here fifteen years ago.

"MARY, MOTHER of Jesus!" Charlie exclaimed. "I need a chief cook and bottle washer, not a captain with sand in his shoes and a radio that's heavier than an anvil."

Beck checked the position of his radio and said he wasn't looking for a job.

"Damn! The tourist season has hardly begun, and we've been run over the way the Wehrmacht marched into Paris. If this keeps up, I'm going to have to call Sam."

"How is he?"

"Don't ask. Anyway, things are good here except that the island is in danger of sinking into the sea if they open one more hotel up there."

"You need one on this side to trim the ship," Beck suggested.

Charlie put up his hand. "Please. That concrete skeleton at the end of the street will be completed the day before never, and then we'll have Norte Americanos down here trying to save souls in the places the rest of us prefer to sell ours to the devil. This I do not need. Not yet. I have some living to do."

Just then, a knock sounded on one of the front doors. Charlie crossed the bar, pulled the door open, and found himself facing a pair of tourists, one of whom had a guidebook in her hand. "Is this Charlie's Bar?" she asked in a thick New England accent.

"It is madam," Charlie replied. "You must be the tax collector."

She giggled and entered the bar with her husband in tow.

Charlie said to Beck, "So it begins, Captain."

"I'm looking for a boat," Beck said.

"You already have a boat."

"I need a fixer-upper. Something for the men to rebuild and keep themselves out of trouble."

"Stay on the small road by the ocean, and you'll come to a commercial port called Barcadera. There's all kinds of derelicts there, people and otherwise."

Following Charlie's instructions, Beck drove to Barcadera on the road that fronted the ocean. As he crossed the low bridge at Pirate's Cove, he looked out at the natural beauty of the place and thought it would be the perfect spot to put a house. However, he wanted a tugboat, not a house, and he wasn't about to squander money on something that didn't float.

At Barcadera, more than a dozen boats of various types and condition sat on the beach or were tied to the wharf. Some others, which seemed seaworthy, appeared to be active in trade and fishing. Beck walked among the worst of them, peeking through holes in the decks, scratching faded paint with a nail he found, and considering which of them would be a worthy candidate for resurrection. No one paid him any mind. He waved to a few of the men working there. They returned the greeting and stuck to themselves.

About thirty yards down the beach, he saw a derelict pulled up on the sand. A frayed rope stretched from its bow to a gnarled Divi tree, though there was no danger of the boat's drifting away. The hull was completely out of the water; the twin propellers hung in front of a pair of rudders, one of which was askew. It took him a couple of tries to climb aboard.

The boat was about forty feet long, maybe forty-two. It had a pilothouse forward and a low stern. The hull and deck were steel and free of significant damage.

He was surprised to find the pilothouse in fairly good shape. None of the gauges were broken, but the compass was missing. Peeling back a strip of chalky paint he discovered a decal on the original surface. He plucked away some more paint to reveal "New York City Police Department" in faded letters on the decal. "What odd chain of events brought this thing to Aruba?" he wondered.

He jumped down and surveyed the hull one last time. It wasn't the most handsome boat, but it would do. He turned to find a man about his age walking toward him.

"¡Un momento!" the guy called and started jogging toward the beached vessel.

Beck stood fast, wiped the sweat from his forehead, and wished he had a hat with a wider brim. "I'm interested in buying this boat," he said.

"Gracias a Dios. My lucky day," the guy bellowed.

"You own it?" Beck asked him.

"Until you pay me for it," came the clever reply.

In Philadelphia, a boat like it was worth little more than scrap value, which Beck pegged at about one thousand dollars. He converted that to florins, took some off to leave bargaining room, and said, "How about twelve hundred?"

"Dollars?"

"Florins."

"That is nothing."

"It's on the beach. It's been there for a while, too."

"The hull doesn't leak."

Beck chuckled. "You'll guarantee that?"

"On the life of my children," the owner said seriously.

"So how much?"

"Fifteen hundred dollars," the guy said.

"And if the hull leaks?" Beck prodded.

"I'll give you one of my children to help you fix it."

Beck stuck out his hand.

After the guy shook it, he exclaimed, "My wife will be so happy!"

They agreed to meet later in the week, at which time Beck would pay the man and haul the boat into the water. He drove to the refinery, where he promptly informed his crew that they had a project.

That Saturday, Beck motored *Kathryn* to Barcadera. Syd waited ashore with Tony. The crew agreed the name of their new boat would be *Huntress*. In her current state, she was more of an old nag, but Beck left the details up to them. He took

Kathryn in as close as he could, which was about two hundred feet off the beach. Ramirez passed a light-duty nylon line from *Kathryn* to Syd, who made it fast to the best cleat on the *Huntress*'s bow. Using the capstan, they shuttled a stronger line ashore, one that could take the stress of dragging the powerless hulk into the water. The process took about half an hour, during which a few locals gathered to watch the action.

When all was ready, Beck eased *Kathryn* astern until the slack was out of the line. Syd rode *Huntress* while Tony stood back, watching for anything that might go wrong. Beck used the least amount of power possible to avoid tripping *Huntress* or tearing the bit out of her deck. It took a few minutes for the hull to start moving, and when it did, it heaved hard to the port side. Syd clung to the wheel, laughing but keeping his eye on things. Half on her side, *Huntress* lumbered back to the sea like a wounded dinosaur. Once her entire hull was in the water, she straightened on her keel and started drifting with the breeze. Wilkie quickly took the slack out of the line until *Huntress* and *Kathryn* were side by side. Beck looked at the beach and realized he'd left Tony behind. The deckhand leapt into the sea and swam for his boat. The crowd on shore gave him a round of applause.

They took their prize to the refinery, where Herzog had granted a small piece of land for them to use as a dry-dock. One of the cranes working in the refinery picked *Huntress* out of the water and set her atop blocks that would keep her upright until she was refurbished.

"Let's celebrate," Beck said when everything was secure.

"Lead the way," Wilkie told him with a wave toward Charlie's.

Koch served them and warned everyone that they should enjoy the moment because of the old adage about the happiest days of having a boat being the day it is purchased and the day it is sold.

Beck leaned his chair against the wall. The afternoon breeze felt hot but soothing on his face. He daydreamed about his future on the island. Would he spend it docking tankers, drinking at Java Bar, maybe bedding a few of the whores if he felt so inclined? Would he take up fishing with the rest of the crew? Would he buy a piece of land, build a house, find a different hobby like Charlie had found in painting? He didn't know, but he was pleased to be away from what had once been the center of his life. It was the way Sam had told him it would be: comfortable, easy going, and fun.

A soft voice came to him, not in a dream, but through the same open window that let in the breeze. "Wake-up, Captain," Frankie said sweetly. "I have a surprise for you."

Beck pried open one eye and directed it at Frankie who hung his arms over the high sill.

"I know things you don't. It will cost you to find out."

Beck started laughing at how a man who literally lived in the street and out of garbage cans could have such a high opinion of himself. It must be the four new teeth, Beck thought.

"You'll have a broken lip," Koch told him with a raised fist, "if you don't move down the street."

Frankie jumped back from the window and danced on his feet with his fists up. Beck leaned out the window. He had two guilders in his hand.

"Two guilders? An insult from a man who has the money to buy a new boat."

"That's hardly a new boat we brought here."

"Not that one," Frankie said, "the other one."

It took Beck a second to figure out that Frankie was talking about *Kathryn*. "She's not mine," he said and pulled out a third guilder.

"You change boats the way I …" Frankie found himself without a witty comparison. He scratched his chin, thought for a second, and took a deep breath. "You have more boats than I have teeth!"

"Not quite," Beck said.

"Hah!" Frankie shouted. "You see that I have the power!" He hustled up to the window and said conspiratorially, "This may be hard for a man to take, so have a drink."

Beck sipped his whiskey.

"Your woman has married another man. He's a friend of Charlie, a painter, too." This caught Beck off guard.

"But don't worry, Captain. This is for money, not love. You still have a chance."

At that moment, Koch came down the sidewalk. "Get lost!" he shouted. "The tourists don't need to see your ugly face in the window."

Frankie winked at Beck and loped down the street like a drunken ballet dancer. Koch returned to his post in disgust.

Having overheard Frankie's revelation, Charlie decided to take action of his own. He cleared the table before Beck and said, "Tomorrow evening we have something to do. Meet me in Savaneta at seven thirty. Dress casually. No radio."

"See you then," Beck said.

❋   ❋   ❋

Seeing that Beck arrived exactly on time, wearing a pair of khaki pants and an open shirt with a collar, Charlie realized it was going to take some time to teach the Captain how to live in Aruba. Time was flexible. Dress was optional. Sobriety was discouraged. Well, it was only the end of his first week, and it was a welcome contrast to Sam's overindulgence. *¡Viva la diferencia!* Charlie thought to himself.

"You drive," he said to Beck. "But I will show you the way."

They followed the road along the sea. The radio played softly. Charlie pointed out a few new landmarks, told a tale of an affair with a woman who used to live in a Cunucu house near the mangroves, and was grateful to have a fresh ear to listen to his stale stories. Of course, he had a surprise for Beck, which the Captain no doubt was anticipating on some level, but there was no way for him to know what a thrill it was going to be.

"We have to make a brief stop," Charlie announced as they rounded a bend which turned them away from a marina and toward the airport. "I want to say hello to a friend at the airport. It's not every day I get to this side of the bridge."

"You're the navigator," Beck replied.

A few minutes after six, they entered the terminal. On the other side of the building, a plane landed. Beck followed Charlie past a security checkpoint. The guards smiled, nodded, and waved them through as if they were the prime minister and a key cabinet member.

"The air conditioning in here is enough to give me pneumonia," Charlie said. "It makes no sense. People come here for the heat."

"Maybe it's to acclimate them before they go home," Beck suggested.

"Good point," Charlie said. "I have an old man's bladder, Captain. Excuse me while I take care of that."

"I'll be here," Beck told him and leaned against the wall. A group of passengers came through the arrival hall doors. He glanced over his shoulder in the direction Charlie had gone. He didn't see the man, so he turned back to watch the people coming through the doors.

A courteous fellow held the door for someone behind him. Using a grand gesture of his free hand, the gentleman ushered Luz over the threshold into the terminal where Beck stood.

Beck smiled for two reasons. He was thrilled to see Luz, and he admired Charlie's cunning. No doubt Charlie's sole purpose for coming to the airport was to reunite him with Luz.

When Luz spotted Beck, she pulled up short. Her gaze met his, and she leaned into his embrace.

"*Tú vives*," she said.

"*Tú también*," Beck replied. With a nod, he thanked the man who had held the door. He saw the guy appreciated the good luck of being with a woman who carried herself with such grace. And then Charlie appeared as if it were pure coincidence that brought them all to the airport at that moment.

"You are in good hands," Charlie said to Luz.

She pressed into Beck's side and grinned.

"I'll give you a ride to Savaneta," Beck said.

Aruba's sovereign waved his hands. "Not necessary. This is my kingdom, and some vassal will have a carriage for me."

"Are you sure?" Beck questioned half-heartedly.

"Please, Captain, I should swim back to Savaneta if only for the exercise. Enjoy yourself, remember to employ a strong offense, and don't, well … you know."

Leaving her family in Santa Barbara had crushed Luz. She tried to explain that their situation was no one's fault but the criminals who had killed their father. However, her mother wouldn't listen, and Anna wouldn't come to her rescue. Since she had given up on Rudi, it was her responsibility to provide for them. They were only moving because they had no choice. From their point of view, it was she who had put them in that position, not Jorgé, not Rudi. It was she, Luz, who had rented the house. It was she who promised them that everything would be better. It was time for her to keep her promises.

Then she told them she had married a man in Aruba.

The drive to the new house passed in silence. Not only had she moved them out of their home without consulting them on the new one, she had married a stranger who was not even Colombian.

Luz delivered the first of her promises when they opened the door in Barrio Santa Barbara. Her mother and sister walked through the rooms, exchanged looks, and said to each other that the place was livable. Luz held her rage in check and spoke encouragingly of the local church, the market, and the availability of jobs. No one wanted to talk about those things, so Luz moved on to the subject of Hernán.

"He will be coming to live with me," she announced.

"My husband and I have a house of our own, and it's only right that Hernán is with me."

"And grow up an Aruban?" her mother said.

"He will grow up my son," she replied.

"And the son of a father who is not Colombian."

"Better than no father at all," Luz managed to say.

Her mother did not say another word to her, not even when the taxi came to take her to the airport. Hernán had asked why the family was fighting. All Luz could tell him was that soon he would be taking his first airplane ride to a place where the sun was always bright.

Now she was in the car with Captain Beck. Behind the happy look she displayed for him, her mind fretted over how she was going to keep her other promises. She accepted that Rudi might never come home. Anna's chances of marrying were slim. Therefore, it was up to her, the way it had been up to her father, to keep them out of the slums.

As Beck parked the car in front of the house in San Nicolaas, she touched his arm with the tips of her fingers. It was men like him, men who paid her for her time and her body, who would keep her out of grinding poverty. More importantly, the money he paid and the favors he bestowed upon her would give Hernán a better chance at life than she'd had.

Before she could ask him to come in, he volunteered to help her with her suitcase. She was frightened to be in the house alone and hoped he would stay the night and pay her for the privilege.

"Your new place," Beck said in rough Spanish.

She resisted the urge to laugh at his accent. "*Sí*," she said and switched on the lights. To her surprise, there was a small refrigerator in the kitchen, as well as a table with two chairs.

"You need some color," Beck commented.

"It's the first layer," Luz said optimistically.

He only understood half of what she said, so Beck smiled and looked around the house in an appreciative way. Nothing could have prepared him for the sight in one of the bedrooms. Here the walls weren't white. A depiction of what could only be Renaissance-era Holland covered the wall. It was a view of a dike stretching into the distance. There were tall windmills along the shore and a sailboat on the sea in the distance. The ceiling was painted sky blue with realistic clouds. It was an unfinished work, but well on its way to being a masterpiece.

When Luz saw the image she nearly cried. She knew Andrés had talent. Charlie had told her so. However, this was something she expected to find in a museum or a cathedral. There it was, in Hernán's room, the enamel fresh and bright. She wondered what Andrés planned for the rest of the house.

"Incredible," Beck breathed.

"Sí," Luz seconded and led him to her bedroom, where someone had placed a twin bed with two cheap nightstands. A full-length mirror hung near the closet.

"I'm tired," she said to Beck.

He smiled and bent over to untie his shoes.

39

LUZ STOPPED counting the nights she slept with Captain Beck. Sometime after the third month she gave up wondering when he would get tired of her. Once in a while she contemplated asking him what he wanted. While she taught him Spanish, she saw the look in his eyes that she thought meant he was in love with her. Yet an offer never came, nor did he stray with another girl. Luz was sure of this because she had asked around, even going to the doctor a couple of times to listen in on what the girls were talking about. They chatted about their clients, their bosses, and their problems back in Colombia. While they behaved respectfully in her presence, there were always a couple of boisterous ones who took a chance by taunting her about her *Americano*. She took the ribbing in good humor. She was a veteran.

Luz understood their situation and knew that most of the time girls just wanted to vent their complaints. It did no good to argue with them or try to help. They either got it or they didn't. Sadly, too many of them didn't. They wasted their money, squandered their good looks among rough clients, and exhausted their youth trying to escape reality.

Luz, on the other hand, applied the lessons she had learned during her first and second tours. She had not reached the level of expertise Inez had achieved, but she was no amateur. She would never admit it, but la Dueña's advice had been correct for the most part. Luz sought out reliable if somewhat boring regular clients. Without exception, the men she serviced paid better than the regular rate. She never acted pushy when a married man took her home early or told her he didn't have enough money this week. Sometimes they were on their way home from work or just didn't have as many guilders in their pocket as they thought they did. She let it pass, and the next week they paid her what they owed and then some. As strange as it seemed, she trusted her clients, and they trusted her, too.

Many of them confided in her. They confessed all manner of sins that would have made a priest blanch. They informed her about the minutia of their lives. They told her what frightened them. They prattled on about lousy friends and ungrateful children. Luz listened, offered no advice, and pleased them sexually to the best of her ability. While they treated her with a wife's respect, it was clear she was a whore and they were her clients.

Captain Beck was the exception. He studied Spanish earnestly, the way she hoped her son would immerse himself in English. He loved to dance to the music on the jukebox. He drifted off to sleep with no more than a *buenas noches*. From his lips came no declarations of grand achievements or excuses for deplorable behavior. He simply spent his time with her, whenever it was available, doing normal things a couple of friends would do. Yet he seemed like more than a friend. He gave her money, bought her gifts for no reason, and found tradesmen to fix things around the house. When they walked down the beach, he held her hand the way she had held the hand of Hernán's father. From time to time, he kissed her as if he meant it as a prelude to something more. She wanted that something more from him, and her feelings surprised her. She ached for sex with a lover as opposed to a client. She longed to experience the mutual satisfaction that comes from genuine caring instead of the physical release that results from biological function. The only man in Aruba who could provide that for her was Captain Beck. However, Beck stopped himself before it went too far. She sensed his frustration as he retreated, but she lacked the courage to ask him why. She feared his answer. What if he worried about catching a disease? What if he found her physically disgusting, which wasn't absurd given how many men had used her body? An answer like that would break her heart. Worse than that, if he told a lie that was nothing more than an excuse to cover those feelings, she would be devastated that he couldn't tell her the truth. So, she didn't ask. She accepted his care and affection and gave back as much as he would take.

Six months had passed since she moved into Montoya's house. Her son's arrival was one hundred sixty-two days past due. These days she counted without exception. She visited the immigration office every week to check on the status of Hernán's paperwork. The answer never varied. "We're working on it," an official named Jerez said. "Be patient," he sometimes added. Luz was losing patience and suspected she had been tricked by Marcela and her fussy lawyer. Her own lawyer, Boedeker, looked into the matter and reported that everything that could be done was being done.

There were three people that Luz figured could help her: Carlotta, Charlie, and Captain Beck. She didn't want to ask Carlotta because the woman had done plenty for her already in finding Herr Boedeker, not to mention the general support she provided during their Sunday lunches. Charlie was another friend, but Luz hesitated to ask him since he always seemed busy with his bar. The only reason she hadn't asked Beck was because she saw him as such a forthright man that he might walk into the immigration office, demand Hernán's paperwork, and if it was not handed over forthwith, proceed to destroy the place. She had heard about what he did in the streets of San Nicolaas, how he beat down those men who had threatened Frankie. His mere presence intimidated the louts who came into Minchi's. None of them so much as cast a sideways glance at him.

But it was the middle of her sixth month since marrying Andrés, and it was time to do something. The new school year was about to start, and Hernán had a spot thanks to Captain Beck's friends at the refinery. Her boy needed to make friends before classes started. She was also anxious to get him away from her family, who were growing increasingly hostile toward her. They blamed her for leaving them behind, as if she had eloped with a millionaire. It was her fault they hadn't heard from Rudi. As if that weren't enough, her mother didn't like her new priest.

Rudi was her brother, Anna her sister, and her mother would always be her mother. She loved them all as such and couldn't bring herself to dislike them. However, she was sorely disappointed that she was the only one supporting the family financially. Anna could have taken some job, anything, to add to their collective income, as her mother could have. They could alternate keeping an eye on Hernán. Thanks to Captain Beck and her steady clients, she was able to pay their rent, their bills, and have money left for them to eat and buy clothes.

One night after a new client was particularly rude to her, she caught herself listening to her boss's voice in her head. It was the speech about how Marcela's own family had accepted her money and never sought work for themselves. Before the words sank in, she blocked them out of her mind. No matter what they did, her family was her family. It was all she had in the world since she didn't own so much as her own body, which was hired out to strangers for a price. She started a silly argument with the client just to distract herself from la Dueña's bitter words.

This morning, as she lay beside Captain Beck, she decided it was time to ask for his help. If he offended the Aruban authorities, so be it. It couldn't get any worse. To hear it from Spanner, Beck was gaining acceptance in the local community, especially in light of his tugboat's assisting the cruise ships in Oranjestaad. The story went that his boat had several water cannons that thrilled the crowds. His tug also saved the government a significant amount of money. The one that used to perform this function had broken down, and no one was talking about getting it repaired so long as Beck was there.

A little after ten o'clock, she slid out of bed and found Beck admiring Andrés's work. The mural was finished. Every bit of visible wall had been painted with such detail it was hard to believe it wasn't a photograph. Bits of white spray blew from the slight chop on the sea beyond the dike. The windmill's blades were grained wood dividing strained canvas. Grass along the dike was a varied green that taunted Beck's eye. Andrés rendered it all perfectly to scale so it gave the impression the viewer was looking out a window. There was more to come. Andrés had started with base colors in the living room and had sketched a few ideas for his next masterpiece.

"Do you know anyone in the government?" Luz suddenly asked.

Beck replied, "Only Charlie, the king."

Luz smirked. She knew that story. "Someone else."

"No. Is there a problem?"

"The papers for my son were supposed to be finished months ago. They still are not in my hand. I wonder if they will ever give them to me."

Beck turned to Luz and asked, "Your son was part of the arrangement you made when you married Andrés?"

"It was."

"The lawyers, what did they say?"

"There's nothing they can do."

The first person Beck thought to talk to was Herzog. As refinery superintendent, he wielded enormous power and rarely used it. At the same time, this was a deeply personal matter, and he paused to consider how Herzog might view him for something like this. It was one thing to arrange for the boy to attend the International School. It was something else to see to it that he got to the island in the first place. Herzog might think he flipped his lid for a Colombiana. While that may or may not be the case, Beck didn't want to be judged as such. The right person for this question was Charlie. He wondered why Luz hadn't asked him herself.

"Let me talk to some people."

"*Gracias*," Luz said, hoping she had made the right choice.

Charlie's Bar was nearly empty when Beck walked in. Koch read the newspaper. Charlie mopped the bar until he saw Beck take a seat.

"Whiskey or water?" Charlie asked.

"Water," Beck answered.

"Balashi Cocktail," Charlie said as he set the glass of ice water in front of Beck. "The desalinization plant is up there in Balashi. We have the Balashi Cocktail for those of you who can't stay out of the sun."

"Or are just plain thirsty," Beck added.

"That too. Tell me what's on your mind, Captain. You're here too late to be early and too early to be late. Therefore, it must be something important."

"Luz tells me her son's paperwork is held up. I'm trying to find out how to fix that."

"How long?"

"Must be close to six months. It was part of her deal with Andrés."

Charlie corrected him. "You mean part of her deal with Marcela."

"You're right," Beck said to Charlie. He swallowed the last of the water and turned to leave the bar.

"What about my tip?" Charlie called after him.

"Put it on my tab," Beck replied and headed for his boat.

Luz tapped her pencil on the ledger page. Each of the girls had paid their casa. Business had been good for them and the bar. Two of them seemed anxious, as if they had an appointment with a particular client. Luz realized she felt the same way about Captain Beck. She found herself staring at the door. Each time it opened, she expected him to walk through. Sometimes he came directly from the boat with a faint hint of diesel hanging from his clothes. His radio bumped her hip each time he hugged her. She had learned to slide it out of the way before easing against his body. After a warm greeting, he sat at the end of the bar for a drink. Luz enjoyed the routine with him. It provided a respite from anxiety created by clients that expected her to perform whether she had a bad day, was worried about her son, or had an argument with her sister.

The door opened and Marcela walked in. She waved with her fingers and stepped up to the bar to collect her money. The boss hardly glanced at the ledger.

She saved her careful inspections for Saturday nights. Marcela left the daily minding to Luz, who was conscientious more out of fear than a sense of responsibility to the business.

"*Buenas noches,*" la Dueña said as she tucked the envelope of cash into her purse and turned for the door.

"*Buenas noches, señora,*" Luz said and watched her boss pass out into the street where her Mercedes was parked in front of China Clipper.

A man came up to Marcela and asked, "*Un cigarillo, por favor?*"

Marcela leaned away from him. He wasn't a bum, nor was he a gringo working at the refinery. His accent betrayed him as Mexican, which was unusual for Aruba. "*No tengo,*" she replied and tapped the button on her key fob that unlocked the doors.

"*Entonces, te ayuda con la puerta,*" the man said and reached for the handle on the car door.

She smacked his hand away.

"*Lo siento, señora. Discúlpame.*"

Without taking her eyes off him, Marcela slid behind the wheel. Just as she started to close her door, she noticed the other side was open and that someone was getting in. She turned her head and saw Captain Beck smiling at her. He pulled the passenger door closed, and as it clicked shut, so did her door. The Mexican smiled and waved at Marcela through the glass. Standing in front of the car were two other men, one older, one about Beck's age. A glance in the rearview mirror revealed a car parked against her bumper. She was trapped.

"*Buenas noches,*" Beck said.

"I speak English better than you speak Spanish, Captain Beck. One of the benefits of being a whore for gringo clients like you is learning their language."

"English is fine," he said.

"I don't think you're here to rob me," Marcela continued. "But you must want something to come out here with your men to bother a helpless woman like me."

"You're right," he said. "I do want something." He nodded to Ramirez, Syd, and Wilkie. The men moved away from the car and strolled down the block to Java Bar.

"A brave man you are to be in here with me," Marcela said. "You know I was one of the most popular whores ever to work in this town. You may find me irresistible."

"I'm a very disciplined man," he told her.

"And good with your fists, if the stories are true."

"There's no reason to be ugly," Beck said. "We're not enemies."

This tack caught her off guard. She expected a fight and had taunted him to get it started. Instead, he pulled back, offered her kind words, and opened his hands to show he was harmless. She gave him a reckless smirk and asked, "What do you want?"

"You're running a business, and I understand what that's like. Let's do some business."

"Good. Get to the point. My husband is waiting for me."

"You made a deal for Luz's son to live here," Beck said slowly. "I want you to finish that piece of business so Hernán is here by next Friday."

It took her a second to register his words. She burst out laughing. Regaining her composure, she turned sideways in the seat, placed her hand on his leg, and said, "You've come to the wrong place. That's the Office of Immigration in Oranjestaad."

Placing his hand upon hers, Beck said, "You are correct. Tomorrow, when you visit the office, I'm sure the man with the authority to approve the boy's paperwork will be more than happy to put his signature where it belongs."

"I'm thrilled you think I have such power … "

Beck cut her off. "I know you have the power. That's why I am asking you do it."

His conviction gave Marcela pause. He wouldn't make such a request without having a threat to back it up. But what could he do to her? He was a gringo. He was a newcomer gringo at that. He may be friendly with Charlie, but Charlie wouldn't want to offend anyone important and thereby risk his own business interests on the island. At the same time, Beck operated that big, expensive tugboat. He worked with the cruise ships in Oranjestaad. His presence saved the government money. And then it struck her. He lived and worked at the refinery, and the refinery was the biggest thing on the island. On the surface, tourism took precedence. However, when it came down to it, the island depended on the refinery for the fuel that ran the desalinization plant, for the electricity it generated, and for the jobs that supported a good portion of the population. Minchi's Bar hosted refinery workers who spent their money on drinks and whores. She enjoyed a lavish life thanks to the money spent there.

"I'll see what I can do," she said. "You must understand, Captain Beck, those bureaucrats were trained in Europe."

"But we share an American sense of how to get things done. Right?"

She held his gaze thinking how fortunate Luz was to have a man like this looking after her. If she were younger and in a less secure position, she would have done whatever it took to make him hers. As she turned the key to start the Mercedes, she thought about how well Luz had taken her advice. She had more respect than ever for the girl who had landed such a catch.

"Next Friday," Beck reminded Marcela, then opened his door, stepped onto the sidewalk, and walked away. He was the captain. He had issued his orders.

Thanks to the two girls waiting for their clients, Luz watched the whole exchange. They waved her to the window when they had seen Beck get into Marcela's car. Luz chewed a fingernail as the conversation unfolded across the street. She knew Beck would do something, but she thought he would go to the government, not to Marcela. When Beck stepped out of the car, she hustled behind the bar where she stuck her hands into the beer cooler. Moments later the girls informed her that the boss had driven off with a smile on her face. Luz felt her knees buckle. She slid down the side of the cooler. Spanner caught her just in time.

"Catch your breath, girl," he said holding her up.

"*Lo siento,*" she said. "I need something to eat."

"I'll call the Chinaman. Get you some soup."

Spanner carried her to the end of the bar, where he placed her on one of the stools. She put her head down on the bar and waited for the soup that was likely to make her vomit.

Two afternoons later, Charlie and Andrés worked on their separate canvases outside his studio. Andrés busied himself with a still life of fishing gear stacked beside a bollard on some forgotten pier. Charlie sat before a landscape of bizarre yet appealing colors.

"We might as well pack up," Charlie said and started to rinse his brush.

"Yes, I have to go," Andrés said. "My father's second wife expects me to bring my wife to the beach today."

In light of what Marcela had done with the money from Ricardo's boat, Charlie found it hard to believe the kid would be seen within a hundred feet of the woman. "What's the point?"

"She thinks we are a family."

Not wanting to start trouble, Charlie held his thoughts in check. He asked, "Where are you headed?"

"To the Hyatt. My father's second wife's husband likes to ride his Jet Skis there.

He shows off with them."

Speaking these people's names was clearly a problem for Andrés. Charlie let him have his foible. He understood the anger. "Make the best of it. Not all the company is bad." He wished he were taking Luz on a date, but he was headed to the bar, where he would sling drinks, bullshit, and dirty dishes for touristas whose idea of an exotic locale was the lobby of their American-owned chain hotel.

Charlie followed Andrés to the first traffic circle, where they went their separate ways.

Luz wore a pale blue swimsuit under a pair of shorts and a white blouse. She heard Andrés pull up and exited the house before he had a chance to get out of the car. Although they were married, they had yet to get to know each other. Andrés typically painted inside the house during the late afternoon hours. Luz was either out doing errands, napping, or getting ready for work. They were friendly but as distant as strangers.

To make small talk, she asked him when he was coming to paint another wall in the house.

"Next week," Andrés said, adding, "I'm thinking of a scene with a boat on the ocean, a boat like my father had."

Luz shuddered at the thought of that boat and what the Venezuelan who bought it had done to her. She had considered telling the story to Captain Beck but then thought better of the idea. If Beck was willing to challenge Marcela, there was no telling what he would do to a man who had effectively committed rape.

"We can have fun today," Luz said to keep the conversation moving. "There will be plenty of tourists to watch, and Montoya loves those Jet Skis. Maybe he'll let us have one."

"I'm not interested."

"Loosen up, Andrés. You're used to looking from the land to the sea. If you go out there on the Jet Ski, you can have the opposite view."

He hadn't thought of that, and now his artistic mind contemplated the value of a different perspective. "You're right," he said. "I'm telling Montoya we want a Jet Ski of our own."

That they took an interest in one of his hobbies delighted Montoya. He was pleased to rent one for Luz and Andrés. He reviewed the controls as if they were taking command of a space ship. He warned them to get the feel of the thing before taking off the way he did himself.

"It's like a wild horse," he said. "I know how to handle such beasts."

His lesson complete, Montoya hopped onto his machine and roared off. Andrés and Luz straddled theirs and motored fifty yards out to sea to stay clear of the tourists who played and swam near shore. Andrés handled the thing conservatively. He accelerated slowly, made wide, looping turns, and never got up to full speed. Montoya raced at them from the north. When he was only twenty feet away, he spun to the side, spraying them with seawater. They bounced over his wake, but Andrés did not give chase. Instead, he headed farther out to sea and toward the lighthouse at California Point.

"That lighthouse looks strange," he said to Luz. "It has to be a mile from the beach."

Luz said, "I thought the same thing, but you can paint it wherever you want it to be."

"I will," Andrés said turning his craft toward the beach.

After an hour on the noisy Jet Ski, Luz was happy to relax on the beach. As she put her head back to doze off, she saw that Andrés had retrieved a sketchpad from the car. The sound of his pencil whisking over the paper lulled her to sleep.

Sometime later, Luz heard Marcela's voice. Her boss was making a comment about a boat to Montoya. Luz sat up and noticed Captain Beck's tugboat steaming parallel to the beach.

"That's a pretty boat," Montoya reflected.

"It's ugly compared to the boat I had to sell," Marcela said.

Reflexively, Luz turned her head to see if Andrés had heard the comment. His eyes never lifted from the paper. She returned her attention to *Kathryn*. From nozzles mounted on the front and back came streams of water that arced into the air. Rainbows, formed in the falling droplets, caused the crowd to point and cheer.

Luz knew it wouldn't be long before her son was with her.

BOOK III
An Island Away

CHARLIE SWITCHED off the television. He leaned back in his chair and spoke to Captain Beck and Chief Calenda.

"You see, my friends, this is why our island is the luckiest in all the Caribbean. Our cousins to the north endure storms, volcanoes, earthquakes, and enough other bullshit to wipe them out. We sit here and sip our drinks, waiting for the tourists to take off their tops."

The men chuckled, but the storm spinning through the northern part of the Caribbean was nothing to laugh about. It was the kind of storm that had put *Patricia* on the bottom. Hurricane season had begun early, and the current storm was the seventh one to have a name and the third strongest on record. From Puerto Rico to New Orleans, evacuation orders were contemplated or already announced. Two earlier storms delivered a one-two punch that destroyed oil platforms in the Gulf of Mexico. Technically, the season was about to peak. That magic time came during the first week in September, the same one as Charlie's birthday, which was only five days away.

"Whatever happens, we're ready," Charlie said patting Screwball's head. "Aren't we?"

Screwball squinted his eyes and strutted to his bowl for a drink.

"The storms are making it difficult for the tourists," Calenda commented. "Their flights are delayed or canceled. The cruise ships have been diverted. They don't know what to do."

Charlie laughed. "They need to learn how to improvise. They are so used to all-inclusive clip joints that they can't remember how to make a reservation on their own. They should go exploring. Invade Canada for Christ's sake. That land of the frozen tundra could use some naked bodies running around. It might give them something to live for."

Beck smiled. "I don't know of any beaches in Canada," he said.

"That's true," Charlie acknowledged, "but who says we have to go to the beach to take our clothes off? We can do that anywhere we like. It just takes a few drinks and the right attitude."

Beck knew this to be the case. On any number of occasions he had walked in the door to Charlie's Bar and found several women, breasts on display, drinking and laughing and not caring who saw them. It was all in good fun. Children rarely entered the place. The big hotels ran daycare programs so mothers and fathers could have all the free time they wanted in order to enjoy such antics as a topless afternoon at the world-famous Charlie's Bar.

In other bars around San Nicolaas, Beck had seen things that made Charlie's Bar appear as sanitary as Disneyland. Caribbean Bar put on strip shows that ended with two burly Colombian's tossing a girl back and forth like an acrobat. When the owner of Guadalajara Bar learned that two lesbians were working at his bar, he hosted a live act that went on twice a night and men still lined up out the door. It was a reprise of what Luz and Inez had done at Minchi's, and there were men with memories long enough to compare the two. There were the drinking contests, the time a quintet of contractors streaked down Main Street for ten minutes, the back room gambling at Las Vegas Bar, and the once-a-week fight that usually ended with one contestant in Calenda's jail and the other handcuffed to a bed in Centro Medico. Such was San Nicolaas, awash in new money from a refinery that was in the midst of a complete reconstruction.

Beck avoided this nonsense by being a witness but not a party to it. Heeding Chief Calenda's stern warnings, he avoided fights at all cost. He explored the island in Herzog's pickup. Violating one of Sam's cardinal rules, he spent many nights on the other side of the bridge. He took Luz to dinner in Oranjestaad or Santa Cruz. If she were occupied with another client, he dined by himself or took Wilkie if *Kathryn* wasn't working. On many afternoons he sat in a spare office at the refinery and called various brokers in search of a tug. He followed several promising leads, but the boats turned out to be too old, too expensive, or both.

Calenda shifted in his chair. He said, "Speaking of the right attitude, where is Sam?"

"He'll be here soon," Charlie answered.

"I doubt that, considering the storm," Beck said.

Charlie belly laughed. "It is my birthday, Captain. Sam may disappoint me, but he has never let me down."

At that moment, Sam stood in the Miami airport debating whether to go out through security in order to smoke legally or to risk the consequences of lighting up where he stood. His flight had been delayed an hour and a half. Judging by the weather report the odds of another hour and a half were pretty good. The hurricane couldn't make up its mind where it was going, and the airlines were afraid to guess.

Sam knew better than to waste his time explaining to the desk agent that a celebration to eclipse all celebrations was hanging in the balance. It was a double header: Charlie's birthday and Sam's retirement party. The desk agent wouldn't appreciate the significance of these events. Several hundred vacationers and a half dozen business people had already harassed her to tears.

Sam's travels had taken him to New York City, where he discovered a shop near the Fashion Institute of Technology which sold an incredible array of art supplies. When Sam explained what he was looking for, the clerk told him he had come to the wrong place. He needed to go to another store farther downtown that catered to painters. A cab ride later, Sam found exactly what he wanted. He informed the woman helping him that a young man he knew was destined to be the next Rembrandt. The kid needed paints, brushes, and anything else Rembrandt would have used, and he needed enough of it to last him years on a desert island, which was in fact where the kid lived. The woman was skeptical until Sam took a book off the shelf, flipped to a page with a picture that looked like something Andrés had painted, and told her, "That's what this kid can do."

"Very well," the woman said and started piling things into what looked like a giant tackle box.

Now that box was under his arm, waiting on a hurricane, the only force powerful enough to delay his emigration. He took comfort in knowing he would make more points with Charlie if he brought a gift for Andrés. After all, Charlie was the man who had everything. Andrés, on the other hand, was just starting out. After he gave the stuff to Andrés, he was going to commission a portrait of *the one*.

Luz Meri Revilla, *the one*, faced a bathroom mirror in the Wyndham Aruba Resort on Palm Beach. It was part of a suite on the highest floor. From here she had been able to see Venezuela the previous afternoon. She applied her lipstick carefully. The client liked lipstick. He told her so. He sat on the corner of the bed, staring at the weather report coming over the television.

"These hurricanes are terrible," he said to her.

"*Sí*," she replied. Hurricanes were terrible, but it was a hurricane that brought Captain Beck to her. And Captain Beck brought her son to Aruba, paid her expenses, and treated her like a dear friend, if not the way a brother should treat a sister. In his company, she was not a whore. She was Hernán's mother, a lady, a respected woman out for the evening or enjoying lunch or walking down the beach. She was a companion of the Americano, *el Capitán*. When people saw her by herself, they asked, "*¿Donde está el Capitán?*" She always replied, "*En la mar.*" They would smile at the answer as if they felt the same joy she did when he returned.

As she zipped her dress, she wondered if one day he would not come back.

Luz had a life that was normal for someone who'd come to San Nicolaas the way she had. She tended bar at Minchi's, where she met prospective clients that hadn't heard about her from someone else. She and Marcela were not exactly friends, but they got along better than strict business associates. La Dueña invited Luz to her family picnics at the beach. Andrés attended most of these, too. Montoya had purchased new Jet Skis, and the two men raced up and down the beach for an hour or so until Andrés motored off to discover a subject to paint. He confided to Luz that he had applied to an art conservatory in Holland. If accepted, he intended to leave Aruba. If not, well, he still had his job at the body shop in Oranjestaad. He made Luz swear she would tell no one, not even Captain Beck, of his plans. The only reason he told her was because he used the address at her house when applying to the conservatory. He came to the house every day to check the mail.

Marcela mentioned to Luz that she was trying to buy the unfinished hotel at the end of Main Street. She invited Luz to a meeting with the old man who owned it, subtly suggesting he avail himself of Luz's body.

"Isn't Luz beautiful?" la Dueña asked.

"Her husband is blessed," the owner replied cautiously.

"Her marriage is flexible," la Dueña explained. "She doesn't have to limit herself to one man."

The old man sensed the trap and retreated carefully. "A man of my age does not have the strength for such a lovely young lady."

Luz received no more invitations to attend these meetings. Still, she heard about Marcela's subterfuge. A lawyer, Herr Diedrik, who happened to be Luz's most generous client, explained how Marcela was manipulating one of the parliament ministers in hopes of obtaining a casino license for the building.

"She doesn't have the looks for it," Diedrik said, "and she's too old."

Luz replied, "Some men prefer older women."

"The man she's after likes them in the cradle."

Luz thought of the underage girls who came to San Nicolaas on false passports. They were supposed to be eighteen, but there were at least four in town who were sixteen. On this small island, secrets were kept only in the cemetery.

Her current client, Jeffery, kept her two nights at the Wyndham Resort. He was an American businessman seeking to develop windmills on the island. Luz asked polite questions about his project. Eager to extol the virtues of his idea, he told her more than she wanted to know. He explained how the windmills generated electricity. Since the wind was free, there was only the cost of maintenance. Aruba was the perfect place for this, he said, and if he struck a deal with the government, in two years the island would get all of its power from the trade winds that never seemed to let up. She imagined the windmills turning away, sending electricity through the cables that bordered the highway leading from San Nicolaas to Oranjestaad.

"I know a man who can help you," she said when he ended his lecture.

"Help me?" he asked quietly.

"With the government."

Jeffery studied her face. Luz knew what he was thinking: how can this whore possibly know the right man to help me? Then his faced changed. Luz knew this was the moment her clients experienced sooner or later. He came to the realization that he had told her too much. He had presented her with all the critical information related to his project that, when fully developed, was worth tens of millions of dollars. He had told her these things as if she had rocks in her head, as if she were making polite conversation to entertain him, as if she knew no one more important than her hairdresser. But the facts were something else. He saw that above those lovely, lipstick coated lips, were a pair of eyes that bore a keen intelligence. They gazed at him conspiratorially. Behind them lurked a mind capable of deciphering what was truly important.

"You know this man who can help me?"

"*Claro*," Luz replied. She was thinking of Herr Diedrik, who knew many of the important ministers. If she played her hand correctly, these men would earn the money of their dreams. Since she was the one who brought them together, she would be rewarded in kind. No, they wouldn't give her millions, but she would never have another problem like the one with Hernán's paperwork or a license to have a business of her own or a visa to go to the United States. They would give her these things, which were mere centavos in light of the value of the windmill project. Any regular agent deserved a greater commission, say ten percent. But for Luz, the ability to control her life was worth a chest full of treasure.

"I would like to meet him," Jeffery said.

"You will," Luz assured her client. "He will call you in a day or two and mention my name."

"Thank you."

"*De nada*, Jeffery."

He took her for a walk along the beach. Luz loved the beach, even the outings with Marcela. She rode the Jet Ski with Montoya or Andrés. She lounged in the sun. She looked at magazines while Hernán snorkeled with Captain Beck. She anticipated the day when Samito would finish his house. He would invite her there and she would go. It would please him, and the time would be fun. No doubt he would try to hold her as a friendly hostage, but she would find a clever way to escape.

Jeffery escorted her through the lobby, where they passed groups of Americans. She understood why they loved Aruba. It was their playground, the place they came to act like children. She appreciated their reasons for this. The Americans she met were mostly like Jeffery: intense, incredibly hard working, and singularly focused on making money. Captain Beck wasn't quite like that, but he was obsessed with his boat. She had watched him playing on the beach with Hernán one afternoon. Beck stood still as *Kathryn* traversed the ocean quite close to shore. He never hid his affection for her boy. Numerous times he knelt beside Hernán and pointed out the features of his boat.

"You see how her bow sticks up?" Beck asked Hernán.

"*Sí*," her boy answered, then added in English, "The business end."

"And what do you do with that?"

"Push!"

"*¡Muy bien!*" Beck said patting him on the shoulder.

Luz appreciated Beck's caring attitude toward Hernán, which she found interesting given that Beck had grown up without a mother. Furthermore, the Captain was a much better father than the one he described as his own. Since her son was old enough to comprehend some things, she'd told him that his real father had died in a coal-mine explosion. Hernán was the last one to whom she had to tell the lie. He took the news stoically. He nodded his head and searched her eyes for a clue to how he should react. Luz hugged him and told him that it only took two to make a family.

"What about Rudi and Aunt Anna?"

"They're your family, too," Luz said, "but here it's just us."

Upstairs at the Wyndham, as Jeffery undressed, Luz sensed he was not in the mood for sex. She knew the reason why. He was preoccupied with his windmills and the possibility that she had shown him a shortcut to success. Seeing how the night was going to unfold, Luz decided her next move.

She asked softly, "Are you angry with me?"

"We had a fantastic time together. How could I be angry with you?"

She pressed him. "I don't know, but you do seem angry."

"I apologize. My mind is on other things."

"Perhaps I should leave," Luz suggested.

Jeffery resisted. "No. No. Stay here. You can watch television or soak in the spa."

She moved close to him, placed her hand on his chest and let two fingers caress the muscles there. "I am not offended. Sometimes it's easier to think when you are alone."

"That's very considerate."

"I don't want to distract you," Luz said. "I'll take a taxi to San Nicolaas."

Jeffery sat still as she gathered up her things. When she was about ready, he sprung off the bed, yanked his wallet from a drawer, and pulled out the cash. He placed the bills in her hand. "Take this," he said.

"*Gracias*," Luz said without looking at the money.

"We'll see each other again?" he asked at the door.

"You know where to find me," she said.

Before the door closed behind her, Jeffery said, "The man you know will call me here at the hotel?"

"He will," Luz answered without looking back. The wadded bills in her hand totaled more than four hundred dollars.

The taxi driver avoided the main road. He drove inland to Noord before turning south, skirting the east side of Oranjestaad, and then climbed the hill toward Santa Cruz. Luz rode up front. As they turned on the road that led out of Santa Cruz, her view of the sea was unobstructed. From this elevation, she could see the ships anchored out there. Closer to shore she saw the deck lights of *Kathryn*. There was no mistaking the boat since the Stars and Strips flew from her mast. Seeing the colors on the tug told Luz more than the vessel's registry. Luz would be sleeping alone because Captain Beck was on his way to assist a cruise ship into the harbor.

Through the window in the door, Luz saw Donna, Hernán's nanny, dozing on the couch. The television flickered, no doubt showing a repeat of the Venezuelan dramas Donna liked. Luz let herself in, making almost no noise. Donna was a light sleeper, though, and she opened her eyes.

"Hernán is a good boy," she said. "He goes to bed when he's supposed to. He never gives me any trouble."

Luz felt her face flush. She was proud but afraid to say it out of fear he would take a sudden turn for the worse and embarrass her.

Donna said, "He can't wait to start school."

"It's all he talks about," Luz said.

"See you tomorrow," Donna finished. She hung her purse on her shoulder and let herself out.

Hernán slept atop the covers. The boy was always warm despite the power of the house's air conditioning system. Luz resisted the urge to cover him up. She went to the bathroom, where she removed her makeup, brushed out her hair, and changed into her pajamas.

Dawn was only a few hours away. Just knowing the day was about to begin for regular people kept Luz awake. She thought about the men and women who were getting ready to work at the hotels, the airport, the gas station on the main road, and the government offices. She didn't envy them. Marcela wasn't the greatest boss, but Luz was mostly left to herself. She picked her clients. She came and went from the bar as she pleased so long as she paid the casa and the molta. She managed her own money, which, since it was all cash, meant she paid no taxes. Spanner watched over her. He intimidated men who gave her trouble at the bar, which wasn't often because Captain Beck's reputation spread throughout San Nicolaas. There was the occasional jerk who was new to town, but the vast majority of men wanted to drink, play pool, and enjoy themselves.

During the weeks when Luz remained in San Nicolaas, this way of life seemed incredibly normal. It was only on the days when she went to the other side of the island, where the tourists dominated the scene, that she noticed how different life was there. The smell of crude oil was not in the air. There was the scent of suntan lotion and constantly cooking food from the outdoor buffets at the hotels. San Nicolaas was a workaday town with shops geared toward whores and local patrons on budgets. No place in San Nicolaas sold three-hundred-dollar bikinis like the one a client bought for her the previous month. Nor did they sell twenty-thousand-dollar watches in the town that hosted one hundred plus working girls. They did sell cheap but stylish clothes, a nice selection of shoes, groceries, hardware, and building supplies. There were no fine jewelry, book, or souvenir shops.

From the outside, the division between the southeast and northwest sides of the island was no different than that of rich and poor, industrial and commercial, that would be found in any other place. However, San Nicolaas was unusual be-cause there were women for sale. This commodity changed the dynamics of everything. In the Zone of Tolerance, the average citizen felt comfortable doing things that anywhere else would be frowned upon. Luz could not walk the streets without having men propositioning her. She was not alone in this. Men propositioned every woman in San Nicolaas, including the ones who worked at the bank and the commercial laundry and the ones who clearly looked old enough to be grandmothers. The offers typically came with a smile and a laugh, but they came nonetheless. Behind the clever slang was a serious intention to pay for sex. Any woman who wanted to sell herself need only loiter in San Nicolaas for fifteen minutes to land a client. Luz knew there were girls working in the hotels on the other side of the bridge, but this was a rarity and extremely risky. The Aruban government was not known for its effectiveness, but when it came to deporting those noncitizens who broke the law, they were surprisingly efficient. She knew this was true because Chief Calenda was making a difference beyond his jurisdiction.

It was Hernán's future that caused her to meditate on the San Nicolaas lifestyle. In less than two weeks, he would be attending school. Mixed in with kids of all ages, it would be only a matter of time before they teased him about his mother. Marcela had warned her about this, and those words haunted Luz now. Maybe she should have left him in Colombia. She tortured herself for half an hour before coming to the conclusion that bringing him to Aruba had been the right choice. The relationship with her family was not the same. They resented her even as they accepted her generosity, something else Marcela had predicted. Sooner or later, Hernán would sense that, and it would alienate him from both herself and her family.

She lived in a complicated world, one full of half-truths, denials, and blatant lies. She admitted she found this a comfortable existence. It was her version of reality. For example, in the morning she would call Herr Diedrik and arrange for him to speak with Jeffery. She knew that connection would bring her more money from Jeffery than her body alone. She would then check the messages on her cell phone. On a typical morning, there were at least five requests for a meeting with her. She would call each man, weigh his disposition, and tell him she wasn't sure when she would be free. After speaking with all of them, she would select one, maybe two, to entertain. Unless he was on his boat, an early lunch was reserved for Captain Beck. In the middle of the afternoon, she would meet her first customer, usually in her room at Minchi's. Her second encounter wouldn't happen until after the bar had opened. She was always there to collect for the casa, to speak with la Dueña, and to see if there was someone new in town. With all the contractors working at the refinery, she frequently shared a conversation with a fresh client who had been told to check out Minchi's and the one who worked on the other side of the bar. These new clients, unless they had experience in other places like San Nicolaas, were reserved, careful, and nervous. Luz put them at ease, gave them a drink or two on her account, and steered the discussion to what they really wanted. She was an expert at this, and Spanner often remarked, "Girl, it isn't fair. They don't have a chance." She shrugged her left shoulder, took the man by the hand, and led him upstairs.

While Spanner strictly enforced the half-hour rule for the other girls, there was no such restriction on Luz. If the man wanted to stay three hours, it was up to her to collect for the time. Luz budgeted the minutes according to the man's behavior. The new clients understood they were only allowed thirty minutes. She admonished them to take their time, to enjoy themselves. She knew these phrases in four languages: Spanish, Dutch, English, and Papiamento. The reward for patience was more money than if she invoiced the standard rate. "The one behind the bar is different," the men told each other. "She doesn't look at the clock."

The hardest thing for Luz was getting rid of a client. After telling them repeatedly that she was *ocupado*, the men took the hint. Typically, they were angry. They did not like to be denied something they thought was their right so long as they paid for it. They didn't understand she had grown weary of them the same way they would eventually grow tired of her. Similarly, if a client who paid more was on the island, she went with the highest bidder. Just as men turned down one woman for another who was better looking, so she turned down a client to replace him with one who had more money. It was her job, and time was her only commodity. She couldn't afford to waste it.

Then there was the exception to her system: Captain Beck. She went to dinner with him when she could have been with a man who paid three hundred guilders for the same privilege. If he walked into the bar, she disengaged politely from the man at hand in order to ask Beck if he wanted a drink. He showed discretion in that he said, "Spanner can get it," or, "I'll come back later." Though he accepted her profession, she always gave him first option to have her company. Without exception, he smiled, waved, and took his leave. It gave her some relief but also pained her. She cared about him with a sincerity set aside for no one else but Hernán.

She prayed every night for her son to become a man like Captain Beck. She didn't want him to be a whoremonger the way so many men were in San Nicolaas. Nor did she want him to be a weakling or a drunkard or a fool. She asked the Lord to guide him through the hazards of life, to grant him intelligence and the wisdom to use it.

At last, she felt her eyes closing. She looked forward to sleep. It relieved her mind of the contradictions that kept her guessing about the future.

41

NEVER HAD a happier man arrived at Queen Beatrix Airport. Sam was Douglas MacArthur returning to the Philippines. He led the crowd off the plane, and his eyes were clear, his stride confident, and his chin up. He carried nothing but his gift for Andrés and another small box. Everything else had been sold, thrown in the trash, or sent to the island a week ago. After an all-nighter at the airport he snatched the last seat on the last flight around the hurricane that separated him from paradise.

He smacked down his passport before an immigration officer who knew who he was.

"One more time, Samito," the officer said.

"For all time, my friend."

"I'll warn the island."

Sam put his finger over his lips. "Don't tell a soul," he said.

"I hear there are some nice girls in San Nicolaas."

"I already have one," Sam replied and scooped up his passport. He winked and headed for the door. The future had arrived.

Since Charlie thought he was still in Miami, Sam rented a car and headed straight for Savaneta. He was surprised to find Andrés there. The young man came out of the studio he shared with Charlie. He had a trash bag in his hand.

"Chico," Sam said, "We're going to party like it's our first day in the Garden of Eden."

"I'm just cleaning up some things in here," Andrés said.

"Need some help?" Sam offered.

"No, thanks."

"Everything okay?" Sam asked. Andrés had always been a serious boy, but Sam got the impression the artist had lost a dog or something worse.

"Cleaning is no fun," Andrés answered.

"Just think about the party we're going to have," Sam said. "What a mess that will be when it finally ends! You know you're always welcome, and bring your friends. There's plenty of food and booze."

Andrés managed a smile. There was always plenty of booze and food when Sam hosted a party.

Sam retrieved the art supplies from his car. He handed the box to Andrés. The kid prized it open and stared wide-eyed at the contents. "I take it you can use that stuff," Sam said.

"Thank you, Sam. You didn't …"

"Listen, chico," Sam interrupted. "You're part of the clan, and we take care of our own. ¿Comprende?"

Andrés sat down on the step with the box on his lap. He rooted through it, then gazed back up at Sam. "These are the best paints in the world," he said.

"The best or nothing," Sam told him. "Speaking of which, I want live music. I'm going to get the Arends Family up here, complete with a stage, dance area, the whole thing. By the way, where's Charlie?"

"Maybe at the bar," Andrés suggested.

"No more afternoon naps?"

"Even with the hurricanes and Luis helping, the bar is busier than ever."

"Luis?" Sam inquired.

"His nephew."

Slightly perturbed that someone other than himself had been granted a key position at the bar, Sam thought of the tourists, the laughter he could stir up, and the thrill of telling them, "I live here, sweetheart." God, he couldn't wait! On the way to the car, he turned back to Andrés. "Two days, chico," he said. "We have two days before the fireworks go bang, bang, BANG!"

Andrés waited until Sam had driven away. When the car was out of sight, he went into the studio to try some of the marvelous things in the box.

Tempting as it was to host the touristas at the bar, Sam avoided Main Street. He passed through the eastern part of town, catching glimpses of the refinery flares between the buildings. He rolled all the way to the southeastern tip of the island, through the now vacant gatehouse that marked the entrance to the former Esso colony, and finally stopped at one particular corner. It was here that he'd grown up in a house provided by Esso, surrounded by similar houses occupied by his littermates and their families. Scanning the area, he saw that there were a few new foundations jutting up from the ground. Someone was building houses here again, and it warmed his heart to think the place was destined for renewal. Waiting for him at the Department of Works was his own permit, fully approved, to build his house by the sea.

He drove down from the heights of the colony to Roger's Beach, which formed a crescent of soft sand around a shallow bay. As he pulled to a halt, a motor launch crossed the bay. It swung into the only pier there, and its occupants stepped out to make the lines secure. Sam immediately recognized them. There was no mistaking Captain Beck with his radio, and the young lady with him could be no one but Luz. As for the boy, he was more than likely Luz's son. Hand in hand, the trio strolled the length of the pier.

"The bad with the good," Sam told himself as he retraced his route to San Nicolaas. He was confident that sooner or later Luz would see him as a worthy candidate for her affection.

He parked in front of Hollywood Bar, took his second gift box from the trunk, and paused for a second to think where Speedy might hide after a free snack from Pueblito Paisa. Somewhere shady, Sam thought. He strolled up the alley until he came to the bombed-out building where he'd found Frankie one night. There sat Speedy, propped against one wall, half asleep and babbling to himself. Sam tossed the package at his feet.

Speedy clawed at the cardboard. It took him five full minutes to get at the contents. He held up a brand new baseball glove, a Louisville Slugger bat, and a chalky white ball.

"Let's get a game going, Speedy," Sam said. "See if you have any of your old moves left."

"I can play," Speedy assured him, smacking his fist into the glove.

Sam picked up the ball and bat and walked to an empty lot where a large gas station used to be. Speedy ran back and forth with his glove up as if he were an outfielder maneuvering to catch a fly ball hit by Babe Ruth. Sam indulged him by tossing the ball high in the air, an easy arc that had the ball falling gently toward the bum. It was a toss any ten-year-old could have caught. The ball plopped down about four feet to Speedy's left side. He shuffled over, tripped on it, and fell.

"Where is it, Samito?" Speedy called from the ground. His glove was still up in the air.

After retrieving the ball, Sam tossed it a second time. The result was only slightly better. Speedy ran under it so that the ball came down behind him.

"The sun was in my eyes," he said.

For half an hour Sam threw the ball. Speedy caught exactly none of them. Frustrated, Sam tried to demonstrate the right technique. He implored Speedy to keep his eye on the ball. "Follow it. Imagine it landing in your glove," he said. Rehab or not, the years of drug abuse had damaged Speedy's brain to the point where concentrating on anything for more than a second or two was no longer possible.

Finally, Sam put his arm around the bum and said, "Speedy. You take the ball and the glove. Practice with Frankie. I'll get him a glove, too. Next time, maybe we can get a game going. Okay?"

"I'll do that, Samito. I will."

"Remember, Speedy, there's only one ball. Don't lose it."

"I won't lose it. I'll sleep with it."

"I bet you will," Sam said and took the bat to Charlie's.

"Planning on joining the Majors?" Koch asked him.

"You have a place for this?" Sam asked.

"Permanent or temporary?"

"Temporary."

"Right here," Koch said pointing to a space atop the refrigerator. Charlie's was a peaceful establishment. He wanted no such weapons easily available to the violently inclined.

Sam went behind the bar, gingerly placed the bat in the space, and stepped back to see how it fit in. It wasn't perfect, but it would do.

It wasn't an opportune time to drink, not with Speedy's disappointing performance on his mind. He looked at the vodka bottle, then at the tourists mingling around the bar. A woman pointed at Beck's life jacket. He heard her say, "Look, that's from Philadelphia."

Sam wished Beck had stayed there and reached for the vodka. A tourist said, "Who are you to walk in and help yourself to a drink?"

"This is my town," he told her with a wink.

"Actually," Charlie said as he approached from the men's room. "It is *my* town, but I grant certain privileges to my special minions."

Sam threw his arms around Charlie, spilling some of his drink on Charlie's shirt. "*Bon dia*, yourself, *padre*. Happy birthday, too."

"It's your birthday?" the tourist asked.

"It is madam, but please, don't ask for a free drink, I'm too cheap."

"I'm not," Sam said. He tossed a hundred-dollar bill to Koch, reached for the lanyard, and rang the bell that hung above the bar. The people who knew what that meant cheered.

"A round for everyone at the bar," Charlie told the interested tourist. "Courtesy of my friend here, who must have won the lottery."

"Thank you," she cooed and turned back to her friends.

"This is the big one," Sam began, "The party of all parties. It's your birthday and my retirement."

"I think we'll be alone," Charlie cautioned. "Our friends are on the wrong side of the storm."

Sam fired up a cigarette. "That's a negative attitude from a master of improvisation."

"I don't control the weather, Sam."

"You don't have to. You have to know how to buy plane tickets."

"I suppose they could fly to Holland, catch a plane to Morocco, then another one to Rio, then one up to Caracas, and finally get here from there."

Sam grinned. "Now you're thinking."

The same tourist turned back to them. "How do we get invited to this party?" she asked.

Sam put an arm around her, planted a wet kiss on her cheek, and retreated just far enough for her face to come into focus. "Lady, with all due respect, this party is not for the uninitiated."

"Can't we join the club?"

All his life, Sam believed in the old adage of the more the merrier. However, for his retirement party he wanted to be surrounded by his childhood pals, his local friends, and especially Luz. Although not on site, he had managed to keep tabs on her through calls to Spanner and Carlotta. Both of them had warned him that Luz spent her free nights with Captain Beck, who now lived and worked in San Nicolaas. Sam didn't care. Sooner or later, sailors returned to sea.

"He's learning Spanish and plays backgammon good as you, boy," Spanner had said, adding, "I don't know what he does behind those closed doors."

"Hah," Sam snorted. "We don't need Chief Calenda to investigate that."

Carlotta was more circumspect. "The Captain is good to her with money and other things. He takes her boy on his boat. She has to pay for her marriage to Andrés and for her family in Colombia. You can't blame her."

Sam blamed no one but himself for going a little too far and thereby raising Charlie's ire. If he hadn't made that mistake, Luz wouldn't need a sham marriage or have to work in Minchi's, for that matter. She could spend her days with him, enjoying a casual island life.

The last word had been Charlie's. During a particular late-night phone call, he had told Sam, "There are more than a hundred other girls in town, and some of them deserve your attention. Share your wealth and charm among the sisters of Our Lady of the Broken Dreams. You may be surprised what you find." While Charlie had been right, Sam wasn't interested in surprises or the chore of finding another girl. Luz and her son fit his idea of the perfect accoutrement to his retired life. They would keep him out of the kind of trouble that had caused his banishment.

The tourist at the bar was waiting for his answer regarding an invitation to the party. Sam pulled his classic move. Without looking away, he fished out a cigarette, positioned it between his lips, and fired the Zippo. He inhaled fresh smoke to the point where his lungs nearly burst. He let the cloud of smoke out slowly so it hung all around his face.

"Buy scissors," he said to the woman.

"Scissors?"

"This one is going to make the papers," Sam explained. "Cut out the article. Put it in your scrapbook. Tell your friends you met the guys who made it all happen."

With that he spun on his heel and left the bar.

"What a character," the woman commented.

"The son I always wanted but could never afford," Charlie added.

Sam left his windows down and the air conditioner off. For reconnaissance purposes, he drove two laps on the San Nicolaas Five Hundred. He wasn't seeking another girl; Luz was still *the one*. He just wanted to see what was out there before he got down to business.

On the subject of Luz, his mind was clear. He wasn't going to push the issue, not on the first day, nor during the first week. He didn't have to rush things now that they were both permanent residents. He could take his time and do it right. After the dust settled from the party of all parties, he was going to implement his strategy to make the woman his own. As for Captain Beck? The man doesn't stand a chance, Sam thought, as he turned the corner onto Rembrandtstraat. I'm going to build my house. I'm going to swim naked when the sun comes up. And I'm going to put my head down on a pillow next to *the one*.

After dropping Luz at Casa Montoya, Beck took Hernán with him to the boat. There was a cruise ship due in Oranjestaad after midnight, and Hernán enjoyed standing in *Kathryn's* wheelhouse during docking operations. Together, the captain and his charge strolled up to the boat and were stunned to see her owner, Jack Ford, sitting on the gunwale.

"Your new first mate?" Ford asked.

Hernán pulled a length of string from his pocket and held it out for Ford to inspect the knots he'd learned to tie.

"Better than you," Ford chided Beck.

"Why didn't you tell me you were on the island?" Beck asked his boss.

"I had to fly down at the last minute for an urgent meeting," Jack explained.

"Meeting about what?"

"The oil business, what else? Lots of people are interested in this refinery and moving product."

They left Hernán with Syd and walked to the end of the pier.

"I owe you one," Ford said as they looked out at the Caribbean. "If you hadn't washed up on the beach, I never would have checked into this place and landed the contract."

"You're welcome," Beck said.

"All's well that ends well, right?"

Beck knew Jack was trying to tell him something. He also knew that it was unusual for Jack to come to the island unannounced. "So what's the bad news?" he asked.

Suddenly, Jack changed the subject. "The crew goes home on a regular rotation, but you stay here. You ever think about coming back? You ever think about Nicole?"

In an instant, Beck forgot about everything, including the lunch he'd just had with Luz. It wasn't as if Nicole had never entered his thoughts during the past year. She had. But he busied himself with things that made it easier to let her fade away. He negotiated the contract for docking the cruise ships in Oranjestaad. He helped the crew rebuild *Huntress*. He explored the island. He made friends with Spanner, Kenny, Charlie, and Chief Calenda. He spent odd days helping the Arends Family patch up their house.

Through all this, Luz absorbed his affection. She gave him the kind of female company he once shared with Nicole. Their times together were as authentic as had been his life in Philadelphia. He understood Luz was a whore. However, she was a whore with her clients, not with him. It wasn't that he hadn't paid her for sex. It was that she trusted him with her son. She made herself vulnerable by asking for help. Other clients would have called those favors in. The two of them discussed that reality. She admitted she counted on him when she could count on no one else. Her confession was genuine, and he never took advantage of it. He was a captain, and the responsibility of the captain was to set an example for the rest of his crew. With him, Captain Beck, she was a woman, a good woman who wanted to raise her son, enjoy a caring relationship with a man, and live her life in peace. He was pleased to serve as a father better than his own.

No less a citizen than Chief Calenda had said, "Captain, I think you are with the one Colombian girl in this town who can tell the truth."

It reassured him that he wasn't an idiot. Of course, from time to time, Charlie looked over his glasses and said warily, "Don't fall in love."

And Jack Ford had mentioned a woman whom Beck had thought he was going to love forever. He'd given her a diamond ring so the rest of the world would know he had made a vow. She had not put it on her finger. He had been devastated but also grateful to be free to make his life what he wanted it to be.

Jack was waiting for his answer.

Did he think about Nicole? Yes, he thought about her. He wondered how she was, how her career was going, if she had found another man. He admitted to himself that he hoped she thought about him as well.

At last Beck said, "I think about her."

"She came to the office one day," Jack said. "She asked how you were."

Beck tilted his head to avoid looking directly at Jack. He saw the ships at anchor, waiting their turn at the dock. The scene distracted him from haunting thoughts.

"Don't lose your sea legs, Captain," Jack said.

Before the sun set, Marcela drove Martin to Luz's door. Standing beside the door was the suitcase Sam had given her. It was packed with clothes, shoes, make-up, and jewelry enough to last several days. Luz herself sat on the couch awaiting Martin's arrival. Marcela had informed her only hours earlier that Martin wanted to be with her. His flight had been delayed, but now that he was on the island, he wanted the pleasure of her company. Luz didn't want to be gone from Hernán and told her boss as much.

"Then he'll have to pay more," Marcela had said offhandedly. "Let the boy with el Capitán."

The lie she told Hernán nearly killed Luz. It hurt that he believed her when she told him she was going to work at a restaurant on the other side of the island. He told her to be careful and said he would miss her. He even wished her luck. He was a sophisticated little boy who trusted his mother, the mother who lied to him about where she was going to be and what she was going to do. As she sat waiting for her client, she wondered how long it would be until Hernán caught her telling a lie.

Marcela didn't knock. She entered the house calling Luz's name. Luz kissed her boss's cheek and smiled for Martin. He gushed that he had been thinking about her for months. Luz held her breath to make her cheeks glow.

"Let's go," la Dueña urged. "I don't want to keep you from your fun."

Martin took her suitcase, which he placed into the trunk. As he did, la Dueña spoke quietly to Luz. "Have you seen Andrés?" she asked.

Luz dodged the question. "Not for a week."

"I'd like to speak with him as soon as possible. Call me when you see him next."

"I will," Luz assured her boss.

Martin held the door for her, and the two of them sat in the back of the big sedan. He held her hand, asked her what she would like to have for dinner, and if she would like to go shopping. Luz knew direct answers made him happy.

"Italian food," she said, "and I heard there is a new shop at the Royal Cabana Casino. Would you take me there?"

"*Claro,*" Martin said.

Luz caught Marcela's smile in the rearview mirror. It reminded her of Spanner's comment. "Girl, they don't have a chance."

Waking up in the dark, when it was too early in the night to be the next day, made Sam grouchy. He looked at his watch. It was only five minutes past eleven. On any previous trip to Aruba, he would have showered, slapped on some after-shave, put on his cane-cutter shirt, and hit the street with both finger-pistols loaded and ready to fire. He would have downed three quick drinks at Java before heading down the street, hunting for the right girl. Tonight he didn't feel up to it. A bad case of heartburn sent him searching for an antacid. On top of that, his body ached like he'd been tossed around the inside of a cement mixer. It wasn't the booze; he'd had only a couple at Charlie's. It had to have been the food on the plane. Whatever it was, he found a roll of Tums in his shaving kit. He chewed two at a time then flushed them down with a glass of water. Although he was still tired, he decided to go for a swim. He had to get his blood moving, and swimming was the perfect thing for that. The young and fashionable called it low-impact exercise.

He left the Dog House wearing only his shorts, which he intended to remove just before he dove into the ocean. As he strolled barefoot through the outdoor bar, he heard voices coming from Charlie's studio. The light was on, and he saw Charlie's silhouette through the window. His friend's voice sounded unusually authoritative. It wasn't like Charlie to issue commands like a general. Therefore, Sam ventured cautiously toward the studio if only to make sure everything was okay.

Suddenly, Charlie was beneath the awning. He said, "Who's that sneaking around like Screwball looking for some strange pussy?"

"*Bon nochi*," Sam replied guardedly.

"Oh, it's you," Charlie said. "And I was hoping it was my girlfriend coming to kidnap me. Well, as I was just telling Andrés, life is full of disappointments."

Sam stepped up to Charlie and saw Andrés sitting inside the studio looking frustrated. The young man stared at the floor and didn't raise his eyes to acknowledge Sam's presence.

"Nothing in town for you tonight?" Charlie asked.

"Giving the horses a rest," Sam said. "If everything is okay here, I'm going to have a swim."

"We're two artistic geniuses having an argument. What could possibly go wrong?"

Not feeling particularly insightful, Sam said, "I'll leave you to find out."

At the end of the dock, he removed his shorts. He stood on the boards for the umpteen-thousandth time. The memory of himself standing in exactly the same spot with a stunning blonde girl from Medellín came to him. He even remembered her name, Camila. She had worked at Caribbean Bar. He met her halfway through a trip after his previous favorite had gone home to some pueblito in the hills near Pareda. Camila taught him to say her name properly. Ca mee la. Ca mee la. She repeated it over and over until he got it right. She did more to improve his Spanish than anyone else. Like a forgiving schoolmarm, she touched his arm and said, "No, Samito, like this." Slowly she would sound out a word, forming her lips and tongue into bizarre features that he found incredibly sexy. It was the oddest foreplay he had ever experienced.

He hung his legs over the edge of the dock. As he looked down at where his limbs magically disappeared into the water, he asked himself if he was willing to give up the possibility of meeting another Camila. His answer was clever and as well reasoned as one Charlie would have given. I don't have to give up the chance of meeting another Camila. I can meet her in San Nicolaas, share some drinks, a turn on the dance floor, and still go home to *the one*. He possessed a pirate's appetite for merriment, and he wasn't about to cut that short just because he had made permanent domestic arrangements. He didn't have to choose between one and the other. Aruba was the one place where he could have it all.

He looked up from his feet, out at the mysterious line where the darker sea met the slightly less dark sky. There among the stars he saw the lights of a boat heading north. Sam thought Nathan Beck had only one bad habit. He showed up at exactly the right time to spoil a perfectly envisioned dream.

THE BAD news came from Charlie himself.

Sam crushed a brand new cigarette into dust when he heard the words, "There's no way they can make it." He refused to accept that his pals couldn't find a way to get to the island in time for the party.

"You and three other planeloads of tourists made it just in time, Sam," Charlie said. "Now the hurricane is running up the East Coast, and all flights have been grounded until it passes."

"We're having a party," Sam vowed. "We're having a party if I have to invite tourists from the other side of the bridge."

"How about a postponement?" Charlie suggested. "Wait until you have Thanksgiving north of the border. Everyone will have free time and hurricane season will be over."

Sam held his tongue. He had all the food, all the booze, all the arrangements made, including live music performed by the Arends Family. Kenny agreed to close Java Bar and bring his girls to the party. Sam convinced Carlotta to take the night off as well. He rounded up ten girls from various bars so his friends wouldn't have to go through the trouble. He laid out some guilders in advance to guarantee the chicas showed. He hired taxi drivers to deliver them to Savaneta and take them back. He hadn't put Doc Van Dam on notice that there might be some injuries. However, he did speak with Chief Calenda, giving him fair warning that there were big happenings at Charlie's Savaneta retreat. Calenda had replied with a circumspect look and asked that Sam do his best to keep things within the bounds of the law, good fun, and common sense.

What angered Sam more than anything was that Charlie wanted to pull the plug in advance of more information. The hurricane might swing out to sea. If it did, planes would be taking off like a reprise of the Berlin Airlift. Besides, Old Man Juárez was expecting him. Was Sam supposed to tell him not to bother with the freshest catch on the island? He couldn't do that. It would be sacrilegious.

"What exactly did the airline say?" Sam queried as if he had missed something in the previous explanation.

"They can't fly, Sam. It's too dangerous. Let's be realistic. You don't want people to risk their lives for a trip to the sunshine. That's ridiculous."

It was ridiculous that his friends had not made the trip earlier in the week when there was an opening. They were secure enough in life to take a few extra days off from work and from what was left of their families. What were they working for? To put in a few extra hours, only to be laid out in their coffins with gold watches, having missed another legendary time of their lives? Now that was awesomely ridiculous! Better they should spend the time reveling in the glory of their island escapades than grinding another day off the office calendar. It was about time they saw the light. If they didn't, well, it was their loss. He was here to stay. They were free to join him or not.

Sam took out his cell phone.

"Give me that," Charlie said snatching the phone. He disconnected the call, then added, "Let's go to town. We'll have our own party. You, me, we'll get Captain Beck and whoever else we can pick up along the way. If we're too drunk, my nephew can carry us home one at a time. He's a strong boy. And, I might add, he's turning into a good bartender. The women love young muscles."

It wasn't what Sam wanted, but it wasn't a bad consolation prize. Charlie rarely let loose in town, at least not in the way Sam had been known to go all out during his own jaunts down the Street of Broken Dreams.

"Okay," Sam agreed. "With one condition."

Charlie waited patiently.

"We buy the fish in the morning. Just in case."

"Good point. Get some money. We're going to need it."

Martin had taken Luz shopping for a dress that afternoon, spent some time by himself in the casino while she lounged poolside, and drove her into Oranjestaad to a Cuban place that featured live music. Luz told him how exciting it was to go to a new place even though she had been there before with a contractor working at the refinery.

The real surprise came at the Hyatt. They were having a cocktail at the beach-side bar when she heard someone calling her name.

"¡Luz! ¡Dios mío!" Inez called out. She scampered over to their table and wrapped her arms around the girl with whom she had made a small fortune at Minchi's.

"I'm sorry," Inez said to Martin in accented English as if he had not taken her to the same hotel during her first trip to Aruba. "My name is Inez. Luz and I are friends from Colombia."

"A pleasure to meet you," he said continuing the charade. He gestured toward the man who slowly approached from the promenade that ran along the beach. "And your other friend?"

"Let me introduce you to Eduardo. He likes to be called Eddie. He is from Chicago."

Eddie remained at a discreet distance. Inez dragged him forward. "Hi," he said raising a shy hand in greeting.

"Vamos, Luz. To the baño," Inez said as she tugged Luz's arm.

Luz rose from her seat and started toward the bathroom with Inez.

Inez looked back and said, "You men talk."

They stopped short of the bathroom because Inez found a pair of chairs tucked behind one of the columns that supported the hotel. She smoothed her skirt under her legs, crossed them, and bobbed a shoe on the end of one set of toes. Luz recognized the brand of the shoe. A pair cost two hundred dollars.

"I heard you were living here," Inez began. "Do you know how much money we can make together? A fortune. We can be rich by doing our shows here at the hotels. Marcela has a deal with the manager." She was so excited she literally bounced on the seat.

Luz was less enthusiastic. "Hernán is with me," she said quietly.

"¡Tan bueno!"

Turning serious, Luz went on. "Listen to me," she said. "I'm married now."

"You can't fool me," Inez interjected. "I know what that marriage is all about."

"No, Inez, please, things are different."

"Different? You're not fucking for money?"

Luz slapped Inez's arm. "Watch your mouth."

Inez was caught without a quick reply.

"I'm sorry," Luz said. "Just because I'm a citizen doesn't mean I can get away with anything. I have to be careful."

"And you have a list of clients as long as my arm," Inez put in. "Do you have any you want to share?"

Indignant, Luz said, "No, I do not, and the ones I do have pay me not to act like a whore."

"I understand. Those things we did together when you were a timid little girl and needed someone to show you how to do it so you could pay the casa and your little boy's expenses — That never happened did it?"

"I'm not saying that."

Inez huffed. "No, you're saying it counts for nothing, that you used me to get to where you are now, which is out of Colombia with your boy, the way every one of us chicas wants to. You have status as an Aruban. You can go to America if you want. Next, you'll send me a postcard from a New York City penthouse."

After gathering her thoughts, Luz said, "You're the one making assumptions, not me."

Inez relaxed a bit. She said, "So, how is San Nicolaas these days?"

"Busy."

"I knew it. From Bogotá to Cali, it is known that there is gold in San Nicolaas. I tried to get a place at Minchi's. The agent told me I am too old. Can you believe that? I am twenty-five!"

"Don't tell me you're here illegally?" Luz said quietly.

"I don't have a passport like you."

"Inez, please, the police have changed. Chief Calenda and his men are looking for illegal girls on this side of the island."

"Don't you mean girls like me as opposed to girls like you?" Inez rose out of her seat and stomped off.

Luz scrambled after her, nearly turning an ankle as she did. They arrived at the table simultaneously. The men were stunned by the flurry of their approach.

Sweet as a newlywed, Inez said to Eddie, "*Vamos, señor*. My friends are very busy. We leave them to their pleasure." She yanked Eddie out of his seat.

Before Luz had the opportunity to sit down, Inez spun away from Eddie and whispered, "When I get back to Colombia I will tell your whole family what you do here."

Easing down onto the plush chair, Luz admitted to herself she didn't care what Inez told anyone. The only person she cared about was Hernán. If her family thought of her as unworthy, they didn't have to accept her money. They could disown her and find a better way to meet their expenses. When she wanted to, she slept in the arms of a captain, an American, a man who had money to give a girl who was sincerely his friend and not his sexual partner. If he wasn't good enough for her family, no one would be.

"Martin," she said, "may I have a Baileys?"

"*Perfecto*," he said, and flagged the waiter.

They started at Java Bar, where Kenny poured double drinks for single prices in honor of Charlie's birthday and Sam's final flight to the island. Sam and Charlie toasted each other twice before the night heated up with the arrival of Roger and several of his pals.

"Get them one on me!" Sam shouted from the jukebox. When Roger came up to thank him, Sam asked, "How is that beautiful wife of yours?"

"She's with her sister in Miami," he answered with a smile. "They can't spend my money shopping because the hurricane is flooding all the malls."

Sam turned serious. "Is she safe, chico?"

"Of course! But angry because everything is closed."

They laughed hysterically as the next song began to play. They danced with each other for a few bars then spun out to gather up two of Kenny's girls. Charlie took the third girl, and one of Roger's pals helped himself to the fourth. Someone shoved a table and most of the barstools out of the way so there was room to move.

Captain Beck walked in before the first song ended. He ordered a round and took his station at the end of the bar. Sam noticed him, ditched the girl, and greeted the Captain with a bear hug that hurt his ribs.

"Don't listen to Charlie. We're having a party!"

Beck shook his head. "I don't know, Sam. The airports aren't open yet."

Sam poked him in the chest. "Be positive! Pray! Make an offering to Poseidon for all I care. Whatever you do, don't tell me we're not having a party. This is it, Capitán, the big hurrah."

"Here's to that," Beck said raising his glass.

"Okay!" Sam fired his finger-pistols in the air. "Whose round is it?"

The gang burst into the street an hour later. No one was sober. No one was thinking about tomorrow. No one cared about yesterday. Kenny stood in his doorway, sorry to see all that money walk down the street.

They banged into each other trying to get through the door at China Clipper. The bartender attempted to hide, but they dragged him out of the bathroom and told him to start pouring drinks or they were going to help themselves. The girls working there knew this crowd was not going upstairs. They stuck to the edges of the room, accepting vinos when they were offered.

The party moved to Las Vegas Bar, where Sam threw the dice for twenty minutes straight. Every man who dared to bet doubled his money. With their wallets refilled, they charged up the street to Carlotta.

"¡Escúchame, hombres!" Carlotta admonished them. "You can have your fun, but I want no problemos!"

They saluted her authority, filled her jukebox with guilders, and drank all the beer out of her ice chest.

"Now what?" Roger asked when the beer was gone.

"We improvise!" Charlie told him.

The next stop was Caribbean Bar. As soon as the last man was through the door, Sam threw the lock. He stood up on the bar and said, "We're having a show."

The bartender took center stage, announced the price of one hundred guilders per man for the girls to strip and the men to drink for forty-five minutes.

"That's more than two guilders a minute," someone noted.

"And worth it!" Sam called back.

The money flew over the bar before the bartender could get down to catch it. There was a brief lull while things were organized. Then the first girl got up to take off her clothes. She wasn't wearing much, so it took barely two minutes before she was writhing around naked. The bartender turned the music loud enough to be heard a block away.

Soon all the girls were naked, and some of the men were, too. It wasn't long before every girl was upstairs making money in her room. However, with the girls gone some of the excitement was as well.

"¡Vamos!" Sam said unlocking the door. Outside was a line of men waiting to see what had been happening.

"I'm hungry," Roger said.

"Then you shall eat," Sam replied.

At the Chinaman's door, they waited for Anything Soup, fried rice, steak on a stick, and enough lo mein noodles to stretch from one end of Main Street to the other. Since there wasn't a chair for every man, some sat on the floor with their bowls in their laps. Chinaman liked that. It reminded him of home.

"What next?" Beck asked.

"Bed," Roger replied.

"Bed?" Sam repeated. "My friend, we have not yet begun to fight! Eh, Captain? Damn the torpedoes! Full speed ahead!"

They roared out of the restaurant and into the first joint they came to, which was Caracas Bar. There they dropped their pants and mooned the television news from Venezuela, which featured dictator Chavez himself giving one of his multi-hour lectures to the citizenry from whom he had yet to steal it all.

"On a night like this, we could go there and have a revolution of our own," Sam said. "Anybody up for that?"

"I can get us there," Beck offered.

"Are the women good looking?" someone asked.

"Let's find out," someone else said.

"We have plenty here. Why do we have to go over there?"

"Good point," Sam said and started chatting up the girl closest to him. She knocked him down a few notches because she was a little ugly, a little heavy, and a little uninteresting. She refused to give him any life details and kept pushing for vinos and a romp in her room. Frustrated with her and longing for Luz, Sam led his ensemble back outside.

He turned the corner from Rogerstraat into the alley that connected to Main Street. By the time he arrived at the next corner he'd lost all his followers but Charlie and Beck.

"Back to Carlotta's," Sam announced. "We can put our feet up there."

To Carlotta's relief, only three men came through the door. It had been a busy night, and she was still open, but in another hour she wanted the doors closed and the lights out. She was shocked to hear Sam order a round of club soda. She had one of the girls bring it to their table while she selected mellow, romantic songs on the jukebox.

"Sweet music, sweet girls," Charlie remarked. "Did you have it this good in Philadelphia?"

"I don't think so," Beck answered.

"You know you didn't," Sam told him. He waved three girls over, explained to them that they were tired and each wanted a massage. He put seventy-five guilders on the table, twenty-five for each girl if she rubbed their shoulders for fifteen minutes. The girls were happy to oblige.

"You see," Sam said to Beck, "It can only get better."

As the girl rubbed his neck, back, and shoulders, Beck nearly fell asleep. He daydreamed of Luz, and when he let his mind wander a little further, he saw a hazy image of Nicole. The twenty-five guilders expired before anything came into focus. He was in San Nicolaas, not Philadelphia. He was drunk but not so much to play the fool. He noticed Charlie eyeing him.

"Don't forget your sworn duty."

"On my honor," Beck said.

Sam was delirious from the booze and the massage. If that was not enough, the reality that he actually lived in paradise struck him with as much force as divine rapture.

"I'm home," he said to the girl who rubbed his shoulders.

"*Bueno, papi,*" the girl said and kissed his forehead.

A while later, the three of them stood before Charlie's Bar. Sam had one more thing to do.

"Until tomorrow," he said.

"*Mañana,*" Charlie replied.

"See you in Savaneta," Beck said.

Sam turned away from his pals. As if he had given a taxi the exact time and place to pick him up, a car stopped at the curb. He was prepared to wave the car out of his way when he recognized the driver. It was Chief Calenda, but this was no police cruiser and the chief was out of uniform.

"I'll give you a ride," Calenda said.

"Yes, you will," Sam responded and pulled open the door.

Having seen Sam get into the car, Charlie strode to the other side of his veranda, where Captain Beck could be seen standing on Rogerstraat. Charlie waved to him. The Captain waved back and walked toward the refinery gate. Charlie flopped into his favorite chair. Screwball gave him a hearty sigh.

"It was worth the hangover," Charlie said to his cat.

Calenda was as sober as Sam was drunk. The chief drove smoothly, hardly touching the brake and keeping an eye on his passenger.

Sam watched the town of his birth go by. It changed dramatically from the days when he washed Stansky the jeweler's car. Buildings had faded and been torn down. Others had their façades remodeled or renamed. The roads were changed from two-way to one-way with the idea of improving traffic flow. The place was as dusty as ever and looking worse for the wear. However, the worst was in the past. Good things were happening, and more were on the way. The price of oil was climbing. The refinery produced more product than it had in years. Didn't one of Roger's friends say something about an expansion? It was coming. In a hurry, too. Best of all, he would witness it the way his father had seen it the first time.

"We have to stop at Zeerovers."

Skeptical, Calenda said, "I think they are closed at this hour."

Sam checked his watch. "They'll be open in exactly nine minutes."

It took Sam two tries to get out of the car, and then only with Calenda's help. He was amazingly steady on his legs, though, and they passed through the open gate without incident. Calenda paused for a look around. Not being in uniform, he was uncomfortable. He didn't want someone seeing him without his official regalia at a business that was closed.

"No worries, chief," Sam said. "They're expecting me."

They found two plastic chairs and sat down to wait. The old tomcat who lived there eyed them. It wasn't ten minutes before the sound of an outboard motor caught their attention. Neither of them got up until they heard the wooden boat knock against the metal pilings. Sam caught the line Old Man Juárez heaved. With the boat secure, Juárez shuffled to the stern, where he opened an ice chest. From it he retrieved a massive fish.

Refusing any help, Juárez struggled onto the dock with the fish in both hands before him. He presented it to Sam, who took it with all the reverence of a holy relic.

"One is all I need," Sam said and walked the last hundred yards to the Dog House.

WHILE MARTIN showered, Luz took the opportunity to check her messages. There were seven: five were clients, one from her family, and one from Captain Beck. It was the first time she had received a message from him. He encouraged her to call him about the party; it may or may not be delayed. She wanted to go, but she didn't want to anger Martin. This was their third outing, and each time he had been more than generous, including the night when he traded her in for someone else. Still, she regretted having to miss the party. Sam would be showing off; the music would be fantastic. Having fun at the party would be easy and natural. For one night, she wouldn't have to pretend she was enjoying herself.

Martin came out of the bathroom, and he asked if she wanted coffee.

"*Claro*," she said with her subtle smile and tried to forget about Charlie's birthday, which marked the end of her first full year in Aruba.

Because he had quit drinking just in time, the headache at the back of his skull was only minor. For this bit of wisdom, Sam gave himself a thumbs-up in the mirror. No doubt the hurricane had moved one way or the other, and the airlines were back in business. He picked up his cell phone only to find the battery dead. He attached the charger, then left the Dog House to use the landline at Charlie's.

At the bar, he found the man himself chatting with Captain Beck.

"Arise, Lazarus!" Charlie called to him.

Sam strolled up and asked about his pals.

"This miracle I cannot perform," Charlie answered. "Look at the sky. The first flight from Miami should be crossing there just now, but not a bird in the air."

Dejected, Sam took a seat with them and lit a cigarette.

"I brought *Huntress* up from the refinery," Beck said. "My crew would like to take you fishing."

Sam poked his head up to peer out at the dock. *Huntress* hung by a single line. "Thanks, Captain, but fishing is a sorry excuse for what I wanted to do today."

"Better than nothing," Beck offered.

"He's right, Sam," Charlie added. "It'll take your mind off things. When was the last time you went fishing?"

It had been a long time, Sam admitted to himself. But he already had fish for the party, a huge, beautiful fish courtesy of Old Man Juárez. What was the sense of catching more? He must have been thinking out loud because he heard Charlie answer the question.

"Because it's fun, that's why. When have you needed a better reason?"

Once again, the King was right. Sam bowed his head, put out the cigarette, and said, "Let me get my hat."

"Bring a change of clothes," Beck suggested. "It's going to be hot out there. You can get a shower aboard *Kathryn*, and we can hit the town directly off the dock."

"You know, Captain, every once in a while you have a good idea."

Soon after, they were underway. Syd steered *Huntress* while Ramirez readied the fishing gear. Beck hadn't done any fishing since coming to Aruba. He was too busy learning Spanish, spending time with Luz, and exploring the island. These things he did when he wasn't on the phone inquiring about various tugs for sale.

Syd took them to a spot off the southeast point of the island where the sea was choppy but where he claimed they caught all kinds of fish. It wasn't long before Sam went into a long story about himself and his father.

"And the old man said to me, 'Sam, you won't catch fish like this anywhere in the world.'" As Sam's father had predicted, they caught plenty of fish, big ones, too. They let them all go since this was sport, not survival.

Like everything Sam did, he jumped into it like a complete enthusiast. He lectured Syd on how to maneuver the boat. He instructed Beck on how much drag to use on the reel. He pointed out his technique for tying and baiting the hooks to Ramirez. Beck was impressed by Sam's encyclopedic knowledge on a subject that Sam himself admitted he hadn't visited for ages.

"This isn't science," Sam told them all. "It's art. Which reminds me, did you see Andrés?"

"Yesterday," Beck said. "Why?"

"The kid is a little out of sorts," Sam said.

"He's young," Beck proposed. "Bound to have something bothering him at that age."

"He's an artist, the real kind. That kid could paint a ceiling that would make Michelangelo's Sistine Chapel look like it was done by a kindergartner."

Beck said, "There has to be a church on the island that could use his talent."

"That's your second good idea of the day, Captain," Sam said. He thought back to the day he'd given Luz a tour of the island. Didn't he enumerate each and every church they passed? Yes, and he knew the church in Santa Cruz was plain as the blue skies over the island. The place needed something as dramatic as what Andrés had done in Montoya's house. It would make the kid a living legend and put the church on the tourist maps. For his part, Sam would call that store in New York City and ask them if they sold paint by the five-gallon pail. It would make him the chief sponsor, the way the doges of Italy supported artists during the Renaissance. Depending on the cost of the project, he could always get money from the refinery, Captain Beck, Charlie, and the rest of his pals. This was just the kind of thing he dreamt of for his retirement.

"Let's head for port," Sam said. "I need a rest before we take on the night."

"Heading for port," Beck replied and stowed his rod.

Sam stretched out in the spare cabin aboard *Kathryn*. The room was tiny but well fitted with bunk beds, lockers, built-in drawers, and pigeonholes to store small things like pocket change and his Zippo. The cabin gave him ideas as to how he would lay out the furniture in his new house. His place would be simple and inexpensive but also functional and comfortable. Those were his instructions to the architect, and the plans reflected his wishes. He fell asleep anticipating a dream about his soon-to-be reality.

"Hey, Sam," a voice said.

"Who's that?" Sam croaked.

"This is your captain speaking," Beck replied.

"Hell, Cap, I was just getting to sleep."

"That was more than two hours ago. The night awaits. Here's a couple of towels. The head and shower are back through the corridor on your right."

"Aye, aye," Sam said as he sat up.

"There's one problem," Beck continued.

"There are no problems in Aruba," Sam reminded his host. "Only opportunities for further improvisation."

"Spoken like the man himself," Beck said. "Charlie called. He sounded jealous about missing the fishing trip."

"He could have come with us."

"Yeah, well, he wants to run out early tomorrow morning. We have to take *Huntress* up to Savaneta because none of us will be in any condition to do it later."

"Sounds like Charlie's planning a run to Venezuela."

"Either way, I told him we'd leave the boat there for him. I was hoping we could use your car to get back to town."

"Fine. Let me take my shower."

While he had been sleeping, the breeze came up. The wind stripped away the heat of the day and most of the humidity with it. As Sam and Beck motored along the coast, they talked about boats and the joy of being on the water. Beck told Sam about his grandfather's admonition to always sleep on his life jacket.

"Sticking to good advice is what got you here," Sam reflected. "Bet you're not sorry."

"I'm not," Beck told him. Though a complete stranger, San Nicolaas treated him like a native son. Even so, it had always been his ambition to have a tug of his own, and he struggled with the idea that he would be forever in port, venturing only as far as the anchorage to meet a ship.

Sam would have thought him crazy for exchanging San Nicolaas for any other place. So Beck kept his thoughts to himself. He wasn't out to convince anyone to join him. Well, there was one person. He had considered asking Luz if she wanted to leave with him. It wasn't just a matter of leaving the island. It was the case of spending her life with a sailor. To him, that kind of life sounded better than the one she had, and it would certainly be better for Hernán. But if he had learned anything in San Nicolaas, it was that life was subject to interpretation.

Twenty minutes later, Beck spotted the lights marking the channel into Savaneta. He ran *Huntress* past them and turned inshore. Sam lassoed the bit on the end of Charlie's dock and made the line fast.

"Next time Tony goes home, you can take his place on deck," Beck said.

Sam winked and stepped ashore. His cane-cutter shirt was without a wrinkle. Moonlight gleamed in the shine on his shoes. He had a fresh pack of cigarettes. Thanks to Ramirez, his Zippo was fully fueled. It was going to be another fantastic night in town. Just the same, he was going to take it easy on the booze. If Charlie thought he was going to Venezuela all by his lonesome, he had another thing coming.

"Come on, Cap," Sam urged Beck. "The night may be young, but we're not getting any younger."

The only lights at Charlie's were the white Christmas lights Sam had strung as a measure of good luck. Now that he was going to be there full-time, he intended to wire a few outdoor spotlights, the kind with motion sensors. That way, he wouldn't stub his toes on anything.

They walked side by side to the end of the dock. Just before they stepped ashore, Beck pulled up short. "Forgot my wallet," he said. "Get the car started. I'll be right there."

"Roger that," Sam said as he followed the path to Charlie's pavilion. All of a sudden, he was blinded by an incredible light. He covered his eyes with his forearm. "What the hell?" he muttered.

A moment later a crowd roared, "Hurrah!" They followed it with a round of applause. Lined up as if for a massive family portrait were all his friends and what seemed to be half the population of San Nicolaas. In the center stood Charlie, grinning like a fool, clapping his hands. Beside Charlie was Carlotta, who blew Sam a kiss. Off to the left, up on their bandstand was the Arends Family. They took their cue and started to play. The crowd sang loud and true, "For he's a jolly good fellow! For he's a jolly good fellow, which nobody can deny!"

For the first time in his life, Sam was caught speechless. He counted down the line of people as they sang to him. Roger was with his wife. George, his child-hood neighbor, stood with a girl he recognized from one of the bars. Tom was next, hugging Carlos and giving the thumbs-up sign. Kenny raised a glass. No less a dignitary than Chief Calenda stood at the far end. He saluted Sam, then touched a match to a fuse on the ground. The fuse raced out of sight. A moment later, several rockets launched into the air. They burst into red, white, and blue clusters that sparkled overhead.

Truth be told, Luz was bored. Martin related a story about something he was doing in America, a business deal, or buying a car, she couldn't remember which. She was thinking about Charlie's party and how much fun it would have been to be there. It was already ten o'clock, and the party was probably more than half over. She recollected when Sam had taken her the first time. She had been terrified of Marcela but desperate for the money. Sam's was the first hundred-dollar bill she had ever seen. A stack of them was now hidden in her house, several stacks in fact, one of which was going to be sent to her family. Of the messages on her cell phone that morning, one had been from Anna requesting money to purchase a new re-frigerator for the house.

As if he could read her mind, Martin asked about her family. "When was the last time you visited them?" he wanted to know.

"Not since I moved to Aruba," she answered.

"I have a friend at the airport who can get you a cheap ticket."

Martin's eyes were bright, his smile sincere. However, he knew nothing about her family and their relationship with Luz. They were as distant as second cousins at this point. On the rare occasions that she actually spoke to her sister, the con-versation was always about the same thing: how much this thing cost or the price of that thing had increased. She had not spoken to her mother since she left Colombia. Would they be happy to see her? Probably not, Luz thought. They had to tell their friends that their daughter was married to a foreigner, that she lived on an island with a strange language, and that she did whatever it was they did there to make a living off the tourists from America and Europe. They were uncomfort-able telling people their daughter had married a man with money. They prayed for Rudi, who was the solution to their problems.

"They could visit you here," Martin suggested.

"Hernán is with me. He is my family," Luz said bluntly.

Martin caught her tone and looked away.

At once, Luz felt irritated and brave. She rapped her spoon softly on the table in hopes it would dissipate some of the emotions that were overcoming her. It did not. Her leg started to wiggle. She tapped her feet to try to distract herself a second time.

"Are you okay?" Martin asked.

"No," Luz said. "I'm leaving." She dropped her spoon to the floor with a loud clang. Their waiter rushed to retrieve it. Martin rose to his feet too late. Luz was already halfway across the room. He dropped some money on the table and hurried after her.

In the vestibule, he caught up to her. "I'll take you home," he said nearly out of breath.

"Send my things to Minchi's," she ordered, then turned to the doorman. "*Un taxi, por favor.*"

"*Sí,*" the doorman said and escorted her to the curb.

A better party Sam could not have wished for. Charlie employed all his kingly powers to create the ultimate night of celebration and entertainment. Most importantly, everyone was there. As it turned out, his friends had arrived in plenty of time. Charlie had isolated Sam by keeping him occupied with other things, like fishing with Beck, so it would be impossible to know what was really going on. How could Sam be furious when the result was such a wonderful surprise? Still, he swore friendly revenge.

"I can only hope so," Charlie said to him. "You see those lights up there?"

"You think it's a UFO?"

"No, you idiot. It's the last plane of the night. All the tourists are here. The clip joints will be full tomorrow, including mine, which is a good thing because I have to pay for all this."

"God bless the touristas!" Sam said.

George and Tom teased Sam incessantly. They had watched him getting drunk the night before from the back rooms at different bars. They drank their fair share, too, laughing at the absurdity of their deception. Some of the girls were in on it as well. Their reward for silence was to attend the party where they ate, drank, and danced to their hearts' content. None of them turned any tricks unless they wanted to. Some of them did. There was no reason to pass up an opportunity to cut expenses and make money.

Sam enjoyed himself more than ever since he didn't have to worry about doing anything. Charlie's crew, including Herr Koch and Luis, tended the grill and the bar. Chief Calenda took care of the fireworks. Kenny and Carlotta supervised the comings and goings of the girls. The Arends Family provided a soundtrack that should have been broadcast around the world as The Sound of Aruba. He moved from group to group, shaking hands, slapping backs, and downing drinks in honor of Charlie's improvisational skills and his own achievement of permanent residency.

After more than four hours of industrious merriment, the crowd settled into a calmer state. The most senior Arends announced their last set. They began a romantic song that featured the work of their youngest member, the one who played the guitar Beck had given him. Since receiving the guitar, he had grown into it the way young boys sprout at that age. It rode high on his chest as he played in the Spanish style.

Beck marveled at the boy's talent. He was grateful for the coming end of the party. As much fun as it had been, the constant eating, drinking, and dancing wore him out. He looked forward to the comfort of his bunk. He wished for it to be Luz's bed, but she was with her client. No matter, she would be back in a few days. He downed his drink and got up for the final dance of the night.

No sooner had he risen from his seat than he thought he saw a familiar face moving across the patio. He stopped short, peered into the crowd, but couldn't find it. He noticed the movement of a man he hadn't seen earlier in the night. The guy was also looking for someone. Beck met his eyes, and the man raised his finger and pointed directly at him. A step behind and slightly to the left stood Nicole Reston. Her gaze fell upon Beck, and she smiled.

Beck found himself stuck in place, unable to turn away from Nicole. He remained where he was as she weaved through the crowd to him. Her hands gently pulled him close, and she pressed her face to his. Their lips met. The kiss was one he knew so well it felt as if they had parted only earlier in the day instead of more than a year ago.

"You're not hard to find," Nicole said. "El Capitán is what they call you. 'At Charlie's,' they said. The taxi driver knew where the place was."

Beck continued to hold her. "I told you it's a small island," he said.

"These are your friends?"

"Mostly Sam's and Charlie's, but they don't mind having me along."

"I guess not," she said impressed by the size and quality of the celebration.

Beck had yet to look up from her, and he still couldn't as he said, "That's the ring I gave you."

Nicole touched the ring that hung on a gold chain around her neck. "Dance with me, Nate," she said.

The song was a home-crafted bolero. They remained silent, letting the music carry them past the awkwardness of parted lovers reunited in a future neither might have expected. Both of them had plenty to say, but each recognized the sanctity of the moment. The past didn't matter, and what was coming had yet to be determined.

"Who's that?" Sam asked Charlie.

"Good question," Charlie answered. "Too healthy to be anything but an American girl."

"Too close to be anything but the Captain's first mate."

"That makes us two for two," Charlie said.

The arrival of this strange woman in the arms of the Captain gave Sam welcome relief. It meant there was someone else in the Captain's life, as in someone other than Luz. In the morning, he would question the sailor about her and have the critical details. Whatever they were, he knew it would help him in his quest of securing *the one* as his own. He raised his glass to toast the good luck that always seemed to come his way.

"What's that for?" Charlie asked.

"To us," Sam said. "Luckier men never walked the earth."

"I'll drink to that," Charlie said. "Now I need to release some of the pressure from my bladder before an embarrassing puddle forms between my happy-go-lucky feet."

The bathroom was located in one of the front corners of Charlie's house. From the window he looked out onto the street, which led in from the main road. There were few cars except those driven by workers returning from San Nicolaas.

Instead of returning to the party, Charlie exited his front door and sat down on the step. He helped himself to a cigarette. Had he been in town, he would have shared a drink with Screwball. The two of them would have surveyed the fools who were out of energy, money, and brains enough to go home. Tonight the scenery was a little different. The stars were brighter here. The trees along the street waved back and forth to the music of the breeze. A stray dog sauntered around the corner of a darkened house.

For a moment, he considered quitting smoking. He hated the habit: the stink of stale smoke, the cost, the irresistible urge to do it. He was addicted, and he'd read once that nicotine was more addictive than heroin. He thanked God he never tried heroin. He would have been a junkie lying in the street with Speedy.

A car motored down the lane, slowed, and stopped at the edge of his property. He saw it was a taxi and shook his head as Luz got out. Sam had been right. Luckier men had not walked the earth, at least not this part of it. Charlie let her pass without catching her attention. He wanted to finish his cigarette before the excitement began.

The sound of music rejuvenated Luz. It meant the party was still going. She might be able to get in a few dances with her favorite partner.

Under the big Divi tree, she nodded to the men playing dominoes. They hardly looked up from the game. A girl whom she had met several times at Western Union waved to her. Carlotta didn't see her, but Kenny smiled over his drink. Then Luz saw Captain Beck. He faced her but his eyes were closed as he danced with a woman. She stopped where she was, watching as he slowly rotated away from her. The woman with the Captain was not one of the girls from San Nicolaas. She could only be a tourist because even in the dim light her complexion was too fair.

The song ended. To Luz's horror, the Captain bent down and kissed his dance partner. It was a lingering kiss on the lips, one the woman relished. She held on to him for a long moment before releasing her grip. She touched something that sparkled on her chest, took his hand, and pulled him out of the dance area. Luz observed their progress through the couples that remained for the next song. They walked across the road that separated Charlie's pavilion from the beach.

Luz knew immediately that the Captain and this woman were not strangers to each other. She was the reason he had never slept with the whore who'd found him on the beach.

Luz pinched her eyes shut. When she opened them, Beck and the woman were out of sight. She closed her eyes again, holding the lids down with her fingers. She refused to cry. She denied herself the self-pity that crushed her heart. Not since the father of her boy threw her into the street had she felt as lonely.

She wanted to be away from the party as quickly as possible. She didn't care if she had to walk to San Nicolaas, so long as she didn't have to see Captain Beck with this woman. Walking from the pavilion, she bumped into Charlie.

"*Un favor, señor,*" she said. "*Me llevas a mi casa.*"

"Of course I'll take you home," Charlie told her. He didn't have to ask her why.

"THIS IS where they found me," Beck said.

Nicole looked down at the sand, then out at the ocean. "Incredible," she told him.

Had he been a casualty instead of a survivor, he would have avoided the pain of this night. It was nearly the same as the day in Philadelphia when Nicole had not put on the ring.

"Do you ever think of coming back to Philadelphia?" she asked.

"No," Beck answered honestly. He thought of going to many places. Philadelphia was not among them. Most of all, he thought of going to sea, of traversing the ocean on a boat of his own. It was where he belonged, always between two places and never in one for too long.

"Are you going to stay here?" Nicole wanted to know.

"Not forever."

"I'm sorry," she said.

Her apology hung between them. Beck tried to discern if it was a statement of regret, an admission of guilt, or an act of contrition. She had yet to make her reason for coming to Aruba clear. It wasn't to see how he was doing or to reminisce about old times.

"I still want my own boat," he said.

Nicole put her hands on his hips. "I understand, but you have to come home sometime."

"Once in a while," he admitted.

"You've been gone for a year, and it took me that long to realize what was special about us. I missed the anticipation of seeing you when you came home and sometimes the sadness of your leaving. I didn't understand that we were living one long first date. I feel that way right now. Don't you?"

He did. If she had said those words last year, then everything would be different. He would have a regular schedule aboard Jack's new boat. He would be sleeping next to her two weeks at a time instead of on odd nights with Luz. They might have been married. They might have had a son. As things were now, he would have to surrender Luz if he wanted to win Nicole. Unlike the men in San Nicolaas, he was the type to have a woman he loved and no other.

Beck had no reason to believe that Luz was actually his. Many times he had considered asking her to give up her life as a prostitute and to live with him. He knew Sam wanted the same thing. Sam and a bunch of other guys. Who was he to think Luz would choose him? He wasn't so arrogant to believe himself capable of deciphering a woman's heart. Nicole was proof of that.

He was left to choose between a woman who might want him and a woman who might not.

Far to the southeast, at the edge of the horizon, gleamed a set of lights brighter than anything else in view. They belonged to the cruise ship that was due to dock in Oranjestaad in three hours. Wilkie was to have the honor of assisting her since Beck was at Charlie's party. Beck decided to change the plan.

"You see those lights?" he asked Nicole.

She peered out in the direction he pointed. "Yes."

"That's *Empress of the Seas*. She's due in Oranjestaad in a few hours."

"Good place to be," Nicole said. "Away from the hurricane."

But in the middle of the storm, Beck wanted to add. "I have to leave," he said. "I'm helping her to the dock."

"That's who you are, Nate. I accept that now."

At a loss for words, he said, "Thank you."

Nicole pulled him close. She said, "I'm flying home in the morning, weather permitting. If you get to Philadelphia, I'd like to see you again. Maybe another first date."

Beck let his arms fall away.

She kissed him and squeezed both his hands in hers. "You have a ship to meet, Captain. Don't be late."

Beck walked the length of Charlie's dock to *Huntress*. No sooner had he untied the lines than the boat drifted toward the open sea. He allowed her to move with the wind until he was through the gap in the reef. If he allowed it to, the wind would have carried him all the way to Venezuela. Instead, he pushed both starter buttons simultaneously. Satisfied with what he had to do, he pushed the throttles ahead one notch. With her propellers engaged, *Huntress* responded by bucking the wind. Beck shoved the throttles forward, cut the wheel to starboard, and raced toward San Nicolaas.

Angry and exhausted, Luz awoke to the sound of someone coming through the front door. Only la Dueña and Andrés had keys. She sat up, listened for a moment, and determined it was Andrés. He was quiet and respectful, unlike Marcela, who would have awakened the entire neighborhood by now. Luz put her feet into the slippers that forever waited beside her bed.

"Sorry to wake you," Andrés said. "The last couple of days there has been no mail. I came to check again."

Wiping her eyes, she asked him if he wanted a glass of orange juice. He said he didn't as he sorted through the stack of envelopes that came only the previous afternoon. Luz took out a cup and filled it from the carton in her refrigerator. She remembered she had to go to Western Union to send her sister the money for the refrigerator her family supposedly needed. Suddenly, she found herself in a crushing embrace. She dropped the carton onto the counter.

"I've been accepted," Andrés declared. "I'm going to Holland!" He shoved a piece of heavy paper into her hands.

The language in the letter was nothing Luz could read.

He clutched Luz by the shoulders. "Don't tell anyone."

"I won't," Luz said.

"No. This is different. When I didn't get a letter last week I thought they forgot about me. It must have been delayed. Now I have my chance. I have to get out of here before she finds out."

The she he referred to was Marcela. Luz knew better than to say anything.

"Luz, tell no one. Especially do not tell Sam, not even the Captain."

In light of the fact that the Captain was with his American woman, the chances of her speaking with him were very small. "Congratulations," she said.

"I'm so happy!" he said. "I should have celebrated last night at Charlie's party. Let's go out tonight, Luz. Come on, we'll go dancing in Oranjestaad."

She wasn't in the mood to dance or to go out or to celebrate anything. "I have to work," she said. She did have to work. No doubt Martin was not going to have her back. She would have to explain herself to la Dueña, another challenge as difficult as accepting that Captain Beck had another woman. To forget it all, she intended to spend the night at Minchi's, pushing vinos, looking for a new client, and avoiding the other girls.

"Take a night off," Andrés urged. "It's okay. We're husband and wife."

His enthusiasm inspired her desire to escape it all. A night in Oranjestaad with Andrés appealed to her, especially since he was neither a client nor a lover.

He was only a friend, no matter what the official paperwork said about their being married. Just the same, it only delayed the inevitable.

"Another time, Andrés," she said.

Andrés left the house with his fancy letter.

Luz fought a bout of jealousy. Mostly she lost. She wished she was the one leaving the island, going to the place she most wanted to go. But where was that? It wasn't Holland. There was nothing for her there. It wasn't Bogotá, not the way her family had been treating her. It wasn't America. She hardly spoke English, and Captain Beck was not going to be her translator. She was lost and envious of those who had a place where they both belonged and wanted to be.

She told herself there was Sam. He wanted her last year and she knew intuitively that he still did. Although more than twice her age, he was spry and eager to please. To this point, she had never considered him a possible suitor for the long term. Nevertheless, it seemed as if he might be better than the others. With him she could live a somewhat regular life. Still, she would be forever dependent upon him to support her and her family. If he grew tired of her, she would be back to working as a prostitute, a position no better than the one she now held.

She rinsed her glass and placed it on the rack to dry. Sam or not, she was going to work. Money, after all, gave her more freedom than any man.

The pavilion appeared to be in pristine condition. There were no broken chairs, no overturned tables, no trash in the corners. The bar contents, organized and clean, awaited the next party. The barbecue was void of ash, its iron grate scrubbed and stowed.

For Sam it was a beautiful sight. The guest of honor need not worry about a thing. He wasted no time beginning his next day in paradise. He lapped the pier a couple of times, floated on his back, and swam a few more laps to prove he could do it better than ever. The breeze dried him as much as the sun. Both were strong, the way they were supposed to be in Aruba. "Hurricanes be damned!" he thought. This place is immune from such disaster. He hoped more people did not discover the fact. He didn't want it to get crowded.

The boys awaited his direction. Sam said they were going to Charlie's, where they would humor the tourists and then head over to Carlotta's. They arranged times with girls in town and complained of hangovers and general hunger pains. Sam chided them for being amateurs and said, "You know where I'll be. Catch me if you can."

He rolled to town with his windows down. The warm air felt as good as Luz's skin against his. To think all he got from her was a massage! In the old days, he would have done everything published in the *Kama Sutra* by the end of the third day. He reminded himself that this one was different. She was *the one*, and as such, deserved respect.

Once again, there were no parking spaces on Main Street. Sam drove a lap on the Five Hundred in search of another spot and put his eye on a few girls in the process. They were nothing compared to Luz. He came down Rogerstraat along the refinery wall when he noticed someone backing into the street. He waited with his turn signal on, thinking about Captain Beck. Sam had seen the woman who'd come to the Captain at the party. Everyone he asked, including Chief Calenda, had never seen her before. Sam guessed she was the Captain's woman from Philadelphia, the one who had left him the previous year. Whoever she was, she had done Sam a miraculous favor. Word would spread, from the San Nicolaas girls at the party all the way through town, until Luz was hit full force with a rumor storm that left her with no doubt the Captain was no longer the man of her dreams. He was nothing but another client. That left him, Samito, to step in to save the day.

He locked his car, crossed the street, and found himself staring at Frankie, who was propped against the wall.

"I'm not talking to you," Frankie growled.

"Not even for a guilder?"

"Not for all the guilders in China," Frankie retorted. He shoved himself off the ground and shuffled toward Main Street.

"What's your problem?" Sam asked, following him.

"My problem is you," Frankie said looking back over his shoulder. "You treat me like a bum."

Sam laughed out loud. "You are a bum."

"Rub it in, rich guy."

"Come on, Frankie, you know I love you."

"The whole town was at the party, but you didn't invite me. You didn't invite Speedy. We're not talking to you, so don't waste your time."

Stunned, Sam stopped where he was. All these years, Frankie had looked out for him, and he had been denied the courtesy of attendance at the most important of their Savaneta bashes. Sam felt terrible, bad enough to make Frankie an extraordinary offer.

"You, Speedy, the boys and I, we'll have a baseball game," Sam said. "How's that sound?"

"Sounds like bullshit," Frankie replied.

"Bullshit? I bought you guys gloves, a ball, a bat. Now we're going to have a game. When was the last time you played a game?"

"Doesn't matter."

"Frankie, that's the best I can do," Sam pleaded. "Think about it. The rest of town will be cheering you on."

"They hate me."

"They love you, chico. You're part of what makes this place great. You and Speedy, you're characters."

"In a horror show," Frankie whined. "Look at my teeth. I only got four."

Sam looked at Frankie's mouth. Despite the four false teeth, a disaster lurked behind his lips. "Okay, final offer for peace, I'll pay for a couple more teeth."

"Four more," Frankie demanded. "Double or nothing."

"Double it is," Sam agreed.

"And a beer, too."

They walked up the street to Charlie's, where Frankie knew better than to try to go inside. Sam threaded through the crowd, took a Heineken from the cooler, winked to Koch, and returned to the street. He took a sip, then handed it to Frankie. "That's five guilders," Sam said.

Frankie held the bottle up, took stock of the contents, and replied, "Looks like four-fifty to me."

"It'll be a lump on your head if you don't find Speedy and start practicing."

After flashing his horrendous smile one last time, Frankie shuffled down the street.

Sam faced the crowd at the bar. Every person was a potential mark, someone who hadn't heard his stories, someone who would buy him drinks for the pleasure of his entertainment.

❊   ❊   ❊

After docking a cruise ship, *Kathryn* normally motored along the coast to California Point where the lighthouse stood before returning to San Nicolaas. At various places along the way, her crew would fire their water cannons to thrill the tourists who covered the beaches.

This morning was different. Something had happened to their captain. On their lives they couldn't figure out exactly what it was. He did his job as always, with skill and courtesy, but he was short on small talk and not hungry for breakfast. They whispered among themselves as to what might have transpired at the party. The Captain showed no signs of a fight, which they knew him prone to start or finish from time to time. He wasn't hungover, though he looked dejected and worried. For Syd and Ramirez, it came down to two things, his health or a woman, and Captain Beck looked like the healthiest man they knew.

The more they talked, the more they ruled out this probability. The Captain seemed well adjusted to his prostitute friend. He slept on the boat when she was with her clients, even mentioned the fact to all of them. A man bothered by such a notion would lie about it or at least not admit it. After a year of such a lifestyle, why would it suddenly affect him? Syd and Ramirez didn't know. They agreed to venture into town at their first opportunity to see what they could learn. After all, he was their captain, the man who ruled their tiny floating kingdom. If something happened to him, it happened to them, too.

The tourists loved Sam. He was nothing like the entertainment at their hotels. He had no script, no orchestra backing him up, no time for the show to end. He gave them everything he had, which was more than they ever expected. When he finally looked at his watch and told them he had to go, they begged him to stay. Couldn't he tell them one more story? What did your father say when you called him after running away to Venezuela? Didn't your mother kill you when you gave her favorite dress to a girl in San Nicolaas? They got no answers. He made his smoking-gun exit. He had things to do.

First on his list was a stop by Carlotta, just to see how she was doing and what had become of his friends. None of them had shown their faces at Charlie's, which meant they either were still recovering or were in the arms of a girl. They were still visitors, amateurs who squeezed the most they could out of their time like the touristas at Charlie's. Sam was well pleased to be free of that burden. He coasted, letting the breeze carry him along.

Turning the corner onto Helfrichstraat, he saw Speedy standing in the dirt lot with his baseball and glove. Sam hustled down the sidewalk to meet the choller. A coughing fit overtook him as he arrived at Speedy's side. He bent over, hacked violently, and nearly vomited.

"Samito!" Speedy greeted him. "Frankie says we're going to have a game."

Breaking into a sweat, Sam gasped. "Sure, Speedy, let's practice a little."

"We need the bat. We need the bat."

Catching his breath, Sam stood upright, coughed one last time, and drew a lungful of air that cleared the redness from his face. "Let's see how well you catch," he suggested.

Speedy gave him the ball and backed into the dirt lot. Sam tossed an easy one, a floater. Speedy rushed under it, put his glove up, and the ball fell right into the pocket. So excited was Speedy that he forgot to close the glove around the ball. It fell out and landed at his feet.

"I had it, Samito! I had it! You saw me!"

"I saw you," Sam agreed. "Let's try it again." Sam launched the ball into the air, but Speedy kept looking at Sam and the ball dropped behind him several yards.

"Sorry," the bum said.

After the tenth try, Speedy started to catch them. Pleased with Speedy's progress, Sam moved on to Carlotta's, but her substitute bartender told Sam the madam was gone for the day.

With no intention of rushing things, he stopped by Luz's house. She opened the door with a warm smile. He asked her if she wanted to go for a ride, maybe take a look at the plans for his house.

"*Nos vamos*," she said and went for her purse.

Sam nearly collapsed. He wasn't prepared for her to accept. But wasn't that the way it always happened? Charlie would have said, "You have to improvise."

"I have to work tonight," Luz reminded him as they rode out of town.

"*Claro*," Sam assured her. He wasn't about to push for more than an afternoon of her time. He had learned to go easy on the booze, and he had transferred the lesson to his love life. "I'll have you home by seven thirty," he said.

"Thank you, Samito," Luz said in English.

"You missed the show," Charlie said to Captain Beck. "Sam was here telling stories all afternoon." He waved to the empty room. "It seems he took his audience with him."

"I'll have a drink," Beck said. "Nothing strong."

Charlie eyed him carefully. "We have nothing weak." He made the drink and helped himself to a glass of water. He watched Beck sip his whiskey and look out at the street.

At last, Charlie spoke to Beck. He said, "Among my many powers, I am psychic."

"Amazing," Beck reflected.

"It is, but sometimes a heavy weight to carry when you know what is bothering your friends."

"What's bothering me?" Beck asked.

"A question, my friend. You have a question that you cannot answer. This is worse than a blocked intestine or a kidney stone that won't pass, both of which I have experienced."

"And you know the answer to the question."

Charlie laughed. "No. I'm only psychic, not clairvoyant. There is a difference."

"So what's the question?" Beck wanted to know.

"Simple," Charlie said with a nod. "You want to know if she is *the one* for now or *the one* forever."

"Close," Beck said.

"Close?" Charlie scoffed.

"The question is which is which," Beck said and stepped out into the breeze. He didn't know it, but the guard at the bank, the woman waiting behind the glass at Western Union, and a pair of refinery workers drinking beer under a Divi tree all knew how confused he was. They didn't know what had caused it, but they saw his consternation as he walked along Main Street. Just before he turned for the refinery, Frankie came out of the alley and noted the dismay on Beck's face. Instead of begging for a guilder, Frankie slipped down the alley, thankful that the only thing he had to worry about was his next meal.

JACK FORD waited on the pier. It was a front-row seat from which to view the refinery in action. *Kathryn* held a tanker named *Persian Explorer* into place while the linesmen secured the vessel to the dock. He was surrounded by the sounds and smells of the refinery, which awaited the contents of the ship. To his right, the new catalyst unit was ready to be tested. Within weeks the refinery would be capable of producing a full range of products from gasoline to jet fuel.

When *Kathryn* was tied off, Beck climbed over the gunwale and greeted Jack with a solid handshake.

"Imagine finding you here," Jack said leading them toward the refinery gate and Charlie's.

Beck hadn't been expecting any visitors, not since his last surprise, which had been Nicole showing up at Charlie's party two nights ago. She hadn't tried to contact him again. Beck assumed she had returned to Philadelphia. He spent two days working as much as he could in order to avoid Luz, collect his thoughts, and figure out what to do next. He made little progress. Yet he was going to Minchi's tonight. By now, Luz had heard about Nicole's appearance. If he delayed any longer, more damage would be done than he could explain.

"Off duty?" Koch asked Beck as he sat in his usual booth.

"Until midnight," Beck replied. "I'll have my usual."

"Same as him," Ford said.

When Koch brought their drinks, they toasted the oil refinery and the climbing price of oil that was rapidly making Jack more money than he ever dreamed of having. His boats and barges were in constant demand to shuttle product from the places that produced it to the places that needed it.

"So what's going on?" Beck asked. "You don't fly between the storms two weeks in a row for a social call."

"I'd like you to go home," Ford said.

Beck asked, "Should I ask Koch for another round before you explain?"

"Not a bad idea," Jack said.

Beck looked Koch's way, and the bartender got the message. "Why would I go home?" he asked Ford.

"Because it's on your way to sea."

"I think it's the other way around," Beck said. "The sea is between here and there."

"Geographically. I have something else in mind."

"Let's hear it," Beck said.

"You're going to bring *Kathryn* back to Philadelphia," Jack told him.

"Who's going to dock the ships here?"

"The new guys. The place is going to be sold. Officially and off the record, it happens next week." Ford said this as if he were talking about a used car, not a major industrial facility. "When I was here two weeks ago, Herzog and I tried to get them to renew the contract. They thought about it and decided to use their own boats, which arrive next week."

"I guess I'm leaving whether I want to or not."

"Very perceptive. Let's skip the long story and cut to the important part. Do you still want a boat?"

"As long as I'm the captain," Beck answered.

"Good. I have one to sell you," Jack said.

"You're selling a boat?"

"I'm selling it all, Nate. The accountants tell me I should sell when things are good. Besides, I'm old enough to be your grandfather and too tired to argue with people like Shahann."

"*Kathryn?*" Beck asked hopefully.

Jack smiled. "She's already spoken for. I was thinking *Marlena*. She's more affordable for a guy with your budget."

Beck liked the sound of that. He stuck out his hand. "I'll take her," he said.

"Good," Ford told him. They toasted the deal, the minutia of which would be worked out later. Before Koch brought their third round, Ford continued. He said, "I'm glad you took the offer. When I get to Philadelphia the first thing I'm going to do is fire Shahann."

Of all the people to find at the ticket counter, Charlie never expected Andrés. He saw the young man standing before the desk, talking with the agent. He waited a few minutes to satisfy his curiosity as to what Andrés was up to. When he saw a wad of bills come out of the boy's pocket, he extrapolated this event to the only logical conclusion.

"Congratulations," Charlie said as he approached.

Andrés whirled to see who was behind him. At the sight of Charlie, he was visibly relieved. "*Danki*," he said.

"When did you get your acceptance?"

His hesitation betrayed him to the point where he couldn't lie, especially to Charlie. "A couple of days ago."

"Better late than never. You're off to Holland. When?"

Andrés glanced back at the ticket agent, then returned his eyes to Charlie. "Saturday," he said.

"Me, too," Charlie informed him. "If they have seats."

The agent smiled affirmatively.

"You see that, we're both in for a trip."

"I should have told you," Andrés said suddenly. "But I didn't want anyone else to hear. My father's second wife …"

"Don't apologize," Charlie told him. "An opportunity like this comes rarely in life. Make the most of it."

"I will," Andrés assured him.

Andrés stood there for an awkward moment, as if he awaited a priest's blessing to leave the confessional. In his hand was his ticket, proof the life he dreamed of was going to happen. He tucked it into his pocket, looked one more time at the agent, and turned for the door. The only two people he cared to tell, Luz and Charlie, knew that he was leaving the island.

Caribbean Mercantile Bank sent Luz's money to Colombia with exceptional efficiency. She appreciated the service even as she wished her family would find a way to support themselves. She refused to accept that they needed a new refrigerator. She resented the fact that they were lying to her. Why couldn't they tell her the truth regarding the true purpose of the money? She knew the answer, which was that then she would be in control. She would be the one to say yes or no to their purpose. That was unacceptable to them since she had always been at the bottom of the family hierarchy. Papa had been first, and as the youngest, she had been last. It was the natural order of things, just as it was typical of them to expect that someday Rudi was going to come home.

As she walked to her house, she found herself in the foulest of moods. The combination of Captain Beck's woman and the business with her family had left her hurting and bitter. She deserved better. She had been honest with Beck; he should have returned the courtesy. The same applied to her family. She began to understand why Marcela behaved the way she did. The world forced her to. It made her into a defensive, vigilant brawler. Then again, Carlotta wasn't like that. Still, Luz could not deny she was less optimistic than she had been. Economically she was well off, and that was what bothered her most. The money wasn't making her happy the way it should have.

She arrived home to find Andrés waiting for her. His suitcase stood in the living room, while he sat on the couch watching television.

"I have to leave this here," he said. "I don't want my father's second wife to find out. Charlie knows. He saw me at the airport."

"You can trust him."

"I have to go to the bank to get my money. It is the last thing."

Luz understood. She nodded her head and turned for her bedroom. It irritated her that Andrés pleaded for her silence when he knew she had no reason to tell Marcela anything about his affairs.

Sensing her disposition, Andrés asked, "Are you angry with me?"

She spoke to the empty doorway to her bedroom. "No, I am not angry with you. I am frustrated that you can leave this place to live your dreams when I am here working as a whore. I am jealous and that is a sin. I should be happy that my son has a good school and a nice house and friends, and that he and I are together. I should be happy, Andrés, and I am."

He resisted the urge to tell her that he felt sorry for her. He allowed her to retreat to her bedroom without a word. Since she faced away from him, his mind's eye imagined the expression on her face. Her eyes squinted slightly with a few tiny lines, faint as old pencil marks, at the corners. Her lips were pressed tightly and her chin was up in defiance of her fate. He pushed his suitcase behind the couch, switched off the television, and let himself out by way of the front door.

✹   ✹   ✹

A round of applause was not what Beck expected when he walked into Java Bar. Everyone was there: Sam, George, Tom, and Carlos, among others. Kenny tended bar, putting a drink out for Beck before it was requested. Beck wondered why they were clapping. Was it because they'd heard about the refinery deal? Did they know he was leaving the island and this was his final salute? Or were they simply happy that their number had increased by one?

"You're a little behind, Cap," Sam said patting him on the back. "And you have some explaining to do."

Tom turned from the bar. He said, "American women are expensive. Stick with the Colombianas."

Beck picked up his drink, downed it, and placed the glass on the bar for another.

"Oh, no," Tom said. "Someone's drinking to remember or to forget."

"Because he's thirsty," Beck told him.

"Who was she?" Sam asked.

The question was as difficult as the one Beck had pondered at Charlie's that afternoon. He answered with simple facts. "I was going to marry her," he said as Kenny set down his second drink of the night.

"What happened?" Sam pried.

"It doesn't matter," Beck replied.

Although not satisfied with the answer, Sam left it at that. He shrugged, sipped his own drink, and considered that, whoever the woman had been, he owed her a word of thanks. She had split Luz from Captain Beck. Sam knew it wasn't right that this pleased him, but he was human and couldn't resist the joy of a second chance at *the one*.

"Can you believe these guys?" Sam asked Beck. "They're going home tomorrow."

"Short stay," Beck commented.

"I'm finished lecturing them," Sam continued.

George raised his glass, "Peace and quiet. I'll toast to that."

Ignoring the comment, Sam said, "Chico, let me tell you, they're pouring the slab for my house next week. When that dries, I'll be laying up block."

"Stay off the vodka," Carlos warned, "Or you'll have zigzag walls and toilets that flush uphill."

"I hear you," Sam muttered. "You'll be the first one looking for a free room."

"Only if it comes with a fridge full of food, a cook, a maid, and a girl better looking than Kenny," Carlos said.

Sam turned to Beck. "You get bored and want to get some exercise, stop by. I'll give you all the food and booze you can handle if you lend a hand building the place."

"I won't be here that long," Beck said.

"What?"

"The refinery's been sold. The new company has tugs of their own."

There was no way for this to be true, Sam thought. Charlie would have said something. What Sam didn't know was that there would be an announcement in the morning papers. Since it had been a stock sale, the Aruban government need not be involved. The transaction was as simple as transferring one set of papers for another.

"You're talking about serious business, Cap," he said. "We don't joke about that pile of pipes over there."

"I know," Beck went on. "I sail next week."

✻   ✻   ✻

Luz expected to see one of her regular clients, a contractor working at the refinery. He called to cancel at eight thirty, a courtesy she appreciated. She dialed Herr Diedrik's number. He was always in a good mood, which is what she needed.

He answered the call on the second ring.

"*¡Amiga!*" he said. "You are free tonight?"

"*Sí*," she said brightly. "*¿Y tú?*"

"I'm sorry. I cannot break away. Let me tell you that Jeffery and I are doing business together. I owe you for that."

"You are very generous," she told him.

"I'm a big spender, eh?" he joked. "However, this is the future, and I'm going to have a part in it thanks to you." He then asked her to hold the line. When he came back he said, "I have to go. There is big news about the refinery. Call me tomorrow."

She said she would and closed the line. Spanner served a beer to the only patron at the bar. When he came back to her side, she asked him if he knew of anything happening at the refinery.

"No," he said. "You want to play cards?"

"Maybe later."

"Ah, here comes the Captain. He is always ready for a game."

When Luz tilted her head up and saw Captain Beck, she could not help but smile. It was a sincere reaction, one brought on by the goodness of the man and what he had done for her. Her mind filled with only the best thoughts of him: how he had moved la Dueña to stop blocking her son's paperwork, how he'd given her money with no demands for service, how he treated her like a decent woman when he could have had her as his whore. It was as if she had never seen him with that American lady. He came to her, kissed her cheek, and asked her how she was.

"*Bien*," she answered, "Now that you are here."

Luz brought his drink and a Baileys for herself.

"By this time," Beck began, "You heard about ..."

"This is San Nicolaas," Luz interrupted. "Explanations are not necessary."

For a moment, Beck considered what she had said. They were in San Nicolaas, and in this town feelings beyond sexual pleasure and a completed transaction were not supposed to exist. But they did. Beck experienced an uncomfortable tightness in his chest as he contemplated what he had to tell Luz. It was critical he do it immediately, before word spread through town via Sam or the refinery workers, of whom Luz knew several important ones.

"The refinery has been sold to another company," he said for the second time that night.

Luz felt her eyes widen.

Beck did not hedge when he continued. He said, "I am leaving the island."

"Leaving?" Luz repeated.

Before she had time to react, Beck said, "I want you to go with me."

In a reflexive burst of energy, Luz found herself clutching the Captain. He held on to her so that her feet were off the floor. She pulled her face back from his cheek, looked over at Spanner, and saw the bouncer smiling at her. Whatever the American woman meant to him, it wasn't enough to keep him out of Luz's arms.

"Poor boy don't have no chance," Spanner said, shaking his head.

"Hernán ..."

"There's room for him on that boat."

Her faith in Beck and herself had been restored. "¿Cuando?" she asked still clutching him.

"Lunes, martes," he was saying. "The other tugs will be here by then. Wednesday at the latest."

"So soon," Luz said.

"I wanted to tell you right away," Beck went on. "I have to go now. There's a tanker due in a few hours. I want to get some sleep before the job. We can talk more tomorrow."

"Okay," Luz said. "Hasta luego."

When the door closed behind the Captain, Spanner gathered up their glasses and rinsed them in the sink. He returned to Luz, who had remained in her seat.

"No gambling with you, lucky girl," Spanner said.

Luz put her hand on his arm. "Why not?"

"The man asks you to go with him and says your son can come, too. That happens once in ten years in San Nicolaas. Maybe less than that."

"But I didn't say I was going with him," Luz added as she dumped the cards out of the box.

"When were you planning on telling me?"

"I'm going to Holland to visit my daughter. Does that require a stamp in my passport from you?" Charlie retorted.

"I didn't mean it like that," Sam said.

"Good, because I have no inkpad for Screwball to put his paw on. Have a drink. Relax. You haven't been this tense since you got yourself wrapped up in *the one* from Minchi's."

"She's still *the one*," Sam reminded Charlie.

Charlie took his time making their drinks. He looked out over the refinery, then back at Main Street. Both were busy. The refinery flares roared fiercely against the night sky while packs of men dodged each other on Main Street. This was how things were supposed to be, fire in the sky and money in the street. It was good for everyone but the environment, and no one gave a damn about that, not when they were growing rich and having so much fun.

"I think she's going to be living with me," Sam said.

"That's news," Charlie replied. "This secret you keep even as you accuse me of holding out on you."

Back on point, Sam said, "You're going to Holland, the refinery has been sold, and Captain Beck is leaving."

"This is life, Sam. People come. People go. Let's thank God they do or else the island would be either deserted or overrun. Which would you prefer?"

"Neither. I just want my house and *the one* with me in it. Do a little fishing. Picnic a few times a week out in the Cunucu. That's not too much to ask, is it?"

"Not too much," Charlie agreed but didn't add that it might be more than Sam received. The gods had a funny way of denying mortals what was rightfully theirs. Sam, although currently on good behavior, had tempted the gods more than any mortal dared, including Charlie himself.

The two men settled into their chairs. Screwball relaxed on the parapet. The breeze and the hiss from the refinery surrounded them in a hush of white noise. It blocked out the rest of the world — the touristas on the other side of the bridge, the cruise ships approaching the island, the hurricanes that spun away from it.

"This is the life I always wanted," Sam said, "to spend forever right here."

SHE HADN'T made up her mind whether or not she was leaving with Captain Beck, but Luz took stock of what it would take to make the move if she did.

Of the many things she had purchased since coming to Aruba, a larger suitcase was not among them. If she was going with Captain Beck, she needed a device to contain her clothes and anything else she wanted to take with her. Then there were Hernán's belongings.

It occurred to her that she could sell most of her clothes. She figured some of them might not be appropriate. Then again, she had no idea where Captain Beck lived or how the women there dressed. Certainly they did not dress like whores, but nor did Luz. Yet most of her clothes were more revealing than they needed to be. Furthermore, did she expect Beck to buy her a new wardrobe? Did she want to use her precious savings for this purpose?

There was also the question of supporting her sister and mother. He had shown all the affection of a true father to Hernán, but did she expect him to support her mother and sister as well? More importantly, what if the American woman caused trouble? What if he ultimately decided to reunite with her? Was she better off with Samito? Or should she keep working in San Nicolaas, where she was dependent on no one in particular but rather the steady demand of pleasure seeking men?

She had less than a week to decide.

It was a good day to go to Hop Long, the day before all the girls went to the doctor. She hauled the bag off the floor and turned toward the living room when she heard the front door slam open. She was about to chastise Hernán when she heard Andrés calling her name.

"I'm here," Luz replied. She dropped the laundry and quick-stepped into the living room to see why he had burst into the house.

"I can't go to Holland!" Andrés cried. "Marcela has ruined me!"

"How?" Luz asked putting her hands on Andrés's shoulders.

He puffed his cheeks several times. "She talked to the bank. They won't give me my money, the money my father put in the account for me," he said. "She says it is hers."

"How can that be true?"

"When my father died, I was underage. She was named custodian and has power over my accounts."

"But you're old enough now."

"Tell that to the bank. The manager, that bastard, is her friend. He says he will have to review the history of the account."

Carefully, so as not to offend his pride, she asked, "How much do you need?"

"How much?" he repeated. "All of it. The money you paid me is in there, too."

"I understand, Andrés. How much money do you need to go to Holland?"

He stared at her. "I can't take your money."

"I'll loan it to you," she said. "The bank will release your money eventually. You can pay me back later."

"No," he said defiantly. "She is the problem. She never cared about my father. She only wanted his money."

Instinctively, Luz took Andrés by the arm the way she did Hernán when she wanted her son to know she was serious. Andrés shook her off. He started to say something, slammed his mouth shut, and hurtled out the front door.

Luz bolted to her bedroom. She took her cell phone off the nightstand and dialed the only man who could do something in a situation like this.

☀   ☀   ☀

George was the last one to go to the airport. He took a late flight to Boston, while the others took the earlier route through Miami. The hurricane was somewhere in the Canadian Maritimes, threatening none of the tourist flights coming from or going to Aruba. The whole world was on schedule.

Sam was glad time no longer mattered to him. He wanted his house completed in short order but knew it wouldn't be. What did it matter if it took three months, or four, or six? In the states, a house like his would be built according to a schedule, a budget, and the harried pace of people desperate to get rich. He was beyond that on to the good life.

In a way, Sam felt sorry for Captain Beck. The guy came to Aruba by the worst possible circumstances. A shipwreck for God's sake! Beck had barely tasted what Sam had feasted upon. And just when it looked like the Captain was going to be there for the long haul, the refinery was sold out from under him, his contract canceled by the buyers. He was being replaced, thanked for his service but still asked to find his way out. It was a tough break, made worse by having to leave Luz behind. Such was the life of a sailor, a woman in every port but none of them your own.

Sam had found his final port of call, and during the previous two afternoons invited Luz to share it with him. He made it clear she was welcome and that she could give up her job at Minchi's.

For her part, Luz had asked polite questions. She wanted to know if there would be room for Hernán. She inquired about the specific living arrangements. Who would sleep where? Who was cooking, cleaning? These questions came only from someone making a decision. For each of his answers, she gave him a pleasing smile, an indication she liked what she heard.

It was a challenge not to force the issue. The last thing he wanted was for her to equate him with every other gringo who walked into Minchi's, fell in love, and offered her the world. He stayed within the realm of the realistic. He thought of himself as the Crown Prince, but he knew that his kingdom was not the richest and that his castle was rather small. For all its defects, it was a world better than anything Luz had either in Aruba or in Colombia.

With his friends gone, Sam got down to business, which meant he headed straight for Charlie's to see how many tourists needed to have an original Aruban experience. About a quarter mile from Savaneta, he saw two police cars on the side of the road. Between them sat a third car, the driver of which waved his arms and shouted at the police. Sam recognized him. It was Andrés. He pulled over and approached the scene with his trademark casual smile.

"You were speeding," the cop doing the talking said.

Andrés shouted at the sky. "Since when does anyone get a ticket for speeding?"

"The chief is coming. Explain it to him," the cop said.

"*Hola*," Sam interjected.

The cop recognized him. "*Bon dia*, Sam," he said.

"Anything I can do?" Sam asked.

Andrés said, "You can tell these guys to let me go. I have things to do."

Sam put both hands up. "Easy, chico," he urged. "Let's take a deep breath."

"Ahhhh! You're as bad as them!"

"Why is the chief coming?" Sam asked the cop.

The cop gave him a look.

"Okay," Sam said. "Andrés, let's take a step under the Divi tree. Cool down a little, okay?"

Having no other choice, Andrés went with Sam. The midday sun beat on them like an angry master. What little shade the Divi tree provided, they were happy to have. Sam crushed out his cigarette and spoke to Charlie's protégé.

"A traffic ticket has you screaming mad?" Sam began.

"And other things."

"I'm your friend," Sam said. "I can help."

"I'm doing this myself."

Chief Calenda pulled up. He got out of his car, put on his hat, and advanced on Sam and Andrés. "You two come with me," he said.

Startled, Sam pointed at himself.

"You, too," Calenda said curtly.

Knowing better than to question the chief's authority, Sam put his hand on Andrés's shoulder and directed him to the back seat of the car. No sooner had the doors closed than Calenda's driver switched on his siren and off they went.

They rolled into San Nicolaas, past the police station, and down Main Street. The driver turned at the end of Main Street, then weaved through the back streets until they stopped in front of Luz's house.

Luz held the door as everyone filed into the living room.

"You're part of this?" Andrés barked at her.

"Listen to them," she said.

"Have a seat," Sam told Andrés. "I'll get us something to drink."

Luz dialed another number on her phone and handed it to Chief Calenda. He spoke to the person on the other line, thanked him, and closed the connection. Luz impressed Calenda to such a degree he didn't know what to say. If this matter concluded the way he expected it to, she deserved a medal.

At last, Chief Calenda spoke to the room. "My colleagues in Oranjestaad are on the case," he began and proceeded to explain why.

The crew met in the galley. Beck informed them they were leaving Aruba. Before they had a chance to absorb what he said, Beck told them they were going back to Philadelphia. It wasn't to be the usual homecoming. Jack Ford was selling off his boats and equipment. They would have a chance to come with him aboard *Marlena* if they wanted it. He was elated when they accepted. These men trusted him enough to follow him wherever he went.

The only question was what they wanted to do with *Huntress*. They couldn't take her to Philadelphia, not without putting her on a ship. After some deliberation, they agreed to try to sell her to the refinery. She was well suited as a survey boat. No doubt her new owners would find time to take her fishing as well.

Under Wilkie's direction, the crew set to work readying *Kathryn* for sea. Beck went off to see Herzog about *Huntress*.

The superintendent greeted him with a pat on the back. "I won't be far behind you," he said.

"You're leaving, too?"

"The hard part is about done. I'll stay on for another three or four months, make the transition with whomever comes to take my place. I'll be off to the next pile of junk."

They went on to discuss *Huntress*. Herzog said he would like to buy her himself. "Always wanted a boat, just like you," he laughed.

"You won't be able to steam her out of here," Beck warned.

"She'll make it to Venezuela or Colombia."

"Is that where you're going?"

Herzog shrugged. "That's where they need the most help."

They wished each other luck and parted ways. Beck walked past the unfinished hotel. He heard loud noises coming from inside. Someone was hammering and cutting. However, in the year he had been on the island it seemed no progress had been made on the structure. In places it was possible to look straight through it. He turned onto Main Street and walked to the hardware store.

While he waited to pay for the items he selected, Beck thought about what he was doing. Kenny might have said, "The girl is after a free green card and the rest of your money." On one hand, Beck didn't blame the girls for that. There was nothing wrong, in a business sense, with their seeking out the highest bidder. On the other hand, he had as many reasons to doubt Nicole as he had to doubt Luz.

It came down to which risk he wanted to take. It was Luz or Nicole or living alone with his boat. By asking Luz to go with him, he had put his money on the table. He was gambling that she was the real thing. Strangely enough, he took comfort knowing Sam felt the same way. It was he who had originally decided Luz was *the one*. Yes, Sam had done that, and Beck felt guilty about taking her away. Well, Beck told himself, now that Sam was living on the island, he would have plenty of time to find another girl.

More than anything else, Beck was enthusiastic about guiding Hernán through life. Whatever the legalities, Beck would figure them out in order to give the boy a fair shot at the world. He would spend the time with him that his own father never had. And when the time was right, he would show him the world as viewed from the wheelhouse.

At eight forty-five, the neon light above China Clipper's door was not yet on. Over the past several months, the girls worked steadily and the bar sold plenty of beer and liquor. The jukebox spit florins like a slot machine. Times had not been this good for as long as Montoya could remember.

He stepped out of the bar with the cash Luz had collected for him. He noticed a police car had stopped across the street directly in front of Minchi's. The police were a common sight on Main Street, especially since Chief Calenda had taken over. In fact, Montoya believed Calenda actually helped the bars since the increased police presence made the Zone of Tolerance feel safe. Even nervous American college students ventured down from the hotels to check out San Nicolaas.

In the back seat of the cruiser, Montoya saw a girl's face. He studied her for a few seconds. She was a girl he had seen before. She had worked at Minchi's more than a year ago, maybe two years ago. He had given her a try. She was good in bed, very physical. That she was in the back seat of the police car was not a good sign for her. Calenda was not known for his taxi service. Montoya waited for his wife on his side of the street.

Inside Minchi's, la Dueña took her time looking around the bar. Not surprisingly, the place was in good order. What was the English phrase Captain Beck would have used, "Ship shape?" It was the same thing her first husband, Ricardo, had said. She smiled to herself as she realized how hard it was for a native Spanish speaker to pronounce.

"*Muy bien, Luz,*" la Dueña said. "If only you could make Spanner look as good as this place. That would be a real accomplishment."

Spanner chuckled at the jibe. Nothing upset him.

"You see girls," la Dueña said to the four chicas standing at the bar, "If you are clever, like Luz was, you can end up running a place like this. Not all of you, but maybe one of you. And if you're very intelligent and ambitious like me, well, then you can end up owning it. That means there is a place for two of you on the ladder to success."

The girls shifted nervously. Above all, they wanted to make some money, not catch a disease, and get home to their families. They had no interest in operating a brothel. Then again, nor had Luz when she first came to Aruba.

"I will see you next week," la Dueña said finally. "*Buena suerte.*" She pushed through the door and found herself toe to toe with Chief Calenda.

"Do you want to talk in the street?" he asked. "Or would you prefer inside?"

"What is this about?"

He refused to yield. "Answer my question first," he said.

"Inside," she drawled. As she came back in the bar, she waved at the chicas. "Go upstairs!" she ordered. Then she faced Luz and Spanner who were standing behind the bar. "Mind your own business."

Spanner and Luz retreated to the farthest end of the bar where they took out their cards.

Another man entered the room. Luz recognized him from the Office of Immigration. His name was Jerez. She had spoken to him about Hernán's documents on several occasions. He was wearing his uniform, which was neat and pressed for a change.

"What is he doing here?" Marcela wanted to know.

"He has some things to tell you," Calenda answered.

After clearing his throat, Jerez spoke in a reedy voice that cracked between every second word. "Chief Calenda will be taking you into custody," he said.

"Into custody," Marcela scoffed. "For what?"

"For obtaining citizenship under false pretenses, among other things."

A few seconds passed while Marcela worked out her attack. She began cautiously. "I became an Aruban citizen more than five years ago. I was married to an Aruban then, and I am married to an Aruban now. That makes me as Aruban as you are."

"This may be true," Jerez acknowledged.

"It is true. My husband is across the street this moment."

"He may be."

"You know my lawyer, Herr Salinas?"

"I know him."

Frustrated, Marcela said, "I did everything correctly. You can take it up with Herr Salinas."

"I will," Jerez told her. "First, you will be remanded to the custody of Chief Calenda and then deported tomorrow morning."

"Deported? You can't deport me. I'm a citizen."

Calenda stepped forward. "That is in question," he said. "It seems your documentation from Colombia may have been invalid. You used these documents, documents in the name of Marcela Mendez, to obtain citizenship here in Aruba and thereby committed a crime which can be punished by forfeiture of your citizenship."

"After a trial," Marcela reminded everyone in the room.

"You are correct. However, it is in the power of the Office of Immigration to deport you while these matters are sorted out. If you are found innocent, you can return to your life here. If not, then you will be home in Colombia. You see, you cannot lose in this situation."

"I am not leaving this room without my lawyer," Marcela told Calenda. She took out her cell phone and started dialing.

Calenda said, "There are other charges you should mention to him."

"Do you think you're Fidel Castro or Hugo Chavez? You're a tin-badge cop in a stinking whore town."

"But still I enforce the law, señora." He waved to a patrolman who signaled another one in the cruiser. The two of them escorted the girl who had been seated in the car through the door. Marcela closed her phone.

Inez wiped her face, glanced from Marcela to Luz to Chief Calenda.

"Tell me who you work for?" Calenda asked her.

Her eyes fixed on Luz, but Inez pointed a weak finger at Marcela.

"And did she provide you with false documents to return to Aruba under a name other than your own?"

"*Sí*," Inez whispered.

"Better proof I could not ask for," Calenda told Marcela. "You operate a prostitution ring outside of the Zone of Tolerance, which is punishable by time in jail. Would you like to go to the airport in the morning or to jail tonight? The choice is yours."

Grinding her teeth, Marcela gestured toward Luz. "She is also here illegally. She married my stepson just for the papers. She takes clients to the hotels."

"Let me see your passport," Calenda ordered Luz.

Luz took her purse from under the bar, fished out her passport, and handed it over. Calenda gave it a cursory look then handed it to Jerez. Jerez made a show of double-checking the photo and the contents.

"It's valid," Jerez said.

"I have one of those rags," Marcela muttered. "What's the difference?"

"You lied to get yours. She did not."

"Hah!"

"Come with me," Calenda said. "I'm sure you'll want to get some things together at home before you go to the airport."

"Can I have a moment with Luz?" Inez asked.

"One minute," Calenda answered.

Inez crossed the room with her head down. Luz met her at the end of the bar as Spanner backed away.

Softly, as if she were speaking to a baby, Inez said, "Help me, Luz."

Luz stared at her hands, which she folded on the bar. It distressed her to see Inez in so much trouble. They had been friends, and together they had made enough money for Luz to keep a roof over her family's head.

"Talk to them," Inez begged. "They'll listen to you."

Luz had warned her at the Hyatt, and now she lifted her shoulders to shrug at advice that had not been taken.

"I'll tell …" Inez hissed.

"They know," Luz lied. "Don't waste your time."

Inez stood up straight and walked to the door. She didn't look back as she passed through it ahead of the patrolman who followed her out.

Chief Calenda was the last one to leave. He straightened his hat, nodded to Luz, and left.

"What's going to happen, girl?" Spanner asked.

"We're going to sell some drinks," Luz replied. "I'll bring the girls down. Shift change is only an hour away."

Down the block, Sam and Andrés watched Marcela get into the police cruiser. She said a few words to Montoya, who crossed the street to her. He drove off in the Mercedes when the police were out of the way.

From Charlie's veranda they heard the barman calling out to them. "Over here, gentlemen!"

They came down the block until they were standing directly beneath Charlie. "You have a flight to catch tomorrow night," he said, "and I won't hold the plane for you."

Andrés jogged to his car, leaving Sam standing alone.

"What about you?" Charlie asked his lifelong friend.

Looking down at Minchi's, Sam saw Captain Beck toss Frankie a guilder and then enter the bar.

Sam looked up at Charlie, "I think I'll play catch with Speedy," he said.

HER BED was empty when she awoke. As was his custom, Captain Beck had slipped out sometime before dawn. There always seemed to be a ship to dock at that hour.

By the time Luz finished her orange juice and started to make breakfast for Hernán, her cell phone rang.

"Ah, Luz," Herr Diedrik said. "So good to hear your voice. It means you didn't get caught up in the things that happened last night."

She hedged. "Not yet."

"Not ever!" the lawyer admonished her. "You are safe, but it would be wise to stay out of sight for a while."

"I will."

"By the way, Jeffery and I are working out the details of his deal with the government. We must get together to celebrate."

"When?" Luz inquired.

"Soon. I'll call you."

"*Gracias*," Luz said. "For everything."

"For you I can move mountains," he told her.

"I would like to see you."

"My heart leaps, Luz. I don't know when, but I will definitely see you soon."

What would she tell the Captain next week? She didn't know because she hadn't made up her mind.

Hernán came out of his bedroom looking for Beck. Luz told him he had gone to sea. It was what she told him every time he asked. It was the truth. Her boy gradually woke up, ate his breakfast, and changed to go play with his friends.

After Hernán's friends came, she cleaned her bathroom and the kitchen. As she put her supplies away, there was a knock on the door. She expected Sam, but when she opened the door, Montoya stood on the step. She welcomed him into his old house.

Smelling the cleaning fluid Luz had just finished using, Montoya said, "You keep a nice house."

She nodded slowly, waiting for him to broach the subject of Marcela.

He gazed at the mural on the wall for a long time. Something in it held his attention. He said, "Ricardo's boy did this to her."

Again Luz told the truth. "No," she said. "She did it to herself. She knows how this town works."

Montoya's attention returned to the mural. "Andrés is very talented," he said.

She agreed. "He deserves to go to school in Holland. He will be famous someday."

"And rich," added Montoya.

"Perhaps."

"He will have the money from his father's bar. The lawyers are writing up an agreement for the bar to remain in trust for him until this is settled."

"He doesn't want the bar," Luz said.

"He said as much," Montoya admitted. "I do not believe Marcela will be coming back to Aruba. I am an Aruban, and I know that once my people decide they don't want you, it is the end of the matter."

Luz nodded her head.

"You are his wife," Montoya stated. "You can run the bar and work it out with him later. I won't get in the way."

The law of unintended consequences seemed to be ruling her life. It was never her plan to inherit the bar. She only wanted to help Andrés. This was the reason she had called Chief Calenda the previous day and mentioned that Señora Álvaro knew Marcela by another name and that Inez happened to be working outside the Zone of Tolerance. Now Montoya, Andrés, and the lawyers had her operating Minchi's. Sam expected her to be his wife. Captain Beck proposed to take her to America. What was she supposed to do?

She refocused her attention on what Montoya was saying.

"Salinas has spoken to Boedeker. There are papers to sign, bank accounts to authorize."

"*Yo comprendo*," Luz said, knowing what she did about the business.

A blank look spread across Montoya's face. Luz knew he was in shock that Marcela had been sent away so quickly. It was nothing he'd ever expected, yet it was real. She knew the feeling well. She experienced the same thing when Hernán's father threw her out of his apartment, when her father died, when her brother disappeared, and when she arrived in Aruba the second time with the idea she only needed to make some more money to return to normalcy. But normal was something that didn't exist. There were opposite extremes, and between the two was a place she never managed to find.

With absolute sincerity, she put her arms around Montoya. "You are a good man," she said. Her ability to reassure him bolstered her own resolve to persevere in a difficult world.

"*Gracias, Luz*," Montoya said pulling back from her. "You remind me of Carlotta when she was younger. She was more flamboyant than you, but you are both strong women."

Comparing her to Carlotta was the highest compliment Montoya could have given her. She thanked him and said she would check in with him from time to time to see how Marcela was doing. He smiled and left her to decide what she was going to do with the rest of her life.

☀   ☀   ☀

Despite a modest amount of alcohol, a full night's sleep, and a healthy break-fast, Sam felt significantly less than one hundred percent. He attributed it to a bad attitude brought on by the rapid departure of his friends. There was also the matter of a delay in the building of his house. The contractor was not at fault. A delivery of reinforcing steel had yet to arrive on the island.

He drove to San Nicolaas in search of inspiration. The crowd at Charlie's was thin, but he stopped anyway.

"Good of you to come," Charlie greeted Sam. "You can help Luis so I can pre-pare for an all-night flight to the other side of the world."

Sam considered a leap over the bar. On second thought, he wasn't up to it. "Where's Herr Koch?"

"A day off," Charlie answered.

Sam accepted that and smiled at Luis. "Who needs a drink?" he asked as he stepped up to the rail.

Two people put their beer glasses forward. Sam slid them under the tap as Charlie backed out of the way. Looking over his shoulder at Charlie, Sam asked, "You see what's going on in the colony?"

A tourist leaned forward for another drink, "What's the colony?" he wanted to know.

It was all the prompting Sam needed to begin a legendary tale of his youth. "To the east there, up on the hill behind that wall was where we used to live."

"Where you lived," Charlie corrected him. "I had to climb the wall to make a visit."

The tourist smirked.

Sam said, "He tells the truth. Anyway, Charlie would come over the wall and I would meet him at the bottom."

The crowd gathered close to the bar so as not to miss a word. Sam and Charlie passed the story back and forth like a couple of professional footballers. Like every good tale, it ended with a police chase, a narrow escape, and a pretty girl with both of them. And it was true.

"I want to talk to you!" shouted a voice from the street.

Everyone turned to see who it was.

Frankie stood on the sidewalk, his crooked finger pointed directly at Sam.

Sam lacked the energy to vault the bar so he quick-stepped around it and up to Frankie as the crowd applauded his tale. "*¿Qué pasa, amigo?*"

"*No amigo,*" Frankie said. "You promise me and Speedy a baseball game, and your friends go away on the plane. We never going to play."

"Ah, we'll play."

"You lie, Samito. You are no longer the Prince. I watch your back. I drink half your beer. I look out for your woman of the week."

"There's only one, chico," Sam interjected.

"Says you. You say we going to have a game, too. No people to play, so no game. No girl with you so you have nothing."

Rather than argue Sam went to the bar for a Heineken and brought it back to Frankie. "Peace, chico," he said.

Frankie held the beer up for inspection. "Full," he said. He gulped the entire contents in three swallows. After belching loud enough for everyone in the bar to hear, he pointed at Sam. "This is your last chance. If you want to be my friend, we play ball before the week is over."

"You're on," Sam said, "At the field in the colony."

"How am I going to get all the way there when I have only these rags for shoes?"

"I'll give you a ride," Sam said.

Frankie ran down the street in search of Speedy. Neither of them had ridden in a car since they were boys.

Andrés told Luz she was the last one he would visit. His friend waited outside in his car, ready to take him to the airport.

"You can use the car," he said. "I was going to sell it, but the way things worked out I don't need the money."

"Sell it anyway," Luz advised. "I don't go so far that I need to drive."

Andrés shook his head. He wanted to give her something as payment for what she had done. He didn't know exactly how, but he was certain it was Luz who set things in motion to have Marcela deported. To his amazement, Marcela blamed it all on him, which was ridiculous because Andrés was no one but a parentless artist who worked in an auto body shop. Then again, he was Luz's husband and her friend, too. Because of that, he had the munificence of her benefactors, among whom numbered some important people.

"Please," he pleaded. "Keep the car."

"Have your friend park it here. I will take care of it."

"Be careful, Luz. Stay close to Carlotta and Charlie and Captain Beck. They are people you can trust."

"I will," she promised. "Go now, before you are late for your plane."

He took a last look at the living room mural and then left the house. Luz went to the bathroom to shower before starting another night in San Nicolaas.

* * *

Glasses pinched to his nose, Kenny studied his new cellular phone. The fully charged battery provided power for the thing to light up like a yule log, but the tiny buttons were a problem. His fingers were too big and his eyes too bad to operate it with ease. Barbara, one of the two girls working in his bar, tried to help him, but the model was unknown to her.

In walked Sam, his own cell phone clipped to his belt. "Give me that thing," he said.

Kenny handed it over. "I just want to program some numbers so I can dial with one touch. The kid who sold it to me said that's possible, but I can't get it done."

In a few seconds, Sam set it down on the bar. "There you go," he said. "Charlie is number one. I'm number two. What other numbers do you need?"

Kenny examined the phone. "How do I make it work?"

"Push pound, then one, then send. Boom. You're calling Charlie."

Peering down at the screen Kenny pressed the buttons slowly. Holding the phone to his ear he heard the line ring. He quickly disconnected.

"How about a drink?" Sam asked.

"Sure, Sam, first one on me. Charlie at the airport?"

"Dropped him off myself a few minutes ago."

Kenny's phone rang. "Who the hell could be calling me? I didn't give anyone the number."

"This is Charlie," the voice on the other end said. "Who's this?"

"Kenny."

"*Bon nochi*, Kenny, what can I do for you?"

"Nothing. I bought this new phone, and Sam programmed it for me. Sorry to bother you."

"These phones don't let us hide. Your number shows up when you call. Anyway, the plane is delayed, two hours at least, maybe you can send a girl or two to entertain me."

Kenny laughed. "How about Sam?"

"He's done enough." Charlie rang off, and Kenny put the phone on the shelf behind his cash register.

After toasting each other and the modern technology that kept them in contact, Sam and Kenny settled into a mellow evening of drinking and bullshitting.

"Captain Beck leaves next week," Kenny said. "Sorry to see him go."

"Poor guy," Sam put in. "Nearly dies finding this place, comes back to make a name for himself, and leaves to live another life's adventure. If I were his age, I'd be doing the same thing."

"Never too late," Kenny said.

"I got what I want. Charlie always says to chew the bite you have before taking another one."

"Good advice," affirmed Kenny. "I have a bit of wisdom of my own if you care to take it."

"What's that?" Sam asked.

"That girl there, Barbara, she doesn't know anything about that cell phone, but she can work her body like a magician. You should give her a try, Sam. You won't be sorry."

Sam checked out Barbara's figure. He told Kenny to send her and the other girl a vino. He played the nice guy, but he wasn't going to do anything that would find its way down the San Nicolaas telegraph to Luz. His reputation around town had to be maintained as the man who diddled with no one. He glanced at his watch and realized *the one* was about to start work. It was his cue to leave.

"See you in a little while, Kenny," Sam said and waved to the chicas as he exited the bar.

Hotfooting it up the street, Sam dodged a gang of refinery workers still wearing their stained coveralls. They stank of oil, burnt metal, and body odor. These guys will never learn, Sam thought. All it took was a quick shower, a change of clothes, and a dash of cologne to make themselves more appealing to the chicas. Sure, the men were paying for the service, but why not make it decent for the chicas, too? He knew he was wasting his time on such thoughts, but he was always interested in making San Nicolaas that much better, not only as a place but also as an experience. Every little bit helped, he reasoned.

He entered Minchi's, where the pool table was full, the bar overflowing, and no girls in sight. He searched the room for Luz but didn't see her either. He inquired with Spanner as to her whereabouts.

The bouncer informed him of the facts. "She's her own boss and my boss, too. She goes out when she wants to."

"Okay," Sam said, "but where and with whom?"

"I don't know, Sam. Pablo's off, and I'm busy here like three men and I have only two eyes to watch like six."

Sam pushed. "She go with the Captain?"

"No," Spanner said curtly. "The Captain is on his boat because the other captain, the older one, he was just here."

"Fair enough, chico. See you later."

Spanner waved him away as he bent into the cooler for beer bottles requested by men at the bar.

His choice of places to go was unlimited, but Sam ambled about town for over an hour. He peeked in shop windows, down empty alleys, and up dusty stairways. At la Bonanza, he bought a candy bar for the hell of it. He sat on a bench watching the men pass by on the street in search of their female entertainment for the night. As much as it had changed, San Nicolaas was still the Wild West boomtown of his youth. There were rough men and dandies, as well as pretty girls and ugly whores. There were bars and saloons, two banks, and a gambling den, and there were more than a few nicely appointed houses of ill repute. In Sam's eyes, it was a gem of the Caribbean, an authentic masterpiece for those seeking a bit of living history. San Nicolaas took the visitor back to an era before the banality of copycat resorts with homogeneous menus and as much surprise as the toy at the bottom of a cereal box.

He wished his friends hadn't left him. In their presence, he was the master of ceremonies. He needed to round up some new ones, people with whom he could share as many nights as were on the calendar.

He strolled down Main Street, toward Java. He passed Charlie's balcony, looked up, and saw Screwball sitting there on the parapet. Sam gave the cat a thumbs-up and continued down the block. He checked his phone. The display showed the current time as ten past eleven. He dialed Charlie's number.

"Not yet," Charlie said. "They have to wind the rubber band."

"I'm coming up there," Sam said.

"Don't bother," Charlie told his friend. "The food is lousy. There are no women but the ones in uniform, and I think they take their jobs seriously."

"I'll keep you company," Sam offered.

"Find a girl and think of me. *Bon nochi*, Sam."

"*Bon nochi*." Sam disconnected and took Charlie's advice. He peeked in Minchi's, where the place was still packed. A line formed near the pool table. Spanner hustled drinks like an octopus. The one girl in the bar was surrounded by five guys.

He retreated to the street, where he jingled the florins in his pocket. He selected a cigarette from his pack, lit it, and studied the street. A bus approached from the northwest. It was decorated with flashing lights and garish colors. He waited while it rolled slowly toward the end of Main Street. As it passed, he watched the touristas inside gulping drinks from plastic cups, dancing to the music, and pointing out the different bars. This development did not please him. San Nicolaas hosted the red light district, but it didn't deserve to be treated as the joke of the island. The fools on the bus had no idea they were looking at a snapshot of reality, not a bad TV show. They could have learned something if they took the time to get off the bus and talk to someone like him or one of the girls or a bartender like Kenny. But to do that was like sticking their hands in a bucket of grease. They were frightened of the mess they'd make.

Sam sucked in a lungful of smoke, let it out slowly to calm his nerves, then moved down the block to Java.

"When did that bus start making the rounds?" Sam inquired.

"Tonight," Kenny answered, "I saw the advertisement in the newspaper. The gringos come for a look at the other half."

"They're treating us like zoo animals," Sam complained.

Kenny proffered no solution aside from a fresh drink. Sam tasted it, then toasted the two of them.

"Cheers," Kenny said. "You think about Barbara while you were out?"

Sam spun on his stool. Barbara waved at him with her fingers.

"You should give her a try, Sam. It would be good for both of you."

"How's that?"

"You need some cheering up, and she needs some money."

"Fair enough," Sam agreed. He put both feet on the floor and pushed off the stool. As he stood up, he coughed several times before catching his breath. He felt as if he had smoked a whole pack of cigarettes at one time. Then his throat cleared, his eyes came into focus, and he felt fine. Still, he drank the glass of water Kenny drew for him.

"You okay?" Kenny asked.

"Strong as an ox."

"That's a man. Now prove it to her, my friend."

The rooms upstairs at Java Bar were not as nicely appointed as those at Sayonara. They were foxholes compared to what Luz had at Minchi's. Yet when the girl waved him into the room, Sam thought a bed never looked so good. He sat down heavily, relieved to have the weight off his legs. Barbara pushed him back on the mattress, then slid her body up the length of his. Nibbling on his ear, she whispered how she was going to please him.

He said, "I think I'll have a *siesta*."

"*Papi*," she replied tapping her wrist, "*treinta minutos*."

Ah, the old argument about time and money. This is why he wanted *the one*. No more haggling about how much dinero for how many minutos. He slipped a hundred-dollar bill from the center of his bankroll and placed it on the bed.

"*¿Está bien?*" he asked patting the money.

"*Por una hora*," she answered taking the bill into her hand.

"*Una hora*," he repeated.

"Okay, poppie," she said getting off the bed. "*Duermes bien*."

Sam knew he would have no trouble sleeping. Through closing eyelids he watched the girl take a seat near the sink in the corner of the room. By the time she took out her nail file and started to work, he snored softly at the ceiling.

Kathryn departed Oranjestaad at half past midnight. A Carnival Lines cruise ship, bound for Jamaica, left the harbor. Another liner belonging to Royal Caribbean took her place. Beck and his crew assisted the ships, then headed for San Nicolaas. From the wheelhouse, Beck watched the island glide past. Headlights traced the main highway, as well as the connecting road which led up the hill to Santa Cruz. On the other side of the tug there were ships' lights. Some were container vessels making a quick stop in Aruba. Another was a car carrier delivering new vehicles. Then there were the tankers. Some were not bound for San Nicolaas but on their way to ports farther north, just as he would be within a week's time.

He heard Captain Upton say, "Keep a firm hand on the wheel or some mother's son will turn it for you." Both of Beck's hands were on the wheel of his life. He was plotting his course and sticking to it. He was leaving Aruba and getting a boat of his own. He was anxious to have his chance in business. For that reason, he told Upton's ghost, "I'll steer us home if you can handle the weather between here and there."

Upton's ghost laughed. "Heavy weather? That's nothing compared to the trouble you can't see when you get your head stuck up a whore's skirt."

Beck shook his head at how Upton's voice hadn't faded after so many years. It nagged him in good times and bad but was strangely silent during the regular days. Beck said aloud, "I don't have my head up anyone's skirt." And he didn't. He was neither kowtowing to Nicole nor delusional about Luz. Luz was a woman like any other in the sense that she had a past that could not be denied and a present that was subject to change. And Nicole was who she'd always been.

He cut the throttles and eased the rudder to port. *Kathryn* rolled gently into the turn as she slowed against the slight chop that swept out with the breeze. The bow fender bumped the dock as Tony heaved a line to the first bollard. The deckhand set the stern and spring lines before signaling to Beck that the boat was secure. Beck switched off the radios, the radar display, and the compass light. He completed the page in the logbook and placed the book in the rack where it belonged.

Although quite late, Beck wanted to go into town. Luz was out, which caused him some anxiety. He was also too excited about the future to sleep. He showered hurriedly, put on fresh clothes, and left the boat in trust to Syd and Tony.

"Can you believe Sam has been up there for almost an hour?" Kenny asked Beck as soon as he was seated at the bar.

"He never does anything halfway, Kenny."

Kenny bobbed his head. The Captain had a point. After all, Kenny himself recommended the girl. If Sam went into extra innings, it meant she had to be all she was advertised to be. "Friend or foe," Kenny stated, "He's paying the extra."

"Everyone pays," Beck agreed. "Chief Calenda sees to that."

Kenny raised his glass. "He tossed Marcela off the island with less ceremony than a seagull shitting in the sea."

Kenny's wit and Charlie's admonitions were two things Beck would miss most. They augmented Upton's repertoire.

"Ah, what the hell," Kenny moaned. "You'll be back."

"As long as there's a port," Beck said.

"That refinery is cooking like never before, Captain. The port is busy the way it should be, the way this bar has been for twelve months running now. The exception is tonight, being a slow night only because these chicas milked the guilders out of every man from the wall to the police station."

"You got your share," Beck observed.

"Thanks be to the queen," Kenny said. "I'm taking a vacation this Christmas, a whole week."

The door at the back of the bar opened. Kenny and Beck turned their heads expecting to see Sam come through, but Barbara alone entered the room.

"What the hell," Kenny whined. "Where is your client?"

"En mi cama," she answered.

"In your bed and you're down here?"

"Dormiendo."

"He's sleeping? You wore him out?"

She shook her head.

"Go get him," Kenny ordered.

"Un momento," interjected Beck. "Here. Take this and let him sleep." He put fifty guilders on the bar for Kenny and put his hand out with fifty more for Barbara.

"You're buying the man a hundred guilder nap?" Kenny asked Beck.

"Why not, Kenny? Let him sleep."

"It's your money."

They conversed about their usual topics: boats, the refinery, the cost of booze, and how Kenny wanted a place in Colombia. Hardly a man came into the bar. Frankie loitered at the door hoping for a free drink or a couple of guilders.

When an hour had passed, Kenny instructed Barbara to go wake Sam. She lingered by the jukebox, hoping the Captain would give her another fifty. When that didn't happen, she pouted and shuffled through the door to a salsa beat. Kenny used the remote control to turn down the volume on the jukebox. He and Beck listened to Barbara's heels click up the stairs. They heard nothing for a few moments and then the sound of Barbara's heels clicked in their ears again.

She stood in the doorway alone for the second time that night. "He won't get up."

"Tell him I'm coming to get him," Kenny said.

Barbara folded her arms, "Tell him yourself." There was still the possibility of earning more money for nothing.

Kenny ruined it for her. He said, "Watch the bar, Captain. I'll be right back."

Kenny came back with his head down. He took his new cell phone off the shelf with one hand and his glasses with the other. He pressed pound, then the number 1. As he waited for the connection, he thought how nice it would have been to retire to Colombia early when he had the chance.

Charlie sat with Andrés in the departure lounge. They talked about Holland and the school Andrés was to attend. It had been more than twenty years since Charlie was to Holland. He liked the country but found it too cold, too gloomy, and too formal for his taste. He liked the casual atmosphere in Aruba. A king and a bum lived on the same street, as he and Frankie did, without any problem.

The delay was four hours old when the announcement came that the plane was boarding.

"Come with me," he told Andrés. "I'm sitting in the front, but they won't say anything if you join me in an empty seat."

Just as they were about to walk down the new Jetway to the plane, Charlie's phone rang. He cursed it but looked at the display and saw it was Kenny and not Sam.

"At last I can say *bon nochi*," Charlie said into the phone. He listened for a few seconds then disconnected. He reached into his carryon bag and took out a pack of brushes. These he gave to Andrés. "Sam forgot to give these to you."

Frankie and Speedy, the second and third most observant souls in San Nicolaas, witnessed Chief Calenda's car turn the corner by the unfinished hotel and enter Rembrandtstraat at an easy pace. He stopped where their alley connected to Main Street.

The two bums stuck close to the walls as they ventured to see what the chief was up to. Shadows protected them from their subjects as the second vehicle arrived in the alley. Kenny emerged from the side door to his bar. With him was Captain Beck. Speedy and Frankie looked at each other, wondering whether or not they should reveal themselves and beg for breakfast guilders. A pickup truck stopped on Main Street, and they stayed where they were. This was a meeting of too many significant individuals for them to risk an approach.

"Where is he?" Charlie asked Kenny.

"Upstairs."

"If it has to be done, it has to be done," Charlie sighed. "Give me a hand."

They entered Barbara's room, which was barely large enough for all of them to fit. Sam was on the bed. In his shirt pocket bulged his cigarettes and his lighter. His head tilted slightly, as if he were looking at the crashers that had interrupted his leisure.

"I'm here!" Doctor Van Dam called from the hallway. The three men pressed into each other to make room for him.

"I have the stretcher there," Kenny said pointing to the bathroom.

"Take your time," Van Dam advised. "He's dead."

It took them a few minutes to position Sam's body on the stretcher. Charlie draped a clean sheet from Barbara's inventory over Sam. With some difficulty, they carried him down the stairwell to the street. In the hallway above, Barbara cried at the tragedy that had come her way.

Frankie and Speedy lurked at the alley corner. Having avoided the destructive drugs that polluted Speedy's body, Frankie possessed the better vision. He knew there was a body on the stretcher and that it was no longer alive because a sheet covered the face. He also saw a flicker of light and heard a tinkling clatter on the street. The object that fell off the stretcher was a Zippo lighter. That instant Frankie knew Sam was gone.

"We're never going to play that game," he hissed at Speedy.

"Why?" Speedy wanted to know, but Frankie sobbed too hard to be understood.

Beck retrieved Sam's lighter from the street. He gave it to Charlie who struck the flint, allowed it to burn a few seconds then snapped the lid closed.

"Be careful, my friends," Charlie said, "or your wish will come true."

TOURISTS AT the hotels examined the picture on the front page of the newspaper. Some of them recognized the guy with the dashing smile under the white mustache. He was the one who told those fantastic stories at that bar on the other end of the island.

One visitor tapped the picture as he told another, "I met that guy several times. If half the stuff he said was true, it's a miracle he lived as long as he did."

Someone else said, "He was always there, drink in one hand, cigarette in the other."

A woman blushed. "He winked at me when I took my top off last week," she said.

Her girlfriend put a hand on her arm. "I was there, too," the girlfriend said. "We drank for free."

People on their first trip to Aruba asked waiters, bartenders, and hotel staff who the guy was. The answer was universal: the Crown Prince of San Nicolaas.

It was Carlotta who decided what time Sam's funeral procession would begin.

She requested a 5:00 PM start because she didn't want to commence such a sad affair in the morning, and her black dress was too hot for the midday sun. So it was that San Nicolaas shut down soon after lunch in order to give the populace time to prepare for the event. There was one exception, the refinery, which continued to operate without interruption.

For the first time in history, a San Nicolaas parade started promptly. It began at Charlie's bar, ran to the unfinished hotel, turned the corner, and doubled back on Helfrichstraat. At the end of Helfrichstraat, they turned left at Bar Sayonara for a block and then right again. From there, it was a straight run through the west side of San Nicolaas to the cemetery.

With the help of the bar owners, shopkeepers, and refinery workers, Charlie organized a world-class procession for Sam. At the head of the line, just in front of Calenda's police car, Frankie marched to a beat that only he heard inside his head. Charlie had found a drum major's uniform among the junk in his bar. It hung off Frankie's shoulders so that the epaulets were halfway down his biceps. The bum managed to find a pair of shiny black shoes on his own, though Charlie suspected they were a gift from someone in the police department. Using Sam's baseball bat as a baton, Frankie swaggered up the street, his chin high, his four good teeth on display.

Charlie drove the big convertible he kept under a cover except for the most important occasions. In the passenger seat was Captain Beck. Behind them, Carlotta wept for the death of the son she never had. Beside her sat Luz, who glanced from side to side at the people who lined the street to see Sam's funeral procession.

The second group was a quartet of military trucks from the Dutch marine base in Savaneta. Two platoons of soldiers strutted beside their equipment. Then came fire trucks from the airport. Next was a contingent of contractors with heavy equipment that was not working that day in the refinery.

The Arends Family played to the crowd from their mobile bandstand. Roger and a group of guys, all dressed in their carnival outfits, danced beside the truck. Another trio of flatbeds, also decorated in carnival themes, carried most of the girls from San Nicolaas.

Then came several cars loaded with Sam's friends, including George, Tom, and others, all of whom had flown down for the funeral. The night before, there were rounds of drinks in Sam's honor but no shows, no gambling, nothing crazy enough to qualify as a party. The girls worked but not very late. It seemed the whole town wanted to talk about nothing but their fallen prince.

It took a little more than three hours for everyone to make it to the dirt lot outside the cemetery walls. The last man was Speedy. Although he was clean and sober, he hardly knew where he was.

"Give me the bat," he said to Frankie.

"Wait just a minute!" Frankie hollered. "I'm in the middle of something important."

Speedy sat down against the wall, his head on his chest.

The cemetery was the last piece of real estate within the bounds of San Nicolaas. It was situated between a mangrove and a vacant lot on the main road. Only Sam's closest friends and the priest went inside the wall. The graves were closely packed, and no one wanted to stand on someone's plot.

George, Tom, and Roger, with the help of Charlie and Captain Beck, carried Sam's coffin to the crypt where it was to be interred. As the priest had his final say, they pushed it into the designated space. A pair of workers inserted the end piece, which had been finished only earlier in the day. The inscription read, "Samito, el Príncipe de San Nicolaas. In paradise I dwell."

Luz and Carlotta retraced their steps to the gate. There they stood with Charlie, Beck, and the others from the United States. As the sun set, they exchanged a few last words about their departed friend. Frankie and Speedy interrupted the conversation with an argument over who was going to pitch the ball and who was going to hit it. Charlie settled the matter.

"Give me the ball," he said. Speedy put the ball in his hand. "Frankie, take your glove and stand over there." Frankie walked toward the mangrove, his figure silhouetted by the ever-reddening sun.

Speedy figured out he was going to do the hitting. He took up the batter's stance near the corner of the cemetery wall. Behind him, he heard the roar of a crowd, but it was only the sound of the trucks heading out of the area. He waved to the imaginary fans on both sides, then looked back at Charlie, who was winding up the pitch. The ball came in straight and fast. Speedy stepped into it, swung the bat, and connected the way he had when he was a teenager. The ball flew over Charlie's head, out toward the mangrove, past a galloping Frankie, and disappeared.

"Did you see that?" Speedy shouted. "Did you see that?"

"We saw it," Charlie replied.

"It went to the ocean!"

"It did, Speedy. I saw the splash," Charlie told him.

Frankie was less enthusiastic. He ambled up to Speedy, snatched the bat away from him, and looked at Sam's assembled friends. "That was a short game," he muttered and started walking toward town with Speedy at his heels.

The next day, Carlotta and Luz sat together at Sayonara. Neither of them wanted to talk about Sam. Carlotta congratulated Luz on the tactics she had employed to remove Marcela. Luz insisted she only did what she had to do. Carlotta recognized that but did not downplay the seriousness of what could have happened.

"Not only Andrés, but all of us are better off for what you did. *Gracias a Dios.*"

"I worry that she will come back."

Carlotta waved both hands in the air. "And then what? If she returns, she will find that you have many friends. She had only enemies. Tell me who is stronger."

Luz thought about what Carlotta had said. It was satisfying to know she was no longer alone. Her circle had grown from Carlotta and Charlie to include a dozen others. She had people who cared about her, who did her favors, who trusted her. Luz herself was as much a fixture in San Nicolaas as any of them. She was the girl behind the bar at Minchi's. She was for hire but only to gentlemen, and the price was not cheap. She tolerated no bargaining nor boorish behavior.

It pained her to think that she had not told Carlotta about Captain Beck's offer to take her away. She was lying by omission, which a priest once told her was as bad as the real thing. She had told no one, and unless Beck had mentioned it, the only other person to know was Spanner.

Luz enjoyed her times with Carlotta, but the longer she spent with the woman, the harder it would be to keep the secret. She felt as if she had betrayed Carlotta, that she had left her out of an important decision. This wasn't fair to either herself or Carlotta. She had her own life to live, and the consequences were her own to bear. However, Luz didn't want Carlotta to find out until it was too late, until nothing could go wrong.

"I'm going to play with Hernán," Luz said.

"Give him a kiss for me," Carlotta said with a pat on her leg.

The men and boats that came to replace Beck and *Kathryn* were assembled at Berth 2C. They introduced themselves to each other, took time to inspect the facility, and swapped stories of their journeys to Aruba. Beck drove the two captains to Oranjestaad, where he introduced them to the port captain and the cruise ship agents. With that piece of business completed, they rendezvoused with Herzog at Charlie's.

"You leave in a few hours," Herzog said to Beck. "All the best with your new venture."

Beck nodded his head. If he'd had his choice he would have left Aruba already. However, it was only proper that he handed things off to the new boats in the correct manner. He felt the crew's anticipation as well. They were ready to move on to a bigger place with more exciting work. It wasn't that Aruba was boring; it was that the sea was out there waiting for them.

Charlie came from behind the bar, holding a glass of rum in his hand. "The death of our dear friend and the departure of you, Captain Beck, call for an exception to the rule," he said. He grasped the bell's lanyard. "To friends, old and new! To friends, absent, present, and overdue." The clang was heard at both ends of the street. Charlie and everyone in the bar raised their glasses and drank.

"*Vaya con Dios*," Charlie finished.

Beck left the bar and returned to *Kathryn*. Wilkie, Syd, Ramirez, and Tony bustled through the passageways and around the decks. Beck knew they were only keeping busy to pass the time until they left. He went to the wheelhouse, where he found the charts for the United States. The one for the Delaware Bay was on top. He looked at the approaches to Cape Henlopen and Cape May. His mind's eye saw Brandywine Lighthouse shining out at him. He wondered if anyone there remembered his voice on the radio. Since he was to stand the first watch, Beck stretched out on the settee and dozed.

No one bothered his dreamless sleep. He awoke to find the wheelhouse exactly as it had been, only darker. After sliding the charts back in the drawer he stepped up to the window. Peering through the glass he saw the guard at the refinery gate leave his shack. Two people were waiting to pass. They were Luz and Hernán.

Beck met them at the edge of the pier. Luz wore her blue dress and a pair of heels that would be dangerous on a boat. He didn't care. He was elated to have her there. He looked at Hernán and the little suitcase beside the boy. It was too worn to have been his, too banged up to have been his mother's either. He glanced at Luz and noticed there was no suitcase beside her.

"You're not coming," he said.

"This is who I am," she told him.

"You're not …"

She would not allow him to stop her. She said, "I don't understand the sea, and you don't understand this town."

"Luz …" he interrupted.

She cut him off again. "I never expected to stay here. I loved my country, my family, and my son. I still do, but this place has given more to me than you think it has taken away. I would never have had a life like this in Colombia. Hernán would never have had a chance to go to the United States. That means more to me than anything in the world."

"It's no reason for you not to leave," Beck told her.

"Yes, it is," she said. "This place is for me, and my son belongs with you. I want him to be a man, a man like you. He cannot become that here."

She handed Beck the drawing Andrés had made of her on the day of Montoya's marriage to Marcela. "Show this to him. Tell him it was his mother."

"It is his mother," Beck insisted.

"And always will be. I am not ashamed of who I am, but he will be. Not today, but when he is older. He will hate me for what I am and what I did."

"You will be here. He will want to see you."

"Someday you can bring him to me, but not before he is a man. I don't want him to meet me again until he has seen the world and learned to appreciate what sometimes must be done to live in it. You can teach him this, and I beg you to do it. Promise me you will."

Beck heard the deckhouse door open. He knew Syd was standing there, waiting. Beck hoisted Hernán's suitcase over the gunwale into Syd's hands.

Luz stooped down to speak with her son. "Go with Captain Beck," she said. "He will bring you back to me soon." She kissed his cheek and pulled him close to her chest. Hernán hugged her back. He touched her face, then looked over at Beck. The boy helped himself over the fender onto the deck. He stared for a long moment at his mother, then glanced up at the boat. He then ascended the ladders to the wheelhouse, where he opened the door and went inside. Everyone's eyes followed his progress. Syd smiled and left to start the engines.

Beck realized that Hernán might grow up just as he, himself, had. He had always wondered about his mother. The mystery of her identity haunted him. He longed to know why she had left his father, why she had never come to see him, why no one was willing to tell him anything about her. Now he asked himself if she had been someone like Luz. Had she lived a life that she didn't want her son to know about? These questions Beck could not answer for himself, but when the time was right, he could answer them for Hernán. Still, there would be no mother in the boy's life. If Beck allowed it, Hernán would come of age among men, boats, and the sea. But he worried that as Hernán grew older he might come to despise his mother for sentencing him to a life away from her. It was how Beck sometimes felt about his own mother.

"You should be with him," he said.

"It is better for him if I'm not," Luz replied.

"He won't have a mother."

"Yes, he will. The same as you."

Beck didn't understand. Although he never mentioned it to anyone else in San Nicolaas, Luz knew how he had been raised.

Gesturing with her arm, Luz said, "There is your mother. She will be good to my son, too."

His eyes saw past the tips of her fingers to the name boards on *Kathryn*. As far as he knew, *Kathryn* hadn't been his mother's name, but boats like her had been his mother. Aboard them he had become the man he was, the man who was entrusted with the future of another woman's son.

Beck raised his eyes. "Goodbye, Luz," he said.

"*Adiós*, Captain Beck."

Luz put her lips to his cheek and pressed gently. She shuddered as her hands clutched his shoulders. Then she released him and took a step back. She saw he was smiling sadly and that his eyes were fixed on hers. She returned the smile, turned on her heel, and walked to the gate.

The sound of the tug's engines carried her beyond the gate and across Rogerstraat to the corner where Charlie's father had built the Lido Nightclub. Behind her, on the other side of the refinery wall, Beck maneuvered *Kathryn* away from the dock.

The crew was on deck, taking a last look at what had been their home. They saw the lights of the refinery and those from the houses on the hill beyond it. Main Street had not yet opened for the night. It was a dark strip in the otherwise sparkling landscape.

When *Kathryn* was in the center of the channel, Beck swung the rudder amidship and slowly brought the throttles to full power. He gave two short blasts on the whistle and then one long one. He was clear of San Nicolaas.

FROM HIS balcony, Charlie saw Luz and her son go into the refinery. He watched the conversation with Captain Beck. Although he couldn't hear the spoken words, he imagined what they were. And then her boy climbed aboard the boat. He almost cheered.

A man of his age and experience should have been able to observe all this through dry eyes. However, Charlie recognized that romantics like himself expected something other than that which history predicts for them. He was humble enough to accept his delusional thinking and understood why tears fell from his cheeks.

At the sight of that girl going in there, he hoped that things would go a certain way. Yet he was neither surprised nor disappointed when she walked back to town. Whether it was dictated by God or not, Charlie didn't know, but had it worked out differently, a secret axiom of the universe might have been broken.

He turned away from his view of the sea. On the street below, Luz paused to allow a car to go by. The breeze tugged at her skirt as she stepped off the curb. Before she entered Minchi's, Frankie called out to her. She waved to the bum and went into the bar. The light came on over the door a minute later. Down the block, the neon sign at Java lit up, followed by those at Black & White, Roxy, and Pianito. So it went, one by one, until the street was a carnival midway of dancing colors.

Charlie settled into his chair. He took a sip of rum, put a gentle hand atop Screwball's head, and said, "Don't fall in love, my friend."

Acknowledgments

I WOULD LIKE TO THANK my loyal analysts Diane, Tami, and Linda who pored over early drafts of this book to weed out the worst of it and Cheryl who helped spread the word. My editors Susan and Joe have sharp eyes and honest hearts. All my friends in Aruba deserve mention, but it is impossible to fit them all on this page. Doc Steve, thankfully, knows how to handle an emergency. Captain Eric Silva is the best tugboat operator I know or have known, and even if he can't always explain what he's doing, it's awesome to watch him in action. My parents took a chance bringing me into this world, and I'm grateful they did so I could have the opportunity to write. Of course Heather is a constant source of guidance and support. Mr. Vernon Fletcher is not to be forgotten for his wary countenance.

About the Author

Captivated by Aruba's cultural diversity, Daniel Putkowski divides his time between the island, Spain, and a suburb of Philadelphia. He is a graduate of New York University's Tisch School of the Arts. His wife and cat tolerate him well enough as he works on *Under a Blue Flag*, his next novel about Aruba. In 2008, *An Island Away* was the #1 bestselling book in Aruba.

To learn more about the author, visit
danielputkowski.com